# THE QUICKENING

*The Quickening Trilogy*
*by Fiona McIntosh*

BRIDGE OF SOULS
BLOOD AND MEMORY
MYRREN'S GIFT

Forthcoming
*The Percheron Saga*

ODALISQUE

# BRIDGE OF SOULS

## THE QUICKENING Book Three

# FIONA McINTOSH

*An Imprint of HarperCollinsPublishers*

This book was originally published in a mass market edition in 2004 by Voyager, an imprint of HarperCollins Publishers, Australia.

EOS
*An Imprint of* HarperCollins*Publishers*
10 East 53rd Street
New York, New York 10022-5299

Copyright © 2004 by Fiona McIntosh
Excerpt from *Odalisque* copyright © 2005 by Fiona McIntosh
ISBN: 978-0-06-074761-9
ISBN-10: 0-06-074761-7
**www.eosbooks.com**

First Eos paperback printing: January 2007
First Eos trade paperback printing: March 2006

HarperCollins® and Eos® are registered trademarks of HarperCollins Publishers.

Printed in the U.S.A.

10  9  8  7  6  5  4  3  2  1

*GH . . . this one's for you*

# ACKNOWLEDGMENTS

I'm aware that a great number of people have traveled this long and traumatic journey with Wyl Thirsk, so special thanks to the booksellers for recommending the series—especially Steve Hubbard in Minnesota and Jonathan Asay in Georgia, and my gratitude to all readers for giving The Quickening and this new writer a go.

The list to thank continues to extend: Gary Havelberg, Sonya Caddy, Pip Klimentou, and Judy Downs; the ever-increasing gang at the Heartwood Bulletin Board for their support and conversation; and Trent Hayes for a new Web site to make our international readers feel so welcome and appreciated.

Heartfelt thanks to Robin Hobb—quietly in the background, always full of encouragement, ever inspirational through her own work. And to Guy Gavriel Kay—not just for *Tigana*—but for his frequent and funny e-mails across the oceans. Also to Lynn Flewelling for such strong support and encouragement.

To my partner in crime, Kate Nintzel, a terrific editor whom I love working with, and to Jennifer Brehl, both at Eos. You're a wonderful team to be part of.

Sincere thanks to Chris Lotts at Ralph M. Vicinanza Literary Agency, for all the work on my behalf and for the regular laughs.

Finally, to Ian, Will, and Jack—who make it so easy for me to disappear into worlds beyond our own and yet are the trilogy of reasons I always return.

# BRIDGE OF SOULS

# PROLOGUE

It felt like an eternity to Fynch.

There was brightness, unbearably sharp, and combined with a hammering pain. He squeezed his lids tightly but the dazzling gold light hurt his eyes all the same as he helplessly relinquished control of his small body to the vast agony exploding through it. He believed he felt his body writhing uncontrollably, but in truth he was rigidly still, his teeth bared in a grimace as the force of magic gifted from Elysius radiated painfully into him.

At one point he thought he glimpsed the sorcerer passing through him to his death, like a distant memory he could not quite bring into focus. Elysius appeared whole again and he was smiling. Fynch vaguely sensed him offering thanks but was unable to lock on to it as the pain claimed all of his attention.

The sickening throb of power began to pulse through his body in time with his escalating heartbeat, each push harder, each more breathless in its intensity, until he lost all sense of himself. He no longer knew who he was or where he lay; he had to relinquish all to the excruciating pain until, finally, he glimpsed its end. The agony ebbed gradually but steadily until he realized he was bearing it. His pulse was fast but his heart no longer felt as though it might explode through his chest. The blinding light had dimmed to flashes of gold, as if he had been staring at the sun too long, and his breath was no longer panicked and shallow but came in deep, rhythmic drafts.

His wits returned. He had survived.

Trembling from the chill that now gripped him, Fynch

opened his eyes to slits. He registered a new layer of pain and closed them again; this time it was a headache that prompted instant nausea. He felt like crying. But where other youngsters might have had the comfort of a mother's voice and love, there was no such consolation for Fynch. He was alone. Wyl had gone.

Fynch hated the way they had parted. He knew Wyl had wanted him to leave the Wild immediately and he had watched his friend battle his inclination to say as much. Ylena's face was too expressive to mask what her brother was thinking. And yet Wyl had said nothing, had permitted Fynch to make his own decision and remain a little longer. Fynch felt a profound sadness for his friend who had suffered so much loss already and would suffer more yet, he sensed. He wished he knew of a way to spare Wyl more pain, or at least to share some of it with him.

He sighed. The nausea had passed. His eyes were still closed and he realized the pain had dimmed considerably. But the loneliness remained. There would not even be Elysius to offer solace. No. The boy suspected he was alone in the Wild, save for the four-legged beast who was his constant companion.

Full consciousness sifted through his shattered nerves and Fynch became aware of a pressing warmth at his side. Having sensed he was alert again, the source of warmth moved and growled.

"Knave," Fynch croaked through a parched throat.

*Never far,* a voice replied in his head. The unexpected sound made him flinch.

The boy turned toward the great black dog. "Did you speak to me?" he asked, tears welling. "Can I finally hear you?"

Depthless eyes regarded him and again he heard Knave's reply in his mind. *I did. You can.*

The friendly voice—one he had never thought to hear—was too overwhelming. Fynch managed to command his reluctant arms to obey him. Slowly, painfully, he wrapped them around the big animal's neck and wept deeply and without shame.

*Elysius?* Fynch asked after a long time, testing his newly acquired power.

The dog's response was instant. *Dead. It was quick. And he was glad to go.*

*Where is his body?*

*Everywhere. He became dust. The massive transfer of power disintegrated his physical being and then dispersed him.*

*Did he say anything before . . . before he passed on?*

*That you are the bravest of souls. He agonized that he might be wrong to force this burden upon you,* the dog admitted. *He regretted the pain you would experience and the journey ahead, but he believed there is no one else who can walk the path but you.* The dog leaned closer and spoke very gently. *In this I know he is right.*

Fynch pulled away from his friend, eyes still wet. There was so much yet to learn. *Knave, I don't know how to use this power. I have no—*

*Hush,* the dog soothed. *That is why I am here.*

The boy took the beast's huge head between his tiny hands. *Who are you?*

*I am your guide. You must trust me.*

*I do.*

The dog said no more, but Fynch sensed that he was glad, even relieved.

*But there is something I must know,* he went on, his tone almost begging.

*Ask it.* Knave's mental voice was so deep that Fynch suspected that if the dog could speak aloud, he, Fynch, would feel the sound rumble through his own tiny chest.

*Who is your true master? Where do you belong?*

Fynch sensed Knave's smile. *I have no master as such. But I do belong.*

*Where? Please tell me.*

*I am of the Thicket.*

Ah. Fynch's tensed muscles relaxed as understanding flooded through him. The neatness of the dog's answer pleased him. *Are there others like you?*

*I am unique, although there are other enchantments within the Thicket.*

*So Elysius didn't send you to Myrren?*

*Elysius did not know me by flesh until we both came here, although he knew of me. And Myrren was not the person I sought.*

This was a revelation. Fynch pressed his hands against his eyes in an attempt to ease their soreness and clear his swirling thoughts. *Then why didn't you just search out Wyl?*

*Because Wyl was not the one I sought either.*

Fynch looked up sharply. *Who, then? Who must we now search for?*

*The search is over. It was always you, Fynch.*

*What?* The dog's unerring gaze told Fynch Knave would never lie. *But why?*

*You are the Progeny and I am the Guide.*

*I thought I was the Wielder,* Fynch asked, confused.

*That, and so much more,* Knave said reverently. *You are many things.*

*The Thicket sent you to find me?*

*The Thicket sent me to find the next Gate Wielder. It did not know that would be you.*

*But it must have known Elysius was dying in order to send you in search of his replacement?*

*Yes.*

*So your role has never been about Wyl or Myrren . . . or protecting Valentyna?* Fynch sent wonderingly.

Knave's response was measured. *My task is to protect you. When the magic of the Quickening entered Wyl, the Thicket believed he was the next Wielder. Elysius wondered the same.*

*Are you saying that it was pure coincidence you came into Myrren's life?* Fynch asked, desperately trying to piece the puzzle together.

*Not exactly. She was Elysius's daughter. Magic was part of her even though it was not strong in her. It was she whom the Thicket decided to keep a watch over. When Myrren made such connection with Wyl, we thought he might be the one. It was only when I met you that I realized it was you we searched for.*

*How can you tell?*

*There is an aura about you, Fynch. Unmistakable, and invisible to all but those of the Thicket.*

Fynch sighed. *I was born with this aura?*

*Yes. Your destiny was set.*

*Elysius never mentioned it.*

*Elysius didn't know. The Thicket told him who you are only as he died.*

*It talks!?*

*Communicates,* the dog corrected.

Fynch held his head and groaned. These revelations were causing fresh gusts of pain to surge through his already aching mind. *It hurts, Knave. Will it always be so?*

*You must control the pain. Don't allow yourself to become its slave. Master it, Fynch.*

*Is this how it will kill me?*

The dog held a difficult silence between them.

*I would know the truth,* Fynch insisted. *If you are my friend—my Guide, as you say—then tell me honestly.*

He sensed the dog's discomfort as he began to explain. *This is the beginning. You must use your powers sparingly. Talk to me aloud whenever you can, although hearing my response in your mind will not sap your energies. The pain and other weakenings will only occur if you send the magic yourself.*

*How long have I got, Knave?*

The dog raised his head to look Fynch directly in the eye. *I don't know. It depends how strong you are, how sparingly you use this power.*

If Knave expected despair it did not come. Fynch wiped his eyes and, using his companion as support, raised himself wearily on unsteady legs. *I must rest,* the little boy said gravely.

*And then we must go to the Thicket,* Knave said, equally somber. *It awaits you.*

# 1

T HE VINEYARD SPRAWLED BEFORE THEM, THE LAND SUDDENLY sloping down in the distance to a small shingle beach and the channel of sea. The tang of salt in the air was invigorating and the bright day with its cloudless sky and sharp light reminded Aremys of how much he had missed the north all these years. He inhaled the air now and smiled. It felt good to be alive, despite the new and sudden complexities in his life.

With his memory now blessedly returned, Aremys felt much better equipped to accept the King's invitation to "walk the rows" of vines at Racklaryon. The mercenary learned that it was one of Cailech's great pleasures to see his vineyard bursting with new life each spring, showing the spectacular results of the savage pruning his vignerons insisted upon.

King and mercenary looked out now across the neat rows and Aremys could almost taste the wine this field would produce at summer's end. Bright green leaves, like the protective wings of a mother hen, shaded their yet-to-mature babies, bunches of fruit that hung like tiny green jewels, fattening and ripening daily as the plants sent out fresh tendrils to weave and curl their way along the special lines that supported the vines. The Mountain People had pioneered this method of support. In the south, the vines were left to themselves, to grow tall at first, stooping over when heavy with fruit. It made for a ragged, untidy vineyard but, in truth, did not affect the quality of the wine. In the north, however, vine support lines had been developed to air the fruit, as some months were humid and damp. It also looked more spectacular.

Cailech's people took pride in the ordered appearance of their vineyards. Not only were the rows straight but each vine was sung to as it was planted—a small prayer to Haldor that each new beginning might yield life of its own. At each row's end, the Mountain People planted a flower called a trineal. It was beautiful but fragile, very susceptible to lack of water or other natural attacks. Cailech's vignerons maintained that if the trineal foundered, they would have but a few weeks to find the solution to prevent the vines from following suit. It was an ancient tradition but one still faithfully adhered to. The bright rainbow colors of the trineal bushes were an attractive feature in this, Cailech's favorite vineyard, and they stood proud, colorful, and healthy at the heads of the rows. It would be a bountiful harvest, the men murmured.

The King was rarely alone; today he was flanked by Myrt and Byl. Aremys had come to know these particular fellows well since his curious arrival in the Razors. He felt comfortable in their presence and over the past few days had started to view them as companions as much as captors. Nevertheless, he had chosen not to reveal that his memory was fully restored. It suited him that these Mountain Dwellers knew only as much as he was prepared to share, until he could learn more about their intentions for him.

The small company had ridden to the vineyard beyond the lake and Aremys was sorry to see that the King had not chosen to bring the intriguing black horse that had caused him such fright on their previous ride. He mentioned his disappointment to Cailech.

"Ah yes, Galapek," the King replied softly, and Aremys felt the weight of the green gaze upon him. "I had the impression that he disturbed you somehow the last time we rode together."

It was said without accusation but Aremys felt the scrutiny couched within. Wyl Thirsk's warning burned in his mind: Only a fool took any comment by Cailech at face value. *Everything he says has a purpose,* Wyl had impressed upon Aremys during their journey together from Felrawthy. *He misses nothing.*

The mercenary thought back to the moment of disturbance the King spoke of. It had occurred only a few days ago. Aremys had initially admired the King's mount but, on casually touching the horse's strong neck, had felt a blast of dark, tainted magic surge through his hands. It had been an intense shock for Aremys—not only that the creature was alive with magic, but also that he could sense it—and he had jerked back in distress. Worse, he had been unable to regain his composure and had been forced to excuse himself from the party of riders. The entire scene had been embarrassing to Aremys, but, more important, no doubt had also appeared suspicious to his keepers at a time when he was striving to convince them that he was not a Morgravian spy or a threat to any of the Mountain Dwellers.

The only positive outcome was that the shock seemed to have caused his amnesia to dissipate and he had been able to piece together what he was doing in the Razors. He remembered following Wyl Thirsk, who now walked in the guise of his sister, Ylena, courtesy of the powerful gift, the Quickening. Together they had entered the mysterious region in the far northeast known as the Thicket. Aremys recalled Wyl asking him to whistle so they would not lose each other among the tangle of this dense landmark. He had obliged, could even remember the tune he had chosen, but then all had gone black and he had woken, disoriented and without his memory, on the frozen rocks of the northern mountain range. Cailech's men had discovered him there, and aided by his genuine confusion, he had managed to muddle his way through those early and dangerous stages. He felt convinced now that he had carefully won not only the trust of the Mountain warriors but that of their king as well. Wyl had warned Aremys that the Mountain King was changeable, capricious even, and had recounted the terrible night of the feast when Cailech had threatened to roast alive the Morgravian prisoners his men had captured and feed them to his people. This was definitely not a man to second-guess and so Aremys had been as honest as he could with the Mountain King, even disclosing his identity when it finally returned to him.

He had not, however, told Cailech anything about his connection to Wyl Thirsk, the former General of Morgravia, or that Wyl was possessed by a magic that had already taken the lives of three people—one of them Romen Koreldy, in whom Cailech had shown a keen interest. Aremys vowed that if the Mountain Kingdom held its own secrets, he would learn them and at least be useful in some small way to Wyl, who had promised to return to the Razors someday in search of his friends Gueryn and Lothryn, both of whom had offered their lives to save his.

Nor had he been honest with Cailech about his arrival in the Razors. It had taken Aremys hours of musing to accept that the Thicket must have somehow repelled him. It was a difficult notion for him to get his mind around. Until recently he had neither particularly believed nor disbelieved in magic, but growing up in the far north, on the Isles of Grenadyn, meant he held a loose acceptance that such a power might exist and was not necessarily something to fear.

Loose acceptance and indisputable proof were entirely different matters, however, and now—since he'd met Wyl and shared the sorrow of his plight—the legend of the Thicket had taken on a sinister character. Acknowledging that this enchanted place had purposefully separated him from the very person he had sworn to protect was disturbing enough, but accepting that the Thicket had also affected him in such a way that he now possessed the ability to sense magic was terrifying.

The horse itself couched a darker mystery. Just touching the animal had made him feel ill. It reeked of evil—and yet also of despair. Aremys needed to see the horse again, reach toward it once more. Perhaps his captors had no idea of the darkness in Galapek? But how else could Cailech know the horse was the reason for his disturbance?

Aremys realized Cailech was still watching him carefully. The mercenary, practiced at subterfuge, stretched a lazy smile across his generous mouth. "It had nothing to do with the beast, my lord. I felt very off-color that morning and I slept for many hours after that event."

"Probably out of your discomfort at almost spewing on

the King's boots!" Myrt added, safe in the knowledge that Cailech encouraged a more casual atmosphere when he was away from the fortress and the formalities of being their ruler.

Myrt's jest gave Aremys the opportunity he needed to navigate himself from the King's scrutiny. It suddenly occurred to him that Cailech knew more than he was giving away. His instincts had rarely let him down, so he listened to them now.

"It reminded me of the time," he said, seizing the opening, "when a very aged and strict aunt of mine came to visit the family." His companions, sensing a tale in the making, came closer. "She was a cantankerous woman who despised social gatherings, yet insisted on everyone celebrating her name-day each spring. Oh, how we hated that day and her arrival with all of its pomp and ceremony. But our family was obliged to her, for the rich crone had gifted much money to the town, and I would be lying if I said we had not benefited from her gold."

Aremys saw with relief the loose, expectant grin on the King's face as he bent to inspect a vine of juvenile grapes. He continued with his tale: a dare by his brothers that went horribly wrong and culminated in his tossing the contents of a chamber pot over the head of the town's special guest.

The men roared with laughter. Aremys noted that Cailech was less responsive but nonetheless amused; a wry smile crinkled the weathered face and sparkled in his eyes. "I would never repeat such a tale if that had been me," he said.

"Nor will I again," Aremys admitted, rather impressed himself by his telling of the story, which was wholly fabricated. "But I am trying to impress upon you, my lord, the level of my dismay. This sorry tale has now been relegated to the second most embarrassing moment of my life. I hope you can guess the first."

"You are forgiven, Farrow, and it's forgotten," the King said as the other two men began to wander away through the rows.

Aremys did not believe him. "Thank you, sire."

"Perhaps you would like to ride Galapek?"

Aremys had not expected this and he knew his hesitation was telling. The King was testing him and both of them knew it. The mercenary quickly gathered his wits. "It would be a privilege, my lord."

"Good," the King replied, his steady gaze unfathomable. "I will arrange it."

He looked beyond the mercenary. "Ah, here comes Baryn. He is head of the vineyard." The previous topic seemingly forgotten, he strode toward the man, calling back over his shoulder, "Don't you love the Thaw, Aremys? Spring unfurling her fronds, pushing through her shoots, warming the ground, and melting the ice?" Cailech pointed as Aremys caught up. "Just look at these vines, fairly bursting with joy as tiny green buds and tendrils begin their life journey."

"You should write poetry, sire."

The King smiled at the compliment. "I have a proposition to put to you, Farrow."

Cailech's sudden twist took Aremys by surprise. He would have to be careful; Wyl had warned him of this. "Sire?"

"I have been thinking about our conversation."

"Oh?" Aremys thought back over the past few days; he and Cailech had had many discussions.

"Regarding Celimus," Cailech clarified.

Aremys nodded. "I recall suggesting a parley."

"There is wisdom in what you advise and I have decided to act upon it."

Aremys raised his eyebrows but managed to keep the surprise from his voice. "Really?"

Cailech nodded. "Yes. I am going to Morgravia, and not under cover of disguise or stealth. Actually, let me correct that. *We* are going to Morgravia."

"You and your chosen men, sire?"

"Me and you, Farrow."

Aremys searched the King's face for any signs of guile, then realized that he would not be able to tell if Cailech was bluffing. The man was a master at hiding behind a granite expression—although on this occasion Aremys thought he detected the barest hint of amusement.

"Then I am honored, King Cailech," Aremys said diplomatically.

Cailech simply nodded. "You will set up the meeting, as you know Celimus. You will act as my emissary."

And with that the King strode away, leaving the newly appointed envoy for the Mountain Kingdom openmouthed.

"Close it, friend," Myrt said, returning to Aremys's side.

"He can't be serious," Aremys murmured, watching as the King's broad figure joined the vineyard manager among an ocean of green leaves.

"He never jests about such things. Take it as a compliment, Farrow. He must trust you."

"Do you know when we leave?"

"As soon as the streams run with the Thaw, he told me."

"But that's now!" Aremys turned to look at Myrt.

The man grinned. "True. Come on, we'd better head back—apparently you are to ride his prize stallion this afternoon."

A remys's stomach had clenched when he caught sight of the magnificent horse being led out of its stall by Maegryn, the stablemaster. The stallion flicked its tail constantly, as though angry. A weak sensation of nausea rippled through the mercenary. He forced himself to relax, for he had been holding his breath and was ashamed at himself for allowing this animal to have such a dramatic effect on him.

*It's only a horse, damn it!* he berated himself, but to no avail; the sinister feeling intensified.

"He's a beauty, this one," Myrt commented by his side.

Aremys fought the swirling dizziness. Did no one else feel it? "Is Cailech not joining us?" he asked through clenched teeth.

"No. Rashlyn will be riding out, though."

"Who is he?" Aremys asked innocently. He recalled Wyl's description of the man who seemed to have an unnatural influence over the Mountain King.

"The King's barshi—a detestable creature," Myrt said. "But if you ever claim I said that, I'll deny it first and kill you later."

Aremys grinned. "A man of magic, then?" he asked, watching as Maegryn saddled Galapek.

His companion nodded and Aremys felt his stomach twist again. "Can he sense other empowered people?" He hoped Myrt would not hear the anxiety in his voice.

"I have no idea. Why do you ask?"

Aremys forced a shrug. "Oh, no reason. I've always been rather intrigued by those with the power, that's all."

"To be honest I wish he'd leave the mountains. His influence upon our king is too strong. There are times . . ." Myrt's voice trailed off.

Aremys glanced toward his captor. "Go on."

The Mountain Man shook his head. "No, I speak out of turn."

Aremys could see it would not be wise to push Myrt further right now, although it pleased him to note that Myrt felt comfortable enough around him to be candid. Perhaps Myrt could become a source of information, or a key to escape.

It looked as though Maegryn was satisfied with Galapek. He was barking orders now for the other horses to be led out.

"Where did Cailech find this magnificent horse?" Aremys asked brightly, noticing that he seemed to be growing more accustomed to the nearby magic.

"It's the strangest thing," Myrt replied, clearly relieved to have moved away from the previous conversation. "I really don't know."

"What do you mean?"

"Well, the very best horses come from Grenadyn—as you would know—but this animal just turned up one day. He certainly isn't from our stock."

"You mean it just appeared out of nowhere?" Aremys asked, astounded. Perhaps the stallion had also been cast here by the Thicket.

Myrt laughed. "No, I didn't mean that. But Maegryn knows all the foals born here. And if we bring horses over from Grenadyn then it's quite a big event because they have to be shipped in. I don't recall this animal being brought across the channel—it would surely have caused a stir if he had."

Aremys was intrigued. It was not his imagination, then.

There was something mysterious about the King's horse. "What does his handler say?"

"Maegryn's very tight-lipped on the subject. I've tried to find out more but he's refused to discuss it. I get the impression that Rashlyn might have gifted the horse to Cailech, though I couldn't guess at where he would find such a beast. Perhaps the King has asked both to keep it quiet. Cailech can be quite unpredictable on occasion—in case you hadn't noticed." Myrt grinned.

"I have," Aremys said wryly.

"He is a great man, but he can be contrary at times," Myrt warned, before adding softly, "I know that worried Lothryn."

Aremys took a careful breath at the name of Wyl's friend. "Lothryn—that name sounds familiar. Who is he?" he commented absently.

"A friend. Formerly second in command to our king. A man I would have followed without question into any situation—but who betrayed us all."

Maegryn was leading the horse toward them now and Aremys again felt the sickening pull of magic. He forced himself to focus on Myrt's words. "Betrayed you? Where is he now?"

"Gone," Myrt said, ending the conversation. "Your mount is ready—and here comes Rashlyn. Be warned—he is a strange man."

The barshi was already mounted on a chestnut mare. He stopped just steps from the mercenary and gazed down upon the tall foreigner. "You must be Aremys," he said in his strangely hesitant manner. "Cailech suggested we meet. I hope you don't mind if I join you?"

"Not at all," Aremys lied, instantly taking a dislike to the wild-looking man with the dead eyes and unwilling smile. He raised his hand in salutation, deciding to avoid all physical contact with the barshi. If Aremys himself sensed the horse's magic through touch, perhaps Rashlyn could do the same with him. He wondered whether Cailech had specifically asked Rashlyn to watch how he reacted to the horse today.

*Which would mean they are definitely suspicious of me,* he thought. The stench of Galapek's magic buffeted his senses as the handler halted the stallion alongside the mare.

"Master Aremys, you'll be riding Galapek this afternoon," Maegryn said. "Be firm with him, sir. But also give him his head on the flat. He likes to gallop. Could use a good run today."

It was all Aremys could manage to nod agreeably and take the reins from Maegryn. How had he backed himself into this situation? Nausea threatened to overwhelm him, but he fought it and deliberately turned his back to Rashlyn as he mounted. He could not allow the barshi to read his fear.

Waves of revulsion pulsed through him as he took his seat in the saddle. It required all his courage not to leap from the horse immediately. "You lead," he said tightly to Rashlyn, hoping to get the magic man ahead of him.

Unfortunately, Rashlyn had his measure. "Myrt—you know the best paths," he said. "You lead. I'll bring up the rear."

The party of three set off, with Aremys now fully convinced he was under observation by the King's sorcerer.

2

MYRT SUGGESTED A PATH VIA THE LOWLANDS SURROUNDING the lake. Aremys grunted his agreement, still struggling to dampen his revulsion for the horse beneath him. Myrt did not linger for a comment from the barshi and set the direction. Once the horses were moving at a steady canter, Aremys felt better, and when they set them at a gallop, the exhilaration and the wind in his face alleviated some of the sickening taint permeating his body from below.

For the first half of the ride the men said nothing and Aremys was happy to be lost in his thoughts and the pure pleasure of being out in the breathtaking valley. The lake was mirror calm and he marveled at how it reflected the lower rises of Razors. The cacophony of the waterbirds drowned any potential for conversation, which suited him perfectly. Although the sun was high overhead, there was no real fire in it, and the riders were glad to feel its gentle spring warmth upon their shoulders, loosening winter's firm grip on the land.

Now that Aremys had been touching the stallion for some time, he was able to control his reaction to the horse. Whatever had initially caused him to gag wretchedly in front of the King had diminished to a constant queasiness, which he was mastering. His revulsion had given way to an intense pity for the animal. The beast moved beneath him with superb grace, all muscle and power, eager to respond to his rider's urgings, but Aremys sensed something beyond the physical, something he would almost equate with human emotion.

"We can stop over there and rest the horses." Myrt butted into his thoughts, pointing toward a cluster of rocky outcrops that formed a loose semicircle and a natural sun trap.

Aremys nodded. He would have preferred to keep going but was helpless, certain that this entire afternoon was all being carefully orchestrated.

They settled themselves against the boulders while the horses grazed contentedly on some tender grass, far enough away that Aremys could converse without the magical stench threatening to upset him. Still, he felt Galapek's pull. The more confident Aremys became in his resistance to the revulsion, the more strongly the horse pleaded to his senses. *What did it want him to do? What was this creature that it could generate such loathing as well as sympathy?*

A new thought struck Aremys: not *what* was this animal but *who*? The notion was so striking that it washed away his fear. *Who was this animal? Who was calling to him using the magic of the Thicket? Could the beast be under an enchantment, like Wyl—a man trapped in another guise?* The thought revolted him.

As he shook his head clear of such a shocking notion, the barshi embarked upon the expected interrogation.

"The King tells me you have lost your memory," Rashlyn said, without any preamble.

"I have," Aremys answered. "It is a terrible feeling not to know anything about oneself."

"I gather it is returning gradually?" the man replied, reaching to unwrap the hunk of cheese and hard biscuit Myrt had packed.

Aremys noted the man's grubby fingers and looked away. The Mountain Men were tough and capable of living rough, but he knew they bathed regularly. The King led by example: He was always scrupulously clean. As it had struck Elspyth not so long ago, Aremys had realized that the people of the Razors were a sophisticated race with great artistic and creative skills as well as a love of the land and a deep respect for one another. Since Cailech had stopped the tribal fighting and drawn the people together, that respect had extended beyond simple courtesies to living alongside one another in a manner that promoted cleanliness and protected them from disease. Aremys had noted with surprise the special ablution blocks that were built around the fortress, proof of how highly Cailech rated the importance of proper sanitation. The King was convinced of a link between human waste and disease, and so it was rare to see any Mountain Dweller squat in the fields or in a corner of the fortress to relieve himself. Instead, carts rolled away from the many ablution blocks daily to deliver the waste into pits dug deep in the ground, far from the main living areas, where it would harmlessly break down and return to the earth. It was part of the modern thinking—along with education and the maintenance of the old languages—that Cailech was beginning to impress upon his people. But this man, Rashlyn, with his dirty hands, his unkempt appearance and offensive manner, did not fit the Mountain folk's mold. How did they tolerate him?

Rashlyn was staring at him. "Yes, slowly," Aremys answered finally. "I know my name, at least, and where I hail from."

"Would you like me to check your skull for any damage?

I am a healer," Rashlyn offered, along with some of the cheese.

Aremys could not risk that the sorcerer might sense through his touch the Thicket's trace of magic. And Shar alone knew where those filthy fingers had last been. "Thank you, no," he replied. "I'm not hungry and my head is fine."

The man frowned. "It must have been a firm blow to knock your senses so. You really should let me examine you."

"No need," Aremys replied briskly, glancing toward his quiet companion, hoping to be rescued. "Myrt here has already looked me over. There is no sign of any damage."

Myrt did not deny Aremys's claim but did not support it either. Aremys suspected that he too was fighting a battle of loyalty. It was fairly obvious from his body language alone that the warrior despised Rashlyn.

"This business of your lost memory is odd, then," Rashlyn said. He spoke through his food and bits of the cheese crumbled and fell from his mouth into his tangle of a beard. Again Aremys looked away, disgusted. "How could a blow strong enough to cause you to lose your wits be entirely healed?"

"I have no idea," Aremys said, shrugging. He found the barshi's probing stare most unsettling; there was madness lurking there, he was sure of it. He stood and said politely, "Excuse me whilst I take a drink," glancing again at Myrt, this time for permission to sip from the stream.

Myrt nodded and Aremys walked as casually as he could to the stream's edge and bent down. He splashed freezing water over his face, enjoying the refreshing trickle of droplets that found a way into the front of his shirt and slid down his chest. As he straightened, flicking water in all directions, he sensed someone directly behind him. The thrill of fear that passed through him nearly unbalanced him into the stream. He turned abruptly, expecting to see Rashlyn reaching toward him, sinister and threatening.

Yes, Rashlyn was standing behind him, but instead of reaching out for the mercenary, he was digging in his pockets. Aremys felt stupid. He was definitely becoming paranoid, he berated himself silently and angrily.

"Apologies, I didn't mean to startle you," the man said, a little slyly, Aremys thought. He retrieved a tiny jar from a pocket. "Here—this will ease the headaches I believe you have been suffering."

"What is it?"

"A soothing blend of herbs for rest with a dash of laudanum. It won't harm you, or dull anything but the pain, I promise. Sip it every hour as you need."

Aremys was trapped. Rashlyn's filthy hand was extended toward him with the small bottle in its palm. He had to take it, or risk throwing yet more suspicion on himself. If the King was waiting to hear that Aremys had vomited again or had refused to ride his stallion, then he would be disappointed, but this moment might yet be his undoing. Aremys saw the healer's eyes narrow at his reluctance but still he hesitated.

"I can easily make up some more; you're not denying anyone by taking it," Rashlyn assured, the softness in his voice almost threatening. Aremys was sure the man was daring him to refuse.

He took a moment to shake his head free of the water droplets, then paused to wipe a sleeve across his face. "Thank you," he replied, reaching out slowly, hoping Rashlyn would simply drop the phial into his hand.

Before that could happen, Galapek alarmed all three men by rearing up behind them, screaming loudly as though in pain. Myrt reacted first, running toward the horse. Aremys took his chance, moving swiftly away from the healer. "Let me help!" he called.

The horse clearly wanted Myrt nowhere near him, rearing and screaming even more wildly as the warrior approached. To Myrt's surprise, however, the stallion calmed a little at the sound of the big mercenary's voice and allowed Aremys to sidle up to him.

Aremys reached for the reins and called again to the horse. "Galapek, there, boy. There, now. Settle, big fellow," he whispered. The horse stilled now, trembling and frightened.

"Poor Galapek, whatever has happened to you, I shall rescue you, I promise," Aremys said, stroking the animal's broad, magnificent face. "Be calm now, boy." He rubbed the stallion's neck, and for the first time, the stench of the magic did not turn his stomach. Whatever this curse upon the stallion was, it was somehow communicating with him, flowing through him and around him, begging him to keep his promise.

And then a word came into in his head. It was faint and desperately called but he sensed it clearly. *Elspyth,* he heard, just once, and then it was gone, like a sigh given to the wind and borne away.

Aremys was so shocked he stood rigid against the horse's neck, trying without success to recapture the word. Elspyth. Surely that was the name he had heard? Myrt's urgent voice broke through his haze of confusion.

"Farrow! For Haldor's sake, man!"

Aremys turned, surprised by the anger in the man's voice. Then he saw Myrt's expression—not angry, but distraught— and followed his friend's pointing finger. By the water's edge, where he had left him, Rashlyn writhed on the ground, shouting gibberish as spittle foamed and flew from his mouth. His arms and legs flailed wildly, then, suddenly, fell completely still.

"Check that the horses are secure," Aremys called over his shoulder as he ran to the prone figure. He hoped Rashlyn might be dead, but luck was not with him. He lifted the small man's chin to ensure a clear breathing passage, but stopped short of breathing any life-giving air into the barshi's mouth. "He has a pulse, I'm sorry to say," he risked to Myrt, who had come up behind them.

Myrt did not smile but something akin to a twitch of amusement flitted across his face. "What's happened?" the Mountain man queried.

"Is he prone to fits?"

"I don't know. I've not heard of any occurring before."

"Could it be the cheese?" Aremys asked.

"No, it's fresh. Nothing wrong with it."

"Something else, then. It seemed to occur at the same time as Galapek took fright."

"What are you saying?" Myrt squatted, saw the indecision in his companion's face. "Speak freely—I have protected you before."

Rashlyn lay rigidly still at their feet. Aremys lifted back the man's lids. The dark, madness-filled eyes had rolled back into his head. The man was unconscious; he could hear nothing.

"I'm not sure I should air my views. You're a loyal Mountain warrior, after all."

"Not to him!" Myrt spat disdainfully on the ground. "Like you, I wish he was dead. He's a danger to all of us."

"Because of his magic?"

Myrt nodded reluctantly. "He uses it for evil, I'm sure of it."

"I think it's his magic that has prompted this episode."

"I don't understand."

"I don't either, entirely." Aremys sighed and decided to take a chance on Myrt. He hoped his instincts would serve him truly. "Were you given any instructions about me and this afternoon's ride?"

Myrt frowned. "Nothing special. I was briefed to give you a chance to enjoy Galapek because you had expressed such interest in the horse."

"The King didn't tell you to keep a special eye on me?"

"My job is to keep an eye on you, Farrow. You're our . . ." —he hesitated—"our guest, after all."

Aremys grinned ruefully. "Myrt, you are more friend to me than most people I have met over the past decade. But let's be honest here: I'm a prisoner. I have to accept that. However," he went on, scratching his head, "your king is entrusting me with a very serious task, which means he has faith in me. Sadly, I can't be quite as honest with him as I can with you."

"Why not?"

"Because I suspect he is in the thrall of this man. You've told me as much yourself, and spending just an afternoon with Rashlyn has convinced me he's not someone to trust."

Myrt said nothing, merely frowned again.

Aremys pushed on. He glanced toward the horse. "I could be aiming completely off target here, but I think there's something very odd about Galapek. No, not odd. Enchanted."

Myrt rocked back on his heels as if slapped. "Magic?"

Aremys nodded. "Worked by Rashlyn, I'm guessing. And known of by your king." There, it was said.

Myrt stood and began pacing. He said nothing for a while and Aremys kept the silence, watching Rashlyn for any signs of consciousness.

"I don't believe this," the warrior hissed eventually, pointing at Aremys.

"You don't have to," the mercenary replied calmly, having anticipated the anger. "I'm just offering my own thoughts. I'm not suggesting that your king—whom I like and respect—is in complete agreement with Rashlyn."

"Then what *do* you mean, mercenary?" Myrt asked brusquely.

Aremys was sorry that he had pushed his friend so far. It was obvious from his anger that Myrt had suspected something not so far from what Aremys had suggested. But the blood of the Mountain People ran thick with loyalty. Wyl had warned him as much and he should not have presumed that friendship might override that loyalty—although, of course, it had in the case of the man Lothryn, who had chosen love and friendship over his monarch.

"I'm sorry if I've given insult, Myrt. It was not intended, especially not to you. I meant that I think Cailech—under the spell of Rashlyn, as you have pointed out—has permitted something unnatural to be wrought upon this horse."

"And how for the love of Haldor's arse would you know, Grenadyne? Are you a practitioner yourself, now, who knows when magic is being wielded?"

The harsh words bit at Aremys, as intended, but he could not ignore the truth. Could he risk divulging it to Myrt?

"Myrt, do you trust me?"

The man passed a weary hand over his eyes. "I'm not sure."

"What does your gut tell you?"

"That you are reliable."

"Good. That is enough for me. Now, we have to get Rashlyn back to the fortress. Help me lay him across his horse and I will tell you everything I know as we travel."

\* \* \*

They took the same route home, although more slowly. Aremys had tethered Rashlyn's horse on a lead some distance behind them, so if the healer regained consciousness he would not be able to hear their conversation and would have to alert them by calling out. "An old mercenary trick," Aremys had said, winking.

On the return journey, Aremys began to share with his friend all the information he was prepared to risk bringing into the open. He cast a silent prayer to Shar that he had this man's measure, that he could trust him not to betray him. He said nothing of Wyl, of course, simply explaining that he had been in the employ of the Morgravian sovereign. Myrt accepted that the mercenary would not explain what specific task he was employed to do for Celimus, merely nodding when Aremys assured him that it was nothing connected with the people of the Razors.

"Let me simply say that I was tracking someone of interest to the Crown," Aremys offered.

"And that's what brought you so far north?"

"Yes. I've remembered that I came to a place called Timpkenny in the far north east of Briavel," the mercenary lied. "I believed the person I was following had passed through there."

"And these people who set upon you—just common bandits, you think?"

"Mmm." Aremys nodded. "Added a little something to my ale to make me feel sick so I would stagger outside the inn late at night. I'm guessing now—all of this is a little hazy, thanks to the drug—but they must have thrown me over a horse to remove me from prying eyes. They led me to the fringe of a region called the Thicket. Have you heard of it?" Aremys held his breath.

Myrt was staring at him intently. He nodded. "They say it has powerful magic."

"It does, my friend, or at least I think it does. The bandits left me there after robbing me. Something must have frightened them, because I expected to be beaten, at the very least." Aremys steered himself toward the truth. "The last thing I remember is a strange noise coming from the Thicket itself."

Myrt's eyes were huge. "A creature?"

"No creature I know makes that sound. No, I can still hear it—it was a sort of humming sound—and then the air became thick and oppressive," Aremys replied.

"Then what?"

Aremys made a gesture of apology. "Then nothing. I woke up to the sound of your men's voices and no memory of what had occurred or who I was. You know the rest. My memory came back gradually over the next couple of days, and it's still returning slowly." He shrugged, then added for effect, "I can even remember the faces of my family now."

Myrt, stunned, shook his head. Finally he spoke. "I believe you, Aremys. No one could make up such a tale, and we know of the Thicket's legend. It's just a shock to hear that its magical reputation is more than myth."

"For me too, Myrt. But I've been over it and over it and the only explanation I have is that the Thicket, or something inside it, had something to do with me appearing at a location in the Razors it would take days to reach by normal means. You checked the area; there were no signs of other people or animals, so I couldn't have been kept drugged and led in by horse."

"I believe you," the big warrior repeated, his hands raised in defense.

"Well, I don't want to put any strange ideas in your head, but my only explanation is that this place called the Thicket is enchanted—I too have heard the old tales—and it did not like my being there, let me tell you. I felt its animosity. I think it got rid of me."

"That's impossible, man!" Myrt said, desperate to cling to something rational.

"I agree, but there's no other explanation. You understand now why I had to keep this part of my story to myself? Obviously I couldn't tell that tale to the King. He would have laughed first and had my throat slit a moment later. As to how the Thicket rid itself of me—it repelled me. I can't think of any other way to describe it. It would be great to believe a nice family of tinkers found me, picked me up, and carried me with them on their journey through the Razors, but I think you'd agree we'd only be making up an explanation to help ourselves feel better about a notion we don't want to accept or understand. No, Myrt, I am convinced that magic has been wielded upon me. I have other reasons to suspect as much as well."

Here it was, the very core of his tale. Myrt would either give himself over entirely to Aremys now or brand him a madman and go running to Cailech. Aremys took a deep breath and waited for Myrt's inevitable question. He risked a glance behind. Rashlyn lay draped over his horse, still unconscious.

"What do you mean by that?"

The fortress was all but upon them now. Aremys could see the people working the orchards, driving carts and going about their chores. He shivered, noticing for the first time that a chill had descended into the valley and a slight breeze had picked up, sending ripples across the surface of the formerly mirrorlike lake. The disturbance matched his own mood.

"Aremys, what did you mean?" Myrt repeated.

Aremys reined Galapek to a halt and the other horses followed suit. He knew Myrt could tell this was difficult for him and was giving him time to find the right words. There were no right words, though—so he just told it as he saw it.

"I think I've been touched by the magic of the Thicket. It temporarily knocked out my memory with the force of its power, but it gave me something in return."

Myrt drew back warily and opened his mouth, then closed it again. Aremys hurried on. "It left me with the ability to sense magic." He held up his hand. "Before you jump in— no, I can't wield it. I just sense it. And magic is with us now."

"Where?" his companion whispered.

"Right here, beneath me."

Myrt looked toward the ground.

"Galapek," Aremys said. "This horse is not natural, Myrt. It is riddled with magic, bad magic. It's tainted—it smells evil and repulses me as effectively as the Thicket transported me all those leagues. This horse reeks of enchantment and I think Rashlyn is responsible for it."

"That's why you were so keen to avoid his touch," Myrt finished, tying together the threads of all he had noticed but had not been able to understand.

"That's right. That's why I disgraced myself on our first ride together when Cailech rode Galapek. The magic assaulted me and I had no control over my reaction to it. I didn't even know why I was behaving so strangely. It took me a while to work it out, but I know I'm right."

"And now?"

"The magic still revolts me, but I have it under control now."

The warrior whistled through his teeth. "So that's why you seemed nervous riding out this afternoon."

Aremys nodded. "I was terrified. I had no idea how I'd handle it, but I knew that Rashlyn had been sent to watch my reaction and so I had to be very careful."

"So you're saying the King sent him?"

"Of course. Cailech's too smart to allow my behavior on that first ride to go unnoticed. He's testing me."

"He speaks well of you, Aremys, you should know that," Myrt defended.

"Thank you. I've grasped as much, and yet I know he is suspicious of me—understandably so, because if he's got something to hide with this enchantment, anything that threatens it is a danger."

"You're risking much by telling me this."

Aremys nodded gravely. "My life is in your hands, Myrt. I trust you, and Shar knows, I had to tell someone. I was about to go mad."

"What do you want me to do?"

"Nothing. Just keep my secret for now."

"I cannot be party to anything disloyal to Cailech," the man said carefully.

"I wouldn't ask it of you. I just want to learn more about the horse—and Rashlyn, whom I wouldn't trust if he were the last man alive in this land."

"None of us would, except the King," Myrt replied, disgust lacing his tone. "And you think the horse's rearing and shrieking and Rashlyn's collapse are connected?"

"Yes. Something has tampered with their magic or disturbed the link between the two. I'll admit to something else . . ."

"Yes?"

"I felt it too, but only lightly. As Rashlyn was holding that medicine out to me, I became light-headed, slightly dizzy. I thought it was the fear of him touching me, but I think I know better now. The magic of the Thicket was resonating again . . . perhaps warning me. Or maybe something has happened, something connected with the Thicket that has also disturbed the horse. I don't understand what, or how. Maybe the Thicket can disrupt the actual enchantment on Galapek—why else would Rashlyn also react? They must be connected."

"But you don't know how?"

"No! It's frustrating!" Aremys frowned. "But I intend to learn more. Will you keep my secret?"

Myrt nodded unhappily. "I will keep it."

"Thank you. I won't betray you or your people—you have my word." Aremys banged his fist on his chest in an oath only another northerner would understand.

Myrt mirrored the movement and then the two men banged fists together in the traditional northern oath of loyalty.

After they had ridden on some time in silence, Aremys decided to push his luck with the Mountain Man. "Now that you know my secret, perhaps you would share with me whatever it was that you held back earlier about your great friend Lothryn?"

Myrt looked taken aback and uncomfortable. "It was nothing of importance."

Aremys shrugged. "It seemed to me that you were troubled by the mention of his name. I thought you might want to share your burden with someone who would not judge you for it—an outsider you can trust."

Myrt glanced back at the barshi's unconscious figure,

then looked around surreptitiously, his expression uncertain. *Come on, tell me,* Aremys urged silently. He knew if ever there was a moment to learn about Wyl's savior, it was now, while Myrt was in a fragile state of mind and the bond Aremys had built between them was new and strong.

"Lothryn . . ." Myrt spoke the name as if in veneration. "Brave Lothryn was brought back to the fortress after the Morgravians escaped—well, all but one."

Aremys bit back the question that leapt to his throat. He must not disturb the man's flow of speech. There would be time to learn about Gueryn le Gant later.

"Koreldy and the woman, Elspyth, managed to get away—because of Lothryn's aid and the fact that we were facing several zerkons. Lothryn and I fought back to back together on Haldor's Pass, a dangerous escarpment. We killed three zerkons that day and lost several men. When the battle was over my great friend turned to me and held his wrists out to be bound. He didn't ask for mercy or even a quick death—both of which I had expected, and might even have given him. I loved him enough to give my own life for him, and I knew Cailech would execute me if I showed such mercy. But Lothryn knew Cailech would have instructed me to bring him back to face his ruler. He allowed me to keep my faith with my king."

It was Aremys's turn to whisper. "What happened?"

Myrt's expression became distraught. His voice shaking with tightly held-back tears, he continued. "I delivered him to Cailech. It was a private meeting and I was not permitted to be present. I have no idea what passed between them. Later, all the King would tell me was that Lothryn was undergoing a special punishment and we would not see him again. I asked whether he was to be killed and I'll never forget the King's reply. He said, 'He probably wishes I would kill him.' I saw a mixture of pain and regret in his face, Aremys. The King loved Lothryn like a brother, and his betrayal cut deeper than any other wound ever could."

Aremys sighed. "And there's been no sign of Lothryn since?"

Myrt shook his head, deeply upset. "We've tried. I know

Rashlyn knows something, but he's as mad as a pit of burning snakes. He makes little sense at the best of times."

As if on cue, they heard a sound behind them, a weak cry from the man slung across the trailing horse.

"He's stirring. We've tarried long enough. We shall speak again when we next get a chance alone," Aremys said and, as Myrt dropped back to check on Rashlyn, he clicked Galapek on toward the mammoth arch that swallowed them into the great stone fortress.

3

WYL'S PROGRESS ALONG THE DARKSTREAM WAS SLOW AS HE traveled against the current back toward the Thicket. His mind felt burdened rather than lightened by his meeting with Elysius and his heart was especially heavy at leaving Fynch. Further, his emotions were still in turmoil at the loss of his sister, Ylena, whose body he now inhabited, and by the disappearance of Aremys. He had precious few friends in his life now. To lose one so soon—especially one he trusted as he did Aremys—was devastating.

But it was leaving Fynch behind that troubled him the most. As he inched his way toward the Thicket, Wyl realized how important the youngster had become to him. Others, such as Elspyth and Aremys, had accepted the strangeness of his life, but Fynch had guessed his secret from the start and had protected him. Little Fynch, so humble and yet so wise, had saved not only Wyl's life but also that of a sovereign with his ingenuity. And then, following his own path, he had left the safety of Werryl, first to track down Romen's killer, and after obeying the pull of the Wild. The boy was deeply enmeshed in this whole business of Myrren's Gift, or at least in the curious life that Wyl was now leading, and Wyl was angry at himself for not insisting that Fynch leave Elysius and travel with him.

The truth of it was, he suddenly felt he needed Fynch. Their lives, strange though they both were, were entwined, and it suddenly occurred to Wyl that Fynch's involvement might be more than pure coincidence. Fynch had been at Myrren's burning; was it possible that he was magically tied to her gift, too?

Wyl sighed. Fynch aside, he was concerned about so many people that his only plan at this minute was to return to Timpkenny. He would stay overnight there before making a decision on his next move. The remainder of his journey up the Darkstream was curiously and happily uneventful—Ylena's fears mercifully remained at bay—and Samm was nowhere to be seen when he alighted, relieved, from the small craft. His intention had been to avoid the boatman and so it suited him that the cottage appeared deserted.

Wyl did not relish the notion of passing again through the mysterious Thicket, but he knew he could not wait too long to find the courage. Dark fell heavily and fast in this place, and he did not want to risk Samm coming across him. He walked briskly toward the dark line of yews that marked the border of the Thicket. Wyl was convinced that he could hear a dim buzz emanating from the enchanted forest; it frightened him, but as he had been allowed to pass through once before, he was counting on similar generosity again.

Wyl took a deep breath, closed his eyes reflexively, and pushed into the tangle. The Thicket's cool atmosphere chilled him instantly. The silence was disturbing. It was clear that the forest knew he was there, and the thought that this place could sense, think, and make decisions for itself was the most disconcerting notion of all.

Oddly, this time there were no snagging branches and no confusing pathways. Previously, when Knave had led him through, Wyl had felt sure that alone he would have lost himself among the yews for good. This time paths seemed to open themselves up to him. He shook his head with wonder. The Thicket was guiding him swiftly through its depths. It wanted him gone, was as glad to be rid of him as he was to have his back to it.

"Thank you," he whispered in genuine relief. Whether or not the Thicket heard he could not know, but he felt better for having offered his gratitude.

It was then that a terrible thought struck him: If the Thicket could guide him out, it was just as able to keep Aremys in. Was the mercenary still blundering around in the forest, trying hopelessly to escape?

Wyl overcame his intense fear, took the chance, and began to call to his friend. The somewhat desperate edge to his voice carried loudly through the dense overgrowth but did little more than scatter small animals he could not see. As if in response to the tension his concern for Aremys had created, Ylena's fear of enclosed spaces began to threaten again. He felt it first as a tightening in her chest, and recalled the identical tautness of emotion that had occurred just before he'd lost control of himself during his first journey on the Darkstream.

The familiar shallowness of breath hit him and he stopped moving. Was the Thicket's magic acute enough to sense this change in him? Instinctively, he began breathing into his cupped hands. He could not imagine how he remembered this trick, but it was something his father had taught Ylena when she was an infant. Panic, he recalled, had often overcome his young sister, prompted by any suggestion of being enclosed or hidden: the game hide-and-seek, looking into the dark depths of the well, or playing under Wyl's bed. To his knowledge, Ylena had not experienced this terror since she was a child, but obviously its ability to strike had traveled with her into adulthood. Wyl was grateful now for his memory of Fergys Thirsk's trick to calm his daughter; he quickly noticed a marked change in what had been steadily rising panic levels.

Whether or not the Thicket was aware of his discomfort, Wyl was fairly sure it deliberately steered him toward what might, at a stretch, be described as a clearing. His relief—or, more to the point, Ylena's—at the space was evident as her legs buckled, dropping him to the ground. It remained cool beneath the yews, but the oppressive atmosphere was not as marked, and Wyl knew that if he could get his breathing under control he would feel less anxious. He put Ylena's pretty head between her knees and forced her lungs to breathe slowly and deeply, as foot soldiers, suddenly overcome by fear of battle, were taught to do before the command to charge. He held this position for several minutes and was relieved that he could feel the anxiety lessening.

A soft sound above prompted him to raise his head and he was confronted by the largest owl he had ever seen. Strikingly marked, the majestic tawny blinked slowly and deliberately in the way owls do. Wyl watched it as intently as it was regarding him, wondering which of them would turn away first, if that indeed was what was expected.

He lost the staring contest. "And you are?" he said, feeling ridiculous but reminding himself that he had spoken to Knave without embarrassment. Why not this curious owl with such intelligence lurking in its large yellow eyes? He was rewarded for his faith.

*I am Rasmus,* the owl said into his mind, startling him.

"I hear you," Wyl replied, in awe of the splendid creature before him.

*That was my intention,* Rasmus said somewhat disdainfully, rotating its head in a disconcerting manner.

"How is it that we can communicate?" Wyl persisted. "Is it because of Myrren's Gift?"

The owl made a disgusted sound. *It is because I allow it, and because you are here.*

"In the Thicket, you mean?"

*Where else could I mean?*

Wyl felt an apology springing to his lips but resisted it. This creature was either baiting him or simply did not like him. "What do you want with me?" he asked, his tone direct.

Again the owl blinked. *We want you to leave,* it said firmly.

"Well, can't you just rid yourself of me?" Wyl replied, determined not to be cowed by this strange creature.

*If we choose to.*

Wyl sighed, irritated by the owl's superior manner. "Then choose it, owl, for leaving here is what I want too."

*If you want to be gone from here, why do you linger?* Rasmus asked, his tone suggesting he too was losing patience.

"I am not lingering," Wyl snapped. "I was guided to this spot, and if you're as magical as I suspect, you can probably sense the sorcery that has touched me."

*I can.*

"Then you know that this is not the body I was born with."

*And so?*

"And so this particular body does not care for the density or fearsome atmosphere of your Thicket."

*It is not mine,* the bird countered.

It was Wyl's turn to blink—with exasperation. He took a steadying breath; showing his fury would not help here. "The person whose body I walk in is scared of this place and was having breathing difficulties."

*We gathered.*

"Was this clearing deliberately created for my benefit?" Wyl was determined to find out the extent of the Thicket's abilities.

*Yes. Are you ready to leave?*

"Not until you answer a question."

*I am not beholden to you.*

Wyl took a gamble. "If you trust Knave, then you should trust me, for he and I are friends. I mean you and the creatures of the Thicket—or indeed the Thicket itself—no harm. The secret of your magic is safe with me."

There was a long pause. Wyl stood up, frustrated by the owl's stare and its silence. "You have let me pass through before. I know you have no intention of killing me."

*Ask your question,* the owl finally said, irritably.

Wyl curbed his enthusiasm and took a moment to consider how best to phrase his question. He sensed the owl would answer, at worst cryptically, and at best literally, so his question would have to be very clear.

"Where is Aremys living?" he asked carefully.

There was no hesitation from the owl. *He lives in the Razors.*

Wyl's relief spilled over. "Is he safe?"

*I have answered your question,* the owl replied, fractious now.

"Please," Wyl beseeched.

Rasmus made a peevish clicking noise. *Aremys is safe.*

Wyl wondered how much more the owl knew. The Thicket held many secrets; perhaps they could help him as he journeyed on. He had nothing more to lose other than the owl's patience, and that was already fast depleting. "Rasmus," Wyl began reasonably, "you have shared your name. Mine is Wyl. But then I'm sure you know that. Can we not be friends?"

*Yet another tiresome question?*

Wyl sat down deliberately. "Yes, I have questions. I know what you are concerned about, and I will not betray the Thicket. I owe it for keeping my friend Aremys safe and for helping me so far. I am your friend also."

*The Thicket has no friends of your kind, save one. You are not he.*

Wyl assumed the bird referred to Elysius. "Then let me ask what I need so I can help the others you do trust—Knave and . . . Fynch."

He had intended to say "Elysius," but "Fynch" came to his mind and slipped out first. He saw the bird react as he spoke his young friend's name, and the shrubs around him seemed to shudder. Was it the boy who interested the Thicket?

"I will protect Fynch always," he risked.

And was rewarded with a testy reply. *He does not require your protection. He has the protection of the Thicket.*

"I see," Wyl said, not really seeing anything but harking back to his earlier suspicion that Fynch had some special purpose in this dangerous game they were playing. Then a notion came to him as suddenly as a wasp sting and causing similar pain. "He's not coming to Werryl, is he?"

The bird said nothing at first, then sighed. At that soft sound in his head, Wyl felt hollow. He had lost Fynch. *Fynch has his own path to follow now,* Rasmus confirmed.

Although he had suspected as much, Wyl felt his heart sink at the owl's sorrowful words. Fynch's new path must be a dangerous one, he realized, or the owl would not have mentioned protection. Wyl also realized there was precious little he could do about it. The Thicket would not permit him to return to find Fynch, he knew. It obviously had its own reasons for helping the boy to follow this new road.

"Knave will be at his side, of course?" he ventured.

*Always,* Rasmus said.

"Thank you," said Wyl, and meant it. "I shall leave now. I am grateful to you, Rasmus, and the 'we' you speak of, for allowing me this time and for answering my questions."

He stood and bowed to the huge bird with marked respect, then walked away, presuming the Thicket would now guide him quickly to its fringe and toward Timpkenny. He was surprised to hear Rasmus call to him.

He turned. "Pardon?"

*I said, where are you going?* the owl repeated.

"I must make my way south to Werryl as quickly as I can."

*We will send you there.*

Wyl looked at the large bird quizzically. "Send me?"

*Come back to the clearing.*

"I don't understand." Wyl felt a thrill of fear run through him.

*You will. Stand before me and close your eyes. Do not open them.*

"I won't."

*If you disobey us, we shall never allow you to leave,* the owl warned.

Too much depended on his safe departure from this place. Wyl did as asked, wondering if this "sending" business was a small show of friendship after all.

*Be still,* the owl cautioned. *It will feel strange but you must trust us. Do not resist. Just let your body float. Remember, do not open your eyes.*

Wyl understood none of it but obeyed as a man used to taking orders.

*Farewell,* Rasmus said, and then Wyl felt a vast, chest-crushing pressure against his body. He wanted to open his eyes but fought the urge, having given his word. Breathing was all but impossible, but he refused to panic. He had to trust the owl.

Had he disobeyed the owl's strict instructions, he would

have seen Fynch before him. Wyl could not see the tears on Fynch's face or the goodbye the boy mouthed to his friend, but he felt the touch of the Gate Wielder as Ylena's trembling body was pushed through a thickened disk of air and disappeared.

*It is done,* Rasmus said. *Be at rest, Faith Fynch.*

Why do they refer to me as Faith?" Fynch whispered to Knave, who sat tall and imposing beside him in a special sunlit divide. Had he not seen it with his own eyes, Fynch would never have believed such a clearing existed in the Thicket. Curiously, the small light-drenched space added no particular cheer to the dense, dark, and brooding atmosphere, but Fynch was nonetheless glad for the brief respite from the chill.

*It is how we think of you.*

"What do you mean?"

*We have faith in you.*

Fynch wanted to ask more, but the words stilled in his mouth as creatures—many known to him only from folklore—began to gather at the fringe of the clearing.

"These are your friends?" he asked, his voice filled with wonder.

*They are the creatures of the Thicket.*

Fynch's attention was caught by a magnificent lion that watched him from the shadows. The animal shook itself and Fynch gasped to see wings extending from the proud cat's shoulders.

"Knave, that's the winged lion of legend."

*No legend as you can see, son. He exists.*

"I only know of him from the old tales and the carvings at Stoneheart. He . . . he is Wyl's mythical animal, who protects him."

*And yours?*

"Mine?" the boy said, awed as he caught sight of the equally legendary great bear. "My creature is . . ." He hesitated as a different animal invaded his mind, demanding to be named. He felt treacherous and pushed the thought away. "My animal is the unicorn."

*He comes to you now,* Knave said.

The other creatures fell silent as the beautiful animal emerged into the light. Its coat had a hue of the palest of blues, but the overall impression was of a pure, dazzling white; even its famed horn was a silvery white. It walked slowly and with such grace that Fynch held his breath, utterly captivated.

Tall and broad, the unicorn towered over the boy and his companion. *Child,* it said in a deep, musical voice. *It is my privilege to welcome you among us.*

Fynch was so overwhelmed that he began to weep. The unicorn bent its great head, careful not to touch the boy with its lethal horn, and nuzzled Fynch, who put his small arms around the creature's neck in worship. *My name is Roark,* it added, for his hearing alone.

"The privilege is mine, great Roark," Fynch whispered.

*Be bright, Faith Fynch. You are our hope,* the animal returned into his mind.

Fynch gathered his composure and dried his eyes. He looked about him uncertainly, registering the expectancy that hung in the air, and tried not to gawp at the amazing troupe of creatures gathered around him.

As one, they bowed, including Knave and the graceful Roark.

*You must acknowledge them,* Knave whispered into Fynch's startled mind. *Put your awe aside, son. You are to whom we give our loyalty. Assume your birthright.*

Fynch did not understand. He was a gong boy. A child of low birth and even lower rank. How could he acknowledge homage from these majestic creatures of legend? Who was he to assume such a role?

It was as if Roark could hear his thoughts. *Fynch, will you accept our obeisance and loyalty?*

Elysius's words echoed in Fynch's memory: *Perhaps the Thicket needs you for more than simply watching over a Gate.*

He could not escape his destiny, he knew this. His life was no longer his own to direct or to make decisions about. Choices had already been made and promises given.

Fynch steadied himself and found his voice. "Creatures of the Thicket," he called, "I will make myself worthy of your faith."

He bowed, low and long. When he stood upright again, he felt a new strength pulsing through him, from his toes through to the tips of his fingers. He realized that it must be the Thicket communicating with him, sending him nourishing power. He felt charged with it, and could not help the radiant smile that broke out onto his face.

"Tell me what it is I must do," he asked the creatures. "I am your servant."

It was Rasmus who spoke on behalf of the creatures and of the Thicket itself. *Be seated, Fynch,* he offered from his perch.

Fynch lowered himself to the ground. Knave and Roark remained standing, flanking Fynch on either side.

*Child, you already know what it is we ask of you,* the owl said.

"I do?"

*Elysius shared the same desire.*

"Rashlyn," Fynch murmured.

The creatures and trees all shuddered their shared hatred for the man.

*Yes,* Rasmus concurred. *You must destroy him.*

"What is it that frightens you so about this man?"

*He is tainted, and he wants to use his power to corrupt all that is natural about the world. His evil is born of his jealously at being unable to manipulate Nature. More than anything, he passionately desires the power to control all creatures. With this at his disposal, he would rule all realms. Imagine him being able to call upon eagle or zerkon alike? Imagine him commanding them to do evil, the other animals powerless to refuse him? You must destroy him!*

"I don't think I am capable," Fynch protested.

*The Thicket and its creatures will help you.*

Strengthened by the thrum of power that bristled through him from the ground of the Thicket, and emboldened by the love and loyalty that surrounded him, Fynch took a deep breath. "Then I ask for nothing more than your faith in me."

It was the right thing to say. Knave confirmed as much with a gently uttered *Bravo, child* into his mind while the creatures showed their trust and delight, some leaping into the air, others rearing to stand on two legs, still others squawking or braying.

Fynch laughed. He was filled with a joy he had never known before. He suddenly felt he belonged to all of them. He reached for Knave and touched the great dog's head.

*I don't believe it,* Knave said, his tone humble. *The King comes.*

"King?" Fynch repeated, puzzled. Since they had begun communicating via this special mindtalk, Fynch had found Knave's manner to be mostly serious, like himself. The dog was not one for jests or shallow thoughts. He spoke only when there was something to say, and during most of their conversations it had been his role to counsel Fynch. The boy knew of Knave's graveness, and the dignity that emanated from his solid, dependable presence, but never had he seen the dog show humility. And this was no small humility: Knave sounded filled with reverence for whatever it was that was arriving. "Knave—"

*Hush,* said the dog, and a powerful beating sound made Fynch raise his head and squint into the light above. Something plunged toward them—a suggestion of a shadow at first, that darkened until it cut out the light entirely and Fynch no longer squinted but was wide-eyed with both fear and awe.

"The warrior dragon," he breathed.

*Our king,* Roark said softly, veneration in his voice, as the mighty creature alighted in the clearing.

The creatures bent low to exalt the hallowed creature that stood before them, its famed, darkly shimmering colors gloriously filling the clearing.

Fynch needed no prompting. He fell to his knees immediately, then prostrated himself. Closing his eyes, he cast a prayer to Shar in thanks for the blessing of this day and what it had brought him.

*Fynch,* said a voice, as rich and mellow as treacle.

"Your majesty," Fynch replied, not daring to raise his head.

*Come stand before me,* the voice commanded. Fynch summoned his courage. With Knave and Roark's whispered encouragement, he opened his eyes and looked upon the King of all the beasts. There was no doubting that royalty stood before him, no wondering if this glorious creature was worthy of such exaltation. Fynch held his breath as every fiber of his being suddenly felt newly alive, restored somehow in the presence of such grandeur.

Like everyone else who looked upon the dragon pillar in the Pearlis Cathedral with awe, Fynch had believed the warrior dragon to be just legend. Associated with the Morgravian sovereign, it was the most impressive of all the mythical creatures but no more real than the winged lion. But now the King of Kings stood in all his glory before him, as real as Fynch himself.

*Faith Fynch,* the King said. *Be welcome.*

"Thank you, your majesty," Fynch stammered, bowing. "I am proud to serve you."

*And we are indebted for that service, child, which is given so bravely by one so young.*

Fynch said nothing. He had no response to such generous praise.

The warrior dragon continued: *And still we ask more of you.*

"I will give my life if it is so required."

The King regarded him through dark, wise eyes. *We shall do everything in our power to prevent you relinquishing something so precious.*

"Please tell me, my king"—*my true king,* Fynch thought to himself—"what it is that you ask of me."

The beast wasted no further time. *The King of Morgravia brings shame to his kind. He is of the warrior clan—of my blood, you could say—but he disgusts me.*

"Celimus is indeed shameful," Fynch agreed quietly.

*That said, there have been Kings before who have disappointed and we have ignored them. The Thicket and its creatures do not meddle in the affairs of men, child. We have watched you kill one another for centuries and we have not involved ourselves. But on this occasion we have been drawn into the struggles of mankind because of the misuse of magic.*

"You speak of Myrren's Gift, your majesty."

The King hesitated briefly. *That included, yes. It was wrong of Elysius to channel his power through his daughter to such a vengeful end. His power, once we granted him access to the Wild, was to be used only for the good of the natural world.*

Fynch felt compelled to defend Elysius. "I don't think he fully realized what the repercussions would be, your majesty."

*Magic is always dangerous, Fynch, even when used with the best of intentions. There are always repercussions, although sometimes we are unable to see what they are until it is too late. That is why the Thicket and its magic have been deliberately shielded from men. Myrren's Gift has already claimed four lives. Wyl Thirsk should have died; instead he is abroad and carrying a deadly enchantment. None of us knows where it could end.*

"Wyl didn't ask for Myrren's Gift, your majesty," Fynch mumbled, trying not to sound petulant.

*I know, my son,* the King replied gently. *I feel great sorrow for Wyl, who is one of the best among men—as was his father. It is the magic that troubles me, and how it will reverberate through the world of men. I mean to end it here.*

"You don't mean to destroy Wyl?" Fynch exclaimed.

*In a way he is already dead,* the creature answered.

Fynch did not like the resignation in the Dragon King's voice. He grasped for placation, desperate to prevent this powerful being from hurting Wyl. "The Thicket and its creatures have asked me to kill Rashlyn, your majesty, and with their help I will endeavor to rid the land of the destroyer. Both brothers will be no more. The magic will end."

*Not really, child, for now you possess it. Rashlyn wishes to control the natural world. He is a corrupter of natural things. He wants power over the beasts. But Celimus is just as dangerous. He too wants power, although of a different kind. I fear that if we do not destroy Rashlyn, these two ambitious men might join together. I know how the minds of greedy men work, and should they claim the Razors and Bri-avel, they will almost certainly turn their attention toward the Wild. With Celimus's help, Rashlyn will try to destroy the Thicket.* The King sighed. *We do not wish to engage in such a confrontation.*

"What can I do to help, your majesty?" Fynch asked, desperation seeping into his voice.

*I grant you permission to use the magic of the Thicket to aid Wyl Thirsk in his bid to rid Morgravia of its king, for without Celimus I do not believe Rashlyn's madness can be fully unleashed.*

Fynch nodded thoughtfully, relief flooding his small body to learn that the Warrior King did not mean to attack Wyl directly. He recognized that the dragon warrior had not offered his own mighty strength or powers, only that of the Thicket. Fynch also knew that the creatures of the Thicket would insist on keeping their secrets. He already felt a part of this mysterious community and knew he would do everything in his power to protect them and their magic.

"Celimus has no heir," Fynch cautioned, even though he presumed the royal creature knew as much.

*Morgravia will survive. Do what you must. Knave is your guide—use his wisdom well, child, and your own powers sparingly. I presume Elysius explained the price you may be required to pay?*

Fynch nodded. "He did."

The King waited, wondering whether the child would expand on his brief answer. A plea for mercy perhaps, a query as to whether his life could somehow be spared. But no further words came. The King beat his wings in appreciation of the boy's humility; he was prepared to give everything of himself for those he loved and asked for nothing in return.

The warrior dragon's gaze penetrated deep into Fynch's heart and he was surprised to see there a startling and precious secret regarding this boy. He had not expected it, but the discovery warmed him. Should he share it? The child's life was already forfeit; what could be gained from adding more confusion? The King felt sorrow well up that they would use this boy so. But there was no other way. Fynch was the sacrifice, though it cut him deeply to send his own to die.

*Then we remain in your debt, Fynch. The Thicket and its creatures will always hold you in their hearts. We bless you and hold our faith in you with reverence.*

There was too much emotion swirling through Fynch for him to risk another word to this mightiest of beasts. Instead he bowed to show his complete acceptance. The royal creature acknowledged it with another powerful flapping of his wings, driving Fynch to the ground as he lifted effortlessly into the air and disappeared.

Roark and Knave were at his side again.

*He has not appeared to us in an age,* Knave said, the awe still evident in his voice. *He came to pay homage only to you, child.*

Fynch, overwhelmed by this fateful meeting with the King of the Beasts, was unable to respond. Knave understood and nuzzled his friend's small hand. *Come, Faith Fynch, we have a journey to begin.*

# 4

❦

OST IN BLEAK THOUGHTS, QUEEN VALENTYNA LEANED HER EL-
bows against the cool whitestone of the walkway that linked two of the palace towers. It was her private place, one she rarely shared. The last person she had permitted to spend time with her here was Koreldy, and before him, Fynch. She could not help but think of those two friends now, both lost to her, both keenly missed. With her face cupped in her hands she stared out across the Briavellian moors she loved so much and marveled at a hawk hovering far ahead in the distance, watching patiently as it waited for its prey. Suddenly it plunged, arrowlike, toward the ground,

making the Queen breathless for the small creature about to lose its life.

That was how she felt. Vulnerable, and now suddenly exposed and helpless. Celimus of Morgravia was the hawk and she the creature giving up her life to him.

Rumblings of war were filtering back from Briavel's spies in Morgravia. By all reports, the Legion was preparing for battle and Valentyna did not have to ponder too hard to guess at their enemy. Was it a ruse? Just an empty threat? Her instincts told her it was, but she would still need to tread with the greatest of care. Her relationship with Celimus teetered on a knife edge and all that stood between peace for her subjects and almost certain slaughter was her written consent to marriage with the Morgravian King.

For that tenuous security, she owed thanks to Chancellor Krell, who had forced her hand and made her send the letter. And yet Valentyna could only hang her head in despair at the damage done by Krell's subsequent well-meaning but short-sighted interference in writing to his counterpart in Morgravia, Chancellor Jessom. Oh, she could scream just thinking about it. In fact, she was still so angry at the old man's actions it had taken all her willpower to maintain her composure at Krell's funeral. He had been quietly buried in the palace cemetery. No family had come for him; he went into the ground as lonely as he went to his god, believing he was despised.

Krell had diligently and tirelessly worked for the Briavellian royal family for nigh on twoscore years. He was like a piece of old furniture: comfortable, reliable, always there in the same place. Valentyna had grown up knowing that her father relied on him, and had come to appreciate his loyalty and advice herself. Despite her anguish that he had invited such ruin with an ill-considered move, Valentyna could not help but feel a keen sorrow that the good man would be remembered for that one poor decision among a host of wise ones during a solid and devoted career serving the Crown.

Now, in a quiet moment of reflection and private recrimination, she regretted her harsh words to him. She had no doubt that she had prompted his suicide and it was something she knew she would have to live with. Valentyna had shed her tears for him in private and she would be lying if she did not admit to herself that she missed his steadfast counsel. But she had also spoken the truth when she told him she could never forgive him for his terrible error. He had overstepped his authority and in doing so had risked the lives of all Briavellians.

Morgravia's king was vain, avaricious, and cruel, but he was not a dullard. Because of Krell's poor judgment, Celimus would now know about Alyd Donal's remains being smuggled into Briavel, and that the Queen he thought he had well and truly cornered was consorting with his enemies.

A man cleared his throat quietly at one end of the walkway to interrupt her musings. She looked toward him, knowing who it would be—one of the few she allowed to come to her here if duty called. All other servants were banned from tracking her down to the bridge.

"Liryk. Please join me," she said. He bowed in respect and walked to the center of the bridge.

"It's beautiful, isn't it?" Valentyna said, indicating the view before them.

"More than that, your highness," her army's commander admitted. "It feeds the soul."

"Liryk," she said, unable to help herself, "you're a poet."

Liryk smiled. It was good to hear her playful. That tone had all but disappeared these past weeks. "No, your majesty. I just never get tired of these moors. I'm always happy to see them when I return to Werryl after being away."

"And so how are you and I going to give this up?"

"My queen?"

"This," she said, moving her hand in a sweeping arc. "We will be giving this to Morgravia." There was a note of anger in her voice. "It will no longer be ours."

"Not giving, your highness," Liryk proposed gently. "I'd prefer to think of it as sharing."

"Celimus is forcing us to give Briavel to him," Valentyna said coldly. "He is blackmailing me, Commander, and there's not a thing I can do about it. If I want our young men to live, I have to give up the realm."

"Pardon me, your highness, but I—and I think I can speak for all your loyal subjects in this—do not view it that way. We applaud this move."

The Queen sighed. "And I am grateful for that," she said. "But will you thank me when King Celimus starts to stamp his own brutal form of authority across Briavel?"

Liryk had no answer, and in truth, the Queen did not expect one. "What news did you come here to tell me, Commander Liryk?"

"The Legion is preparing for movement east now, your highness. If we are going to placate our neighboring King, we need to do it soon."

Valentyna closed her eyes and took a deep breath. She cast one more fond glance toward the moors and then gave brisk orders.

"Have Crys Donal summoned, please. I will meet with you both in my study. Elspyth too."

"At once, your highness."

Valentyna watched him leave, hating what she was about to do.

The Queen dismissed the servant and poured the two men a glass of wine herself.

"Where is Elspyth?" she inquired of Liryk as he took the goblet from her.

"Your highness, she is nowhere to be found," he answered, silently happy for the woman's disappearance. He had agreed with Krell that Elspyth's influence on the Queen was dangerous. The Morgravian woman had fired their queen's spirit—made her feel strong and encouraged her to defy Celimus.

Valentyna glanced at Crys, who shrugged. "I haven't seen her for a couple of days, if truth be known. I thought she was with you, your majesty."

"Strange," Valentyna admitted. "Your search has been thorough?" she asked her commander.

"I've sent several runners to comb the palace, your highness. She's certainly not in any of the usual places."

"Has anyone checked her chambers?" Crys asked. "You

had lent her some garments, your highness," he added. "Are they still there?"

"You think she's fled?" the Queen exclaimed.

"Did she tell you about a man called Lothryn?" Crys replied, calmly sipping his wine. He suspected that they would not find Elspyth. She had mentioned several times to him that she was no longer needed here. He also suspected his own stay had worn thin, and who could blame the Briavellians with the Legion gathering in force across the border?

The Queen nodded slowly. "Only vaguely."

"There's a story attached to him," he explained. "It involves Koreldy." Once again it pained him to see the Queen react to that man's name. Wyl had given firm instructions that Valentyna was not to learn the truth about Koreldy, but it seemed to Crys unkind not to let her know that the person she obviously loved was not dead as she suspected but roaming the land in a new guise. Crys felt a lurch of despair as he remembered that terrible night at Felrawthy. The day after had been worse, but he knew he must not think on that now. *Bury your hurts,* his mother used to say. *Bring them out only when you're alone and strong enough to look at them.* And so he had somehow buried the despair of losing his family so cruelly and was trying not to dwell on their deaths.

"Crys?"

He was embarrassed to realize both the Queen and Liryk were watching him.

"I—I'm sorry. Lost myself there," he said, not wanting to say more.

"You were telling us about Elspyth and Lothryn," Valentyna prompted, deliberately avoiding mentioning Koreldy by name.

"That's right," Crys continued. "The Mountain Dweller Lothryn saved the lives of Elspyth and Koreldy in the Razors. No one knows if he survived Cailech's wrath at his betrayal. Elspyth is determined to learn his fate."

Neither of them referred to their knowledge that Elspyth was in love with Lothryn. "And you think she's gone back?" Valentyna suggested.

"I think she's capable of doing something that bullheaded, yes," he said, and smiled gently to reassure the Queen that he admired Elspyth for her courage.

"Into the Razors?" Liryk queried. "Alone?"

"I don't know, sir. She's a passionate girl. I don't think fear stops her from doing anything. If not for Elspyth, I would be dead with the rest of my family."

The new Duke of Felrawthy could refer to his loved ones now without threat of anger or tears. His brief time in Werryl, offering distance from all things familiar, and the new title by which everyone seemed determined to address him, had made the difference between his collapsing into inconsolable anguish or rising to the challenge of what he was born and bred to do. It was what his fine parents would have expected of him.

A knock came at the door. Liryk put his glass down. "Shall I see to it, your highness? It may be the messengers."

"Please," the Queen said, distracted as she pondered the business of Elspyth's disappearance. "I miss Krell," she muttered.

Crys held his tongue. No one had heard the exchange between the Queen and her chancellor that had preceded his death, but Valentyna had openly admitted that she had driven him to anguish with her harsh criticism. Crys had to admire the Queen for her forthright manner; she refused to shrink from blame but accepted and dealt with it as best she could. Krell's death had been a shock for everyone, most of all Liryk, but the doughty soldier had kept his feelings to himself and remained stoic throughout the funeral and the ensuing mourning that had gripped the palace.

Crys sipped his wine quietly, wondering why he had been summoned to what appeared to be a formal meeting. It would be better for Valentyna, he knew, if he were to leave Briavel. Perhaps he should offer and save her the trial of asking him to do just that.

Liryk returned to disturb his thoughts. "Your majesty, we found this note in Elspyth's chamber."

"Anything else?" Valentyna asked as she broke the wax seal. "Clothes?"

"Nothing, your highness," he replied, watching her frown as she quickly read the note's contents.

Valentyna looked up and sighed. "Your hunch is correct, Crys. She believes she has done what she came here to do and has taken her leave."

"Gone to the Razors?" Crys inquired.

"It doesn't say but I suspect you're right. I know how fond she was of this man Lothryn. If I were her, I too would want to know the truth of his fate."

There was another knock at the door. Valentyna could not disguise her frustration at being interrupted again. She stuffed the note into her pocket and stood. "Gentlemen, I'm going for a ride. We shall continue this meeting this evening, please, when we can talk without disturbance. There are many things to discuss and I need to think. Liryk, would you see to that?" She nodded toward the door. "I'll leave by the back way."

The two men stood and watched her go.

The highest point of the moors was the farthest Valentya could get from her subjects—or so she liked to believe—and the ideal place to vent her fears or frustrations. Her ever-present escort, however, was hovering nearby, so she swallowed the bloodcurdling shriek she longed to let rip. She gave a deep groan instead. Too many of those she loved or trusted had been taken from her or left her. She stared back toward the palace and counted them off softly to herself.

Her father: murdered. Wyl Thirsk: murdered. Romen Koreldy: murdered. Fynch, her little rock of strength: disappeared, and with him the strange yet somehow reassuring presence of Knave. Now Elspyth, her new friend and confidante, had disappeared as well, almost certainly advancing toward her own death as she ventured into the Mountain Kingdom to discover the fate of her beloved Lothryn.

Valentyna paused in her account of her personal sorrows to think on those of Crys Donal. An entire family slaughtered in one evening. So much death. And now, in order to protect Briavel, she would have to banish her latest friend too. That was what she needed to discuss with the new Duke of Felrawthy, but this afternoon, with all of its interruptions, conversation had proved impossible.

The Queen of Briavel shook her head with despair. Almost all of this destruction swirling about her was the work of one man. One cruel, scheming, greedy man. The man she would have to marry if she wanted to prevent further death.

She cast a disconsolate glance toward the soldiers shuffling in the shade of the copse a short distance away. Three were now being sent to shadow her every move. She hated it, but put up with it. Liryk's caution was well founded, but she missed her freedom. She inhaled the sweet air of the moors and felt even more despondent. Everyone seemed to be worrying about her at the moment. She sensed her advisers observing her, could feel their concern tightening around her like a bandage, constricting her free will. Valentyna knew what they feared—and they were right to fear it, for if she could find a way out of this marriage, she would renege in a blink. She knew such a dream was impossible, though. No one was going to save her. The nobles had told her to find Ylena Thirsk, but that was pointless. How could it make any difference? Ylena's word might convince them that Celimus was a cold-blooded murderer, but she knew it would not make them change their minds about the marriage.

She thought about Ylena Thirsk and the terrible things the young woman had experienced. Crys had explained to Valentyna what Ylena had been through just to get herself to Felrawthy. It had made the Queen shudder to imagine how Wyl's sister had coped with yet more terror after what she had already suffered at Stoneheart. Ylena was younger than she and had shown such courage. She would have to find similar courage now and face her destiny. Her father had fought to keep Briavel safe. She must do the same, just in a different manner. She would buy its peace with her body. Give it over to that hateful man, let him parade it before his minions and use her for his pleasures. But he would not have her love—ever. That belonged to one alone, and he was now dead. In giving her body to Celimus, however, she might still attain something untainted, something good. They might produce a child. And into that child she would pour all of her love, everything she denied Celimus and had hoped to give to Romen Koreldy. She would raise a proud sovereign to take the joint throne of Morgravia and Briavel one day.

Valentyna sighed as the soft breeze tousled her already messy hair. "Give me a sign, Shar," she said to the gentle wind, hoping it would carry her plea to the god. "Show me that marrying Celimus is the right decision."

She felt like weeping at her pathetic words. Instead she wiped away the single tear that had fallen, rubbed at her other eye just in case, and willed herself to be strong. She would live up to the woman her father believed she had become. She strode back toward the soldiers. They had already spotted her movement and busied themselves with preparing the horses to ride again.

Squinting into the sun, Valentyna did not see the bird at first. It was its gentle song that attracted her attention and she looked around for the music maker. It was perched on a low branch of the great elm she was about to walk beneath. She recognized its family immediately; King Valor had been a keen bird spotter and had gone to some pains to school his only child into recognizing various species. This bird was a beautiful little chaffinch and its pretty music made her smile. She whistled back at it as she passed by, and heard it continue to sing as she departed the copse.

It was only as Valentyna guided her horse onto Werryl Bridge some half hour later that she realized she had been humming a tune to herself on the journey back. The bird-song had reminded her of a traditional Briavellian ballad: "Wait for Me, My Love." Valentyna had always loved its melody and its lyrics were beautiful; in fact, her fondness for the song was well known throughout the kingdom and the court minstrel had serenaded her with it on her nine-teenth nameday. She began to sing it now privately in her mind and the words stayed with her as she ascended into the palace proper.

Ranald, a stableboy, bowed and reached for the Queen's reins.

"Thank you, Ranald," Valentyna said, and found a smile for the eager boy.

"Your highness." He beamed, unable to mask his pleasure at serving the Queen so directly.

"It was a lovely ride," she said to him, enjoying his enthusiasm, wishing she could be a child again, without a care in the world.

"I'm glad, your highness. Bonny's a beautiful girl. My favorite," he chirped, ignoring the scowl from the stablemaster, who had come out to watch his young charge receive the horses correctly and no doubt thought him far too chatty.

"Mine too," Valentyna said, winking at Ranald. As she turned away from the boy the refrain of the ballad filled her mind again—and its resonance struck her.

> Wait for me, my love;
> I shall return one day.
> Accept not another's words;
> With me only, I pray.

Valentyna froze in the courtyard as the words played over in her mind. Men walked around her and horses neighed. Dogs growled over a bone and busy servants crisscrossed the yard on various errands, calling to one another. Among the activity, their queen stood still and silent, deep in her own thoughts. What had sounded so poignant and charming when sung on her nameday now sounded like a message from the dead. A warning.

"Romen!" she whispered fearfully, her breath catching in her throat.

"Your majesty, are you unwell?" she heard someone inquire.

"I'm fine," she stammered, coming back to the present and almost running from the courtyard. She flew into the palace and up the beautiful staircase, and up the next flight and the next. Servants watched, perplexed, as their sovereign ignored their salutations and curtsies, rushing past them toward her study on the topmost level, her boots clicking loudly on the flagstones. Finally she came to her father's former chamber and slammed the door behind her.

Leaning against its solid wood panels, she held her head as her breath came in great sad wrenchings. *Wait for me, my love.* Was this Shar's sign? Was this a message? What had prompted the song and its lyrics to come into her head? The bird! A chaffinch! Was this a warning from Fynch? Was he asking her to wait? For whom? Romen was dead! Cold, lifeless, bloodless . . . gone.

She realized she was sobbing and felt ashamed of herself for losing control. What was happening to her? Storming out of meetings, crying violently, listening to birds, believing in magic. She was going mad.

But she had asked for a sign. Perhaps this was it. She could be imagining it, of course, clutching at anything to save herself from Celimus, but it felt so right to believe it.

"But who am I waiting for?" she asked the quiet of her room.

She was startled by a knock at the door. "A moment, please," she called, instantly embarrassed at being found in such a discomposed state. She quickly splashed water over her face from a basin in a tiny closet and dried herself with a linen cloth, then smoothed back her hair as best she could.

She touched her fingers to her father's desk and drew strength from the solid wood, then took a steadying breath. Her mind was racing in all directions, but she had duties to perform. She needed to be steadfast. Briavel still looked to her for leadership, even as it collectively cast her to the wolves—or wolf, she thought bitterly.

Valentyna cleared her throat. "Come."

One of the older pages opened the door and bowed. "Your majesty, forgive my disturbance."

"That's all right, Justen. Who has sent you?"

"Commander Liryk, your majesty. He asked me to find you the moment you returned from your ride. He says it is urgent."

"Oh? A problem?"

"A visitor, your majesty."

Valentyna frowned. "Another one? Can't Liryk handle it?" she said irritably.

The page blinked, uncomfortable, and she felt immediately contrite. "Did Commander Liryk give you the name of this visitor, Justen?" she asked, more gently now.

"Yes, your majesty. It is a woman by the name of Ylena Thirsk."

# 5

MAEGRYN MET THE RIDERS AND WAS ALARMED TO SEE THE state Rashlyn was in.

"He'll be all right," Aremys assured the anxious stablemaster as he handed him the reins of Galapek and Rashlyn's horse.

"I couldn't care less about him," Maegryn said, and the vehemence in his voice surprised Aremys. "But the King will be alarmed and that makes us all uneasy. Did you have any problems with the horses?"

"Galapek got himself a little rattled over something, but he calmed quickly. Just skittish," Aremys answered, skirting the truth. The fewer lies he told the better. "He's more incredible to ride than I could have imagined. Thank you, Maegryn."

The man could not help himself; he smiled widely at the praise. "Yes, he's a beauty, this one. A real find."

"Where did he come from?" Aremys put the question casually.

"The barshi gave him as a present to the King. Had the horse sent in secretly from somewhere, apparently. He won't tell anyone from where."

"That's a little odd, isn't it? You'd think that if there were more like this one, the King would be keen to know."

Maegryn shrugged. "We're not allowed to ask too much about Galapek, sir." He looked embarrassed. "I'll be off, then, sir. I'm glad you enjoyed the ride."

Aremys knew there would be little further information to be won from Maegryn today. "Thank you. I hope you won't mind if I look in on him again?"

"I'm sure he'll be glad to see you, sir. You're one of the very few he permits near him. I think he's taken a shine to you." The stablemaster smiled.

Aremys stroked Galapek's twitching withers as the horse was led away. He was hoping for another sign from the animal but got nothing.

Myrt was barking orders for Rashlyn—who was lying on the ground still mumbling his strange nonsense—to be taken to his private quarters and attended by a physic. Then the Mountain Man turned to Aremys. "Come on," he said. "The worst is still before us."

Aremys sighed, needing no confirmation. Cailech.

They tracked the King down to his wine cellar, cata-comblike chambers dug into the ground beneath a separate stone building. Descending the flagged stairs into the musty darkness, Aremys smelled earth and spice; mixed with the aroma of yeast and the oak of the barrels, it was a comforting blend. It was cool down here but not cold; the temperature would remain much the same year round, he guessed, and the vaulted ceilings combined with the peace and stillness to give the cellar a chapellike quality.

"We're sorry to interrupt you, your majesty," Myrt began.

The King turned from his discussion with the cellarmaster and grinned at the newcomers. *He's in a good mood,* Aremys thought. *What a pity we're about to ruin it.*

"Farrow, you have to try this!" Cailech called over the barrels. "It's to be our best vintage yet." The King slapped his cellarmaster on the back in praise, then lifted the long-handled tasting cup to his lips and drained it. "Ah, nectar," he said, delighted.

"Sire," Myrt bowed. When he straightened, his expres-

sion in the diffused light of the beeswax candles was sufficiently somber to win Cailech's attention. The King's smile
faded.

"You look like you've swallowed bad meat, Myrt. What's
wrong?"

"It's the barshi, sire," the warrior began. Cailech handed
the tasting cup back to the cellarmaster, who stepped aside.
"He's unwell," Myrt added.

"Oh?" Cailech looked toward Aremys. "Farrow, what's
this all about?"

Aremys was surprised to be brought into the conversation.
He wanted to clear his throat but knew this might make him
appear nervous, so he just began talking, sticking as closely
to the truth as he could. "We were resting, my lord, after a
ride around the lake."

"We were at the Ring, sire," Myrt interjected.

Cailech nodded. "Go on." Again he looked to Aremys.

"I was drinking at the stream and Myrt and Rashlyn were
leaning against the boulders. Rashlyn was eating, and was
seemingly in good health. We had been discussing my
headaches and he had just approached me at the water's
edge to hand me a small bottle of a concoction he said would
ease my discomfort—when the horses distracted us." Aremys had decided that the plain truth, rather than a version of
it, was the only course with Cailech.

"It was Galapek, sire," Myrt said. "Something startled him;
we don't know what. We couldn't see anything near him."

"And?" Cailech said, the hard green gaze impaling Aremys where he stood.

"Well, as I recall, I rushed over to help Myrt calm the stallion. It was over as quickly as it began—perhaps he was
stung by a bee or something irritated him. When we turned
back to Rashlyn, he was lying on the ground, seemingly
having some sort of attack."

"Attack?"

"Like a fit, sire," Myrt qualified.

"He lost control of his body for a few moments," Aremys
said, "and then he became rigid. I checked immediately for
a pulse—it was strong—but by then he was unconscious."

The King's face showed nothing of what he was thinking. "How long did this episode last?"

"It was over almost as soon as it began," Myrt said. "We laid him on his horse and got him back here as fast as we could." He dared not look at Aremys as he said this. Hurrying back to the fortress had been the last thing on their minds.

"And where is Rashlyn now?"

"He has regained his wits, sire, so I had him carried to his room and ordered that a physic attend him," Myrt reported.

"You have no idea what this is about?" The King looked between the two men.

Myrt shrugged and shook his head. Aremys figured the King needed more than sheepish shrugs. "I thought it might have been the cheese sticking in his throat, but his passage was clear," he fabricated. "And Myrt tells me the food was fresh, so we know he has not been poisoned. Does he suffer from fits, my lord?" he added innocently.

"It seems he does now," Cailech growled, the breezy mood blown through and replaced with what felt like a gathering storm. "I shall go and see him. How was Galapek, Farrow?"

The King switched subjects and moods so adroitly that Aremys was sure he would never learn to prepare himself for it.

"Even more magnificent than I'd hoped, thank you, sire. A truly beautiful creature. I hope you will let me ride him again sometime." He sensed, rather than saw, the glance Cailech and Myrt exchanged.

"I'm glad to hear it," the King replied. "Myrt, you can accompany me to the barshi's chambers. Farrow—"

"Sire?"

"I'll see you later. You will be leaving in the early hours of tomorrow for Morgravia."

Back in chamber with the familiar guard outside, Aremys sighed in frustration. He was not going to attempt an escape and felt sure Cailech knew this. But it seemed the King was keen to remind him that he was a prisoner and under the control of the monarch; hence the armed guard.

"Not for long," Aremys muttered under his breath as he flung his water flask into a corner. He would gladly leave for Morgravia in a few hours, and from there he would win his freedom. He liked the Mountain People. He did not even mind living here in the fortress among them, could almost see a pleasant life in the Razors stretching out before him, but he was beholden to no man, not even a king, and certainly not one who stopped just short of shackling him.

It irritated him that Cailech could be so friendly one moment and so domineering the next. Surely the King knew that Aremys would far rather give his help to him than Celimus? In truth, though, he could not blame Cailech entirely for remaining suspicious. One didn't become—or remain—a king if one trusted everyone, especially strangers who appeared out of the blue with no tangible explanation for how they had arrived. Especially strangers who reacted strongly to the King's own enchanted horse.

Aremys replayed the afternoon's events in his mind. Rashlyn's collapse had definitely coincided with the animal's shriek, he was sure of it, which meant something had disturbed them both. There had been nothing in the vicinity to alarm them or it would have created a similar reaction in himself and Myrt. No, this was something else. More like a disturbance in the strange magic that riddled the horse. Could it be that the wild-looking healer was bound to the stallion in some way? What if Rashlyn himself had cast some sort of spell upon the horse? Why, though? Why would he interfere with the animal?

Because Cailech had asked him to?

But why would the King ask something like that? Aremys thought it unlikely that Cailech possessed the cruelty that would prompt the idea of hurting an animal the way Galapek had so obviously been injured.

But what if the idea had come from Rashlyn? "Because Rashlyn could and Cailech allowed him to," Aremys said quietly into the silence of his chamber.

The notion took a firm place among his thoughts. He nodded. Yes, that made more sense. Aremys thought back to Wyl's account of Cailech's horrific actions during the feast, when he had presented the Morgravian prisoners as a dish to his people. Wyl had been sure Rashlyn had been behind that hideous episode, but that suggested the barshi was capable of persuading the King to do things not of his own volition. How could Cailech, usually so dominant, be so weak in the company of Rashlyn?

Aremys had no answer for that. He returned to his original puzzle. Something had disturbed the magic linking the barshi and the horse. It couldn't have been the Thicket or he too would have felt the effects, but perhaps it had resonated through the Thicket, thereby explaining his more subtle reaction. Had Wyl done something to disturb the balance? Unlikely, or the Thicket would probably have protested more strongly.

Aremys put his head in his hands, frustrated by his swirling thoughts that took him nowhere. *Think!* he commanded himself. Could it have something to do with Elysius? Had Wyl made it through and met the manwitch? Was that it? "Possibly," he muttered, but that did not help him get any closer to the riddle that was Galapek.

And then he remembered the most chilling moment of the whole sorry afternoon. How could he have forgotten it? The horse had somehow communicated a name to him: Elspyth. He began to pace now. It could be a coincidence, of course, but an unlikely one. The horse must have belonged to Lothryn, or somehow held the secret of what had happened to Lothryn.

Frustrated, Aremys punched the wall. If Cailech wanted to punish Lothryn, why hurt his horse? And how would a horse know about Elspyth, for Shar's sake!?

*You're going mad, Farrow,* he told himself. *Now you've contrived a magical talking horse.*

He decided to clean up and go in search of Myrt and more answers. Something else had begun to niggle at him and he wanted to find out if it had any basis in fact. Discovering he was right might not advance his cause, but it might provide some leverage if and when required.

Aremys opened his chamber door and explained to the guard, a nice young fellow with an unfortunate harelip, that he needed to find Myrt. The guard nodded, a shy smile emerging on his deformed mouth, when Aremys said, "After you." It was a joke they shared from the time when the guard, Jos, had first been assigned to Aremys; he had made the wry comment that if he proceeded first, the mercenary might bash him on the head and escape.

This, of course, had made Aremys laugh. "Look at you, lad," he had replied, grinning. "I'd need an ax just to dent you. You're built like an ox." He could see that Jos had taken the remark as a rare compliment coming from the bear-sized man. They had never spoken at length, but Aremys had been sure to keep the words they did share lighthearted and friendly and Jos always responded, albeit cautiously. The guard was only just into manhood and still establishing a reserve of confidence to draw upon, a process probably made more difficult by taunts about his affliction, Aremys figured. When they walked shoulder to shoulder, as now, the mercenary was careful always to defer to his guard in the hope that the young man might take some self-assurance from it.

They found Myrt at the main stables. The Mountain Man nodded when he saw them. "Go get your meal, Jos. Leave him with me. I'm getting our stuff ready anyway. We leave soon."

Aremys grinned at his young keeper. "Don't forget what I said about that young lady," he said, referring back to an earlier exchange. "You should tell her, for I sense from what you say that she doesn't trouble herself over your mouth— it only matters how you use it," and he winked.

Jos chuckled, a hand flying up to cover his crooked smile.

"What have you been filling that lad's head with?" Myrt asked.

"Nothing that didn't fill yours when you were his age, Myrt," Aremys replied, helping him to lift a heavy crate into a cart. "Why aren't you with a woman, Myrt?"

"Who says I'm not?" the man countered, somewhat sharply.

Aremys shrugged. "You haven't mentioned a wife . . ."

Myrt reached for another crate. "I have no wife."

"I see."

"Oh? And what do you see?"

"Nothing, my friend. What's wrong with you?"

The warrior flicked away what sounded like an apology. "Cailech's furious about what happened. Kept asking me what you were doing when Rashlyn passed out."

"Mmm, I thought he might. I told you he suspects me of knowing something."

"He's not so suspicious that he's not pressing ahead with the journey. In fact he's brought our departure forward—we leave at sundown. You, me, Byl, and two others."

"So what's all this stuff?"

"Gifts for the Morgravian King."

"Ah, goodwill."

Myrt grunted. "Help me load the rest of it."

They worked quietly and quickly for the next few minutes.

Maegryn appeared. "I've picked out the animals you'll be taking, Myrt. I've assigned Farrow Cherub."

"I'm a better horseman that that," Aremys protested. "I'll feel ridiculous calling out 'Whoa, Cherub.' "

"That's the joke, Farrow," Maegryn said, grinning. "He's anything but!"

The two Mountain Men laughed and Aremys joined in briefly, until Myrt gestured that they should leave.

"We're expected at the King's chamber," said the warrior. "He wants us to sup with him before we leave."

Aremys nodded. "Are we finished here?"

"Yes, I'd say so. Thanks, Maegryn. Be back later, then."

"As it suits you, Myrt. I'll be waiting." The stablemaster turned back to the stables.

"I need to talk to you first," Aremys said as they made their way toward the fortress.

"I reckoned you might. Follow me."

They walked in a companionable silence through several courtyards toward a part of the fortress he had not been to before.

"Where are we going?" he said.

"My home," came the brief reply.

Myrt stopped a few times to share swift words with various people. He asked one youngster to find Byl and have him call at Myrt's home after dusk. The big warrior generously introduced Aremys to all those he spoke with and the mercenary noted how they deferred to Myrt. He presumed the man had taken on a stronger leadership role since Lothryn's disappearance. He mentioned as much.

"I suppose so," Myrt replied. "I don't really want it, but Cailech finds it easier to rely on me to pass on his orders. I'd prefer everything to be back to how it was."

"With Lothryn as the King's second, you mean?"

"Yes, he was worthy of it and good at it."

"Why was he better than you?"

"Because he understood Cailech, and because he was not afraid of him. They grew up together, they were friends first and foremost. A bit like how it was between the old Morgravian King and his general, that Fergys Thirsk. They were great friends from childhood, I was told."

"So I've heard," Aremys said.

"Well, friendships made young like that have longevity and there's great affection there too. I'll never have that kind of relationship with the King. And when a relationship like that is broken, it hurts."

"You sound like you're speaking from experience, Myrt."

"In a way," the man muttered, hurrying Aremys down a short flight of steps.

"Did you know Lothryn from childhood as well?"

Myrt glowered at Aremys and his persistent questions. "Yes, as a matter of fact."

They emerged into the open again, into what appeared to be a walled community. The place took Aremys by surprise. "Shar! How amazing."

His obvious delight broke the tension. Myrt grinned. "More of Cailech's dreaming. This is his great social experiment."

"Explain it me," Aremys said, gazing around at the hive of activity.

"Well, not everyone chooses to live in and around the fortress, as I'm sure you've gathered. Originally the Mountain Dwellers were different tribes, spread throughout the

Razors. Cailech not only united us into one people but dreamed of forming a small city—he wants the fortress to become the true heart of the Razors and he is encouraging people to settle inside it. He dreams of his own Pearlis or Werryl, I suppose you could say. He has built homes for the settlers and has encouraged markets to be held regularly. He's even set up a school, which is very popular and getting bigger and bigger. Our king encourages education and at his urging more people are bringing their children to the classroom. Cailech has organized special rewards for families who set up home here permanently. It's really quite a new experience and a lot of our folk are watching to see how it goes. I think it will work. I believe Cailech will have his city in years to come."

"It looks like this community is thriving," Aremys said, unable to keep the awe from his voice. "I can see from the layout that it's been thought through very carefully."

"It has." Myrt smiled. "The King didn't want it emerging too haphazardly, so he put together a group of people who could plan a village, grow it into a town, and envision a city emerging one day. I was one of the first to live here and that encouraged others to come too. Lothryn lived not far from here, among a smaller group of senior people—formerly tribe leaders and family members distantly related to Cailech."

"Does Cailech have family?"

"Oddly, no. We Mountain folk tend to have large family groups, but Cailech was an only child. His mother died by accident, in a fire. Cailech was about thirteen when it happened. He was away with his father at the time, settling a dispute among the tribes."

"Does he blame himself?"

"No, I don't think so. He knew it was an accident. But Lothryn told me the King never really got over the loss. That's why he's keen on keeping families together, and he loves the youngsters. Part of his belief is that children thrive when they have elders around them and big family groups to teach them the right ways, and I agree with him."

"I would have thought he'd have a wife, then, his own family."

Myrt shook his head and Aremys thought he saw something painful flicker across his expression. The Mountain Man fought down whatever demon was rising. "He hasn't had time to take a wife, I suppose."

"And you, Myrt? What of your family?"

"I have a sister. I live with her. Her husband was one of those killed in the Grenadyn disaster. He was seventeen; they'd only been married a few weeks. I suppose you've heard of that incident?"

Aremys nodded. He knew only too well the story of Grenadyn's unwarranted attack on the Mountain People and the slaughter that ensued.

Myrt sighed. "Well, my sister never got over her loss. She all but raised me. Now, I suppose, I look after her."

"No love of your own, Myrt?"

The Mountain Man walked on. "One. That person did not want me," he answered in a thick tone, and prevented any further conversation by stopping to chat with a shopkeeper selling candles.

Aremys stared at Myrt for a few heartbeats. He was sure of it now, sure that the Mountain Man had a secret. Perhaps it could be exploited toward his own ends of helping Wyl. As Myrt finished his chat with the shopkeeper, Aremys took a moment to marvel again at Cailech's embryonic city. The laneways had been cobbled with stone from the mountains and more building was already under way, with more streets leading off the main one. It certainly was not Pearlis, but it was bigger than any village he had encountered, and there was a sense of sprawl about it; the place seemed well on its way to developing into a bustling town. He could not help but be impressed by Cailech: He was still a relatively young king but he had enormous vision. It was then that Aremys decided to give his all toward helping the Mountain People. If somehow he could influence the attainment of a working peace between the two prideful monarchs of Morgravia and the north, then he would. For Cailech and his ambition, yes, but also for Myrt and Byl, for Myrt's sister, for Maegryn and young Jos, and yes, even for Lothryn, wherever he was.

Like Wyl, Aremys wanted to believe that Lothryn was still

alive. And if he was, he intended to find him. He was convinced that the horse and its magic would lead him to the man it seems everyone had loved—even the King.

"Everyone except Rashlyn," Myrt cautioned, when they were sitting in his small house a short time later and Aremys brought the subject back to Lothryn.

"Rashlyn didn't like him?"

"More to the point," Myrt said, busying himself with a pot of tea at the hearth, "Lothryn despised Rashlyn and the barshi knew it."

"Why?"

"Cups are over there," Myrt replied, nodding toward a dresser. "Lothryn objected to the influence Rashlyn has with the King. He admitted to me not long before he disappeared that it had gotten to the point where he felt something had to be done about it."

Aremys almost made the terrible error of mentioning the cannibalistic feast. He stopped himself just in time and covered his near blunder by turning his back on the Mountain Man to reach for the cups.

He brought them back to the small wooden table. "What made him say that?"

Myrt poured boiling water over the leaves. "Let that brew, shall we," he said amiably. "Well, there were many reasons. Cailech had been making erratic decisions, out of character for him—there was one particularly disturbing incident involving some Morgravian prisoners. He wanted to make an example of them to send a message to the Morgravian Crown. They weren't even the culprits, for Haldor's sake, they were just a raggle-taggle group of farmers who were sent into the Razors with one old soldier as a leader."

Aremys held his breath. Myrt was almost certainly referring to Wyl's friend Gueryn le Gant. He kept his voice casual. "And?"

"The King's method of making an example of them was terrifying, to say the least. I don't want to go into the details, but it never sat right with me, or any of us, for that matter. Don't get me wrong, Cailech doesn't hesitate when harsh punishment is called for—as you know from the repercussions of the episode at Grenadyn—but he's not a cruel man by nature."

Aremys nodded; he remembered the events on his island home only too well. He had had a crush on Lily Koreldy for several years, but she was older than he and no doubt had never even noticed the lumbering boy who looked older than his years and who turned a beetroot color if ever he was in her presence. "That was a terrible business."

"Yes, but Cailech spared Romen Koreldy, even gave him a home and looked after him for a while. They actually became quite good friends by the end of it, despite the trauma that sat between them."

"I'm surprised Koreldy could forgive him."

"Don't be fooled. Koreldy never forgave Cailech and the King knew it, which is why he warned him when he left that if he ever set foot in the Razor Kingdom again, he would lose his life."

"So Koreldy was like me, eh? A very well-treated prisoner."

Myrt turned the pot three times and grinned at Aremys's perplexed expression. "Tradition," he explained. "Yes, Koreldy was dealt with in much the same way as we're treating you, except he was never entrusted with a mission for the good of our people."

"Did you ever see Koreldy again?" Aremys asked. Myrt poured the tea, not answering. "You know he was working for Celimus, don't you?" Aremys pressed. "In name only, though. Actually he was working against him."

That won the Mountain Man's attention. "What do you mean?"

"Koreldy hated Celimus, with good reason. The Morgravian King double-crossed him in an agreement they had. I know Koreldy stuck to the mercenaries' code of honor: He did his job and kept his counsel, but Celimus tried several times to have him killed for what he had learned in doing that job."

Myrt's eyes narrowed. "You're talking about the death of the King of Briavel now, aren't you?" he guessed, and was glad to see Aremys nod. "What do you know about that?"

"Plenty. What are you prepared to swap for it?"

"What?" Myrt said, astonished. "Swap information?"

"Yes," Aremys said, reaching for his cup. "Listen, Myrt, you know things and so do I. I would give you my knowledge happily, but getting information from you is like trying to get milk from a zerkon. Dangerous at best and fucking hard to boot!"

Myrt exploded into a rare laugh. "All right," he said. "All right, Grenadyne, you win. I haven't laughed like that in a while."

Aremys arched an eyebrow. "I can tell," he said. "Your turn, Myrt. The Morgravian soldier you mentioned—is he still alive?"

"Yes," Myrt said, serious now. He sipped from his steaming cup. "Your turn. Whose side are you on?"

"Cailech's. I will negotiate for him and will do all I can to help win this peace he pushes for. Understand this: I hate Celimus and will do everything in my power to undermine him. I am no enemy to the Mountain Kingdom."

Myrt said nothing, but Aremys saw something blaze in the man's eyes and sensed it was relief.

"All right, next question for you," the mercenary continued. "Is the Morgravian soldier called Gueryn le Gant?"

Myrt balked at this. "How do you know that? How do you know him?"

A little fib would help here, Aremys decided. "I know le Gant's niece. She's been distraught since he disappeared and I said I'd keep my ears and eyes open for any news on my travels north. Thank you for confirming it."

"He's in our dungeon."

It was Aremys's turn to flinch. "I have to see him, Myrt."

"Not until you answer my questions. Koreldy—where is he, do you know?"

"Probably scattered to the four winds by now."

"Dead?" Myrt could not hide his astonishment.

Aremys nodded. "Killed by one of the King's hired assassins. A woman," he said.

"Cailech must be told."

"Why? Did he want to kill him by his own hand?"

"He was certain that Koreldy, after his recent escape, would return to rescue le Gant."

"What will the King do when he learns of Koreldy's death?"

"Kill the Morgravian soldier."

"Then he cannot know of Koreldy's demise," Aremys said urgently.

Myrt scowled. "Says who? I've told you, I'll do nothing that smacks of betrayal of Cailech. Now answer me this if you want any more information or help: Why are you so interested in Lothryn? It makes me suspicious of you."

Aremys shook his head. "Don't be. Elspyth of Yentro is known to me—you could say we are friends, although we've not known each other long. I met her soon after she escaped from here and she was hoping to return to the mountains to discover Lothryn's fate. You know they were in love, she and Lothryn?"

Myrt grimaced. "I guessed as much. There would be no other reason for Loth to betray us as he did, and without sharing his decision with me."

Aremys was glad that the Mountain Man had not blinked at the coincidence that he claimed to know two separate women who just happened to know Gueryn and Lothryn. He could slap himself for such clumsy contrivance, but fortunately the big man had not been paying close attention. Aremys took his chance. "Myrt," he said gently, "I know that you loved Lothryn too, perhaps more than in just a brotherly fashion—"

The Mountain Man reacted as if burned. He stood up, pushing his chair away, eyes blazing with sudden hatred. "Fuck you, Aremys."

Aremys kept silent and did not so much as flinch when Myrt threw his cup and its contents into a corner and then kicked at his chair, smashing one of its legs. The big man turned to glare at the Grenadyne, daring him to make a move so he could punch him as well. But Aremys remained calm.

"I don't want to fight you," he said. "I want to find him for you."

Despite the warning, he was prepared for a fight: a black

eye perhaps, maybe broken fingers. So he was ill-prepared
for tears, and when they came he hated himself for shattering the barriers that had kept Myrt strong. He sat there a moment bewildered, then did the only thing one person can do
for another who is hurting: He put his arms around the
Mountain Man's big shoulders and held him.

Eventually he spoke. "He's alive, Myrt, I know it. From
all that you've told me, I don't believe Cailech would have
killed him. That's why his reply to you was so cryptic.
Lothryn lives and our only clue is Galapek. Help me and
we'll find him together."

The tears were brief, dried away almost as soon as they
had dared to arrive. They were replaced by wrath. "I can't!"
the man roared.

"You can. We're all he's got. If you love Lothryn—as I
know you do—then fight for him. Let's at least find out if
he's alive and what state he's in."

Myrt stomped around his small cottage, a new battle raging within him now. Aremys had noticed that the dwelling
showed a woman's touch—a jar of fresh hill flowers on the
humble sideboard, dishes neatly stacked, floors swept, and
surfaces dusted. It was as neat as a pin. He wondered where
the sister was and asked Myrt.

"Due back shortly," the Mountain Man answered, distracted. "Listen to me, Aremys. I'll help you because of
Lothryn, not because I'm threatened by what you've learned
about me. If you ever repeat what has occurred here or been
mentioned between us, I'll kill you. I might be in love with
a man, but it doesn't stop me being capable of killing one. I
want you to understand that."

"Your secret is safe with me. Whether you prefer men or
women is of no consequence to me. I've trusted you with my
life—I shall go on doing so. I'm only sorry that you have to
be so unhappy."

"Don't trouble yourself. I've lived with it all my life," the
Mountain Man said gruffly. "More to the point, what can we
do? We leave in a few hours and I don't think Cailech plans
for you to return here." Myrt's anger had dissipated, to be replaced with despondency.

"Well, that does change things. It might be that you must track Lothryn down without me." Aremys looked toward the ceiling, racking his brain for the best step. "Can you take me to see the horse again? I think it was trying to communicate something to me on our ride."

"You're jesting, aren't you?" When Aremys returned his gaze evenly, Myrt scoffed. "You expect me to believe the horse tried to tell you something?"

"Weren't you listening when I told you about the Thicket's magic? No, I'm not saying it talked, exactly," he lied, "but I felt something, and if there is more to learn, this is my last chance. I also want to see le Gant."

"No."

"Yes! He is not loyal to Celimus. He's like Koreldy and all the others that bastard has coerced and tricked, double-crossed and had killed. What do you think a soldier of that caliber was doing blundering about in the Razors anyway? Did you really think he wanted to be here with a gang of farmers who wouldn't know a sword from a threshing fork?" Myrt bit his lip. "Come on, man. This was set up by the Morgravian King. He wanted Cailech to kill Gueryn, but I have to see him to find out why."

"Because it might help in your mission?"

"Of course, why else would I want to see him?" Aremys lied again, and hated himself for deceiving this good man. "Keep the secret of Koreldy, I beg you—just a little longer. The King will learn of his death anyway once he enters Morgravia, or if you insist, I'll tell him myself."

"I do insist," Myrt said, staring hard at Aremys.

"All right. Just keep it quiet for now until I can learn some more."

Myrt nodded. "Where to now?"

"The dungeon," Aremys replied grimly. "Then Galapek."

# 6

GUERYN FELT FORGOTTEN. IT HAD BEEN DAYS SINCE MYRT AND his friend had walked with him and he had begun to think he would never smell sweet air again. Food and fresh water were being delivered daily, however, so he knew he had not dropped entirely from the Moutain People's consciousness. The jailer, Haz, offered no news or even conversation and Gueryn had given up trying to elicit any. In truth it was his own fault. Haz had made the effort to talk in the early days, but Gueryn's refusal to eat had brought the King's wrath down on his head. Now he ignored the prisoner, taking care of only the bare necessities.

Rashlyn had looked in on him twice since Gueryn had been returned to the dungeon, and was satisfied that his health was being maintained. The Morgravian had greeted the soft-spoken healer with only an icy silence on each occasion.

Having decided that he was fighting a losing battle in trying to kill himself, and realizing that he could do more good by regaining his health and learning as much as he could about the Razor King and his intentions, Gueryn had tried to keep himself fit. Once he felt strong enough, he had begun doing push-ups; now he was up to three hundred daily. As a result, his upper body was muscled again. And he walked. His cell was relatively narrow but quite long and he had used this length to pace relentlessly up and down. He lost count of the times he met each wall at either end because he had given up keeping track after a thousand. And with his physical health restored, he had begun to speculate on his situation.

The hated Rashlyn knew something about Lothryn, that much was clear. And he was smug about it. This suggested to Gueryn that perhaps the brave Mountain Man might not have perished as they had all assumed. Gueryn also knew the King was keeping him alive so that Koreldy would return to save him, but he had no idea why Cailech should believe there was any attachment between them. Gueryn had never met Koreldy until that time in the fortress. The odd thing was that until Gueryn's sewn-up eyes had been released of their stitching, he had believed Koreldy to be Wyl Thirsk! He had gone over it time and again in his mind, realizing that he had just wanted to believe it was Wyl. Nevertheless, something deep down told him there was more to the puzzle than what his eyes had confirmed. Even when he saw the unfamiliar face, he had still believed Wyl was somehow present. And how could Koreldy know the family battle cry? Or speak to him in the way Wyl would? Nothing added up, and the King's belief that Koreldy would return to rescue him further muddied the waters of his thoughts.

Gueryn was sitting in the corner of his cell, once again remembering Elspyth's death, for which he could never forgive himself, when he heard the key turning in the lock.

"You're early, Haz," he mumbled. He had no real knowledge of time, but his body and its regular functions gave him reasonable clues. And his body was not yet hungry.

A huge man stepped into the cell, a man he had never seen before. "Gueryn le Gant?"

Gueryn nodded, searching for a pithy rejoinder—any attack on his keepers felt good. "Who else did you expect?"

The man grinned, which confused him, and turned to nod to another person outside. Gueryn was sure he heard Myrt's voice saying that he would keep watch.

"What's going on?" he asked, alarm bells suddenly klaxoning in his mind.

"I have very little time, so you must listen as I explain something quickly. And you're going to have to trust me."

"Why would I trust you?"

"I'm a Grenadyne, not one of the Razor People. And

there's a single word I can say that I believe will make you trust me."

"Oh yes? What's that, Grenadyne?"

"Thirsk," Aremys replied abruptly. "Now hear me out. No interruptions. I am friend, not foe."

The name Thirsk was like a slap in the face. The big man had Gueryn's full attention.

"My name is Aremys Farrow. I am a mercenary and was employed by your king to hunt down and kill Ylena Thirsk."

"What?" roared Gueryn, pushing himself to his feet.

"I said, don't interrupt, soldier," Aremys warned. "I found Ylena, but instead of killing her, I took her to safety into the north of Briavel, where we parted company. I hope she has made it south to Queen Valentyna. I won't go into how I got to be here, but rest assured, although I might look like a free man, I'm as much a captive as you are. Cailech plans to use me to negotiate a parley with King Celimus. If I'm successful I might win my freedom, in which case I'll go looking for Ylena again and offer my protection. There is another woman—someone you know—who holds strong affection for a man called Lothryn. I understand that Lothryn betrayed the Mountain People in helping you, Koreldy, and this woman, Elspyth, to escape. Now that I've found you, as I promised Ylena I would," Aremys lied, "I'm determined to find Lothryn as well. My instincts tell me the King has kept him alive in order to make the punishment—whatever it is— of aiding your attempted escape the sweeter. You should know that Koreldy is dead." Gueryn closed his eyes as he heard this. "And that somehow I am going to get you out of here."

Aremys stopped. It was obvious he was sharing too much information; the prisoner looked too shocked to respond.

Then the Morgravian began to laugh. It was not the reaction Aremys had expected, and he gritted his teeth in annoyance. "A word of thanks might be more appropriate," he suggested.

"Thank you for coming, Grenadyne. Thank you for what you're trying to do, but I'm as good as dead, man. If Koreldy is no longer alive, that's my death warrant," Gueryn said, painful resignation in his tired voice.

"No one knows about Koreldy but myself and Myrt," Aremys assured.

"Myrt is a good man, but he is a loyal Mountain warrior. The King will already know."

"The King does not know. He doesn't even know we're here now. Myrt is outside keeping watch. He is protecting you."

"Why?" Gueryn demanded.

"It doesn't matter why."

"It matters to me. It doesn't make sense. Myrt has no reason to betray his king."

"Let's just say I have something on him that encourages him to help me."

Gueryn shrugged, suddenly tired. "Fine. Really, there's no reason for me to care. Everyone I have ever cared about is dead except Ylena, and it sounds to me like Celimus will kill her too."

"No chance."

"If you've met Ylena, as you claim you have, then you'll know she is a pretty, indulged, and fragile creature. She will not outwit Celimus—not without her brother's protection or mine."

"She has the protection of a queen . . . and mine."

"Oh, that's right, the protection of a new, inexperienced queen—by now under siege from King Celimus, I imagine—and a Grenadyne mercenary who is a captive of King Cailech. Forgive me if I don't hold my breath."

"I don't know why I bothered," Aremys muttered, stung by le Gant's ungracious manner.

"Neither do I. Save yourself if you can. I watched Cailech kill Elspyth with his own hands and enjoy it. He will do the same to me, and to you if he so chooses."

Aremys frowned. "Elspyth isn't dead."

"Yes, she is, mercenary. I'm sorry to upset you further. See this on my boots? That is her blood. Her life became forfeit when I refused to capitulate to Cailech's interrogation. I might as well have stuck the knife in her myself," he finished bitterly.

Aremys moved for the first time since entering the cell.

He crouched by Gueryn and dared even to place his hand on the soldier's shoulder. Hardly daring to breathe, he asked, "When did this happen?"

Gueryn shook his head. "I've lost track of time here. It was weeks ago, I'm sure."

"Gueryn, look at me. I saw Elspyth so few days ago I could count them on both hands and probably have a finger to spare. She, Ylena, and I were all together in Felrawthy."

"You lie! Why are you lying to me, you bastard?"

It was Aremys's turn to shake his head, but with compassion. "I'm not. We drank tea together, for Shar's sake! Elspyth is alive and determined to return here to discover Lothryn's fate. She was on her way to Briavel the last time I saw her. She'll be there right now, I'd wager."

A barrage of emotions raged openly across Gueryn's face as he considered what he was hearing. Aremys watched him take a deep breath. "Farrow, I watched Elspyth of Yentro die horribly. Now, one of us has been taken for a sap. I know your time is short, but I want you to tell me everything you know."

So Aremys did, as quickly as he could, while leaving out everything relating to Wyl's magical metamorphosis. The gruff old soldier would never trust him if he began to talk that sort of nonsense.

When Aremys had finished his story, Gueryn struggled to his feet and began to pace, deeply shocked by what he had heard. "The Duke of Felrawthy is dead?" he said, so disbelieving that he repeated it. "Dead? Jeryb?"

Aremys nodded. "I only discovered this piece of savagery myself a day ago from Myrt, when the news filtered into the Razors. It seems Celimus is making Cailech's people the scapegoats, but it was his men, his killing rampage—I presume punishment for the family's harboring Ylena. And no doubt it quashed any thoughts of an uprising from the northern duchy."

It did make horrible sense. "All of them?" Gueryn asked.

"So I'm told. Crys was seeing Elspyth to the border, so I'm not sure about him, but the Mountain People said the whole family perished."

"This is monstrous. That poor girl. Her husband, Alyd . . ." Gueryn closed his eyes in despair, then his courage rallied and he opened them again. This time they were flinty. "And you're now going to negotiate a parley between these two Kings?"

"To buy my freedom, yes. What about Elspyth? Do you believe me?"

"How can I disbelieve what I saw with my own eyes?"

"Because I'm guessing Rashlyn was involved, wasn't he?"

"He was, in fact."

"You do know he's a man of dark magic?"

"I've been on the receiving end of it," Gueryn replied bitterly, remembering the hideous sensation of being suspended in midair.

"Isn't that enough evidence?"

The Morgravian turned on the big Grenadyne, eyed him quizzically. "What do you mean?"

"Gueryn, he fooled you. Whether it was Cailech's idea—or, most likely, Rashlyn's—they duped you into thinking you were watching Elspyth die."

"Don't be stupid," Gueryn roared. "It was her, I tell you."

Aremys bit his lip in thought. He had not realized just how powerful Rashlyn was. "Yes, to all intents and purposes it was Elspyth. Have you ever heard of a glamour?"

"No. What is it—some kind of magic?"

"Yes, and I'm guessing that's what Rashlyn used against you. We northerners are more accepting of magic than you folks in the south and growing up we tend to hear about spells and sorcery of days gone by. My grandfather once told me about a powerful enchantment that can make one person look like someone else—a glamour. Only the most gifted can wield such power."

Gueryn wondered how many more shocks his heart could take in one day. He stared at Aremys in a stunned silence.

"Elspyth was alive and well when I left her," the mercenary went on. "I hugged her goodbye. I bet you didn't touch her."

Gueryn shook his head numbly. "I could only watch her die."

"It was another woman, le Gant. They took some poor

woman and placed a glamour on her. You said they were trying to get information from you. What was so important that they would murder a woman in front of you?"

"Cailech wanted to know about my connection to Koreldy. I have none, but it appears Koreldy had some connection to me." Gueryn barked a harsh laugh. "They stitched together my eyelids as part of my torture and I was blind when I met Koreldy. But do you know something, Farrow, I thought he was Wyl Thirsk." Gueryn began to weep, all his pent-up emotion spilling over. "I failed the boy. I failed the Thirsks."

"No, you didn't," Aremys countered helplessly, feeling the depth of Gueryn's emotion. "There's so much I'd like to tell you, but there's no time," he whispered. "Look, I have to go. You're safest here until I can work out how we're going to rescue you. You must hang on. Give nothing away of what we've shared."

He reached out and grabbed the man's hand, putting it against his own heart in the way of the Morgravian Legion. It was the highest form of commitment one soldier could make to another.

Gueryn was astounded by the action. There were only two men he had ever given such a signal to. Both were named Thirsk; father and son. Both were now dead.

"Wait!" he said, suddenly remembering. "Lothryn—you think he's alive?"

"I do."

"That horse has something to do with it, the horse called Galapek," Gueryn murmured, almost to himself, disgusted that he had not yet worked out an answer.

"What?" Aremys whispered, almost raising Gueryn's feet from the floor as he lifted him to standing.

Gueryn shook his head. "I don't know what I'm saying. I just have a feeling that the horse Galapek, Cailech's new stallion, has something to do with Lothryn."

"Why? What exactly do you know?" Aremys asked urgently.

Gueryn frowned. He had no idea why the Grenadyne was so excited. "Rashlyn knows the truth of what's happened to

Lothryn. I overheard him jesting smugly to Myrt and Byl that Lothryn was closer than they knew. And he went on to make some joke about the meaning of the word 'Galapek.' "

Aremys looked blank. "I don't know the word. Sounds like the old language," he mused.

"It is. And I do know it. 'Galapek' means 'traitor.' Cailech has named his new stallion Traitor, which, in my opinion, is just about the worst name you could give a horse."

Aremys looked stunned. Then he spun on his heels and called over his shoulder, "I'll be back, le Gant. Say nothing of this!"

The huge man all but ran from the cell, slamming the door behind him. Gueryn heard the lock turn. He had nothing but his sorrowful thoughts for company now.

W ell?" Myrt asked, startled by Aremys's rapid exit from the cell.

"Let's get out of here first," Aremys said, his head swirling with fantastical thoughts, every nerve tingling with terror. It could not be true, could it?

Fortunately Haz was not in attendance at the jail. Myrt thanked the young, completely disinterested guard, who was obviously posted in the dungeon as some sort of punishment, judging by his scowl. He merely nodded when Myrt reminded the lad that Gueryn was to be walked daily.

Outside, Myrt grabbed Aremys's arm. "You got something, didn't you?"

"Do you know what the name Galapek means, Myrt?" Aremys asked, his voice hard and low. When Myrt shook his head, Aremys closed his eyes with a mix of anger and despair. What a cruel fate. "It's the ancient language of the north," he said. "Cailech's schoolchildren would probably be able to tell you. It means 'traitor.' "

Myrt looked perplexed. "All right, a curious name for a horse and even stranger connotations, but what's that got to do with Lothryn?"

"You fool. You poor sad fool," Aremys said, unable to help himself. "The horse is Lothryn," and his voice almost broke on those words. "Rashlyn has somehow worked his vile magic on Lothryn to turn him into an animal, and now your oh-so-proud King can keep his former friend as his servant until he's no good for anything but the knacker's yard."

Myrt opened his mouth to speak, but no words came. No sound at all, in fact. Aremys had once seen a man suffer a heart tremor; it had come quickly and gone as fast, leaving one side of the man's face paralyzed. That was how Myrt looked now: paralyzed. His facial muscles had gone slack and all color had drained from his cheeks, his eyes were like dull black buttons.

Finally he found some lucidity. "Cailech broke him. We all watched it. He did it in a special corral he'd had built. It took days. Days of painful, heart-wrenching breaking of this horse's spirit until it bowed its head before him."

Myrt began to weep. Aremys could feel tears stinging his eyes too; he could not remember the last time he had cried over anything or anyone. His sister perhaps, when he had seen her tiny corpse laid out, the vicious gores of the forest boar covered by a beautiful silken dress. He tore himself away from the memory.

"He said he would break him using trust," Myrt finished. "It was Lothryn all along. Lothryn who fought for days until he was too weak to resist his king anymore."

Aremys shook his head in wonder. "And that's why the horse made me feel so sick. The Thicket's magic sensed the sheer power and evil of the sorcery that had been wielded to turn a man into a horse."

Myrt's red-rimmed eyes stared at him. "Aremys, don't lie to me now. You said something earlier that I scoffed at—that the horse communicated something to you. Did it really say something?"

Aremys nodded miserably. "It whispered a name. Elspyth."

Without another word, the Mountain warrior turned and walked away to deal with his pain alone.

# 7

It WAS THE FIRST TIME SINCE CHILDHOOD THAT CELIMUS HAD set foot in his father's beloved war chamber. Magnus had always loved the room, even in times of peace. Its windows faced east, toward the traditional enemy, and when Celimus had paid one of his few visits here, he had believed its views went on forever. He recalled now how his father had laughed a little indulgently when Celimus had voiced that notion. It had been a rare moment of shared enjoyment for father and son, and had passed all too quickly, Celimus forgotten the moment a messenger had arrived with a missive for General Thirsk, who always seemed to be at his king's side. Celimus was briskly told to find his tutor—although no one appeared to care where he went, as long as he left. He had understood with a sour realization that he had no place among these men. He had been nine years old, ready to watch and learn about kingship, but Magnus had not cared enough to teach him. That much had been obvious; Celimus had not returned to the chamber until this day.

It was here that men had smoked and argued with one another, plotted and schemed against Briavel. In this place many a war had been invented, but peace had also been designed. It was a room of ancient waxed timbers and leather smoothed from years of use, where, if you concentrated, you could still smell a hint of the sweet tobacco King Magnus had favored. A once magnificent, now faded tapestry depicting a famous battle scene from centuries previous hung across one wall, and a hand-twisted rug, threadbare in places, lay across the wooden floor, whose dusty boards had recently enjoyed a polish.

King Celimus held no sentiment for this chamber so loved by his father. He hated it, in fact, equating it with the reason he and his mother had never felt Magnus's love. But this war room of his father's was where detailed maps of Morgravia, Briavel, and other realms were stored. And Celimus needed those maps now. He also needed to give the impression that he was preparing to declare war on his neighbor, and this was the place from which to do that.

In not appointing a general after Wyl Thirsk's death, Celimus had effectively claimed full leadership of the Morgravian Legion. This had shocked many of the noble families, who had assumed that Jeryb Donal, with his brood of sons, was the most likely successor. But Donal had refused when such ideas had been suggested. His focus, he had assured all, was firmly on the border between Morgravia and the Razors. There was no better defense than Felrawthy and he had no intention of moving to Pearlis. Celimus had made it equally clear he did not require a general as such. He preferred to work through the captains, leading the Legion himself.

To most Morgravians' despair, Celimus had recently given the directive to mobilize the first few divisions of the Legion. People had prayed that war between Morgravia and Briavel was for the history books now. The coming marriage had promised so much for the two realms' prosperous future together. Still, no one could argue with this King. He was a law unto himself.

It was Celimus's intention that his men start departing for the Briavellian border today.

"That should give our queen something to think about," he said to Jessom, who was standing nearby, pouring his sovereign a cup of wine.

The war room had been freshly cleaned, waxed, and aired for Celimus. Someone had even placed a bowl of fruit and vase of exquisite tannika buds in one corner. Celimus did not particularly care for either, but he liked the splash of color in this dull and dreary place. His mother, he recalled, had adored the famed buds, which only flowered for a few short weeks in spring. It afforded him an ironic amusement that his mother's influence now held sway in Magnus's once firmly private, men-only chamber. If he had any of her perfume, he would dab it over every surface so that Adana's scent permeated every corner and overwhelmed any lingering essence of Magnus. He smiled grimly at the thought.

"What are their orders, sire?" the Chancellor replied, handing the goblet to the King.

"Merely a show of strength at this stage. They await further orders," Celimus said distractedly, looking toward the flushed, dusty messenger being led into the war room by one of his aides. "Yes?"

The aide bowed, as did the messenger. "Sire," the aide said, "a courier from the north."

Celimus did not mask his irritation at being disturbed. "I take it this is urgent?"

"I'm assured it is, your highness, and to be given to you directly," the aide qualified. He would never dare interrupt the King and his chancellor unless it was important, although of course he did not mention this fact. "Say as little as possible" seemed to be the new creed among the palace servants when faced with their king.

The courier bowed again, overwhelmed to be in the presence of the King. It was clear that since arriving at the gates of Stoneheart, he had not even paused for a cup of water to quench his thirst.

Celimus leaned against the huge table where he remembered his father poring over maps and looked at the newcomer expectantly. With his arms folded and legs crossed at the ankle, the King suggested this was all most inconvenient and he offered no words to allay the messenger's obvious nervousness.

The man licked his dry lips. "Your highness, I was dispatched from the midlands checkpoint, having taken a message from another messenger, who had been sent by your captain at our northern base between Deakyn and Felrawthy." He paused to take a breath, not noticing the flicker of irritation across the King's face at the preamble.

The Chancellor did. "Get to the point, man, if it's urgent," Jessom warned, hoping to prevent Celimus from erupting. He had sensed his king's brittle mood that morning and experience suggested it would not do to test his flexibility right now.

"I apologize, sire," the man stammered. "The message I am asked to deliver direct to you is that King Cailech of the Razors seeks a parley."

A stunned silence filled the war room, then evaporated as exclamations ensued from both King and Chancellor.

"A parley with Cailech!" Celimus blustered. "Preposterous! Whatever for?"

The courier reddened. "My king, I am not privy to any background to this missive, other than to report that it was originally delivered to the Legion by a man called Aremys Farrow." He bowed, his task concluded. Celimus ignored him, glancing angrily toward the Chancellor. Before anything further could be said, Jessom dismissed both courier and aide. He stilled the King's coming explosion with a guarded look and both waited impatiently for the two men to leave.

As soon as the door shut, Celimus erupted. "Farrow!" he raged. "Working with Cailech?"

Jessom deliberately kept his expression clear of all emotion, although he too was startled by the news. "We don't have all the details yet, your highness. We cannot know what has occurred here."

"What secrets has he passed on?" Celimus demanded.

Jessom shook his head. "He knows nothing, sire. Besides, he will not share details of his paid missions with Cailech. Mercenaries of his caliber never let one hand know what the other is doing."

"Precisely my point, you fool," Celimus said. "How do we know that he hasn't been working for Cailech all along?"

Experience had taught Jessom to ignore such offense. "To what end, sire? What benefit has he gained? What secrets could he have learned during a few hours at Stoneheart? Both he and Leyen were watched on my instructions. Farrow did not leave his chamber, even washing up there. He did not emerge until supper with you, and during your meeting the only matter of note discussed was Ylena Thirsk—and presumably she means nothing to the Mountain King. Farrow returned to his room and was gone within two hours. With respect, my king, I think we are jumping to conclusions."

"Then what is Farrow up to?" Celimus roared, only mildly placated. "What is Cailech up to?"

"Well, let's think it through," Jessom said in a soft voice meant to calm his sovereign's rage. "An ambush, possibly?"

"Hardly," Celimus countered. "By all accounts, Cailech is not stupid. He's not going to risk himself on the vague chance he could hurt me. No, there is another reason."

"I have to wonder what he thinks the Razor Kingdom and Morgravia have in common, sire," Jessom said airily, about to expound further when the King cut him off.

"A mutual distrust of Briavel perhaps," Celimus replied, his mind now working its agile way around various scenarios. "Let's presume Aremys has no loyalty to either party— that he is working purely for personal gain. Perhaps he was captured by Cailech while he was on business for us, although that is unlikely; as you suggest, however, there could be other reasons he found himself in the company of Cailech. Let's give him the benefit of the doubt for now, shall we?"

"All right, your majesty," Jessom agreed, as if the more rational approach were all Celimus's idea. "So?"

"So, I agree to meet with Aremys Farrow on Morgravian soil. I am intrigued as to what Cailech has in mind with this parley."

"What do you propose, sire?"

"I shall see him somewhere that can be properly guarded. It will take too long for him to be brought to Stoneheart." The King began to think aloud. "Perhaps halfway—Rittylworth?"

"Felrawthy, my king," Jessom said in a tone of rich satisfaction. "What better spot?"

"Indeed," Celimus agreed, warming instantly to the notion of personally taking over the rich estate. "Who cares if Crys Donal is alive in Briavel? He is a traitor now, and Felrawthy belongs to the Crown. Make immediate arrangements. Send a message for Aremys Farrow to be brought to Tenterdyn. We shall meet him there."

"At once, your highness. And Briavel?"

"Can wait for now. Let Valentyna stew. Perhaps the sight of our men will soften her resolve. She would be a fool to go into battle."

"You would still marry her, sire?"

Celimus looked at his chancellor as though he were conversing with a dullard. "I don't want war, Jessom. I want her to capitulate. I don't want her as my equal—which is, tragically, how she sees herself—but I do want her as my queen. I want an heir from her. I want Briavel, man. And then I shall have the Mountain Kingdom too. I want it all!" he bellowed, storming from his war room, his energies charged.

Aremys found the company of the Legionnaires easy and comfortable. With the Razors behind him, he was relieved to be back in Morgravia—and suddenly the chance of finding Wyl again felt possible. He still felt touched by Myrt's sorrow, Gueryn's imprisonment, and the shock of realizing what had become of Lothryn, but there was nothing he could do about any of that right now. He had a job to carry out for the Mountain King and his freedom to win.

He liked Cailech, in spite of it all. The man had a deep intelligence and quick mind, and Aremys was impressed that the King—who he sensed was capable of arrogance and too much pride—had not been too proud or arrogant to appreciate the benefit of a parley with the southern King. That Cailech despised Celimus was obvious, but he also had the capacity for pragmatism. He had admitted to Aremys that if he could stomach a meeting with Celimus and form some sort of loose bond, the long-term benefits were immense.

They had talked over a sumptuous supper before Aremys and his escort left. Myrt had been quiet, but then Myrt was always quiet. Only Aremys seemed overly sensitive to his silence; the King was focused on the coming meeting with his southern couterpart.

"Can he be trusted?" Cailech had asked bluntly.

"I doubt it. Can you?" Aremys had inquired, which had made the King bellow with amusement.

"You'll do well, Aremys. Go and set up this parley for me."

"And in return, Cailech," Aremys had risked, "what is my reward?"

"I allow you to live," the King had answered. The gregarious mood did not fool Aremys. He knew only too well that the King still held deep suspicions about him, but no mention had been made of Rashlyn other than to assure the two men that the barshi was well.

Aremys had not replied to the King's flippant comment. Instead he had held his ground, refusing to flinch under the King's scrutiny.

"All right, mercenary. I understand your need for an exchange of some kind," Cailech said, relenting. He smiled. "What would please you that I could provide?"

Aremys had decided to risk it. "I would have Galapek."

The King's reaction was dramatic despite his efforts to shield it. The eyes narrowed and Aremys saw the man's jaw tighten. His barb had hit home.

"What is your interest in my horse?" Cailech had asked, his tone bordering on anger.

"Only that I wish he were mine, sire," Aremys had lied. "He is the most beautiful stallion I have ever encountered— and that's saying something, coming from a Grenadyne."

"He is still new for me. I am fond of him."

"I see," Aremys had observed, keeping his voice light so no offense could be taken. It was time to pull back. "King Cailech, I will attempt to set up this parley for you in good faith. I need nothing from you in payment—not even your fine stallion. All I ask is that you grant my freedom once you have had the opportunity to work out a peace agreement with Celimus."

Cailech had instantly offered his hand, palm up. Aremys knew this was a rare show of friendship from a man who no doubt believed he had no equal, and once again he was struck by how quickly the King's mood could change.

"I will gladly seal hands on that, Aremys," the King had said. "I like your confidence that Celimus and I will find common ground."

Aremys had placed his own hand on top of the King's.

"You alone will make it happen, my lord. I have complete faith in you."

Cailech had smiled and this time there was no guile in his face, just open warmth. "I hope you will choose to stay among us, Grenadyne. But I will grant you your independence as soon as this deal is done."

Aremys had opted for a lighthearted response. "I must be free, your highness. My memory tells me I have a woman to find," and he had winked, much to the King's delighted amusement.

And so Aremys Farrow of Grenadyn had been provided with an escort, a fine horse, and a message to deliver to Celimus, which he had duly done, emerging out of the Razors with his hands held high, insisting that Myrt and his other two companions do the same.

Aremys had deliberately asked Myrt to lead him as close to Felrawthy as they could get, having learned from Wyl that these Legionnaires were the least likely to shoot arrows first and ask questions later. They had entered Morgravia via a pass known as Haldor's Tooth, which had led them into the duchy of Felrawthy, to a village mainly inhabited by soldiers about ten miles from Brynt proper. Captain Bukanan's men were well drilled to take prisoners for interview. Aremys believed he could thank Jeryb Donal for this mercy.

He had nodded gently at Myrt to allow the Mountain Men's hands to be bound. His too had been tied, and while the men of the Razors were led into a small dwelling, Aremys had been taken before Bukanan, who had listened to his story with an intense interest.

"A parley, you say?" the ruddy-faced Captain had repeated.

"Yes, sir. That's the message I bring," Aremys had confirmed.

"You understand how odd this is?"

"I do, sir. It's why I was chosen to deliver the message. I am known to the King and he will trust me."

Bukanan had studied him closely and finally replied: "You will remain in our care until we hear back from Pearlis."

"I understand," Aremys had said, smiling at the nicely couched words that really meant they were prisoners of Morgravia. "You must understand, however, that these men of the mountains are not to be harmed in any way and are to be released the moment you receive word from King Celimus."

"Who makes these conditions?" the captain had inquired politely, although Aremys had heard the edge in the tone.

"Cailech of the Mountain People. He insists his men are not to be compromised by King Celimus."

"And he's in a position to make such demands?" the Captain had asked, somewhat surprised at the audaciousness of the Mountain King.

"Captain Bukanan, I am merely the go-between for two powerful men. If my attempt to bring them together succeeds, you and I can continue our lives in peace. I think Morgravia wants peace, and what I want is to return to my life as a free man. Let us make this happen, you and I. If Cailech's men are harmed or kept longer than he considers fair, he will call off the parley and you may well be fighting a war on two fronts—with the King of the Mountains and the Queen of Briavel—which would be a shame, don't you agree?"

When it was put like that, Bukanan most certainly had agreed. His wife had just given birth to a son and the Captain had every intention of remaining alive to raise the child he loved with such ferocity. "We'll accept these terms, Farrow. Although you will have little to bargain with once Cailech is on Morgravian soil—for you may be sure Celimus will not agree to go into the Razors."

"Leave that to me," Aremys had said cryptically.

The Captain had shrugged. "As you wish. We will dispatch our rider this instant. Make yourself comfortable among us. It will take a few days."

# 8

LIRYK HAD PERSONALLY ESCORTED THE WOMAN WHO CALLED herself Ylena Thirsk to a small reception room. She was disheveled and spoke little, insisting that her business was with the Queen, who was expecting her. Liryk, despite the woman's high rank, had her thoroughly searched for even the smallest of weapons. The woman gave no protest and, in fact, carried nothing with her except the riding clothes she stood in. She certainly did not resemble the famed Thirsks. Apart from the golden hair—an obvious difference—she was beautiful, not a quality the Thirsk men had been known for. Liryk noticed that she carried herself erect and proud—clearly of noble status—and her defiant gaze when he tried to question her at the guardhouse had told him she was not intimidated by him or his men. Finally he had agreed to send a runner to the Queen.

"It is up to her majesty whether she will see you," he had cautioned.

"Rest assured, your queen will see me," the woman had replied, and had followed the soldier in silence to the chamber. The commander recognized that this sudden visit was fraught with danger for the now precarious marriage plans. The nobles had called for Ylena Thirsk and it seemed Shar had answered Valentyna's dearest prayers.

"Lady Ylena, my men tell me they found you in the woodland bordering the palace?"

"Yes, that is true," Wyl replied. "I was lost, Commander Liryk, and grateful for their guidance. I have already explained that my horse fell lame in Beeching," he lied, still a little shaky from his magical arrival into the Werryl woods.

"I left it there," he added, realizing too late that the Commander could easily check up on his story.

"And you walked from Beeching? Could you not buy another horse?"

"To tell the truth, sir, I did not have sufficient funds in my purse for that purchase. It wasn't so far."

"Most noblewomen would find five miles a difficult journey on foot."

"You forget I am a Thirsk," Wyl parried. "Even our women are tough," he added, working hard to keep vexation from his tone.

Before Liryk could reply, the doors of the chamber burst open and Valentyna strode in, her complexion slightly flushed from her hurried passage through the palace. Wyl had been anticipating her arrival with a hammering heart, and he felt it lurch now at the sight of her. He hurriedly dropped a low bow, glad that he had the excuse of riding breeches to avoid the more feminine curtsy. "Your highness," he murmured, his feminine voice catching in his throat. He could smell her soft scent of lavender. All he wanted to do was hold her, kiss her. He could do neither.

"Please, Ylena," Valentyna said, equally nervous but for different reasons, "be at ease."

Wyl looked at Valentyna's extended hand. He could not help himself; he took the Queen's hand in his own elegant fingers and kissed it—an unusual action for another woman. He saw her frown slightly as he looked up. Was it from consternation or had she recognized something in his eyes? He knew he was clutching at straws with such a notion. Surely all she saw before her was a ragged noblewoman.

"Thank you, your majesty, for permitting me an audience," he offered. It was all he could trust himself to say, and he was relieved to be rescued by the arrival of a servant with a tray of refreshments.

"Truly the pleasure is mine, Ylena," the Queen said, bafflement still evident in her expression. "Let us move to the balcony, shall we? It's a lovely morning." Valentyna led the way outside. "Liryk, you're most welcome to stay," she added, which of course was his cue to depart.

"I shall take my leave, your highness," he said, and saw the Queen's face relax at his decision. "I will leave a man outside the door should you need me again," he added, glancing toward Ylena Thirsk. His couched message was unmistakable. The Queen nodded at him, smiled her thanks at the servant, and offered to pour her guest a glass of sweet wine; Liryk was already forgotten. The Commander departed unhappily, his mood evident in his sour expression.

If Wyl's own sense of awkwardness was anything to judge by, Valentyna was equally unsure where to begin. He decided to take the lead.

"You have been expecting me, haven't you, your highness?" he asked, taking the cup of wine.

"Well, yes," Valentyna began, then shook her head slightly. "It's an odd thing, Ylena—may I call you that?"

*I'd prefer you to call me Wyl,* he thought. "Of course, your majesty. Please go on."

"Your letter said to wait for you and to trust you would come. My nobles insisted that without you they could not believe any of the recent claims against the Morgravian King, so I prayed for your arrival. And, curiously—please don't think me silly—"

"I would never do that," Wyl confessed, leaning forward and taking her hand. It felt so natural to do this and yet, he realized, it would strike the Queen as odd for her guest to be so instantly familiar.

Valentyna did not appear to be discomfited by his forwardness. "Even disheveled, you're really so beautiful—not at all like Wyl!" she exclaimed, and then burst into embarrassed laughter, covering her mouth. "My apologies, Ylena. I'm so surprised to see you my manners seem to have fled with my wits."

Wyl laughed. How could this woman say words that would normally offend and yet coming from her they seemed like playful affection? "Wyl was not handsome, your highness . . . and he knew it," he admitted.

"Ah," the Queen interrupted, "but Wyl, even though I knew him so briefly, was probably one of the most beautiful people on the inside that I will ever have the good fortune to meet."

Wyl felt himself glowing at the words. "I think if my brother could eavesdrop on this conversation, your highness, he would be more thrilled than you could ever know."

"He was so generous to my father and me," the Queen said somberly. "I can't quite shake the guilt of his death, knowing that he could have saved himself."

"It's probably not right of me to speak so openly, your highness, but Wyl was in love with you."

Valentyna felt a hot blush stealing up her throat. "How can you know this?"

"Romen told me," Wyl answered, and watched the Queen blink at the mention of her lover's name. It was wrong of him to do this, but he felt a little out of control in her presence. It was dangerous, though, feeling that anything was possible. He reined in his spiraling emotions.

"How well did you know Romen?" the Queen asked tentatively.

"We were together for several days, traveling to Rittylworth and its monastery. I got to know him well during that time, as people do when they eat together, ride together, and share thoughts that two strangers might not otherwise."

"Romen spent time here too. Did you know that he made a promise to your brother?"

"To protect us both. Yes, he told me."

"I—I would be honest with you," Valentyna struggled to say. "I was in love with Romen—I am still."

Ylena would have no way of knowing this and so Wyl framed an expression of gentle surprise on her face. He nodded, wanting to make it as easy as possible for Valentyna. "I can understand that, your highness. Romen was very tender toward me and I know he was a good man despite his occupation. I can see what a fine match the two of you would make."

Valentyna's eyes shone at the compliment. "Truly?"

Wyl nodded, hating himself and yet loving that he could lift her spirits so.

"No one else would agree with you, Ylena," the Queen admitted drily. "Romen might have been noble, but my realm has its collective heart set on a union between two royal households. But forgive me bleating on like this. I'm aware of your shocking losses, Ylena, and am ill at heart for you."

Wyl lowered his head but Valentyna reached over and clasped Ylena's hand. Her touch sent a tremor of joy through him.

"I have also heard about your courageous trip from Rittylworth to Felrawthy and know your brother would be so proud of you."

"How have you heard this, your highness?"

"Through Crys Donal."

Wyl moved free of her touch, surprised at such news. "Crys is here?"

The Queen nodded. "I'm sorry; perhaps I should have mentioned it earlier. There's so much to tell."

Wyl sat back, his pulse racing not with love now but with fear. What had occurred? "Please, tell me," he said.

"The Donal family was murdered."

Wyl stood abruptly, staggering slightly and gripping the balcony rail. He forced himself to breathe deeply. "You have proof?" His voice came out as a groan.

Valentyna's reply was soft. "Yes. Their deaths were confirmed by a witness." She paused to allow him to collect himself before she continued. "Crys was escorting Elspyth to the Briavellian border, which is how he escaped being killed too." Valentyna's voice was trembling. "It was Pil— the novice . . . You know of whom I speak?"

Wyl nodded without turning to look at her. He could not bring himself to explain that Ylena and Pil had traveled together.

"It was Pil who found Elspyth and Crys and alerted them to the tragedy, and Elspyth insisted the new Duke of Felrawthy accompany her to Werryl."

Wyl could not make his throat respond. It felt closed and as dry as tinderbush.

"My apologies, Ylena, I should have started from the beginning," Valentyna said. "It has been a shock for us all."

"Was it Celimus?" Wyl croaked.

"Apparently so. The men wore his colors, according to Pil and Lady Donal."

He swung around. "Lady Donal lives?"

Valentyna shook her head sadly. "I'm sorry, no. She died of her wounds, but the brave woman got herself as far as Brackstead, bringing the—" She stopped abruptly, realizing that what she had been about to say would only upset Ylena more.

"Bringing what?" Wyl insisted.

Valentyna stood, offered her hand, and ended up gently embracing her guest. She spoke softly. "Ylena . . . let me start again and tell you everything I know."

Wyl nodded glumly.

"Let's walk. I'll find it easier to revisit this painful story if I'm moving." She found a thin smile, but it was not returned by her guest. "Come, let us stroll in the gardens . . . if you're not too tired?"

"I'm not," Wyl said, numb from the shocking news but still glad for any time he could share with Valentyna. "Where is Crys now?"

"I'll send for him so you two can meet after our walk."

"And Elspyth—she's here too, I presume?"

At this the Queen paused and searched for the right words. She found nothing of comfort. Instead she spoke to Ylena in a straightforward fashion. "She disappeared during the night. You missed her by hours."

Wyl could no longer be shocked. He raised weary eyes to meet the searching blue gaze of the tall woman before him. "She's gone after Lothryn, then," he said, resigned.

"You know of him?"

He nodded. "What a mess," he murmured. "What a shocking mess my life is."

Valentyna did not understand the depth of his comment, but she nodded gently and took her guest's thin arm. "Come, the gardens will revive you even though what I have to tell you might not."

The two women, strikingly different in appearance, strolled quietly through the peaceful herb gardens. The dark of Valentyna's hair contrasted with the gold of Ylena's. Both were in riding clothes and Valentyna was quietly delighted that the noblewoman walking alongside her had not so much as blinked at her appearance. It struck her as odd, because most women she met were surprised that she preferred this masculine garb, and Ylena seemed the kind of fragile beauty who would be horrified to appear in anything but a perfectly tailored outfit. Yet here she was, entirely unself-conscious in dusty trews, her hair tied back, her face smudged and fingernails hastily but not successfully cleaned. It did not match up with the woman she had imagined. Fynch had given her such a detailed description of Wyl's beautiful sister, how elegant and sophisticated she was, that it hardly seemed this could be the same person walking beside her. Of course, Valentyna reminded herself, Ylena had been through considerable trauma in recent weeks, and she was of Thirsk stock. The bloodline had to prevail, she reasoned. And it was true that Ylena reminded her more and more of the Wyl she had known so briefly.

She spared the young woman none of the details, telling her everything she knew of what had happened in Morgravia.

"Where is Alyd's head now?" Ylena asked. Valentyna was surprised by both the forthrightness of the question and the young woman's control. She had expected an outburst of grief, but Ylena had shed not a single tear.

"Ylena, I know this is very difficult for you," the Queen began, trying to step gently around the tender subject of Alyd Donal's remains. "I will do whatever you wish."

"Bury him here," Wyl said without hesitation. "Tenterdyn is soiled with enough blood of its own. Let him lie alongside his mother."

Valentyna nodded. "That's how Crys felt about Aleda. He wanted her to belong here for the time being." They had made several revolutions of the herb garden now. "Are you tired?"

"I must be but I couldn't sleep anyway," Wyl replied, shaking his head. "All of this news is shattering, but there are plans to make. Tell me about Celimus, your highness."

Bemused by her enthusiasm to share her anxieties with this woman, who could do little to help her, Valentyna told Ylena everything she knew.

"I can't believe Krell would do such a thing," Wyl said, alarmed at how rapidly the situation in Briavel had deteriorated.

"If you had known him, you would understand how very accurate your comment is," Valentyna agreed. "It was foolish beyond belief and so out of character for him to do something so rash. Celimus now knows everything."

"Not everything, my queen," Wyl cautioned, and Valentyna could hardly believe the thrill the fighting words sent through her. "He has no idea where I am. We must keep it that way."

"But it will soon get out. If I have spies in Morgravia, Briavel is surely riddled with his watchers."

"True. It was a mistake for me to announce my real name," Wyl admitted. "But it was the only name that was going to get me through the palace gates. I need some time to think, your highness. Perhaps I might take that rest now, if you will permit it?"

"Of course. I'm glad you're here, Ylena," Valentyna said, surprising herself with such naked truth. "You may not look like your brother, but your personalities are devastatingly similar. He made me feel safe, as you do, curiously enough."

Ylena's face shone with Wyl's pleasure. "I am your servant, your highness. As my brother once pledged his allegiance to Briavel, so I do too."

"I accept it with gratitude, Ylena, but what can we two women do against that treacherous King to the west? I marry him shortly, do you know that?"

"Perhaps you must, your highness, but not without a plan," he said reassuringly, even as his stomach clenched at the thought. "Gather up all the latest information you can—everything your people can report."

The Queen wondered at what point in their conversation Ylena had assumed such authority, but she nodded her agreement. "My intention was to ask Crys Donal to leave Briavel," she added.

"Yes, he cannot remain here. It will only inflame the situation now that Celimus knows he has survived. Besides, Crys may be far more help to our cause in Morgravia."

"What do you mean?"

"I'm not sure yet, your majesty. May we talk again in a few hours?"

"Surely," the Queen said, and then, unable to help herself, added: "It's uncanny . . ."

"What is, your majesty?"

"Either I'm going mad or Shar himself is conspiring to confuse me." She gave Wyl a long, searching gaze and he watched, discomfited, as her eyes misted. "It sounds so foolish, but not only do you echo your brother, you remind me keenly of Romen Koreldy in the way you talk to me. He and I plotted together not so long ago on how to keep Celimus and his marriage proposal at bay. I feel as if I am reliving that moment." A tear escaped and ran down her cheek. "Oh, forgive me, Ylena. I know I'm making no sense."

"Don't be sorry," Wyl said, reaching into a pocket and handing the Queen a handkerchief.

Valentyna gave a small, harsh laugh. "No, you don't understand. Our mutual friend Elspyth asked me just a couple of days ago to keep an open mind on people who might pass through my life."

"You're right; I don't understand," Wyl admitted, trying to lighten the moment with a grin.

Valentyna dabbed at her cheeks with the handkerchief. Something tweaked at her mind, but she paid it little attention. "I hate feeling this weak. A mention, a reminder of Romen, anything that resonates of him can undo me."

"Then use his memory to make you strong. If he was able to make you feel safe, call upon that feeling to give you courage rather than allowing it to undo you," Wyl urged.

The Queen sighed, handing back the beautiful square of linen. Once more she felt a tug at her thoughts, but again she dismissed it as Ylena spoke.

"What were you going to say about people passing through your life?"

"Oh, nothing really." Valentyna pulled at a stalk of lavender, crushing the flower between her hands. Wyl had to look away; it was a painful reminder of happier times, when Valentyna had crushed a head of lavender and held up her palms to Romen for him to inhale the scent.

"Elspyth is determined that I should lock Romen away and open up my heart to others who might love me," the Queen continued, shyly now.

Wyl heard alarms klaxoning in his head. "And what else did the wise woman Elspyth advise, your highness?"

Valentyna smiled at his gentle sarcasm, not knowing how terrifying this conversation was for her guest. "It was an odd moment—she was most intense about her words. We were in this very place actually, and she begged me that should someone ever remind me strongly of Romen to take notice of it."

Wyl felt his stomach twist with relief. Elspyth had obviously danced around the topic. She had learned the lesson of a loose mouth in the harshest way at Tenterdyn—and his sister had died because of it. Elspyth would not make the same mistake again, although it had not stopped her from alluding to his secret.

He needed to get away before the conversation became even more dangerous.

"I am proud indeed that I remind you of someone you loved so much, your majesty," he said, and bowed to kiss the Queen's hand and take his leave. As he did, he inhaled the scent of lavender as he had done not so long ago in the guise of Roman Koreldy, and felt a rush of adoration and desire through his body.

W yl fled from the herb garden with its painfully sweet memories and was fortunate to bump into young Stewyt, the page who had looked after his needs when he was last in the palace, as Romen. He schooled his expression to show no recognition.

"Excuse me," he said, touching the youngster on the shoulder.

"My lady?" the lad said, bowing.

He had grown in the short time Wyl had been away. "What is your name?"

"Stewyt, my lady. May I help you?"

"I hope so. I'm a guest here and—"

"Yes, the household staff has been informed, Lady Ylena, and I have been appointed to wait on you, if that pleases?"

The boy had struck Wyl as sharp on their first meeting and it seemed this intuition had not been misguided. The page had been very sure of himself then and it had occurred to Wyl that Stewyt might be a spy for Chancellor Krell.

"It does please me," he replied now. "I was wondering where my chamber is."

"Let me take you there, my lady. Please follow me."

They engaged in small talk on the journey through the formal reception rooms of the palace, making their way up the beautiful marble staircase and then another flight—less ornate this time—toward the guest rooms. Stewyt was a competent guide, pointing out items of interest as they entered the western wing of the palace—a place Wyl had not been previously.

"We have arranged a suite for you, my lady. I hope you find the accommodation comfortable. Please let me know if there's anything I can fetch for you."

"Thank you," Wyl said, impressed by the lad's composure. He stepped past Stewyt into a freshly aired sitting room.

"The door over there leads into your sleeping chamber, my lady, and that other door is a dressing room where you might take your ablutions. Shall I send up a bath?"

"Please."

"Would you like a maid to help with your toilet?"

"Er, no, thank you, Stewyt. I would prefer to be alone right now." Wyl knew he should order some fresh clothes, but this new existence was hard enough. The riding clothes made him feel comfortable.

Stewyt nodded. "As you wish, my lady," and he bowed formally to take his leave.

It seemed to Wyl he would never escape the fragrance of lavender. A fresh bunch had been placed in a jar by the window and a light breeze carried the scent through the room. The stalks were mingled with mint, of all things. So typically Valentyna; he sighed. She'd probably ordered the arrangement herself.

He looked out from the window across Werryl Bridge. It was a magnificent sight from this high perspective. A procession of people crossed to and fro, in and out of Werryl city, and he noticed they all paid quiet homage to the newly erected statue of King Valor, who had taken his place among the other, more ancient royals who stood guard, made welcome and bade farewell to all who traveled the bridge. The people's love for Valor was evident in the way they paused to nod at his likeness or touch the statue's foot. It was poignant to watch and Wyl wished a similar tradition were followed in Morgravia to honor its revered dead. Then he stifled a nervous laugh at the mental picture that sprang to mind of the folk of Pearlis spitting on a statue of Celimus.

*I must not falter now,* he berated himself, knowing that being so close to Valentyna while trapped as Ylena was dangerous for him. He decided he should lie down, even if rest eluded him. Wyl was asleep in moments.

Fynch came to him in his dreams.

*I cannot stay long. I am traveling with Knave into the Razors.*

*Fynch! Is it really you?*

*Wyl, sending to you is hard for me, so don't talk, just listen. I know what troubles you. Offer to go to Pearlis on Valentyna's behalf. Buy her more time.*

*Celimus will have me killed.*

*But you are already dead, Wyl. Farewell. I hope we shall speak again.*

*Fynch? Fynch!*

Wyl woke trembling and disturbed.

# 9

YNCH SAT DOWN HARD ON THE SMALL MOUND OUTSIDE THE cottage that had been built by Elysius. "My head throbs."

Knave prowled nearby. *It will. Each time you use the magic, the pain will become a little worse.*

"I had to."

Knave did not comment. Instead he offered some advice. *Take some sharvan leaves from the pot in the cottage. Elysius used them to alleviate the pain.*

Fynch nodded and forced himself to stand, despite the lingering ache. "Do we leave immediately?"

*As soon as you feel strong enough.*

"I wish we didn't have to leave this place. I feel safe here."

*I understand, Fynch.*

"Why did he come, do you think?"

Knave knew to whom the boy referred. *To thank you.*

"Something odd happened."

Knave remained quiet, although the silence was filled with unspoken questions.

Fynch touched the dog on his large head as he moved toward the cottage. "Maybe I imagined it, but I felt connected to the King somehow."

*We all do.*

"No, it was more than that. I felt like I belonged to him," Fynch said softly, slightly embarrassed. "Even though I know my creature is Roark, the unicorn."

The dog offered no explanation and Fynch sensed his friend was confused when he replied: *It cannot be a bad thing to feel connected to the King of the Beasts.*

Fynch understood he would get no more insight from Knave. He knew the Warrior King had also sensed something between them. He had seen recognition flare in the creature's dark eyes. But the King had gone now and there was no point in teasing at that problem.

Not when there was a journey to make, a man to kill, and another to save.

Despite his sleep, Wyl did not feel rested in the slightest, and Fynch's words had so disturbed him that he could not face putting his head back on the pillow. Soon enough, a gaggle of servants arrived to deliver the bath, hot water, fresh clothes, and a tray of welcome food and wine.

He took his time luxuriating in the steaming water and staring at the trio of gowns Valentyna had sent for him to choose from. He hated the sight of them, despised having to climb into a dress and curtsy before the woman he loved. And what was more, something terrifying was occurring in Ylena's body. At first he had been alarmed by the creeping hurt that had begun low and deep, almost at his groin. Sharp needles of pain had stabbed regularly at him since he had woken. The heat of the bath had soothed them but not taken them away, and then a fresh ache across his back had begun. When the dull throb of a headache gathered, he knew he was ill, but it was only as he was considering how to explain the discomfort to a physic that he understood what this was all about. He had Ylena's monthly bleed. A new wave of sickness passed over him. How much more humiliation could he take? Did he truly have to contend with this?

He took his mind back to easier times, when life was bright and happy for Ylena. He recalled how she would withdraw each month for a day at least and rest, but he had hardly been privy to much more information than, "Your sister is indisposed. She leaves a message that you should visit tomorrow when she will be feeling better." He smirked bitterly in the warm waters. *The first day is always the worst,* she had told him when he had dared to ask more than was polite. So he had to deal with this pain for one day—and then what? How long would the bleed last? He knew there was something about linens and regular changing, but that was a woman's world. *His* world now. He dipped deeper into the warmth of the bath.

Fynch's words haunted him. His friend was right: What did it matter if Ylena died at the hands of Celimus, or anyone else? Her death would buy Valentyna time. Wyl Thirsk would go on living anyway, he thought grimly. Perhaps he could persuade Celimus to do the ugly deed and end it once and for all. But just as he began to work out a plan, he remembered Elysius's warning that if he attempted to contrive his own death, the repercussions would be savage. He could not risk another person he loved suffering and he felt sure the penalty would be leveled on someone else rather than himself.

He dropped Ylena's head to her hands in deep frustration, but in truth his mind was made up. Fynch's advice was wise. Wyl could represent Valentyna to Celimus. The King of Morgravia would hardly turn down the opportunity to welcome Ylena back to Stoneheart—and no doubt directly into her former cell in the dungeon . . . or worse. He cared not. The sooner he was rid of Ylena's body, the better. He felt sick at heart that he would lose her again, but he would be glad to no longer walk in her skin.

Wyl pondered a plan as he washed Ylena's hair and readied her for dinner. A small glow of luck saw a maid arrive to clear his tray. He begged a favor and it was taken care of in minutes. She brought him strips of linen and a strange brown liquid that smelled awful and tasted worse.

The young maid smiled at him as he thanked her. "The pain will go quickly, my lady. I'll have some more linens delivered."

The Duke of Felrawthy crossed the room and swept Ylena into his arms. "Wyl," he whispered into his prisoner's ear, "thank Shar you're safe."

Wyl felt self-conscious at the show of affection and yet knew it would appear perfectly normal to the Queen, who stood regally nearby, delighting in the reunion of her Morgravian guests. She looked dazzling in a dark brown gown

of the simplest design. Figure hugging, with no frills or
flounces, ruches or tucks, it flattered her tall, slim frame, the
deep color accentuating the brightness of her eyes against
her creamy complexion and the dark hair she had twisted up
behind her head with a tortoiseshell comb.

When he was placed back on the floor, Wyl took the
Duke's hand in his own and placed both their fists against his
own heart. It was the gesture of a Legionnaire, and in Morgravian society would have looked not only odd but vulgar
when performed by a woman. Fortunately, Valentyna had no
understanding of the gesture, although Wyl knew Crys would
instantly understand its intent. For Wyl, it was the only way
he could show his true self and convey the depth of his feeling for what had occurred.

"I'm shattered by the news of your family," he said softly.

Crys momentarily lost his tight grip on the sorrow he kept
locked away and Wyl saw it march slowly, painfully, across
the handsome Duke's features.

"I can't—" Crys began haltingly.

"I know," Wyl said, fighting down the lump that was closing his own throat. "I understand. Stay strong, Crys. Their
lives will not have passed in vain."

All Crys could do was gather up his hurts quickly and
hide them again. It was either that or break down completely. He nodded as he turned away.

Valentyna rescued them both. "Ylena, Crys, come, I've
had a table set up by the fire. Let us break some bread together."

Had the Queen deliberately chosen to entertain them in
the same chamber in which Wyl had first met her father,
with its secret doorway and huge tapestry covering the
privy? He could not guess but it felt strangely comforting to
be here again—as though he had come full circle. Nothing
much had changed in the room, save a few Valentyna-esque
flourishes. A jar of blooms, some fresh lavender and herbs
scattered on the floor that would release their scent as they
were crushed underfoot, a thick rug, and a charcoal-
sketched likeness of Valor done by his daughter that hung
unobtrusively in a corner. It was not a great work of art but

had obviously been done with raw emotion and she had somehow captured the spirit of the man. The final brightening touch was a tiny puppy, gamboling about near the warmth of the hearth, teasing at a bone.

Valentyna saw Wyl's amusement at the little fellow as they seated themselves and shrugged. "I miss Knave." Then she whispered, "I hear you have the curse. Have you taken some raspberry-leaf tea?"

Wyl nodded, though he had no idea whether he had taken such tea or not. He was startled by her candidness. Did women discuss these maladies openly with one another?

Valentyna's smile was all sympathy. "The first day is always the worst."

Wyl wondered if his face was flushed red with the embarrassment he was feeling and was glad when Crys claimed his attention, drawing him away from the Queen's conspiratorial gaze.

"You've heard that Elspyth has gone?" Crys inquired of Wyl, the young Duke fully composed again.

Wyl felt proud of him. Morgravia could recover with young men like this to lead the future. If only he could rid the realm of its present monarch, there was hope. "Yes, into the clutches of Cailech, I suspect."

"What can we do?" Crys asked, not really expecting a response.

"I shall have to go after her."

"What?" Valentyna cried, and Wyl could understand how strange his comment must have sounded. "What can a tiny creature like you do against Cailech and his Mountain Men?"

"Oh," Wyl said, finding a lazy grin he was certain Romen would be proud of, "you'd be surprised, your majesty."

"But you've never been there. You have no idea about this man!" Valentyna spluttered, the noblewoman's arrogance reminding her of someone she had once loved.

"True," Wyl lied. "But Elspyth decided to risk it," he continued, "and we have time on our side. Presumably she is on foot?"

The Queen nodded. "She took nothing, not even the horse she rode in on."

"She'll be a while getting into the Razors, then. In the meantime, there's a realm at stake."

Valentyna found a sad smile for her new friend. "I was measured for my wedding gown this afternoon."

"As you should be," Wyl said, suppressing the nausea that rose in his throat at the thought. "You must be seen to be progressing with your plans for the wedding, your highness. Let the spies report that you are preparing as any imminent bride would be."

Valentyna put down her goblet, her expression one of disgust. "And in the interim allow him to intimidate my people by setting up his arrogant Legionnaires in camps along our border?" She briefed her guests on everything she had gleaned from recent reports.

Wyl considered this information, sipping quietly from his own wine, as a poultry course was laid before them. Valentyna's fare was simple but delicious, as was her choice in most things. He stared now at the roasted chicken before him, the heady scents of lemon and rosemary wafting up to tantalize him.

"The Legion's movements are purely that," he said, looking up from his plate and sounding nothing like a pampered young noblewoman.

"Pardon me?" the Queen inquired, a fork speared with meat balanced halfway to her mouth.

"You think it's a ruse?" Crys chimed in.

Wyl shook his head. "No ruse. Celimus would not hesitate to send in his men, if pushed, but he has a good soldier's brain. And he's a king now with designs on broadening his empire, not losing his subjects. No, I think this is what you might call stage one. I would do precisely the same in his shoes."

"Which is what, exactly?" Valentyna asked, stunned by Ylena's sudden likeness to Liryk or, indeed, her own father. The girl's brother, Wyl Thirsk, had sounded just as straightforward in the final few moments she had known him as he had helped her escape the fate both he and her father had met that afternoon.

"Parade the might of the Legion, remind Briavel of the power that lies across the border. He knows you are aware that war with Morgravia would be insanity and that you will not permit it."

"Won't I?" she said, suddenly contrary. She sounded as if she would rather fight. Ylena's presence, fragile though it appeared, seemed to have given her a new rush of hope.

"No, your majesty," Wyl answered. Ylena's voice was high-pitched and very feminine, but the tone he managed to hit left no room for argument. "You will send him a declaration of your affections instead. A reinforcement, if you will, of your commitment to the marriage and peace for the region."

A hard blue gaze riveted Wyl to where he sat. He swallowed to loosen his throat, which felt suddenly tight. Oh, how he would love to take her in his arms and kiss her, declare his love, and tell her everything, to hell with whether she believed him or not. A roll of pain in his belly reminded him that the Queen saw a woman across the table and certainly did not harbor the same sentiments. What was more, her expression demanded an explanation of his statement.

He was about to continue when they were interrupted by a knock at the door. Valentyna called for one of her aides to enter and Wyl saw the irritation flicker across her face. He realized how much she would be missing Krell's competent presence, knowing how much he had screened from her and dealt with himself.

The man bowed. "Your highness, Commander Liryk said you would want to have this information immediately." He handed her a document.

"Thank you," the Queen said, standing as she took the paperwork and nodding to dismiss the messenger. She moved to the fire to read it. "Excuse me," she murmured to her guests.

Both watched her expression grow more serious as she read, then darken. She let out a harsh sound, half laughter, half despair. Wyl pushed his chair back and, despising the swish of his gown and girlish click of his heels, was at her side.

"Your highness, what is it?" He could see her pale before him. Crys too was on his feet. "Your majesty?"

The Queen shook her head, eyes closed, jaws firmly clamped together as she gathered herself. She opened her eyes and they were filled with tears. "Our spies report that King Celimus of Morgravia is on his way north to Felrawthy, where he will meet for a parley with the Mountain King."

"Cailech and Celimus?" Wyl murmured in disbelief.

She nodded. "It's a reliable source too."

"What on earth would they have in common?" Crys said into the tense silence.

"Briavel!" Valentyna banged her fist against the mantelpiece and let out a sound of deep anguish. "They mean to destroy us."

"Wait, Valentyna!" Wyl cried, forgetting himself and all protocol. "Let me think." He began to pace.

Anyone who had known Fergys Thirsk, and perhaps his son, would be aware that this was a family trait. It had always amused Magnus to see his general pacing as he formulated battle or peace plans, and if Ylena or Alyd were alive, they would be able to confirm that Wyl was hewn from the same block. Neither of the two people watching Ylena pacing now had known Fergys or Wyl Thirsk that well, but Valentyna had known Romen and she had watched him perform this very action when thinking and plotting. It struck her so resoundingly she felt her breath catch in her throat. Even more disconcerting was the fact that Ylena was pulling at her ear as she paced, a habit Valentyna had teased Romen Koreldy about on several occasions during their short time together. There it was again, the tugging at the right ear, the relentless slow pacing, the face lost in thought. *Shar!* She was going mad. She looked away and reached for her wine, swallowed it in a single draft. The liquor helped steady her but did nothing to alleviate the shock of the news or the bewildering sense of Romen's presence.

Suddenly she was reminded of Fynch's strange suggestion that Wyl Thirsk and Romen Koreldy were of one mind. The boy had stopped just short of saying they were one person. How could it be that Wyl's sister now seemed to reflect similar traits? And then Elspyth's words blew through her mind:

*I believe that some people are reincarnated. Perhaps you should listen more carefully to your friend Fynch. It is to this which he refers, I am sure. And you must promise me that should another person look at you and perhaps touch you emotionally as Romen did, reminding you uncannily of the man you loved, that you will permit it.*

*Permit them to love me, you mean?* Valentyna remembered saying in amusement, almost teasing.

But Elspyth had nodded seriously and added, *Perhaps even a woman.*

Valentyna looked back at Ylena. *Perhaps even a woman.* She gasped, turning away to hide the sound and the frightened look on her face. What was happening here? What was Shar's plan? Something else nagged at the edges of her mind, something urging her to recall it. But it remained on the fringe, hovering and niggling, and her anxiety over this latest action of the Morgravian King won the battle and banished the thought. Valentyna had to focus on Celimus and his intentions, not her spiraling emotions and deranged thoughts that Ylena Thirsk was the embodiment of Romen Koreldy! *Fool!* she screamed at herself inwardly.

Crys urged Wyl to speak his thoughts.

Wyl swung around, the swish of his gown annoying him again. How he wished he could at least be Faryl, tall and strong in her masculine clothes. "I know Celimus," he said, just pulling himself back from blurting out, *I know Cailech too.* "And I have traveled with someone who knows Cailech," he lied.

"And?" Valentyna prompted, pushing away her own confusing thoughts.

Wyl raised Ylena's delicate hands. "Celimus despises Cailech. He is quietly obsessed with the Mountain King, your highness, and nothing would prompt him to organize a parley with a sovereign whose realm, I'm sure, he entertains visions of destroying."

"At least Celimus is consistent in his ambitions," Valentyna commented bitterly. "Go on."

"Everything I've heard suggests that Cailech hates Morgravia's new king just as energetically—has more reason to, in fact." Wyl's mind was racing. "So in truth, I can't see either of them making such a move of their own volition. Something has prompted it."

"As the Queen suggests, then—joining forces against Briavel," Crys argued.

Wyl shook his head, felt Ylena's hair bob from side to side, and grimaced to himself. "No. Celimus doesn't need the Mountain King to overwhelm Briavel. The Legion could crush the Briavellian Guard resoundingly. If he were of a mind to do so, he could take Briavel by force and then combine the armies to take on Cailech. That's the more logical scenario—no offense intended, your highness."

"None taken," she replied, frowning. There was no doubting it: She felt as if she were being briefed by a soldier. "Why the parley, then?"

"Does the letter say any more?"

Valentyna scanned it quickly again. "No, just the name of the man who brought the original message out of the Razors and delivered it to Celimus's people."

"Who was it?" Wyl said. No doubt someone reliable like Myrt, he reckoned.

Valentyna squinted at the page. "Dreadful writing," she murmured. "I think it says his name is Farrow. Yes, Aremys Farrow."

# 10

USING FRESH HORSES AT INTERVALS, KING CELIMUS HAD SWEPT through the gates of Tenterdyn earlier than he'd expected. He was impressed by the sprawling estate of Felrawthy's duke and delighted to see that the manor itself was exceptionally well appointed. For a provincial family, the Donals had not lived without creature comforts. Freshly bathed and changed now, and having taken ownership of Jeryb's magnificent study with its view over the heather-laden moors, Celimus nodded at his chancellor. "Bring him before me."

Jessom entered the small antechamber where Aremys Farrow had been asked to wait. "I trust there are no tricks up your sleeve, my friend," he cautioned the mercenary.

Aremys eyed the hook-nosed Chancellor. "Just earning my living, Jessom," he replied. "Lead on."

The man turned and showed Aremys into the main chamber.

"Farrow," Celimus said from the window where he had been admiring the vista.

"Your highness," Aremys returned, dropping a low bow.

"You are quite a surprise."

"That is not my intention, sire," the mercenary replied, straightening.

"Will you tell me how it comes about that you are working for my enemy?"

"Your highness, I am a man available for hire by anyone with coin to pay. I am always loyal to my employer, as your chancellor would know. You must not fear that I have shared any secrets with Cailech, just as he need not fear I will share any of his with you," Aremys said smoothly.

"So you admit he has secrets?" Celimus said, moving in his fluid, elegant manner to sit on the corner of Jeryb's old desk.

"We all have secrets, your majesty," Aremys said carefully. "It does not mean they necessarily impact on one another."

"Farrow, I would know how you came to be in the Razors when you were on paid business for the Crown of Morgravia," Celimus replied testily, tiring of the banter.

Aremys was prepared for this question. "Your majesty, I was following the trail of Ylena Thirsk, as instructed."

"Did you meet up with Leyen?" the King interrupted.

"No, sire. But I believe she may have discovered that our prey had visited this very house."

"Is that so?" Celimus said, olive eyes narrowing.

Aremys moved into the critical area of his fabricated story. He would have to be convincing. "I don't know what happened to Leyen. I presume she must have given up her pursuit because I haven't found any trace of her since Tenterdyn. Perhaps she had other tasks to perform?" he prompted carefully, and pretended not to see the glance between Chancellor and King.

"I gathered Ylena Thirsk had already left Tenterdyn before Leyen's arrival," Aremys continued, "and found myself giving chase to the eldest son of Felrawthy and the Thirsk woman, who seemed to be heading north to the very rim of the Razors before veering east."

Celimus nodded. "Into Briavel."

Aremys hesitated, a question in his expression. Perhaps the King knew something he did not.

"We have heard reports that Crys Donal is at Briavel's palace. Perhaps Ylena is with him."

Aremys wondered how in Shar's name the heir to Felrawthy had found himself in Werryl, although having heard with horror of the slaughter of Jeryb's clan, he wasn't terribly surprised that the young man had fled Morgravia. "Not necessarily, your highness," he said into the lengthening silence.

"What do you mean?" Celimus queried.

"Your spies have not reported a sighting of Ylena Thirsk, have they?"

"Not yet, no."

"Hmm," Aremys said, quietly theatrical, as though thinking through something complex.

"Farrow, you still haven't explained how you come to be with Cailech's people," Jessom prompted.

Aremys understood now why Wyl had disliked Jessom so deeply. He felt his own hackles rise at the interruption.

"I was getting to that, Chancellor. I overnighted in a border village, preparing to cross into Briavel the next morning to see if I could pick up the trail of Ylena Thirsk. There was no inn, just a shorrock house, and perhaps I had one too many, I don't know. I suspect my nip was spiked with something in order to make it easier for thieves to set upon me later. It seems I wandered away from the main village in a stupor, and I do remember stumbling onto a track which I presumed would lead me into the Razors proper. I was very cold, I recall, and desperate to lie down. I remember men following me from the village, which is what drove me toward the mountains. But I'm afraid I remember very little else, sire."

The King shook his head. "So what occurred next, Farrow?"

"I've pieced together that the thieves did attack me but were fended off by some men from the Razors, obviously using the track to enter Morgravia. They dealt with the villagers swiftly, by which time I was unconscious, and then decided to take me with them."

"Why?" Celimus demanded.

"I don't know, sire. Perhaps they knew I would die in the cold if they didn't. They could see I was drugged and had been set upon by bandits. They felt obliged." He shrugged.

"Obliged!" Celimus roared. "To help a Morgravian?"

Aremys was determined not to be intimidated. He kept his voice low. "They are not all murderers and thieves, your highness. The people of the Razors have scruples, families, a desire for peace—"

"Ah, you sympathize with the Mountain horde, Farrow?" the King interrupted, a definite barb in his tone.

"My king, I am a Grenadyne, so my soul is of the north. I like the notion that realms may prosper in peace rather than conquering one another through war."

"Is that what this is all about, then?"

"Yes, your highness."

"Cailech is holding out the olive branch to Morgravia?" Disbelief was thick in the King's voice.

Aremys nodded slowly. "You would like him, your majesty, if you'd agree to meet with him."

"This is rich beyond words, Farrow. When did the leap from drugged captive to King's counsel take place, might I ask?"

"King Cailech naturally wished to meet the stranger who had been picked up lurking on the fringe of the Razors. He learned that I was from the north, working as a mercenary in the south, and on business for the Crown of Morgravia. He does not know the details of my task for you, your highness. When the King interviewed me our conversation led us toward discussing the future of the Mountain People. When he said it was his greatest desire to create peace in the region, I asked him what was stopping him from discussing the same with the King of Morgravia. I mentioned that you were preparing for your wedding, sire, and that the two great realms of Morgravia and Briavel would soon be joined in peace. It fired his imagination, I think. He asked me to set up this meeting."

"That's it?" Jessom posed. "You are merely a go-between?"

Aremys did not look at the Chancellor but addressed Celimus. "Yes, sire, that is precisely what I am. Because I had been employed directly by you, Cailech thought it would be easier for me to seek an audience and set up this parley. He believed you were more likely to trust me than him."

"I don't trust anyone, Farrow, least of all mercenaries who have no loyalties."

Aremys said nothing but he did not shrink under the hard gaze of the King. He understood that Celimus was used to staring down others. *He must practice it in his mirror,* Wyl had once commented caustically. Aremys remembered that now and had to stop himself from smiling.

"King Celimus, I sell my services, not my soul," he finally replied, determined to stand his ground. "Cailech certainly does not own me—no one does. I am here to respectfully suggest that you, the reigning sovereign of a powerful kingdom, might consider it worthwhile to listen to what your northern neighbor has to say. Far more can be achieved around the dinner table, sire, than on the battlefield."

"So now you're a philosopher and peacemaker, Farrow? I could have you killed for your insolence."

"Yes, you could, sire," Aremys said in a tone that made it clear he knew that worse had happened to innocents around this man. "But I ask your forgiveness if I have given the impression of presumptuousness. What you need to understand is that my own life is at stake, sire."

That seemed to win the King's attention. He gestured for Jessom to pour some wine. "Carry on," he told Aremys.

Jessom offered Aremys a cup of wine and the mercenary was relieved by the gesture. Perhaps he would make it out of this meeting alive after all.

"Thank you," he said before continuing. "I give the impression of being a free man, sire, but I am in fact Cailech's prisoner. I have bought my freedom with the promise that I would attempt to set up this meeting. No money will exchange hands."

Celimus held his cup up toward Aremys in an ironic toast. "You play with your life freely, mercenary."

"It is mine to give, although I'm not sure I had any choice, your majesty."

"And did you think I'd just say yes?"

"I could only hope so, sire."

"In order to save your life?" Celimus mocked.

"No, my lord. To save Morgravia from war. I presume you'd like your marriage to be conducted in peace."

Celimus arched a perfectly shaped eyebrow. "So the Mountain upstart believes he can wage war on Morgravia—is that right?"

Aremys was tired of this but knew he was treading a fine line. Celimus walked his own knife edge of madness and would just as easily snuff out a person's life as swat at a fly. He needed to be careful. "No, your majesty. I think he believes he can achieve peace between his realm and yours."

Celimus smiled slyly and walked around Jeryb's desk to sit down. As he did so, Aremys had time to notice a child's engraving in the wood of the desk. The letters carved clumsily into the timber said ALYD and the mercenary was reminded of how that young man had been treated by this very King—his life taken on a whim, in front of his new wife and his closest childhood friend. That same friend who was now considered friend by Aremys. The mercenary felt a charge of anger as he considered that the two great families of Morgravia—the Donals of the north and the Thirsks to the south—had been all but wiped out on the command of the cruel man before him.

He watched Celimus lean back in Jeryb's handsome chair and sip from Jeryb's cup what was presumably a refreshment from Jeryb's cellar. Anger settled in his gut. He joined Wyl in hating Celimus more than any other man, alive or dead, and determined to bring about his demise.

"Farrow," the King began in a voice filled with tedium, as though explaining something obvious to someone stupid, "you know full well that I will not risk myself by going into the Razors to meet with your cowardly captor, a man who sends one of my own people—if I dare call you that—to do his dealings for him."

"I realize that, your highness."

"So I must presume that he is prepared to risk coming here alone, for I will not brook his men setting foot on Morgravian soil."

"They would set up camp at the border," Aremys replied, as though he and Cailech had already anticipated as much from Celimus. He felt relieved that the Captain had not reported that Aremys had been escorted into Morgravia by men of the mountains. Aremys inwardly saluted Bukanan's foresight at not risking anything that might turn this situation ugly. Presumably the man knew how vicious his king could be and that an opportunity to make an example of Cailech's men would prove irresistible.

"I see. So that means Cailech is perfectly comfortable about coming to meet me, in Morgravia, with no protection other than the sword of a Grenadyne mercenary who is in my employ and presently under my guard?" Celimus's tone was filled with ironic amusement.

"I am not his protector, sire. I am purely his emissary."

"Excellent. The situation is even more precarious, then, for Cailech is all alone and on Morgravian soil. What is to stop me from simply killing him?"

"Your desire for peace, sire," Aremys offered as reasonably as he could. "The men of the Razors can be damnably elusive and they do not forgive, my lord. I am guessing they would wage systematic attacks on your borders until their last man fell . . . the last woman, even."

"That does not scare me, Farrow," the King replied, lazily twirling his goblet. "Frankly, I'd prefer his head on a spike at Stoneheart to holding talks in my court."

"Of course he does have some insurance, sire."

Celimus laughed, genuine enjoyment spicing the mirth. "Of course he does! Now what could Cailech possibly offer me that I don't have and could possibly want?"

Aremys felt a tremor of fear pass through him. He was about to weave his most audacious lie yet, the only trump card he could produce from up his sleeve, and to a king who would have his throat slit from ear to ear this very second if he even suspected the ruse. "I believe there is one item you desire more than anything else, sire."

"I didn't know you possessed such magical insight into my desires, Farrow. Perhaps I should have you tortured and burned as a warlock?"

"No enchantments, sire," Aremys replied calmly. "Simple logic tells me what you covet at present."

"And that is?" Celimus said, a sarcastic sneer on his face.

"Ylena Thirsk, your highness."

The sneer vanished instantly, as did the casual posture. The King sat forward, suddenly alert. "You have her?"

"I will deliver her, your majesty, on the promise that both Cailech's life and my own are ensured your complete protection. We will come to Morgravia for the parley and you will allow him an escort of his men. Your two best captains, including Bukanan, who I gather is currently indispensable in the north, will stay at the border with the Mountain warriors. When the parley is complete, we will be escorted safely to the border of the Razors and permitted to depart into the mountains. When this promise is in writing and announced publicly to your people, I will arrange for Ylena Thirsk to be delivered to you."

Celimus ignored everything Aremys had just listed. "Do you have her, Grenadyne?" the King bellowed.

"I do, sire," Aremys lied, schooling his features to show an expression without guile. "Although I am not at liberty to tell you how that came to pass or where she is." He smiled. "I do not require payment for her capture, sire. I would not consider that fair," he added, and chanced a soft grin.

The idea to use Ylena as bargaining power had only occurred to Aremys when he had stood before Captain Bukanan and had arrogantly claimed that he had something in store that would keep Cailech's life safe. He had no idea where Wyl was or how he might reach him, but he reckoned Celimus would go along with the notion that Aremys was holding Ylena, not just because he was a mercenary paid to track her down, but because the King wanted her. Celimus's own greed and cruel desire to visit more torture on this last remaining member of the Thirsk dynasty far outweighed any doubt of Aremys's honesty—at least, that was what Aremys was counting on. How he would deliver on his promise or, more to the point, wriggle out of it, was a whole new problem, but for now he was bargaining for his life and Wyl was all he had. If he could win Celimus's nod with the lie, he would also win his freedom from Cailech. He reassured himself that he had no intention of betraying Wyl; he was simply using Ylena's name as the lure to buy some time and his own safety.

Celimus leapt to his feet. His eyes were dark and stormy with wrath, and Aremys wondered if he had misjudged the monarch. But he had not. The impending storm cleared as swiftly as it had gathered and the King began to laugh as he applauded Aremys.

"Bravo, Farrow. Bravo indeed. I shall guarantee your life and that of King Cailech for the duration of his stay on Morgravian soil. Is that good enough?"

"With all the other provisos in place, sire."

"Yes, I agree. When?"

"When it suits you, your majesty. You are the host."

"Where, Jessom?" Celimus asked.

"Here, of course, sire. Tenterdyn offers easy access to and from the border, plus the ambience of a provincial palace. I would suggest a feast and entertainment, your highness. Show Cailech that you are a magnanimous host and prepared to extend the hand of fellowship while you hear what he has to say."

"Good. See to it all, Jessom." Celimus turned back to Aremys. "And Ylena?"

"I will start making preparations, sire," Aremys said, feeling very nervous now.

"Waste not a minute, Farrow. Return to your captor and pass on your news. I expect the Thirsk woman to be delivered as soon as our talks are done."

Aremys bowed and departed, eager to be out of the King's sight.

# 11

SO HOW DID THIS AREMYS FELLOW END UP IN THE RAZORS IF HE was with you in Briavel?" the Queen asked, having discovered why both her guests had reacted so dramatically to the mention of the man's name.

"I have no idea," Wyl replied, feeling both relief and delight that Aremys was alive. "We lost each other in the north."

"How does one lose someone?" Valentyna said, sipping her wine.

It was not a serious question and Wyl opted not to answer it. "Long story," he murmured. "I have an idea," he added hurriedly when it seemed the Queen might want to hear the long story. Fynch's suggestion would work now, with this latest news about Aremys.

"A plan?" Valentyna repeated, fractionally sarcastic. She folded her arms.

"Yes. But you won't care for it much."

"What's this about?" Crys queried.

"We have to buy some time with Celimus," Wyl explained, and Crys nodded. "So we buy it with me."

"He'll kill you!" Valentyna exclaimed.

"No, he won't," Wyl said, not believing it himself.

"He razed Rittylworth Monastery and its village, killing dozens, before turning on Tenterdyn and slaughtering my family," Crys said, his voice cold, "all to hunt you down. Don't tell me he won't kill you the moment he sees you." Then he added, quietly, "You know what will happen!" He was stilled from saying anything further by a dark glare from Ylena.

"What will happen?" Valentyna asked, sensing a new tension.

Wyl shook his head, ignoring the Queen's question. "He won't kill me because of Cailech," he said. "I'll make sure to time my arrival when the King of the Mountains is present. If they're planning some sort of treaty, Celimus won't be so stupid as to demand the death of a noble before his newly formed partnership, will he?"

"Won't he?" Valentyna said, an appalled expression accompanying her query. "You're gambling an awful lot on his sense of courtesy."

Wyl was relieved she had been diverted, and replied, "I know Celimus. I grew up around him. If he has one outstanding quality, it is his charm. No, I don't think he will harm me while he needs to maintain outwardly calm relations."

"And what about afterward, when Cailech's gone? Why will he care then?" she demanded.

"Because I shall be gone too. Aremys is there—he will help me escape."

"No," Valentyna said from the fireplace, her voice raised. "I can't let you do it. It's ridiculous and of no substance. I won't permit it."

Wyl took a silent breath. He would not enjoy this next statement. "I am not yours to command, your highness."

The words hit her as effectively as a punch. She struggled to control her expression as pain battled with her defenses. "My apologies, Ylena. I think I misunderstood our talk earlier," the Queen replied, her tone as tepid as the congealed gravy around the chicken they had all forgotten to eat.

"No, your highness. There is no misunderstanding. I am loyal to you and to Briavel. That will never change. But I will make my own decision on how to serve."

"You will be going to your death, Ylena!" the Queen snapped.

"I don't believe so, but I choose that path come what may."

"Not on my behalf! I will *not* have your blood as well as your brother's on my hands."

"I'm sure you tried to order Wyl around too, your highness, but it seems you lost that argument as well. I am just as stubborn when it comes to protecting those I love." The bit about love had slipped out. Wyl felt Ylena's face color afresh at the error.

Valentyna missed the slip. "Ylena, you are barely into your womanhood!" she exclaimed.

"And it is my womanhood which demands I leave your table, your highness. Please forgive me," Wyl said, suddenly feeling a most unpleasant release to the build-up of pain that had accompanied him all day. Still, it was a welcome excuse to get away from the Queen's commands.

Crys looked baffled but the Queen, still angry, could only nod. She understood precisely Ylena's predicament. "By all means."

Wyl fled toward his chamber, clean linens, and a fresh brew of raspberry-leaf tea. He hated being a woman. And he especially hated the disdain shown to women by others of the same sex. How dare Valentyna consider Ylena unworthy? *Well, that's not really fair,* he told himself as he ran up the last flight of stairs. Not unworthy, but certainly ineffective. He thought of Faryl and wished Valentyna had had the opportunity to meet her. Then the Queen would have seen a woman hold her own against a man.

He spent the next few minutes with an expression of disgust on his face as he sipped at the raspberry-leaf tea and replaced the linens. He felt quite worn out by the end of it all and, in a fit of pique, changed into his favored trews and shirt, although he had to admit the skirt was easier to wear in his current condition.

*Shar, please deliver me from this,* he prayed as he drank the bitter tea. *Let me be a man again.*

A knock at the door interrupted his plea. He was not surprised to see that it was Valentyna, but he was embarrassed.

"May I come in?" she asked.

"Of course, your highness," Wyl said, clearing his throat. "I'm sorry, I—"

"No, it's quite all right. It is I who should apologize. Forgive my interruption," Valentyna began. "Oh, good, I see you've brewed more leaf. How are you?"

"Oh, you know, first night," Wyl said, offering a half smile like an old hand.

"Had you hoped you were pregnant?" the Queen startled him by asking in her most gentle tone.

"No, your highness. I knew I wasn't," Wyl lied, unable to think of anything more enlightening.

"I'm sorry. I shouldn't have asked. I just thought that, newly married, you and Alyd had probably . . . well, you know . . ."

"Yes," Wyl interjected, disturbed by where the conversation was headed. He had never felt more of an impostor. "No baby, though."

Valentyna looked wistful. "You know, Ylena, there are moments when I wish more than anything that I had joined with Romen and that his seed had quickened my womb."

Wyl had to look away. This was too painful. He busied himself with tidying his discarded clothing.

Valentyna rallied a smile and changed the subject. "I see you've changed out of the gown. Not to your liking?"

"It's lovely, your highness. I just got so used to these comfortable clothes while traveling."

Valentyna nodded knowingly. "I often prefer my breeches myself. Men have it good. I often wish I was a man, don't you, Ylena?"

"I do, your highness. I'm wishing it right now in fact." Wyl had never spoken a truth with more passion.

She took his intensity in a different light. "Ah yes, I can understand why. You presumably get a lot of pain. I must admit that I escape the cramps. Shar is merciful with me."

"Do you look forward to children of your own?" Wyl asked, desperate to push away from the subject of women's ailments and yet not doing so very successfully.

"I do. I've decided it's the one good thing that might come out of this hateful marriage. Celimus won't have my love, but he can have my body. He will give me something far more precious than he takes."

Wyl grimaced as the fresh ache from his side joined with the pain of the image of Celimus siring a child upon Valentyna.

Valentyna filled the difficult pause. "I came here to apologize for my heavy-handed tactics earlier. Even as a little princess, I bossed everyone around," she said, trying to lighten the mood swirling about them. "I know I cannot permit or deny you anything, Ylena. I just don't want you to forfeit your life in order to save me from Celimus."

"I don't think I can save you from the marriage, but I can give you more time to get used to the idea," Wyl said, the resignation in his comment agonizing in its truthfulness.

"But you can't guarantee that you will escape."

"There are no guarantees in life, your highness. I have lost too much in too short a time to care anymore."

"But I don't want to lose you as well," the Queen said, her tone plaintive.

"You won't."

"What exactly is your plan?" Valentyna said. "No, wait, let's have some warmed milk sent up. We can lace it with some liquor to help you sleep and forget your pains."

Wyl nodded. Valentyna looked outside and called to

Stewyt, who had been positioned for the night outside the door, sending him to the kitchens.

"Now, tell me everything," she said, curling up next to Ylena on the deep sofa near the fire.

She was unbearably close but Wyl would have slashed his own throat sooner than ask her to sit apart from him. If this was all he could have, it would have to be enough.

"I shall go to Felrawthy, present myself before King Celimus—ensuring that King Cailech is in attendance—and beg Morgravia's indulgence."

"But what is your aim? I can't see the point if I have to marry him anyway."

"Well, among other things, to get the Legionnaires redeployed from Briavel's border. Their presence is making your people very nervous, and rightly so."

"But you said it was only a ploy."

"I am assuming that, your highness. I can't truly speak for Celimus's whims. Regardless, I would see the physical movement of the Legion away from the border."

"And you think he'll do it?" the Queen asked, amazed.

"Yes. I'll tell him that you are nervous, that you feel intimidated and threatened—which is, of course, his intention. I'll assure him that your personal preparations are well advanced and I'll give him a token of your loyalty to him and the truth of your claims."

"And what's that?"

"Me."

"So he can kill you!" Valentyna exclaimed, exasperated again.

"He won't do that in front of Cailech, your highness. But he will be appeased. He will realize that for you to relinquish me, you have been duly intimidated. The plan is perfect in its simplicity. My presence will confirm not only your commitment to peace and the marriage, but also your desire to appease him—you have gladly turned over his enemy who had run to you for protection."

"And how does that save you, Ylena?"

"It doesn't—but please, your majesty, let me worry about saving myself. I have a few tricks of my own."

"Oh, you're so frustrating!" Valentyna replied. "You sound like Wyl and Romen rolled into one." Then she stopped, shocked at what she had said without thinking.

"Do I? How odd," Wyl replied.

They stared at each other, the candlelight and flames from the fire combining in a soft glow across their beautiful faces. They were so close, Wyl realized. Too near. Close enough to kiss. A madness came over him and smothered his judgment. It was the move of a lunatic and he knew it, but still he leaned across the few inches separating his mouth from the Queen's and placed Ylena's lips to Valentyna's.

The Queen reacted as if burned by a spitting coal from the fireplace. She leapt to her feet, wiping frantically at her mouth. "Ylena!" she spluttered, shock and anger combined on her face.

Wyl felt frozen with horror at his actions. "I'm sorry," was all he could manage. "I beg your forgiveness, your highness."

The Queen appeared uncertain whether to flee or slap the woman before her. Then she gathered her wits. "No," she said, holding up a hand. "I must have been giving off all the wrong signals. Forgive me, Ylena, I should not have come to your chamber tonight. All this talk of babies and changing into men . . ." She laughed awkwardly and then that awful expression of disgust crossed her face again.

Wyl stood, feeling sorry for both of them. "The apology is all mine, Valentyna. I don't know what came over me. I've been through a lot these few weeks and the emotions have got me all confused," he offered. It was pathetic even to his own ears, but he pressed on, desperate to fill the vile and difficult silence that would surely prevail if he did not keep talking and backing her toward the door. "It's been a very long two days for me, without much sleep, and I shall put it down to the raspberry-leaf tea clouding my judgment, your highness."

"Yes," Valentyna stammered, none of her mortification dissipating. "I've heard it can make one hallucinate."

"You don't even look the tiniest bit like Alyd," Wyl said, hating himself for the weak jest at the expense of his beloved sister and friend.

There was a knock at the door and the Queen started, her hands wringing each other. "That will be the milk," she said, and Wyl heard the slightly hysterical note in her voice. He lowered his head, ashamed of himself as never before. "I'll leave you, Ylena," Valentyna managed with some grace.

"No, I'll leave you, your highness," Wyl said, bending to kiss her hand. He could feel her fingers pulling away with revulsion at the touch of Ylena's lips and could have wept at his own lack of control and stupidity of moments earlier. He would never forgive himself and she certainly would not.

The Queen, flushed and agitated, pulled open the door and pushed past the same serving maid who had helped Wyl earlier.

"Thank you," he said wearily to the girl as she placed the milk on a small side table. "Can you ask the page to bring me parchment, quills, and ink, please?"

There was not anything to pack, and nothing other than his memories to keep him here a minute longer. He lifted the letters from the desk and blew out the flickering candle, leaving behind the debris of his hurried toil—sealing wax, broken nibs, ink blotches, as well as various letters begun and crumpled on the floor, where he had tossed them in frustration. He bent now to pick them up and threw them into the embers of the fire he had not bothered to tend. The paper sputtered and curled before catching and burning quickly in a brief eruption of flames. He watched until his awkward words of explanation to the woman he loved were nothing but blackened flakes—just like the fragile relationship he had clung to and now ruined.

He cast a glance at the letter in his hand. After several attempts he had finally settled on being Wyl and the words were brief and to the point. There was nothing of Romen's charm, Faryl's cunning, or Ylena's courtesies, merely a simple apology for his unforgivable behavior and a reiteration that he was making for Felrawthy. No honeyed farewell, no promise of return, no attempt at reconciling their awkward parting. He would be gone from her life once and for all. Wyl had wished her well for her upcoming marriage and encouraged her to be brave and stoic in what she faced. To never forget who she was and to remember her promise to bring forth a babe who would rule both realms with honor and love. Wyl could not save her this trial or the destiny of an unhappy life with Celimus, but he could let her know that he had listened to her soft words and wished her the joy of loving a child. He suspected that this part of the letter might make her cry, but he knew she would read the rest with only relief that he had gone. "So be it," he muttered to himself as he strode across the room to the door.

Stewyt was sitting outside, straight-backed and wide-awake. No need to rub the sleep from those alert eyes, Wyl thought.

"Thank you, Stewyt, for waiting up," he said.

"A pleasure, my lady. I am here to serve," the page said, sounding mature far beyond his years. "May I take those for you?"

"Please," Wyl said.

"I will personally deliver them immediately, my lady."

"No, Stewyt, I would prefer if you would arrange their delivery in the early hours of the morning. I don't wish either recipient disturbed tonight and there is nothing of such import that it cannot wait until tomorrow."

Stewyt nodded, then hesitated, and Wyl saw him take in the change of clothes from gown to breeches. "Is there anything else I can do for you tonight, my lady? Perhaps I could send up some refreshment, have the fire stoked?"

Wyl cut him off with a gently raised hand. "Nothing, thank you," he said, forcing a smile. He had no intention of letting the curious page know of his movements. "I am very tired and sleep calls."

"I shall see you're not disturbed again then, my lady. Good night and sleep well." Stewyt gave a solemn bow and moved swiftly off into the shadows of the corridor.

Wyl waited for what felt an interminable time, making sure the inquisitive page did not see his departure. Eventually, he tiptoed from his chamber and made his way quietly down the various flights of stairs. At one landing he noticed a portrait of Valentyna he did not recall having seen before.

In the low light of the sconces, the tall figure seemed to be pulling away from the wall, advancing on him. Her expression struck him as accusatory, the faint smile mocking. If only she knew the truth, he thought, and regretted bitterly that he could not share it with her. He extended his hand toward the painting, hoping he could reach high enough to touch her on the lips, but Ylena's fingers only stretched to Valentyna's chest. It would do.

"Farewell, my love," he whispered, and then he was sprinting down the final flight of stairs and running toward a doorway he remembered from his time as Romen. It took him through the scullery, where he saw one sleeping attendant who should have been stirring the porridge that simmered continually through the night. The young girl looked exhausted; her lips were parted and a light snore punctuated the silence as she slumped on the table. Wyl smiled. Oh, for a simple life with only a dressing-down from cook in the morning to worry about.

He slipped out of the door into one of the many vegetable gardens, disturbing two cats fighting over a struggling rat. One took off, the dying creature still in its jaws. The other shrieked at its loss of the feast. Wyl looked around to get his bearings and made for the stables and his journey north.

# 12

ALENTYNA BROKE HER FAST EARLY AND PRIVATELY ON THE balcony of her bedchamber. She had changed rooms not so long ago. At first, after learning of Romen's murder, she had wanted to cling to his memory, to remember every word, every smile, every touch they had shared together, so briefly, in her bedroom. More recently, however, with her marriage looming, she had decided she must bury those memories and put aside anything that prompted their return. Hence the move into the new quarters. Her new room had been her mother's. It was from her mother that she had inherited a taste for simple, fine things, and this chamber and its suite of rooms used natural light and space to achieve a sense of calm. And calm was what Valentyna needed right now. She was still deeply upset from the previous night's events, and although not hungry after her fitful sleep and fretful awakening, she had adhered to her father's long-held advice that bad news and bad moods were best dealt with on a full belly. Nevertheless, she had ordered only the lightest of meals, consisting of a small sugared roll, a single lightly boiled egg, a sliced pear, and a pot of dark, strong tea.

She had left the letter from Ylena unopened by the side of her tray until she had picked over the fruit and egg, neither of which she tasted, and downed her first cup of tea. Valentyna suspected the letter would contain an outpouring of beautifully crafted yet cringing apologies and hated the thought of reading them, let alone facing the woman who had so misread her affections. She was sure her face still burned from the combined horror and embarrassment of Ylena's error, although Valentyna was uncertain whether this intense discomfort was for herself or on behalf of Wyl's sister. Both probably, she thought glumly.

She poured a second cup of tea, this time with a slice of lemon instead of sweetening honey, and waited until she had sipped from its steaming contents before breaking the seal on the letter. It was a sharp surprise to discover that it was not even close to what she had imagined. A brief and succinct apology for what Ylena called her unforgivable behavior was followed by an equally concise confirmation that she was already on her way to Felrawthy. She specifically asked not to be followed, and urged the Queen to write immediately to Celimus with news that she was sending Wyl Thirsk's sister as a token of her loyalty to the King of Morgravia.

The second half of the single sheet was softer in its intentions, if not in its words, and reminded Valentyna of things her father might say. Unlike her father, though, the words felt as though they had been written by someone not used to being openly affectionate, yet who cared deeply for her well-being. Frankly, Valentyna thought, drumming her fingers on her seat, Ylena simply did not know her well enough to write with such tender, albeit awkward, familiarity.

Tears stung her eyes and she hastily rubbed them away. She had not intended to cry, but weep she did, hating herself for these last days of such hysterical behavior. From Wyl's description of his sister all that time ago, she had expected Ylena Thirsk to be a gentle, fragile sort of character. Despite hearing how she had overcome such enormous trauma, Valentyna had still been stunned by the confident and direct woman who had presented herself at the court of Briavel.

She put down the letter, picked up her cup, and let the steam from the tea warm her face, which felt chill from being outside on this still brisk spring morning. It struck Valentyna that Ylena had behaved in a fairly masculine fashion throughout her short time at Werryl. This had occurred to her well before the kiss, even before the supper; it had begun to resonate as early as their stroll in the gardens. Ylena had showed all the poise and upbringing of a noblewoman, but she appeared to think like a man. Valentyna prided herself on being an adept judge of character, but Ylena's disposition was not easy to explain yet unusual enough to notice. At first she had thought she was imagining it, but during supper Ylena had taken over the conversation and led the discussion to Celimus and Cailech as though they were sitting in a war room. She had heard her father conversing with his soldiers for too many years not to recognize the similarity of the situation.

That aside, she wondered about Ylena's uncanny habit of pacing while she was thinking. That had rocked Valentyna only marginally less than the wretched kiss. The likeness to Romen was too painful to bear. Valentyna remembered how she had had to look away and how shallow her breathing had become as she watched Ylena. And then the worst part—that terrible incident in Ylena's chamber. Valentyna blamed herself for it. Ylena had lost so much—parents, brother, husband, the family friend Gueryn le Gant. And then she had learned of the tragedy at Felrawthy. The emotions had all boiled over, presumably, and she had sought affection from someone who seemed to be offering it. Valentyna made an involuntary sound of disgust. And yet the explanation sounded too neat and tidy, as though she were contriving every excuse to explain the curiosity that was Ylena Thirsk.

Far more likely, the practical voice in Valentyna's head suggested, the girl had a liking for women. But even that did not make sense. A woman who wanted to lie with other women surely did not have a male childhood sweetheart; nor did she marry that man as soon as they were both old enough. When Wyl Thirsk had told her and Valor about Alyd Donal's death, he had also described the great love between Alyd and his Ylena.

Valentyna closed her eyes in frustration. And then the nagging thought, which had called from the edges of her mind almost since Ylena's arrival, filtered to the top of her consciousness and set a new and chilling problem before her. Ylena's handkerchief—the one she had handed Valentyna when she had wept in the garden—was the same linen that she herself had given to Romen! How could Ylena possibly own it?

The Queen put down her cup, stood, and leaned against the balcony railing. Was she imagining things? No! It was her own handkerchief. She had even mentioned it to Elspyth at Aleda's funeral. Elspyth had been weeping for Aleda and Valentyna had put an arm around her petite companion and handed her a beautiful square of embroidered linen. She closed her eyes to remember the words she had shared with her friend: *I gave Romen an identical kerchief,* she had whispered. *You keep this. Now both my best friends own one.*

She repeated the words in her mind as she gazed down onto Werryl Bridge and its endless stream of activity. Romen had died in a brothel in Briavel, and Ylena's only contact with him had occurred between Pearlis and Rittylworth, she calculated. Then they had parted, and as she understood it, they had not seen each other again before he died. Valentyna had given Romen the handkerchief long after he had left Morgravia and the Razors, and he had lived the rest of his numbered days in Briavel.

A new thought struck the Queen. Perhaps that hateful woman, Hildyth, had stolen it from him. But why take a square of meaningless linen? And even if she had stolen it from Romen at the Forbidden Fruit, how could Ylena now have it in her possession?

Wyl, Romen, Ylena, and Hildyth—what did they have in common? Why was she even linking them in her mind? Wyl and Ylena were related; that one was obvious. Romen and Wyl had fought together in vain to save her father and had certainly saved her. Romen had rescued Ylena, keeping a promise to her dead brother, Wyl. And Hildyth? Hildyth was connected only to the man Valentyna had loved, through death—a blade in the heart.

But no. There was another link, was there not? She shook her head in a futile attempt at denial, but it whispered through her raging thoughts. A shining, clear notion that traveled brightly through the maelstrom of her mind and landed as sharply and painfully as an arrow. A notion that had been voiced by two separate people: Fynch subtly, and Elspyth more insistently.

Fynch had claimed that he believed Wyl and Romen were of one mind. Valentyna was immediately reminded of Knave and the talk of magic that swirled about the dog. She recalled Fynch's confusion when Wyl's cantankerous dog had taken so easily to Romen, and how Romen had called out the dog's name in Stoneheart, though he had never met Knave before. Even more baffling for Fynch was how playfully Knave had greeted the stranger. The Queen remembered Fynch describing how Wyl's eyes had changed color at the witch burning— more talk of magic she had ignored. And then along came Elspyth with similar murmurings. She had urged Valentyna to accept the notion of reincarnation, all but saying that she too believed Wyl somehow resonated within Romen, and that the Queen's beloved might well be spiritually present in a new person—a woman, even. Wyl . . . Romen . . . Ylena.

Valentyna startled herself by being sick, turning just in time to avoid soiling her clothes. She sank to the floor of the balcony, upending the crockery on the tray, and gave way to deep, dry sobs. Nothing made sense anymore.

She remained curled on the balcony until the cold and the smell of her vomit brought her back to the present and the one stark reality she could not escape: marriage to Celimus. Today was the all-important fitting for her gown. She must attend to her toilet, and tolerate the seamstresses' chatter and annoying pins and requests. The time between now and the night when the King of Morgravia would legally bed her could be counted on her fingers.

Valentyna collected her shattered wits, put all thoughts of reincarnation and magic to the back of her mind, and steeled herself for her regal duties in the coming days. Forging peace was all she would permit herself to focus upon. She had a war to prevent and a wedding to prepare for. She would do as Ylena Thirsk suggested and write a letter of appeasement to King Celimus using Ylena as barter. She might as well, now that Ylena had made her sacrifice.

Crys had risen later than Valentyna but read his letter before he dressed. Wyl suggested two options for him to consider. The first was that he try to catch up with Elspyth, who Wyl felt was on a foolhardy mission, although he did not believe she was in any immediate danger. Both he and Crys felt protective toward Elspyth and it was only right that, with so few allies, they all look out for one another. Failing this, he suggested Crys don a disguise and infiltrate Pearlis, particularly the Legion, spreading the word of Celimus's betrayal of Jeryb and his family. Wyl listed a few names of reliable men Crys should single out in particular. He was to tell them about the treatment of Ylena and Alyd as well. *Take the head of your brother,* he urged; *give them proof.* Crys was to be patient, though. He was to avoid doing anything rash and to encourage a similar self-control in any angry Legionnaires. Wyl asked him to lie low among the Legion until Wyl himself somehow got word to him. He reinforced the point that Crys was not to even hint at the truth should the Queen ask questions about Ylena. He signed off, wishing Crys luck and hoping that they would meet again soon. He added a note to Crys to remember the password, for he could not promise he would return as Ylena.

Crys smiled grimly at the postscript. Any stranger could walk up to him in the future and claim to be Wyl. *How frightening it must be for him,* he thought as he turned his mind to departure. Frankly, he would be glad to be on the move again, doing something constructive. He would leave today—this morning, in fact—and was sure the Queen would quietly sigh with relief when he did so.

Valentyna gritted her teeth and got through the gown fitting. As she had expected, the seamstress and her assistants tittered around her for almost an hour. Sadly, they did not poke her with a single pin, which might have at least given her an excuse to vent some of the frustration she was feeling. Somehow she found a smile when they stood beaming at their finished creation.

She had demanded simplicity, and simplicity she had been given. Madam Eltor was used to Valentyna's likes and dislikes, having designed gowns for the new Queen since she was old enough to attend formal engagements, but this time the dressmaker had surpassed herself. The gown had long, clean lines in a fabric that fell so beautifully into its natural folds that it took even the designer's breath away when she saw it hanging on Valentyna's elegant body.

"You're a woman now," she had whispered to Valentyna, whose eyebrows had raised slightly when she saw the plunging neckline. It revealed not only the shapely top of her arms but displayed the flawless creamy expanse of her chest, fabric meeting flesh just before any cleavage might show.

"You will have to be sewn in, of course, my dear," Madam Eltor warned through the pins in her mouth. Having known the Queen since childhood, the dressmaker had long ago been excused from the formality of using Valentyna's titles. "It's the only way we'll get this perfect fit across your bust."

Valentyna nodded distractedly. "Finished now?"

"No," came the reply. "Be still, child," and the Queen of Briavel could not hide the ghost of a grin at the reprimand Madam Eltor had been giving for so many years now they had both lost count.

The gown's only adornment was a tiny row of pearls sewn

along the neckline and around the cuffs, which ended three-quarters of the way down Valentyna's long arms.

"I'll wager all of Morgravia and Briavel will be wearing this new length and slim sleeve by summer's close, your highness," one of the assistants commented eagerly.

Valentyna and Madam Eltor shared a glance in the mirror. They had been setting new fashion trends in Briavel for years, despite Valentyna's lack of interest in her wardrobe.

"Would you like to see it with the veil?" Madam Eltor inquired, already knowing the answer.

"Not today, Margyt," Valentyna begged. "Next time, I promise. Right now I have some urgent things to attend to and a realm to run." She gave the older woman a beseeching grin.

The seamstress nodded, a look of long-suffering patience on her face. "Next time, then," she said kindly, adding firmly: "Which, your highness, will be in four days. Be warned."

Valentyna groaned. "Thank you, everyone," she said, wriggling hastily out of the dress.

"Flowers?" Madam Eltor asked.

The Queen sighed. "It is in hand. Your colleague Madam Pern is designing open creamy white roses and fairy's breath for the posy and a wreath of white buds for my head," she answered. "I'd prefer lavender."

"It wouldn't work," Madam Eltor commented, quite used to Valentyna's contrariness. "The white buds will echo the pearls and enhance the Stone of Briavel, which I presume you'll wear?"

Valentyna nodded. She had to admit the gown suited her, with its sleek look and sharp lines. She was not one for the rounded, softer look many of the court women preferred. The Queen liked the way her dressmaker had echoed her slightly masculine edge in the sharp plunge of the gown's neckline, and the lack of affectation and adornment made her feel she could almost get away with wearing her riding boots beneath it. She smiled inwardly. Her people graciously accepted her tomboyishness without reading all manner of sinister connotations into it—why could she not accept Ylena's masculine contradictions? "Because it doesn't add up," she argued.

"I beg your pardon, dear?" Madam Eltor said, the wedding gown held reverently across her outstretched arms, ready to be placed into clean muslin for the journey back to her chambers in Werryl.

"Nothing," Valentyna murmured, embarrassed to realize that she had spoken her last thought aloud. "Thank you, Margyt. I'll see you soon." She saw the seamstress and her chittering assistants to the door and called for a page.

"Find me Stewyt, please, Ross, and also summon the Duke of Felrawthy to a meeting in my solar. I will see him in an hour."

The boy bowed and ran off on his errands. Valentyna hurriedly tied back her hair. She wished she could wear it just like this at her wedding—combed off her face and plaited. She pulled at wisps she had not quite managed to incorporate into the main plait, then made a sound of disgust at their waywardness and left them alone. A soft knock heralded the page.

"Stewyt, thank you for coming so quickly."

"Your majesty," he said, bowing low. "How may I help?"

Stewyt often unnerved her with his mature manner. Talking with him often felt like speaking to Krell or someone of similar age and ilk. She saw that Stewyt would make a fine chancellor in years to come; he encompassed all the right qualities, from discretion to intense curiosity about everyone and everything. He was a superb listener and rarely needed to have anything repeated.

She cleared her throat and her thoughts. "I wanted to talk to you about Lady Ylena."

"Yes, your highness. You received her note, I presume?"

"I did, thank you. But you didn't deliver it. I was given it with my breakfast tray."

"That's right, your majesty. Lady Ylena did not want you disturbed last night. She told me the contents of the letter were of no immediate import and I was to ensure both were delivered this morning."

"Both letters?"

"The other was for the Duke of Felrawthy," Stewyt quali-fied. "Is there something wrong, your majesty?"

"No, not at all. I've been informed that Lady Ylena left the palace during the night. Did she seem upset when you saw her?"

Stewyt frowned. "No, your highness. She was very alert, as I recall, and somewhat intense, if I might hazard that thought."

Stewyt looked as though he had more to say. Valentyna nodded, impressed as always by his composure. "Is there more?"

"Forgive me, your majesty, but I took the liberty of watch-ing Lady Ylena."

"Oh?"

"Yes, I felt her manner was a trifle odd. She went to some trouble to impress upon me how tired she was and in need of sleep, yet throughout our conversation she struck me as being very much awake and caught up by a sense of ur-gency."

"And you were right, of course," Valentyna prompted.

"Yes," the lad said, not meaning to sound smug. "I set off on my errand as requested but doubled back, just to see if my instincts were right. Chancellor Krell taught me to fol-low my instincts, your highness," he added. "I watched Lady Ylena hurry out of her chamber."

"She did mention in her letter to me that she intended to depart last night," Valentyna replied, determined that this lad should not think Ylena was up to any mischief. She could not have gossip of that kind going the rounds and providing any future ammunition. "You recall, Stewyt, I asked you to keep her presence between ourselves, which is why I hand-picked you as her page."

He nodded solemnly. "I have told no one of her presence, your highness."

"Did anything else occur that you think is worth men-tioning?"

"Well . . ." The page sounded uncomfortable.

"Yes?"

"She—" He stopped, and started again. "On her way past

your portrait on the first landing, your highness, she paused . . . rather deliberately."

"And?" Valentyna queried, not understanding the boy's hesitation.

"She touched it, your majesty. Touched your . . . er, your breast, your highness."

Valentyna felt a new thrill of alarm. "Did she say anything?"

"She murmured a farewell to you, your highness. In all truth, I would say that she was trying to reach your face but wasn't tall enough."

"I see. Thank you, Stewyt." The Queen quickly dismissed the page, following him out of her chamber and heading to her solar to meet with Crys Donal.

He was waiting for her. "Good morning, your majesty," he said, and bowed.

"Crys, you look readied for travel," she said, noting the cloak as she walked toward him, and surprised him with a brief kiss.

He blushed. "Yes, your highness, I've decided to leave. I think it's only right, what with your troubles with the Legion and so on. I know I'm a thorn in your side and I agree with Ylena that I can probably be of more use back in Morgravia, being a thorn in the King's side." He grinned but it looked hollow.

"You've spoken with Ylena about this?" the Queen asked, surprised.

"No. She sent me a letter which I received this morning. She suggested I infiltrate the Legion and start spreading news of the slaughter at Tenterdyn to help turn the army against their king, your majesty."

"Is that her plan?"

Crys shook his head. "I don't know what her plan is, your highness."

Valentyna sat down in her favorite window seat with her back to her guest so he did not have to look at her in the eye. "Crys, since when did the Duke of Felrawthy—or any Duke of Morgravia, for that matter—take orders from a young noblewoman?"

There was a difficult pause, as she had anticipated, and then an equally awkward laugh. "Your majesty, Ylena Thirsk is no ordinary noblewoman. The surname alone tells you the stock she comes from."

He was going to say more, but she cut him off. "The fact that she is the daughter of the famous Fergys Thirsk and sister to the revered Wyl Thirsk does not necessarily make her a military strategist, though, does it? I would have thought a woman like Ylena would have been taught to embroider beautifully and make polite conversation with strangers while making an elegant tour of a room, not the art of warfare."

"Just like you, your highness." Crys immediately regretted his gentle sarcasm as Valentyna turned to fix him with a stare. "Forgive me, your majesty, I meant no insult. I admire you tremendously for the dazzling way you balance being a beautiful woman and a strong ruler. It's not easy, your highness; anyone with half a brain can see that such skill requires both a feminine and a masculine side."

Valentyna dug deep and found a smile to show no offense had been taken—it was obvious that Crys was genuine in his praise, although just as obvious that he was protecting Ylena. "I don't know, Crys. I was under the impression that Ylena was a gentle, pampered young woman."

"Which she was, I'm sure, your highness. But plenty has happened to change that, and they do say blood will win out."

"They do indeed," Valentyna said cryptically. "If you'll forgive my digging into a painful subject—her relationship with Alyd, did you know much about it?"

"Only that they were madly in love. His letters were filled with his adoration of both Thirsks. They were his family during his time in the south. What's troubling you, your highness?"

She struggled. Could she tell him? She needed to share her secret with someone and Crys was as reliable as any of her own counsel. "You don't think she had leanings toward women, do you?"

The Duke looked shocked. "Ylena? No! Whatever gave you that idea?"

Valentyna made a face. "Oh, just something that happened last night between us. I don't really want to talk about it."

"Except we are," he said, grinning, understanding what must have occurred. That would now explain why Wyl had fled in the night. "No, Ylena used to write to us as well, your highness, and she was intensely in love with Alyd. It was all she could do to talk about anything other than him, their marriage, and children. They were planning a large brood."

"So they wanted babies immediately?"

"Oh yes, even Alyd said they would begin a family as soon as they could." He laughed. "They even married before we expected—couldn't wait for us."

Valentyna shook her head, baffled, recalling Ylena's confusion when she had mentioned pregnancy. "Well, she's not pregnant, I can vouch for that. It's why she left the table so suddenly—her monthly flux had arrived."

Crys tried unsuccessfully to stifle a laugh at the thought of Wyl dealing with women's ailments.

"I can't imagine what's so amusing, Crys," Valentyna said in a vaguely injured tone.

"There is nothing funny, your highness. My apologies."

Valentyna was sure he knew more than he was telling her, but she could not fathom what. "Is there anything else you know that could help me, Crys? Please, I feel like I'm navigating through a quagmire."

He gave her a look of tender sympathy. "Your highness, Ylena is true to you. After all that Celimus has perpetrated on her family and the family she married into, her loyalties have changed. We all love Morgravia, but we would rather fight on the side of Briavel as long as King Celimus sits Morgravia's throne." He surprised her by going down on one knee. "You can trust me and you can trust Ylena. She is fearlessly casting herself into the lion's den. Whether Celimus has her killed or not, it doesn't matter—we will never see Ylena again, that much I can assure you." The last was said bitterly.

Valentyna reached to touch his bowed head, moved by what he had said. "Oh, Crys, I don't want her death on my hands."

"She has nothing else to give. Your highness, Ylena doesn't want to live anymore—can't you see that? That is why she can give it up so recklessly for someone she loves."

He felt he had gone too far in mentioning the word "love," and Valentyna's anguished response confirmed it.

"I don't want her love, Crys!" The Queen was shocked by the pain that moved across the Duke's open face at her words.

"Then take her sacrifice graciously and use it for your own ends, as she asks."

"I don't even understand her intentions in going to Felrawthy," Valentyna replied bitterly.

Crys stood. "I imagine she means to disrupt those talks in the north," he said. "And somehow bargain for the deployment of the Legion back to Pearlis so your people can breathe easily again and get on with celebrating a royal wedding." He took her hand. "And about the wedding—I don't think you can escape that, your majesty, but you can demand equality. You can influence how this new era for Morgravia and Briavel will be felt by people. Believe me, if we can find a way to overthrow Celimus, we will, but you must proceed with this marriage."

She had heard it before from others and given herself the same sound advice. It was time she got on with living it now. "You're right. No doubt we shall see each other in Pearlis."

"I might not go straight to the Morgravian capital, your highness," Crys said, as if the decision had only just arrived in his mind.

"Not Felrawthy?" she asked, fear in her tone.

"No, that will have to wait, your highness. The time to seize back my family estate is not yet ripe. I've actually been thinking about Elspyth."

Relief softened Valentyna's expression. "You're going after her?"

"I think I should. She's a resilient woman and knows her mind, but she's still only a girl alone in a strange realm with no weapons or protection—"

"Heading off into the Razor Kingdom to rescue a prisoner of its king," the Queen finished, shaking her head. "I'm glad, Crys. Thank you."

The Duke shrugged. "Elspyth was good to me when I needed to be reminded who I was and what needed to be done. If not for her insistence, I would have gone tearing back to Tenterdyn."

"And lost your own life, and Felrawthy would have lost its duke."

"Yes," he admitted. "She saved me from my own stupidity and anger."

"Well, you still have every right to be angry, to want vengeance, Crys, and because of Elspyth's advice, you might yet get it."

He sensed the sorrow behind her encouraging words. "I'm sorry that you don't have the same opportunity, your highness."

She forced a small smile. "Oh, I'll find my own way."

Crys knew as well as she did that her comment was mere bravado, but he returned her smile with a squeeze of her hand.

"How will you follow her?" Valentyna asked, changing the subject.

"I'll start with Liryk, I suppose. I suspect your commander is rather gratified that Elspyth is out of your life, your highness"—he grinned as she nodded conspiratorially—"but he might help by asking his guards if they saw her leave."

"What good will that do?"

"Well, I imagine Elspyth was in a hurry to leave Werryl. That being the case, I believe she might have hitched a ride with someone." He shrugged. "It might help me follow her, that's all."

The Queen nodded. "Be safe, Crys. We shall meet again soon, I hope."

He kissed her hand with feeling, and then the last of her allies left the Briavellian monarch to her loneliness and bleak thoughts.

# 13

AFTER LEAVING WERRYL, WYL MADE STRAIGHT FOR A HIDE OF
Faryl's in Crowyll and dug up a pouch of money. He
was pleased he could still remember some of the locations
of her stashed coin, and although he did not care for using
blood money, he was in dire need of it.

He galloped his horse as far and hard as the beast would
permit, then traveled on through the night more slowly and
spent most of his coin on a new horse the following morning. Although he had not slept, he was determined to press
on and the replacement animal was fresh and happy to be
given its head. His plan was to follow the border as closely
as he could, entering Morgravia only when he believed he
was far enough north to cross directly into Felrawthy. He
could not risk stumbling upon any Legionnaires and being
recognized.

At around midday the next day it was his good fortune to
ride into the village of Derryn at a time when he not only
had to rest his horse but needed food and sleep himself, and,
most important, a chance to bathe. The pain had gone and he
felt as well as could be expected, considering his fatigue, but
it seemed that the bleeding would continue for a few days
yet. How inconvenient and messy it all was.

Wyl hoped he would never be a woman again. The
grooming, the curtsying, the requirement to be elegant and
gracious at all times—these were merely a few of its annoying aspects. He pitied Valentyna, and yet he admired her too.
Somehow she managed to balance the demands of being a
woman with a strength of her own. Ylena, much as he had
loved her, had delighted almost exclusively in her feminin-

ity—but then that was all that had been expected of her since the day of her birth. A daughter born into a wealthy noble family, particularly one as distinguished as the Thirsks, had one main task: to marry well. To achieve this she was educated in every possible pastime that could enhance her opportunities, from the effective running of a household to the art of embroidery. King Magnus had employed a small army of women to teach Ylena such niceties from her arrival at Pearlis at a tender age. And his sister had proved herself to be an adept student.

Fresh sorrow overcame Wyl as he pondered yet again how little Ylena deserved what had befallen her. She had always been ready with a kind word for everyone and her smile could banish even the gloomiest of moods. She had truly been a beauty in every sense of the word. That her mind had been empty of the thoughts and ambitions that drove Valentyna was not Ylena's fault. She was merely following form, whereas Valentyna was one of a kind. Yet Ylena's life had unraveled over a matter of weeks; what should have been the happiest time of her life had instead been the most cruel. Wyl felt a familiar nausea grip him and he knew he must stop grieving like this over his sister. Ylena was dead and no amount of soul-searching or tears would restore her.

Wyl knew his exhaustion and the monthly flux was contributing to his morbid feelings and was convinced that a decent meal and some rest would help to lift his spirits. As he walked the horse through the main street, he found there was no inn but discovered by asking a young woman passing by that a widow by the name of Mona Dey ran a guesthouse in the village. After stabling the horse, paying for its care, and making sure he could retrieve it with ease whenever he wanted, Wyl headed for the widow's place.

He paid Mona in advance, much to her delight, and was shown to a small, neat room at the back of her large dwelling. He learned from the chatty widow that her husband had been a wealthy though miserly trader with a wandering eye for other women, especially whores. According to Mona, her husband had died between the legs of a buxom twenty-year-old, a blade driven into his back up to the hilt.

She told the chilling tale with a sly relish and it brought back hideous memories for Wyl.

"A pocketful of silver—that's all the slut got for her trouble," Mona said smugly. "I got the rest." And she beamed. From then on she had lived her life to the full, deliberately spending her dead husband's money with abandon in revenge for his meanness, until there was virtually nothing left. "I held back just enough to keep me off the streets," she told Wyl, with no trace of bitterness, "and now I take paying guests and live a quiet life."

"I can't imagine it gets much quieter than Derryn," Wyl commented, surprised at the widow's candor.

"You're right there, my lady," Mona cried, and laughed as if he had cracked some great jest.

As open as Mona Dey was about her own background, Wyl appreciated that she showed not the slightest interest in his. Either she was entirely self-centered or she was very canny, knowing that most strangers preferred not to discuss their business. Wyl thanked the widow and paid her some extra coin for her discretion, for she had not even inquired why Ylena was traveling alone.

The evening meal, Mona told her guest, was served at sunset and no later. Wyl grimaced and politely asked whether there was any possible chance of a tray in his room now. He explained how tired he was and that his flux had fair drained him of all energy. A look of deep sympathy had come his way—definitely a special sorrow only women could share, he realized—and no doubt the generous coin rattling in her skirt pocket had encouraged Mona Dey to look kindly on the young noblewoman.

"I'll see what I can rustle up for you, dear," she said. "Oh my, I used to suffer it something awful at your age. And my Garth, he had no sympathy at all, still claiming his marital rights." Wyl quailed inwardly at the turn the discussion was taking but adopted the right expression and paid attention. "And pain! Shar save me, I thought I was fit to die," the widow continued. "My mother had no sympathy. She said I should get used to it, for it would curse me for most of my life—my mother was a bitter woman, you see. My father died on her young and left her with a brood of children and no money. Her bleed was bad too and left her in poor shape one week of each moon, and it meant she couldn't work during some of those days and we went hungry."

The widow looked set to carry on discussing her mother's moon cycles, but Wyl feigned a swoon, which effectively stopped the monologue and had Mona rushing for cold flannels and smelling salts. When he seemed recovered, the widow suggested the young lady take a soak. There was a room in the house already set up for bathing. "I have some herbs that will ease the pain, dear," she offered kindly.

Wyl was grateful to her and said as much, winning a wide smile from the widow. "And I'll fetch you some raspberry leaf," she added. "Chew straight on it, my lady. Tastes like hell but is far more effective for your condition than a weak brew."

Wyl stammered his thanks and allowed her to guide him to the bathing room, which had a huge old tub that more than swallowed up Ylena's exhausted body. He would have been happy to wash in cold water, but Mona wouldn't hear of it. "Heat is what you need, dear, for the ache."

Wyl did not want to start explaining that the ache was done; he just wanted peace and privacy now. So he let her fuss and organize for steaming jugs to be brought up by a small army of lads she paid to run to the smithy's where a huge cauldron of water was kept on the fire permanently. The joy of finally closing the door on Mona's chatter and climbing into the tub was second in Wyl's mind only to kissing Valentyna for the first time.

Afterward, he ate a meal of cold roast meat, potatoes simmered with cream, and some cheese, before slipping between the well-worn but fresh sheets on Mona's guest bed and drifting almost instantly into sleep.

When he awoke he was disoriented. It was black outside and as quiet as a tomb. Mona had kindly left a candle in his room, but it had burned down to a sputtering nub. He had been asleep for at least twelve hours, he estimated. Careful to make no sound to disturb the household, he relieved himself in the chamber pot and hurriedly dressed in his dusty but

comfortable riding clothes. Wyl did not like to sneak away
without thanking Mona but had no means to scrawl a note;
the only way he could show his appreciation for her care
was with money, which he left on the remade bed. He
thought it unlikely she would think further on the young
woman who had passed through her house, but if she did,
she would remember Ylena kindly for her generosity.

He could not risk making his way through the house, so,
thanking his lucky stars that he was on the first level, he
climbed out of the window and dropped silently to the
ground, rolling as he had been taught when he was a lad. He
must have startled a badger or some night creature on the
fringe of the small wood that skirted the town, for he heard
the animal blundering disgruntledly back into the trees. He
remained still, listening for any other sounds, but it seemed
there was no one about. Nevertheless, he took the precaution
of making his way to the stable via the back lanes. As he had
anticipated, there was a sleeping stableboy in one corner
who could barely rouse himself from his slumber at the
young woman's oddly timed arrival. When he did, he recognized the noblewoman, pointed toward a stall, and mumbled
something incoherent. Wyl was just glad to find his horse,
saddle her, and be off as quickly and quietly as he could.

He ignored the fresh hunger pangs that gnawed at his
belly and was out onto the open road again, Derryn behind
him, moments later. One more day's riding, he guessed, and
he would be able to cut into Morgravia and enter Felrawthy,
back into the lair of Celimus, and perhaps have a chance to
get into a new, more suitable body.

Cailech sat in a secret cave in Haldor's Tooth, pondering
the situation that was about to unfold. The Grenadyne's
suggestion to forge an alliance with Morgravia had touched
the very core of everything the Mountain King believed. He
was privately miffed that such an obvious idea had not occurred to him in the past, for treating with Magnus and his
general, Thirsk, would surely have been easier than dealing
with Morgravia's current monarch. But he had always de-
rided any suggestion of forging links with Morgravia—wait,

no, not always. In his early days as King, he had had notions of living as neighbors alongside the bordering realm, but had put them aside in more recent years. Rashlyn had always said the stones did not auger well for negotiating attempts, and eventually Cailech had stopped asking.

Nevertheless, when Aremys returned to the cave and reported on the meeting with Celimus, Cailech felt a surge of anxiety. "You're sure there is no trap?" he asked Aremys.

"No, sire. But I have made our way as safe as I can under the circumstances. Celimus is organizing for the hostages to be delivered as required, and I have taken out some additional insurance."

The mercenary explained that his bargaining tool was one Ylena Thirsk, daughter and sister of Morgravia's two previous Generals. The name carried weight with Cailech, and he had no qualms about using a Morgravian noblewoman to barter for their safety. He just had one question: "Well, where is she?"

Aremys startled the King by laughing and shrugging. "I have no idea, sire. But that is a worry for another day. You will be back on your own soil before I have to consider what to do."

Cailech smiled. He liked the way the large Grenadyne thought. Farrow had impressed him from their first meeting, and even though the mercenary clearly knew more than he was telling and had an uncanny interest in Galapek, Cailech privately considered the man a friend. He had never said as much, but they both knew it; there was mutual respect and admiration between them. Perhaps it was simply that, with his clear thinking and dry humor, Aremys reminded him of Lothryn. He missed Lothryn so deeply it actually pained him to dwell upon it.

It had been the most agonizing of discoveries to realize that his closest friend and confidant had betrayed him. How could Loth have chosen the Morgravians over his own people, over his own king? Cailech had ranted as much to Myrt, who had kept a dull silence throughout, but whose lack of words said much. Cailech quietly admired the man for his loyalty to his friend. Loth could have learned much from Myrt about brotherhood, honor, and trust. Cailech's pride would not permit him to show any mercy to his childhood friend, no matter how in love with the woman of Yentro he might have been. It made no difference why Lothryn had made his choice; it mattered only that he had made it, and made it incorrectly.

When news came that they were bringing Lothryn back alive, Cailech had wanted to slay him on the frosted stones of the fortress's threshold. He could not bear to see his lifelong companion—now a traitor—step even one foot across it. But then Rashlyn had persuaded him to exact a higher penance.

Somehow the King had been persuaded down the path of magic. Burning with a feverish anger, he had listened with fascinated horror to Rashlyn's suggestion that there was a far more subtle operation than an easy death by the sword. The barshi's repetition of the words "traitor" and "treachery" had fired the King's anguish into a white heat of vengeance. He had agreed to Rashlyn's plan, believing that by owning Loth, by breaking his spirit and forcing his subservience with Rashlyn's dark magic, he would somehow win his respect. His former friend and comrade would suffer the humiliation of knowing he would forever carry the King on his back, ever be subservient to Cailech, never forgetting who ruled whom.

Now, thinking about it, Cailech saw how distorted and poisonous such punishment had been. If he could reverse the magic he would do so, especially now that Aremys seemed to have such a dogged interest in the stallion. The truth was, his victory over Loth felt hollow. Painful, in fact. As with the threat to make cannibals of his own people, it had shown him to be base, led by anger rather than by his clever mind. How had he permitted Rashlyn to guide his hand toward inflicting such horrors? He shook his head.

"A silver for your thoughts, sire," Aremys said, approaching Cailech where he sat on a rock ledge with a clear view into Felrawthy. He brought with him a clay flask of wine and poured a cup for the King and one for himself. Myrt and the rest of the Mountain warriors were sharpening blades and checking the supplies of weapons, which everyone prayed would not be required.

"I was just thinking of Lothryn and how much you remind me of him."

"I shall take that as a compliment, sire. I have heard people speak highly of your second, despite his final actions."

"As they should," Cailech said, unable to hide the sorrow that had him in its grip.

"No one can tell me what happened to him, sire. I presume you executed him?"

Aremys heard the hesitation. "Yes, he is dead," the King replied flatly.

"Doesn't stop you missing him, though, I see."

Cailech nodded. "I miss him every day. We grew up together. We understood each other, we protected each other. That was what made his betrayal so shocking. We loved each other, Farrow. We were brothers in all but blood."

"With such love between you, could you not find a way to spare him?" Aremys prompted, hoping to lead the King into revealing more about Galapek.

"Only the barest thread separates the most passionate of opposites, Grenadyne."

"What do you mean, sire?"

"I mean that because I loved Loth so much, his betrayal stirred in me intense hatred."

"I understand." Aremys knew he would not get the admission he had hoped for. Instead, the silence stretched between them, before Cailech roused himself from his private thoughts and addressed the question that was no doubt troubling his men too.

"Is this a wise undertaking, Farrow?"

"Many would consider it foolhardy, given the Morgravian sovereign's reputation," Aremys replied. "However, I do believe that once he meets you, you, more than anyone, have the ability to convince him that an alliance is preferable to these regular skirmishes that could so easily escalate to war."

Cailech nodded, reassured by the Grenadyne's faith. "And his marriage?"

"Is still planned to go ahead shortly, which is why timing is of the essence. With Briavel's army at his beck and call, who knows what delusions might suddenly cross his mind?"

"I am told the Legion has been deployed to the Briavellian border. Hardly a loving wedding gift."

"Scare tactics," Aremys guessed. "There is no benefit to Celimus starting a fresh war with Briavel when he can conquer the realm through marriage."

"Intimidating the bride is a grand way to start a historic treaty between the two realms," Cailech replied.

"It seems Celimus knows no other way. From what I can gather, he has been a bully all his young life. Why should he change now that he is King?"

"Mmm—my thoughts exactly," Cailech mused.

Aremys could not work out what the King meant. Dismissing it, he reassured Cailech. "Nothing will go wrong, sire. Just don't tarry. Say what you have to say and plan to use emissaries to do the rest. The main thing is that you and Celimus meet and like what you see in each other."

Cailech nodded. "When are we expected?"

"Tomorrow. He is planning a feast in your honor. I suggest that only Myrt, Byl, and I accompany you, sire."

Cailech's green gaze narrowed. "A lean force."

"It shows trust."

"Even if I don't trust him."

"Exactly."

The Mountain King laughed again. "I hope, for your sake, Grenadyne, that you do not leave this meeting with my blood on your hands—or you will have hundreds of my warriors baying for yours."

Cailech raised his glass to Aremys, who followed suit. "To unions, sire."

"And friendship, Farrow. Thank you for your help."

"Does that mean I am a free man now?"

Cailech drained his cup. "It does, but I hope you will return to the fortress with us."

"If we are all still alive after this adventure, your highness, I would be honored to."

Celimus was riding on the moors that surrounded Tenterdyn and surveying what he now considered Crown land.

"It is beautiful, your majesty," Jessom said from his own horse, echoing the King's thoughts.

"I was thinking I would make Tenterdyn my summer palace and Argorn could become the royal winter retreat," Celimus replied with a smug smile, looking toward the majestic Razors, which reared up a hazy purple in the distance.

"Crys Donal and Ylena Thirsk might have something to say about that, your highness," the Chancellor cautioned, careful to hit a tone that did not suggest either reprimand or contradiction.

"Not from the grave they won't," his king snapped testily.

The notion had crept up on the Chancellor so quietly he had not realized it existed until this moment, but now it dawned on him that he had tired of the King's waspish manner and complete disregard for those who strove to accommodate his whims. Jessom's commitment to Celimus stretched to killing—and for no extra reward, certainly no thanks. Jessom was no fragile soul who shirked the meting out of death, but Celimus's settling-in period of brutality was, in Jessom's estimation, prolonged. The bloodshed seemed to be escalating, not diminishing, with the King's expanding power.

Celimus was young and brash, and his eagerness to stamp his own mark on his kingdom—and indeed beyond—was understandable. But since Jessom had first arrived in Celimus's life, he had hoped he might mold this brilliantly sharp young man into one who could be relied on to be subtle. Jessom had put all of his life experience and extensive range of talents at the King's disposal so that Celimus might learn from him.

Maris Jessom was the seventh son of a rich man, a moneylender who was involved in a number of ventures from bridge building to breweries. But even with such wealth, a son so far down the family's hierarchy was never going to be favored highly in the shareholding. His eldest three brothers were carving up the empire among them, and everyone else, including his three sisters, had to find their own way. In the case of his sisters, they had used their status to marry well. But Maris, thin and hook-nosed, had long ago accepted that he would never be a handsome man and so had decided from an early age to use his only real asset—his incredible intelligence—to get on in life. If the combined wits of his siblings were distilled into one, they still would not hold a candle to the speed, agility, and vision of their youngest brother. Although Maris kept this weapon a secret, it was obvious to him that his father should have chosen his seventh son to run his financial empire; it seemed that he alone had inherited the shrewdness, perceptiveness, and cunning that had helped his father to become one of the wealthiest men in all of Tallinor. But Jessom senior had never taken much notice of his gangly youngest son, and as soon as Maris was old enough, he had been encouraged to leave the family home to seek his own fortune. His mother, who loved him well, had given him a heavy pouch of gold. "Use it wisely, Maris," she had said, her eyes beginning to tear as she hugged her youngest farewell.

And he had, roaming the towns and villages of Tallinor from north to south and east to west as a traveling moneylender: an innovative and supremely lucrative scheme, and convenient for borrowers, who were surprised and pleased to have money coming to them. Perhaps people thought he would never collect on his lendings. But collect he did. Borrowers learned the hard way that Maris Jessom did not extend his loans. And because he never called in his loans early or was so greedy as to make the terms so cumbersome that they might be considered cruel, he always had the law on his side. The young Jessom was also ruthless, a characteristic that contributed to his rapid success.

It was not long before he had to travel with a bodyguard, and then two, for fear of being set upon by the new breed of bandits who seemed to think it was perfectly reasonable to steal from the rich, as they could afford to lose the money. This made Jessom's anger, normally slow to stoke, boil and he was soon traveling with a small company of his own paid mercenaries, who killed bandits for a hobby and kept all the spoils.

Jessom enjoyed two decades of this life, during which time he built a network of contacts and knowledge from all over the region, before deciding to settle down in Tal, not far from his original family home. Here he planned to establish his own permanent moneylending empire, using mercenaries to do the dirtier work of collection around the realm. By this time both of his parents had died and his less fortunate siblings were scattered across the realm.

It was around this time that King Sorryn of Tallinor declared moneylenders—whose number seemed to have tripled in Jessom's lifetime—to be "a pus-filled carbuncle on society that needed to be lanced" and systematically set about dismantling their terrible grip on the poor. Jessom saw the crackdown coming and fled Tallinor well in advance of the Purge, as it came to be known.

He fled to Morgravia, a wealthy man but homeless as well as landless and without the ties of family. Disillusioned, Maris Jessom decided on a change of career. He was too old to find the energy to establish a new empire and so he watched and waited. Garnering information, observing trends, and identifying needs were Jessom's talent. He saw an opportunity within the Morgravian royal family long before it occurred to anyone else that a king might need more than his general to be his closest counsel.

The position of Chancellor did not even exist during Magnus's reign, for he was a King who preferred the companionship and advice of his military strategist in all matters. But it was obvious to Jessom that the new King would not accept the guidance of Wyl Thirsk upon Magnus's death. Maris Jessom fancied himself a kingmaker; he had a network of messengers, mercenaries, informers, and spies who could help shape a kingdom, plus he had years of experience in finance as well as a shrewd understanding of human nature.

He watched Celimus for long enough before he became King to know the young man was problem-riddled and it would take years of smoothing and guidance to educate him on how to run an effective realm. Jessom saw the charm too, though; he sensed that Celimus could easily turn that talent toward his kingdom and use the energy he squandered in despising people into making them loyal to him. Jessom had to admit the proposal of marriage to Valentyna of Briavel was a masterstroke, but the killing of her father, Valor, had been plain stupidity. It was the act of an arrogant man, too inexperienced to realize that a suggestion of his power was more than enough. Jessom knew King Valor would have supported a union between Celimus and his daughter, which made his death pointless.

The murder of Thirsk had been another senseless move, although Jessom realized that there was a history there that affected the King's judgment and prevented him from being objective. Jessom had watched Thirsk too, long enough to realize the young General was loyal to Morgravia. Celimus could have molded that loyalty to his will—and the execution of the youngest Donal, the razing of Rittylworth, and the slaughter at Tenterdyn, not to mention various other deaths, including that of young helpless Jorn, need never have occurred.

Murder was dangerous. It had a nasty habit of coming back to haunt the perpetrator and Jessom could not help but think that there were too many corpses at the King's feet— with the Chancellor's involvement—for either of them to escape the outcry that was surely coming. All it would take was one voice of dissension. One voice that counted—be it that of Ylena Thirsk or Crys Donal or even Aleda Donal, wherever the hell she was. A few rumblings from Lord Bench could set off a catastrophic series of questions for the King to answer . . . and Jessom knew who would shoulder the blame. It would not be Celimus.

And yet, if only he would listen to Jessom, Celimus could still be a strong, powerful king who ruled prosperous realms. Not one or two, but three—the very empire the King dreamed of. All was not lost yet. Perhaps they could use Ylena Thirsk to their advantage—there was always a way— instead of simply murdering her.

He realized he was shaking his head and that Celimus, wearing a quizzical expression, had turned his horse to face his chancellor.

"Your majesty, may I speak candidly?"

"Of course."

"Well, sire, with the alliance you may well forge with the Mountain King, and what could only be described as the fairy-tale union with Briavel that is about to occur, you will have achieved what most sovereigns do not dare dream of, let alone attempt."

"And your point is?"

"My point, your majesty, is that you are now in the enviable position of essentially controlling three realms without resistance, without bloodshed, without the other two sovereigns realizing how powerful you actually are."

"Why is that a good thing, Jessom?"

"Your highness, there is a saying that holds good in almost every facet of life: Never allow one hand to know what the other is doing."

"Don't give me riddles, you fool. Speak plainly."

Jessom drew a deep breath to stop his disdain from showing. "Once married, Valentyna is beholden to you as wife, so she will be unable to rally any forces against you, which effectively leaves the Mountain King in the cold, should he suddenly decide the alliance is not working for him. I suspect he is much too canny for that, though—he will maintain the peace and enjoy the benefits of trade and free movement as well as increased prosperity. My lord, it is obvious to me that, handled with care, you will have the empire you have always dreamed of."

"Did you think, Jessom," Celimus replied, "that I could not work that out for myself? Is it your belief that I need you to spell out every scenario for me because I am too dim-witted to see beyond what is in front of my nose?" The tone was sarcastic and menacing.

"Not at all, sire," Jessom replied, with equal calmness but also with courtesy. "But with such an alliance so close to completion, I just think that killing Ylena Thirsk or Crys Donal might be . . . well, shall we say hasty, for want of a better word."

"So you would have me leave two dangerous mouths on the loose?"

"All I suggest, sire, is that you wait. You will have Ylena Thirsk in captivity shortly. Don't do anything too soon.

Think on the various situations that will inevitably present themselves. I imagine that Ylena Thirsk is feeling extraordinarily isolated these days. She has no parents, she has lost her guardian, and her beloved brother is dead. Her new husband and his family—her only allies—are fodder for the worms. Apart from Crys Donal, she has no one to turn to. She is a beautiful, vulnerable young woman who no doubt craves the security of being pampered again: her own private chambers, servants to wait on her, fancy gowns on her body, and money at her disposal. Think about it, sire. You could be her savior. You could put all this behind you and lavish your care and riches on the lonely girl—until she becomes your supporter."

Celimus listened this time without the smirk on his face. "She always was a spoiled little thing. I used to think she'd jump at shadows."

"That's exactly what I mean, sire. She may boast the name of Thirsk, but she is merely a girl. Her world has crumbled and been destroyed. What she needs now is resurrection from the rubble. If you provide that, it doesn't matter what excuses or tall stories you weave to excuse your behavior of the past; she will believe them all because what she will want is her life back again. Marry her off well—to your gain. I would go so far as to suggest you find her a high-ranking warrior from Cailech's brood. She will be no more trouble to you then."

The King's horse was restless. "Interesting idea, Jessom," Celimus replied. "I will think on what you have said. What time is the Mountain King due?"

"Midday, your highness. We had better make for the house."

"My summer palace," Celimus corrected, and smiled.

Jessom saw no warmth in the smile; if he was honest with himself, he would admit that he had never seen any genuine warmth in Celimus. Why it should bother him now was a surprise. This mood of dissatisfaction had taken him so unexpectedly that he recognized it as dangerous. He, like the King, had some thinking to do.

The King galloped on ahead, but Jessom rode back to Tenterdyn more sedately, silent and distracted.

# 14

VALENTYNA CRAFTED HER LETTER TO CELIMUS THE AFTERNOON of Crys Donal's departure. She wrote with great caution, outlining her decision to release Ylena Thirsk into his care. The words suggested her expectation that he would look after Ylena even though she was being given into the captivity of the Morgravian Crown. The Queen expressed her understanding that any known enemy of Morgravia could not be considered a friend of Briavel and that, as helpless as Ylena painted her situation, Valentyna did not wish to go against the express wishes of her husband-to-be. She felt sick writing the lies but pressed on, detailing her progress with her own arrangements for the wedding, not describing her gown but telling him a little of how well it looked. She discussed the party that would accompany her into Morgravia, which was not inconsequential, and then lightly touched on her desire to return to Briavel soon after the ceremony so that a second celebration could be held for her people. Much to her distaste, Valentyna felt she should ooze some special compliments here about how much the Briavellians were looking forward to seeing their queen with her new king.

By the end of it she felt revolted by the smooth way in which she lied to protect her own life as well as at how easily she was giving away Ylena's precious life. As terrible thoughts filled her mind about the ways Celimus might choose to kill Wyl Thirsk's sister—and kill her he would, she knew—the guilt of remembering how generously Wyl Thirsk had sacrificed himself for Briavel's heir nearly overwhelmed her. She was repaying his sacrifice with disdain for his family. Valentyna's fingers twitched with the desire to rip up the parchment with its treacherous contents.

But the memory of Ylena's hard words stayed her hand. It was Ylena's decision to give up her life and Valentyna realized she would probably aggrieve the young woman more if she did not carry out her wishes. Her life was forfeit anyway, Valentyna told herself. One way or another, Celimus would hunt Ylena down and complete his annihilation of the Thirsk line. Ylena seemed to feel that her sacrifice for Briavel matched that of Wyl's and would give some point to all the deaths that surrounded her tragic family.

"Too sad," Valentyna murmured at her desk. "Your life is given too cheaply, Ylena, for the gain is so little. I cannot escape marrying him."

She had the letter dispatched immediately, for fear of changing her mind, going so far as to take the parchment to the stables herself, placing it into the courier's hand.

"How long?" she asked. Briavel also used a relay network for messengers and she felt sure that once they were across the border, the Morgravian couriers would respect the urgency of this missive.

"Two days if we all ride hard, your majesty," the young man said.

"Then use as many couriers as you can. It is extremely important that King Celimus see this message as quickly as possible."

"I shall personally ride like the wind, your highness," he said, and with a bow from a saddle he was gone, clattering over Werryl Bridge and heading northeast as fast as his horse would go.

Valentyna turned away, feeling hollow and more lonely than she had ever felt in her life. Growing up as an only child had taught her to be self-sufficient and imaginative, but nothing could have prepared her for this complete loss of family, friends, and allies. And still, she realized, she could not begin to reach the depth of loss that Ylena must surely be experiencing. No wonder Wyl's sister was throwing her life away with such abandon. It might also explain why she was indulging in such curious affections. The Queen had not been able to shake the memory of Ylena's kiss; it seemed to haunt her every moment. There had been such tenderness in it . . . no, more than that. It had been filled with love. Valentyna had been kissed only once before in such a manner and that had been by Romen. Although this was a different mouth, different face, different *everything*, there was an aching familiarity to the passion behind that affection. But the memory of that physical love made Valentyna angry. Angry enough to want to fight: not Ylena, but the person who had perpetrated all the pain. On her way back into the palace, in a state of resentment at the way her life was turning out, she sent a runner to find Commander Liryk.

He arrived slightly out of breath at her study door. "My queen, you wished to see me?"

Valentyna was struck by how old Liryk seemed to be all of a sudden. She had taken his and Krell's presence around her for granted, as if they would always be in her life, but this man was surely well into his seventh decade. The notion of him not being around one day bit deeply into her thoughts, reminding her that she might lose yet another of her supporters soon. It hardened her resolve.

"Yes, Commander, thank you for coming so quickly. In the absence of a chancellor, I would like you to summon the nobles for me."

"Of course, your highness," Liryk said, frowning despite his courteous manner. "All of them?"

"Yes. It is urgent. How swiftly are you able to gather them for a meeting?"

He paused and she wondered whether he was considering her question or her state of mind. He obviously anticipated that she was about to do something dramatic. "Three days, your majesty, if I get the couriers sent immediately."

"Do it please, Liryk. I'd appreciate it if you would give this the utmost priority."

"Of course, your highness." She waited, and of course the gentle objection came. "It is unusual, though. Perhaps I might give them some inkling of what you wish to discuss so urgently?"

She smiled. She had expected this. "State security, tell

them," she answered, and turned away, not unkindly but with sufficient firmness that Liryk knew he had been dismissed. "Thank you, Liryk," she added, just in case he thought to try to dissuade her.

Valentyna heard the soft sigh, the protest of his knee as he bowed, and then the sound of the door closing.

Wyl allowed himself to be picked up by Morgravian soldiers and was relieved to see that they were genuine Legionnaires and not mercenaries. It was a young company; although he recognized none of them, they certainly recognized his name. An awkward silence spread through the group of men as Wyl finished his introduction.

"You are General Wyl Thirsk's sister?" the startled leader qualified.

"I am," Wyl replied, his spirits soaring. He knew it was unlikely he could change the outcome of what was going to happen, but hearing his own name uttered with such reverence restored his confidence. And perhaps he might live to fight another day in another body.

He wondered whether Valentyna had taken his advice about writing to Celimus, claiming she was sending Ylena to him. Their parting had been so awkward and painful, he supposed the Queen was just glad to be rid of Ylena Thirsk.

The young officer could not help himself. "But what are you doing here? We heard you had disappeared."

Wyl was certainly not going to start explaining any more than he wanted to give away. "What is your name?" he asked.

"Harken," the young man replied. "Er, Captain Harken, I hope, by year's end."

"Well, Harken, firstly please remember whom you address. I am the daughter of General Fergys Thirsk, Duke of Argorn, and the sister of General Wyl Thirsk. Please treat me in the fashion you would any noble."

Harken flushed with embarrassment at the stinging rebuke. Blotches of red appeared on his cheeks and ears. "I . . . I apologize, Lady Ylena."

When he saw his reprimand had worked, Wyl deliberately

looked behind him as if suddenly fearful. He might as well continue with his planned charade and hope that the Queen of Briavel had complied with his suggestion. "Thank you, Harken. Have they gone?"

"Who, my lady?" the man asked, desperate to please. He looked over her shoulder and his companions followed suit, suddenly nervous.

"The Briavellian Guardsmen who brought me to this crossing point." Swords were drawn instantly, the ring of steel loud in the silence of the morning. "Fret not, gentlemen," Wyl assured. "They have no quarrel with you. They were concerned only with me." Wyl held his breath, hoping his detached manner and confident explanation would trick the Legionnaires into believing he had been brought to this point under armed escort.

"Why have they brought you here, my lady?" Harken asked sensibly.

"I am a gift," Wyl said, taking some grim amusement from the irony of his words. "For your king."

The aspiring Captain looked appropriately baffled as well as rattled. "I don't understand."

"You are not meant to. Your sovereign will and you will raise his ire if I am not taken to him immediately. I have no intention of trying to escape," Wyl added, glancing toward the rope that had appeared in one anxious pair of hands. "All you're required to do is escort me into Tenterdyn, gentlemen. Restraint will not be necessary."

"Put that away," Harken snapped at the lad, who was not much younger than he. "You do know who this is, don't you?" he added, more angry with himself, Wyl suspected, than with the youngster. "Lady Ylena! She is to be treated with respect."

"Thank you, Harken. I'm sure my brother would be proud of you."

"I never met him, my lady. He passed away the very week I entered the Legion. But your family's name means everything to me. All I ever wanted to do was join the Legion and be commanded by General Thirsk."

"Are you Laud Harken's son?" Wyl asked in surprise.

"Yes, my lady. I am surprised you know of him."

Wyl realized his error. "My brother spoke well of Laud Harken. How is he?"

"Dead, my lady. He fell in the north recently."

"How?"

Harken shrugged, embarrassed by the sorrowful tremor in his voice. "I was told it was a Mountain warrior's arrow, but, my lady, he was outraged by the Rittylworth scandal and no doubt said too much, too loudly."

Murmurings erupted within his group, reassuring Wyl that the name of Thirsk still resonated loudly within the Legion. He was counting on this very fact to help Crys to stir up trouble in Pearlis.

"I understand, Harken, and I am deeply sorry for your loss. Now you must take me to Tenterdyn."

The company remained on patrol while the young Captain-to-be provided the escort alone. This pleased Wyl, for it gave him a chance to learn as much as he could from the gullible youngster. They traveled in silence for a while before Wyl began to ease out some information.

"I imagine the missive from Briavel has arrived by now?"

Harken frowned. "I'm sorry, my lady, I'm not sure what you speak of."

Wyl felt disappointment slice him. "Apparently there was a courier coming from Queen Valentyna about my arrival."

Harken shook his head. "We can find out. I will make some inquiries as soon as we arrive."

"Who is your general now?" Wyl asked. He could see Tenterdyn sprawling in the distance. They would be there soon.

"The King is our general, my lady."

Celimus had finally gotten his wish and taken over the Legion.

"I see. And I hear he is expecting a parley with the Mountain King?"

"Yes—today. King Cailech arrives by midday."

"You sound excited, Harken."

"I am, my lady. If our king marries Queen Valentyna and this parley achieves a truce between Morgravia and the Razor Kingdom, there will be peace at long last."

Wyl made Ylena smile. "I thought most young men of your age dreamed of going to war?"

"I am engaged to be married, my lady. I dream of Alys more than I do killing for my realm." He returned her smile with a shy one of his own.

"Good for you. It is a worthy dream. So you trust your king to achieve these two coups?"

Harken smiled ruefully. "If anyone can, King Celimus can." Wyl suspected that Harken, young as he was, would not be drawn into saying anything openly traitorous, although his tone suggested he felt it.

"Peace for the region would be a rare achievement."

"Is the Queen as beautiful as everyone says she is?" Harken asked suddenly.

Wyl nodded. "More exquisite than you can possibly imagine."

"I was told you were a beauty, my lady," Harken began, then pulled himself back. He looked stricken. "Forgive me, my lady, I meant no offense."

"None taken. I imagine I look a real fright, dressed like a man and having ridden for days," Wyl admitted. "It is not easy to feel pretty in this situation."

"I'm sorry, Lady Ylena, that was tactless of me. Do you mind my asking why you are presenting yourself to the King? There was a rumor that . . ." He struggled to say more.

"That he tried to kill me?" Wyl finished. The young man nodded. "It is true, Harken. Your king is not a good man, I'm sorry to say, and I think you know it. You suspect your father's death was not as cut-and-dried as it was painted to be, and you are most likely right. If Laud stood up to the King's treachery at Rittylworth, then he would have paid in the most dramatic way. I am truly sorry for your family."

Harken's eyes were wide, the first hints of fear creeping across his innocent face. They were just a few yards from the compound of Tenterdyn now. Wyl spoke quickly. "Listen to me. I am here to frighten the King, but not to prevent peace. I hope the King's marriage to the Queen of Briavel will herald the beginning of the great union of our two realms, and that he will forge a peace with King Cailech, but

Celimus is not a man ever to be trusted. Remember that, Harken."

The young man heard the desperation in his companion's voice. "I don't want to take you in there, my lady," he said, further stricken. Both of them saw the gatekeeper stepping out.

"You must. But you must also do what your heart tells you."

"I don't understand," Harken urged.

"You will. You are Legion, used to taking orders, but one of the defining characteristics of an officer of the Legion is that he will never harm another Morgravian unless that person is a betrayer of the realm. Keep that in your heart. Do not allow Celimus to lead you and your men and the rest of the soldiers down the path of darkness. Be true to the Legion first."

"Ho, who comes?" The gatekeeper's voice ripped through the tension of their whispered conversation.

"Tell the truth," Wyl encouraged. "You cannot save me."

Harken spared an anguished glance toward the woman beside him. Wyl felt sorry for the youngster. He clearly sensed that he was involved in something deeply wrong by escorting Ylena Thirsk into Celimus's clutches.

"Come on, boy, we haven't got all day!" the soldier urged, irritated. "Who do you bring here?"

Wyl cleared his throat. "I am the Lady Ylena Thirsk, sir. I wish to speak to King Celimus."

The gatekeeper laughed. "Yes, and I'm the Lady Twinkle and plan to marry him. What is this?" he roared at Harken.

"Watch your manners!" Harken commanded, and the soldier glanced toward the badge on the youngster's uniform. This was an officer in the making and Wyl quietly smirked at the older man's error.

"This *is* the Lady Ylena Thirsk," Harken said, firm of voice now. "She has already been searched, but you may do so again if you are required."

The gatekeeper, far less chirpy now, signaled to another guard, who asked Wyl to alight from his horse. He was searched and Harken's papers were checked for authenticity.

They were permitted to enter the gate by the now slightly sheepish keeper. Another, more senior soldier arrived to ask questions and his eyebrows arched immediately at the name of the woman standing before him.

"Call the Chancellor," he said to his second. Then to Wyl, politely: "We wait, my lady."

He turned to the Legionnaire. "Thank you, Harken. We will take it from here. You may return to your men."

Wyl offered his hand to the young man. "Thank you for your escort," he said, although he hoped his gaze communicated far more. "Again, I am sorry to hear about your father," he added.

Harken looked distracted and anxious. "Sir, has a missive arrived from Briavel concerning the Lady Ylena?"

The man shook his head. "Nothing has arrived from Briavel. I am the first point of contact for all deliveries."

"Perhaps I should wait—" the young man began.

"No, Harken. A company of men without their leader stands at the Briavellian border. Return to your post," the senior man said, this time firmly enough that it brooked no further argument.

Harken bowed. When he straightened, Wyl alone saw the anger and concern in his eyes before the youngster saluted and departed the compound.

"Ah, here we are," the older soldier muttered, and Wyl turned to see Chancellor Jessom emerging from the the main house, a look of pleasure on his face. He swiftly adjusted it to a thin smile, but Wyl saw the satisfaction all the same. The Chancellor's reaction confused him. Surely astonishment, or at the very least irritation, would be more fitting, considering Jessom and Celimus must have hoped Ylena was dead by now?

Jessom's stride was confident and he covered the ground between the main dwelling and the gatehouse with surprising swiftness. "Ylena Thirsk. Almost perfect timing."

*What?* Wyl kept his expression deliberately blank as his mind raced to understand this new development. Jessom continued, "Our king was wondering when you would be delivered. This will be a special name-day present for him and no doubt he will reward Aremys royally for the gift of your life into his hands."

They were expecting Ylena's arrival? How could this be if no message from Valentyna had arrived—and what did he mean about Aremys? Wyl played for time. "I'm sorry. Do I know you?"

Jessom's smile thinned even further. "My apologies, we have never been introduced. I am Jessom, Chancellor and King's Counsel of Morgravia."

"Since when did King Celimus take advice from anyone?" Wyl replied as acidly as he could, watching the crease across Jessom's face, which passed for his smile, fade entirely.

"Thank you, Bern. I will take the Lady Ylena from here," Jessom said to the officer nearby. The man nodded and left their company, happy to pass on responsibility, but not before both Jessom and Wyl saw his raised eyebrows at Ylena's cutting comment. Wyl unhappily allowed Jessom to guide him away from the gates, but he noted that they were not heading toward the main house. The Morgravians must have other plans for Lady Ylena.

Jessom's voice was biting when it came. "You are in a perilous situation, Ylena Thirsk. I suggest you not make it worse on yourself," he advised.

Wyl made Ylena's beautiful face smirk. "How much worse could it possibly get, Jessom? The snake that sits upon the Morgravian throne is hardly going to show me mercy. I do not fear him."

"Nevertheless, I recommend you don't openly insult King Celimus. It could go very badly for you."

"You don't understand, Chancellor. I am not afraid of dying. I am not afraid of Celimus and his savage tortures. Any opportunity I get, sir, I will openly insult him and the bitch Queen who spawned him."

Jessom was normally in control of his emotions, but he drew back in surprise at the young woman's words. "When Aremys said he could deliver you, Ylena, I'm not sure our king understood how heroic you have become. It seems your struggles to survive have toughened you. That only means he will enjoy hurting you all the more. I am not a cruel man and I certainly do not condone the torture of women. Let me suggest again that you make this easier on yourself."

Wyl was happy he had managed to sting the man into losing his composure, even slightly. But more important to him was the second mention of his friend. *Aremys said he could deliver me? What is going on?*

"I am glad I have impressed you, Chancellor, but, frankly, that was not my intention. I will not plead for the King's mercy. He can do with me as he wishes."

"Then I wonder, what is your intention? What can you possibly gain through your defiance?"

"All will be explained, I am sure," Wyl answered cryptically. Valentyna's letter had definitely not arrived, then.

The Chancellor's face betrayed his bafflement. Wyl smirked internally. Jessom was used to knowing everything about everyone. Ylena's inexplicable behavior must be unsettling.

"The King will see you in good time," Jessom said, businesslike now. "But for the meantime, you will remain in here." They had arrived at an outbuilding: a storage hut built in the shade of a huge oak where Aleda had kept her cool pantry. "I'm afraid you have timed your arrival a little prematurely, Ylena. King Cailech is due any minute."

Wyl made a sound of disdain.

Jessom pointed to bucket of water. "May I suggest you clean yourself up. I can have a gown found for you, if it pleases."

"It does not please. I will see the King exactly as I stand before you, Chancellor. And by the way, your new status as servant to the King"—Wyl emphasized the word "servant" and was pleased to see that it struck home—"does not permit you to address a noble by anything but a correct title, sir. You will refer to me as Lady Ylena Thirsk or Lady Ylena Donal—take your pick—but you will accord me the small measure of respect I am due, prisoner or not."

The Chancellor was taken aback by the attack but composed himself smoothly and was quick to retaliate.

"Morgravia has forgotten you, young lady, and your family's name is being dragged through the mire at every opportunity. Climb off your pedestal, Ylena. I am not intimidated by your noble line. I'm wondering how long they will respect you when your head is rotting on a spike outside Pearlis. In fact, I'll do you a kindness—I'll hunt down Alyd Donal's head for you so you can both rot together. Romantic, eh?" he said, uncharacteristically cruel, as he finished tying her ankle to a huge timber post in the hut. "Now clean yourself up, woman, and make ready to meet your sovereign."

For the first time in his life Wyl spat at someone. It was the only comeback he could think of to show his hatred for this servile creature of the King's. He half hoped Jessom would kill him in a blood rush of anger. The Chancellor's body would accord him serious power.

But Jessom was not a man of violence; he was far more subtle in his methods. Instead he made a clicking sound of reproach, as a parent might do to a naughty child. "And you want to be treated like a lady?" He laughed; the sound was harsh and filled with hate. "I have been spat on all my life, Ylena," he said, wiping her spittle from his robe, "and I have always beaten my enemies."

He turned at the sound of the bell from the gatehouse, signaling that King Cailech's party had arrived.

"Farewell, Ylena. We shall summon you in due course."

# 15

**F**YNCH AND KNAVE STOOD AT THE FOOT OF THE RAZORS, about to step onto the tiny, unguarded track that would guide their ascent into the mountains. They had seen no soldiers and their journey from the Wild had been uneventful, and enjoyable for Fynch, who had needed time to think. Knave was not a companion who made conversation—he replied to questions, and prompted them if he considered them important, but otherwise he was silent.

"Why are we walking? Surely the Thicket could send us?" Fynch wondered.

*You can send us,* Knave said, a rare tone of amusement in his voice. *Too dangerous, though. We cannot take the chance of Rashlyn sensing a powerful spelling. Sending Aremys might have registered with him, but he would not have known what the magic was and we can only hope he dismissed it. However, since then we have had the transfer of Wyl to Briavel, the death of Elysius, the arrival of the Dragon King, and you coming into your power. So many surges of magic are not easily dismissed.*

Fynch nodded seriously. "Do you think he knows Elysius has died?"

*I suspect he might have felt something. More important, I am wary that he would have felt the transference of power.*

"How would he sense it? Would it be like a pain?"

The dog led them onto the narrow track. Neither of them looked behind, even though they were now officially leaving Briavel.

*Possibly. More likely he would feel it as you might a seizure. Not pain so much, but loss of physical control and perhaps consciousness. It would bewilder more than hurt.*

"But would he know what it was?" Fynch persisted as he pushed aside the branches of overhanging trees.

*Who knows, Fynch? It would shock him to learn that his brother has been alive all this time, if indeed he did work out that the disturbance was Elysius dying, but I can't imagine he could begin to consider that his sibling's magic had been passed on.*

"You are guessing, though."

*Of course. But remember, your sensitivity to magic and your ability to embrace it and use it are known only to those of the Thicket. Rashlyn may be a sorcerer, but he is not sensitive to the natural world.*

The track rose sharply ahead of them and they began to climb in silence, Fynch concentrating on the challenging, slightly slippery surface of decaying leaves. Many hours later they reached a plateau of rock, the trees below them now. It was cold in the open and a breeze had whipped up. Fynch shivered through his breathlessness. He did not like the cold; he felt it before most others because of his thinly fleshed body and he was glad of the thick fleece jacket Knave had found in Elysius's home and insisted he carry.

*We must be wary, now that we have no cover for a while,* Knave cautioned.

Fynch squatted on his haunches to take some deep breaths and rest for a few moments. He put on the jacket, relishing its instant warmth, then took a sip from his water skin.

"Are you hungry, Knave?" he asked, wondering if the dog should be allowed to hunt.

*I don't need food, Fynch. I ate with Wyl to maintain a pretense of normality.*

"No food at all?" Fynch was incredulous.

*None. I am of the Thicket.*

"You are real, though, aren't you, Knave?" There was a plaintiveness in the boy's voice.

*Real enough; fret not.*

Fynch sighed and confessed, "I rarely feel hungry either. I eat because I know I should, never because I want to."

*That is because of who you are, what you belong to. The powers you have.*

"How can that be? I didn't possess magic until the day Elysius died."

*Fynch, you have always had the capacity to wield a certain magic. You just didn't know it until now.*

Fynch shook his head, too distracted and surprised by Knave's assured claim to argue the matter. He took another draft of water to calm himself. "How long will it take us to get to the fortress?" he finally asked, wiping his mouth with his sleeve.

*Yes, the fortress. I've been thinking about that,* the dog replied. *It occurs to me that if we do our resting by afternoon, we might cover more ground at night.*

"Using magic, you mean?"

The dog did not answer immediately. Instead, he sniffed

the air and Fynch kept the silence, knowing Knave was pondering the most difficult of decisions.

*Yes,* the dog said at last. *I am hoping that if Rashlyn follows a normal pattern, he may not sense small bursts of power as he sleeps. In truth I don't believe he will know what it is even if he does feel it, but I have been reluctant to take any chances.*

"But you've changed your mind now?"

Knave's voice was gentle. *I think I overlooked how slight you are, Fynch. I don't believe we will be able to cover as much ground as I had hoped. It is a long way from Briavel's side of the Razors to Cailech's fortress on their western rim—I realize now it would take us too long. We shall have to take the risk.* He said the last few words with regret.

"But keep the distances small," Fynch added with trepidation.

The dog's dark eyes regarded him sorrowfully. *I am sorry to ask it of you. You will need to chew on the sharvan leaves regularly now.*

"Don't be sorry, it's my burden," Fynch replied, wishing he felt more brave than he sounded. He attempted a brighter tone. "This is how we traveled before, isn't it . . . from Baelup to the Thicket?"

*Except then I had to rely on the Thicket and Elysius. This time we travel with all the power we need.*

"Are you sure?" Fynch had no idea how he was supposed to effect such a magic. He had thought that after the transfer from Elysius he would feel a reservoir of power gurgling within, a well of magic at his beck and call. But he could detect no change within himself. He mentioned this to his friend.

Knave considered the question. Again Fynch waited patiently. The dog sighed. *It is different for me. I am of the Thicket, therefore I rely on it to feed me its magic when it needs to use me, and I feel an energy buzzing within. Anyone touched by the Thicket would feel it, I'm sure. I imagine Wyl might sense it echoing within him somehow and Aremys too. They have both been touched by the magic of the Thicket.*

"Then why not me?"

*I think, Fynch, because you are more than us*, the dog said gravely.

"More than you?" the boy repeated, not understanding.

Knave tried again. *I belong to the Thicket. Wyl, Aremys—and others, no doubt—have been touched by it, not empowered by it but affected somehow. But Elysius, and now you, are connected to it in ways I can't explain. We have no magic without the Thicket to feed it. You do.*

"Oh," Fynch replied, still feeling baffled.

*But I think, my friend, there is far more to you.*

"What do you mean?" Fynch frowned.

Knave gave a low growl of frustration, as if he could not put into words what he was trying to say. *It's as if you and the Thicket are one. While Elysius was merely passing through—for want of a better way of describing it—you belong to the Thicket and it to you. And the King of the Creatures never visited Elysius. I have never seen him before—most of us haven't.*

The gravity of Knave's explanation hit Fynch like a blow. The words and their intent terrified him. There was a finality to what Knave was suggesting; it was as if the Thicket had a hold on him that he would never escape. He did not want to think about it any further. Neither was he ready to consider the implication of the Dragon King's visit. That knowing in his eyes—it was all too bewildering and frightening.

"So what is your plan again?" he said, deliberately forcing the fear away by changing the topic.

Knave must have sensed Fynch's terror, for he switched smoothly from their previous discussion. *We travel on foot by day, then sleep from late afternoon for as long as you wish. We cannot travel by sending until the early hours of the morning, by which time I'm counting on Rashlyn being asleep.*

"But what if he's not?"

Knave shook his head in a doglike shrug. *If he can sense your magic, there's not much we can do about that. We will keep the sendings short so he never feels it quite long enough to tease at it. He cannot see you, Fynch. Not even with his own magic.*

"But he might feel me coming, is that what you mean?"

*Perhaps; I don't know. But he won't know who or what it is, I believe.*

"All right," Fynch said, giving up the train of conversation. To be honest, he had never been one for farseeing plans. He had taken each day as it presented itself and enjoyed all that life gave him during those days. He had been a sunny child and his mother had said often enough that he was destined for something special. He thought of his mother now. She had often disappeared for days, but she would always return, and when she did, she would be withdrawn, a little moody. One evening, returning late from his toil at Stoneheart, Fynch had overheard his parents arguing. His father had called his mother a slut. Fynch did not know what the word meant, but the vehemence behind it had shocked him. His mother had laughed in her tinkling manner and given some retort which had enraged his father further. A year or so later Fynch had learned the meaning of the insult and asked his sister about it. She had looked embarrassed and even pained by his query, but was a truthful person like her brother, so she had explained to him that their mother was a free spirit. "A sort of madness overcomes her," he remembered his sister saying.

"And what happens?" Fynch had asked, not really comprehending.

"Well, it takes her away from us," his sister had replied gently, ruffling his hair. "Sometimes she needs space and freedom."

Fynch was a child who needed clarity in all things and so he persisted. "What does she do when she goes away?"

He recalled now how his sister had sighed. "She allows men to take her, Fynch. It means nothing. Dad says it is a madness and best we leave it like that."

The little boy had finally understood. He knew his mother was fey—she saw things in her dreams and heard voices whispering to her. Most of the folk around their way thought she was bordering on insane, but in truth he could not imagine his mother any other way. He loved her just as she was, with all her curious ways, and although deeply troubled to hear of this new side of her life, he said no more about it. But he thought on it, wondering which men had taken their pleasures with his mother. She was pretty, there was no doubting it, with her petite frame and elfin looks. And when she let her golden hair down, and bathed and put on a fresh dress, she still took his father's breath away. He loved her so, which made her inclinations all the more hurtful. His father would drink himself into a stupor each time she disappeared, no doubt hoping the liquor would take away the grief.

Soon after learning his mother's secret, Fynch had become troubled by thoughts that perhaps he had not been sired by his father. Fynch did not resemble any of his siblings closely—they were all dark and solid like his father, while he was fair, golden in fact, with the same elfin qualities as his mother. Though he had worked hard at convincing himself that he simply took after his mother, the thought still troubled him. He had never shared this anxiety with anyone. Well, not with any person. The Dragon King had seen it in him, though—Fynch was sure of it. The dragon's eyes had flared as they penetrated the boy's soul—had seen the truth of Fynch's secret fear.

As he climbed farther into the Razors, Fynch thought about what the King of the Creatures had asked of him. Perhaps, in his heart, he had always known that his life would be brief and so had given his energy to enjoying the moment he lived in. So be it. He was not scared of dying anymore, but he would make his death count. As much as the Dragon King saw destroying Rashlyn as his priority, Fynch knew that his own loyalty lay with Wyl. Somehow he had to help Wyl defeat Celimus. It was why he had risked more headaches in sending Wyl to Werryl. And, against Knave's counsel, he had sent Valentyna the chaffinch to whistle a tune he hoped would prompt her to wait for Ylena. He had even risked more pain to send dream thoughts to Wyl, urging him to face Celimus and to die again, if necessary.

Fynch was utterly committed to the cause of ridding Morgravia of its present king while also protecting Valentyna and

Wyl. Deep down he believed Valentyna would have to marry Celimus—she could not both prevent such a union and secure peace for her realm. He wondered whether she could survive such a marriage, for he knew the cruelty of Celimus. But far worse was his deeply held belief that Wyl would fail in his bid to become Celimus. When he tried to interpret this chilling thought, the only explanation he could come up with for his fear was that Wyl hated Celimus so much he would never be able to live with himself in that guise. If Wyl could not achieve the end of the Quickening by becoming Celimus, however, it could mean an infinite lifetime of changing bodies. Or perhaps Wyl would die in the body of some lonely guard, an arrow through his back. Fynch grasped—perhaps more than Wyl did—that in any of his guises Wyl could be killed through an accident or natural causes. The Quickening, as Fynch intuitively understood it, only worked if the killer was still connected to Wyl via a weapon or touch, which was why Myrren could not have used the magic to save herself. She had died at the stake; the flames had taken her life.

Knave interrupted his thoughts. *We had best keep moving. We are too exposed here.*

Fynch stood, adjusted the sack across his shoulder, and buttoning his fleece, followed the dog.

*What were you thinking about?* Knave asked.

Fynch was surprised. The dog rarely asked questions on such a conversational level. "Myrren," he replied.

*Oh?*

"She must have known that the Quickening could not save her, that she would be consumed by the flames. So she took revenge instead. If only she hadn't," he finished, more bitterly than he had intended.

*It wouldn't have changed Wyl's fate,* Knave said softly. *Celimus would still have sent him on the journey of treachery into Briavel. Wyl would have died by Romen's sword; Ylena would have wasted away in the dungeon; and Gueryn would have died in the Razors.*

Fynch nodded wearily. "Yes, you're right."

*I don't approve of what Myrren and Elysius did, Fynch,*

*but Wyl's life was forfeit from the moment Celimus took the throne. It might be worth your looking upon the Quickening as a gift rather than a curse.*

Fynch rubbed Knave's great head to acknowledge the kindness in the dog's voice. No one could approve of the Quickening, but perhaps some good might yet come of it. He thought about the zerkon that could so easily have killed Wyl in the Razors. If the beast had succeeded, that would have been the end for Wyl, for Elysius had told him the magic worked only between humans. They had a lot to thank Lothryn for, if he still lived. The fate of a kingdom had shifted on that one man's bravery.

Fynch was not aware that he had voiced this thought aloud in his mind. It was only when the dog responded that he realized he needed to learn how to control his new abilities more thoroughly.

*Fynch, do you not realize yet that the destiny of all three realms rests with you?* the dog said. *It is your actions—not Lothryn's or Cailech's, not those of Celimus or Valentyna, not even what Wyl might achieve—that will save the land. You will decide the destiny.*

Tears rolled helplessly down the small boy's face. *I am the sacrifice,* he thought privately, hauling himself up another small ledge. *So be it.*

# 16

RASHLYN AWOKE FROM HIS STUPOR, ANGRY AT FEELING HANDS at his brow, wiping away the sweat of his ragings. He swung at the person tending him, hitting her in the face and drawing blood at her mouth. "Begone, woman!" he roared, searching his wits to identify his location. He was in a strange chamber; it was dark outside.

"Wait!" he called to the woman, who had turned her back on him.

She looked at him then, a line of red trailing from the corner of her lip to beneath her chin. Rashlyn could see the hate in her eyes and dismissed it, used to such a reaction.

"Where am I?" he demanded. "Why am I not in my own chambers?"

"The King said we were to watch over you here until you fully recovered," the woman replied sullenly, touching her mouth and bringing away bloodstained fingers. "He said you would not like anyone in your rooms."

He ignored her injury. "How long have I been here?"

"Two days."

That shocked him. "Where is the King?"

"Gone." She spoke the word as a threat. "He left with the Grenadyne the night of your seizure."

She called to someone and a man entered the chamber. He took one look at the woman and glanced darkly toward Rashlyn.

"I suspect I am no longer welcome," Rashlyn said to the man, hoping to unnerve him.

"You have never been welcome, barshi," the Mountain Man replied, not at all intimidated. "We permitted you in our house only because our king asked it. My wife has taken good care of you."

"And I regret my odd form of thanks, Rollo," Rashlyn answered, recognizing the pair now. She was a midwife, a capable nurse, and the husband, Rollo, was a senior and trusted warrior of Cailech's. It would not be wise to insult them further.

"My apology, Kaylan," he said, getting slowly to his feet. The dizziness was still there. "I must have been dreaming. I am sorry for your wound."

"Leave, scum," Rollo growled.

Rashlyn was not surprised. Without Cailech around, the people of the mountains did not maintain the deference they attempted to show him in the King's presence.

"Be careful, Rollo. I understand your daughter is with child. We wouldn't want anything untoward to occur to the infant, now, would we?" Rashlyn said conversationally as he pushed by the couple.

The man roared, lunging toward the barshi, but his wife held him back. "Don't, Rollo. Who knows what he is capable of," she said, terrified now, her bleeding lip forgotten, her pride tattered as her pleading eyes beseeched Rashlyn to leave the family be.

*That's better,* Rashlyn thought, smirking at the cowed Rollo, pleased by the fear in Kaylan's tone. One day he would make them all pay for their disdain. He left the stuffy dwelling and gulped deeply the fresh air of the mountain night. Limping across to the nearby well, he drank two long refreshing cups of the clear water. It revived him sufficiently that he could make his way, without staggering, to his lonely chambers.

Once inside, he bolted the doors, double-checking the locks. Only then did he begin to relax; only then, in the safety of his isolation, did he permit himself to release his fright at losing two full days of his life. What had happened? He was aware that his periods of darkness, when he spiraled into his other self, were extending, but had no idea they could stretch so long. Until now, the longest he had lost himself to such madness was half a day, and that had frightened him enough. But two days! Usually during these black periods he functioned reasonably well, but it was as though he was someone else. Rashlyn did not dislike that other self; at such times he was confident, flamboyant, certainly creative. His mind was at its most sharp and great innovations often came to him. He felt invincible in this state. No drug he knew of could induce such a constant euphoric sense of power. But when he was able to think clearly, Rashlyn understood that the euphoric moods were dangerous too. During these times he was unpredictable, capable of anything. The surge of power forced him to relinquish control over his actions. It was a madness, he knew. It had been creeping up on him for years. His brother had seen it in him first and his father not long after. Curse their souls!

And yet this time it did not feel quite the same. His body was still trembling from the seizure. Normally he would emerge out of the darkness, realize he had lost himself, and discover what had occurred in his "absence"—there was no better way to describe it. But this occasion was different. It sounded as though he had simply collapsed. Cailech must have seen him in a considerably weakened state to have ordered his care. Who else had seen him, apart from the King and the two who cared for him? Where had he been when the seizure overcame him?

Rashlyn was famished but ignored the growling plea of his belly. Using a spell to summon a flame, he lit a fire and brought some water to boil. He added verrun bark and a handful of arkad petals and tried not to think about anything but the brewing and cooling of the infusion. As soon as he tasted the first bitter sip of the brew, he felt his mind begin to clear.

He sat at the window, inhaled deeply of the numbing air, which also helped to freshen his thoughts, and continued sipping. The tea began to work; the blurriness cleared and he was able to move backward through the past days.

It came to him. He had been riding with the Grenadyne and Myrt. His suspicions about the stranger had not lessened for knowing him; Rashlyn was convinced there was a mystery attached to the foreign mercenary. If he could make physical contact with the man, he was sure he could find out more. It had unnerved Rashlyn to hear from the King that Farrow had reacted strongly when he had stroked Galapek. Clearly he had felt the magic in the stallion, which could only mean the mercenary owned power himself or had been touched by it somehow. Cailech had wanted to dismiss the incident, but Rashlyn was not convinced such a reaction could be passed off as coincidence. And so the King had agreed to force Farrow into riding Galapek with the proviso that Rashlyn accompany him to observe him.

The barshi recalled now how the mercenary had not reacted in the manner described by the King on his first meeting with the enchanted horse. Either the Grenadyne had wrestled his emotions back under his control, or the King had been mistaken and the man's claim of being fatigued from his adventure in the mountains was true. And yet Rashlyn was sure Farrow was hiding something. The stranger seemed too confident, too aware that he was being tested. He had parried Rashlyn's questions smoothly and then, just when Rashlyn had gotten close enough to touch him . . . something had touched Rashlyn instead.

The barshi closed his eyes and took himself back to the moment. The shrieking of the horse had echoed his own instinctive reaction to the immense pressure he had felt throughout his body. There had been no pain, but the experience had been followed by intense nausea . . . then darkness. The woman, Kaylan, had called it a seizure, so presumably he had thrashed about in his unconscious state.

"It was not my madness that caused this," he murmured. "So what did?"

"Magic," he answered himself, and laughed briefly. "Powerful magic," he whispered, remembering it more clearly now.

Galapek had felt it and had screamed. The barshi wondered if the horse had experienced a similar weakness. But there was more to the strange event than his physical reaction . . . there was also a sense of dread. The ominous notion that something was coming toward him was strong indeed. For the first time in a long time Rashlyn felt very fearful.

Elspyth had decided to slip away from Werryl Palace when everyone's attention was diverted toward Brackstead and Lady Donal. She felt bad about leaving without a farewell to both Crys and the Queen. Valentyna had welcomed them warmly when they were in need, had sheltered and protected them without hesitation. Elspyth's secret departure would surely be considered a slight and this bothered the woman of Yentro. But she wanted to leave with no fuss, no teary farewells, and definitely no one trying to talk her out of it—which the Queen most certainly would attempt. It seemed right to go quietly, taking nothing, not even the horse she had ridden into Briavel.

What she regretted most was the seemingly sly departure, which might be construed the wrong way, and not leaving a note for Wyl. She owed him that much. Why could she not have taken a few extra minutes and scribbled a second note for the Lady Ylena Thirsk? Elspyth was sure Wyl would find his way to Werryl, and she could have given him an assurance she would not do anything rash, along with a promise of her return. But her head had been filled with Lothryn and seizing her chance to leave without creating a commotion. She knew Liryk would be glad to see the back of her; his and Krell's surreptitious glances and grimaces had left her in no doubt of their displeasure at her presence. She knew they did not appreciate her speaking her mind about Celimus. There were moments Elspyth had been sure either one of them would have gladly silenced her with something more painful than stares.

So, as soon as she saw the royal party depart across Werryl Bridge, she grabbed her small sack of goods and fled via a small, barely known courtyard gate which Valentyna had admitted making good use of as a child. She stepped out of the palace grounds and walked through the town of Werryl rather than across its beautiful bridge. The main township was walled and Elspyth intended to make her escape by blending in easily with the traffic that drifted into and out of Werryl daily through its most northern gate. She felt confident she would find someone to hitch a ride with into Crowyll, and perhaps from there she could buy a nag and use four legs instead of two to get to Banktown in the far north, before turning west and crossing the border into Felrawthy.

It was the brewery driver's child who spotted her first. The cart rolled level with Elspyth as the big horse's ponderous tread caught up with the slow-moving crowd passing through the gate. The guards did not seem to be paying close attention to those leaving town and Elspyth was confident she was unlikely to be stopped or questioned. It wasn't as if anyone would be looking out for her at this early stage of her journey. Nevertheless, her previous adventures had taught her to take precautions. She needed an innocent cover—just like this family here, she thought, eyeing the little girl, who smiled tentatively.

"Where are you going?" the child asked.

Elspyth smiled brightly. "I'm going north," she replied.

"And what will you do when you get there?" the child said.

"Well, I'm going home actually," Elspyth lied, and cast a gentle rescue-me expression toward the driver, who shrugged his apology for the youngster's inquisition.

"Do you have a family?"

"No," Elspyth said, surprised at the question. "I have no one in my life who worries about me, but north is where I come from and where I feel comfortable."

"The north of Briavel?"

"The north of Morgravia," she said theatrically.

"And where's that?"

Elspyth laughed. "A long way away. I come from a town called Yentro."

"And you have to walk all that long way?" the little girl exclaimed.

"Hush, Jen. Let the lady be," the man said, embarrassed. "I'm sorry, miss," he added, looking at Elspyth shyly. "She gets bored easily on these trips and we've hardly begun."

"It's all right, really," she replied, making a swift decision. This was her ride. She looked toward the girl again. "I once knew a pretty lady called Jen and she had beautiful red hair like yours." It was a lie, but Elpsyth needed any leverage she could create and quickly.

Jen's eyes grew wide with pleasure. "Am I pretty?"

"I think you are. I'm sure your father does too."

"Would you like to ride next to me?" Jen asked.

Elspyth swallowed her delight. It was the invitation she had hoped for. She looked deliberately toward the man. "Oh, I don't think your father would . . ."

He reacted precisely as she had intended. "You're most welcome to ride with us, miss," he offered kindly. "We're going as far as Coneham, if that helps?"

"Oh, I'm sure it will." She smiled. "Where is that, exactly?"

"North of Brackstead. Hop up."

Elspyth climbed into the back of the cart, near the little girl. "Thank you," she said, with relief. "Will we be stopping in Brackstead?" she added as innocently as she could, not liking the idea of running into Valentyna and Crys.

"No. We don't stay in inns or the like, miss," the driver said. "We just curl up in the back. We carry everything with us."

Elspyth smiled. It was perfect. "That sounds wonderful. I'm sure I can help to keep your Jen amused on our journey."

"My name is Ericson," the man said, an expression of gratitude sweeping across his tired face. Elspyth felt a tiny pang of guilt at how adroitly she had manipulated the kind fellow.

The cart rumbled through the northern gate, Jen chattering incessantly about anything that came into her head and Elspyth doing her best to agree where necessary and answer when required. She pulled her blue cloak more tightly around herself, for the morning was chill. As they passed the soldiers at the gate, she tried not to catch anyone's eye, but she had never quite grasped how attractive she was and her dark hair and pert features could not help but win attention.

"Shar guide you," the guard said to her. It was a common blessing used by Morgravians and Briavellians alike to bid others a good journey, but it was the wink that came with it that made her grin. "Don't stay away too long, now," the guard added, encouraged by her smile. "I won't sleep until I see your pretty face again."

Elspyth made a gesture of admonishment, as if to say it was improper of him to talk like that in front of her family, but the cart had already rolled on and the young man missed her mock annoyance.

It had been a long time since Elsypth had felt as light-hearted as she did at that moment. *I'm coming, Lothryn,* she silently cast. She hoped Shar would take pity on her and she might soon be reunited with her beloved.

As Elspyth was privately celebrating her escape, Gueryn was arguing with Rashlyn, who, now recovered, had decided to visit the prisoner.

"Who would it hurt?" Gueryn demanded.

"No one, but I don't understand your request," the barshi said.

"Because I am rotting here."

"Why is that my problem?"

"Because you're meant to take care of me," Gueryn said, his tone as acid as he could make it. "Either you make it possible or, I promise you, Rashlyn, I'll find a way to kill myself, even if it means banging my head against this wall until I knock my senses clean out!"

Gueryn knew he sounded desperate; he could hear as much in his tone, and he also knew it was highly unlikely he could fashion any genuinely expedient method to cause his own death. Still, he had made the threat and the barshi looked thoughtful. Gueryn decided to press his luck. "The King insisted that I be looked after. I refuse to sit here day after day in your stinking dungeon."

"Isn't that what prisoners do?"

The man's light voice irritated Gueryn further. "Let me work, damn it! I'll provide an honest day's toil for the chance to breathe fresh air and work my muscles. You can keep me chained if you must."

"Oh, I will," Rashlyn murmured.

Gueryn felt himself losing his temper; the only thing that stopped him reaching for the barshi's throat was the memory of the magic Rashlyn had once used on him.

He tried again, a little more humility in his tone. "The King agreed to allow me daily walks so I can remain as healthy as possible considering my situation. I am prepared to work for them, for Shar's sake."

"Where?"

That took Gueryn by surprise. He stopped his pacing and turned on the healer. "Where what?"

"Where would you work?"

Gueryn knew he had to negotiate carefully now. He forced himself to keep the exasperation in his voice, as if the chance to escape the loneliness and despair of the dungeon were all that mattered. No one, especially Rashlyn, must guess his true intent. "Where? Anywhere! The kitchens, the vineyards, the stables . . ." He ran an unsteady hand through his tangled graying hair to give himself an air of distraction.

"Your preference?"

"Does it matter?" he retaliated, wondering whether Rashlyn was testing him. "I'm good with horses; I'm not afraid to work in an open field; and if you want me scrubbing pans, I'll happily do that. Why don't you choose?"

"The kitchens would not want you, Morgravian," Rashlyn mused. "And I don't want you around knives or any potential weapons." He scratched at his wild beard and something fell out of it. Disheveled as Gueryn himself looked and as dirty as he felt, Rashlyn's grubbiness revolted him.

"Then let me work in the stables," he said. "I'll muck out, rub down, water, exercise the animals—whatever the stablemaster wants."

Rashlyn stared at him. The eyes were tiny and dark; no evidence of warmth flickered in that cold gaze. "I shall speak to Maegryn," he said, after a long pause. "Remember my lesson, soldier. With the King gone, you have no protection to count on, other than what my rule deems fit."

"I had no idea you hailed from royal blood," Gueryn risked.

"Be very careful, le Gant," the dark man warned, his lips twisted in a cruel sneer beneath the filthy beard.

Gueryn emerged into a sharply bright spring morning, his eyes stinging from the sunlight but his body rejoicing in its warm caress and the chance to breathe the opposite of the stale mustiness of his cell. He stood between two guards, neither of whom he knew, and watched a man approach. Rashlyn was nowhere to be seen.

"I'm Maegryn, the stablemaster," the man said, coming to a halt.

Gueryn nodded. "Thank you for allowing me to work in the stables. I'll not let you down."

Maegryn made a low sound of disdain. "You wouldn't want to, soldier. Come with me."

Gueryn followed as fast as the rope binding his ankles would allow.

"You're not going to make him wear that all day, are you?" Maegryn complained to the guards.

"Rashlyn's orders," one said, shrugging.

"And who is he to be giving orders?" Maegryn said, adding under his breath, "Haldor spare me."

Gueryn took a chance. "He told me he is the King's voice when his highness is not here," he said to Maegryn, who was now slicing through the rope with a blade.

The stablemaster stood, his deep-set eyes giving away little of the man inside. "And I'm the fucking King of the Stables, so Rashlyn had better look out when he gives orders in my domain."

The guards laughed.

Gueryn bowed. "Your highness," he said, and knew he had made a fragile conquest when Maegryn grinned in response. "Thank you," Gueryn added, looking toward his unshackled feet.

"Don't get too excited, soldier. Jos here will be hanging around to keep an eye on you."

Gueryn eyed the huge, lumbering lad beside him. "Nice to meet you, Jos."

The big guard nodded, a sloping grin pulling at his deformed mouth. "Don't give me trouble now," he warned, the words slightly mangled.

"You have my promise," Gueryn assured, looking toward Maegryn too.

"But is it worth anything?" the stablemaster teased.

"As an officer of the Legion, most certainly."

"I wish your king showed similar manners."

"My king is a ruthless, lying, cowardly murderer."

Maegryn gave a low whistle. "Well, I hope our king watches his back, then."

"What do you mean?"

"I gather our people are about to make a peace alliance with your people, soldier."

"What?" Gueryn's eyes narrowed; surely this was a jest.

"If our Cailech has his way, then the Razor Kingdom and Morgravia are soon to be allies," Maegryn clarified.

Gueryn was shocked. "Celimus cannot be trusted."

Maegryn shrugged. "So long as you can, le Gant. I'm only King of the Stables, remember? What happens for the greater good of our realm is not something I have any control over. Now, I think you need exercise as much as my horses do—follow me."

Jos stayed with Gueryn all afternoon and the Morgravian noted that Jos followed his orders dutifully, taking his responsibility of watching over his prisoner seriously. The deformity was a pity—it gave the impression that Jos was a dullard when he was anything but. It also gave the other guards reason to tease him, as Gueryn learned from the lad's shy admission. He found the youngster pleasant, courteous, and charming. Jos laughed at Gueryn's small jests and even made a few of his own. Gueryn made a promise to himself to make a special effort with Jos. Confidence was all the lad needed. The harelip would fade to invisible if Jos's personality were allowed to shine through.

Gueryn had to admit he was enjoying himself after so many weeks of despair. He had walked, rubbed down, and watered six horses now and was pleased with himself, despite the twinge from aching muscles and tired limbs. He had not counted on being as weak as he felt.

"A good afternoon's work, soldier," Maegryn said, offering him a linen rag. "That's good honest sweat there."

"Call me Gueryn," the soldier offered. When the man nodded, he added, "Can I come again?"

"Tomorrow's fine. I'll be glad to see you. Perhaps Jos can bring you this time."

"What about Rashlyn? Will you speak with him?"

"The man's insane. No one follows his rules. We won't say anything—he probably won't even come looking."

Gueryn's relief showed. "Until tomorrow, then."

He nodded at Jos to let the guard know he was ready to be returned to the dungeon and gave him a grin. He was building tenuous friendships here, and was a big step closer to Galapek. That made the aches all the more satisfying. Tomorrow he might see the horse the stranger, Aremys, had claimed was Lothryn. It still seemed too incredible to contemplate, but Gueryn could not forget the touch of Rashlyn's evil magic on his own body or the murder of a woman made to look like Elspyth. There was no knowing the limits of Rashlyn's power.

*Until tomorrow, then,* he said privately as he fell into step with Jos.

# 17

RYS ADMIRED THE WAY THE BRIAVELLIAN COMMANDER, DEspite his busy duties, offered his help. If Liryk minded, he did not show it.

"Forgive me for dragging you away from important affairs, Commander Liryk," Crys said. "I'm just a little worried about Elspyth, as is your queen."

"And rightly so, your grace," Liryk said sharply. "She is a young woman abroad alone. No matter how I tighten the net around bandits and cutthroats, they still exist, and she makes the softest of targets."

"Too true. Where should we start?"

"Let's find out who was on duty first during our absence in Brackstead."

"How many gates are there?"

"Five main ones, but as you rightly point out, she was leaving as anonymously as possible, so I imagine she would have used the busiest outlets—Werryl Bridge or the northern gate."

It took them an hour to find and question the relevant men, drawing a blank until one young man was hurried back from a meal. He wiped his mouth in haste, concern on his face. His superior introduced him. "This is Peet. He was one of three guards on the northern gate for the morning watch."

Liryk and Crys had already questioned the other two from the morning and all from the afternoon rotation. Crys was sure this man would offer no further insight and had resigned himself to a fruitless search following a trail that was already stone cold.

"Sir," Peet said to his commander, nervously nodding at Crys. "My lord."

Liryk cleared his throat. "Relax, man, you're not in any trouble here. We're seeking your help."

"Oh?" the guard replied, none of the anxiety leaving his tone or expression.

"We're hoping you might remember a young woman who left Werryl yesterday. We think she might have departed via the northern gate and we're pretty certain it would have been on your watch, the early-morning guard."

Peet nodded, relieved, looking between both men. "I'll try, sir. Can you describe her?"

Liryk looked at Crys, who obliged. "Well, she's petite. She has dark hair and is comely. Very pretty, in fact." He grinned at the young man. "She stands about yea high to me"—he measured a point halfway between his elbow and shoulder—"and I'm guessing now but I think she might have been wearing a soft brown skirt, pinkish sort of blouse, black boots. I really can't be sure, but that was what she was wearing when she arrived in Werryl." He knew Elspyth had not taken any of the items Valentyna had given her to wear.

Peet's expression became forlorn and he sounded embarrassed. "Hundreds of people pass through that gate each day, my lord. That description could be any of a dozen women from yesterday." He held his hands out in a gesture of helplessness. "So many people, you don't really scrutinize anyone unless you've been ordered to."

Crys nodded, understanding. "I know, it was a long shot."

Liryk sighed. "I'm sorry, my lord." He was genuine in his commiseration; he did not like the antagonism the woman of Yentro had stirred up, but he certainly was not happy at her going off alone into the mountains. He thought Crys had been far too flippant about her disappearance when it had been first discovered; obviously the Duke had had a change of heart, but a little too late, he thought privately. "Thank you, Peet, you can return to your meal," he told the guard.

"Oh," Crys said suddenly, "she did have a cloak with her. The morning was cold, so presumably she had that on. It's blue, if that helps."

Peet, who had been turning away, swung around. "Blue cloak?"

Crys nodded. "Does it jog anything?" he asked, noticing the man's keen attention.

"Why yes, my lord, it does. I do remember a woman in a blue cloak. Her hair was dark, I think, though she had it covered though with the hood, so I can't be sure."

Liryk stepped forward. "Well, tell us, man. Hurry now."

The soldier bit his lip in thought. "I wished her Shar's speed, my lord," he said, looking toward Crys. "I added something along the lines that she should hurry back to Werryl because I wouldn't be able to sleep until I saw her pretty face again." He shrugged. "It was harmless really—I was just passing the time of day with a lovely girl."

Crys smiled. "That's all right, Peet. Was she alone?"

"No, as I recall she was with a family. I thought it was hers."

"Come on now, son. What do you remember?" prompted Liryk. "Bring the scene back. Remember all those exercises we've been doing about how to recall a moment in detail?"

"Yes, sir, I do," Peet said. "I can remember it well now. She was traveling with a little girl and a man who was driving the cart they were in. They—the woman and the girl—were laughing. It was a cart with one horse."

"Did she say anything?" Crys asked.

"No. Seemed happy, though."

"The man—what do you remember about him?" Liryk added.

"Not much, sir. He said he was going to Coneham. His cart had brewery barrels on it, which, come to think of it, strikes me as a little odd."

"Why is that odd?" Crys asked.

Liryk turned to him. "Because our brewery is situated northeast of the city. There would be no need to pass through Werryl itself, let alone the northern gate, for deliveries to Coneham. It does sound suspicious." Liryk addressed the officer. "Find out whatever you can on this fellow—if there's any information among the men. Get Peet here to give as detailed a description of him as possible. Anything at all he remembers, record."

"Is the lady in trouble, sir?"

"No, lad. But we need to find her and your information can help us track her down."

Peet nodded and took his leave, following his superior officer.

"Not much to go on, I'm afraid," Liryk admitted to Crys.

"It's something, though. I'll wait around a little longer—Peet's information might jog someone else's memory."

"Let's give it another hour."

"And then I'm heading for Coneham, come what may," Crys promised.

The cart slowed to a stop and Elspyth was roused from the snooze she had fallen into. She presumed they were breaking for something to eat and felt embarrassed that she had no food to share with her hosts. She did, however, have some coin Crys had insisted she keep during their journey to Werryl. "You may need it if we get separated," he had cautioned, and she was grateful now for his generosity. At least she could offer to pay for her keep while traveling with Ericson and his little girl.

Elspyth noted a hut not far away. She knew they had taken a route off the main road, which Ericson had said was a shorter route with less traffic. "How long have I been dozing?" she said, stretching. She didn't recall feeling tired, or falling asleep, but apparently she had needed rest more than she thought.

"Oh, hours," Jen said in a singsong voice. "The tea always makes the women drowsy."

Elspyth smiled at the youngster without understanding. They had shared some tea at the roadside not far out of Werryl. She had thought it odd, because they had only just left the city, but Jen had insisted she was thirsty and hungry and Ericson had said tea and a hunk of cheese would satisfy his daughter, who rarely ate breakfast. Elspyth had been happy to go along with them and had enjoyed the curious-tasting brew. "Where are we?" she asked, imagining they might be a couple of hours north of the city.

"Just outside Sharptyn," Ericson replied, jumping down. Jen followed.

Elspyth was taken aback. "Sharptyn! No, wait," she said, frowning. "That can't be right." Her mind raced across her imaginary map of Briavel. Sharptyn was to the west, almost into Morgravia, and many hours from Werryl. She shook her head free of the befuddlement of sleep. Perhaps she was mistaken in her mapping. "Are you sure?"

He grinned and there was something unpleasant in it. "Oh yes, very."

"But Sharptyn is far west. You said you were heading north," she said, a pang of fear tingling through her body.

His nasty smile remained. "Did I? Well, we're here now, Elspyth."

Ericson no longer looked tired or kind. He looked predatory and smug. "Jen?" Elspyth looked toward the child, bewildered and frightened.

Again the singsong voice. "Sorry, Elspyth. So, so, sorry," Jen chanted, not even looking at the woman. "Ericson chose you. I didn't want to. I liked you."

"Ericson!" Elspyth shrieked as men appeared out of the hut. "What's this all about?"

"It's not personal," he said, acknowledging the new arrivals with a nod. "Just business. Get her, lads," he added.

Elspyth had no time to think; she lifted her skirt and ran. She forced her legs to move faster than they ever had before, and she screamed, unleashing every ounce of her strength and spirit. Even escaping from Cailech's fortress had not been as terrifying as this. She could hear the shouts and taunts of the men chasing her. They were laughing at her.

She thought of Lothryn. Her pathetic attempt to rescue him had achieved nothing more than getting herself trapped, and probably killed. He would never know that she had tried to reach him. She screamed one last time as she sensed a man about to launch himself at her. He crashed from out of the bushes, knocking her sideways and crushing the breath out of her. The others arrived panting, some laughing still. And then Ericson forced her to swallow more of the tea she had drunk earlier. It all made sense now: She had been drugged. Elspyth tried to spit out the liquid, shaking her head from side to side, deliberately gagging. Ericson hit her, which shocked her into opening her mouth, giving her attacker the chance to pour the drug down her throat.

The men let her go. She just had time to count six of them, including Ericson, before the sky began to reel. She sensed something reaching toward her, something powerful trying to connect with her—or so she imagined—but it was too late. Elspyth lost consciousness again. There would be no more screaming now.

Fynch had felt Elspyth's fear as she fled from the men, sensed it when she fell. He had never met this woman of Yentro, and yet somehow her terror and helplessness assaulted him. He reached toward her and could see her now: prone, presumably unconscious, with men standing around her.

Knave looked back to where Fynch stood rigid on the small ledge. The wind was whipping around them and Knave wondered whether he and the boy should be harnessed together somehow. Fynch was so slight, Knave feared that a stiff, rogue gust of wind would blow him off the ledge.

Bewildered by the boy's closed eyes and fixed stance, the dog returned to him. *Fynch! What happens now?* he asked. When Fynch did not respond, he nudged the boy, suddenly disturbed that he could not lock on to whatever was troubling his companion.

Fynch staggered and finally opened his eyes. "It's Wyl's friend Elspyth. She's in trouble," he said, holding his head.

Knave knew it hurt to use the magic. Elysius had been very careful about the power. His channeling to Myrren had near enough killed him, for she had needed his company and strength for a sustained period. But Fynch was so small and inexperienced and seemed to be opening himself fully to the magic. He did not know yet how to shield himself from it. He must have accidentally latched on to this woman's plea for help. Well, she was not Fynch's problem. He had a task to fulfill.

*We must press on, Fynch,* Knave began.

"No. She's hurt, in trouble. Elspyth is the woman who escaped with Wyl from the Razors. She helped him. I cannot forsake her," Fynch murmured through his pain.

*Chew some sharvan,* Knave suggested, determined not to show his annoyance at this new setback.

Fynch poked into his sack and retrieved a handful of the dried leaves he had taken from Elysius's stock. He sat down and quietly chewed as suggested.

*How do you know this?* Knave asked.

"I have seen her," the boy answered.

*I'm not sure I understand. Is Elspyth empowered? How can she reach you otherwise?*

Fynch shook his aching head. "I don't think she's empowered. Wyl did not mention her having any sentient ability. I'm not sure, to tell the truth, whether she even knew I was there."

*What do you mean?*

"She did not call to me, exactly. I felt her fear and then I heard her scream. I followed her trace." Fynch looked at Knave with large, serious eyes that were full of pain and the dog felt grief for the small boy. "I think it's the Thicket."

*Sending you her message, you mean?*

Fynch nodded once, carefully. With the pain slowly clearing, he did not want to reawaken it. "You said something earlier about Wyl being touched by the Thicket and therefore sensitive to magic, even though he cannot wield it?"

*I remember.*

"Well, Elspyth is the niece of the Widow Ilyk—the seer Elysius knew and used once. Do you recall that?"

*Yes.*

"So perhaps Elspyth, though not empowered herself, has a vague awareness of magic's touch. Wyl mentioned that she once dreamed of Lothryn calling to her."

*And?*

Fynch shrugged. His head felt better, the dizziness gone, with just a reminder of the pain lurking. He spat out the pulp of the sharvan. "I'm guessing that she cast out her fears without realizing she could, and it just so happened that the Thicket was listening. The Thicket has connected us all, you might say."

It was plausible, Knave thought. *So what are you thinking now, Faith Fynch?*

"I have to find out more about what's happening to her."

*We cannot be diverted from our journey,* Knave warned gravely, hoping to impress on Fynch once again that nothing mattered but what the Dragon King had asked of them: to destroy Rashlyn and rid the world of his evil.

"I know. I'm going to send a spy," Fynch said, and chanced a grin at his black friend.

*Then use a fast one. We must get on.*

Fynch looked out across the hazy landscape. He knew what he was searching for and sure enough he found the kestrel, high on the wing and hovering, staring down toward the ground. He closed his eyes and drew on his magic to summon the bird of prey.

Knave saw the bird tilt its wing and knew that was the moment Fynch had connected with it. The kestrel swooped and banked high again, turning in their direction, and then dived toward them fast, no doubt curious. When it arrived it perched itself on Fynch's outstretched arm and even permitted the boy to stroke it, in thanks for answering the summoning. Knave was impressed. He had been told that Elysius had achieved something similar once before, but not as easily; according to the creatures of the Thicket, he had cajoled and beseeched them when he needed help. But the answer to Fynch's call had been immediate.

Knave would not normally be privy to what passed between boy and bird, but Fynch generously opened his mind so the dog could listen in as well.

*I need you to find someone for me,* Fynch asked.

*Who?* the bird replied casually. Knave wondered if the kestrel knew who Fynch was.

*It is a woman—this is what she looks like*, and Knave saw the mental image Fynch gave to the kestrel.

*Where?*

*Two miles east of Sharptyn.* Another picture was given: an aerial map of Briavel. Knave was spellbound; was the Thicket supplying Fynch with this practical information?

*And when I find her?*

*Let me know what you see. I will send help.*

*With your powers, can you not look for yourself?* the bird asked cheekily.

*I could, my friend, but I lose strength and a portion of my life each time I draw on my powers. You can save me some of this loss if you will make that journey and be my eyes.*

*I shall do what you ask if you will give me your name and tell me who you are.*

*Gladly. My name is Fynch. I am from Morgravia and was a cleaner at the castle of Stoneheart.*

*Oh, but you are much more than that, surely,* the kestrel said, scorn lacing its voice at the boy's humility. *I must know the truth before I make this journey.*

*All that I have said is true,* Fynch replied evenly.

*But there is a secret,* the bird encouraged. Its inquisitiveness was infectious and Knave realized he too was holding his breath. Fynch said nothing. The silence hung between the three of them, heavy with the knowledge that one of them was reluctant to share.

*You must tell me,* the kestrel urged. *I am like you, Fynch. I need facts . . . and I need the truth.*

The boy hesitated, and then, *I am Fynch,* he replied, his voice filled with a power Knave had never heard before. *And I am the King of the Creatures.*

At the last word, he passed out, crumpling to the ground. The kestrel lifted from the boy's arm just in time to avoid falling with him and launched itself into the air and away from the mountains. Knave was too stunned by Fynch's words to move. He gazed after the bird until it was no more than a tiny speck on the horizon. Then, as it disappeared from his far-reaching sight, he roused himself from his disquiet and lay down, curling around Fynch to keep his friend warm until he regained consciousness.

## 18

AILECH WAS FLANKED BY ONLY TWO OF HIS OWN MEN AS HE slowed his horse at the gates of the Tenterdyn Estate of Felrawthy. On one side of his rode his loyal warrior Myrt, and on the other a man he now called friend: Aremys Farrow.

Despite certain misgivings, the King had decided to trust Farrow. Cailech considered himself an able judge of character and his instincts about people had rarely let him down. Lothryn had been his only error—but it had taken almost forty years of friendship to discover his mistake. His mouth twisted at the thought of Lothryn's betrayal.

"Sire?" Aremys said, noting the expression on Cailech's face.

"I'm all right," the King replied. "Just wishing Lothryn were here." He expected Myrt to agree and was surprised by the grim silence at his right. He did not miss the sly glance his warrior gave the Grenadyne. What did that look mean?

"You don't need him for this, my lord," Aremys assured him. "Only you can achieve what we're setting out to do today."

"He had a way of making me feel calm."

His companions remained silent. What was there to say? Aremys believed Cailech had no right to feel sorry for himself after what had been perpetrated on Lothryn, but he was hardly in a position to comment.

Myrt saw the Morgravian guard approaching. "Are you ready, sire?" he asked.

"As I'll ever be," Cailech replied, glancing toward his new friend, who nodded encouragement.

"Lothryn would be proud of you for this," Aremys said.

"He would, wouldn't he, Farrow. This is something he would applaud."

"Then you honor him by it."

Cailech smiled. There was gratitude in his expression and something unreadable in his eyes—sorrow perhaps? Aremys hoped so.

The guard arrived and the mercenary addressed him. "I am Aremys Farrow. You're expecting our party, I gather?"

The guard nodded. "We are. Wait here, please." He whistled to the gatehouse and gave a hand signal.

"You might care to bow in the presence of a king," Aremys suggested while they waited for the gates to open.

He was relieved to see the man looked abashed, had worried for a moment that due respect was not going to be accorded to Cailech.

"Forgive me, sire," the man stammered, and bowed low. Cailech and his companions exchanged satisfied glances.

An officer met them. "Welcome, your highness," he said with appropriate respect. Then he looked toward Aremys and nodded. "Farrow," he acknowledged.

Aremys gave his reins to the men who had arrived to take care of the horses. "Captain Bukanan, sir. Good to see you again. This is Myrt, Second Warrior of the Mountain People."

Celimus was watching as the King of the Mountains arrived at the gate, exchanged a look with Farrow, and then jumped gracefully from his magnificent stallion. The Morgravian sovereign was surprised. For some reason he had imagined that the Razor King would be dark, stocky, and bearded, with hooded eyes and a secretive countenance. He had not expected this golden-haired warrior, tall, clean-shaven, and artless of dress. The man wore no jewelry to proclaim his royal status, and his clothes were simple and yet frustratingly elegant. Celimus would have liked to own the cloak that hung so magnificently across the broad shoulders and seemed to shimmer in the daylight. And yet for all the understatement in his presentation, the Mountain King oozed confidence. Celimus suddenly felt like a strutting peacock in his bright courtly clothes. He pulled angrily at the circlet around his head.

"I don't think I need this," he muttered to Jessom, who, as ever, was nearby.

"I'll take it, sire," the man replied, nothing in his tone to suggest that he was inwardly smirking at the insecurity one glimpse of the Mountain King had provoked in his king. "It is time," he added.

Celimus remained silent, distracted by his thoughts. He turned from the window and strode past the Chancellor toward the main steps of Tenterdyn, where he had intended to arrange himself so the Mountain King might come cringing toward him. But there was absolutely nothing in Cailech's demeanor to suggest he would comply with that idea. In fact, if anything, he seemed utterly assured. It was the opposite of what the Morgravian had expected, and baffling.

Celimus forced away his puzzlement, replacing it with a beautifully contrived bright expression, as he emerged to meet his fellow sovereign.

*So far so good,* Aremys thought as he looked toward the movement at the front of the large house, which not so long ago had been filled with the Donal family. He felt a sudden flurry of fear as he saw the King, flanked by his chancellor and various other military people, emerge from the huge main doors.

"Your majesty, King Celimus is here to greet you. May I accompany you?" Captain Bukanan offered.

Aremys thanked Shar that Celimus was playing this out according to strict protocol. It was a heartening sign that the King of Morgravia was treating his sworn enemy with courtesy and equality, although Jessom no doubt had been a guiding hand.

"Thank you, Captain," Cailech said. He threw a final glance toward Aremys, who noted the glint in the King's eye and read it as a combination of pleasure and mischief. He truly admired this man who walked so boldly into his enemy's camp, unarmed and with nothing to offer but promises.

Aremys closed the gap between himself and Myrt to fall into step behind the King. He admired the superb cloak that the King had donned for this most formal of occasions. It was a pewter color, made from the softest of wool, spun repeatedly until it shone, from the coats of the shaggy polders—a rare cross between goat and sheep, found only in the mountains. Cailech's people took good care of the two large flocks they had gathered. The animals' long hair was impervious to moisture and felt like silk to the touch. The women of the Razors had done their king proud with this beautiful garment, which kept the natural silvery gray of the polder as its background while yarn dyed crimson and black had been woven into an eye-catching, intricate pattern along its entire length. Aremys marveled at how the clever design made the already tall man look even larger. Cailech was certainly a match for Celimus in height and looks, although the Razor King was older and more rugged than the vain southern monarch.

Myrt nudged Aremys out of his thoughts and they stepped forward for the party from the mountains to be introduced to King Celimus.

The dance of Kings had begun.

"King Cailech, welcome to Tenterdyn, our summer retreat," Celimus said, his tone full of largesse. He noted a twisted expression flicker across Farrow's face and wondered what it meant.

"King Celimus, it is a true honor to meet you." To the Morgravian's astonishment—and indeed to all who were privy to this historic meeting—Cailech bowed his head and shoulders toward his southern foe. "Thank you for this parley."

For once in his life Celimus was at a loss for words. He had not anticipated such graciousness from his northern foe. He was irritated further by the man's surprisingly deep voice, which made him feel like a boy greeting his father. His stomach clenched.

Everyone waited for Celimus's response. Finally it came. "I am intrigued, King Cailech," he said, reaching for the right words, "by this opportunity for Morgravia. Come, we are here to talk." He gestured for Cailech to enter the Donal estate.

Captain Bukanan, already briefed on the format for the day, returned to where Myrt stood. "I believe I must accompany you; is that correct?"

Myrt nodded. "We will return on horseback to a spot of my king's choosing and await word of his safe return. There are others coming with us, of course." He stopped himself from using the word "hostages."

It made little difference. Bukanan knew he was a hostage. The Captain nodded his understanding and took his leave from his king, as did Myrt from Cailech.

Inside, the party was led by their regal host to a huge chamber Aremys had not seen on his previous visit to Tenterdyn. At each end of the large space was a glorious stone fireplace and a long table stood in its center. Tapestries softened the walls, as did huge windows with bench seats and elegant shutters, each one crafted with the Donal sigil. Aremys realized that the room's simplicity deliberately allowed the dazzling scenery of the distant Razors to do all the work of impressing visitors with the beauty of the chamber.

"I thought you would be most comfortable seeing your home from here," Celimus said, his charm more evident now that he had taken a minute to gather his thoughts.

Cailech smiled in return. "Having never witnessed its beauty from this vantage point, I thank you for such a treat."

The response pleased Celimus. He indicated the thin man at his side. "I took the liberty, King Cailech, of retaining only my chancellor, Maris Jessom . . ."

"Your majesty," Jessom said on cue, bowing his head to the Mountain King.

" . . . to match your Aremys Farrow. I believed we would be most comfortable with the fewest ears."

"I am grateful for the consideration, your highness."

"Please, be seated," Celimus continued. "Let us offer you some southern refreshment."

Jessom nodded toward a waiting servant, who brought drinks and wafers to the large table. Celimus gestured for Cailech to be seated at his right so the Mountain King could see the Razors through the magnificent picture windows. Aremys was offered a seat at his left.

"I will bear witness alongside the Chancellor," Aremys said, as deferentially as he could manage, and moved to stand beside Jessom.

"As you wish, Grenadyne," Celimus said, unfazed.

"Smart move, Farrow," the Chancellor murmured under his breath. "You would fare well in court."

"I don't belong here, Jessom, and you know it," Aremys shot back, relieved to be out of Celimus's gaze.

"Shall we dispense with our regal titles, Cailech?" Celimus said brightly, raising his goblet.

"I thought you'd never suggest it," the Mountain King replied, grinning and raising his own cup.

"To us, then," Celimus said with a flourish, tapping his goblet against his guest's and noticing the glint of humor in Cailech's light green eyes.

"To Morgravia and the land of the Razors!" Cailech responded, and both men drained their goblets.

"Again!" Celimus called to the servant. His cheeks were suddenly flushed with the gravity of this historic moment.

"Would your father be proud of this parley?" Cailech asked as their goblets were refilled.

The Morgravian was unprepared for such a disconcerting question. "My father?" he repeated, angry at himself for doing so.

Cailech nodded and again Celimus saw amusement sparkling in the man's eyes, although his facial expression gave nothing away.

"Er . . . I'm sure he would."

"I think he would be shocked," Cailech said.

"Why do you say that?"

"I believe he did not see such a vision of peace as you have, Celimus."

Aremys silently congratulated the King of the Mountains. With a neat twist of words, he had given Celimus credit for bringing together two enemy nations.

Celimus searched for a hint of guile behind the words but saw nothing except openness on Cailech's rugged face.

Again he was not ready for the man; such praise from the enemy was something to be savored. "I would like to think that I can bring together our realms, Cailech," he began, warming to the vision of himself as peacemaker, "as well as Briavel."

"Indeed. In the space of a just few days, you could achieve such an amazing feat that your jongleurs will recite great tales about it, bards will sing stirring songs of homage, and I have no doubt your artists will record the events so that future generations will understand this momentous time in Morgravia's history."

Aremys felt Jessom shoot a warning glance his way. Cailech's praise was honeyed, but it was in danger of sounding insincere. So far, however, Celimus was lapping it up, Aremys noticed, certain that the Morgravian King would personally commission the songs, plays, and artworks should they not arise unprompted. Wyl had told him that the man was vain, but Aremys also recalled Wyl's warning that Celimus was clever, that behind his charm and looks was a stunningly sharp mind. Yes, Aremys thought, Cailech would have to be a bit wary.

The servant had been dismissed now. It was just the four of them.

"And tell me how you fit into all of this, Cailech," Celimus said, leaning back in his chair.

"Quite simply, I wish us to stop being enemies. I see no reason for it other than our own stubbornness and I am offering you the hand of friendship and alliance from hereon if you wish to take it. My people will respect your boundaries utterly. There will be no further threat of raids, no incursion into your lands without your permission."

Celimus nodded. "And what will your people gain from that?"

"Freedom of movement without harassment or threat of injury. We wish to have permission to trade freely with the people of Morgravia and Briavel. I would also suggest you sanction a delegation of your people to visit the Razor Kingdom in order to gain a greater understanding of our people, our culture, and our living standards. Perhaps you will allow a similar delegation from the Razors into Morgravia? I firmly believe that the more we can appreciate each other's culture, the more peacefully we all will live."

"Interesting. I am not averse to anything you have suggested, Cailech. There would have to be a governing body made up of delegates from both realms to supervise the . . ." —Celimus searched for the right word—"the melding of our kingdoms."

"Of course. My thoughts entirely. But I don't believe we could ever live as one, King Celimus," Cailech cautioned, addressing his counterpart with highest courtesy. "Our ways are too different from yours. By the same token, there are many areas in which we are similar. I want the same things for my people as you want for yours. I want our young to be educated and literate; I want free trade so commerce can flourish between our realms; I want my people to eat and sleep well, secure in the knowledge that their own are safe no matter which borders they are moving across."

Aremys could have applauded Cailech for building his case so eloquently. He doubted Celimus could find fault with anything Cailech was presenting and it seemed the Morgravian King was paying genuine attention and not just lip service. Aremys listened as Cailech continued.

"Nevertheless, my people don't want to be Morgravian and I know you have no intention of taking your people into the Razors. Let us agree that we are different—but will tolerate each other's differences. We will learn to admire these subtleties that make us the people of the Razors and your people the sophisticated Morgravians."

"Bravo," Jessom whispered to Aremys under the guise of softly clearing his throat.

Before Celimus could respond there was a knock at the door. The King looked toward his chancellor, irritated. "See to it, Jessom," he said unnecessarily, for Jessom was already making for the door.

The other three remained silent as the Chancellor listened to the hurriedly spoken message. He turned. "My king, apologies for the interruption. There is an urgent missive from Queen Valentyna. Apparently you have insisted that anything arriving from Briavel be delivered to you immediately."

Celimus nodded. "Forgive me," he said to Cailech.

"Never keep a woman waiting, Celimus—least of all a bride, and a queen at that," Cailech responded with mischief.

Celimus laughed. "Bring the messenger in," he ordered.

The man was permitted to enter. He bowed and moved toward Celimus. "Your highness, this was sent in haste."

Celimus waved his hand at him, saying nothing, having already broken the wax seal. He scanned the letter. Jessom shooed the messenger out of the door. He, along with everyone else in the room, was holding his breath. Aremys had not realized how much tension had been created by Cailech's proposition; it was only now that he saw that he had been hanging on Cailech's every word, waiting for Celimus to agree once and for all to a formal union. This messenger could not have come at a worse time.

"Nothing wrong?" Cailech queried, his voice casual, although he glanced toward Aremys for guidance. Aremys shook his head, glad that no one noticed the exchange.

"Farrow," Celimus said, taking Aremys by such surprise he almost jumped.

"Yes, sire?"

"The delivery of Ylena Thirsk . . ."

Suddenly the King's tone sounded cunning and his body language was sly. Aremys felt the first stirrings of alarm.

"Yes?"

"It is in hand, as agreed?"

"It is, sire," Aremys lied, resisting the urge to tug at his collar, which suddenly felt a tad tight.

"Interesting," Celimus said, standing. "Listen to this," and he read Valentyna's letter aloud.

When he finished, Aremys was convinced he could hear his heart pounding, the silence in the room was so profound. He made himself look directly at the King. "That's right, sire," he confirmed. "I sent a message to the Queen to release Ylena."

Celimus frowned. "*You* did!"

Aremys nodded.

"You know Queen Valentyna personally?"

"Not personally, sire."

"Well, how exactly do you know her, then?"

"I'm sorry, sire, I can't divulge my sources. You understand that, I'm sure."

Jessom could see that his king's ire was stoking frighteningly fast, but there could be no scene right now with Cailech quietly watching this event unfold. Jessom felt abashed that he too had been caught out by this missive. He had presumed Ylena had been brought to Tenterdyn via whatever means the mercenary had at his disposal. The fact that Queen Valentyna had become involved was something of a shock.

"Your majesty," Jessom interrupted as gently as he could, "Ylena Thirsk is already here."

"Here?" Celimus repeated, a storm gathering in the olive eyes.

"Yes, your majesty, she arrived just minutes before your guests. Circumstances prevented me from bringing her before you."

The King gave his chancellor such a murderous look that even Aremys, who could not have cared less about the conniving servant, felt his blood run cold. But Aremys also realized that the King had been diverted: His wrath was directed at Jessom now, rather than himself, and he pressed that advantage.

"As we know, sire, Ylena went to Briavel. I have contacts there, and before I was attacked in Timpkenny, I sent word to follow her and keep her under observation."

"Why, by the hairs of Shar's arse, would you do that, Farrow, when I wanted her in Morgravia? Why not have her captured, man?"

Cailech laughed openly at the curse. "I shall have to remember that one, Celimus."

The King of Morgravia caught his famous temper, the laughter reminding him that he was being watched carefully by another sovereign.

Aremys, smoothing an innocent expression across his face, began to embellish the lie, his mind already racing toward how he might get to Wyl before anyone else to ensure that their stories coincided. If Wyl told a different tale, they were both as good as dead. "I figured that the noblewoman would be dangerous wherever I held her in Morgravia, your highness. And as I didn't have her in my own hands, I thought it best just to have her watched. I knew I could get to her whenever I needed to so long as I knew where she was based. I also felt she was a captive of her own fears, sire. If she felt safe in Briavel, she would not leave the realm and I would not have to give further chase."

"But when did you plan to carry out your mission for me?" Celimus asked, following the Grenadyne's line of thought.

*Good question,* Aremys acknowledged silently. Again Wyl's warning about Celimus's sharp mind nudged him. "Immediately, sire. I was in the north, and Ylena Thirsk was presumably well south by then, which meant I didn't have to hurry and run unnecessary risks of being discovered. I knew my people would pick up her trail and keep watch until I was ready to make my move. I didn't expect to be carried into the Razors, sire. That was a surprise." He glanced at Cailech, whose mouth was, as he had expected, twisted into a wry grin. "And a good thing too that I had people on task in Briavel."

"So then what?" Celimus persisted. The mercenary began to wonder if the King was simply toying with him before calling for the death squad.

"My people are tactically placed, sire. It was simply a matter of getting word to them from the Razors."

Celimus switched his attention to his royal guest. "You were aware of this word being sent, presumably, Cailech? If Aremys is your prisoner, as he tells me, surely you didn't give him such freedom as to pass messages out of your realm to enemy states?" It was phrased as a question, but no one could miss the challenge in the Morgravian's words.

To his credit, Cailech did not so much as hesitate. Aremys had told him about his plan to use Ylena Thirsk as bait; he would have to trust his new friend. "I permitted him a message, yes. It was to Briavel, to a dignitary in the Queen's court. You must remember, Celimus, that you and I were enemies until just moments ago. I would have done anything to undermine you. Allowing this man to send a message into Briavel did not disturb me. Had I known at the time that he was working on your behalf, I might not have been so generous."

Satisfied, Celimus returned a steely gaze to Aremys.

"Anyway, Celimus, has this not achieved the outcome you wished for?" Cailech's question surprised everyone.

"Pardon me?" the King of Morgravia managed.

The Mountain King waved a hand in mock disgust. "It's just that we seem to be wasting time over petty details. You wanted this woman, you have her. Aremys has delivered as he said he would. Why is there a case to argue?"

There was no accounting for the moods of Celimus or the shifts in his thinking. His whole body seemed to relax as he considered Cailech's question, and Aremys could not help but compare the two kings' capriciousness. They made a good match.

"Why indeed, my friend?" Celimus echoed. "You are right," he added, nodding slightly at his guest and then returning his attention to the mercenary. "Thank you, Aremys, for delivering Ylena into my hands. To be honest, I hadn't thought you would trust me sufficiently to hand over the bait you dangled in front of my nose *before* you and your new employer left my realm for the safety of the Razors. After all, it was to be your insurance." His last few words were not lost on anyone in that chamber.

Aremys took the moment to bow, covering his relief. Straightening, he said, "Your majesty, as I have explained before, I am a mercenary and always for hire. You have shown me nothing but generosity and I would have been foolhardy not to trust such a powerful monarch." He nodded at the King. "I would like to be able to work for you often, sire. Ylena Thirsk is nothing to me. My communication to your queen simply suggested that the person to whom she offered sanctuary was your open enemy, and that she would be wise not to risk her new king's wrath by sheltering her."

"And it worked, by Shar!" Celimus said. "You are a cunning man, Aremys Farrow."

*As are you, you snake,* Aremys thought; instead he said: "I am simply a man for hire, my lord. I take opportunities where and when they present themselves. Do you still wish me to kill her, sire?"

"I think I can manage that myself if and when needed," Celimus said, a cruel smile flitting over his mouth. Cailech frowned but held his tongue. "So where is she?" the King continued, looking at Jessom.

"In one of the outhouses, sire. I said you would summon her at your pleasure."

"And how is she?"

"Surprisingly feisty," Jessom commented.

"The Thirsk girl has found some spine, has she? I shall enjoy seeing this. So will you, Cailech. Do you know of the Thirsks?"

"Only by reputation," the Mountain King said. "This is the daughter of General Fergys Thirsk, I presume?"

"Mmm, yes, the sister of Wyl Thirsk—finally back in my care." Celimus laughed. "Have her presented to me during this afternoon's feast, Jessom. I should like Cailech to see how we deal with treachery in Morgravia."

Aremys felt his blood run cold. He needed to warn Wyl. The thought that his friend would probably die again in a few hours disturbed the Grenadyne so much that he could not breathe. He loosened his collar.

"May I see her?" he said, shocked that he had spoken without thinking it through.

"Why?" Celimus looked at him sideways.

Aremys thought quickly. "She knew I was following her, sire. I just want to remind her that I always catch my prey."

Celimus clapped. "You have a nasty streak, Grenadyne. By all means. Jessom will go with you. Get her ready for us," he said to his chancellor.

He turned to Cailech. "Let us get some air. How about a ride—just us? That horse of yours looks splendid. I should like to try him out for myself."

The Mountain King smiled. "Delighted. Am I to assume that we are done here? Formalities concluded?"

"Well, my friend," Celimus replied, Cailech noting this

was the second time the southern King had addressed him in this way. "I am about to be married to the most beautiful woman of our age. Aremys here has just kept his word and delivered to me the last of the Thirsks, whom I shall see die before my eyes shortly. I can't think of anything I feel like dealing with less right now than the threat of war between our realms—which is what I presume is the alternative to an alliance?"

Cailech watched his counterpart carefully as he spoke. This man had no intention of honoring a union. What he wanted was sovereignty over Briavel and the Razor Kingdom. The marriage achieved the first, and the pretense of friendship would achieve the second. The green gazes of two powerful men met and each understood the other very clearly.

"It would mean war, yes," Cailech finally answered, realizing what a sham this whole event had been. His thought that he could charm this man or appeal to his good sense amused him suddenly. He had been carried away by the vision of the Grenadyne, but both of them had misunderstood the main point: Celimus did not want friendship or even harmony. All the King of Morgravia wanted was absolute authority over his neighbors. Neither Cailech nor Aremys had factored in the southerner's avarice or his self-delusion of might. They had entered into the parley like excited boys, stupidly believing that Celimus would also be seeking peace, trade, community. How innocent and how ignorant they had been. And now he was trapped. Would Celimus allow them to leave here alive? He might not care for the lives of those he held prisoner, and Aremys had delivered Ylena Thirsk early. Why? What had he to gain from that?

"That must be avoided, then," Celimus commented. Cailech had to remember what he was referring to. *Ah yes, war.* It was time to unleash his final trick then, all that stood between him and certain death at the end of this man's sword—or more likely, that of one of the King's henchmen. It was unlikely Celimus would dirty his hands with Mountain blood.

"King Celimus," Cailech said, standing now to look at his

enemy eye to eye. "My emissary here, Aremys Farrow, may be far too trusting, but I am not. Until now I could not be sure you would see things in a similar way to me. I had to take the precaution that your desires might differ from mine."

Aremys felt the temperature in the hall drop. The gently crackling fires at either end of the room had no effect on the cold that descended. He had to admire Celimus when the southern King barely twitched at the couched threat that now lay between the two monarchs. What had Cailech kept up his sleeve?

Celimus asked the question that burned at Aremys's and Jessom's lips. "Ah, further insurance, I gather. Tell me, King Cailech, so that I understand clearly, why is it that, although you don't trust me, neither do you fear me, even though you are on my land, in my house, under my guards' watchful eyes?"

"Please don't take it personally, Celimus. It's simply the caution of a king who knows how easy it is to give trust too quickly."

Celimus nodded indulgently as if to say he truly understood.

"There are two thousand Razor warriors currently gathered in the foothills," Cailech said.

"Two thousand!" The number clearly took the Morgravian's breath away.

Cailech grinned good-naturedly. "And another two thousand camped a little bit higher."

Aremys closed his eyes. He had definitely underestimated Cailech—as had Celimus.

"And what are their instructions?"

"To hit Tenterdyn with full might if my second, Myrt, does not give the all clear by nightfall."

"Nightfall? You hadn't factored in much time for the feast, my friend."

"I wasn't sure I'd make it to dinnertime."

"Bravo, Cailech. You are a man after my own heart. You will make your rendezvous with your men."

"Alive?"

"Alive," and Celimus laughed, genuinely now.

Aremys felt his stomach unclench. He took what felt like his first breath in minutes.

"I hope you and Farrow will at least agree to dine with me," the King went on.

Cailech nodded, green eyes ablaze with triumph. "And our union?"

"Begins today," Celimus lied. "My men will be instructed that people of the Razors are no longer targets. I will put together a delegation, to be led by Jessom here, and I suggest you do the same. They can hammer out the details of how we shall run this union. Let us clasp hands, before our two witnesses, to signify the formal alliance of our two realms."

The King of Morgravia held out his hand and King Cailech of the Razors gripped it firmly. "To peace," he said, although he did not believe it could happen as long as this King sat upon the southern throne.

"To peace," Celimus echoed, privately laughing.

# 19

Wyl heard the approaching footsteps but had anticipated soldiers arriving, not the two men who entered the hut.

"Look, Ylena," Jessom said, a note of triumph in his voice, "I've brought you a visitor."

Aremys spoke before Wyl could answer; it was his only chance for a warning. "I thought it would be polite of me to introduce myself, Lady Ylena, as I was the one pursuing you on behalf of King Celimus. It was I who encouraged your protector to hand you back to Morgravia."

He watched the surprise leave Ylena's face. There was a

momentary hesitation before she replied, but so slight he was sure he alone had been sensitive to it.

"Congratulations, sir," Wyl said. "Do come closer and allow me to spit on you and the trade you ply."

*Bravo, Wyl*, Aremys thought. *Thank you for saving my life. Now how am I going to save yours?*

"You high-and-mighty Legion wives and daughters are all the same—don't think your men are any different. I've heard what happened at Rittylworth—"

Aremys was interrupted by the arrival of a Legionnaire at the doorway.

"Chancellor Jessom, the King wishes to speak to you before he leaves on his ride."

"I'll be just a minute, Farrow," Jessom said. "Try not to make the wildcat too angry—her claws are sharp." He smiled thinly as he left the hut.

"What are you doing here?" Wyl whispered.

"Listen to me, Wyl!" Aremys urged in an equally terrified whisper. "They are going to kill you."

"And that's supposed to frighten me?"

The big man frowned. It had not occurred to him that Wyl might welcome the next stage of the Quickening. "I . . . I suppose not."

"That's why I'm here—I want him to kill me."

Aremys shook his head. "This is all too much for me," he groaned. He stole a look over his shoulder to the courtyard, where Jessom was conversing with his sovereign. "Look, I used you as a bargaining tool. I told Celimus I could deliver you to him—it was my insurance to get Cailech and myself out of here alive."

"I gathered as much," Wyl said, just a touch of sarcasm in his tone.

"I had no idea you would deliver yourself. It was just a ruse—to buy us time."

"Well, I'm here now. What intrigues me is how you and Cailech come to be here together."

"It was the Thicket. It separated us."

Understanding dawned on Ylena's face. "Ah. I suspected as much. Any plan in mind for yourself?"

"None," Aremys said, and looked at Ylena's lovely face with despair.

She nodded. "When do you leave?"

"Tonight," Aremys replied, then heard Jessom's footsteps approaching. He gestured to Wyl, who quickly switched Ylena's expression to one of rage.

"Get out!" he screamed.

Jessom entered to hear her shriek. "Oh dear, I did warn you, Farrow."

"Don't worry, I'm going. What are you going to do to her?"

The Chancellor looked thoughtful for a moment. "Well, the King wants her dead, as you know." It was a callous comment designed to frighten Ylena.

"Good, I can't wait," Wyl said.

Jessom was unable to hide his astonishment at Ylena's reckless statement. "I was going to say that I was hoping to persuade him otherwise, but the young lady seems determined to die." He shook his head. "I imagine King Celimus will make an example of her."

"That's risky, isn't it?" Aremys queried.

The Chancellor sighed. "He will want to impress his regal companion."

"He won't—not in that manner," Aremys said, desperate to prevent Wyl's death, no matter how much his friend wanted it.

"We shall see. Come, Farrow, I trust you have gloated sufficiently. Farewell, Ylena. Prepare yourself to meet your king."

"He is no King of mine, Jessom!" Wyl called out after the two men. A memory of kneeling before King Magnus filled his mind, and he recalled how he had pledged his life for Celimus. "And gladly will I give it," he muttered now. He hoped Shar would hear and let Magnus know.

Cailech allowed Celimus to ride the exquisite white stallion that had been bred in the Razors. The Morgravian King's silence as they guided their horses toward the back of Tenterdyn where the lush plains stretched toward the mountains, attested to his enjoyment of the beautiful beast.

"He's extraordinary," Celimus finally said when they halted beneath a small stand of trees.

"He is yours."

"I could not—"

"No, really. Let me gift him to you to seal our historic union. It is appropriate. I reared this one from a newborn foal. He has a twin brother, identical. His mother is one of my most treasured broodmares and his sire is a tough old rogue with perfect bloodlines. He suits you as much as he does me. Now we shall both have white stallions of the same family. Fitting, don't you think?"

Celimus gave Cailech one of his dazzling smiles. This gift pleased him more than anything the Mountain King had brought with him; it meant more than the alliance itself. "Thank you. I will think of you whenever I ride him."

"His name is Wildfire, like the falling-star trails we see on a clear night in the Razors."

"And what can I give you in return?"

Cailech shrugged. "Oh, I'll think of something," he said. Both men laughed.

"Whatever you want, it is yours."

"Be careful. That promise sounds wide reaching. I might choose your bride-to-be."

Celimus gave a wolfish grin. "Whatever you want that is here in Felrawthy, then."

"I know I mentioned this before, but I feel compelled to repeat it: Our fathers would be proud of this alliance," Cailech said, his voice suddenly wistful.

"Not mine. I never made him proud."

"What you have done today, and what you have achieved between Morgravia and Briavel, should make him sit up in his tomb and applaud."

Celimus liked the notion. He laughed, respecting his companion despite himself, despite his plans to betray him. He and Cailech were similar. Not in looks of course but in . . . what was it? He reached for that intangible something he had recognized in Cailech. Texture, that was it. They had a similar texture. Both Kings, both ambitious. Celimus believed the Mountain King was as ruthless as he himself was. The likeness pleased him. Cailech's personality, though less flamboyant, was just as large and domineering as Celimus's own. His father had seen these facets of his son's nature as flaws, and yet here they were reflected in a man his father had considered powerful, talented, intrepid. Celimus shook his head.

"My father hated me, Cailech. We hated each other, in truth. He killed my mother—I'm sure of it—and were I not his only heir, no doubt he would have seen me dead too."

"You will carve your own way for your own realm, my friend. Forget him. He is dust. Not forgotten, I grant you—you will always feel his shadow falling over you—but remember, that is all it is. A shade, no substance. He cannot hurt you now, or command you. You rule Morgravia and you have vision. Your people are fortunate."

Celimus's chest swelled with pride to hear his fellow sovereign speak of him with such respect, but it deflated as he pondered the last few words. "No, they don't see it that way. They fear me."

Cailech reached down to stroke the neck of the borrowed horse he was riding. "Is that such a bad thing?"

"Your people are in awe of you. My people are just frightened of me."

"You have the power to change that, Celimus. And within weeks, not just your people, but the citizens of Briavel, and even my people, will see what you have achieved: peace throughout the whole region. What an extraordinary time this is—and you are the one who has brought it about. I am proud to be a part of it."

Celimus searched the Mountain King's face for guile, suspecting this man was simply oiling him up, but he saw nothing but the hard green gaze of a man determined to forge peace. In that moment he made a decision that went against everything that made Celimus who he was. Charged by this man's encouragement and pride, he decided to maintain the alliance. He would not betray Cailech as planned; he would keep his promise and spare lives. He would ensure that the union worked, even though it meant compromising his grand plans of imperial domination. In one of the rarest moments of his life, Celimus smiled and meant it. "Let it be so, then," he said, his voice almost catching with the emotion he felt.

Cailech saw the change and realized that he had just saved hundreds of lives and ensured a new peace for his kingdom. He felt invigorated by what had been achieved by a simple conversation on horseback. "Remind me to gift you a horse more often," he said, his eyebrow arching.

Celimus threw back his head and laughed boyishly. "I'll race you across the fields and show you how fine this stallion is."

Wildfire sprang forward and Cailech followed. But inside he felt a tinge of regret, for the Morgravian's words had reminded him of Galapek and his growing sorrow at what had been worked upon the poor beast.

G ueryn was permitted to walk without being shackled this time. Even his hands were free to swing at his side as he luxuriated in the warmth on his back from another beautiful morning.

"How are you today, Jos?"

"Just fine," came the mangled reply, but Gueryn understood.

"Only one of you today?"

The big man nodded. "We trust you," he said, offering his crooked grin.

"I won't run away if you have more important duties to attend to," Gueryn assured.

"You're my most important duty. I can't let the King down by losing you."

"All right, I do understand. But you have my word," Gueryn offered. It was crucial now to build a friendship and some trust. His chances at escape were increased if he could lull his captors into believing he would never make such an attempt. Descending the Razors was no easy prospect, and vivid memories of the arrow thumping into his body discouraged him from such an idea, but it was spring and there would never be an easier time, with the King and Myrt away.

"Morning," Maegryn called, stepping back from a horse whose hooves he was inspecting.

"And what a fine one it is," Gueryn replied.

"Did you ache from your work?"

"Yes, but it felt good."

"A treat for you today. A ride, with Jos here and another guard."

"Oh? How come?"

"Three of our stallions need some proper exercise."

Gueryn could see his own pleasure reflected in the grin from the stablemaster. "A ride." He said it as though the words were brand-new on his tongue.

"I'd come myself but one of the King's broodmares is in labor and I have to be around for the delivery. She's struggling a bit, so I can't risk not being close."

"Can we help?" Gueryn asked reflexively. He had been around horses since he was a child and had been involved in enough births to be useful.

"I appreciate it but I'm hoping the little one will be born before you lot return. And the mother's best with fewer fussing around her." Gueryn showed his understanding with a slight nod. "Jos, you'll be on Charger—he's out sunning himself over there in the paddock. He's a fiery character but let him loose. He needs a good run. Rollo will be accompanying you. He's on Dray, the older stallion."

"And me, Maegryn?" Gueryn asked.

"Well now, Morgravian, I thought I'd allow you to ride something very special. You might have to prove your worth as a horseman today because you'll be calling on all your skills."

Gueryn grinned. "Do your worst, Maegryn. I'd ride a donkey right now just for the chance to be back in a saddle again."

"This is no donkey, le Gant. This is the King's most prized horse and he's a flighty one. That's him you hear right now making all that noise."

Gueryn frowned. "He does sound agitated. What do you call him?"

"Galapek."

The joy of learning he would be on horseback, however briefly, had temporarily sapped Gueryn of his wits. It had not occurred to him that one of the mounts could be the very horse he was trying to track down.

"Galapek," he repeated, taking a moment to gather himself and ensure no recognition showed in his expression. "That's a sorrowful name indeed for a fine stallion."

"Oh? I've been told it's from the old language. How could you know old Northernish?" Maegryn asked, intrigued.

"My ancestors on my maternal side were from a place even more north than here. The old language stayed alive in our family. I learned some of it as a child."

"So what does it mean? We've all been dying to know," Jos chimed in.

Maegryn grimaced. "I think Rashlyn said that none of us know what Galapek means."

"It means 'traitor,'" Gueryn answered, surprised. So none of these men had an inkling about the stallion, not even the irony of the King's choice of name.

"Traitor?" Maegryn repeated. "What sort of a name is that for a horse?"

Gueryn shrugged. "Perhaps your king has a sense of humor."

"Stupid name, if you ask me. This is an extraordinary beast, le Gant. You Morgravians have never clapped eyes on anything so remarkable. He's the most beautiful stallion I've ever seen."

"Grenadyne?"

Maegryn's eyes seemed to sink into his skull even further, if that were possible. "He was a present. I have no idea who sired him."

Gueryn sensed the withdrawal. He had worked too hard to forge this precious friendship, however fragile it was, and didn't wish to lose it. "Well, let's see this splendid beast. You've made me feel envious already."

"Here he comes now," Maegryn replied, forthcoming again. "Admit it, le Gant. He's the finest horse you've ever seen."

Gueryn felt his breath catch in his throat. The horse was massive through the chest. He came toward them, proud and majestic in gait. He shook his head and his long mane flicked in a shiny wave of fluid movement while his black coat sparkled in the bright morning. He was beautiful, there was no denying it, but Gueryn saw the ugliness in the horse's eyes. They were wide, as if in permanent fear, and his flesh appeared to twitch incessantly.

"Ah, here's your other companion," Maegryn said. "Rollo is one of the King's most trusted men, le Gant. No tricks, eh? He's also one of our best archers and won't hesitate to sink another arrow into that shoulder of yours."

Gueryn smiled at Rollo. Rollo did not smile back, and Gueryn recalled with vivid intensity his aborted escape, the arrow ripping through skin and nerves, muscle and bone. He was in no hurry to feel that sensation again, yet knew he would risk it if the opportunity for escape presented itself. "Have no fear," he assured, lying easily.

Maegryn gave some final instructions regarding the horses and Gueryn submitted to having his hands loosely strung together.

"You can still handle the horse with ease. Just a precaution, you understand?" Rollo said.

Gueryn pulled a face to suggest it was of no consequence to him and then made use of Maegryn's offered leg up to hoist himself into the saddle. The other men followed suit, and after a nod from Rollo, the party eased itself away from the stable compound.

# 20

HEY HAD TRAVELED A SHORT DISTANCE THROUGH THE NIGHT using magic. The boy had performed the magical transportation and then slept restlessly, sometimes crying out, presumably in pain. Now awake, he squatted, pale and quiet, chewing sharvan leaves.

Knave wanted to ask Fynch what he had meant the previous day when he answered the kestrel's question so audaciously, but he did not dare. When Fynch had finally roused himself from the curious stupor he had fallen into after the bird's departure, he had been withdrawn and Knave had sensed it was no time for talk. Movement was best and so he had suggested they walk for a time and then sleep until the early hours, which they had done. When the time came, Knave had marveled at the speed with which Fynch had conjured the spell to create what could only be described as a bridge to the Thicket. When the Thicket responded, Knave felt a pulse like a thick plume of air punched into his side. The next moment he landed, breathless, alongside Fynch on a safe ledge deeper into the Razors and closer to their prey.

"All right, Knave?" Fynch had whispered.

*Yes,* he had replied, and that had been the end of the conversation. Fynch had settled immediately and slept. Once again, the dog had lain down beside his companion and kept the youngster's body warm with his own.

Now it was time to move again. *Are we waiting for something?* Knave risked.

"For Kestrel. I feel him."

*How is the pain?*

"Not unbearable," Fynch answered. "Thank you," he added, and Knave knew he meant it. Then: "Kestrel speaks," and Fynch opened his mind to share the communication with Knave. *Where are you?* he asked the bird across the leagues that divided them.

*Just outside Sharptyn. I have found her.*

*Good,* he replied calmly. *What can you see?*

*She seems to be a prisoner—she walks with shackled hands and feet. There are others, all women. Men guard them. And there's a child—a small girl belonging to one of the men, I think. The girl talks to your friend.*

*Is Elspyth injured?*

*Pretty name.* There was a pause. *Not injured, but she looks frightened.*

*What are they doing now?* Fynch pressed his temples and Knave knew the pain was back.

*I can't really tell. I would guess that they are stretching their limbs because they came out of a shed a short while ago.*

*Fynch. You must stop,* Knave urged.

Fynch nodded. *Kestrel, I am so grateful to you. Can I trouble you to remain there awhile longer?*

*No trouble.*

*Thank you. I'll talk again shortly.* Fynch closed the link.

*You cannot keep doing this,* the dog cautioned.

"We must save her." Fynch's tone was stubborn.

*How?*

"You must go to Valentyna and get her help." The dog's silence made his exasperation clear. "Please, Knave."

*We have a task to complete.*

"And I will finish it as promised. But I also promised that I would help Wyl's cause. I will not forgive myself if Elspyth perishes."

*We are helpless.*

"Not helpless. Just distant. I can fix that."

*No, Fynch.*

"Yes. If you won't go, I will."

A difficult silence lengthened between them as the huge dog regarded the trembling yet implacable boy. Knave knew the suffocating pain Elysius had suffered, even though the sorcerer had used his magic infrequently and with utmost care. Knave could not imagine the burden Fynch was bearing right now.

*You'll send me?*

"And bring you back when you've delivered her a note."

*That will still take days.*

"Not if I send you the entire distance."

*Fynch! It will kill you.*

"Trust me. I am stronger than you think."

The dog felt helpless. He had no doubt his companion would send himself back to Werryl if he did not comply. *And you will promise to continue on alone?* he asked.

Fynch covered his face, pushing his fingers against his eyes. His answer was mumbled and weak. "Yes, of course."

*Rashlyn will sense the magic,* Knave warned.

"I don't care. Elspyth could die."

*So could you.*

"I am already sacrificed."

*Oh, Fynch.*

"I'm sorry. I don't mean to sound cruel, but you must do this for me. I will prepare a note. Valentyna can send help."

*Can you write?* the dog asked, looking for a reason to prevent this madness.

"I know some letters . . . enough to convey the urgency."

Knave looked at him gravely. *There is a cave over there. You must rest for a while before you travel on.*

"I think you're right," Fynch admitted. He dug into his sack for a scrap of parchment he had had the foresight to throw in, but although he had brought a quill, he had forgotten ink in his rush. "I'll use blood," he said matter-of-factly, and, without hesitating, dragged a small knife across his palm.

He scrawled five words only, spelled incorrectly but clearly enough: Elspyth, Sharptyn south, huts, danger. He had to dip the quill frequently into the pool of blood in his palm. Knave could not watch, disgusted with this turn of events but also feeling helpless.

"For Valentyna only, you understand?"

*I understand.* Knave allowed Fynch to tie the parchment around his neck with some trailing grass vines. It was fragile but would make the journey.

"Ready?"

*Do it!* the dog instructed, unable to conceal his dissatisfaction any longer.

"I'll wait to hear," Fynch said, hugging the dog briefly. Without wasting another word, he sent Knave tumbling through a magical tunnel arcing from the Razors to Werryl.

Knave landed softly on all fours, checked that the parchment was still in place, and then took his bearings. He was in the woodlands just beyond Werryl city, where the Queen liked to ride. Sighing to himself, he set off at a lope toward the palace.

Back in the Razors, Fynch retched pitifully, but there was nothing to be expelled. He curled up, exhausted, in his cold

but dry cave and, chewing on his decreasing supply of sharvan leaves, drifted toward sleep—the only place where
respite from his aching head was to be found.

It was late afternoon of Elspyth's second day as prisoner.
The first had passed in a blur caused by the drug and the
shock of her situation. She was still too stunned to take in all
that had happened to her, but she had been able to realize
that she was among women only; there were no male prisoners. Released from the huts, she found the courage to
speak to one of her fellow prisoners.

"What are we doing here?"

"Finally found your voice, then. Don't worry, we're all
the same when we first arrive."

"What is this place?"

"We're prisoners. They trick us, trap us, and keep us
here."

"What for?"

"Who are you? You're not Briavellian, are you?"

"My name is Elspyth. I'm from Yentro, northern Morgravia."

The woman raised her eyebrows. "You're a long way from
home, Elspyth, and you'll certainly wish you'd never been
duped by Ericson. I'm Alda, from southeastern Briavel."

"He's trapped us, you say?"

Alda nodded. "For his sport."

Elspyth gaped at her companion. "Sport?" she repeated.

"Well, it's for all of them, really. He just gets paid a lot for
finding us."

"Alda," Elspyth said, her voice shaking now. "What do
you mean?"

A bird screeched in the tall trees. Both women glanced up
but neither could see the kestrel perched there.

"We fight and they bet on us. After three wins, we're sold
on. I've got one more win to go to get out of here."

Elspyth opened her mouth to speak but had no words. Finally she croaked, "Sold?"

"There's a good slave trade out of Morgravia's south.
Didn't you know?" the woman asked, clearly surprised.

"I had no idea."

"Oh yes. A very good trade. Ships from the Exotic Isles slip in and out of a tiny bay called Cheem, east of Ramon, west of Argorn. They pick up slaves regularly." She shrugged at the disbelief on the newcomer's face. "At least it's an escape from this—but you have to survive three bouts, of course."

It was too much for Elspyth to take in. "What sort of fighting is it? Bare hands?"

Now the woman laughed harshly and Elspyth heard a hint of despair in her voice. "Blades, you fool. To the death. You will be fighting for your life tonight, my girl, and for the right to be shipped off as a slave. Forget your former self—it doesn't exist anymore." Then she became wistful, the bravado shattering. "Perhaps one day I'll see my family again, track down my son, but right now I have to make it through one more fight."

Elspyth grabbed her companion's arm. "Alda, I don't know how to fight."

"None of us know, girl! It's pure animal instinct that has kept me alive. I suggest you find some of your own or your blood will be splashed across the main hut's dust tonight."

Elspyth, shocked and upset, could not help the tears that began to trickle down her cheeks.

Alda pushed Elspyth's hands from her sleeve. "Expect nothing from me, or anyone else, for that matter. No one has friends here. We don't know who we'll have to kill next to survive. Two days ago I killed someone I liked. I don't want to know you or feel sorry for you, because you might be the woman I have to kill tonight." She paused, and her tone softened slightly. "Ericson dreamed it all up apparently. Did he use the young girl to lure you?"

Elspyth nodded blindly through her tears.

"No good blaming yourself. I fell the same way, accepting a seemingly kind offer of a lift, trying to get back from Werryl to my family more quickly than I could on foot. They're experts at picking the perfect mark."

"What were you doing in Werryl?" Elspyth asked, desperate to prolong any conversation that might take her mind

off what was hurtling toward her. She heard the shriek of the
bird again but ignored it, finding herself on her knees in the
dust, clinging to Alda's skirts.

"It doesn't matter. I don't want to share anything more
with you. Don't think we're friends. I can't help you—won't
help you. You'd best prepare yourself. It's either kill or be
killed. Get that straight now."

Alda ripped herself away and hurried to the other side of
the compound. No one saw the tears she shed there over her
own cruelty. What sort of monster had these men turned her
into?

Wyl too was preparing for death, except he welcomed it.
Dying again would be his salvation and he wondered
who he would become. In truth he did not care; all he knew
was that he could not bear to be Ylena for much longer. He
knew that ultimately he would have to become Celimus, but
he clung to Fynch's quiet belief that random acts could
change the course of Myrren's Gift. He desperately wanted
to believe in anything that might spare him living as Celimus. As much as he loved the idea of marrying Valentyna,
the notion of walking in the body of the present King of
Morgravia was repulsive. Every time he saw the vision of
Celimus's face before him, he had to draw on all his strength
to force it away.

In the end, to distract himself from his downward-
spiraling thoughts, he washed Ylena's face and combed her
hair. Wyl tied it back once again, not prepared to allow the
soft waves of golden tresses to pool around her narrow
shoulders. He also refused to change out of his riding trews.
There would be no curtsying today. He did, however, dust
his garments as best he could, having decided that Ylena
should not die looking ragged and filthy. Wyl knew appearance and presentation had been high on his sister's list of
priorities and looking pretty was the least he could do for her
considering that he was contriving to bring about her
death—a second time.

He glanced at the small tarnished mirror that Jessom had
provided. Not even its rusted surface could hide the ethereal

radiance that shone from Ylena's visage. She was gaunt now, but somehow that only added to her ghostly beauty; it reminded Wyl of how their mother had looked when she was laid out following her death.

The wasting fever had shrunk his mother's willowy figure to a skeletal state, and she had died gasping for one more lungful of air, but in her death repose Helyna of Ramon remained breathtakingly lovely. Ylena would be the same, Wyl promised himself as he stared out through eyes that were so full of sorrow that they looked even larger than usual.

Wyl threw the mirror down, shattering it across the flagstones, glad that it would never reflect that sad, haunting face again.

He turned at the sound of footsteps. It was Harken, together with the older officer from earlier in the day.

"I thought you had gone," Wyl said, gathering his unraveling emotions.

"Our company was called back this afternoon to guard the arrival of the Mountain King."

"You have been summoned," the older soldier cut across them both. "The lad here seemed determined to see you again."

"And how kind of you to let him," Wyl said, bitterness lacing his tone. "It is a pity you don't feel the same loyalties to General Thirsk that I would expect from a soldier of the Legion."

"He's dead, or hadn't you noticed?" the man answered with a cruel grin. "Thirsk is no good to us now. We're stuck with the nasty royal brat and the only way any of us will survive is to follow his orders."

Wyl mustered as much contempt as he could on Ylena's face. "You sniveling coward! The Legion could overthrow him in a blink if it would only find its spine. What has happened to all of you?"

The man did not bother to reply, simply held out the manacles to be put around Ylena's wrists. Wyl obliged; there was no point in wasting energy on a man like this. He turned his attention to the dumbstruck Harken.

"I'm so sorry," the young man finally stammered. "I just had to see you again."

"And I'm happy you did. There is nothing you can do for me, but I urge you to rally your men against the Crown."

He expected the old soldier to strike him for saying something so treacherous, but the man simply laughed. "Don't be daft, lad. These are the ravings of a condemned woman. Follow orders—that's the Legion's way, isn't it? And you have yours."

"Harken, look at me!" Wyl commanded. "Do this, if nothing else. Throw your support behind Celimus's bride. When he marries Valentyna of Briavel, she will be your queen. Help her. Don't let him crush her as he has all of you. Make your men pledge their allegiance. She is your only hope against his brutality."

Harken, stunned, could only nod. His companion gave Ylena a shove. "Come on, lass. Let me follow my orders. I've got just another winter to get through and then I'll be out of the Legion and off mending fishing nets in the northwest. After that I don't care what the young bloods do. Right now we have instructions to bring you to his majesty and that's what we're going to do."

Wyl rubbed at Ylena's burdened wrists. "Let us go then," he said.

Elspyth stood with about sixteen other women in what was akin to a cattle pen, which Ericson and his cohorts had built inside the main stone building. She had been forced to strip herself of clothes and given a grubby length of linen to cover whatever she could. One end of the cloth was stained with blood and it was all Elspyth could do not to scream at the testimony of another's injury, perhaps her death.

The men had been drinking for most of the afternoon. They were well and truly intoxicated now, eager for the naked women, for fighting, for killing. The volume of noise in the building rose noticeably when the women were herded into their pen, clutching at the useless fabric that barely concealed their modesty.

The smell of liquor, combined with sweat, vomit, and the unmistakable scent of congealed blood, made some of the jumpier women gag. Others began to wail. They knew what was coming and that, in the next hour or so, they could be taking their last breath. Elspyth could cope with the stench, but her rising fear would surely undo her. She had learned that the men had not found "fresh meat" for a week or more, and one kind soul had told her she would be a definite item on tonight's menu. There were no more tears to cry and there was no one coming to save her. If she was to survive this, Shar help her, it would be because she managed to kill three of her fellow captives.

Elspyth looked around the pen and wondered who she might be partnered with tonight. She noticed all of the women were in relatively good health, no one older than around thirty-five summers. She smiled grimly. Of course they wouldn't choose anyone much older—the naked bodies would not offer the same spectacle.

"I've heard they sometimes rape the winner," a woman nearby murmured, no doubt awaiting her first bout, her eyes panic-stricken.

"They're not here just to look, you fool," her neighbor warned.

Elspyth gritted her teeth and turned away, her glance catching that of Alda on the opposite side of the pen. The other woman looked calm yet menacing, as if violence lay just behind that expressionless exterior. Madness and the threat of death whirled around them all, but Alda's attention was riveted on Elspyth alone. It was unnerving. When Elspyth saw torches being lit around the central area, and a man approaching to get the first fight under way, her emotions frayed. She would not let the men see her fear, but inwardly she screamed her pain toward Lothryn, knowing he too was helpless, but needing to say farewell.

She reached Fynch instead.

The boy woke, consumed by Elspyth's anguish. *Lothryn, I love you, I'm so sorry! Shar, help me!* Her scream came through a gossamer-thin link that threatened to tear away at any second. But this time Fynch was quick enough. *We're coming. You must hold on,* he reassured her, and then the link was ripped away, her terrified voice a memory. But her fear was contagious and it remained like a bad smell, festering around him. Fynch shivered. The pain was back in his head; he was not sure it had ever left or that he would ever be free of it again. He wanted to chew on more sharvan but resisted, knowing he was turning to the leaves too quickly. Knave had counseled him to fight the pain, not let it control him.

He focused on Knave now. *Where are you?*

*At the palace gates. I believe I've just enraged a number of Briavellians with some ferocious barking.*

Fynch smiled despite himself. *Thank you for going, Knave.*

*How are you?*

*I'm all right. I've just woken. Elspyth reached me again. She sounds in desperate trouble.*

*The note is intact. Here they come now. I hope they remember me.*

*No one could forget you.*

*We'll speak again soon. Chew some leaves—you'll need them after this.*

Fynch did not reply. He broke the bond and cast a silent prayer to Shar to guide the message into Valentyna's hands. She alone had the power to save Elspyth.

Knave barked again, for good measure, as the guard limped toward the gate. "Shar's mercy, look at the size of that thing," he muttered to his younger companion. "I'll send an arrow into its heart if it doesn't quiet down."

"Wait! That's that black dog of the boy's, isn't it?"

"Which boy?"

"You know—that Fynch lad. One of the Queen's favorites."

"Shar spare us, so it is. I must be going mad not to have recognized it."

"Do we let it in?"

"Search me. You take a message to the Captain."

"Looks like it's got a note tied around its neck," the young soldier said, nodding toward the dog as he left.

"You'd better hurry," his companion called after him.

Several minutes passed, during which Knave stalked the breadth of the gate impatiently and the older guard watched, mesmerized. Knave was convinced the man was half-asleep. He barked, just to make sure he had the fellow's attention, and the soldier nearly leapt out of his skin.

"Bastard animal," he murmured, then turned to see his superior approaching. "Captain Orlyd, sir," he said, nodding stiffly.

"Barnes," the Captain acknowledged. "Ah, the dog. Yes, I believe that's the same one. Commander Liryk says it's to be given entry."

"Right-o, sir. You're sure it's not dangerous?"

"It's a dog, Barnes. Haven't you seen it playing around these very grounds with the young lad Fynch?"

"Er, once or twice, sir."

"Then you'll know it's harmless. Move, man. Let's see what the note is about."

When the gate was raised, Knave padded in and obediently sat so that Fynch's note could be taken from his neck. Fynch had taken the precaution of scrawling a "V" on the outside, as he had seen on some of Valentyna's personal items.

"This is for the Queen," Orlyd said as he patted Knave's large head. "Good fellow. You'd better come with me." He shook his head as Knave stood to follow him. "Smart too, eh?"

Man and dog took the quickest route toward the royal apartments, where the Captain knew Liryk had been having a meeting with the Queen and the Duke from Morgravia.

Orlyd gave a message to the man acting as the Queen's secretary and wondered again at how sorely missed old Chancellor Krell was. If Krell had been at his desk, Orlyd would probably have been taken directly into the Queen's chamber. The former Chancellor had had an uncanny knack of knowing when something was important enough to warrant such attention. Orlyd was sure this was one of those occasions.

Liryk emerged with a quizzical expression. "I trust this is urgent, Captain?"

"I believe it is, sir." He held out the note.

"Shar strike me. It's Knave," Liryk said as he took the note, and at that moment Valentyna appeared at the doorway, looking for one of her servants. She squealed with delight at seeing Fynch's dog and their reunion was filled with licks and joyful sounds.

"Is that a note?" the Queen asked, still grinning from Knave's particular form of salutation.

"It appears so, your highness," Liryk replied, handing it to her.

"It will be from Fynch, of course. I've been dying to hear news of him. I presume he is nearby if Knave is with us," she said, unraveling the parchment from its leafy twine. It took only seconds for her to read it. "Shar save us!"

Liryk, who was in the process of dismissing his Captain, turned back in alarm. "Your highness?"

"It's Elspyth. She's in trouble."

"How does the boy know?"

"I have no idea. But I'm glad Crys was lingering over his farewells. He won't have gone yet, will he?"

"At the stables still, I imagine. Captain Orlyd, please prevent the Duke of Felrawthy from leaving until the Queen has spoken with him."

"Right, sir."

"I'll be straight behind you," Valentyna called after him. She looked toward Liryk. "She's in Sharptyn. You know what this is, don't you?"

He nodded, his expression grim. "It ties up with a few other disappearances we can't explain."

"I'm sure of it," she said, eyes blazing. "And now we have the location of where these scoundrels are holding the women. Come, Liryk, Knave. We'll send the guard with Crys."

The old man broke his usual sense of protocol by grabbing the Queen's arm. "I trust the Duke is not to be put in charge of my men, your highness? We have been chasing clues regarding these men for many months now."

Valentyna realized that in her excitement she had overlooked something important. She reminded herself to learn

from it. Her impulsiveness could make her careless—her father had told her this many times, even though he was usually referring to her horse riding. "No, Liryk," she said,
covering his hand with her own. "You are in charge." Her
voice was gentle. "I will send Crys because Elspyth is his
friend and she trusts him. It will give him a reason to leave
us too." Liryk nodded. "It also means I send one less man of
our own."

"Thank you, your highness."

Valentyna continued speaking, her voice serious. "Commander Liryk, I cannot do all that is ahead without you. I
hope you understand how much I rely on your counsel and
support. I don't see myself as an island."

It was an odd comment and yet a timely one for the old
soldier, long in need of assurance from his sovereign. He
found a smile. It felt like his first in a long time.

"I am obliged, your highness," he answered in a thick
voice. "I sometimes feel we old fellows are no longer much
use to you."

She frowned. "You've been part of my growing up, which
makes you all the more important to me now. I hope you understand I will never do anything that is not in the interest of
Briavel." Valentyna knew the statement referred to virtually
everything that had happened since she had taken on the
monarchy—from her relationship with Koreldy to trusting
the Morgravians and dismissing Krell.

"I don't doubt you, your highness. But you are under
more pressure than most royals face in their first year of
rule. Let us get this girl rescued before it's too late."

"I know you don't like her, Liryk," Valentyna added, determined—while they were talking so candidly—to take this
opportunity to discuss Elspyth. She wanted to exert her authority as the ultimate decision maker for the realm. She
often felt as if she were serving some sort of apprenticeship,
with Krell and Liryk guiding her, smiling benignly at
choices they considered wise and grimacing when she went
against what they thought was right. Elspyth came under the
latter category.

"It's not personal, your majesty," Liryk began. He

searched her face, as if the words he looked for were written across her forehead. She gazed back at him intently, giving nothing away. "It's just that Chancellor Krell and I felt she was a dangerous influence here."

"A dangerous influence on me, you mean?"

He sighed. "We felt she was driving you to say and do things that might put the realm at risk."

"Never, sir. Never!"

"I'm sorry, your majesty."

"You're entitled to an opinion; indeed, I'd be troubled if you didn't have one." She raised an eyebrow. "But I am also entitled to like whomever I choose without sanction from the people around me." Valentyna saw her words bite; she had meant them to. "Elspyth knows things we don't. This marriage with Celimus is not as cut-and-dried as you think. My instincts are screaming at me that it is wrong, that it is a bad decision for Briavel, and yet I can't convince anyone of it. The nobles refuse to hear any dissent, from any party, and the rest of Briavel can speak of nothing but the years of peace to come. I seem to be the only one concerned by the fact that the Legion is breathing down our necks on the border, seemingly preparing to invade. I know I have no choice in this, Commander Liryk," she said, deliberately lowering her voice to just above a whisper. "I have to marry Celimus. And yet people like Crys Donal, Elspyth, and Ylena Thirsk truly believe it is the worst decision I could make."

Liryk felt it was his turn to be forthright. "Your majesty, with all due respect, if you don't continue with your preparations for the wedding, we will go beyond the point where a marriage can save any of us. The King of Morgravia is threatening war. It is a war we cannot win, your highness, not even if we recruited every man of able body. The sheer weight of the Legion will crush us, your majesty." His voice wavered as emotion swelled through his words. "This is not King Magnus, your majesty. Celimus is not a man of compassion. He will brutally slay every Briavellian man and his son, and his son's son, if necessary, if we choose to go to war against him. What we are seeing now is only the threat. He is making sure we understand the consequences of your back-

ing out of this marriage, your highness. If you love Briavel
and you love its people—"

Valentyna stepped back, aghast that he could think otherwise. Liryk continued, ignoring her shock. "If you love Briavel and its people," he repeated, more gently this time, "you
will hurry up and marry the King of Morgravia."

He bowed, refusing to react to the telltale glisten in the
Queen's eyes. "I shall prepare to leave for Sharptyn, your highness, and I shall bring back the woman of Yentro for you. I give
you my word that I will achieve this for you or die trying."

Valentyna was unable to speak. She watched Liryk's
broad back go down the corridor and she felt hollow.

# 21

❦

**E**LSPYTH WATCHED THROUGH HER TEARS AS THE BODY OF THE
woman who had been wailing earlier gushed its
lifeblood steadily into the sawdust. The killer, an older
woman, stood bowed above, bleeding from several wounds
and no doubt in shock. The victor had struck a lucky blow at
the top of the wailing woman's thigh, which had hit a major
artery in her groin. Death had followed not long afterward.
The men did not even give the woman the grace of a peaceful death; instead they cheered hysterically while the win-
ners gleefully collected on their bets.

The women in the pen watched in silent horror as another
soul was collected by Shar's Gatherers. Most did not know
the dead woman's name. As Alda had cautioned Elspyth,
there was no point in getting to know one another; it only
made the killing harder. The corpse was dragged away by the
hair, to be burned later with the rest of the dead, their bodies
piled up from the evening's entertainment. The victor, still
frozen, her eyes glazed over, was led roughly out of the arena.

"It's her first kill," a voice said close by.

Elspyth started, unaware that Alda had sidled up beside her during the fight. "And the dead woman?"

"She was on her third fight. If she'd won tonight, she'd be on her way to the boat. Stupid fool—she could have won easily. Still, one less for me to kill."

Elspyth looked up at the taller woman. She felt sorrow that a mother had become so hardened. And yet it was because of her child that this woman plotted to win at all costs. Elspyth shuddered in disgust. "Get away from me."

The Briavellian made a sound of disgust. "I hope you're next!" she said, nodding her head toward the man approaching. "Time you found out what it's like out there."

Elspyth ignored her, her gaze fixed on the obese fellow waddling toward them with his hated parchment of names.

"Next up, ladies, is Olivya," he said in a jovial voice.

No one moved. Terrified gazes met the more resolute ones of those succumbing to a sense of fate.

"Come on, now. Small, pretty, dark. Ah, there you are, my dear. Cast off that sheet now," he said to Elspyth. "It's your turn."

Elspyth had forgotten she had given a false name. Her legs felt too weak to hold her body up, let alone carry her across the pen and into the arena. She began to weep.

"Come on, lass. Haven't got all night," the man urged, scowling now.

Alda pushed Elspyth forward viciously. "Who's she fighting?"

"Ginny. Where are you, Ginny?"

"Let me fight her instead."

"You're not down to fight tonight, Alda," the fat man replied. "We're going to make you lose some sleep over your third." He smiled without kindness, sweat running down his oily face.

"I'll make it a real spectacle," Alda said desperately.

Elspyth felt her chest constrict, trapping her breath. What was Alda thinking? She could see the bloodlust in her face, and knew the Briavellian was looking forward to an easy kill.

The idea that she was considered a pushover dragged Elspyth from her stupor. She sucked in air with a huge angry gasp and suddenly the noise, the smell, the woman's blood still wet and gleaming on the floor, and now, the fat man and Alda bargaining over her death, galvanized her. Elspyth felt the fear leave her in a tingling, angry rush. It pushed upward through her throat and exploded in a cry of fury, and something she had never felt before oozed from every fiber of her being. It was rage, bubbling through her as a white-cold flame, torching her thoughts, sparking her emotions, scorching her with its devouring wrath. The fear that had left a puddle of urine around her feet only minutes earlier fled.

Elspyth stepped away from her own mess, cast aside the flimsy linen, and addressed the man in a voice that was animalistic and predatory. "Let me fight Alda!"

The fat man looked at her. This was new. Normally the women fought one another under protest, all but helping their opponents into the ring, apologizing for having to hurt one another, then weeping over each death. But these two women were eager for the fight; with those sorts of emotions, the spectacle was sure to be especially entertaining for the men.

His thick tongue flicked out to wet his rubbery lips as he considered this option. "My, my," he said, unpleasant smells wafting toward Elspyth as he moved closer to her. "You must be confident."

"Just announce it," she answered, eager to get the fight done. If she was going to die, she'd rather do so now than spend further hours agonizing.

Alda clapped her hands with pleasure. The Morgravian had admitted she did not know how to fight. It was going to be easy.

"All right, then," the man replied. "Don't say I never give you girls what you want," he added with a lecherous chuckle. "Off with your linen, then, Alda. Both of you oil up. I'll make the announcement."

Wyl walked between the two men, his arms in front of his body and tied at the wrist. He did not feel scared. This was the death he wanted; he just wished he could somehow spare Ylena's body from being mistreated in the process. He spent the time during the frigidly silent walk toward the main hall contemplating what would be the kindest death for Ylena and decided a blade into her heart was ideal—just as Faryl had killed Koreldy. That way, when her body was cleaned, covered, and laid out in Argorn, as he fully intended it to be, no one would have to see the ugly wound that had felled her. She could remain beautiful for eternity in their minds.

But it nagged at Wyl that Celimus was unlikely to have in mind something as straightforward as a knife. He would draw this out as if it were a game; in the same way that he had taunted Wyl—forcing him to witness Alyd's death and Ylena's suffering—he would now mock Wyl's sister in front of his honored guests. Except he was in for a surprise. This Ylena walked to her death with a light heart.

"Are you all right, my lady?" Harken whispered.

"I am fine. Remember all I have told you. If you think well of the Thirsk family, be assured they would have sworn their allegiance to Valentyna the moment she became Queen of Morgravia as well as Briavel. Do the same, for all of us."

Wyl sensed Harken's fear but also his pride at being singled out. "I will do it for you, my lady."

"Then I am glad to have met you."

"Be quiet," the older soldier warned. "We're here now."

Dusk had fallen so quietly Wyl had not noticed. The north draped itself with evening's calm without the south's cacophony of noisy birds telling the world it was time to roost. There was still sufficient light, however, that Wyl had no doubt as to the identity of the man waiting at the grand doorway of Tenterdyn.

"Good evening, Ylena," Jessom said, all politeness. Wyl did not reply. "As you will," the Chancellor replied, not at all offended.

"Thank you, gentlemen," Wyl forced out of Ylena's lips. It was meant only for the young soldier and he qualified his words with a brief glance toward him. He was careful not to name Harken. Jessom was far too sharp to let the soldier leave if he thought any sort of alliance—no matter how tenuous— had been formed.

"We'll take her from here," Jessom said to Ylena's escort. Two burly guards stepped out from behind the Chancellor and took position on either side of Ylena. "Follow me."

Wyl was led past familiar rooms toward a part of Tenterdyn he had not seen on his former visit. He heard the murmur of voices and small explosions of laughter, which grew louder as they approached a wing that he recalled had been shut off by doors. They were wide open now, the corridor lit by torches and guarded by yet more soldiers. Two kings were present; it was little wonder that the level of security was so high.

"Wait here," Jessom commanded, touching Ylena's arm. Wyl shook off his hand and the man's thin smile returned. "I must let the King know his lamb has arrived."

There was no mistaking his meaning. If Ylena's mouth had not been so dry with tension, Wyl might have tried spitting again at the Chancellor, for the amusement of soiling his robes, if nothing else.

Jessom disappeared around a corner. The sounds of men eating and entertaining themselves filled the frigid silence between Wyl and his guards. The aroma of food wafted toward them and one man's belly acknowledged it with a growl. Wyl turned toward the sound and met the culprit's abashed expression.

"Do you know that I'm being brought here to be killed for sport in front of your king?"

The guard shrugged, although Wyl sensed there was embarrassment hidden behind it.

"We just follow orders, my lady." It was the man on his other side who answered.

Wyl looked at him. "And as a Legionnaire, you are comfortable with the notion of slaughtering an innocent woman—a noble no less—from a fine family that has given its life to the Legion? You are old enough to have known my father."

The man did not respond, but the pity in his eyes betrayed him.

Jessom rescued him. "Come, Ylena Thirsk. Your king awaits you."

\*      \*      \*

Elspyth stood at the fringe of the rough circle mapped out with string tied around small stakes in the earth. She was naked but no longer cared, ignoring the sounds of appreciation from men enjoying the sight of a lovely body. All that mattered right now was the person on the opposite side of the ring, also naked, also breathing hard, and no doubt hoping that her cold stare would be enough to intimidate her opponent into submission without a blow.

The fat man was stirring up the excited crowd, but Elspyth ignored him too. She knew where Ericson was sitting and briefly entertained the idea of flinging her knife, Koreldy-style, at his bulk. She had a vision of him flailing in shock as the blade hit him squarely in the throat. She sighed, knowing she could never throw true. The blade would probably make it only half the distance and then clatter pathetically on the ground, undoubtedly to wild applause, leaving her defenseless, to be slaughtered by Alda. A bell sounded and dragged her back to the insanity before her. She knew her knuckles were white as she clutched the single small blade that was her weapon.

She heard the fat man remind her that this fight was to the death, then his explanation that Alda was fighting for her third win and her right to be given over to slavery. The men cheered, no doubt imagining profit from her sale as well as her win. Elspyth forced herself to withdraw completely into her mind. She recalled the long night journey to Deakyn with Wyl—he walked as Koreldy then—and how he had told her that a warrior preparing for battle must draw every ounce of his conscious self into a closed section of his mind that no one could penetrate. She had smiled a little indulgently at his description at the time; now she understood completely what he had meant.

The bell sounded again and Alda began moving, circling. *This is it,* Elspyth thought. *Kill or be killed.*

"To you, Lothryn, my love," she murmured, remembering how he had given his own life in order to save others. She suddenly felt sure that Lothryn's feelings at that moment of decision—the knowledge of certain death, the grief of losing his

new son, the sorrow that their love had remained unspoken—
were identical to her own. It was a tearing free of all ties, a casting loose of all fears in the pursuit of one thing: kill or be killed.

Alda lunged and Elspyth's mind went blank.

Wyl stepped into a large chamber that was warmed by
fires at either end. A few men milled around, holding
goblets of wine. He recognized none of them, which meant
there was no one who might object to Ylena's mistreatment.
His boots crunched on the floor and he realized he was
walking over the remains of Aleda's fine cranberry-colored
glassware. Like the loyal family of the north, it was now
shattered, forgotten.

And then he laid eyes on the man responsible for it all.
Celimus, brimming with self-importance, sat at the head of
Jeryb's oak table, goblet in hand, making some toast, his
cheeks slightly flushed from the wine and the general jovi-
ality. To his right sat Cailech; the Mountain King looked less
comfortable and there was less debris about him, as though
he had been more cautious in his enjoyment of the repast.
Wyl knew the man well enough to recognize that the smile
fixed on his face was fake. Cailech raised his glass in answer
to whatever Celimus had said but did not drink; meanwhile
his penetrating gaze soaked up all around him as effectively
as a sponge. He was bare-armed; the muscles sculpted and
tensed, as if he was ready to leap to his feet and charge, like
an animal disturbed. No, Cailech was not happy here, but he
was pretending well enough. Next to him sat Aremys, un-
smiling and rigid, no sign of wine or food about him.

The three men noticed Ylena's arrival at the same time.
Celimus looked savagely delighted, his eyes darkening with
pleasure at what he knew was coming. Cailech, however,
looked taken aback. His roving gaze settled intently on
Ylena and the contrived smile faded. Her beauty had taken
him by surprise, Wyl realized. Poor Aremys looked like a
chained dog; one that knew it was about to take a hiding. He
paled, his already unhappy expression settling into a blank
mask, as if he was steeling himself. He could hardly make
eye contact with Wyl, such was his despair.

The room quieted as people noticed their presence, but Jessom allowed the hush to settle fully before he spoke. "Gentlemen, may I present Lady Ylena Thirsk, daughter of the late General Fergys Thirsk and sister to the much loved General Wyl Thirsk, may Shar bless their souls."

Some repeated the last few words and Wyl took bitter delight in seeing the Morgravian King's mouth tighten. The smile turned acid and Wyl knew he would pay for that loyalty to his family with blood.

"Ylena Thirsk, how enchanting to have you back among your fellow Morgravians," Celimus said, flashing a bright smile toward his honored guest. "Come, Cailech, you must meet the woman who escaped my punishment through the aid of a mercenary who goes by the name of Koreldy."

Cailech turned a cold green gaze onto his fellow king. "Koreldy?"

"You know him?"

"I will flay the skin from his bones when I find him again."

Celimus, fired by the excellent wine from Jeryb's cellars and feeling very pleased at being about to do away with the final member of the hated Thirsk dynasty, threw back his head and laughed with delight. "Then I have done you a service, my friend. Koreldy is dead."

The Mountain King did not react. His face was set in stone, his eyes unreadable.

"Well, actually," Celimus continued, noticing the lack of reaction and pleased by it, "I think we have my bride-to-be to thank for his death."

"How so?" Cailech asked tightly.

Celimus drained his goblet of wine and slammed it down. Droplets of red launched from his mouth like blood as he shook his head. It was fitting, Wyl thought, for blood would flow tonight. "Koreldy fled to the safety of Briavel, pretending to be a champion to my queen." He made a gesture of nonchalance. "She was unaware of his identity, of course, until I revealed it to her."

"Why don't you admit it was the only way you could escape

death from Koreldy's sword, you sniveling coward," Wyl shouted.

Exclamations rang out in the hall and Celimus's eyes shone with hatred. He walked toward Ylena until he towered above her. "The Thirsk bitch lies. She wasn't there; how could she know? Where were you, Ylena? At Rittylworth, wasn't it? Cringing in the cellar of a monastery before your flight to Felrawthy. It is fitting that your journey ends here. No one can save you now."

"Nor do I want them to, you son of a whore. Thank goodness your father killed your mother. The only pity is that he did not do it before she birthed you—"

He got no further with his insult. The punch to Ylena's face was expertly leveled and the room went dark for Wyl. Everyone else was frozen in shocked silence. Jessom was the first to gather his wits; he nodded toward one of the guards to pick up the woman sprawled across the flagstones, her head bleeding from where she had gashed it on the table.

Cailech glanced toward Aremys and saw his stricken expression. He didn't know what was going on here, but he didn't like it one bit. There was clearly a connection between Aremys and the woman. More than that, and perhaps more disturbingly, it seemed that Celimus was putting on this whole charade for his benefit. If Celimus thought his northern neighbor would get pleasure from watching a noblewoman humiliated and injured in this fashion, however, he had entirely misjudged. Cailech was the first to admit that he was no softhearted monarch; he had not flinched at having the Morgravian woman staked out for roasting, or killing her later to trick Gueryn. But she had been a prisoner of battle. This Thirsk woman struck him as a pawn in whatever game was being played out between Celimus and the Thirsk family, and Cailech wanted no part of it. He raised an eyebrow in silent question to Aremys, who glared back at him, as if demanding that he do something.

Celimus turned to his guests and rubbed his knuckles. "Don't worry, she has a head as hard as stone—like all the Thirsk trolls." Nervous laughter sounded in the room. "Get her ready!" he ordered Jessom, who escorted the guard holding the prone woman out a side door.

Cailech wanted to bring the evening to a rapid close. It was time to get away from here. But the sight of the golden-haired beauty and her magnificent defiance of the man everyone in Morgravia feared compelled him to learn more. He knew Celimus was watching him and so he said smoothly, "You were telling me about Koreldy," as if the interruption had been of little consequence.

Celimus continued with similar aplomb, seating himself and bidding everyone do the same. "Yes, forgive the disturbance. I revealed Koreldy's true identity to Queen Valentyna, who was mortified—as you might imagine—for the mercenary had killed her father, King Valor."

"I see. And?"

"Well, she banished him, which made it possible for one of my assassins to deal with him. I had no intention of allowing Koreldy to roam the land after he had betrayed me."

Cailech sucked in a breath. "You have proof of Koreldy's death?"

"A finger, still wearing a signet ring with a deep bloodred stone and marked with the family insignia."

"I know the ring," Cailech replied, feeling suddenly empty. He had been looking forward to dealing with Romen Koreldy himself, it was true, but he had not expected the acute sense of sorrow that pervaded him. In spite of their differences, not to mention the bad blood, he had respected the man, and felt sure Koreldy would have preferred to be felled by a Mountain warrior's sword than a Morgravian assassin's blade. "I always thought the man had lives to spare," he commented, trying to hide the bitterness in his tone.

"Well, he used them all up once he crossed me, my friend," Celimus boasted, and urged more wine to be poured.

Cailech had tired of being referred to as friend by the Morgravian King. He gave a subtle nod toward Aremys, who understood its meaning but made no move; instead he glanced again toward the door beyond which the woman had been taken. Cailech frowned. What was it between those two?

"That woman—what is to happen to her?" he asked, twirling his half-empty goblet.

"She will be executed in your honor, sir," Celimus answered.

Cailech spilled some of the wine in his surprise. "Certainly not in my honor!"

The King of Morgravia shrugged. "Well, she is to die anyway—I'd like her to be my gift to you. You're not squeamish, are you?" It was a challenge.

Cailech had had enough. He liked neither the sound of the gift nor the suggestion of his gutlessness. "Celimus, we have enjoyed your hospitality long enough. You will forgive me if I take my leave now."

"I could not forgive you if you did, my friend."

"Why is that?" Cailech asked, gritting his teeth.

"We still have time before the appointed rendezvous and I would like you to partake of the evening's entertainment."

"Which is?"

Celimus's voice was sly. "Tell Jessom we are ready," he said to a waiting servant.

It was terrifying. Elspyth had never fought in any sort of hand-to-hand combat in her life, not even as a child, enacting pretend sword fights and mock battles with other children in the pursuit of laughter and competition. Now she found herself facing a woman who seemed utterly determined to kill her. Elspyth had no tricks to draw upon, no skills that might help her protect herself.

Alda's lips was drawn back in a tight snarl. There was no doubt in Elspyth's mind that Alda saw herself as the predator and her opponent as the cornered, helpless prey. The older woman laughed, springing forward and feinting toward her right. Elspyth fell for the bluff and tried to dart in the opposite direction, but found that path cut off, a blade slashing toward her. She shrieked and twisted away, feeling the knife cut cruelly down her back.

The men roared; more bets were exchanged in Alda's favor. The cheering and jeering continued without respite as the audience insulted Elspyth, shouting that Shar's Gatherers were running toward her so fast, she might as well give up now.

Again Alda pounced, this time trying to slash her opponent's face—which was all the prettier, many men in the audience conceded, for its pleading expression. Elspyth reacted instinctively and put both her arms up, which won her a nasty gash on the arm, where bright blood bloomed instantly. The arm she held her blade in began to go numb almost immediately. She cried out in despair.

Alda was enjoying herself. Elspyth realized the woman was simply playing with her. She had promised the fat man a spectacle in exchange for being allowed to kill the opponent of her choice, and she was delivering on that promise. How many more slashes would she make before the killing blow came? Elspyth wondered through her tears as Alda leapt again, missing so slightly that Elspyth heard the whistle of the blade through the air. Alda laughed again. Elspyth's exertions were making her blood flow more freely. She could feel it was running down her back, and her front was splashed with blood from her arm wound.

The numbness made it hard to feel her hand gripping the blade. That was probably Alda's intention, she realized, impressed. Not all for show, then. Her would-be killer was making strategic wounds, designed for disabling as much as for exhibition. No wonder Alda had made it to her third fight. No doubt she would make it to the slave boat.

Elspyth felt the sadistic bite of the blade again, this time expertly delivered across one breast, and rapidly followed by the wet sensation of blood spouting forth in concert with the vicious pain. Elspyth staggered, hardly daring to look down at the ruin of her body. When she did she saw only red, running freely and draining her of strength and the will to remain standing. Opposite her swaggered Alda, free of cuts or injuries but covered in blood nonetheless . . . Elspyth's blood.

And then Alda did something she had no idea would awaken the primeval instinct in her opponent. Responding to the chanting of the male audience, now calling for an end to the ragged young woman, Alda slowly licked at the blood that spattered her mouth. The men, driven into a frenzy of lust and greed, shouted all the more fiercely for the killing blow.

But Elspyth, watching that theatrical gesture, as if Alda thought Elspyth was hers to consume, felt the searing white flame of anger once more. She straightened, threw back her greasy hair, and screamed. And her fury traveled and hit its mark, cutting through the shields of sorcery, streaming loudly into the consciousness of a man trapped in the body of a horse.

It was as if, for just a moment, he saw it all.

*Kill her, Elspyth,* he cried. *Survive!* And then he was gone, slipping away from her mind like sand through fingers.

"Lothryn!" she shrieked, but silence was all she heard. Thick, dark silence and Alda's sinister presence.

"It's time, Olivya," the woman called sweetly, like a mother to her child. Except the sweetness was tainted and false.

"Do it, then, bitch! End it!" Elspyth screamed back over the excited clamor of the audience, who knew the blade would fall only once more.

Alda was not prepared for this. She had anticipated begging and weeping, but not aggression. Then she frowned; Elspyth was crouching as if in disabling pain, placing her blade in the sawdust.

"I have no more to give," Elspyth whispered, "no more."

Her opponent became angry. "You gave nothing! You didn't even try to defend yourself, you weak fool. At least now I have my escape from here. Thank you, Olivya—your life has bought something precious." She sneered as she quickly covered the ground between them.

"Make it swift," Elspyth pleaded.

"I will," the woman said, wiping blood from her mouth, hardly able to see flesh through the red liquid covering her opponent's body. "Bare your throat!"

Elspyth turned her head slightly sideways, knowing she looked like a lamb with its neck exposed for a quick killing slash.

In her excitement, all Alda saw was the girl giving herself

willingly to death. She did not notice Elspyth's hand reaching slowly for the blade by her side. Some of the men did, and began screaming for Alda to beware, but she could not hear them in the cacophony. She had eyes now only for Olivya's creamy throat and raised her blade high into the air.

Elspyth watched the weapon reach the zenith of its arc . . . Now! She moved faster than she ever had before. It was a once-only effort and it had to be accurate. Wyl had told her that in battle, when you sense the opening in someone's defenses, you have to strike as fast as your body allows and put your full strength behind it, as a cat does when it pounces. Elspyth was that cat now. She felt her legs push up hard as she poured every ounce of her courage and love for Lothryn into one savage leap. Propelling herself upward, she thrust the blade before her and, unbelievably, saw it embed itself in the center of Alda's throat.

Elspyth felt pain as Alda's knife, intended for her neck, missed its mark and sank deep into her shoulder. It hurt, more than she cared to think about, but it would not take her life . . . unlike her blow. Alda's spluttering surprise was cut short by a horrible gurgle, and she fell to the sand.

Elspyth, trembling with shock, knelt beside Alda's slumped figure and took her hand. She did not want her to go to her god amid hate. The woman tried to speak, but her eyes were already glazing over. Did she feel regret that she had lost her chance for the slave boat or sorrow for the cold-blooded actions that had brought her this far? Elspyth would never know, but she felt the slightest squeeze of her hand as the dying woman struggled not to release her soul to the Gatherers.

A hush blanketed the audience in eerie silence. Much money had been lost this evening; the underdog had won against the odds.

Alda's blood mixed with Elspyth's, forming a pool between them. "I'm sorry," Elspyth whispered, unable to control her tears. "May Shar guide you to his peace." Alda died with a crooked smile, as if in thanks for Elspyth's blessing.

The strangled silence of disbelief was broken by the angry shouts of soldiers bursting into the building. One of them was Commander Liryk, roaring orders, but it was Crys who saw Elspyth first.

The sight of the two bloodied figures in the middle of the makeshift arena horrified him, stopping him in his tracks. One woman was obviously dying, perhaps already dead, and the other was sobbing.

"Elspyth," he called into the rabble. She did not hear him. "Elspyth!" he yelled, fury overtaking him as images of his own dead family scorched a path to the front of his mind.

She looked up, her body trembling. "Crys?" He saw her mouth move hesitantly, as if she was unsure she could believe what she was seeing.

He was at her side in a few angry strides and scooped her into his arms, the blood that covered her body wet against him. Unable to force out another word, all Crys could do was bury his face in her lank, bloodied hair and weep with her.

Kind arms finally loosened his grip on Elspyth and a blanket was thrown around her shivering body. Liryk squeezed Crys's arms. "Steady now," he said, and Crys was grateful for the reminder that he must hold his strength in front of the men. He nodded, communicating his thanks silently to the senior soldier. "She's hurt," he said, at which point Elspyth sank to her knees.

"Get her out of here," Liryk barked to one of his men.

"No, wait!" she begged. "Have you got the leaders?"

Liryk shook his head. "Are you up to helping us with that?"

"Can't you see her wounds—"

Elspyth interrupted Crys. "It's all right. Please. Ensuring their heads roll at the swipe of an ax means everything to me."

"Good girl," Liryk said, impressed, for he had seen the woman of Yentro's injuries and knew they must be extremely painful. "Point them out."

Crys helped Elspyth to her feet and wiped her face with a damp towel a nearby guard handed him. The cool water and the cleaning away of the blood revived her slightly.

"Come," Liryk encouraged. "They're rounded up outside."

"What about the women?" she asked.

"They're being taken care of," Liryk assured her, then gave a low whistle. "I'm shocked by this. We had no idea of its extent."

"You knew about it?" Elspyth could not help the accusation in her tone.

"Suspected it," Liryk corrected. "But we've been waiting for something or someone to give us a lead to follow."

Elspyth made a sound of disgust but said no more, feeling Crys's slight pressure at her shoulder, suggesting she hold her tongue. She turned to follow Liryk, but when she tried to walk unaided she fell down.

Crys picked her up gently and Elspyth felt warmed by the sad smile on his face. "Let me support you, Elspyth, if you won't permit me to carry you," he said, and circled her waist loosely with his arm so she could lean against him as she needed to.

"Thank you," she whispered. "How did you find me?"

"Later," Crys replied. "Let's get this ugly business done."

Outside, Elspyth pointed out the men who had led the betting and then took much pleasure in asking Crys to take her to where Ericson was trying to stand unnoticed in the mob.

"That's him," she said. "He calls himself Ericson. He is the leader of this rabble, the one who acquires the women for his sport." She said the last word as if it was poison in her mouth.

Ericson was dragged from the crowd and bound and shackled alongside seven other men who had been involved.

"Is this it?" the Commander asked.

"Yes. The rest are just cruel onlookers."

Liryk nodded wearily. "Right, men, hear me." He addressed his soldiers. "I want proof of the name of each man here. If he has no proof, he will be executed. Those who provide proof are to receive forty lashes each. If they survive the whipping, they can drag their sorry arses home and explain it how they will. Remember," he said, turning back to the prisoners, "we will have a record of your names and the towns you hail from. If you err again, at any time, your family will be stripped of its assets—homes, land, money, belongings. Is that clear?"

Elspyth saw the men blanch with fear on hearing about the physical ordeal ahead. Perhaps now they might understand a tiny measure of what they had put the captured women through. She had no sympathy in her heart for them, and wondered what Liryk had in store for Ericson and his band of followers. She did not have to wait long.

"The leaders will have their heads removed from their bodies," Liryk said, glaring at the cowardly Ericson, who visibly staggered at the sentence.

Silence gripped the crowd, soldiers and prisoners alike too stunned to make a sound.

"What are you waiting for?" Liryk said calmly to one of his captains.

"I'm sorry, sir. Do you mean now?"

"I do. All of these men are to watch, as a reminder that Briavel's queen does not show mercy to those who break the most sacred laws of life."

Despite her flagging strength, Elspyth had the energy to feel sorry for the Captain, who, to his credit, gave a crisp salute despite his sudden pallor. She stayed conscious long enough to bear witness to Ericson's sobs as he was forced to kneel and lay his neck across a log. She looked around for his daughter, but the girl with the singsong voice was nowhere to be seen as the ax fell and her father's head rolled from his body.

"They say the head knows it has been removed from the body for several seconds afterward," Crys commented blandly, still supporting her with his arm.

"Good," Elspyth mumbled, and, her strength gone, slumped against his shoulder.

# 22

YL WAS BROUGHT BACK INTO THE HALL OF THE ÐONALS, where an air of expectancy greeted him. He glanced at Aremys's stricken face and wished he could reassure his friend that death did not frighten him anymore. Any escape from the sheath of Ylena's body was welcome.

At Jessom's bidding, and with an awkward silence prevailing, he was taken by the two guards to a spot at one end of the chamber where his hands were tied to a timber framework, no doubt hastily erected for his benefit. His ankles, still manacled, were unnecessarily tied to the timbers as well. *This is novel,* he thought. Celimus was obviously getting more creative. He stared defiantly at the Morgravian King.

Celimus took a swig from his goblet. "The last of the great Thirsks, strung up for our pleasure, gentlemen. Call in the archers," he said, then glanced toward the stony-faced Mountain King. "Come on, Cailech, I thought you people were . . ." He paused.

"Barbaric?" Cailech offered.

Celimus smiled, sly and cunning. "Fun loving, I was going to say."

Cailech did not reply. He turned to look at the intriguing woman and was met by a hard blue gaze, fiery with hatred and anger. He felt his breath catch, as it did each time he looked at her. He admired the defiance, her complete disregard and indeed disrespect for the company she was in, and the lack of fear for what she surely knew was coming. She had the courage of the Mountain People in her soul, he thought fancifully, caught by the golden hair that had fallen loose. Ylena Thirsk looked dirty and disheveled, but she was nonetheless desirable, he admitted to himself.

He had to look away from her fierce stare. "No trial?" he asked as two archers were brought in.

"None required," Celimus said. "She pays the price for the treachery of the men of her family."

"Shar won't grant you forgiveness for this, you evil scum, Celimus. This is like the witch Myrren all over again, isn't it?" Wyl forced out a laugh as the similarity of the situation struck him. He saw that it struck home with Celimus too and took pleasure in seeing the King flinch. "She got the better of you and so will I. I won't scream, I won't give you any satisfaction, you cowardly—"

"Shut her up!" Celimus ordered a soldier.

But Wyl was going to have his say, even as the embarrassed guard moved toward him. "Your father wished many times that my brother could be King, so you got rid of both of them—and the King of Briavel, Romen Koreldy, and the Donal family. Watch out, Cailech, he'll be planning to kill you next. And no doubt his bride. He'll slaughter everyone until—"

Ylena's mouth was bound. Although he could not make himself understood, Wyl continued to rage at the man who had destroyed the lives of so many good, loyal people of Morgravia. He saw Cailech shake his head, noticed that the Razor King wore an expression of wonder.

"Where are you going, Aremys Farrow?" Celimus asked loudly over Ylena's accusations. "Be quiet, Ylena, or I'll slash your mouth so it can't move properly."

Wyl quieted. He had promised himself he would keep Ylena as unmarked as he could. There was nothing more to be achieved anyway by his unintelligible ravings. He joined everyone else in the chamber in looking toward the mercenary.

Aremys had hoped no one would notice him slipping away from the hall. He could not witness this. "Apologies, sire. I thought I should go and check on the horses so that we would be ready to move out after the . . . entertainment."

"Everything will be readied for your departure, Farrow.

I'd prefer you to stay. In fact I rather thought you'd like to see your prey be felled."

"Not in this manner, sire," Aremys risked.

Celimus did not react as Aremys thought he would. In truth, the King was enjoying everyone's discomfort. "Your king has remained, and as this is in his honor, I expect you to share in this gift," he ordered.

"Of course, sire. As you wish," Aremys said, glancing toward Ylena and privately agreeing that it was probably for the best. He would need to know which of these men Wyl would become. And then a chilling thought occurred to him. Did Myrren's Gift work only if Wyl was slain by hand—that is, if someone was physically connected to the weapon? His mind raced. Wyl had never mentioned it, but then perhaps Wyl did not know! Koreldy had been killed by Faryl, who had plunged a knife into his heart with her own hand. Faryl had been killed by Ylena, who had held the blade that slashed the assassin's throat. If Celimus was planning to loose arrows into Ylena, no one would be connected to the weapon when it landed in her body. Ylena would surely die . . . but perhaps so would Wyl.

The sense that he had stumbled across something important so terrified Aremys that he shouted into the thick, expectant silence: "Sire!"

"Yes, Farrow?" the King said, his temper rising.

Aremys looked at Ylena and then at Cailech—saw the Mountain King frown and knew he suspected something between him and the woman. "King Celimus," he began, clearing his throat nervously, "this is a messy end, sire, particularly for a celebration. Why don't I just take her out the back and kill her for you?"

"You had your chance, Farrow. Now I will show you how to finish a job."

"But, your majesty . . ." His words died away and he felt a twinge of fear as Celimus turned to stare at him, no longer indulgent toward the emissary of the Mountain King, no longer prepared to be generous.

"Don't push me Grenadyne, or you'll find yourself staked out like the Lady Ylena there."

"I would have to object to such treatment of a protected guest," Cailech warned icily, nodding at Aremys to continue.

"Let me finish what you asked me to do, King Celimus. I will cut her throat here and now before you." It was his last desperate try. At least he could be sure Wyl would live on.

Celimus found himself cornered. He wanted to have some fun with Ylena's death, but he could tell he had overstepped the mark where Cailech was concerned in threatening Farrow. He knew from the expression on Jessom's face that the Chancellor was urging him to take the easy way out: have the mercenary finish off the woman. He was angry but this was not the time or place to make a scene.

"Well, at least her blood will not be on my hands." He smiled. "Go ahead, Farrow. Finish the job I paid you to do."

Aremys risked a glance of thanks toward Cailech, convinced that without the Mountain King's timely comment and brittle tone, Celimus might not have relented. Cailech returned the gaze with an expression of utter bafflement.

"I will need a blade, sire," Aremys said.

Celimus gave an order and one of the soldiers at Ylena's side pulled a mean-looking knife from his belt. "It's sharp," he murmured. "Make it quick."

Aremys nodded. Everyone wanted this ugliness done with. He took a deep breath. This was it. He was about to die, to sacrifice his body to Wyl. He stood close to Ylena. "As One," he said, and grinned sadly at the irony of the words. He saw the tears well in her eyes as she heard the Thirsk family motto.

Aremys raised the blade, knowing precisely where to strike to slash the jugular for a swift death. As he did, however, Ylena began to scream and struggle desperately.

"Arrow! Arrow!" Wyl shrieked in Ylena's high voice, determined to stop his good friend from giving up his own life.

"What's she saying?" the Morgravian King inquired, determined to drag out the agony.

"She's simply yelling my name," Aremys answered.

"Er, I think she's saying 'arrow,' sire," one of the guards objected.

"Oh, perhaps she'd prefer to be killed by the archers?"

"No, sire," Aremys said as firmly as he dared. "This is best."

"Wait!" the King replied. "Let's ask her. It's the least we can do, isn't it?" He cast an appealing glance around the hall, playing the magnanimous sovereign.

Aremys glared at Wyl. "You fool," he said angrily, under his breath.

The guard ripped away the bindings around Ylena's mouth.

"Step aside, Farrow," Celimus said, enjoying himself hugely. The big man did so reluctantly, but not before glaring at Cailech, who frowned again, taking in all the strange nuances of behavior on display here.

"Ylena," Celimus said; it sounded almost tender. "As a final act of generosity toward your family, I'm going to allow you to choose how you die: by Farrow's blade across your throat or by an arrow fired by one of my expert archers?"

"By the arrow," Wyl said fiercely, not daring to look at Aremys.

"As we suspected. Good choice, Ylena," Celimus replied, stopping just short of rubbing his hands in glee. "Thank you, Farrow. It seems your job is complete. Move away."

This time Aremys looked at no one as he returned to his spot near the door. He stared at the ground. He would not watch Wyl die.

"Ylena, my dear, I did have some sport planned with the archers, but as everyone here seems to want you to have a speedy end, I'll send them away and instead I will do the necessary."

"As you wish," Wyl replied without blinking, knowing he was spoiling Celimus's fun by being so accepting. It worked. The King's face darkened with a scowl.

"Give me a bow!" Celimus said, his tone furious. "Let's finish this."

"Why don't we?" Wyl said, in the most bored tone he could achieve. He could hardly believe his luck that Celimus had chosen to do the deed. He would become the Morgravian King within the next few moments, and much as he hated the thought of living as Celimus, what pleasure it would be to finally kill him. "Hurry up, sire! I am eager to be gone from here." He saw Cailech give a grin of astonishment at Ylena's bravado. Celimus took aim. Wyl switched his attention briefly to Aremys, but his friend refused to look at him. Wyl could not understand why: Aremys knew he would live again, this time as King.

"Farewell, Ylena Thirsk. May Shar send you to wherever your predecessors have ended their days." Celimus stretched the bowstring taut. "Heart or eye? Or shall I let it be a surprise?" he asked with a cruel smile. Everyone could hear the slight strain in his voice caused by holding back the string so tightly.

Wyl refused to answer and instead closed his eyes. Celimus was an excellent shot.

Cailech's astonishment erupted. This woman was extraordinary; she should not be wasted in this manner. Ylena Thirsk stirred more emotion in him than any woman had in his entire life. Cailech had been accused of being cold toward women, but that was not true. He liked women well enough; he just had never met anyone who truly excited him. But Ylena Thirsk provoked in him a swirl of inexplicable feelings. He wanted this woman! And he was not about to let her die trussed like an animal at the end of one of Celimus's arrows.

He moved fast as a pouncing cat and pushed the Morgravian King's wrist up just as the arrow was loosed. It shot high into the air of the hall, burying itself with a resounding thump in a solid beam overhead. Everyone followed the quivering motion of the shaft, not sure whether to be horrified by Cailech's action or relieved. Wyl opened Ylena's eyes with angry disbelief. Aremys had to ball his hands into fists to stop himself from clapping.

Celimus turned the darkest of stares onto his fellow king.

"I've just decided about that gift you offered me, Celimus."

The Morgravian's expression did not change, nor did he utter a word in response.

"I want her," Cailech said, pointing toward Ylena.

"What?" Celimus roared.

"You heard me," Cailech replied calmly. "I shall take

Ylena Thirsk from you. She will travel with us high into the Razors and will never trouble you again."

"What possible interest could you have in her?"

"I'm sure if you think about it long enough, you'll work it out," Cailech said, winking.

Impossibly, Celimus began to laugh. Jessom slowly let out his tightly held breath. Cailech had certainly taken a risk, but the Chancellor could not think of a better way to handle this situation. Had he not suggested to Celimus that he marry Ylena off to a Mountain warrior? There would be little chance of her escaping the Razors, and once the royal marriage was complete, no one would care about the Thirsk name, so deliriously happy would they all be that Morgravia and Briavel were unified. "My lord, this is an opportunity," he risked.

Cailech grinned. "You see, Celimus, even your own counsel likes the idea."

Wyl began to rage, Ylena's voice becoming hysterical. "You bastard! You killed my brother and I'll see you in hell for that. Let me die. I want to die!"

"Oh, someone get her out of here," Celimus said, more exasperated now than angry. He could not help but like Cailech's idea as he watched Ylena being dragged away.

"You did promise me a gift. Anything, you said," Cailech reminded him.

"That's true, I did," Celimus agreed, looking at Cailech. "There would have to be conditions, though. Koreldy tried something similar."

"I am not Koreldy." Cailech bristled.

"Why do you want her?"

"Why would any red-blooded man want her? Does she not affect you so?"

"No. Her mere name sickens me."

"All the better for me, Celimus. I think she's a beauty. Let us truly bind ourselves in our treaty—I will take a Morgravian as my wife."

"Your wife?" Celimus exclaimed, unable to hide his incredulity.

"Yes, why not?" Cailech was grinning widely now. He

glanced at Aremys, who could hardly keep his own smile in check.

"You jest, surely?"

"I never jest about anything so grave as the sacrament of marriage. If you can marry a Briavellian, Celimus, why shouldn't I complete the triangle of our realms and marry a Morgravian?"

"Why not indeed, sire?" Jessom said, daring to join the conversation. "It is indeed a perfect union." His eyes pleaded with his king. This was better than any of them could have dreamed. Surely Celimus could see that?

"There would be conditions," Celimus said again, frowning as his agile mind ran through this new turn of events.

"As you said," Cailech replied. "Although I can put your mind at rest. Ylena Thirsk would not be permitted to leave the Razors. I make that pledge to you now."

"Ever?"

"Ever."

"And as your queen, she would not be permitted to make any decisions that might affect Morgravia—or our treaty will be nullified and I will wage war on your people. Not just the Legion, Cailech, but the full might of the combined Morgravian and Briavellian armies."

"She will be Queen in title only. I am the power in the Razors."

"Done. Now how do we effect this?" Celimus asked, looking toward his chancellor.

Cailech took the lead. "I will take her with me now. Your men can escort us to the border and see that she is safely transported into the Razors, from where she will never emerge. Your chancellor here can draw up the paperwork and your delegates can talk with mine. I will sign whatever you need to effect our treaty and this new understanding regarding the Thirsk woman."

Celimus shook his head. He could find no ruse; Cailech seemed earnest in his desire for Ylena. "All right, I agree. Ylena Thirsk is yours to take. She is my gift to you."

"Thank you," Cailech said, surprising himself by how delighted he felt. He turned to his companion. "Come, Aremys. Ready the Thirsk woman for travel. She rides with me."

# 23

IN THE END, WYL WAS GIVEN HIS OWN HORSE FOR THE FIRST part of the journey. He sat sullenly astride the bay next to Aremys, a thick and uncomfortable silence between them as the two Kings made their official farewells.

"You have no idea how angry I am by what's happened tonight," he finally said in a low voice to his companion.

Aremys bristled. "This was Cailech's idea, not mine, but I'd be lying if I didn't say I'm not ready to kiss the ground he walks on because of it!"

Wyl glared at his friend. "What's that supposed to mean?"

The Grenadyne cast a glance around to check that they were not being eavesdropped upon, particularly by the Chancellor. "It occurs to me," he muttered, a bite in his tone, "that perhaps Myrren's Gift only works when the killer is still in touch with you somehow."

Wyl frowned. "I don't get you," he replied.

"Did Elysius explain how the gift works?"

Wyl shrugged. "What's to know," he said, bitterness underpinning his reply as he watched the sovereigns clasp hands and shoulders in the tradition of parley and peace.

Aremys sighed. He understood Wyl's angry mood; it would be ludicrous even to pretend he could imagine what it felt like to be trapped as Wyl was, or how much courage it must have taken to welcome the agony of whatever form of death Celimus had wished upon Ylena Thirsk. "I began to wonder, back in that hall, whether whoever killed you had to be connected with you through the weapon."

That won Wyl's attention. He paused in thought. "I've never considered that. You mean if the arrow had been shot

I might be fully dead, but if you'd slit my throat I would be you?"

"Exactly," Aremys muttered beneath his breath. "You might truly have died and then all would be lost. That's why I acted as I did."

Ylena's face looked newly distressed. "So I do owe Cailech my life."

"Possibly, is all I'm saying. I don't care to test my own theory," Aremys admitted. "And I'd prefer it if you didn't either."

Wyl glanced at Aremys again and this time Ylena's expression was chastened. "Thank you," was all he had time to say before Cailech was striding back to their party.

"My lady," the King of the Razors said. Wyl did not understand the soft tone or the gentle expression on Cailech's face. All he could do was nod.

Aremys felt a new fear thrill through him. He had not had time to explain that although Cailech might have saved Wyl's life, the new situation was just as dire. Although he knew Wyl had to be told, he was relieved that he had not had to give that explanation just yet or deal with its consequences.

When Cailech was seated on his horse Celimus strolled up. "Safe travels, my friend." Cailech simply nodded. The Morgravian turned to his prisoner. "Another lucky escape, Ylena Thirsk, but this time I fear it is your last. I won't be seeing you again."

"Oh, you'll see me, Celimus," Wyl promised, a determined, somewhat sly smile touching Ylena's lips. "In a place I call hell."

Celimus laughed. "Good luck with her, Cailech—as I understand it, her husband plowed the furrow only once. She'll be nice and tight for you. Remember your promise to me."

Celimus's words shocked Wyl, but he put them aside in order to take his final opportunity to have the last word. He had never heard Ylena's voice sound as cold and threatening as he made it now. "And you remember my promise to you, Celimus. When we meet again, you will die and I will bear witness to it. Just you and I, Celimus—as it should be."

The words sounded strangely prophetic to Chancellor Jessom. The threat felt so very real on this cold night in the north, and yet how could it be, coming from a helpless captive, a young woman at that? Nevertheless, a chill passed through him as he watched Ylena Thirsk stare at the Morgravian King. She was too confident, too unfazed by Celimus—she had demanded her own death, for pity's sake. It did not make sense. He glanced at Aremys and was surprised to see the mercenary watching him. The clue sat between Aremys and Ylena; Jessom was convinced of it. He narrowed his gaze in thought and saw the Grenadyne nod toward him as the party, escorted by Legionnaires, moved out of Tenterdyn.

Jessom watched them depart in silence, seized by an unshakable notion that, despite what both Kings promised, they had not seen the last of the Thirsks.

The journey back to the border was uneventful and mostly silent. That suited Wyl; he was content to let his horse follow the party while he contemplated this new turn of events. It was frustrating being pulled farther from Celimus, but then Fynch had warned him of the randomness of Myrren's Gift. Perhaps this was one of those occasions. He expected to meet Celimus again—and next time, as he had promised, he would not fail. His mind turned to what the King of the Razors might have in mind for him. Why had Cailech stayed the hand of Ylena's would-be murderer? He felt a sudden gratitude to the Mountain King, for perhaps Aremys was right; so far all his deaths had involved someone killing him with a weapon they held. He noticed Cailech beckon to Aremys, who nudged his horse to draw alongside the King, but he could not hear their conversation and lost himself in his thoughts again.

"What lies between you and the Thirsk woman?" Cailech asked Aremys, direct as usual.

"Sire?"

"Don't play the innocent with me. I'm sure I deserve better."

Aremys sighed. "It's true, my lord. I did not want to see Ylena Thirsk murdered."

"That much is obvious. But why?"

"She is innocent of all that Celimus lays at her feet."

Cailech made a soft sound of exasperation. "I worked that out for myself, Grenadyne. Tell me something I don't know, something that accounts for that look in your eyes that fairly begged me to step in and halt the proceedings."

Aremys knew he would have to skirt the truth as carefully as possible. "When I was picked up unconscious in the eastern part of the Razors by Myrt and his companions," Aremys began, "I had lost my memory, as you know." The King nodded but said nothing. The horses slowed to a walk. They could see flaming torches being waved in welcome from a distance. It would not be long now before they were reunited with their men. "As my memory returned I remembered the task I was involved with at the time of being set upon by the thieves in northern Briavel."

"I'd like to hear the end of this before we actually reach the others, Aremys," Cailech admonished gently.

Aremys nodded and got to the point. "I was hired by King Celimus to track down and murder Ylena Thirsk."

"Right. So I gathered."

"Celimus has, as I understand it, my lord, designed the deaths of Wyl Thirsk, Romen Koreldy, King Valor of Briavel, perhaps even his own father, and no doubt countless others."

"You knew about Romen?" Cailech interrupted.

"It only came back to me recently. I didn't know him, my lord, only of him."

"Why do you think you mentioned him when you awoke from your stupor?"

Aremys was reminded again that Cailech missed very little. "I suppose because Ylena Thirsk mentioned to me that he carried a blue sword."

"So you did actually meet up with her?" Cailech said, his mind moving swiftly now.

"Yes, sire. I met with her at Felrawthy, but had no intention of killing her as instructed. We talked of Koreldy because she was so grateful for his help in saving her life the first time. Having learned all that had befallen the Thirsks, and realizing that the girl was obviously an innocent, I followed Koreldy's lead and decided to help her. Mercenary I may be, sire; cold-blooded murderer I am not. It was I who took her into Briavel, where I felt she would be safe. We lost each other at Timpkenny when I wandered out for some air and got set upon." His story sounded horribly thin. He continued quickly. "We'd already discussed her going to Werryl and throwing herself on the mercy of the Queen, so she must have followed the plan in my absence."

"But the note to Valentyna of Briavel that you claimed to have sent to Celimus, correct? Despite what I told Celimus, I would never have permitted you to send a missive to Briavel, certainly not without knowing what you were sending."

Aremys nodded. "Right. I had to lie—I was trapped. But who would have thought the Queen would give her up in the fashion she did? I had both your life and my own at stake, as well as Ylena's. You'll recall when I told you about my insurance that I said I had no idea how to deliver the Thirsk woman."

Cailech nodded. "It does seem that Ylena Thirsk wishes to die. Do you think she forced the Queen's hand?"

"Perhaps, and frankly, who could blame her?" Aremys offered, not wanting to say much more, cautiously grateful that he had gotten this far on lies.

"And your need to rub salt in the prisoner's wounds was actually your way of warning Ylena—am I right?"

"Again, yes, sire. I needed Ylena's story to match mine, or I feared none of us would leave that hall alive."

"The Chancellor knows nothing?"

"Nothing, my lord. He watched Ylena and me argue, nothing more. I was fortunate that a message came for him during that time in the outbuilding. I had but a few moments to brief Ylena."

"I see," Cailech replied. He fell silent. They were almost at the rendezvous point, could see Captain Bukanan and the other dignitaries being brought down to be exchanged. "One more thing, Aremys."

"Yes, my lord?"

"Why do you care about Ylena Thirsk? What hold does she have on you?"

*And here we come to it,* Aremys thought, struck suddenly that he had no answer to this question. Cailech waited as the mercenary's mind raced to find something to offer the King. The carefully constructed web of lies could all fall apart now if he said the wrong thing.

"What is it, Aremys? Why do you hesitate?" Cailech pressed, more pointedly. "Are you hiding something I should be concerned about?"

"No, my lord. It's not that—"

"Then what!" Cailech demanded. Aremys saw Wyl glance behind at the disturbance of Cailech's raised voice. "You will tell me, Grenadyne, before we meet our men . . . before I permit you to enter the Razors again, before I—"

It was Aremys's turn to interrupt. "Because I love her!" he blurted, shocked by the vehemence in his voice. But the last thing he wanted was to be separated from Wyl again and this was the best reason he could manufacture. It was not so far from the truth: He had come to love Wyl Thirsk like a brother, regardless of the guise in which he walked.

Cailech looked at him, astonished. For a moment neither man spoke and Aremys knew he must hold the Mountain King's hard gaze no matter what. To look away now would be interpreted as weakness or deception.

"You jest," Cailech said eventually.

"I do not, sire," Aremys said sadly.

"But—"

"Let us not speak of it anymore, my lord," Aremys said, glad for the cover of darkness. "I have not yet expressed my deepest thanks for what you did today for Ylena. Let me do so now."

"By Haldor's arse, man, I didn't do it for you," Cailech said, still rocked by the Grenadyne's admission. "I did it for purely selfish reasons. I would be lying if I did not admit here and now that I desire her more than I have desired any woman. I meant what I said."

Myrt arrived. He took one look at his king and knew

something was awry. He nodded to his sovereign. "Welcome back, sire."

"Get rid of the Morgravian escort, Myrt, and make the official exchange," Cailech said abruptly, turning back to Aremys.

Myrt accepted the salute of the Legion's senior officer and the departure of the men. When he returned, he glanced uncertainly between Aremys and the King, sensing the new tension.

"We'll be right with you, Myrt," Cailech said. "Take good care of the noblewoman we've brought with us."

Myrt took the reins of Ylena's horse and led creature and woman into camp without another word.

"I mean to make her my wife, Aremys."

"Without even knowing her," the mercenary replied softly, careful not to sound judgmental.

Cailech looked toward the stars and gave Aremys the truth. "I've never been so affected by a woman and I've barely shared a word with her. She is disheveled, dirty, angry. She is magnificent. I want her."

"She is certainly different from any woman I've ever known," Aremys admitted, unable to help himself. "Be careful, sire."

"Of what?"

"Of getting your heart broken."

Aremys meant it sincerely. He knew Wyl would shout loud and long when he heard of the King's intentions and Aremys only wondered how long Ylena would keep her life once Wyl set his mind to losing it again.

Cailech, however, took the mercenary's meaning a completely different way. A dawning realization spread across his expression. "Oh, poor Aremys. The Lady Ylena has rejected your advances."

"No, my lord," Aremys corrected. "I have never made them."

"She doesn't know?" the King asked, aghast.

The Grenadyne shook his head. "I prefer it that way, sire."

"Then what do you mean about getting my heart broken?"

"Only that she loved her husband, Alyd Donal of Felrawthy, passionately and completely. She will never love another."

"We shall see," Cailech said confidently, then: "We have cleared this between us, then?"

"My lord?"

"I can't have you mooning around the woman while I'm wooing her, man! I don't want us to fight over her."

Aremys smiled for the first time in a long time. "Good luck to you if she will have you, Cailech."

The King of the Razors grinned and held out his hand palm up in absolute sincerity. Aremys laid his own palm over it. Cailech grinned. "You constantly surprise me, Grenadyne. Now, if you'd be so kind, I'll ask you to introduce me to my bride-to-be."

E lspyth was laid out on a makeshift pallet on the ground, blankets piled over her small frame to keep out the bite of the cool spring night. A nearby torch lit her face a ghostly color.

"Am I dying?" she asked Crys.

He mustered the crooked grin she loved. "No, but we've got to get those wounds closed up. Drink this," he said, helping her to sit up slightly. "It's warm, sweetened tea. Good for shock, my mother always says." He sighed. "Said."

"Crys, take me home." It was a plea. She squeezed his hand. "I know you've probably got better things to do than travel to Yentro, but I just want to get back to the north."

"To Lothryn?" he asked, his voice gentle.

"Both. I can get well more quickly at home and I feel closer to him with the Razors in sight. I've had enough of roaming the land. The last time I slept in my own bed, ate in my own cottage, did something simple like go to the market, seems like a lifetime ago. I need to see if by chance my aunt is still alive, and I need to return to my life. Wyl doesn't need me now."

"Will you promise me that you won't go off into Cailech's lands if I do take you home?" Her pause was telling. "I won't let you waste yourself, Elspyth. You know how I feel about you—"

"Don't, Crys," she begged softly.

"I don't mean it like that," he urged. "I know where your heart lies. But I care too much about you to let you risk yourself, and Wyl would kill me anyway if I did."

She found a smile for him. "He'd be wrathful, for sure. You saw him in Werryl?"

He nodded and then laughed. "Supremely cranky too. He'd got the flux and he made an inappropriate move on the Queen."

Elspyth spluttered into painful laughter and then groaned at the way it tore at her wounds. "Oh, I mustn't laugh at him," she said, "but I can't help it. I wish I'd known Wyl before Myrren's Gift."

"It's true what they say—he was no painting," Crys commented, determined to see her smile again. His timing, as always, was perfect and she found herself giggling once more.

They were interrupted by Liryk. "Well, this is heartening."

Crys cleared his throat. "Anything to keep her conscious and her mind off her woes," he said to the soldier, winking at Elspyth.

Liryk nodded. "Elspyth, I am so sorry for all you have been through."

"Please, Commander Liryk, the fault is all mine. It was stupid of me to leave as I did and even more naive to fall for that man's cruel trap. Did you find his daughter, by the way?"

"We did. We'll take her back to Werryl and see if we can find the rest of her family."

"Good. She was part of the scheme, I know, but she's so young. Her father used her as much as he used the women."

"Well, he's gone to Shar to answer for his sins now. Now, on another note, we need to get you stitched up, my girl. Those wounds risk infection and that could be life threatening even if the injuries aren't."

"Do you have a physic in the company?" Crys asked.

Liryk gave a nervous smile. "No, but as it happens a Master Rilk passed through an hour ago. One of my men recognized him and hailed him."

Elspyth nodded. "Physic Rilk?"

The Commander looked sheepish. "Well, not exactly. He's a tailor." At Crys's exclamation of protest, he held up a hand. "Hear me out. Next to Madam Eltor, there isn't a more adept person with a needle and thread in the whole of Briavel. Rilk crafts for the top nobility in Morgravia too."

"A master tailor to sew me up?" Elspyth queried.

"He has the finest silken thread and a light touch, Elspyth. It's the best we can do. Those wounds need to be sutured, and rather than let one of my men do a hack job, I'd far prefer a talented craftsman to work on your skin."

Crys was frowning. "I suppose, under the circumstances, this is the best option."

Liryk nodded; he had already motioned to the soldier behind him to bring the tailor forward. "This is Master Rilk," he said, and looked at the craftsman. "This is Crys Donal, Duke of Felrawthy, and our patient, Elspyth."

Crys shook the tailor's hand. "She's got four major cuts." The little man was already perspiring, even though it was a cool night, and Crys had to wonder if he was up to such a grisly task. "Can you stomach it, sir?" he added.

"Oh yes. I've done something similar for my son's beloved pet. I'm sure Miss Elspyth will have far finer skin." He chanced a grin but no one returned it. Rilk's tone became brisk and businesslike. "Can we have her gently moved to a table, please? I'll need lots of light and clean linens and hot water. I presume you have some antiseptic?" Liryk nodded. "Good, I'll need plenty of it. Do you have any shorrock or liquor with you?"

"We'll find some," Liryk said.

"Do it quickly, please, and get some down Miss Elspyth's throat to dull the pain. Not too much, mind, just enough to help her drift off a bit."

Elspyth had already drifted, frightened yet too exhausted to keep her attention on what was about to happen.

K nave was back at Fynch's side. The boy was pale and trembling from his efforts to return the dog to the Razors. *This is exactly what I was afraid of,* Knave growled.

"I'll be all right soon. I just need to sleep."

*Have you taken some sharvan?*

"No. Just let me be."

Knave looked around, quietly exasperated. Fynch had made no progress since they had parted. He was obviously too weak to send himself anywhere.

"How was Valentyna?" the boy mumbled.

*Worried about you. Liryk and company left immediately.*

"Good . . . ah, wait, here is Kestrel." It took Fynch some pain to open up his mind, but he wanted Knave to share this.

Kestrel's thin voice entered their heads. *Elspyth is safe. Quite badly injured from what I can tell, but alive and talking to some of the men who arrived.*

*What are they doing?* Fynch asked.

*Perhaps I can show you?* Kestrel replied.

*Yes, let's try,* the boy said, a new excitement cutting through his pain.

Knave sighed. If Fynch did not stop exerting himself unnecessarily, he would die before they even left this plateau.

Fynch concentrated. His eyes were squeezed tightly shut. *That's right, Kestrel. Open your mind completely to me. I won't hurt you, I promise. I just want to see through your eyes, if I may.* There was a pause and suddenly a picture appeared in Knave's mind.

*I see it,* he admitted grudgingly to Fynch.

An awning of sorts had been set up. Torches burned brightly around it and some men held candles as others bent over a prone figure. Kestrel must have perched himself on a low branch nearby; his sight was keen and they could clearly see all that they needed to.

"They seem to be sewing her," the boy said. "There's Commander Liryk. And . . . oh, wait, is that Master Rilk?"

*You're right,* Knave said. *It's the tailor.*

"He's mending her," Fynch said in wonderment. They watched Rilk snip a thread and then step away and arch his back. *She's pretty, isn't she?* Fynch said absently. *I'm glad we were able to help. She's going to be all right.*

*Is that enough, Fynch?* Kestrel asked.

*Enough,* Knave answered, determined now that his charge would rest.

*Perhaps I'll follow the pretty lady,* the bird added. *I've got nothing better to do.*

*Thank you, Kestrel,* Fynch replied weakly, his head pounding.

*We'll speak again soon,* the bird said, taking to the air.

Knave bristled. *I can feel the echoes of your pain, Fynch. You've got to stop using magic for a while.*

"I can't," the boy moaned, retching helplessly into the bushes.

*We have no choice. You must recover your strength before we proceed. We'll make camp here. I'm going to find you some food. You may not feel like eating, but your body is mortal, Fynch. It needs nourishment.*

The boy did not reply. He had fallen asleep, collapsed into a small, curled shape like a tiny animal.

# 24

ALENTYNA LOOKED AT HERSELF IN THE MIRROR AND GLUMLY permitted a brief, silent admission that the dress was exquisite.

"Oh, my queen, you make the most glorious bride," Madam Eltor said. "The fit is perfect." She looked at the breathtaking woman before her and sighed. "A smile would help."

"I'm sorry, Margyt."

"I have to ask you to try on the veil now, my dear," the woman continued, affixing the confection of cream gauze and seed pearls to Valentyna's dark hair. She stood back and looked at her finished creation with satisfaction and pride.

"Thank you, it's lovely," was all the Queen could force out.

"You know, Valentyna, perhaps it's not my place to speak, but we would all like to think that you enter this union with some joy."

The Queen and her seamstress had known each other too long for lies. "I'm sorry that I cannot," Valentyna said. "I bring it about for Briavel, Margyt, because I know it brings us peace and, I hope, new prosperity, but I cannot love him."

"Because of another?" the woman risked.

Valentyna shook her head gently. "No. Simply because I don't love him. We can't help our feelings, can we?"

"No, child. In that you're right. My husband and I could never claim to have loved each other as I know other couples do."

"But you have a good partnership," Valentyna said.

"More than that, to be honest. We are the closest of friends. But yes, we also have a great partnership—as you will with King Celimus. You will make it so. You will give us heirs and make us proud."

A smile ghosted across Valentyna's mouth. "That is my fervent wish."

Margyt Eltor patted her queen's hand. "Let me snip those threads now and release you."

"Are all the preparations in hand?"

"Yes, your majesty," Madam Eltor said, back to her formal role. "I shall be taking two dressers and a couple of other girls for errands and any other needs we might have. The various gowns we spoke of are also ready."

"And the new riding clothes?"

"Completed. You didn't want new boots too, did you?" the seamstress asked, frowning, her mind already racing toward how quickly the cobbler might work.

"No, I like my comfortable old ones," Valentyna replied.

"As I understand it from our earlier discussion, your highness, we depart for Morgravia in ten days?"

"Yes. The wedding was supposed to be at the close of spring, but I see no point in holding off and will send a message today to King Celimus. It should please him. I'll have one of my assistants confirm everything with you shortly. We'll take it slowly with a view to four days' journeying. I can visit some of the towns and villages along the way to pay my respects to our people."

"I imagine the party will be quite large," Margyt commented as she sliced through the threads that had ensured the gown's perfect fit.

"I suppose so," Valentyna said, not really caring. "Perhaps Commander Liryk will split it into smaller groups and send them by different routes."

"Yes, that would be sensible," the seamstress agreed. Then: "Are you giving the King a ring, your highness?"

The Queen nodded. "Studded with jewels in the colors of Briavel."

"Lovely," Margyt said, helping her sovereign to lift the gown over her head.

"Why are you alone this time?" Valentyna's voice was muffled from beneath the garment.

"Because I don't want my girls twittering that our queen goes to her marriage as if to a funeral," Madam Eltor admonished. "I sensed from our last fitting that you were not getting any pleasure from the preparations. I thought privacy was best, your highness."

"Thank you again, Margyt. Your sensitivity always makes you my favorite," Valentyna said, finding a playful tone.

The seamstress responded, glad of it. "Oh? I hear Master Rilk gets plenty of your business, your highness," she said archly.

"He wanted the wedding gown," Valentyna replied, tugging her more casual day gown over her head.

"The cheek of the man!"

The Queen laughed. Madam Eltor and Master Rilk had been married for as long as she could remember. And between them they crafted everything Valentyna wore.

"I will take my leave, your highness. There's still plenty for me and my girls to do."

"You're a treasure. I promise to be smiling next time we see each other."

"Make sure of it, child. You will be preparing to take holy vows in the grand Pearlis Cathedral the next time I stitch you into this gown."

Madam Eltor's words remained with Valentyna long after she had departed, reminding the Queen that there was no way off the path she was now on.

Nothing and no one was going to save her from Celimus. She wasted no further time in sitting down at her desk and crafting, with her own hand, a message to her groom to set a final date for their wedding ceremony.

Wyl recognized Myrt and several of the Mountain warriors, all of whom treated Ylena courteously. He was not sure what to think of this new situation. It felt dangerous—all his senses told him so—but at the same time it was reassuring to be back with Aremys.

Someone handed him a bowl of broth. "My lady." It was Myrt, Wyl realized, when he lifted Ylena's chin to glance at the owner of the soft voice. "The King tells us you have been treated inhospitably in Morgravia."

"He speaks true," Wyl admitted.

"I'm sorry there is still a long journey ahead, but he hopes you will eat something before we leave."

"We leave tonight?"

"Yes, my lady. We wish to be deep into the Razors by midnight."

"So you travel comfortably in the dark?" Wyl wondered.

"We need no light but the moon," Myrt said, with a polite nod, then left.

The broth was surprisingly good, hearty and rich with the flavor of meat. As Wyl finished the bowl, glad for the warming nourishment, Aremys arrived in the cave, holding a candle. He looked distracted and hesitant; Wyl figured it could not be easy for the mercenary to find time alone with the Mountain King's new captive.

"We're breaking camp now, leaving immediately. How are you?"

"Fed," Wyl said. "Myrt brought me food."

"Does he know you recognize him?" Aremys asked, alarmed.

"No, I've been careful about it."

"Good. He's sharp."

"How much aren't you telling me about this turn of events?"

Aremys hesitated. "Cailech insists on knowing why I have aided you."

Wyl nodded and Aremys paused, embarrassed. "I was cornered and had to come up with something."

"So you told him . . .?"

"That I loved you." He watched uncomfortably as Ylena's face transformed into a look of incredulity. Fortunately, whatever Wyl was going to say was cut off by the arrival of a messenger announcing the party's imminent departure. Aremys asked the man if scouts had checked that Celimus had sent no tracking party. The man confirmed that they had done so and there were no spies trailing them.

During this exchange, Wyl had composed himself. "So, are you going to tell me the rest?" he asked. "We don't seem to have much time."

Aremys scratched his head. It was best to give it to Wyl straight, he decided. "Cailech's taken a fancy to you."

"Oh, Shar save me!" Wyl groaned. "You're serious, aren't you," he said, and it was no question.

"It gets worse," the big man continued.

"How can it?" Wyl asked, letting Ylena's head drop between her knees.

"During your absence from the hall, Cailech declared to Celimus that he would make you his wife." Wyl looked up sharply. His horror was reflected in the Grenadyne's despondent expression. "It took everyone by surprise. There was nothing I could do."

"I understand, Aremys," Wyl admitted, bile rising in his throat. "You were helpless back there. But we're not helpless now," he declared, standing to Ylena's full height, which barely reached halfway up the mercenary's chest.

"Please, Wyl," Aremys said, cautiously glancing around. "Go along with this for the time being."

"Go deeper into the Razors, back to that fortress?" Wyl hissed. "Are you mad? I've escaped it once. I don't think I'll be able to do it again."

There was nothing for it but to tell Wyl all that he knew. "I've found Gueryn," Aremys said firmly, knowing it would stop Wyl's tirade.

It did. Wyl grabbed his shirtfront angrily. "You're sure it's him?"

Aremys nodded. "We spoke briefly. I said I'd come back for him. He's in the dungeon and, considering his situation, looks quite good for it, but now that Cailech knows Romen Koreldy is dead, I fear for his life. And then there's Rashlyn, the most unpredictable factor in all of this. Apparently he's used magic on Gueryn a few times now."

"What do you mean?"

"Too long in the telling now. Suffice to say it's been used for good in healing the arrow wound, but bad too, and it's rattled your old mentor."

Wyl paced, pulling at his ear, thoughts racing as to what would be the best course of action. He did not want to go with Cailech—the Mountain King's intentions for him were just too revolting to contemplate. But Gueryn's needs called strongly. He could not desert his dearest, oldest friend, not after the sad way they had parted.

Aremys sensed that Wyl needed a final push and gave it. "I've also found Lothryn."

Ylena's eyes blazed in the soft light. "He's alive? I knew it!"

"But not how you remember him, Wyl," Aremys cautioned.

"How so?" Wyl asked. His frightening dream at Felrawthy, of the man's voice screaming from behind a barn door, returned to haunt him.

Before Aremys could reply, Cailech appeared at the mouth of the cave. "I hope I'm not interrupting anything."

"I can't imagine it would matter if you were," Wyl replied, flustered by his friend's various revelations and the discomfort of seeing his captor—his husband-to-be—smiling so disarmingly at him.

"No, I suppose it wouldn't," Cailech agreed, his smile broadening. "I hope my men have treated you deferentially, my lady?"

"Thank you, sire," Wyl replied, remembering Ylena's manners, but aiming a glare toward Aremys.

Cailech did not miss the glance between them. "Ah, I suppose Aremys has explained why you're here."

"He has, King Cailech." Wyl was at a loss for words. He understood his friend's reasons for wanting him to return to the fortress, but this was a perilous situation for him now.

"Don't be frightened, my lady. In the south you know us as barbarians, but we may surprise you."

"Romen Koreldy spoke highly of you, my lord. He told me much about the ways of the Mountain People and I have an appreciation for your sophistication," Wyl said, believing it best to reveal now that he knew something of the culture. Any misjudgments he made in seeming too familiar with the Razor Kingdom he might now be able to hide behind Romen's teachings.

"Did he now?"

"He liked you," Wyl offered.

"I hope you will too, Ylena. Come now, we must journey."

There was nothing for Wyl to do but follow the King's guiding hand. "You will ride with me, my lady," Cailech added, and it was fortunate indeed that the King did not see the look of despair that swept across Ylena's face.

Wyl gritted his teeth and allowed Cailech's strong hands to help him into the saddle, tensing uncomfortably as the King climbed up behind him. Cailech's arms passed around Ylena's tiny waist and took the reins from her.

"Allow me," he said graciously.

Wyl grimaced toward Aremys, who looked away in embarrassment.

"Comfortable, Ylena?" the King inquired.

"May I not ride a horse of my own, sire?" Wyl risked.

He sensed the King's wry grin. "It is good for my men to see me take ownership of you, my lady. It is critical they understand how highly I regard you. Life in Morgravia is no longer possible, Ylena, you surely agree?"

"I do, my lord," came the grudging reply.

"And it seems your life is now worthless in Briavel too, where a queen must bow to the whims of her powerful neighbor and soon-to-be husband. So the only realm where your life can be protected—and, might I add, revered, my lady, is the Razor Kingdom. My men are surprised by your presence, I'll not lie." Cailech's mouth was so close to Ylena's ear that Wyl felt sickened. "But in seeing us together like this, they will now offer you the highest respect, my lady, as befitting a noblewoman and my future wife."

Gueryn was still smiling from the thrill of riding Galapek. Not even the sound of his cell door hammering closed or the key turning in the lock could tarnish the day's experience.

He, Jos, and Rollo had taken the horses around the lake and beyond for several hours, returning late in the afternoon. Gueryn had felt exhilarated. He had not had a chance to confirm his suspicions about Galapek, unfortunately, but the joy of being in the open and on a horse again was exquisite. He had wept as they neared the stables at the close of the ride, embarrassing himself.

Jos had given him a consoling pat on the shoulder. "I'm sorry you are our prisoner, Gueryn," the young man had offered.

"I too am sorry," Gueryn had replied, "but thank you for this wonderful escape, however brief it has been."

"What do you think of our fine stallion?" Maegryn had asked on their return.

"That I wish he were mine," Gueryn had answered truthfully.

The stablemaster had laughed. "Everyone does."

"Can I rub him down?"

"Most certainly," Maegryn had said, but sadly for Gueryn, who had hoped to be left alone with the horse, the head of the stable had remained.

Despite Maegryn's presence, Gueryn had managed to whisper once to the horse, begging the animal to give him a sign that he was Lothryn, but nothing had occurred. And yet he could not doubt the sincerity of the stranger, Aremys. As the incredible words had tumbled from the big man's mouth, horror lacing each one, Gueryn had believed them. His brief but terrible experiences with Rashlyn were all he needed to draw upon to believe that the mercenary had hit on the truth.

Being Morgravian, Gueryn had always been scornful of magic—frightened of it too. Along with most Morgravians, he had accepted the persecution that had not so long ago been visited on anyone perceived as a witch or warlock. But now, after hearing Aremys's story and feeling the effects of Rashlyn's power for himself, Gueryn was forced to accept that magic must be at the heart of the mystery surrounding the horse Galapek, and indeed Wyl himself.

Myrren of Baelup came to mind and, inevitably, Wyl's attempts to protect her from further suffering. The memory surfaced fresh and clear now. At the moment of the witch's death Wyl's eyes had changed color, reflecting the exact strange hues of Myrren's eyes. The very reason for her persecution was mirrored in Gueryn's own beloved Wyl Thirsk. And he was not the only person who had seen it. The tiny gong boy, Fynch, had shared the experience. They had not both imagined the presence of some magic.

Gueryn's good mood evaporated as the sour thoughts overtook his mind. If he could accept that Wyl had been somehow touched by the magic of the witch, then surely it was possible that Lothryn could be so remarkably changed by sorcery, especially when wielded by one so deeply wicked and heartless as Rashlyn. But what about Wyl? How had Myrren's magic affected him?

He was still wrestling with the question, haunted by the memory of how Romen had tricked him into believing he was Wyl, when the key turned again in the lock. Gueryn was startled. He moved back into the shadows, away from the nub of candle and its light which was now permitted him as a small kindness.

He instantly recognized the figure that appeared in the doorway and his stomach clenched in fear.

"Le Gant," Rashlyn said, in his light, irritating voice. "You can't hide from me in this dungeon."

"Have you come to share my ration of water, Rashlyn?" Gueryn asked, forcing himself to fight back his fear.

The small man laughed. "After tonight's proceedings, I imagine conversation will be the furthest thing from your mind. Take him," he commanded to the two men who now pushed through the doorway. Gueryn recognized neither. His heart lurched with new terror.

"There will be a reckoning with your king over this, Rashlyn," he warned in desperation, all bravado gone now. If he were to die at this man's hand, who would back up Aremys's claim?

"But it was the King who gave me permission, le Gant. He agreed that I could use you for my own . . . interests, shall we say. Come now. I'm sure we'll both find it interesting."

Gueryn did the only thing left to him. He struggled with the guards and bellowed his protestations as loudly as his lungs could manage, in the faint hope that someone might hear and bear testimony to his disappearance at the hands of the barshi.

## 25

FYNCH LAY STILL ENOUGH TO BE DEAD, CURLED ON THE FLOOR of the small cave he and Knave had come to call home these past few days. Knave had worried about the boy's weakness, but Fynch had grown stronger through long healing sleeps and the dog had to assume that this was the way of the magic. No doubt Elysius had done the same. He regretted they had not asked the manwitch more questions about the sickness.

Kestrel had communicated that Elspyth was also healing through long rest periods after her surgery with Master Rilk. Knowing that Elspyth lived and would recover from her injuries had helped Fynch to let go of Wyl's friend and become more focused on the trial ahead and his own health.

Knave understood that the boy had no idea of what they

were up against. Not even he could imagine it, to tell the truth, but he had heard the gravity in Elysius's voice when speaking of his brother and had seen how the manwitch had fretted at the thought of passing the magic, and the responsibility that came with it, to such a youngster. But all of that had paled in comparison to the arrival of the Dragon King. His presence alone had impressed upon Knave the dire task they faced. For the King of the Creatures to come to them from his abode high in the mountains of the Wild, where no man or possibly no other animal had ventured, made it clear that Fynch's trial was more important than any of them could know.

The youngster stirred, his eyelids fluttering as consciousness arrived. Then his eyes opened and he regarded the dog. "You make me feel so safe, Knave," Fynch murmured sleepily.

Knave only wished he could protect the boy from all that was coming toward them. But this was no time to scare him. They needed to be strong together. *I'm never far, remember?* the dog replied.

Fynch sat up and stretched. "I feel better than I have in days."

*You must eat,* Knave said, unable to hide the elation in his voice.

"You sound like my sister."

*Your sister must be a wise woman.*

Fynch reached to hug the dog. "I'll eat for both of you." He was able to start a fire with the smallest trickle of magic and Knave quietly marveled at how quickly his friend had accepted his new powers. Fynch did not talk about the wondrous nature of his new skills, but Knave understood that the lad treated this gift as he treated everything in his life—with serious care. The dog knew Fynch would never be playful with the magic or test its boundaries; he would no more send messages unnecessarily than he would try out his own ability to fly.

The boy refused the rabbit Knave had killed for him. "I can't; it repulses me for some reason."

*You don't like rabbit?*

The boy frowned. "I don't think I like meat anymore. I'll find some berries."

There were some cirron berries growing nearby and Fynch made a meal of them with a knuckle of bread. "I feel well enough to travel now," he said in between tiny mouthfuls.

*It's time we made a move,* the dog agreed. He was about to say that they should travel as far as they could during the morning, and that Fynch should sleep in the afternoon before sending them about ten leagues east, when Fynch cut across his thoughts.

"I'm going to risk Rashlyn today."

He caught Knave off guard. *What do you mean?*

"I'm tired of all this patience. I'm tired of feeling sick and wearied by the magic. If it's going to be this harmful to me, let's not waste more time. Let's really use it."

*What are you talking about, Fynch?*

"I'm talking about sending us all the way. I sent you to Werryl, and I know I can do it now for the two of us. I can get us right to the door of the fortress if we feel that bold." Then he grinned shyly. "Perhaps I should send us somewhere a little safer."

*No!* Knave replied. *Too risky, too dangerous for your health, too—*

"Hush, Knave. I know my limitations."

*I'm not sure you do,* Knave said testily.

Fynch knew the dog's bad humor was a manifestation of his fear. "Trust me. I think I can blur the magic."

*I do not understand.* Exasperation gave way to weariness in the dog's tone.

Fynch shrugged. "Hard to explain, but while I was sleeping I think perhaps . . ." He hesitated.

*Perhaps what?*

"Perhaps the Dragon King spoke with me," the boy finished, embarrassed.

Knave was surprised but he pressed on. *And?*

"I believe I can try to muddy the magic going out, so to speak. Whether Rashlyn senses it or not, I might be able to confuse him sufficiently that he can't lock on to us or what we are."

*That's a big gamble.*

"Yes, but time is not on our side. I'm getting bad feelings about things."

*Things?*

The boy pulled a face. "Just a sense; again, hard to explain. I thought it was my fear for Elspyth, but it's more than that. It's Wyl, it's Valentyna. There's something very bad happening in the Razors, something not right."

*Unnatural, you mean?*

"That's it. That's exactly what I mean. There's a taint of evil on the wind, and it's talking to me in my dreams.

*What do you see?*

"Two men. Both in pain. I can't really see them, only sense them. One I believe I might know, but I can't be sure . . . I mean, how could I?"

*And Rashlyn's behind it?*

Fynch nodded glumly. "I think he's the source of what's bad. I could send a creature to find out more . . . perhaps Kestrel even. But that would just be more time wasting. We should go ourselves."

*Perhaps that's why the Dragon King spoke to you.*

"Yes, that's what I believe. Are you ready?" Fynch said, picking up his small sack and pulling it around his body.

*Now?*

The boy grinned again, less hesitantly this time. "I've already opened the bridge to the Thicket. It awaits us."

Knave suddenly felt the thrum of magic from the Thicket. He took a deep breath. *I'm ready.*

Fynch put his arms around the dog and Knave sensed the pressure of the air thickening around them. As the Razors began to shimmer around them, Knave braced himself for the landing, unnecessarily. Fynch had mastered his sending skills and had summoned a pillow of air to cushion them as they arrived. Knave was on all fours in a blink and hovered protectively over the little boy, who was vomiting violently into the undergrowth.

*Take your time,* he whispered helplessly, wondering what kind of toll the magic would take this time, so soon after Fynch's last use of it.

Fynch grasped for his sack and the sharvan leaves. He forced a handful into his mouth, which tasted sour from the recent meal he had just lost.

Knave rebuked himself for agreeing to this madness when he had just managed to get his charge to eat something. *Sip lots of water,* he advised. *I'm going to scout around.*

Fynch said nothing, chewing intently to start the painkilling juices flowing down his aching throat. Using the magic might have been a good idea, but it had taken a huge toll on him. He felt as though he might die.

Knave saw that the boy's eyes were bloodshot, and for the first time, a thin rivulet of blood ran from his nose. The dog felt uncharacteristically angry with everyone: himself, for not insisting that Fynch spare himself, Elysius for passing on the magic, his king for entrusting this lovely child with such a huge task, even Fynch for insisting on sending them so far. He stalked away, his mood as dark as the fur that covered his body, and blended into the cover of the foliage. When he returned, his companion lay on the ground, still and pale. Alarmed, the dog nuzzled the boy, his fear almost making him whine.

"Knave?" Fynch croaked, his complexion ghostly as he raised his head.

*I'm here,* the dog replied, his relief evident. *There are people coming, and horses, quite a reasonable number of them. We're well hidden, so we just need to remain still.*

"It's Wyl," Fynch said groggily.

The dog was confused. Wyl was in Briavel, with Valentyna. *How do you know?*

"When I sent us, I tried something new." Fynch coughed and blood splattered from his mouth. "I'm sorry," he said, his tone flat.

*No! I am,* Knave said, his anger at last finding its way into his tone. *This is not right, Fynch. You're going to die if you don't stop overextending yourself.*

Fynch looked at his friend with a sad expression. "I'm going to die soon anyway, Knave," he said gravely.

The dog was lost for words, so Fynch continued, wiping his bloodied mouth on his sleeve. "I cast out as we traveled, trying to lock on to Rashlyn and using the magic of the Thicket to shield us. I found Wyl instead. I think the Thicket did that deliberately."

*Why?*

"Probably because Wyl is not meant to be in the Razors. He should be in Briavel with Valentyna. The Thicket is warning me."

*Did it tell you what to do?*

"No, unfortunately. That's up to us, Knave. I think we should just follow at a distance and take stock of the situation. He's surely not here by choice."

*Are you up to following them?*

"I'll manage," Fynch said.

Knave had to look away, unable to bear the pain in the boy's face. *They'll be a few minutes yet,* he said. *Just lie down until then.*

For once Fynch obeyed.

Crys made a sound of exasperation. "It's too soon."

"I don't want to spend another second in this blood-soaked place," Elspyth said, grimacing as she pulled on her cloak.

"Please, Elspyth. At least let me take you to Sharptyn."

"No, Crys. I want to leave the region. I nearly died here and I'm not talking solely about my physical wounds. Before you arrived . . ." Her voice quavered but she steadied it. "Speaking of which, I still haven't thanked you for bringing the Briavellian Guard."

He waved her embarrassment aside. "Master Rilk said—"

"Master Rilk is a tailor!" Elspyth cut across his words. "I'm grateful to him, grateful to you all, but I'm ready to leave."

"Where will you go? Surely not into the Razors?" Crys beseeched. His hurt expression added new injury to her aching heart.

"No. I'm not fit enough for that. I shall go home first." She looked around her. "This place almost looks"—she searched for the right word—"clean again."

Crys risked reaching forward and buttoning her cloak for her. "Liryk and his men have done a good job."

Elspyth smiled at his gesture but wished he would not show his affection for her quite so openly. "They have. When does the Guard move out?"

"Today, I believe."

"Then my timing is perfect. And you? Where will you go?"

Pain flickered briefly across Crys's open face, but he wrestled his expression back under his control. "Not Briavel. I'm a hindrance there and Valentyna will be making preparations for her journey to Morgravia now."

"Poor soul. She intends to go through with it, then?"

"She has no choice. I don't believe it can be avoided, Elspyth. And with Wyl taking himself off to die again at the hands of Celimus . . ." He trailed off.

"She could just say no," Elspyth blazed, then grimaced at the sour look her words won from her friend. "No, I know. She can't. That would mean war. Do you think the next time we meet Wyl, he'll be the King of Morgravia?"

Crys gave an involuntary bark of a laugh. "Oh, I don't know," he said, a helpless tone in his voice. "Wyl's so stoic. Where did he find the courage to march into Celimus's den, knowing he goes toward a horrible death?"

Elspyth sighed. "I think we're all capable of being heroic when it comes to those we love, Crys," she said sadly, and knew he understood by his equally sorrowful nod.

"Well, a happy ending for Wyl and Valentyna perhaps?" he tried brightly.

"But not for us, eh?" she responded in kind.

"It could be if only you'd let it," he said, then wished he had not. "I'm sorry, Elspyth."

She accepted his apology readily. "Come with me," she said, knowing how badly the Duke of Felrawthy needed the anchor of friendship, and truthfully she herself did not feel like traveling alone.

"Really?" Crys asked, hardly believing Elspyth's words.

A smile lit the petite woman's face. "Why not?" She held up a restraining hand. "But there are terms."

"Of course. No kissing, or any attempt at seduction," he listed, grinning. "No suggestion that Lothryn is a wasted cause or that you're too small, too fragile, too feminine to save him."

She laughed openly now. "I like that you use your wit to hide your emotions, Crys," she said, meaning it with affection.

"It's all I have now. I feel so bruised and battered, I need to hide. Thank you for allowing me to accompany you. I won't let you down, Elspyth." They both understood the unspoken words.

"I appreciate that," she said. "Did Wyl have any ideas for us before he left?"

"Well, he did suggest I stir up some trouble within the Legion."

"In what way?"

"Reinforce the name of Thirsk, remind the men that the Donals were true, insist that Celimus is a destroyer of realms." He ran his hands through his hair. "And a slayer of souls."

She touched his arm. It was all the solace she could offer. "Shall we detour past Pearlis on our way north?"

"Could you stand to? I mean, it's not as direct as you probably want."

Elspyth paused to consider his question. "No, but I'm not really well enough to be any good to anyone, and a couple of extra days will not make a difference to my journey."

"Perfect. Can you ride?"

"Let's take Ericson's cart. He's not going to be needing it," she said, feeling ghoulish at her pragmatism. "You have a horse, don't you?" He nodded. "Then we're set. Let's go do some damage to our king."

Rashlyn stepped back to admire the fruits of his toil. He was drenched in sweat; it beaded into his tangled beard and soaked the already soiled shirt he had worn for days. He chuckled. "Better, definitely better," he muttered, and swallowed a cup of the rejuvenating brew he had made before he began his ugly work.

He knew from past experience that crafting this sort of magic was exhausting, but now he believed it actually drained the life from him. A measure of his essence had been used to create the spell. That was his sacrifice, the price he had to pay to manipulate this magic. But he was becoming stronger, more proficient in his crafting. The dog stood on all fours before him, trembling so badly Rashlyn was sure it would collapse. It snarled, despite its obvious suffering.

"I suspect that was none too pleasant for you," he said to the creature. "In fact, I imagine it was nothing short of excruciating. I'm surprised you lived through it . . . and rather pleased you did."

Again the dog growled weakly, baring its teeth, pulling helplessly at the restraining chain that held it to a ring in the wall.

"How does it feel to be a dirty dog, le Gant? A filthy Morgravian dog?"

The dog leapt forward and managed to make the sorcerer flinch. But the chain dragged it back viciously and it fell over. It lay on the ground, panting hard, eyes glazed, its energy spent.

"Oh, don't die on me so soon, le Gant. I do so want to show the King my handiwork. I'm going to give you to him so he can feed you the crumbs from his table, or perhaps break your ribs with his boot if that takes his fancy. I suggest you change your attitude. You are nothing now, you Morgravian dog. You never were."

The dog snapped once, but so weakly that Rashlyn did not even hear its jaws come together. He was lost in admiration at his skill. The dog could hear and react. The horse Galapek seemed nothing more than a void, but le Gant the dog showed spirit. Very good.

He was so close to full control now. He could hardly wait to present his latest creation to Cailech. Together they would rule not only the men of the land but its creatures and birds as well. Cailech could go to war with the south with bears, wolves, wildcats, even a troop of zerkons under his command—it was more exciting than Rashlyn had ever dared to dream.

And while Cailech might be the most powerful man in the

realm, Rashlyn believed he himself would be even stronger. Without knowing it, Rashlyn had come to the same conclusion as Elysius. He believed that Nature was the reflection of Shar, and if he, Rashlyn, could exert control over Nature's beasts, then surely he would achieve godlike stature himself.

The barshi left the semiconscious dog to lie in its own mess, slamming the door shut on yet another tomb. The dog, hurting deeply and wondering how it could bring about its own death, whined softly as it passed into unconsciousness.

## 26

WYL SANK INTO A GLUM SILENCE AS THEIR PARTY NEARED THE higher ground and the inevitability of the fortress. The terrain was familiar and once again he felt the weak but nevertheless sickening pull of Romen's fears as what little was left of him recognized where they were.

Cailech had been generous enough to leave Ylena to herself during the journey. At night she was permitted to sleep alone in a tent made from animal skins that the warriors rigged up for her rest. Fresh water was always found for her ablutions and Cailech had even promised a dip in a hot spring where he insisted she would have privacy. He had been formal and courteous in all conversation and their only physical contact had been during the hours on horseback. Wyl realized that Cailech must be enjoying the feel of Ylena's slim body pressed against his chest, and although he made a huge effort to sit as far forward as he could, ultimately by day's end the journey would wear him down sufficiently that, without meaning to, he would find himself leaning against the King's broad, hard body. There were occasions when Cailech, wanting to show Ylena something, would win her attention by gently touching her arm or speaking quietly into her ear as he pointed out a soaring eagle or a particularly jagged series of peaks, so distinctive to the Razors. And each time Wyl would withdraw just a bit further within, to what was purely him.

This was the third morning and they had broken camp a couple of hours ago. Aremys dropped back to ride alongside Cailech. Wyl had been surprised to find that the mercenary had essentially ignored him these past two days, preferring to keep company with Myrt and a fellow called Byl. He guessed that his friend was anxious and embarrassed by the situation in which Wyl found himself.

"I imagine they're restless to be home now," Cailech commented, nodding toward the men Aremys had just been talking with.

"They are. I don't think any of you Mountain People feel comfortable outside the fortress and its compounds."

Cailech grinned. "That's a good thing." He inhaled the sharp mountain air. "Can you smell that, Ylena? Those are tiny white flowers called thawdrops that burst through at the first hint of spring and flourish toward midspring. The fragrance is being blown here from the valley just outside the fortress, which we'll be passing soon. It's quite a sight. I shall pick you some."

Wyl remembered the valley—it had been bare the last time he had passed this way. His stomach clenched at the thought of reentering the Mountain Fortress.

"Your friend is very quiet, Aremys," the King said, amused, as if Ylena were not encircled by his arms, the prisoner of his desire.

Aremys shrugged, not daring to look Wyl's way. "I hardly know her, my lord, to pass judgment on her silences," he said carefully.

"You have us baffled, Ylena, you see?" Cailech said. Wyl could feel the King's face touching the back of Ylena's head as he leaned forward. "Are you not happy to have escaped Celimus again? Can you not share your pleasure with us?"

"I wanted to die, sire. You denied me my revenge."

"How so?"

"I wanted the blood of both Thirsk heirs on his hands,

your majesty. I wanted it mingling with that of the blood of the holy men of Rittylworth and the loyal souls of Felrawthy he had slaughtered."

"And Koreldy's," Cailech said quietly.

"Yes, Romen's too. And that of King Valor."

"Do you think he will kill his bride?" Cailech suddenly asked.

Wyl flinched. "He is capable of it."

The King nodded. "Is that his plan, though, do you think?"

"No," Wyl admitted. "He wants heirs. Perhaps three, to sit each realm," he added craftily.

It did not rattle Cailech as intended. "I have an heir, Ylena," he replied. "His name is Aydrech, and I am hopeful you will give me more sons."

Wyl felt a fresh wave of nausea, all his own. He fought back, unwisely. "I hear that Aydrech is not truly of your blood, sire."

Cailech's right hand left the reins and raised itself in the air. The men behind obediently slowed and stopped their horses, as did Cailech. Aremys looked uncertain, glancing between King and guest.

"What did you say?" Cailech said, his voice hard.

It was too late to retract it; besides, Wyl had nothing to lose. The threat of being touched by this man was coming closer by the minute.

"You heard what I said, your highness, and your very reaction proves its truth."

Myrt had dropped back to Cailech's side. "My king, is everything all right?"

"Move the men forward, Myrt. I have a private discussion to finish."

The big warrior nodded and shot a surreptitious glance toward Aremys, who also felt the dangerous tingle in the air but hadn't understood Wyl's words. The other horsemen moved by, averting their eyes, and Aremys made to follow.

"Wait, Aremys," the King commanded, leaping down from his horse with agile grace. He walked around to where he could look his bride-to-be directly in the eye. Wyl knew that stare well. "Now, Ylena. Finish what you have to say or I shall slit your throat here and now."

Wyl remained silent. Aremys shifted uncomfortably on his horse.

"What do you know about my son?" Cailech said, and his tone was now edged with a fire that had not been directed at Ylena previously.

"Only what I said, sire."

"And how do you come by such information?"

Wyl considered his options. Romen could be the scapegoat; no one could hurt him anymore.

"It was Koreldy."

The King looked shocked. "How could he know?"

Aremys wanted to know as well, although he feared Wyl's answer and feared even more this nest of vipers Wyl had seemed to deliberately uncover.

"Did anyone mention to you the love between Romen Koreldy and Queen Valentyna, my lord?" Wyl asked, enjoying watching the surprise flit across Cailech's face, to be immediately masked.

"You jest, of course."

"I have no reason to, your majesty. You heard Celimus tell you that Romen was at Werryl Palace, acting as champion to Queen Valentyna."

Cailech nodded. "She fell for his charms," he said, smiling at an old memory of Romen's flirtatious manner.

"She fell in love, your highness," Wyl corrected. "He was not charming her—he was wooing her."

"It sounds like Koreldy," Cailech said disparagingly. "So what?"

"So he told her things—things he would normally have kept to himself. A man truly enraptured can have no secrets from the woman he loves."

"He told her about my son," the King finished.

"He told her about a man called Lothryn whose wife bore a new son, sire."

"Aydrech is of my flesh, Ylena."

"She knew that, my lord, and mentioned as much. Lothryn explained to Koreldy about the boy. I gather it shocked Romen, as it does me, to learn that you would take another man's wife purely to produce an heir."

At this the King found his lazy grin again, infuriating Wyl. "As I am doing with you. Now I understand, Ylena. You were married to Alyd Donal. I'm sure he won't mind if I bed you, although I am sorry that you see me in such a harsh light. I am genuinely intrigued by you. You have kindled a fire in me I have never before felt burn so bright."

"And I'm supposed to be flattered by that?" Wyl asked incredulously. "What about how I feel? You are treating me with the same contempt that Celimus treats Valentyna."

Cailech did not react to Ylena's stinging words but changed the topic adroitly, frustrating Wyl. Cailech was too wise to fall for his baiting. "You sound as if you admire the Queen, Ylena."

Wyl shook Ylena's head in annoyance. He glanced at Aremys, who looked as anxious as he had looked in the hall at Felrawthy. "I do, more than any other woman I've ever met, sire."

Cailech made a sound of disgust. "This is the same woman who sold you out to Celimus, knowing full well he was determined to kill you."

Wyl's anger flared. "And if you believe that, your highness, you are even more ignorant than the southerners believe you to be."

It happened fast. Wyl felt Ylena's body being wrenched from the saddle. Cailech's strength was immense and her body hung from his hand like a rag doll, the tips of her boots only just touching the unforgiving rock they stood on. Aremys was off his horse in a blink, unsure of what to do.

Cailech dragged Ylena even closer. "Don't you dare use that high-handed Morgravian tone with me, Lady Ylena. Remember, you breathe only because I allow it."

"Then disallow it, sire," Wyl taunted. "Kill me now as you threaten. I don't wish to marry you. I would sooner die. Why can't you understand that I went to Celimus to lose my life?"

The light green gaze narrowed and studied her hard. "You went to Celimus? Willingly?"

Wyl nodded as best he could.

The King let go of Ylena and Wyl explained. "Valentyna

was as determined not to release me from her protection as I was to leave it. She could not help me, sire. But I could help her. Presenting myself to Celimus as if I had been sent by his bride-to-be meant I could probably get the Legion called away from Briavel's borders. Celimus is unpredictable and Valentyna is headstrong; their engagement has been threatened by Morgravia's aggression. So I made the sacrifice."

"Why? Why do you owe her anything?"

Wyl had no ready answer to that question. "Because Wyl died trying to save her, to save her father. My brother must have had good reason to swap his allegiance to Briavel, sire. Can you imagine a Thirsk doing that without cause?"

Cailech said nothing, only continued to stare at Ylena. Wyl looked toward Aremys, whose expression begged him to win back Cailech's trust. "I decided to give what little I had to my brother's cause, my lord. I have no reason to live. Queen Valentyna has every reason to. Don't be misled, my king, Valentyna alone is what stands between Celimus and the Razor Kingdom."

"How so?"

"I think she can influence him. If she handles this right, Valentyna might just guide him from the path of war."

"I don't know her but I agree," Cailech admitted. "Although something happened back there at Felrawthy. I can't be sure but my instincts usually serve me true. I believe Celimus might hold to the promise we made to each other."

"And you, my lord?"

"I have no reason to start a war, my lady, or I would not have wasted my own time or breath in meeting with Celimus."

"I would be lying if I said I was not impressed."

"Perhaps we can build on that, then?"

Wyl looked sharply up at Cailech. "What do you mean?"

"I mean, Ylena, that I understand your reluctance to be here and your fear of the Mountain Kingdom, its people, and its sovereign. But perhaps my determination to forge a lasting peace with the south is a place from which we can build this new relationship. Your life is forfeit anywhere outside of the Razors—you do understand that, don't you?"

Wyl nodded.

"Good. Then take my protection. It is mine to bestow on whom I please. I will not rush you, my lady, but I will make you my wife. I have given my word to our neighbor. It is on that understanding that he released you."

Cailech watched Ylena take a breath to interrupt, and hurried on: "I know you wished for death. I could see it in your eyes. But I will not permit such beauty to be wasted, nor such a feisty spirit. You are the last of the great Thirsk family, Ylena. Surely you wish to see its name flourish again?"

Wyl was ill-prepared for Cailech to touch on the very topic that was closest to his heart, one that provoked a storm of emotion and pain in him. He felt Ylena's eyes water and turned away. It was in that moment of despair that he caught sight of a dark shadow that disappeared almost the instant he saw it. Knave! That meant Fynch was here too. Why?

New fears and confusion erupted. He was cold and he was tired. Ylena's fragile body needed rest and it was obvious he could not provoke Cailech into a swift killing. Despite his private anxieties, he could not help but feel his spirits lift at the thought that his friends were close. He would have to go along with Cailech's plan for now and rethink his options once he was inside the fortress.

And so he gave Cailech a response he knew would please the King. "I wish that more than anything in the world, sire. I just cannot see how the Thirsk name can survive."

"Through me, Ylena," Cailech said gently, greatly relieved by her answer and beguiled by her sorrowful beauty. "I give you this pledge: Any child of ours will bear the name of Thirsk. That would also infuriate Celimus, of course, which is really rather satisfying. Does that please you, my lady? I would allow you to call him Fergys or even Wyl to honor your dead."

"It pleases me, sire," Wyl replied, taken aback by Cailech's generosity.

"Then come, my lady. Let me take you to your new home and allow me to show you off to your new people. I will make you a queen, Ylena."

Wyl sighed and dredged up a wan smile for Ylena's face. "You honor me, sire," he said, his mind racing for a way to escape the Razors again, and quickly.

* * *

Fynch could barely raise his head when Knave returned. *It is Wyl, as you warned. I think he is with King Cailech,* the dog said.

The news roused Fynch, although he was too weak to sit up. He squinted his eyes. "How do you know it's the Mountain King?"

*I heard them talking and I saw the men defer to him. Ylena shares his horse and his cloak is far grander than any of the other men who travel with him.*

"How in Shar's name could this have occurred?"

*From what I could gather, Wyl was at Briavel but somehow convinced Valentyna to hand him over to Celimus.*

"Celimus! Where is he?"

*I couldn't tell from their conversation. But I do know Wyl tried to get himself killed.*

"He cannot invite death!" Fynch exclaimed, coughing. Knave saw blood on the boy's hand when he took it away from his mouth. "Elysius mentioned it to us, remember—after Wyl stormed out of the cottage in the Wild?"

*I do. He risks much—the King got angry but fortunately took no action.*

"We've got to see him, Knave," Fynch bleated, feeling helpless.

*You don't seem so well.* Knave deliberately kept his voice toneless.

"I'll be all right," Fynch replied, lying. He did not fool Knave.

*Stand up, then. Let's be on our way.* The dog loped off.

Fynch tried and failed. Tried again. Knave reappeared, looming over him. "I'm so sorry," the boy whispered.

The dog hardly heard the apology. *You can't stay here, Fynch. It's too open. The warrior scouts could pick you up.*

"I can drag myself somewhere perhaps?" the boy offered, feeling ashamed.

*Use what strength you have to climb onto me.*

It was obvious that Fynch understood the depth of his sickness or Knave knew he would have objected. Instead the boy used his reserves of will to drape himself across the large animal's back.

*I'm sorry, Knave.*

*Don't send! Save yourself. Now let me get you somewhere safe and dry.*

Knave moved silently and slowly, picking his way over the rocky ground, careful not to dislodge the child lying across him. He hardly felt the weight. The boy fell asleep and the dog was relieved. With sleep there would be no pain.

Where could he take Fynch? Perhaps the Thicket could send them to a safe spot. It had done so before when they were traveling. He called to the magical place; disappointment knifed through him when it replied and he learned that he was no longer connected to it as he had been before. He could feel its magic but only through Fynch's link. Knave no longer had its powers at his call.

He pressed on toward a ridge and sent a plea to whoever might be listening that there would be some protection here from the elements. He hoped that it would not be the final resting place of Fynch the gong boy.

Kestrel had tried to reach Fynch but could not raise a response. He had followed the pretty woman and her companion as far as the outskirts of the big southern city known as Pearlis. It was obvious they were headed into its center and he would lose them among the crowds. He sighed as he watched the two blend into the constant flow of people either making for or leaving the main city gates; time for him to leave. Kestrel dipped his wing to the right and made a new course. It was warmer here and he would not have minded a few days of hunting with the sun warming his outstretched wings. Here in the south spring was already turning its face to welcome summer, but the north was where Kestrel was headed—to cooler climes and an intriguing young lad who dared to call himself King of the Creatures.

Elspyth had no idea that the bird of prey had just bade her farewell. She was not feeling at all well and, for all her bravado, thanked Shar's blessing that he had seen fit to send her an angel in the guise of Crys Donal. Her injuries reminded her constantly of her ordeal and the pain sapped her energy. She would never have made it into Morgravia without Crys's strong arms and guiding presence. Reaching Yentro seemed wishful thinking, and the Razors and Lothryn a plain impossibility now.

Self-pity was corrosive and pointless. She pushed away the melancholy that threatened to overwhelm her and permitted Crys to use his body to shield her against the sudden crush of people. They had traveled in the cart until they neared the city and then left it at the roadside for some fortunate finder. Crys's horse carried them both from there, but progress was slow because of the stream of people flocking into and out of Pearlis. Still, it was not nearly as crowded as it had been on Elspyth's last journey into the city, when she had arrived with her aged aunt for the tournament. That felt like a lifetime ago, and yet she would have fingers to spare if she counted back in moons. Had it really been such a short period since she had first clapped eyes on Romen Koreldy in Yentro, before she had learned that he was no longer the dashing mercenary but General Wyl Thirsk of Morgravia?

She thought about Wyl as Ylena—felt a pang of sorrow for his suffering and wondered where he was now. Was Ylena already dead and Wyl walking as someone new?

"A regal for your thoughts?" Crys murmured from behind.

"That you're clutching me too close," Elspyth replied.

He squeezed her harder. "My only legitimate chance," he said.

She ignored his jest. "Is the gate into Pearlis always this busy?"

"Yes, so I gather. Still, it was a good idea of yours to abandon the cart and expensive clothes."

"How does it feel to be an ordinary citizen?"

"Better. For the time being the Donal name is cursed."

"We'd better think of a name for you."

"I can be your brother, how's that?"

"I approve. I've always wanted a brother."

"And if you had one, what would you call him?"

"Jonothon."

"Then that's who I am for the time being. I'll hop down and lead you in on the horse. Hopefully we'll slip by unnoticed."

"There's no register at Pearlis," Elspyth offered.

"Nevertheless, some bright spark might recognize me. Alyd and I are . . . *were* incredibly alike in appearance."

"Good idea to tie your hair back like that, then."

"Thank you, sister. Here we go. Don't look anyone in the eye, but don't avert your gaze too obviously."

"Can't we just talk? You're making me nervous with your instructions."

"So how old would Cousin Jemma be now?" Crys replied smoothly.

They were passing through the main gate and Elspyth risked a laugh toward Crys. "Oh, I think she'd be marriageable age. I hear she's very pretty."

"I don't like flaxen-haired women. I like dark haired beauties, as you well know," Crys continued conversationally. He nodded at a guard, who ignored him, and then he laughed. "I am not marrying her even if it does mean you can come and live in the city."

"We're through," Elspyth said, touching his shoulder with relief.

"Well done."

"Now where to?"

"Lord and Lady Bench are old friends of our family, and they will be able to get some medicines for your pain. You look pale."

"Are you sure we'll be welcome?"

Crys grinned his reassurance. "Trust me."

"Famous last words." She groaned, but felt safe for his confidence. She could tell that the wound on her shoulder had reopened and was glad her cloak was dark enough not to give away their secret. "Let's hurry."

It took longer than Crys had anticipated to wend their way into the quieter, more affluent neighborhood where Lord and Lady Bench kept their family home. In the end, he stabled their horse and hailed a carriage to take them the final half mile.

"This is better, Elspyth. If for any reason their house is being watched . . ."

"Why would it be?" she asked, collapsing into the seat.

Crys gave the driver instructions. "I don't know," he said patiently. "But I highly doubt that Celimus would allow one of the most powerful men left in this kingdom to go about his business without some form of observation."

Elspyth nodded. She did not want to talk anymore. It was all she could do just to hold herself together. The pain had stepped up to a most determined throb, she could feel heat at the shoulder wound, and her head was pounding.

"Infection," Crys muttered when she told him. "You need a physic. The Benches will see to it."

"Let's hope they're home."

Fortunately the Bench mansion was encircled by a huge privet hedge and the driver was able to take them into the sweeping driveway and unload them unseen. Crys paid him some extra coin; it might buy silence should it prove necessary. Then he all but carried Elspyth to the door, which was swiftly opened by a dour-faced servant.

"Is the family at home?" Crys inquired.

"That depends, sir," the man said, looking the shabby couple up and down. "Who is calling?"

"If Lord Bench is in residence please inform him that . . ." Crys hesitated; perhaps this fellow could not be trusted. It paid to be cautious. "Tell him it is an old family friend from Brightstone." Crys remembered that the Bench family had a seaside property in the far northwest.

"I will need a name, sir," the servant said with irritating condescension, closing his eyes as he contrived a fake smile.

Crys took a breath. "Just say it's Booty. Now hurry, man, this woman needs medical attention." Elspyth felt like deadweight in his arms, although she was conscious and gave him a brave grin as the manservant disappeared.

"Booty?" she asked.

"My father's old nickname for Lord Bench. Apparently there's no item he can't appropriate if he sets his mind to it."

They stood in awkward silence for a minute, then suddenly a plump, powdered woman came bustling through some double doors, closely followed by a tall, silver-haired gentleman.

"Shar's wrath!" the woman exclaimed. "Is that woman sick?"

"She is, my lady, and urgently requires attention."

Before Crys had finished speaking, the older woman had turned to the manservant. "Arnyld, why are you still standing there? Send a runner for my physician at once! Tell Physic Dredge to waste no time." She turned back to Crys. "Put her over here, son," she said gently, pointing to a long low bench seat.

"I'm bleeding, my lady," Elspyth began, "I'll ruin—"

"Hush, child," the woman admonished. "Do as you are told." Elspyth obeyed immediately, sinking to the bench.

Crys took his chance while there were no servants visible, turning and bowing to Lord Bench. He was met by a grim-faced stare.

"I wondered who had the audacity to use old Jeryb's nickname for me to gain entry," Eryd Bench said in his melodious voice. "Introduce yourself truly now, before I call a Legionnaire."

"Lord and Lady Bench, my apologies for arriving in this manner, but circumstances demand it. I am Crys Donal, Duke of Felrawthy."

The couple standing before him blanched. Lady Bench reached for her husband, who helped her sit down next to Elspyth. Crys, looking at their pale expressions, was relieved to know the physic was on his way.

# 27

NAVE WHINED SOFTLY, HIS GREAT HEAD ON HIS PAWS, HIS body encircling the sleeping boy, whose breathing sounded dangerously shallow. Something was happening to Fynch, but his close companion could not reach him. All he could do was watch, wait, and pray to the Dragon King that this was not Fynch's time.

Fynch was dreaming. He felt himself flying; the wind

whipped through his hair and whistled past his ears. For a dream, the view around him looked awfully real, and the wind was shockingly brisk.

A voice suddenly spoke into Fynch's mind, and he knew it could not be a dream. *Not long now.*

It was the Dragon King and Fynch realized he was riding him, feeling each powerful beat of his wings as they worked in tandem to drive the creature faster through the air.

*My king,* Fynch sent, his voice unashamedly filled with awe. *Where do we go?*

*To a private place, my son. Somewhere safe. Where you will be free from your pain and where no one can hear us.*

*Am I truly with you?*

*Your body is with Knave, Fynch. Your spirit is here.*

*How can I do this?*

*It's my way of honoring you.*

*Honoring me?*

*We ask so much of you.*

*Whatever you ask, sire, I give it gladly.*

*Brave boy. You are more than worthy.*

*Of what, my lord?*

*Of Kingship, Fynch.*

*I don't understand, my king.*

*You will, my son. That is why I have brought you here.*

Wyl felt a sense of despair as they entered the gates of the fortress. Cailech was immediately surrounded by well-wishers welcoming him back, and stealing interested glances toward the golden-haired beauty he had left on the horse. It was Myrt who arrived at Ylena's side to help her dismount.

"May I show you to your rooms, my lady?" he asked, taking her hand to help her from the horse, much to Wyl's discomfort. "The King has requested you dine with him later."

Wyl reached for a gracious smile, though the invitation reminded him of the meeting with Celimus he had been forced to attend while trapped in Leyen. "Thank you, er . . .?"

"Myrt." Aremys appeared at Wyl's side and now offered the formal introduction. "He is a friend, Ylena. You can trust him."

Wyl nodded toward Myrt, who gave one of his rare smiles. Aremys had already explained that Myrt knew about Aremys's suspicions about Lothryn's fate, but as the mercenary obviously could not come clean about Ylena, he would have to remain polite but distant to Wyl's sister.

"I will see you later perhaps?" Aremys said to Wyl, and then to Myrt: "Shall we meet at the stables?"

The big warrior nodded. "Come, my lady," he said, and Wyl had no option but to be guided away, deeper into the fortress of the Mountain King.

Fynch remained curled on the Dragon King's vast back, though the creature had landed. Its darkly vibrant colors seemed to pulse bright one moment and soft the next, illuminating its scales. Fynch felt warm and safe for the first time since leaving the Wild, even though he knew he was not really here. Physically, he remained on a freezing ledge near the home of the Mountain King and he was dying, with Knave's body curled around him.

He twisted to lie on his back, loving the deep connection between himself and the Dragon King. The magnificent beast remained silent while his guest acclimatized himself to the breathtaking scene below. They were on the highest peak of the Razors, but not in the northeast, where Fynch's body lay.

*Are we in the Wild, my lord?*

*Yes, Fynch.*

The boy sighed. *If I died now amid this beauty, my king, I would die happy.*

The King did not reply.

*I am dying, aren't I, sire?*

*You have pushed yourself too hard. The magic you have called upon is so potent it is poisoning you.*

*Elysius managed to live with it,* Fynch said.

*True, my son. But Elysius did not draw upon the magic of the Thicket, nor was he required to use magic for years on end. He preserved himself by using it sparingly.*

*I am sorry I have been so careless with it.*

The Dragon King twisted his sinuous neck and the massive head came close. A monstrously large eye regarded the tiny figure that lay on its back. *You need make no apology to me, Faith Fynch.*

It moved Fynch to hear these solemn words and tears ran down his face. *I am not afraid to give my life, my lord—I hope you know this. But I am so afraid of failing you that I am impatient to reach Rashlyn.*

The Dragon King gave a murmured growl of agreement. *I know, child. You will not fail us.*

*But I am not sure I can recover in time, my king. I will likely end my life where Knave and I lie.*

*That is why I have brought you here, Fynch,* the King said, his voice so deep the boy could feel it rumbling the length of his own body, despite the gentleness of its tone. *I shall restore you. But, as always with magic, there is a price.*

*I will pay it,* Fynch said bravely. *I wish only for my strength to return so I may to do your bidding.*

*I accept your sacrifice, and in return you deserve an explanation. I have seen something in you, Fynch, that you must know.*

*I felt it too, my lord,* the boy admitted. *I sensed you recognizing a part of me I barely know myself.*

*Can you not guess, child?*

Fynch considered the King's question and closed his eyes. Yes, he could guess, but was this something he truly wanted to know? He assumed the price he must pay for the temporary restoration of his health was death, had already accepted as much. If it had to be sooner rather than later, he would not fuss. He made his decision.

*It is connected with my mother, I feel.*

*Go on.*

Fynch felt a breeze break through the protective wings of the huge beast and brush against his cheeks. More tears were falling, but he ignored them. He was not crying because he was sad or frightened; he was weeping because this was the most emotional moment of his life. The Dragon King was about to confirm something he had always known but had held buried within, a secret with far-reaching repercussions. If revealed, it could affect the course of a realm.

*I believe I am not of my named father's flesh.*

A tremble passed through the Dragon King. *You are correct, my son. So who fathered you?*

Fynch did not want to speak the name. He didn't know why he was so sure it was the truth; all he knew was that he had glimpsed it within himself the moment the Dragon King saw it. While it had surprised the King of the Creatures, for some reason it had not surprised Fynch.

The boy looked out again over the majesty of the Razors, hidden valleys emerging from beneath the snows as spring staked its claim.

*I didn't know it would thaw this high up.*

*We are in the Wild, my son. Everything is possible.*

Fynch nodded. The Dragon King was not rushing him to answer, but now it was time. *My mother was fey. At each new moon she would experience a sort of madness. The madness took the form of lust.* He hesitated.

*Go on, Fynch.*

*She would tempt other men. She had no control over it. And?*

*I was conceived during one of those moon times.*

*Yes, you were. Who is your father, Fynch?*

*My father is . . .* He almost dared not speak the name but knew he must. *My father was Magnus, King of Morgravia.*

*Indeed. You are part of the dragon throne line and thus a part of me.*

*Was Magnus aware of who I was during our conversations at Stoneheart?*

*He felt a strong connection to you, Fynch, as you did with him. But no, he never knew you were of his flesh.*

At the great creature's final word, Fynch felt a rush of sadness. It washed over him like a crashing wave but settled finally into peace—the peace that comes with the finality of suspicions confirmed and a puzzle solved. A new sensation took over; a feeling of warmth. He did not know whether it was the dragon himself—but he was aware of some sort of new link between that creature and himself.

Suddenly he felt a sense of intense belonging . . . to both Kings, Magnus and the Dragon.

## 28

LORD AND LADY BENCH SAT WITH ELSPYTH AND CRYS IN THE
Benches' drawing room, which was hung with family
portraits and softened with lush furnishings and drapings.
Elspyth, determined not to miss out on the conversation, was
propped in a comfortable chair. Helyn Bench's physic had
examined her and declared that the wounds were neatly sutured; infection had set in only at the shoulder. Fortunately
it had been caught in time and the physic promised to send
over a special brew that would clear up the problem within
days. Rest and quiet were also integral to the healing. Helyn
had not hesitated in confirming that Elspyth would remain
with them until she was fit and well.

"I cannot impose on you for so long, my lady," Elspyth
had protested.

"Child, you'll be going nowhere until the fever is gone
and the infection has cleared," Helyn had cautioned, and Elspyth understood there would be no arguing with the powerful woman.

Now the Benches and their guests reclined comfortably.
Crys and Elspyth had related the worst part of their tale. A
small porcelain brazier burned gently in the corner of the
room. Elspyth thought it similar to those the Mountain People favored and said so.

"As a matter of fact, it is from Grenadyn," Eryd replied,
"but I'm impressed that you have seen one in the Razor
Kingdom and intrigued as to how you lived to tell the
tale."

Elspyth blushed. "It is a long story, sir, and after the one
we've just told you, I can't imagine you would want more of

the same," she said, hoping to deflect his attention from the story of how she came to be so far north.

"Indeed," he said, eyeing her gravely but not pursuing it. After the story of the murder of the Donals, the Benches were already in a state of shock. "Crys, I regret having to tax you further on this subject, but are you quite sure that the Crown was behind the slaughter at Tenterdyn?"

Crys nodded. "My mother died in my arms and her last wish was for revenge. Her haunted eyes spoke of the horrors she had witnessed—the killing of my father and brothers and then the burning of their bodies. The massacre at Rittylworth was also definitely the work of Celimus—Ylena Thirsk confirmed it and Elspyth happened along quite soon after the raiders had left. She took the message from Brother Jakub to my father."

Helyn handed Crys a goblet of wine. "None for you, I'm afraid, Elspyth. Sorry, please go on," she added, smiling softly at the young Duke.

Crys hoped the tremble in his voice would disappear with the help of the liquor. "As I explained, we have been at Queen Valentyna's court. She offered her protection without question. I hadn't expected the diversion of tracking down Elspyth," he said, "or I would have been here much earlier."

"What can we do?" Lord Bench asked. "I feel so helpless."

"Wy—" Crys stopped himself in time. "Ylena suggested that I come to Pearlis and try to stir up some trouble for the King."

"Ylena Thirsk did? Where is that girl now?" Lord Bench demanded. "To tell the truth, I thought she must have gone home to Argorn after Wyl's death. Now that we know about her husband's murder, all the more reason for her to flee Stoneheart."

"No, sir. Ylena was thrown into Stoneheart's dungeons. A mercenary called Romen Koreldy rescued her." Crys quickly outlined how Koreldy fit into the tale, manipulating the truth by telling them that he had made a promise to the dying Wyl to find his sister. "Then, after escaping Rittylworth, Ylena fled to Felrawthy. She carried proof of my brother's murder there with her—which is why Celimus sent his assassin to find her. Leyen, of course, never—" He stopped abruptly as both his hosts flinched with obvious alarm. "Is something wrong?"

"Leyen?" Lady Bench said, her expression aghast. "Is that the name you used?"

Crys nodded, glancing toward Elspyth.

"Can you describe her?"

Discomfited by Lady Bench's interest, Crys gave a quick summary of Leyen's appearance.

"But that's her!" Helyn exclaimed. "I know this woman. She came to our house, for Shar's sake. I have been protecting her from Celimus since I first met her and he began asking questions about her. She told me she was a messenger—a go-between for the King and Queen Valentyna!" Exasperation rang in her tone.

"She is an assassin, you say?" Eryd said gravely, looking toward his wife to be calm.

"Well . . ." Crys hesitated. He had made a mistake, should have used the name Aremys Farrow. But how was he to know that the Bench family would know Faryl?

"Out with it, young man," Eryd urged. Duke or not, Crys was still a young pup in Lord Bench's eyes. It was inconceivable to him, even after days of trying to accept it, that Jeryb Donal was dead. The old rogue had been stronger than several oxen; he had been destined to outlive them all. Friendship aside, it upset Eryd deeply to think that Morgravia had lost not just such a fine man but also its finest remaining strategist and soldier. Celimus would pay for that loss.

Crys looked helplessly toward Elspyth. She knew he was trapped by duty whichever way he turned: to his parents, to the realm, to these fine people, to a friend. She hesitated, and then impulsively leaned forward.

"My lord, my lady," she interrupted. "I have a story to tell that you will not want to believe—no doubt won't be able to believe once you have heard it. But I am telling you the truth, for I have borne witness to it with my own eyes."

"As have I," Crys joined in, a mixture of terror and relief flooding his body as he saw that Elspyth had made the decision for him. He hated breaking oath with Wyl, but he hated lying to Lord Eryd Bench even more, particularly as the old man reminded him so much of his own father. And the truth was, they needed allies. Someone had to help share the burden of Wyl's woes. It had sounded fair enough at Tenterdyn to keep this terrible secret, but someone in power had to know of Myrren's Gift. Others must be convinced to rally to Wyl's cause.

Eryd glanced between them. "This sounds dire," he said. He had thought he had heard their worst, but it seemed far more terrible information was yet to be revealed.

"Why do I suddenly feel I don't want to hear what you're about to tell us?" Helyn Bench added, surprised herself that she could resist a tantalizing tale.

"You might regret our sharing this with you, Lord and Lady Bench. But once told, you must promise us you will aid us and act upon it."

"My dear," Helyn said, now truly wishing she had joined her daughter, Georgyana, for a day of shopping, "you make it all sound so sinister. What is this about?"

"It is the story of Wyl Thirsk, my lady, and I shall tell you everything I know, even though he will never forgive me for sharing it."

Elspyth began.

As Elspyth was sharing Wyl's story with a stunned couple in Pearlis, Wyl, in the Razors, was explaining to the women attending Ylena that he preferred not to wear either of the two dresses that had been brought to his chamber.

Cailech had commandeered a suite of rooms as accommodations for Ylena. Once again, Wyl was arrested by the simple beauty of the Mountain People's creativity. A fresco of vines and their fruit trailed the perimeter of each room's ceiling and the whitewashed walls were hung with paintings of the stark Razor landscape. A thick rug on the floor and an equally colorful bedspread added yet more brightness to the natural light flooding in through the huge windows favored by the King throughout the fortress; he liked to bring the mountainscape he loved inside.

The last time Wyl had been in this stonghold, as Koreldy, braziers had warmed each room. Only the endless hallways and cavernous spaces connecting the chambers had been left unheated, and those had been freezing, he recalled. But it was well into spring now and the hardy Mountain People had done away with the heating.

Ylena's body trembled from the cold as Wyl tried again to politely decline the garments. "Thank you, but I prefer my trews," he said.

"Both gowns are woven from the coat of polders, my lady," one of the women assured. Her tone suggested that this was equivalent to being spun from gold.

Wyl was none the wiser for the explanation but was courteous enough to touch the dress and smile. "It is very beautiful," he agreed.

"Please, my lady, we will get into trouble if you do not wear one of these dresses."

"Oh, surely not."

They nodded. "Our king told us to dress your hair as well. He has had fresh thawdrops brought up from the valley."

Wyl looked toward where the women glanced. He had not noticed the vase holding the tiny white flowers Cailech had promised to pick for Ylena. He felt more trapped than ever, and wished he could reach Aremys. Perhaps he should just make a run for it. He could hope someone would bring him down—if he were lucky, kill him. It would likely be a Razor warrior and then at least he could inhabit the body of a man again . . . but if he was felled by an arrow, he might not live to avenge those who had been murdered, or see Valentyna again.

Valentyna. His heart ached as he remembered the disturbed and disgusted expression she had worn the last time they were together. If only he could be a man again, he would somehow make it up to her . . . even if only to apologize on Ylena's behalf for his stupidity.

He realized suddenly that the women were staring at him and the silence had stretched embarrassingly long.

*For you, then, Valentyna,* he decided, and nodded to the waiting women. "Which one suits me best, do you think?"

The women beamed. One reached out and touched Ylena's hair. "You are so beautiful, you would do either of them justice." Then she took Ylena's hand. "We have longed for the day when our king would take a woman for his own," she said shyly.

Wyl was touched in spite of the horror he felt. "Do you not mind that I am Morgravian?"

She shrugged and looked toward her companion, who made a similar gesture. "That you have captured his heart is enough. We do not question his choice, and in truth there is no one suitable within our own kingdom. Whoever he chose to marry, it would have caused jealousy among the factions. You have no allegiance to any Mountain family. This way he offends no one. And, my lady, rumors abound that our two kingdoms have signed a peace treaty. This makes your marriage to our king even more special. How could we not accept the woman our king loves?"

"Loves?" Wyl repeated, aghast. "He doesn't even know me."

"The King is a great judge of character," the woman said stubbornly.

"He's told you we are to be married?" Wyl asked, further alarmed.

They nodded. "Oh yes," the other woman said. "The news is spreading like fire around the fortress."

"And has he said when?" Wyl held his breath.

They hesitated, sensing his trepidation. "The day after tomorrow, my lady," the older one said finally. "A gown is being stitched from pure white polder—our most rare color. Animals are being slaughtered today for the feast and people are already gathering to catch a glimpse of you."

They saw the noblewoman's hands fly to her face and press against each cheek in horror. Her look of desperation frightened them.

"He will be gentle with you, my lady," the older one assured, imagining the angelic beauty was fearing for her wedding night.

"Oh, stop, please," Wyl said, determined now to find a way to flee or bring about his own death. He remembered the warning from Elysius with despair. It was not possible for him to invite his own death. But randomness was still possible, as young Fynch had assured him. That was what he needed now to save him. A random act—be it madness, violence, or anger. Whatever occurred, he had to be rid of Ylena's guise within the next few hours.

"You're sure of this?" Myrt hissed in a whisper.

Aremys nodded, trying to look nonchalant as he lifted the latch on the side door leading into the stable. He forced himself not to glance over his shoulder. "Where's Maegryn?"

"He's always around somewhere. You'd better have a story at the ready if we're caught."

"Perhaps you should wait outside," Aremys suggested. "I can't risk you getting into trouble with Cailech. Once you're committed, there's no going back."

Myrt shook his head. "I have to see the horse for myself."

The set of his friend's mouth assured Aremys there would be no further discussion. He nodded and stepped into the darkness. His eyes took a few moments to adjust to the minimal light that filtered through the stable's timber boards. A snort told him Galapek was in the shadows to his right. He immediately began whispering a stream of soft words to the creature.

Myrt closed the door and remained silent behind Aremys. He realized he was holding his breath. He watched Aremys raise his hand and place it on the animal's majestic face, and as man and beast touched, he felt a surge of emotion. Was this really Lothryn?

"Lothryn," Aremys murmured. "If you're there, give us a sign. I've brought Myrt." He nodded at Myrt to step forward. "Say something," he whispered.

Myrt moved from behind the Grenadyne and cleared his throat. "If that's you, my friend, prove it."

"I can feel the magic shivering through his body," Aremys said. "He's fighting it; that's why his flesh is trembling." He turned back to Galapek. "Come on, Lothryn, do it for Elspyth. She's alive. She's coming for you. And Wyl's here too!"

The horse reared up onto its hind legs and squealed. Aremys fell to the floor, pain filling his head as a voice, equally pain-filled, growled into his mind, *Turn me loose!*

"It's him!" Myrt whispered as he tried to calm the horse, which was kicking and pounding at the wall. "Quick! He could hurt you."

"He won't hurt me," the Grenadyne said, disgusted with himself for falling. His head throbbed but his satisfaction was intense, as was the awe this sickening magic inspired in him. "It is him, Myrt. He spoke to me. He wants to be turned loose."

The warrior turned an anxious gaze toward him. "What do we do?"

Aremys frowned, as much with frustration as with helplessness. "Well, we can't just let him go. We have to think this through. There's Gueryn to consider, too."

"Forgive me if I don't lose any sleep over a Morgravian soldier," Myrt said. "I care only about Lothryn."

"Understood. Listen—" He got no further. A sudden shaft of sunlight made them both swing around toward the side door where Maegryn had just entered the stable.

"Myrt? What are you doing here? And that's the Grenadyne with you, isn't it?"

Myrt was not as adept at lying as Aremys and his hesitation, as well as the guilty glance toward his companion, was telling. "I . . . that is, we . . ."

"We got back today," Aremys continued smoothly for his faltering friend. "I was hoping we could go for a ride."

Maegryn looked quizzically at them. "But you've been riding for days."

"That's true," Aremys agreed, mentally kicking himself and giving an embarrassed grin. "A lot has happened these past few days, Maegryn. I felt like being as alone as I am permitted to be. Can't think of a better place than in Galapek's saddle."

"Surely you weren't thinking of taking the King's horse without his or my permission?"

"Of course not," Myrt said, regaining his composure. "We were just passing and thought we'd look in on the animal.

Aremys is fond of him—brought him a red apple because he knows he hates green ones."

The stablemaster was not to be put off so easily. "I heard Galapek. What was all the noise about?"

Both men shrugged and Aremys knew they looked more guilty for that single gesture than for any of their stammered responses or awkward pauses. He could tell from the guarded look in the stablemaster's eyes that Maegryn was suspicious of their intentions.

"Where are you going?" Aremys said when the man turned away. He knew very well where Maegryn was headed, but he was desperately stalling for time.

"The King, if he'll see me. I'm sorry but I have my orders."

"Who from?" Myrt demanded.

"Rashlyn."

"Since when do you take orders from him?" Myrt spat.

"Since le Gant went missing," the stablemaster replied. "The barshi insisted that anyone acting suspiciously around the King's horse would meet the same fate."

Aremys felt a chill move through him. "What do you mean, 'fate'?"

Maegryn shrugged, fortunately not realizing that Aremys had no way of knowing of the Morgravian prisoner. "According to the barshi, le Gant has been dealt with."

"Dealt with!" Myrt repeated. "I thought only the King made decisions about our prisoners?"

"Listen, Myrt," Maegryn began, his anger stoking fast now. "I hate Rashlyn. You of all people should know that. But I won't interfere in the King's business—you should know that, too. Lothryn, Haldor rest his soul, learned the hard way about crossing the King. I don't intend to be given into Rashlyn's keeping because I've invoked the ire of King Cailech. I can't help you."

"Is that what's happened?" Aremys pressed. "Rashlyn took le Gant?"

Maegryn looked down. "I don't know what's happened. I suspect Rashlyn took him from the dungeon, yes."

"What are we coming to, Maegryn, when we are too

scared to speak out?" Myrt asked. He did not mean it as an accusation; it was more a sad-sounding reflection on his own shortcomings.

"Lothryn stood up to the King and Lothryn paid the price!" Maegryn yelled. "I don't have his courage."

"True. And where is Lothryn, do you think?" Myrt asked, advancing on the stablemaster.

"Be careful, Myrt," Aremys murmured. His senses had become highly attuned over the years to the feelings of men in a blood rage, and Myrt seemed close to losing control of his emotions.

"I . . . I don't know. Dead, I suppose," Maegryn answered, stepping back. "Don't threaten me, Myrt."

"An honorable death, do you think?"

Maegryn nodded slowly, uncertainly.

"He's not dead. He's alive!" Myrt boomed, close to Maegryn's face. "Rashlyn told us as much. It's just taken me a while to work it out."

Maegryn's expression was shocked now. "Alive? Where?"

"Here, Maegryn. Right beneath your nose," Myrt said, a cruel tone to his voice that Aremys had never heard before. Myrt was too upset. This was dangerous.

The stablemaster frowned, stepped back again, closer to the door. "What are you talking about?"

"I'm talking about magic, Maegryn. I'm talking about Rashlyn and his sinister ways."

"I don't understand," the man muttered, licking his lips nervously. He looked deeply scared now, as if he too sensed that the situation had turned nasty.

"You'd be right to feel petrified," Myrt went on, noting the man's fear. "Lothryn is in your care."

Maegryn's eyes widened, the nonsense of Myrt's words giving him courage. "You're talking in riddles, man. What's he saying, Grenadyne?"

Aremys hesitated. Myrt's emotions had gotten the better of him. Sharing what they knew with Maegryn, who was as loyal to Cailech as any of his warriors and did not share Myrt's single-minded dedication to Lothryn, was a dangerous idea. "Maegryn," he started, his mind racing, "it's going to be hard for you to believe us—"

"Galapek *is* Lothryn, you fool!" Myrt interrupted, spitting his fury and advancing on the cringing stablemaster. "Rashlyn, with the King's permission, used his dark magic to change him into Galapek. That's why you don't know where the horse came from, and why the King is so careful about who rides him or asks questions about him. And that's also why you've been sworn to secrecy. You've always known there was something odd about the whole situation surrounding the horse. Admit it, damn you!"

"Lothryn?" Maegryn repeated, shaking his head in confusion. He looked at the huge horse and saw the anger in its eyes then returned his anxious gaze to Myrt. "No," he said, his head moving slowly from side to side in denial.

"You know it's true, Maegryn. You've had doubts of your own from the start. Right from the beginning when Cailech said he would break this horse's spirit and earn its loyalty with trust. What do you think that whole charade was about, eh? The King was humiliating Loth, destroying his closest friend, his truest follower, and then rebuilding him in the form of a beast. A mute beast that would have to carry the King on his back for the rest of his life and thus pay homage like any slave or lowlife. An honorable death was too good for our best warrior, Maegryn. The King wanted to make him pay; he wanted revenge and humiliation for Loth's betrayal."

Maegryn retaliated, reacting to the pain of the truth he knew he was hearing. "Lothryn chose the Morgravian woman over his own king, his own people!" he cried.

"And he deserved to become this, did he?" Myrt boomed. "An animal! He still lives, Maegryn. That's the worst of it. He knows. He's trapped inside that body, in agonizing pain."

The stablemaster shook his head again, as though he himself were in pain. "No. This isn't true. Can you prove it?" he demanded, looking between the two men. "Show me how this is Lothryn. How can you know?"

Aremys answered in a tone of such resignation, Myrt knew they had lost the opportunity of convincing Maegryn. "I can feel the taint of the filthy magic."

"That's it, Grenadyne—your word? And what . . . you are gifted with sentient power?" He looked at his fellow Mountain Man. "Have you gone mad, Myrt? You would trust this foreigner over your own king?"

"It's the truth, Maegryn."

The stablemaster gave a harsh laugh, feeling a small measure of control return. "The truth?" he scorned. "Says who? Another prisoner? For that's what he is. I have no gripe with you, Farrow, but don't ask me to take your word over that of my king."

Aremys said nothing, knew nothing he could say would change the stablemaster's mind.

"You don't know anything of substance, Myrt," Maegryn continued. "You're just believing the Grenadyne. Have you heard Lothryn speak? Has the horse communicated anything to you?"

Myrt shook his head, anger trembling through his body. "He spoke only to Aremys."

"To Aremys!" Maegryn repeated, still more scorn in his tone. "No proof, nothing but this man's say-so, and you're prepared to believe that Lothryn has been turned into a horse. Does that not sound ridiculous to you?"

Myrt nodded. "It does, but not when you say that same sentence with Rashlyn's name attached to it. The barshi is evil and you know it. His influence on the king is dangerous. Lothryn felt it and said as much to me. I don't think our king ordered this. I think Rashlyn did. I believe, as Lothryn did, that the barshi is able to sway the King against his own wishes."

"Rashlyn uses magic against the King?" Maegryn clarified, aghast.

"Yes. That's what I now believe. I think he can persuade Cailech to agree to things he would not choose himself."

Maegryn put his hands up in a warding gesture. "That's enough, Myrt. I don't want to hear any more. You speak treachery against our sovereign and it is my sworn duty as one of his men to make this betrayal public. I'm sorry."

The stablemaster had just opened the door when he felt the breath cut off from his lungs as huge, powerful hands closed around his throat. He let go of the door's iron ring, gasping. Fear pounded through his ears and the blood pumped desperately through squeezed veins and arteries. As if from far away, he heard the Grenadyne shouting at Myrt. He found enough strength to twist around to see through his bulging eyes the rage in the bigger man's face, but he could not loosen the warrior's grip to beg for life. "I'm sorry too," were the last words he heard before Myrt intensified the pressure and crushed his victim's neck. Maegryn slumped in his killer's arms, dead.

Aremys, shocked, stood frozen in place. He was angry with himself for not foreseeing Myrt's rage and preventing the killing. But the deed was done. Instead of accusations he offered help. "Where can we hide the body?" he said matter-of-factly. Myrt was in a state of shock, his rage gone the moment Maegryn had died beneath his fingers. He did not reply, crouching instead by the corpse. "Come on, man! It's done with. You can't bring him back. We have to hide him."

"I'm a dead man. We Mountain folk are strict about killing our own kind."

"We're probably both dead men anyway. Come on, help me. We have to hide him and buy some hours."

"For what?" Myrt said hopelessly.

"Everything's going to unravel, my friend. The King is marrying a woman who does not want him and whom he does not know well enough," Aremys responded. "Strange stuff is going to happen—believe me. Time is our enemy now. I know you don't want to, but you have to choose between Lothryn or your king and you have to do it now! This is what I wanted to avoid, why I asked you to remain outside."

Myrt nodded sorrowfully. "I made my choice, Grenadyne. I chose Lothryn."

Aremys continued, more gently this time. "All right, then. We now know we are in the presence of your friend, and we must find a way to release him."

"Can we?" Myrt asked, his spirits lifting.

"By death if necessary," Aremys answered gravely. "We need to find out more from Rashlyn."

"He has Cailech's protection," Myrt warned.

"Not while the King is enamored of Ylena Thirsk, he doesn't. We must get to Rashlyn now . . . and perhaps he will lead us to Gueryn."

"I told you, I don't care about the Morgravian soldier."

"But I do. And so will Ylena Thirsk when she finds out her guardian is a prisoner here."

Myrt looked at him, startled. "Her guardian? Does the King know that?"

Aremys shook his head. "I shouldn't think so but I'm going to tell him. I'll seek an audience with the King. You establish where the barshi is and keep him from Cailech at all costs."

"And Galapek?"

"Will have to be patient a little longer," Aremys said softly, turning to stare at the stallion in the shadows. "Myrt, this choice you've made—you do understand you'll have to leave the Razors?"

"Escape, you mean?"

Aremys nodded. "I won't let you go alone."

The warrior sighed. "This is how Lothryn must have felt. Damned if he did and damned if he didn't. I betray those I love whichever choice I make. I'm sorry, Aremys. I can't promise I'll leave."

It was best not to force the issue, Aremys realized. The circumstances would no doubt make all the decisions for them. "Come on, we've got to hide this body," he said.

Myrt nodded. "I know where."

# 29

LADY HELYN BENCH RELUCTANTLY HELD HER HUSBAND'S jacket as the man she loved slipped his arms into the sleeves. "I wish you wouldn't," she began again.

He turned in her arms and hugged her. "My mind is made up, my dear. I don't like this cloak-and-dagger stuff. I think we must air the grievances tactfully."

"Eryd," she said, fear combining with exasperation, "how tactful can you be when you're about to accuse someone of murder?"

"Indeed," he said, and pointed to a silk scarf. "Would you help me with that, please?"

She flounced to the chair and picked up the length of silk draped across it. "And not just anyone," she continued. "The King!"

"Helyn, in case you haven't noticed over the years, I am not a dimwit."

"Taking witnesses won't stop him!" she cried. "He'll just have you all killed."

"Don't be ridiculous, woman. Kill me and then Lord Hartley? Then I suppose he'd have to kill Lord Jownes and Lord Peaforth because they would follow in our footsteps. And then who else would be left to advise, to cajole, to administer this city? He needs us."

"Please don't go. Don't do this."

"I shall know from the way he reacts whether or not he is lying."

"Eryd!" Helyn pleaded, just short of a screech, hating the way her husband closed his eyes in despair. "Do you believe that the Donals are not dead? Not hacked to bits, raped, burned? Or that the massacre at Rittylworth was a misunderstanding and that the monks are in fact live and well?"

"No, Helyn," he said, and the tone in his voice chilled her. She wished she had not resorted to sarcasm. He was deeply angered now; she had overstepped the mark. "Please do not speak ill of the dead. I am painfully aware of the deaths of my friends the Donal family and the innocent men of Rittylworth."

"I'm sorry, Eryd, I—"

He cut her off, too angry to hear more. "Enough, wife. The three remaining lords of Morgravia cannot disappear! Now hush your ramblings and get this scarf tied, or I shall be late."

"What did you tell the others?" she asked, resigned, understanding there was nothing more she could do to stop her husband from walking into the dragon's den.

"All that we know."

"Not about Wyl Thirsk, surely?"

"No. That revelation I am keeping to myself until I can see this phenomenon with my own eyes."

"Do you believe our guests, though?"

He nodded, slowly, reluctantly. "How could I not? Their tale is so shocking and mysterious, no one could make it up. Jeryb Donal's son would not lie to us, Helyn. You can see it in his face that he is as petrified of this . . . this Myrren's Gift, as they call it, as he is intrigued by it. We have known Crys Donal since he was a babe in arms. He is as open a man as any, I am sure. No, there is no lie there, but I can't accept it fully yet."

"That Wyl Thirsk walks in the body of his sister, you mean?"

"That he was the Koreldy assassin, that he was Leyen, whom you delighted in so much, that, yes, he has become his sister."

"But it does make sense, doesn't it, my love?" she said. "It is odd that a Grenadyne mercenary would bother to rescue his enemy's sister from the dungeon of his benefactor." Eryd nodded. "Then take her to safety before going to look for that Widow Ilyk person."

"Is that the seer's name?"

"Yes. I'm embarrassed to admit that she has done readings for me in the past."

"It's all nonsense, Helyn. You know that," Eryd grumbled.

"I thought so until now," she replied, hurrying on. "Then the Grenadyne is trapped, taken into the Razors, and instead of bargaining his way out—as presumably he could have done with that Mountain King—he risks everything to get Gueryn le Gant and Elspyth away. Does that sound like a hardened mercenary, or like Wyl Thirsk trapped inside the body of one?"

"I agree, Helyn. It's not that I need convincing. I just—"

"So then he makes his way to Briavel to offer his protection to Queen Valentyna. Why? Well, of course, he'd saved her life once before from a potential assassination attempt and had fought to save her father's too, losing his own life in the effort. But then King Celimus comes along and it all goes wrong. Wyl gets killed by the King's own assassin, Leyen—"

"They called her Faryl."

"Whatever her name was. That girl, as much as I liked her—and I guess now it was simply Wyl I was liking all over again—was not used to womanly things."

"What do you mean?"

"Well, the baths. Remember I told you?"

"You must have."

"And you weren't listening as usual," she admonished. "She was so hesitant about going into the pavilion—that's where we first met. She was terribly embarrassed about showing her body, and let me tell you, Eryd, no woman who looks like that is ever coy about her body. She had no idea about the soap leaves, and when I mentioned the razing of Rittylworth, her whole demeanor changed. That's because it was Wyl, fearing for his sister."

Eryd nodded. "I understand, Helyn. I want to believe it, but I believe what I see with my own eyes, not hearsay."

"I know. As you say, though, it's too chilling not to be real. I need no further convincing."

"About what, Mother?" came a light voice, and the Benchs' daughter, Georgyana, slipped into the room.

"Were you listening?" her father asked, anxious that his young, fanciful daughter had heard more than he wished.

"No. But I wouldn't tell you if I had," she answered, and pulled a face at him, at the same time taking his hand and squeezing it. That father and daughter worshiped each other was obvious. Helyn sometimes wondered how they ever found room for her in their lives. "Did you meet our guests, darling?" she said.

"No," Georgyana said, shaking her long golden curls.

"We have visitors downstairs," her father said. "I suppose you came in through the back like a servant?"

"I'm hungry." His daughter pouted. "I wanted to see what was cooking."

"Well, come and meet them," Helyn said, glad of Georgyana's noise and distraction.

"Do I have to?"

"You'll like them," she assured.

"Who are they?"

"The Duke of Felrawthy and a lovely girl called Elspyth, from the north."

"Oh, another stuffy old man like father?" Georgyana said, winking toward Eryd.

"Far from it, my love," Helyn replied. "Crys Donal is one of the best-looking men in Morgravia, and soon to be the most eligible when word gets around of his new status."

"Ooh! What are we waiting for, Mother?" her daughter squealed. "Off you go, Father. Bring me back something small and sparkly."

Eryd rolled his eyes with exasperation. "I am hoping for an audience with the King, Georgyana."

"Well, steal me something from the palace, then." His daughter giggled as she left the chamber.

Helyn gave her husband a searching glance. "My love, please—"

"Don't say it," he warned gently. "You know I will be."

She said nothing and left, fearful of letting herself down with tears.

K nave was amazed at Fynch's recovery. His surprise drew a grin from the boy. "Truly, I am well," he said, stretching. "I'm even hungry."

*No headache?*

"All gone . . . for now."

*How can this be?*

"The King came."

*The Dragon King? Again! He was here?*

The boy nodded. "He came to me in my dreams. I flew with him, Knave. He carried me to the Wild."

*You were here all the time*, Knave said quietly. *I noticed you were restless in your sleep, though. I feared it was pain . . . death.*

Again the boy smiled, gently and without smugness, but Knave noticed something new in his expression. Some knowledge, perhaps.

*I don't mean to pry, Fynch, but you appear miraculously well.*

"I am," Fynch said, laughing. He stood. "And I don't need sharvan either. He healed me."

*The King did?*

"Yes. He said he would restore me so I can fulfill my task."

Suddenly Knave could not look at him; he understood the way of things. *But nothing comes without a price, am I right?* he asked, sadness in his voice.

"Don't dwell on it," Fynch replied softly. "I am at peace, my friend. The King shared something with me that has made me happy. Happier than I have ever felt before."

*And this sharing was a secret?*

The boy nodded.

*I understand, Fynch. I'm glad you feel so well. I hated to watch you suffer.*

"I know. You are a better friend than any I could wish for," Fynch said, hugging the large dog. "Now," he continued brightly, "I must eat something and then we must go. I am strong now, Knave, and ready to face our enemy."

Knave said nothing. When he first clapped eyes on the small gong boy in Stoneheart, he had not anticipated that he would lose his heart to him in friendship. He had never guessed he would come to resent the burden placed upon his shoulders by the Thicket.

It was as though Fynch read his thoughts. "If we don't destroy him, Knave, he will destroy the world we love and the Thicket. The magical creatures will die and the Dragon King will be exposed. We have no choice."

Knave did not respond but Fynch sensed the resolve in the dog and knew that his words had reminded his companion of their duty.

*Eat,* Knave finally said. *We have a journey to finish.*

The Duke of Felrawthy was getting on famously with the unashamedly flirtatious Georgyana Bench. From the moment they had touched hands, the young woman curtsying to the Duke, Elspyth realized Crys might never stare at her in that sad-eyed, wistful way again.

She was surprised how it hurt, tried to shake it off as simply feeling clingy about the person who had rescued her from death, but she knew deep down it was all about her longing for love. She did not want Crys Donal—of this she was sure, for she loved only one person—but she would be lying if she did not admit to enjoying the Duke's attention.

It was embarrassing when Lady Bench dropped in on her private thoughts. "Forgive my daughter, my dear."

Elspyth reddened and smiled awkwardly. "Not at all, Lady Bench."

"Oh, do call me Helyn," the woman insisted, touching Elspyth's arm as they sat together, withdrawn from the animatedly chatting pair.

"Thank you, Helyn," Elspyth said. "Crys and I are great friends. I think terror and fear bring people painfully close, and we have shared much, not the least of which was learning of his family's deaths. But our relationship is platonic, I assure you."

"You have been very strong for him, Elspyth. Don't underestimate how he might feel."

Again Elspyth smiled, sadly this time. "He's made that perfectly clear, actually," she said. "But I love another, Helyn, and I really must make tracks soon to return to him. I'm glad, truly, that Crys and Georgyana are getting on so well. He needs a reason to smile and a woman who will enjoy him."

Lady Bench lifted her eyebrows. "I know I shouldn't speculate so soon, but it's true that they would make a marvelous match. Eryd would be delighted to join our family with the Donals."

"Where is Lord Bench?" Elspyth frowned, not really wanting to discuss a potential love match between Crys and Georgyana.

Helyn Bench grew serious and looked away from her laughing daughter and into Elspyth's soft eyes. "He's gone to the King."

"What?" Elspyth started to rise, alarmed.

"No, wait," Lady Bench soothed. "You need to understand."

"Lady Bench, he is sworn to secrecy about Wyl Thirsk!"

"And that secret will be kept, my dear. Have no fear, we are not about to start broadcasting news of magic in this city. We only stopped burning suspected witches less than a decade ago, as you would know."

"So what will Lord Bench say to Celimus?"

Helyn Bench's face darkened. "I believe he intends to confront the King—in his wonderfully articulate and polite way—about the Donal family and no doubt Rittylworth." She put a hand in the air to stop Elspyth's oncoming tirade, then noted the fear in Elspyth's face. It reflected her own anguish, although she hoped she was disguising it well enough.

Elspyth glanced toward Crys, who was clearly entranced by the vivaciously pretty girl who had engaged him in such lively conversation. She returned her gaze to Lady Bench. "I think his action is unwise, Helyn."

Her carefully chosen words sent a chill through her companion; they echoed her own anxiety. She began to weep, no longer able to hide her worries.

"Oh, Helyn, please don't. Can we reach him?"

The older woman shook her head. "And he is adamant anyway. He would not listen to me earlier when I begged him not to do this."

"What is his reasoning?"

"He believes in sovereignty, Elspyth. He desperately

wants our king to act like the true Crown of Morgravia, to behave with care and compassion and to listen to wise counsel from his own lords."

"Eryd has listened to our horrific story and still believes he can change this cruel King into a compassionate ruler?" Elspyth asked, shocked.

"He believes we must follow the rules of our kingdom. Talk before action. No accusations before all information is sought and gathered. He does not intend to ruffle feathers, Elspyth. Eryd will be careful."

"Listen to me," Elspyth said, enunciating carefully as if talking to a dimwit. She did not mean to act condescending; she was frightened. Petrified, in fact. She knew Crys had noticed her distraught body language when he excused himself from Georgyana and crossed the room. "Helyn, Eryd is in grave peril. His life is at stake. So is yours and that of your daughter. The moment he raises this topic with the King, he will broadcast how much we know and the King will instantly see him for the danger he has unintentionally become."

Helyn was weeping again. "I feared as much."

"Elspyth? What has happened?" Crys asked. She told him briefly and watched him pale. "The King killed my father on a simple suspicion and then had the rest of the family executed just for good measure," he said. "Lady Helyn, forgive me, but Lord Bench has signed his own death warrant. We have to get you out of here. Immediately. I'll ready transport. Pack only essentials, and warm clothes. We're going north."

Helyn Bench, trembling, reached toward her daughter. Georgyana, however, began to protest. "This is preposterous. I have engagements and—"

"Be quiet, Georgyana, and do as you're told!" Elspyth admonished. "We're trying to save your life." Suddenly she could no longer feel the pain of her recent injuries. Fear had taken it away.

Crys tried a different tack. "Georgyana," he said, amazed at how his stomach flipped when she turned those huge eyes on him, "I could not live with myself if anything should happen to you." His expression pleaded with her to follow them without further protest.

Clearly she saw something else in that expression, something Crys thought he had disguised. "Oh? Could you not, Lord Donal?" she replied, and her smile said it all.

Eryd Bench and his colleague sat in a small waiting chamber at the foot of Stoneheart's war tower. Eryd had no idea why they had been escorted here, but Chancellor Jessom emerged just as he began to privately question the logic behind this curious venue.

"Lord Bench, Lord Hartley, it's good to see you on this mild eve. Are you both well?" The visitors made all the right noises and Jessom continued: "My apologies to have kept you waiting. The King, as you can see, is working from his war room tonight—I hope you don't mind meeting with him here?"

Eryd was slightly less anxious for Jessom's warm greeting. "Not at all. I am grateful he could see us at such short notice." He looked toward Hartley, who simply nodded in agreement. Lord Hartley had offered to come along as support when Eryd had confided his reservations about the truth of the slaughters at Felrawthy and Rittylworth.

Jessom smiled benignly. It was not an expression that came easily to him, particularly in the light of the situation. Two lords asking for an audience at sudden notice, and Lord Bench at that—it all smacked of trouble. "Thank you, Lord Bench. As you know, his majesty has only just returned from the north. I'm sure he will be pleased to tell you more when you see him."

"I look forward to it, Jessom," Eryd replied. "I heard he was at Tenterdyn?"

"That's right," Jessom said carefully.

"And rumor has it a meeting of Kings took place there."

The Chancellor attempted another smile. "No smoke without fire, Lord Bench. Perhaps you might inquire of the King for more information. I am a simple chancellor."

"Nothing simple about you, Jessom," Eryd said, deliberately softening his voice to avoid giving offense.

Jessom did not respond; he simply bowed to the two lords. "Not long now, gentlemen." He exited the room, to return several minutes later. "Lord Bench, King Celimus will see you now, alone."

Eryd looked toward Hartley, who stared stonily back. "Go ahead, Eryd. You speak for all of us," he encouraged.

"This is unusual. We are both here for an audience with his majesty," Eryd tried to explain, but the thin Chancellor shrugged.

"My apologies, Lord Bench. The King requests your presence only."

Eryd nodded. Too late now for anything but compliance. He would just have to be especially careful with the slippery sovereign.

"Will you wait?" he asked Hartley, who nodded. "Thank you, Chancellor," he said, gesturing for Jessom to lead the way. At least with Lord Hartley in attendance, he had someone to vouch for his arrival and presence, even if the other man could not bear actual witness to his meeting with the King.

He followed Jessom, filled with intensifying trepidation as his wife's cautions rang in his ears. Perhaps this had not been such a good idea after all. Perhaps Hartley had not been the right person to accompany him. He was an unmarried man, his only son dead of the fever some years back.

Which had been precisely the King's thinking when he heard of the arrival of the two lords. "Separate them and take Hartley down to the dungeon," he had ordered.

"But, sire," Jessom had said, startled. "Could we not wait and see what it is they wish to discuss with you?"

"We know what they're here about, Chancellor!" the King had said, voice rising. "They're here because they don't believe that the noble family of Felrawthy was slaughtered by Razor warriors. They suspect this because word has gotten around that I was meeting with the Barbarian King. It's not hard to follow their thought patterns, Jessom."

"No, sire. But the dungeon is a fairly radical step for someone of Lord Hartley's status."

"So is death, Chancellor. Be careful I don't ask you to kill him for me."

At which point Jessom had kept his thoughts to himself. Experience told him it was the same old argument, one he would never win. Expecting the King of Morgravia to show restraint was a waste of energy. He was a power unto himself, not caring for any advice. In fact, if Jessom was truthful with himself, he was well past the point of believing there was a prosperous future to be shaped under Celimus. His personal dreams of becoming a kingmaker had been cracked by Rittylworth's shame, shattered by Felrawthy's calamity, and, he suspected, were now well on the way to dust, for he did not expect to see Lord Eryd Bench live out the night. Not if Bench was here to question the King's actions and motives, no matter how elegantly couched those accusations might be.

The fragile treaty with Cailech would also be broken soon enough, Jessom suspected, and was saddened by it. The Mountain King had shown tremendous courage and foresight in his actions and the Chancellor rather admired his man Farrow for brokering the meeting. The mercenary had been under intense pressure—especially with that business about Ylena Thirsk—but still he had shown himself to possess a cool head even within the eye of a storm. These men could be valuable to Morgravia and yet Celimus was systematically destroying any chances of retaining their loyalty. How much longer would the nobility put up with his ways? Not long, Jessom suspected, and he was not about to be the King's scapegoat.

Their only chance, in truth, was Queen Valentyna. The marriage presented opportunities, and not just in deflecting attention from Celimus's ugly deeds. Valentyna was bringing something positive and shiny bright into the lives of Morgravians. The people were looking forward to a dazzling queen and the pomp and ceremony of a formal wedding. Valentyna's beauty and composure, not to mention her personal power and wealth, were the sparkle that had long been missing in Pearlis—not forgetting the promise of heirs. She was the ideal diversion from all the death and destruction. These would not go away, of course, but they would be put aside for a while—perhaps long enough to lose some of their potency, by which time Valentyna of Briavel would have worked her own magic simply through her presence. With the people's hearts won, no one—not even the lords—would want to upset the balance between the two realms with difficult questions. Sleeping dogs would be left to lie, as they say, Jessom thought as he guided Lord Bench up the tower stairs. He could hear the old man puffing behind him.

His mind turned again to Valentyna and he had a sudden sharp thought. Perhaps his own loyalties should be aligned with the Queen. She was intelligent and wanted peace and prosperity for her nation; that meant she was open to advice and still young enough to be malleable. Perhaps it was to Valentyna he should dedicate himself; he could be not a kingmaker but an empire maker.

Jessom arrived at the King's chamber feeling far more lighthearted than he'd felt when he began the climb. He looked behind him.

"All right, Lord Bench?"

"Yes," the man wheezed. "I had forgotten the tower was so tall."

"It is deceptive," Jessom answered, tapping on the heavy timber door.

"Come!" the King called.

Jessom swung the door open and announced the visitor.

"Eryd," Celimus said, beaming from behind the desk. "I imagine you are familiar with this chamber, eh?"

The voice was so friendly that Lord Bench felt himself relax momentarily. "Yes, my lord. Your father spent much time here briefing us in years gone."

The smile remained fixed on the King's face, bright, dazzling, and, Eryd suddenly realized, predatory. It was the first time he had seen right through to the heart of the young man. He had always considered him supremely clever and quick-witted and felt these were qualities that would serve him well as King. He had heard troubling stories from years ago, when Celimus was something of a hell-raiser, but had put them down to youth and riches. Like most of the nobility, he had hoped that despite the cool relationship between Magnus and his son, Celimus would shine as King if the right people were around him. He himself had always intended to be a pillar of support and wise counsel for this new King.

But too many of the lords were muttering that, for all their advice, the King was making his own decisions without reference to the council. He did not even show the courtesy of informing some of the most senior people of his plans. The proposed war with Briavel had come out of nowhere and had escalated so fast it had ignited a private war of its own, with many of the senior officials—such as Lord Hartley—quietly declaring that permitting the King to continue in this way was too dangerous. Such treacherous talk, even in private, was seriously disturbing. Civil unrest was the last thing the realm needed.

"Are you all right?" the King inquired, and Eryd snapped to attention.

"Yes, your majesty. My apologies. I think I was taken aback there momentarily by memories."

"But we have a new sovereign on the throne now, Lord Bench," Celimus admonished, and although his manner was genial, there was bite in the sparkling tone. "I know I can count on your loyalty."

Eryd coughed. "Of course, your majesty."

"Which is why," Celimus continued, "I am glad you came this evening. Where is your lovely family, by the way?"

Eryd glanced at the Chancellor, who was handing him a glass of wine. Jessom's expression was blank, giving no clue as to why the King would ask such a curious question.

"Er . . . at home, sire. Why?" Eryd sipped, recognizing a superb southern red, fruity and earthy, with hints of juniper and blackberries. Normally he would relish the opportunity to share such a fine drop, but the King's carefully couched question turned the wine instantly sour on his tongue.

"Oh, no reason. I just thought it would be lovely to see your charming Georgyana again. It would have been a pleasure to have you all here," Celimus replied evenly.

The answer arrived as smooth as silk, but as sugary sweet as it sounded, Eryd was not fooled. He felt suddenly dry-mouthed and the ball of fear in his stomach, which just mo-

ments ago had been almost negligible, suddenly grew expo-
nentially. Unless Eryd was mistaken, the King had just made
a supremely well-disguised threat. Eryd sipped again from
the glass, a bigger, more nervous gulp, but could hardly
bring himself to swallow. His throat suddenly felt as though
it were closing up.

"To your good health," Celimus said, and raised his cup.
Lord Bench was paying scant attention. His thoughts had
fled to Helyn and Georgyana.

"Tell me why you came," Celimus said, suddenly turning
to business.

Eryd was feeling light-headed. He thought it was anxiety,
but he noticed how warm the room had become even though
there was no fire burning. He tugged at his collar to loosen
it. "I wished to talk to you about Felrawthy, your majesty."

He saw the King glance toward his chancellor and the
subsequent twitch of a smug smile was not lost on Eryd. So
the King had expected him. Had anticipated this meeting.
They were lost.

"Oh yes? What can I tell you, Lord Bench?"

Eryd was feeling worse by the moment. His vision was
blurred and his thoughts were swimming. He forced himself
to stay focused. "I heard a rumor, your majesty, that you
have signed a treaty with the Mountain King." He was sure
he was slurring his words.

"That's right, Eryd, I did. We are now peaceful neighbors. I
had hoped to make this announcement at my wedding, as the
icing on the cake, you could say." Celimus laughed softly at his
own jest. "But it seems my learned lords are well ahead of my
news."

Eryd drew a shaking hand across his forehead. "Forgive
me, your majesty, I suddenly feel very unwell."

He heard the King tsk-tsk comfortingly. "Oh, dear. Some
more wine perhaps?"

"No, no, thank you," Eryd said, pulling his goblet away
from Jessom, who was suddenly at his side. "I think I should
go, your highness. Perhaps we could continue this talk when
I am feeling better. Tomorrow?"

"Sit back, Eryd, and listen," the King said. It was said in

a friendly manner but was clearly an order. Lord Bench obeyed, hearing a soft ringing in his ears.

"I think you came here this evening to see if you could shed some light on the slaughter at Tenterdyn. Would I be right?"

As if no longer in control of his body, Eryd nodded his head. The movement felt painfully slow. He could hear the King's voice, but it came to him as though he were deep inside a well, echoing around his mind.

"Good. And I believe you might have heard something along the lines that I ordered the killing of the Donal family? I think I'm right in presuming it might be Crys Donal who told you?" Celimus said, still friendly and speaking softly.

Again against his wishes, Eryd nodded, as if compelled to give the King what he wanted.

Celimus smiled. "Thank you, Eryd, for your honesty. I'm afraid I can confirm that I did give that order, and I regret that my men missed the Donal heir, who, I assume, is now running around Briavel causing trouble and sending people like you these treacherous messages." Eryd frowned. Had he heard right? "Is this not making sense, Lord Bench?" the King asked gently. "I suspect you are wondering now about Lord Hartley, or perhaps about those closer to your heart . . . your wife and your beautiful child? I would forgive you for not paying any further attention to me, for you have good reason to be worried about your family."

Eryd tried to stand, but found himself paralyzed.

"My apologies, sir," Celimus continued, as nonchalantly as if he were discussing the weather. "I took the precaution of poisoning your wine. Won't be long now. I think I'm right, aren't I, Jessom, in that Lord Bench would be experiencing some sort of paralysis now?"

Eryd could not turn to watch the Chancellor's nod. If he had, he would have seen the disgusted expression on Jessom's face, and known that the man had murdered one of the most powerful men in the realm tonight only under threat of his own death. He heard Jessom's whisper, though, as the Chancellor removed the goblet from his catatonic grip.

"Forgive me, Lord Bench," he said, and then was gone, stepping aside to reveal the heinously grinning face of the King of Morgravia

"You are dying, Eryd, in case you hadn't quite grasped it. We shall say it was your heart. I will ensure a proper ceremony for your funeral, you can count on it, and all your noble friends will come and pay their respects. I'm afraid I can't promise the same for your women, although I will make you an oath that they won't suffer, how's that? Pretty Georgyana, such a shame."

Eryd began to growl unintelligibly, the only voice left to him now. His vision had turned dark, and although he could hear, he no longer listened. The cruel words were too painful. He felt his chest constricting and his heart seemed fit to burst from the little space it had left. He tried again to move, but it was useless.

His last coherent thought was that the King had gotten it wrong; for all his smug satisfaction, he had no idea that Crys Donal had returned to Morgravia and was in fact already in Pearlis. Perhaps, Eryd thought as his breathing came in shallow gasps, the young Duke had already taken the Bench women and escaped, for he would surely not have liked the news of this visit to the King. *Please don't let Georgyana die,* he prayed as the paralysis took him and he gurgled a final heaving gasp. He died, eyes wide open, saliva dribbling down the dark robes he favored.

"Check him," Celimus ordered.

Jessom obliged in silence, seeking a pulse at the neck. He shook his head. "Dead."

"Good. That is a most effective weapon, Jessom. I might ask you to use it again sometime. I gather you didn't enjoy that death." Jessom did not reply and the King did not care. "You've already sent the men?"

"They left for the Bench household not long after the two lords' arrival, sire."

"Hartley knows too much."

Jessom knew it was wasted breath to try to convince the King not to kill again tonight. "I shall see to it, your majesty."

"Arrange for him to be dealt with by men you trust, Chancellor. I want no wagging tongues."

"May I ask, your majesty, how we are going to explain the disappearances of Lord Bench and Lord Hartley?" Jessom risked.

"That is what I pay *you* for, Chancellor. Don't trouble me with details. Be gone."

Jessom turned, and as he did, so did something inside him.

## 30

YL ENTERED THE SAME IMPRESSIVE CHAMBER HE HAD BEEN ESCorted to as Romen Koreldy. Once again he was greeted by the Mountain King, who immediately dismissed the two warriors he was speaking with.

"Ylena," Cailech said, moving swiftly from the huge windows where he had been gazing out across the valley. "You look enchanting." He kissed her hand and moved back to the panoramic view, this time with her in tow.

Wyl closed his eyes with revulsion but permitted the courtesy. "Thank you for the fresh clothes."

"Can't have you looking like a man all the time," Cailech replied, his light green eyes sparkling in the dying light. "Are you hungry?"

"Not especially."

"Mountain People are always ravenous," the King admitted. "I'm afraid you'll have to be polite and pretend you're eating plenty. Just push the food around if you must, but let the kitchen know you've appreciated their efforts tonight."

Wyl nodded. "Of course."

"Your hair is so beautiful and soft," the King said, reaching a hand to touch Ylena's carefully dressed hair.

Wyl stepped closer to the window, trying to avoid the

King's caress. "You certainly live in a magnificent place," he said, keeping his voice steady, mind racing. He had to escape. No ideas had presented themselves, save death, and he was not permitted to force that. The Quickening was sinister enough without antagonizing its magics. He thought about those who were still left to him—Fynch, Elspyth, Aremys, Gueryn, hopefully, and, of course, always Valentyna. He was terrified that Myrren's Gift might strike at them if he broke its laws, and he could not risk those precious lives.

"This is your home now, Ylena. I hope you'll come to love it in the same way that my people do."

Cailech watched the Morgravian noblewoman smile wanly at him. "May I ask you a question, sire?"

"By all means. Come, sit, let me pour us something to enjoy while we talk."

Sitting was good, Wyl decided, for there were no chairs in the room that could take the two of them. "Thank you," he said, walking deeper into the chamber toward the hearth.

"I had a fire lit. I presumed you might be feeling the cold."

"Just a bit," Wyl said, and shivered for effect, making the King grin.

Seated, Wyl broached the subject that had burned on his lips ever since meeting Cailech again. "My lord, I have learned that someone very precious to me was sent into the Razors a little while ago with a scouting party."

The King did not reply, simply arched an eyebrow in query as he handed Ylena a small, exquisite glass of a honey-colored wine that looked syrupy and delicious. "This is my personal favorite. Please enjoy."

Wyl nodded his thanks and sipped. It was Romen's distant memory that recalled the wine—a burst of sharp fruit that somehow was also achingly sweet—but it was Ylena's mouth that smiled with pleasure. Again the King grinned.

"He is Morgravian," Wyl continued. "An older man. His name is Gueryn le Gant."

Cailech's expression remained unchanged. "Yes, I know of him."

"Is he alive, sire?"

"I don't know."

Wyl's heart twisted in his chest. He had to be especially cautious here. He could not let on that he knew anything more than Ylena herself could know. "I see. But you had him as a prisoner?"

"That is correct."

"Can we find out if he has survived, my lord?"

"That depends."

"On what, your majesty?" Wyl drew on all his sister's sweet manners.

The King put a finger to his lips at the sound of a knock on the door. "Come," he called.

A servant appeared. "Forgive me, your majesty. Warrior Borc wondered if you could spare a moment. He said it's extremely important."

Borc! Wyl remembered the name all too well—the man had nearly prevented their escape from the fortress the last time.

The King showed his irritation at being interrupted. "Very well. I can spare only a moment, and tell him it had better be vital news." The servant disappeared. "Forgive me, Ylena," Cailech said. "This won't take long."

Wyl nodded, a polite smile on his sister's face.

Borc entered nervously. Wyl stiffened as he saw that the man still carried himself with a limp—the legacy Romen's sword, wielded by Wyl's hands, had left.

"This had better be good, Borc," the King warned. "I have company."

The young warrior nodded toward the noblewoman, embarrassed, and made a low bow to his sovereign. "Please forgive me, sire, but I bring dire news."

"Dire?" the King repeated, not taking the younger man seriously. "Get on with it, then, man."

"Should I speak freely?" the warrior asked, glancing again toward Wyl.

"I would have said so otherwise," Cailech replied, his tone brusque.

"Yes, your majesty," Borc bobbed another bow. "I . . . er, well, I was passing the stable earlier this evening, sire, and there was a terrible commotion from within. It was your stallion, my lord."

"And where was Maegryn?" the King asked.

"That's what I'm here to tell you, sire. Maegryn is dead."

The King paused deliberately in an attempt to steady his erupting emotions. "Killed by the horse?" he asked, mind racing as to whether Lothryn could or would do such a thing.

"No, your majesty. Killed by our own and the Grenadyne."

"What?" Cailech roared, no longer caring for control.

Wyl stood and backed away, his own mind in a swirl of confusion. What could have happened between Aremys and Galapek to provoke such a thing?

"Farrow was there?" the King demanded.

Borc nodded. "It was not Farrow who did the deed, though, sire."

"Tell me." Cailech's face had darkened, his eyes narrow. Wyl knew the look, had seen it through Romen's eyes. A storm was raging beneath the seemingly calm expression. The men had forgotten Ylena in the shock of the news and he frantically scanned the room for a way out. But there was no side door, no entry other than the one presently blocked by Borc. He was trapped.

"It was Myrt, sire."

The room became deathly silent. Even the air seemed to thicken in that moment of dread.

Cailech's voice, when it came, was strung taut. The impact of a second betrayal from a trusted warrior hit hard, and he half whispered, half groaned, "You are sure of this?"

The man nodded, eyes darting toward Wyl and anxiously back to his king. "I was taking a tumble with a girl, sire. Forgive me. We were in the hayloft above your stallion's stable when two men came in. I recognized Myrt immediately, and of course the Grenadyne was easy to distinguish even in the low light of the stable."

"Go on," the King urged, his body tensed like an animal ready to pounce on prey.

Borc looked as though he regretted the whole idea of bringing this alarming news to his sovereign. *Gone is the smugness now, eh, Borc?* Wyl thought, deriving momentary pleasure from the uncertain expression on the warrior's face as he tried to explain something the King did not want to hear yet insisted on being told.

"Myrt and Farrow, they . . ." Borc looked embarrassed.

"What? What did they do?" the King demanded.

Borc took a breath. "They talked to Galapek, sire."

Wyl had not thought the atmosphere in the room could get more potent with foreboding or that the King could hold himself more still or more tense, but he saw he had been wrong.

Borc tried to fill the silence. "The Grenadyne spoke to the horse as if it could hear him, sire, and so did Myrt. They . . . well, I feel awkward about this, sire," he said, looking to his king for help.

"Say it!"

"They called your stallion Lothryn."

Cailech swung around, a sound of anger combined with anguish escaping his throat. He swatted at the clay flagon nearby and it shattered on the granite floor, the smell of honey and syrupy-sweet wine wafting through the chamber.

"Finish it, Haldor damn you, Borc!" the King said, rounding on his warrior. It was the first time Wyl had ever seen Cailech lose his control.

Borc swallowed. "The horse reared when they called to him, sire, then it began to scream and kick at the walls. Farrow told Myrt that the stallion wanted to be let loose."

"Did they do that?" Cailech demanded.

Borc shook his head. "Maegryn interrupted their planning. He questioned what they were doing around Galapek. Myrt seemed unsure at first, sire. The Grenadyne did all the talking, said he wanted to go out for a ride or some such excuse. Maegryn said he had to report them because the barshi had given orders since the disappearance of the Morgravian prisoner that anyone acting strangely around Galapek was to be singled out."

Wyl kept Ylena's gaze on the floor but sensed the King steal a glance toward her at the mention of Gueryn. He worked hard to give the impression that she was embarrassed to be sharing this information and did not react to the mention of the prisoner.

Borc was racing to the end of his sordid tale, clearly uncomfortable and eager to leave. "Maegryn said he was coming to see you, sire, and that's when Myrt grabbed him. Farrow told him not to, but there was blood rage there, sire, Myrt couldn't stop. He strangled Maegryn but I didn't stop to see what they did with the body, your majesty. I jumped from the small window upstairs and came straight here, although I gather the Grenadyne is also on his way to see you." He looked behind him as if Aremys might already be standing there.

"And Myrt?"

"Has gone to find Rashlyn, your majesty. Farrow wants to know what has happened to the Morgravian prisoner. Maegryn mentioned that he thought the barshi had taken him for his own uses."

Cailech twisted away in angry thought, staring out of the window. He could only barely see the great shadows of the mountains in the distance now as darkness fell quickly upon the Razors.

"Borc."

"Sire?"

Cailech's voice was as cold as the ice that covered the Razors' peaks in midwinter. "Assemble the senior warriors. Tell the gatekeeper no one leaves, not even our own. Send reinforcements to the portcullis. Have several guards posted on every gate—even those into the town. Neither Myrt nor the Grenadyne is to be permitted access in either direction. Release the dogs. Understand?" Borc nodded. "Send Rollo to me immediately with one other of his choice—have runners sent for him if necessary. Tell Rollo everything and then find Myrt." Borc bowed and departed.

The King turned slowly to face Ylena. Wyl set her face impassively and took the lead. "I'm sorry, your majesty, that I witnessed that. I'm sure it was a private concern."

"It was not your fault, Ylena. I should have taken more precaution."

"That man of yours was speaking about Gueryn le Gant, wasn't he?"

The King nodded, staring so intently at Ylena that Wyl felt himself falter slightly. Perhaps it was not a good idea to question Cailech right now. But there might never be a better opportunity, and time was their enemy. "Gueryn le Gant is my guardian," he said. "When our mother died, Gueryn was all we had, for my father was away at Pearlis with the King. When I was sent to Stoneheart to be raised as the ward of King Magnus, Gueryn was there too. He is family. He is all I have left." Wyl made Ylena's soft tones beseeching.

The news took the King by surprise, but he had no time to respond, for there was another knock. Once again he hushed Ylena with a gesture. Both knew who it was going to be. The same servant appeared with an expression of apology, but Cailech hardly noticed.

"Is it Aremys Farrow?" he asked before the man said anything.

"Yes, sire."

"Send him in."

Aremys was shown in and Wyl immediately sent him a look of warning.

"Sire, you were expecting me?" Aremys said smoothly, trying hard not to show his surprise.

"I guessed you would come around soon enough," Cailech said, his tone casual and his body language relaxed. Behind him Wyl shook his head toward Aremys, desperately cautioning him against saying anything incriminating.

Aremys faltered. The smile he would normally give to the man he now considered a friend did not arrive.

"Care for a cup of wine, Farrow?"

"No, sire, I came here only briefly to pass on a message. Forgive my interruption, I thought it was important."

"Apparently there are a number of important messages to be communicated tonight," Cailech replied.

The cryptic reponse was not lost on Aremys. "I can come back later, sire." He saw relief move across Ylena's face and then froze as Cailech also glanced toward her.

"No, please, come and join us," Cailech said affably. "I'd like to share some wine with you."

Wyl looked at the shattered flagon and Aremys followed

his glance. Something dangerous had occurred here tonight; tempers had frayed. "Are you well, Ylena?" he asked, suddenly wondering whether Cailech had hurt Wyl.

"I am, thank you, Aremys. I was just about to tell the King about Queen Valentyna and all she told me of Romen's tales of the Razors." Aremys nodded, frowning slightly, and Wyl took the risk of saying more. "You know, about how Romen's escape was aided by Lothryn, and how he later worried about what might have happened to the brave warrior who betrayed his king."

Wyl himself had fast reflexes but Ylena's body moved more slowly than he was used to. He saw the King's sudden action but as Ylena could not avoid the hard, stinging slap. Ylena's small body flew across the room, gashing a leg on a small table and sprawling across a chair before tumbling to the granite floor. Wyl lay still. From the terrible pain, he suspected Ylena's slim shoulder had dislocated during the awkward fall.

Wyl heard Cailech ranting above his sister's body. "Do you think I'm stupid, Ylena?"

Wyl had no choice; he spoke quickly to his friend. "He knows about Maegryn," was all he managed before he felt himself lifted easily from the floor and flung again across the chamber. He glimpsed Cailech's enraged face and heard his roar of anger. Ylena's body crunched awkwardly against the stone fireplace and this time her leg snapped, the bone poking through the skin. Fresh pain klaxoned through her frail body. Wyl released a scream, partly out of helplessness, partly designed to keep Cailech's attention away from Aremys. It was too late, though— Cailech's men had arrived, among them someone Aremys clearly recognized.

"Hold him, Rollo!" the King commanded, pointing at a startled Aremys, who had remained frozen, unsure whether to run toward Ylena or out the door. Either way he left his decision until it was too late and Wyl closed Ylena's eyes with despair. He moved her bleeding, broken body into a sitting position and prayed the King would not hurt her further. He could handle the physical pain, but the battering of Ylena both at Tenterdyn and now here was more than Wyl could bear emotionally.

"Be still, Farrow!" Cailech commanded. "There is no escape."

Aremys obeyed. "What is this about, your highness? I thought I was a free man."

"You were," Cailech said, advancing on his new victim, Ylena forgotten. "Until Borc brought me some dark news."

Aremys wore a confused expression. "What news, sire?"

"You snake!" Cailech spat. "Am I that gullible, Farrow? Perhaps I am," he said, answering his own questions with a weariness in his voice. He smiled suddenly, ruefully. "I trusted you. I thought you were on our side."

"King Cailech—" Aremys began.

"Don't, Grenadyne," the King warned. "Don't begin to spin any lies. Rollo, is everything secured?"

The man nodded. "Borc and some others are seeing to it, sire."

"Myrt?"

Rollo looked uncomfortable at the mention of the senior warrior's name. "He is being followed to the barshi's quarters, sire, as you ordered."

As soon as Aremys heard Myrt's name, he lowered his chin and his body slumped slightly in the grip of the men. They were all as good as dead now. He looked over at Wyl, equally helpless at the other end of the room, and felt something inside him break.

Rashlyn had been experiencing an inexplicable sense of doom for the past few hours. The Stones, which he had cast for himself, kept showing him the coming of a dragon. It made no sense. Dragons were creatures of myth, as were winged lions, unicorns, and other strange beasts worshiped through the ages—and still revered in Morgravia. The Stones had never given him such a picture before and yet they insisted, time and again. Considering that he had cast the Stones only a few times in his life on his own behalf—and had always found them accurate—this was wildly unsettling.

He had been pondering this curiosity for many hours,

wondering at what it could mean for Cailech and, more to the point, himself. Now he felt a light was dawning: Perhaps the vision pointed toward the changing of a sovereign in Morgravia. It had come to him that the King of Morgravia sat upon the dragon throne, and that the King's emblem—and mythical creature of the Crown of Morgravia—had always been the dragon. So did the coming of the dragon shown by the Stones mean a new king for the southern realm?

That made little sense, however, for the present King was young, virile, and seemingly in excellent health, according to Cailech. Perhaps they were suggesting that the marriage of Celimus to Valentyna would change the Crown somewhat, bringing a new queen to the throne. Except the Stones were specific; they spoke only of the dragon and a new coming. Valentyna was not in any way connected to the dragon throne; nor, to Rashlyn's knowledge, did the Briavellians have any link to the mythical creatures in the manner of Morgravia.

No, he pondered, pulling at his tangled beard, this was specifically about the Dragon King. There it was again: change. Before Cailech had left for Morgravia, the Stones had spoken change and Rashlyn had thought they referred to something sinister. As it turned out, Cailech had returned triumphant, not only with a new truce and a peaceful neighbor but with a bride as well. Rashlyn nodded to himself, congratulating the Stones on their accuracy. Change had indeed occurred for the King of the Razors. Everything had changed for the better.

But now this . . . this time it felt sinister, threatening. The Stones pointed toward the coming of the dragon, but he had done this casting purely for himself, not on behalf of Cailech. This foretelling was about him. Was the dragon coming for him?

Deep in his thoughts, he jumped in alarm as the door of his chamber crashed open and Myrt's huge body filled the doorway.

"Good evening, barshi," Myrt said. The words were polite, but the tone and the expression on the big man's face belied them.

"What are you doing here?" the small man stammered, immediately summoning a spell of protection.

"I've come for the truth about Lothryn—or should I say Galapek?"

Rashlyn was intrigued by the big man's discovery; he held back the magic he had prepared to hurl. "What do you know?" he asked, his voice light and taunting.

"Where is the Morgravian prisoner?" Myrt responded.

The barshi gave a mad cackle. "I'll be happy to show you," he said, and pointed to the corner, where a large gray dog was sitting, chained and quivering.

Myrt, aghast, was unsure whether to take the deranged barshi seriously, yet somehow knew he was being shown the truth. "Gueryn?" he asked the dog tentatively.

The dog whined. It was in obvious pain, but it pawed the ground in frustration and strained against its chain.

"Like my work, Myrt? It's so much better than Lothryn, whom I'm afraid I must have killed in the process. As you can see, le Gant is alive within the beast and fully aware of his new status."

"You fucking—"

Myrt got no further. Pain exploded in his head and his nose and ears began to leak blood.

"Shut up!" the barshi screamed. "Or I won't even give you a choice of what I turn you into, you stupid fool." Myrt was moaning unintelligibly and clutching his head. "I guess that hurts, eh?" Rashlyn continued. "Well, listen to me now, big man. I'm going to take away the pain and then you are going to tell me who else knows my secret."

Myrt shook his head vigorously and blood spattered the barshi. Rashlyn seemed not to notice; instead he stepped up the punishment and the warrior's eyes bulged as a fresh wave of pain hit.

"Do just as I say, Myrt," Rashlyn warned. His fingers moved slightly and the warrior was pushed back and held against the wall. "Better?" he asked, dispelling the pain.

Myrt shook his head, refusing to cooperate even as his body was released from its agony.

"Who else knows?" Rashlyn asked, moving toward the warrior.

"Just me and, I presume, the King," Myrt spluttered. Although the pain had lifted, the toll on his body was significant enough to make him gasp still.

"Oh yes, the King knows. It was his choice to punish Lothryn that way, you see. I think it's beautifully subtle. And Galapek is so magnificent—"

Rashlyn suddenly stopped and cocked his head, as if listening to something. He turned slowly, fear coursing through every fiber of his being.

"What?" Myrt asked.

"Shh!" Rashlyn cautioned, swiveling his body from the window to the door, then back again. "It's coming," he murmured.

Myrt, connected to the barshi through the madman's magic, also sensed the approach of something. Stunned by the immensity of power that was being communicated, he whispered, "What is it?"

"The dragon," Rashlyn replied, suddenly releasing his magic hold on Myrt as his own fears got the better of him.

Myrt fell to the floor, hitting his knees hard and yelling in protest. He was forgotten as the barshi began to spin around in the chamber, a look of terror on his face. Myrt took advantage of Rashlyn's confusion to drag himself across the floor to the dog, which cocked its head toward a key on the table. Myrt nodded, reached for the key, and unlocked the chain that secured the dog. It barked once and stretched itself on unsteady, gangly legs.

Blood was running freely from Myrt's nose; he only noticed it now. He tried to wipe it away, but more replaced it. He was thinking he should ignore the weakness imposed by the barshi's magic and somehow make his way to the door, crawling if necessary, when the doorway was filled by a large figure.

"Hello, Borc," he said, disdain lacing his tone. He did not like this young man, whom he blamed for Lothryn's capture and torture.

The warrior looked over at Rashlyn, who seemed to be in

a trance, mumbling to himself. "What have you done?" he demanded of Myrt.

"Nothing. He's off in his own world, muttering about the coming of a dragon or something. Why are you here?"

"Why are you on the floor . . . bleeding?" Borc continued angrily, dismissing the question leveled at him.

"The last time I checked," Myrt began, working hard to ignore the weakening sensations in his body, "I was your superior, Borc. Do I need to remind you of how to speak to a superior?"

"And the last time I checked, Myrt"—Borc sneered—"you were busy murdering someone."

"Ah," Myrt replied, hiding his shock. He would not give this sniveling youngster the satisfaction he surely craved of watching the most senior of the warriors groveling to him.

"I told the King," Borc added triumphantly.

"Yes, I'm sure you have, you arse-licking fuck!"

Borc's reply was cut off as a boy appeared to step through the granite blocks of the high tower's wall. He was surrounded by a shimmering light that momentarily blinded the three men in the chamber before it dissipated. The boy looked around at them and Myrt realized this was no vision; the boy was flesh and blood—scrawny and small but terrifyingly real.

Rashlyn's wildness intensified. "Who are you?" he screeched.

"I am your destroyer, Rashlyn," the boy said.

Then everything happened very fast. Rashlyn leapt through an open window. The drop meant certain death, yet Myrt was certain he glimpsed the barshi hovering in the open air before he disappeared from view. The boy smiled before seeming to dissolve back through the wall. Borc watched him too, openmouthed and filled with disbelief. It was his slowness to recover that gave the gray dog a chance to leap, bringing the man down.

Myrt watched in horror as the dog, its limbs still trembling, struck for Borc's throat. Myrt reached for his dagger, but so did Borc. The younger man was strong and he struck at the dog with the blade, wounding it many times in its side.

But the creature refused to let go. It had the warrior by the throat at last, seemingly experiencing the blood madness that comes over a beast when defending its life or those it loves just as it comes over a man.

Myrt raised himself painfully, still suffering the effects of the magic, and all but fell onto Borc and the dog. The animal was growling fiercely now, its huge jaws locked around the man's neck, tearing at his throat. Borc made one final valiant effort and managed to sink his blade into the animal's chest. The dog screamed and rolled away, but Myrt moved quickly. He would mete out death on behalf of the dog who had saved his, Myrt's, life. Raising his dagger, he struck deep into Borc's lacerated throat and hit the artery he was looking for. The younger man stared with dismay at the plume of blood that erupted, and grabbed his neck in a sad attempt to retain the precious liquid. He even managed to drag himself to his knees before Haldor claimed him and Borc of the Mountain People fell heavily across the prone dog, dead.

## 31

RYS DONAL RODE ERYD BENCH'S CHESTNUT MARE THROUGH the Pearlis town gates, nodding to the watchmen as he passed.

"Shar guide you," they called to the lone rider, who raised his hand in friendly salute but said nothing in return.

Not long afterward a black carriage, like any other public carriage that plied its trade on the streets of Pearlis, also left the gates.

"How long, Gordy?" one of the watchmen cried as the driver paid his toll, recognizing him from the pool of men who entered and exited the city many times a day with paying passengers. The man shrugged and the gatekeepers caught sight of two women in the carriage whom they recognized as Lady Bench and her daughter. "Evening, Lady Bench," one said, showing the right courtesies.

Helyn Bench smiled back, the men never knowing how much courage that gesture took. The younger woman did not look at them at all. "Onward, driver," Lady Bench called.

It was at least another fifteen minutes before a petite figure, cloaked in blue, walked a horse out of the city gates to whistles of approval from the men. It was not dark yet, so they could see her pretty features set in a pale face. Fortunately for Elspyth, they could not see the dark bloodstain on her cloak or the fierce effort it required for her to urge the horse to carry her gently beyond the reach of King Celimus. She forced a smile and said, "See you soon, lads," as if she were only going to be away for a few hours, then she too disappeared down the road. She knew she had two bends to get past before the third one would remove her fully from the watchtower's view. It felt like a lifetime and she wondered if the guards were wondering why she was riding so slowly down the road.

Finally she caught sight of Crys Donal. He rushed toward her, and as much as she wanted to be composed and not show how sick she was, Elspyth all but fell from the horse as she leaned toward him. As they had done before, the strong arms of the Duke of Felrawthy cushioned her and carried her gently to a patch of soft grass. "I'm sorry you had to do that, but—" he began.

"Hush, Crys," she replied. "There was no other way. It would have looked too odd for Georgyana to ride out after her mother's carriage, especially alone."

"We can only hope those guards make no connections. Two of us were strangers and easily forgotten," Crys reassured. Elspyth noticed how his gaze softened when it fell upon the Benchs' golden-haired daughter. She felt another pang and reminded herself that Crys did not belong to her. She had pushed his gentle advances away too often. She was spoken for . . . if, perhaps, only by a dead man, she thought sadly.

Crys glanced toward Lady Bench, who sat on a milestone staring straight out before her, clearly dwelling on thoughts of her beloved Eryd. He walked over and put his arms around her. She was a friend of his mother's, who was about the same age. He tried to imagine how Aleda must have felt watching Jeryb Donal die. Crys was sure Eryd was dead by now too, and knew the effect of his death on Lady Bench would be no less painful than if she had witnessed it.

"I'm so sorry, Helyn," he said softly.

"Are you sure it's useless, Crys? I mean—"

He cut off her teary words; they were too painful to listen to again. "We cannot risk Georgyana, Lady Bench. You must see to her safety first. I promise you I will return to Pearlis, but first I insist on ensuring that you three ladies are out of danger." He hugged her again, suspecting that her inclination was to send Georgyana on with him and take her chances back in Pearlis. "Please, Lady Bench. Celimus showed no mercy to my parents, or my brothers, the youngest of whom had barely reached your daughter's tender years. He will have no qualms about killing you, Lord Bench, Georgyana, and anyone else who looks to be getting in his way."

"In the way of what?" she said.

"Of whatever it is that he wants," Crys replied. "He is mad, Lady Bench. He dreams of empire. The upcoming wedding is a sham. He will destroy Valentyna and Briavel one way or another—it just appears more respectable if he can do it diplomatically. Listen to me," he said, taking the liberty of turning her face toward his earnest one. "If he was prepared to murder my father, who was the most loyal of Morgravians, then he will respect none of his senior counselors' lives. Please trust me."

"So you think Eryd is already dead," she said, her voice flat.

There was no point in attempting to placate this woman with empty words after making her and her daughter flee for their lives. "I do."

She did not break down into sobs as he had expected; she

did not even shed another tear. Instead she echoed the words of his mother. "Avenge him," she said, "for our sakes."

"Celimus has many deaths to answer for, my lady. I intend to make him accountable for each of them, rest assured."

She squeezed his arm, unable to speak for her tumbling emotions.

"Come, we will ride in pairs now," he continued. Elspyth was breathing hard, and Crys reached for her hand. "Can you go a bit farther?"

"Yes, let's go," she said, enjoying, despite herself, his touch in front of Georgyana.

"You and Lady Bench ride together, Elspyth. Georgyana can come with me," Crys said, instantly putting to rest any delusion that he was not utterly infatuated with the young noblewoman. It was fitting that he should align himself with his own kind; they would make the most handsome of couples, Elspyth thought. She scowled privately but convinced herself that her acid mood was caused by the throb at her shoulder.

"Where are we going?" Georgyana asked, unaware of the sour emotions the pretty woman by her side was feeling.

"They will expect us to go north," Crys said, "as we all have homes and links there."

"So we go south?" Georgyana finished for him. He smiled indulgently.

"Yes, my lady. South to Argorn."

Jessom stared at the sputtering candle. Its erratic flame held his attention in the otherwise darkened room. His thoughts were distracted, roaming. A light perfume wafted up from the soap leaf he had used to wash his hands after touching Eryd Bench's body. He had killed twice himself, and had had many deaths carried out at his order, but none had ever felt like this one. Lord Bench's death had been as unpleasant as it was unnecessary. Unpleasant because Jessom had been forced to administer the poison personally and very much against his own will, and unnecessary because it had achieved nothing but another dirty secret to keep hidden.

He linked his newly washed fingers as he contemplated the afternoon's pointless proceedings. To the King, the report of another killing, no matter how high ranking the victim, was akin to hearing that a kitten from the kitchen cat's latest litter had died. *He just kills on a whim,* Jessom thought bitterly. Bench and his fellow lord could have been so easily diverted, sent on some special mission even, but left alive, retaining their importance in the fabric of Morgravian life. "Shar knows, that fabric is wearing very thin," the Chancellor muttered.

If even Lord Bench had been questioning the King and his motives, then this was surely the end of the road, for Eryd Bench would never have considered making his concerns public without much soul-searching. How many others had doubts? Jessom wondered. How many others disapproved of the King's actions?

"Civil unrest is next." Jessom finished the thought aloud.

It would only take someone like Crys Donal, now the Duke of Felrawthy, to stir up sufficient emotion and the civil unrest could turn into an uprising. Jessom was not so naive as to believe that the famous Legion would not follow its instincts, which would be screaming in favor of Lord Donal after what had happened in the north. The Legion had suffered several blows recently—enough to provoke the men into turning against the King they hated.

Jessom listed them in his mind: Alyd Donal, Wyl Thirsk, Ylena Thirsk, most of the Donal family, Rittylworth's holy community. Even the death of King Valor of Briavel was beginning to be viewed suspiciously, particularly given that Wyl Thirsk had been in Werryl on the King's business when he had lost his life alongside Valor. Jessom had heard mutterings that the circumstances of the two deaths were not as cut-and-dried as they were said to be. Then there was Jorn, a popular lad around Stoneheart—his torture and death had hit hard, and for what result? The Legion had not recovered from the deaths of its own men either—all in the pursuit of missing taxes. Too many men had been impaled and left to die long, horrible deaths. Celimus was too cruel, too quick to punish without consideration of the repercussions. As for all the mercenaries who had lost their lives—well, few cared, but Jessom was tired of killing for no good reason. Almost all could have been spared; they had been on the Crown's side anyway.

He slammed his hand down on the table in frustration. And now Lord Bench was dead and Hartley was languishing in the dungeon. Jessom had finally rebelled against Celimus. He would find a way to spare Hartley yet; he refused to kill pointlessly again.

Jessom lit a fresh candle and extinguished the sputtering one with a pinch, hardly feeling its warmth on his fingertips. He was too deep in thought about his own future. He assessed his options. They were few and mostly unpalatable. He could remain with Celimus and stay loyal to his belief that the King of Morgravia was too strong to be challenged. He could raise the Legion himself by telling its officers the truth, but then what? They could unseat Celimus but there was no heir, which potentially meant some distant relative from Parrgamyn perhaps laying claim to the throne. Jessom's experience of the Parrgamyse told him that this was not a wise path. Alternately, he could argue that a new dynasty be created from within—with someone like the new Duke of Felrawthy, perhaps—but such a transfer of power would be messy, full of internal strife, and not guaranteed to be successful or bloodless. Third, he could leave. Disappear tonight and begin a new life elsewhere. But where? And if Celimus survived as King, he would have Jessom hunted down. The Chancellor could not bear to dwell on what the King would do with him when he was caught . . . and he was sure he would be caught, even if it took Celimus years.

That left one last option. And as he reflected on its merits, he realized it was, without question, not only the best of the alternatives but was perhaps his most inspired idea ever. If it worked, he would never have to worry again. If he failed, it meant an horrific death. He must take precautions.

He would need the help of an expert in fashioning a fail-safe capsule of the juice of the Deathbloom, a plant so rare most people had never heard of it. If he was caught in this last and desperate measure, then he would not hesitate to bite down on the capsule, which would deliver death so swiftly that no one would even realize what had occurred. By then, his body would be stiff in the rigor the plant's poison so effectively provoked.

He smiled thinly. "Not that I intend ever to take that capsule," he whispered.

Wyl stared at Aremys through Ylena's glazed vision. He must have passed out momentarily, he realized; he had slumped to one side and must appear dead. It looked as though the fight had gone out of the Grenadyne. The King was pacing before him, poking his finger into his chest, sneering at him with cutting words. The two guards on either side of Aremys looked uncomfortable. Wyl fought the pain back as Gueryn had taught him and righted Ylena's frame against the hearth. No one saw his movement; everyone was intent on Cailech.

Wyl had to move, broken leg and dislocated shoulder aside. Go down fighting—was that not the Legion's way? He rallied his spirit and called upon everything left within him to find the strength to move toward Aremys.

"So you don't deny Maegryn's murder?" Cailech demanded of the mercenary, his anger back under icy control.

"No, sire. It was a mistake."

"Mistake!"

Aremys blinked. There was no way out of this, no possible explanation—except the truth, of course—for the death of the stablemaster. Aremys no longer cared about Cailech and the peace treaty or about the Mountain People. In truth, if he boiled it down, he cared about the man trapped in the broken woman's body in the corner, he cared about a man driven mad with pain and anguish by being transformed into a horse, and he cared about bringing about the death of a southern king.

Nothing much else mattered—not even his own life, it seemed, because it had not occurred to him to include it in his list. He stole a glance at Wyl and realized he had moved. Not dead, then; brave Wyl was forcing his broken body toward him. What could the two of them achieve against two huge warriors and an enraged king who was now reaching for his blade?

"Lost for words, Farrow? Perhaps this will loosen your tongue," Cailech said, swiping his knife across the Grenadyne's face.

Aremys saw the red splashes spatter Rollo's face. The man blinked but said nothing. To his own credit, Aremys hardly flinched. Perhaps it had been too fast. How he found the strength he would never know, but he enjoyed it. "Haldor be praised that your blade is kept so keen, Cailech. I didn't feel a thing."

The King's gaze narrowed as he watched the bright blood drench the face of the man he had called friend, the man he had thought might fill the yearning gap that had been caused by the loss of Lothryn. But this man was now facing death *because* of Lothryn.

"Why, Aremys? You could have had it all with me," Cailech said, a touch of sadness creeping into his tone.

"Because you are a puppet king," Aremys replied, defiance rising in him as he accepted death. He could see the pulse at Cailech's temple beginning to throb.

"Explain yourself, Farrow."

The mercenary shrugged, reveling in his nonchalance. It was amazing to let go of fear; he suddenly felt empowered. This was how Wyl must have felt when he was baiting Celimus into killing Ylena at Tenterdyn—except Wyl had not expected to die, he thought, a rueful grin creeping across his bloodied face.

"Answer me!" the King roared, raising the blade.

"I'm not afraid to die, Cailech, so threatening me will not help you learn what you need to. But I shall tell you anyway. You are a puppet to Rashlyn. Ask your men. Ask Rollo here what he thinks of your mad barshi and the way he controls you. Ask poor Myrt, who would have crawled over the very ice caps for you but hates you now for what you have done to Lothryn at the barshi's whim. You are controlled by the mad sorcerer. He uses magic on you, my king, and makes decisions for you."

Aremys felt the change of atmosphere in the room immediately. The grip of his captors lessened and he saw Cailech's face move through a series of expressions from disbelief to rage.

"You lie!"

"No, Cailech. Look at your men. Ask them. You turned Lothryn into a beast. Galapek is an abomination—abomination—but it was not your idea, was it, sire? It was Rashlyn's. And now the Morgravian prisoner has disappeared. Where is Gueryn le Gant, your majesty? Magically twisted into another abomination, that's where. Can your people trust you with this sort of misery and sorcery hanging over them?"

Before Cailech could respond, Rollo broke in. "My king, is this true? Have you used magic on Lothryn?"

Cailech's hesitation in replying was damaging.

"And now he's going to have Myrt killed, Rollo, because he knows the truth too."

Rollo dropped his hands from Aremys and his second followed suit. "I cannot permit this, sire," he said, shaking his head, disbelief raging in his eyes. "I hate the barshi. But I loved Lothryn like a brother, and Myrt is our leader even though you are our king. You would kill the two men I trust most? Rashlyn is evil, sire."

Cailech's eyes darkened in the granite face. "Do you challenge me, Rollo?"

The warrior backed away. "I don't know the truth, sire. I don't understand any of it. If Myrt killed Maegryn then I wish to hear why. I want his side of the story, not the words of Borc, who would sell his own grandmother to get into your good books."

"I order you to take this man to the dungeons," Cailech said. His words were slowly spoken and chillingly intense.

Rollo shook his head with equal slowness, hardly believing he was defying his own sovereign. "Not until you bring Rashlyn here . . . and Myrt."

The room had become still with tension. Cailech stared at Rollo and then back at Aremys. His silence was telling as he considered his options. Finally he nodded wearily. "Go. Bring them both here."

Relief flooded the warrior at the King's capitulation. He

wasted no time, nodding first to his second to follow and then to Aremys, who would have liked to thank Rollo for his courage. It was pointless, though. As he stared at Cailech and the King returned the glare, both knew the Grenadyne would not live a few moments beyond the warriors' departure.

As the door closed behind the two Mountain Men, Cailech rounded on Aremys.

"I know you don't intend to let me live long enough to clap eyes on Myrt again, sire," Aremys said, playing for time.

"How instinctive of you, Farrow. I'm glad we understand each other."

"Lothryn got to be a horse. Nothing so exotic planned for me, Cailech?"

"Nothing leaps to mind," Cailech growled, stepping closer.

"Or do you have to wait for the puppeteer to arrive to make the decision for you? So he can cast his magic and make you dance precisely as he wishes?"

Cailech shook his head in mock disgust but Aremys could see him grinding his jaw. And then his hopes were destroyed. Cailech turned nonchalantly to gaze down at the figure of Ylena Thirsk, who had painfully and silently crawled the length of the room, a trail of blood behind her.

"Ah, Ylena, good. You've arrived painfully, I see, and just in time to watch your rescuer die. I think Aremys was counting on you to divert me while he took care of me, although I have to wonder what he had in mind, as neither you nor he carries a weapon. Perhaps he was going to bite me to death." The King laughed. "Here, my dear, let me help you," and he reached down almost tenderly to pick her up.

Aremys felt his gut twist. It was over, then. Cailech was right; he had been counting on Wyl to achieve some diversion. Between them they might have been able to get the blade from Cailech and hold him off until the others returned.

"There we are," Cailech said, placing a grimacing Ylena into a chair just in front of Aremys. "Now you have a good view." He lifted her skirt to look at her leg and made a tutting sound. "Nasty. That must really hurt. I'm constantly impressed by your courage, Ylena." He returned a savage gaze to Aremys. "How would you like this done, my friend? Throat? Gut? Heart?"

"May Haldor rot your soul, Cailech!" Aremys said, helplessness washing over him. He looked once more upon Ylena. "I'm sorry I failed you."

"You haven't yet," Wyl answered. "Remember who I am. Use me!" he urged.

Cailech smiled. "Such a brave pair. What is it between you two? I could almost feel jealous. You seem to have each other in some sort of thrall. It's not ardor or lust, for I would have sensed that. It's more than that—"

Aremys was not going to listen anymore. "Get on with it, then, and look to your back, Cailech. Celimus will never allow you or the son you foisted on Lothryn's wife to live." He rolled the die once more. Perhaps in Wyl's fighting words there was a chance yet. "I've already told Celimus about Aydrech. Security in case you did not keep faith with me. He'll come looking for you both. The boy will not live to see a year, I predict."

That was it. That was Cailech's weak spot, he realized. His love for the child and his desire for an heir were more important than anything else in the world to him. Aydrech was his softness.

Cailech's subsequent howl at the biting threat was filled with a venom that Aremys had only previously experienced in battle. It was beyond anger or fear. It was a rage people reach when there is nothing else to care about but the kill. Many hardened fighters spoke of the moment when nothing but blood—the enemy's blood—could cleanse them of that hatred and wrath. Aremys watched the blade rise and closed his eyes, expecting to die. It was up to the gods now.

It was no god that came to his rescue that day but a damaged man trapped in a woman's body; broken and bleeding, he somehow found the strength to push the enraged King still further.

"And Celimus will not spare the child any pain," Wyl said,

watching the blade also. "He'll probably drag Aydrech behind his horse, or simply impale your weeks-old son . . . he might even roast him and feed him to the royal hounds," he goaded the King.

This time Cailech roared as the blade descended and it was Ylena who took the mighty blow that nearly cleaved her in two, cutting flesh and sinew, cartilage and bone, finally coming to rest buried between her breasts.

Her sad, lovely eyes met Aremys's as she fell to her death at last. Her gaze was triumphant.

Cailech groaned. The sound was deep and guttural, and filled with rage. He was bent double, his body shaking and his large hands clutching his head as it swung angrily from side to side, as if in denial. The Mountain King suddenly arched his back and clenched his fists, his expression a contortion of such pain that Aremys took a step back. Cailech let out a final low and desperate growl, slumping forward before he straightened, staring at the bright blood on the hand and arm that had dealt the murderous blow. The King took a deep, shuddering breath and lifted his formerly light eyes to meet Aremys's.

Aremys, hating to have put Wyl through more pain, noted their curious ill-matched color and did not know whether to cry with relief or share the despair of loss. He laid his hand onto the hard, muscled arm of King Cailech and whispered, "Welcome back, Wyl."

Wyl Thirsk, now King Cailech of the Razors, flexed his broad shoulders and sighed. "Let's go find our friends," he growled in Cailech's deep voice.

# 32

FYNCH SAT CROSS-LEGGED, STARING AT THE MAN WHO HAD brought so much hatred and destruction into the world. Now he must die.

Rashlyn did not know Fynch could see him, but he could feel the boy, sensed his powerful presence here among the Razors. He looked so small and helpless; how could a child possess such potent magic?

Rashlyn had fled without thinking, but leading the boy into the small wood behind the fortress now seemed like madness. Perhaps the child would die of cold. Perhaps he himself might. He summoned a spell to warm himself and pondered his next move.

It was not in Fynch's nature to be violent, but he was a destroyer whether or not he cared for the role. The blood of the dragon line pounded in his veins and the Dragon King himself demanded this of him. He would not fail. He might die but he would not let his king down.

Not far away from him sat Knave, silent, filled with dread and powerless. His part in this adventure was over. He had guided Fynch to Rashlyn and now all he could do was bear witness.

It seemed to Knave that the barshi had disappeared, but still Fynch sat and waited.

*How do you feel?* Knave could not let go of his concern.

*Well enough to face what I must.*

*Does your head still pain you?*

*Yes. There is no more sharvan, before you ask.*

*Where is he?*

*Hiding, he thinks. He is confused and frightened, but he will face me soon enough.*

*Are you frightened?*

*No.*

*I am.*

*Don't be. This is what you and I were meant to do.*

*Who are you, Fynch? Please share it with me before . . .* Knave hesitated.

*Before I die?* Knave did not reply and Fynch did not force it. *I am the son of King Magnus of Morgravia, half brother of Celimus. I am of the dragon's blood.*

*Is that what the Dragon King saw in you?*

Fynch nodded.

*What does it mean?*

*Nothing really,* Fynch said, shaking his head gently. *Hardly anyone knows. My mother, and she's dead. The Dragon King, you, and me. Magnus perhaps, but he is cold in his tomb.*

*Shouldn't you tell someone?*

Fynch smiled and shrugged. *Best kept between us. I know who I am now and where I belong. It is enough. That's why the Dragon King took me away as I slept—he wanted me to know the truth before I faced Rashlyn. He restored me temporarily so I could fight a king's fight.*

*Where is the barshi?*

*Over there,* Fynch said, pointing into the wooded area. *He thinks he is hidden.*

*Invisible?*

*Apparently. But I see him.*

*Fynch, what are you planning to do?*

*Nothing.*

*What does that mean? You won't fight him.*

*He must attack me.*

*But you'll then respond?*

*Wait and see. Be brave now, Knave; you've told me that often enough.*

*I don't want to see you die.*

*Hush, here he comes.*

When Jos arrived at the antechamber outside King Cailech's meeting room, he was greeted by a look of disdain from the servant who was manning the desk. "Are they sending half-wits to the King now?"

"Shut up," Jos growled, towering over the man and glad to note that the words sounded perfectly enunciated. "Do your job and let me do mine."

The man sneered but backed away and knocked at the door. Curiously, the King opened it himself. This dismayed the servant. He was not used to talking to his majesty in person. "Er, sire, there is a messenger for you."

Wyl looked over the servant's head to the bear of a lad behind him. No memory of his face registered within Cailech. "Who are you?"

"Jos, sire. I've been sent by Rollo."

The King looked back into the room, spoke briefly, then nodded. "Come in."

Jos entered to find the Grenadyne wiping blood from his face with a dampened linen and a woman, clearly dead, laid out on the floor with the King's cloak covering her face.

The King looked at him with a stony expression. "I believe you know Aremys," he said. Jos nodded, his eyes riveted on the dead girl. "This is Ylena Thirsk. She turned out not to be a good choice as a bride."

"What did you have to tell us, Jos?" Aremys prompted, the blood finally cleaned away, although the wound still seeped slightly.

The warrior turned his confused gaze on his king and bowed. "Apologies, your majesty," he said, remembering his manners and the message he had been sent to deliver. "Rollo sent me. They've found Myrt; he's badly injured. Borc is dead. Rashlyn is nowhere to be seen."

Wyl sighed. "Where is Myrt?"

"In the barshi's tower."

"All right. Jos, I would consider it a personal favor if you would have Ylena Thirsk's body shrouded and readied for travel on horseback. I'm returning her to Morgravia, where she belongs. Please use people we trust; no one with a loose mouth—you understand?"

"Of course, your majesty."

"Good. Then please ready horses for myself and Farrow."

Jos's eyes sparked with pleasure. He was rarely involved in any tasks other than lifting, carrying, and general menial tasks around the fortress. "Certainly, your majesty."

"And Jos, after we depart, I am leaving Myrt in charge. Rollo will be his second and I am appointing you Rollo's deputy."

The hulking lad looked toward Aremys and could not subdue a beaming grin. It did terrible things to his already twisted mouth—which is why he rarely smiled—but that did not matter anymore. "Thank you, your majesty," he repeated, bowing again. "You carry on, I'll fix everything here," he added, hoping the King understood him.

He did. "Good lad."

The King and Aremys left hurriedly, with strict orders that only those whom Jos permitted were allowed to enter the King's meeting room. Jos gave a twisted smirk toward the servant, who was not quick enough with his bow to miss the young man's sarcastic gesture.

"How do you feel—or is that a stupid question?" Aremys asked as they strode through the corridors.

"Shaky, but I'm getting used to Cailech's body. Relieved to be a man again."

"A king, don't forget." Aremys watched Cailech's face break into a reluctant grin. "You wear him well."

Wyl took no pride in knowing he had just destroyed another life. "Cailech fought me. I wasn't sure I could win."

"Inside, you mean?"

Wyl nodded. "Such anger. I don't know what he saw—presumably me, the real Wyl Thirsk, but perhaps he glimpsed Romen as well. Who knows? But whereas the others capitulated in shock, he was savage in his intensity to hang on to life."

"It's a pity he had to die. Cailech had admirable qualities. He was a good king most of the time."

"Without Rashlyn he would have been the greatest sovereign of his time," Wyl agreed.

"We have another king to worry about now," Aremys reminded.

"Poor Ylena. I so wanted to keep her whole."

"You did her proud, Wyl. Don't dwell on it. She's at peace now—and we aren't. I presume we're headed to Pearlis?"

Wyl shook Cailech's proud head. "Werryl. I have to see Valentyna, if I can make it before she leaves for Stoneheart and Celimus."

"You can't prevent the marriage," Aremys warned, knowing it was a waste of breath.

"I know. I just have to see her. Do you know where we're going?"

"Yes. Up these stairs and then out across the courtyard toward that tower over there. And what makes you think the Queen of Briavel will take kindly to a visit from the King of the Razors?"

"Valid question. I'll think of something. Knave is here, by the way; I saw him before we arrived at the fortress."

"Does that mean the boy is here as well?" Before Wyl could answer, Aremys added beneath his breath, "Remember to acknowledge your people, King Cailech." He nodded toward a group of warriors approaching.

Wyl received their salutations appropriately, Cailech's essence guiding his gestures and facial expressions. He answered Aremys: "Yes, Fynch is most likely here too, though I can't for the life of me think why."

More people, more polite salutations, and then Firl, the lad Aremys had allowed to beat him during swordplay when he had first arrived in the Razors, greeted them. "Your highness; Farrow," he said breathlessly, bowing.

Wyl nodded. "How bad is he?"

"I'm not sure, sire. We can't find Rashlyn to help."

"Have any other healers been called?" Aremys asked.

"Arrived a minute ago."

Wyl pushed Cailech's tall body past the young man and ran up the stairs with Aremys directly behind. Rollo's men were guarding the door but automatically stepped aside at the sight of the King. Wyl entered the chamber. He had anticipated the worst but was surprised to see Myrt sitting up.

It was Aremys who spoke first. "I hope you haven't made us run up those fucking stairs for nothing, Myrt."

His jest broke the tension and Rollo and Myrt grinned

while Cailech's face twitched in that way it did when he was amused but thoughtful. Wyl had realized he still had to win Rollo's trust and clear up the business of the barshi and his effect on the King.

He immediately addressed Rollo. "We need to speak."

Rollo raised his hands. "The fact that Farrow is still alive, sire, says plenty. Forgive my insubordination of earlier."

"Already forgotten, though we will speak more about your concerns shortly," Wyl replied. He moved toward Myrt and glanced at the dog lying on the floor, Borc's body next to it. The dog was deathly still and had puncture wounds on its body. For some reason Wyl felt dizzy and nauseous. It was not the sight of the animal's blood, but the feeling that it was tainted with magic.

"Are you all right, sire?" Aremys asked, noting the King's sudden change in demeanor.

"Is that Rashlyn's dog?" Wyl said, fighting an urge to throw up.

Myrt did not understand what had happened, but he had watched Cailech's interaction with Rollo and desperately wanted to trust his sovereign. He glanced toward Aremys now, who nodded reassuringly, then motioned at Rollo, who moved to shut the door. "Best to keep this between ourselves for now, sire."

Wyl frowned. "Speak," he said, moving away from the animal and positioning himself where he could suck in some fresh air from the open window.

"According to the barshi, the dog is . . ." Myrt hesitated, looking embarrassed, and glanced again at Aremys. The mercenary had only just become aware of the smell of magic. He no longer had to touch the beast to know it was there; he could sense it. The reek was not as bad as it had been with Galapek, but it was there all right. He despaired for Wyl at what he knew was surely coming.

Wyl followed Myrt's gaze, sensed the awkwardness. "Say it, Myrt."

"Yes, sire. Um . . . Rashlyn was boasting that the animal is the Morgravian prisoner. He used sorcery to turn him into a dog."

The King's face was suddenly a mask of anguish. "He what?"

Aremys moved to Wyl's side. "Careful now," he muttered. "You mean like Lothryn?" he asked, already knowing the truth as he looked back to Myrt. The big man nodded, his eyes fearful.

Aremys decided to impress some reassurance on these men, now so apprehensive around Cailech—and with good reason. If only they knew who Cailech's puppeteer was now. "We can speak freely," he said to the Mountain warriors. "The King has accepted that he's been entranced by Rashlyn on occasion and magically urged to agree to things he would normally never entertain. We've deduced that the spells only work if the barshi is close to the King, or his majesty would never be free of his hold—as he is now. He will execute the barshi when and if we find him."

He looked directly at Rollo. "It is because of this sorcery that our king was convinced to allow Lothryn to be . . . changed," he said carefully. "It was not his idea. He would never have agreed to something so horrific, so against our law of honorable death."

Wyl spoke up as if in a trance, stunned by the horrifying news about Gueryn. "He will never have that effect on me again. I am free of him. Do you men believe me?"

Something in the ferocious timbre of his voice and his cold, hard gaze had the right effect. Both Myrt and Rollo nodded.

"I will find Rashlyn and kill him," he added, and they believed him. He moved to crouch by the dog and stroked it tenderly, battling the revulsion caused by the magic. "Gueryn still breathes."

"He saved my life, sire," Myrt said. "Borc would have killed me if not for the animal's courage."

Wyl stopped himself from saying all that he wanted to about Gueryn's bravery; he was fighting back tears and took a moment to compose himself. "I will personally deliver Rashlyn to whichever god will accept him," he said.

"No need, sire," Myrt said. "You haven't heard the rest of my story." And he described the mysterious arrival of the boy through the tower walls, bathed in light and claiming to be Rashlyn's destroyer.

Wyl closed Cailech's eyes. "His name is Fynch," he said into the heavy silence that followed Myrt's startling revelation. "He is known to me."

No one dared ask how or why, which was fortunate, Aremys thought, because he could not imagine how Wyl would explain it. Cailech looked haggard, he noted. It had been one shock after another for Wyl: his sister, then Gueryn, now Fynch . . . not to mention another death, another body, another person to learn about.

"And you are recovered?" Aremys asked Myrt, taking the attention off the King so Wyl could gather his thoughts and emotions.

"Rashlyn used his filthy magic on me to weaken me, but the effects are wearing off. I'm ready to do your bidding, sire."

"Good!" Wyl growled. "Because you and Rollo are being left in charge here."

"Where are you going, sire?"

"To Briavel," came the reply. It provoked surprise and confusion on the men's faces, but Cailech's tone suggested it would be imprudent to argue. "Who is Maegryn's second? Call for him," Wyl commanded.

Rollo nodded and opened the door to the guards. "Get Obin. Hurry!"

"Gueryn's life is to be saved, so help you all," the King muttered. Rollo and Myrt exchanged another confused look. "Where did Rashlyn and Fynch go?" Wyl continued.

"Sire, as I said, one floated out of the window, the other through the walls," Myrt said, shaking his head. "I think I may have been seeing things."

"No, you weren't," the King replied, deadly cold. "You were witnessing two sorcerers throwing down the gauntlet at each other in a fight that has nothing to do with us."

It had come to Wyl now what this was about. He sensed that it was related to the sense of doom he had felt for Fynch when he had left him in the Wild. He pieced it together as he paced the room, waiting for Obin, who he hoped could save

Gueryn. Elysius must have died, Wyl guessed, and he remembered now the strange sensation of loss he had felt upon arriving in Briavel, courtesy of the Thicket. He had dismissed it as worry at leaving Fynch and his fretting over Ylena, not to mention being magically tossed hundreds of miles across the land. But perhaps Myrren's Gift had kept him linked with Elysius and he had felt the strange little man's death. *But you didn't die without luring Fynch into your web of despair, did you?* he thought savagely, suddenly hating Elysius.

He addressed the men again, his anger at Fynch's awesome responsibility and what had been perpetrated on Gueryn spilling into his tone. "Everything that has occurred tonight stays between us and a young warrior called Jos, whom I've appointed as your deputy, Rollo. In my absence, Myrt makes the decisions for our people. Agreed?" The Mountain Men exchanged worried glances. "Is that clear?" Wyl shouted.

"Yes, sire," the warriors said in unison, neither Myrt nor Rollo wanting to point out that nothing was clear about tonight. Not the King's strange behavior, nor the incredible sight of a ghostly boy appearing through granite walls; not Rashlyn jumping through an open window and hovering outside, not the talk of sorcery or men being changed into beasts. Nor why Myrt, who really did not want the task, was now leading the Mountain People.

"What about Lothryn, my lord?" Myrt risked.

"I'm going to find Rashlyn. Before I kill him, he will restore Lothryn and Gueryn le Gant." No one wanted to ask what would happen if the magic could not be reversed.

"Aremys," Wyl said.

"Sire?"

"Stay with the dog for me. If he dies . . ." Wyl could not finish. "Just see him cared for. I'll meet you all at the stables in one hour."

Fynch bowed, much to Knave's surprise. "Rashlyn," he said. "I have been sent."

The barshi had appeared as if out of nowhere. He looked rattled.

"By whom?"

"Can you not guess?" Fynch asked, echoing a king, a dragon, who had promised him so much not long ago.

"Elysius?" Rashlyn whispered in wonderment.

Fynch nodded.

"Why could he not face me himself?" the barshi demanded. He sounded deranged, his voice controlled and soft one moment, high and angry the next.

"He is dead."

"Then I do not fear you," Rashlyn cackled.

"You should," Fynch said, unfazed by the madman's baiting. "Elysius was not the only one who wishes you destroyed."

Rashlyn sounded arrogant now. "I know dozens just among the Mountain People who would slit my throat happily, if not for the King. I have his protection."

"Not anymore, I'm afraid."

That won the barshi's attention. "What do you mean?"

"Cailech is dead."

Rashlyn could not speak as he tried to absorb the terrifying news. Then: "I don't believe you. You're just a child."

"My age makes no difference. You have no protection now; Cailech will not save you. In fact, I would imagine the King of the Mountains is stalking you this very minute for the abomination you have imposed upon two men."

Rashlyn stared at the boy through wild eyes. "You just said he's dead. How can a dead man stalk me?"

Fynch simply grinned.

"Why are you here?" the barshi screeched. "If Cailech is dead then I am lost anyway, as good as dead."

"Not good enough. We wish to destroy you."

"We?"

Fynch nodded. "The Dragon King and I."

The sorcerer looked at the boy, puzzled by the riddles he was giving for answers. He regarded the self-possessed child from beneath hooded lids and asked the obvious. "Who is the Dragon King?"

"He is the King of the Creatures."

"And who are you?"

"I am the Dragon King," Fynch replied, and opened a bridge to the Thicket.

Wyl ran on long, muscled legs that covered the hard ground easily. Before leaving the tower, he had taken a deep breath and laid his hand once more on the barely breathing dog. Its eyes were glazed and blood seeped from its nostrils; its tongue lolled on the floor from between its jaws and it was all Wyl could do not to weep as he whispered to Gueryn to hold on. The dog did not move and Wyl left, not risking another word for fear his voice would break.

"Let him live," he prayed to Shar as he ran now. He felt the wood calling to him—sensed the hum of a powerful magic and recognized it as the Thicket. The Thicket and something else, something bright and powerful and good, overlaying an ugliness that he presumed was Rashlyn.

He burst into the clearing, drawing his sword, and pulled to a sharp stop when he saw Fynch standing there, bathed in a fierce glow of golden light. Knave was nearby and instantly covered the gap between himself and the new arrival, nearly knocking the King over with his welcome.

"Hello, Wyl," Fynch said, not turning his gaze from Rashlyn. "I'm sure you know who this is," he added.

"Fynch," Wyl replied, feeling a new sense of awe as he looked at the small gong boy who had so suddenly been infused with power, who was so composed . . . so brave.

"King Cailech, I—" Rashlyn began. He looked still more confused, his gaze darting between boy and man.

"I am not Cailech," the familiar voice said, turning a hard gaze on Rashlyn. "I am Wyl Thirsk."

The man groaned. "The General? You can't be. I . . . I would know it."

"Your eyes deceive you, Rashlyn," Wyl replied. "You didn't know me when I came here as Romen Koreldy either. Your brother's magic has given me the power to possess others. Clever, eh?"

"No! I won't believe this," the man said, shaking his head to deny what he knew to be true. The man looked like Cailech but did not behave like Cailech; worse, Rashlyn could almost taste the magic emanating from his former protector.

"You know I speak the truth," Wyl said.

"Tell me how," the barshi begged. "I must understand it!"

"Not until you lift the spell on Gueryn le Gant," Wyl demanded.

The wild man's mouth split into a thin, cruel smile beneath the tangle of his beard. "I cannot. It is irreversible."

Wyl took an involuntary step toward Rashlyn, his hand going to Cailech's sword.

"Don't," Fynch warned. "It is what he wants."

"And Lothryn?" Wyl demanded, already knowing the answer.

"Even more of a problem. At least with your friend le Gant, I knew what I was doing. Didn't hurt him as much. But Lothryn—that was horrible, even for me. He could not have survived it. You're wasting your time. The barbarian scum is dead."

It was Cailech, not Wyl, whose anger and grief rose now, who raised the sword and ran at the barshi. Wyl could not help but join with Cailech's lust to hack the magic man from skull to feet.

"No!" shouted Fynch, and Wyl felt Cailech's body slammed to a halt, high in the air. "Do not attempt to kill him. That is my job," the little boy commanded. His tone demanded respect.

Rashlyn screeched with laughter. "Now even your own people work against you, Thirsk. Perhaps I should kill you."

"You cannot. My protection will repel anything you cast against him."

Rashlyn sneered at Fynch. He moved his hands and a huge flaming ball roared toward Cailech's suspended body. Wyl held his breath, but the ball of flame bounced against something he could not see and fell away helplessly to extinguish itself in a nearby pool of thawing snow.

"Wyl, I want you to go now," Fynch said.

"I can't leave you."

"You did before and you will again. We walk different paths now."

"Will I see you again?"

"I think not."

"Fynch—"

"Don't, please. There is nothing to say except that I have loved you as a brother. Go now and do what you must."

"I need Knave."

"I know. He will come with you."

*I am not leaving you, Fynch,* the deep voice growled in the boy's head.

*You must. It's the only way we can save Wyl. You are his guide now.*

*I don't understand.*

*You will. Now go.*

*Fynch . . .*

*Knave, go!*

"Rashlyn is running," Wyl warned.

"He cannot escape me."

"Why do you have to do this?" Wyl's tone was pleading.

"Because no one else can."

"Let me go, then," Wyl said wearily, and felt Cailech's body lowered gently to the frosty ground. "What about Gueryn and Lothryn?"

"I do not know," Fynch said, knowing he was breaking Wyl's heart. "I must deal with Rashlyn."

*And you will die,* Knave crashed into Fynch's mind.

*So be it.*

"Do you and Knave talk?" Wyl asked, noting the odd silences and the expression on Fynch's face.

"Yes, ever since Elysius passed his magic to me."

"I thought he must have done so," Wyl said, feeling helplessly sorrowful.

"Wyl, Valentyna is to marry Celimus in a matter of days. You cannot save her that trial; you know that, don't you?" Wyl nodded. "But I know you wish to see her and you have something to tell her."

"I do?"

"Tell her everything. Let there be no secrets between you. She must understand who you really are."

"I cannot!" Cailech's expression became dismayed.

"You must. Please, trust me," Fynch urged. "And in turn she will trust you."

Wyl had no answer to Fynch's request. The boy had never been wrong before.

"Now please go. It is time I faced the barshi."

"Who are you, Fynch?" Wyl asked fearfully.

Fynch's face broke into a beatific smile. His golden hair seemed to radiate a bright glow, which spread to outline his tiny frame. "I am the Dragon King, Wyl," he said, and vanished.

Knave threw back his huge black head and gave a chilling howl, silencing the twittering birds that had come home to roost among the trees and echoing throughout the Razors. It was the heralding of death. Wyl knew he would never see the brave boy again. Somewhere deep inside he felt a part of his heart break. No tears and no amount of time would ever heal the loss.

## 33

OBIN HAD TAKEN ONE LOOK AT THE GRAY DOG AND SHAKEN HIS head. Aremys nodded, sad for Wyl. Another death he had not been able to prevent, and knowing his friend as he did, Aremys was sure Wyl would blame himself for this one too. One man; so much sorrow. Myrren and her father had plenty to answer for in Shar's plane. Aremys thanked Obin and then, wrapping the dog in a sheet he found in Rashlyn's rooms, hefted the animal into his arms.

"I'll take you to Lothryn," he murmured to the dog, who was still breathing in short, desperate pants. The dog whined but its eyes did not open.

When Aremys finally made it to the stable, staggering under the weight of the large animal, he heard Galapek whinny. The horse knew; Lothryn knew. Another man had been broken by Rashlyn's twisted magic.

Aremys laid Gueryn down in some fresh straw and lit a lamp. He explained to the horse who this was, all self-consciousness about talking to a horse gone. The animal reared, angry, and Aremys tried to calm him with soft words and soothing hands. As he touched the stallion he sensed the enormous and agonizing effort Lothryn was making to communicate with him. The horse was begging to be set free. Aremys was torn with indecision. Footsteps approached and the new King of the Razors stepped inside the stable, immediately flattening himself against the wall.

"Fight it, man," Aremys said, realizing Wyl had been overcome by the tainted aura of magic. "You'll get used to it, as I have."

Wyl lost the battle momentarily, gagging and then retching into a corner. "Oh, Shar." He groaned. "What has he done to them?"

Galapek whinnied again, a sound that nearly broke Wyl's heart. He forced himself to find composure, wiping his mouth on Cailech's sleeve, and in so doing, seeing Gueryn lying in the straw.

"Could Obin save him?" he asked.

Aremys shook his head. No point in lying.

Wyl leaned against the wall again, closed his eyes and groaned. The sight of him, so filled with anguish, made Aremys look away. How much more could Wyl take, he wondered, before he gave up on his fight? Or, more likely, found a way to take his own life.

A huge black dog entered the stable, startling Aremys out of his bleak thoughts. "Shar's wrath! I've never seen a dog so big."

"Meet Knave," Wyl said, flat-toned.

"Ah, the famous beast," Aremys replied. "May I?" he asked Wyl, his hand reaching to stroke the animal.

"Knave alone decides," Wyl said, and Aremys detected just a hint of humor in the tone. Perhaps Wyl would get through this, after all.

"Hello, Knave," the Grenadyne said, risking touching the

great head. Knave growled with pleasure as Aremys scratched his dark brow.

"Welcome to the chosen few," Wyl said, coming back from the dark place where he had been moments ago. "Knave is particular about who he lets touch him."

The black dog gave a deep-throated, suspicious bark and walked over to the horse first. Galapek did not flinch. Knave sniffed the creature and whined gently. Then he padded over to where Gueryn lay dying. This time he growled softly and began licking at the wounds of the gray dog.

"Speak to Lothryn," Aremys suggested, wanting to divert Wyl's gaze from the touching but painful scene in the straw. "Breathe through your mouth; it makes it easier."

"That's how Fynch overcame the major hurdle of being a gong boy," Wyl said, his mind going back to a time when he had lived the simple life of a Legionnaire.

"Where is Fynch?" Aremys asked.

The fragile shell Wyl had built around his emotions fractured again. "Gone to his death, fighting Rashlyn."

Aremys regretted his question. "I don't understand."

"You don't have to. None of us do, except perhaps Knave. It is not our battle."

The big man had no idea how to respond, so he left it, turning instead to the problem in front of them. "Come, Lothryn can talk to us."

Wyl stepped up to the horse. "He's beautiful despite that repulsive magic."

"So true. Touch him."

Wyl did so and his eyes widened. Startled, he fought the reek of the evil magic and laid his head against the sleek forehead of his rescuer and friend. "Lothryn," he wept, "it's me, Wyl."

The magnificent horse nuzzled him, as if in thanks, and Aremys too felt the telltale sting of tears.

*Wyl,* the horse whispered weakly into his mind, *I knew you would come. Didn't expect you to look as you do now.*

"I'm sorry I took his life."

*Don't be. He lived it fully. Paid the price for his decisions.*

"We will find a way to restore you."

*Turn me loose, I beg you. Tie the dog onto my back and let us go.*

"Aremys," Wyl gasped, "touch him. Hear what he's asking."

The Grenadyne laid a hand on Galapek and shared the conversation.

*I must save my strength,* Lothryn said, *what little is left. Please, put Gueryn on my back and turn us loose.*

"Why?" Wyl beseeched.

*I don't know, in truth. It seems right. Don't leave us here like this.*

"Do you know how to rid yourself of this guise?" Aremys asked, heart lurching with hope.

*No. But something is compelling me to leave.*

Wyl frowned. "Why take Gueryn?"

*Do you want him to die here . . . in a stable?*

Aremys grimaced at the harsh words. "Where will you go?"

*I don't know. Give him to me. You must leave. Let us do the same.*

"We could lose you forever," Wyl pleaded.

*You've lost us already. Let me try—let me see what or who this is calling to me.*

Wyl nodded, resigned. "Let's do it," he said to Aremys.

They fashioned a sling from the linen in which Aremys had brought Gueryn to the stable and found a sack to hold the dog. Knave finished tending to the gray's wounds.

"Odd that he would do that," Wyl commented absently.

"An instinctive attempt to heal the wounds perhaps?" Aremys offered.

"Or simply Knave's way of showing his sorrow."

"He can breathe easily through the sackcloth," Aremys said.

"He won't be breathing much longer," Wyl said, stroking the dog's face.

"Come on, Wyl. You have to be strong," Aremys warned. "Like Fynch."

The fighting words rallied Wyl's flagging spirits. "Yes, you're right. Fynch is off fighting a lost cause; I should at least try to hold myself together." He hefted the injured dog into the sack and together he and Aremys tied the sack to the sling, then to the saddle on Galapek's back.

Aremys watched the King reach again toward the majestic face of Galapek.

"Haldor protect you, Lothryn," Wyl said.

*Shar go with you, Wyl. We shall see each other again.*

"Elspyth will kill me in an ugly fashion if we do not," Wyl joked, trying to lighten the heavy moment.

Lothryn did not reply, simply waited for Wyl to make his farewell to Gueryn.

Wyl cupped the gray dog's face in his huge hands and kissed it, hoping that love and honor would somehow pour through his touch and reach the brave, dying man trapped inside.

"As One," he whispered to the dog, and then the horse was off, moving through the great doors Aremys had pushed open and cantering off into the blackness of the night.

Rashlyn felt compelled to return to the clearing, even though every fiber of his being told him he should run. But he was too curious about the boy, Fynch, and his self-proclaimed title of King of the Creatures.

"Come, Rashlyn," a voice called, startling him, for he could see no one. Then Fynch shimmered before him. "It is time."

"For what?" the barshi screamed at the child.

"For you to die," Fynch replied, a new gravity in his voice. He had left behind everyone he loved, deliberately cutting himself away from Wyl and Knave. He knew he could not carry out his task, could not offer himself as sacrifice, if they were near.

Sacrifice. He understood now. It had taken some time to ponder its meaning and recognize how he must apply it to this battle with Rashlyn. It meant more than death. It meant yielding.

Faith Fynch. Sacrifice.

The first wave came as Rashlyn hurled a magical avalanche of blows at Fynch, screaming with madness and anger as he loosed his powers.

Around them the creatures of the mountains quietly gathered in awe. They had instinctively known for many hours that something momentous was about to occur, although they had not been exactly sure what. Now they knew. Zerkons, ice bears, deer, snow hares, even the birds who had been spreading the news since dusk, gathered side by side, predator and prey, forgetting their fear or hunger as they witnessed a wild man doing battle with a creature they had never seen before, a creature they knew of only from stories handed down through the ages. A dragon.

Rollo, Myrt, and Byl saw Cailech glance at the muslin bundle that had been carefully tied to one of the Mountain King's most trustworthy horses. They could see past the stern expression to the emotional battle going on inside. Wyl steeled himself not to look at Ylena's corpse again. It was over. Her life was spent and had been given bravely, as all the Thirsks before her had given theirs.

Beside Cailech's horse stood a huge dog. He explained its presence to the Mountain Men. "This is Knave. He is going to help us with what we must do, and is one of the reasons why Rashlyn no longer has any hold on me."

"Where is Rashlyn, sire?" Myrt asked. He seemed fully recovered from the barshi's attack.

"He is dead," Wyl risked, hoping he was telling the truth.

"And Lothryn, your majesty?" Rollo added.

They deserved to know the truth. "I have released him. Aremys here can talk to him and that was what Lothryn wanted."

Rollo gasped. All the talk of magic had been confusing enough, but was the King saying that the Grenadyne could communicate with the magically created animals? "What! How?"

"Myrt knows," Wyl replied. He was not in the mood for further discussion. "He will explain. Right now we ride for Briavel."

"May I ask why, sire?" Myrt said. His tone was hesitant but his manner firm.

"To make a new peace treaty, this time with a queen who needs the support of the Mountain People."

"Against the Morgravian Crown?" Myrt asked, quickly grasping his king's intent.

It was Aremys who replied. "Celimus has no intention of keeping his promise to the Razor Kingdom. Our only hope of peace is with Briavel."

"But, sire," Rollo pleaded. "She is marrying Celimus. Her loyalties stand with him!"

"Not necessarily," the King replied in a tone that discouraged further argument. "I need you to trust me. I have not yet led our people astray. I will not do so now."

"Shouldn't we come with you, sire?" Myrt asked, far preferring to ride headlong into danger with his king than to take over royal duties.

"No. I need you here, Myrt. You and Rollo will keep everyone steady. And in case the horse returns—he will need friends, allies who know the truth." He said no more. It would not serve any purpose to get their hopes up that Lothryn might be restored.

Myrt asked anyway. "Can the spells be reversed?"

"It's my keen hope they can be. According to Aremys, it is why Lothryn asked to be released."

"Where has he gone?"

"We don't know," Aremys replied. "But he took the gray dog with him. We just have to hope he knows more than we do, now that Rashlyn is finished."

Myrt nodded unhappily, a glum Rollo by his side. "Haldor keep you safe, sire."

Cailech nodded back, appreciating the warrior's suffering and his wish to protect his king. "It is better this way, Myrt. We two can slip into and out of Briavel far more subtly than a pile of Mountain barbarians storming Werryl Palace."

"Get word to us the usual way," Myrt said, cocking his head toward a small box fastened to the side of the horse that carried Ylena.

Wyl frowned, taking a moment to delve into Cailech's memories. He understood. "I hope those pigeons are strong fliers," he said.

"The best," Myrt answered. "Rollo's top birds," and he grinned toward his companion.

"All right. Keep faith. Look after Aydrech. If anything

happens, if Celimus sets a raid, the boy must be protected at all costs."

The big man nodded. "I will take care of him personally."

"Good," Wyl said, adding: "Rotate the watches regularly. I have no idea whether Celimus will attempt anything or not."

"Possibly not with a wedding so close," Aremys commented drily.

"Nevertheless," Wyl replied, "the child's safety is paramount." He leaned down and clasped each man's hand in farewell, suspecting that neither of these loyal Mountain warriors would see their king again.

The horse arrived at the edge of the wood. Lothryn was drawn toward the trees, and as he entered their cover he felt the pulse of magic emanating from somewhere deep inside the forest. He also noted that he was feeling stronger, more himself, than he had felt since the change had been inflicted on him. Pain continued to be his companion, but he believed it had lessened ever so slightly.

Lothryn was reassured by the connection between him and the dog. He could feel its heartbeat, weak but still there. *Hang on, Gueryn,* he passed through the link, even though he had no idea whether the trapped man heard him or could even register something as subtle as another's thoughts.

Still following the compulsion, Lothryn pushed deeper into the wood until he came to a clearing. He stood at its fringe and looked in wonderment at the sight that confronted him—a huge dragon coated in a shimmering armor of scales. Its serpentlike neck was twisted and the great head was thrown back, but there was no sound. The great beast was silent as wave after wave of sickening magical power pounded its body. The deathly magic was a sickly brown color, impenetrable by light. And Rashlyn was dealing the blows, his face a twisted mask of hate.

Lothryn was tempted to rush forward and pummel the barshi with every last ounce of strength he could muster from Galapek's powerful body, and yet something stopped him. He stared at Rashlyn and knew that if hate, madness, and despair could be embodied, they would look exactly like the sorcerer before him. Although Rashlyn looked exhausted, he was standing and seemed to be in control of his powers. He muttered a stream of unintelligible words; the dragon faltered.

Looking around, Lothryn became aware of other creatures—dozens, no scores of them—clustered among the trees and dotted around the nearby foothills. He even saw zerkons, and flinched in fear, before he realized they were paralyzed by the same awe that he was experiencing.

A dragon! Who would have thought they truly existed? Lothryn had always considered them creatures of myth.

*Fight back!* Lothryn begged.

*He won't,* replied a voice, startling him.

He twisted to see who it was. A bird on a nearby branch stretched its wings. *Who are you?* the horse asked.

*I am Kestrel.*

*And who is that?* Lothryn tossed his head toward the dragon.

*That is the King. The King of us all. And he is sacrificing himself to save us. He was once Fynch.*

*I gathered Fynch was a child.*

*He is so much more.*

*But I see him as a dragon,* Lothryn persisted. *There's no boy there.*

*He is still a child physically, but the dragon reflects who he truly is.*

Kestrel's explanation served only to confuse Lothryn. He looked back at the dragon, which staggered slightly. *Why doesn't he use his powers? Surely he can topple a man!*

*Oh yes, he could overcome the sorcerer with ease, but he refuses to kill. That is the child in our king. He made a pact with himself, I think. I sensed it when he first spoke to me. There is no violence in Fynch. He agreed to destroy Rashlyn but in his own way.*

Lothryn felt his spirit lurch with grief. Wyl's friend, now—like all of them—somehow changed by enchantment. *So how can he beat the barshi?*

Kestrel's sorrow was immediate and apparent. *By taking everything that is Rashlyn. He will absorb the storm of magic, consume the pain, devour the evil. Already his glow lessens. When they began, the King of the Creatures burned golden bright. See how the murky evil has dimmed him.*

*But then he will die himself,* Lothryn said, aghast.

*I suspect so,* Kestrel agreed, bitterness in his voice. *But not before Rashlyn burns through his power until there is none left.*

Lothryn needed to ask no more. Both creatures fell silent, keeping vigil with the other animals of the mountains, still gathering to pay homage to their king.

## 34

WYLAND AREMYS SET OFF FROM THE FORTRESS IN THE DEAD OF night, Knave trotting at their side. The Grenadyne chanced airing his concern to the grim-faced King at his side. "We cannot travel the Razors successfully at night, Wyl. Surely you know that the way down is treacherous?"

"I do. We won't be going far," came the reply.

"If you're intent on this mad journey into Briavel, why not leave at first light? We would easily make up the poor advantage of departing now."

"I'm sorry, I haven't explained myself," Wyl said, turning to look directly at his anxious friend. "Leaving by horse was purely for appearances."

"What?"

"I have another method, much faster—though horribly unpleasant."

"Has becoming a king gone to your head?" Aremys began to sound truculent. The night's proceedings had worn down his emotional reserves. He was tired, angry at losing Cailech, furious at failing Lothryn and Gueryn, sad for Wyl, and altogether sick to the back teeth of magic. He must have murmured the last thought aloud because Wyl answered him.

"Well, just a little more magic to go. It was you who gave me the idea."

"Me! Whatever are you talking about?"

"I'm talking about the Thicket, Aremys. We will use the Thicket to travel."

That won the Grenadyne's attention. He felt his belly clench and could not speak for a few moments. Finally he said, "How?"

"Knave. It's why I insisted he come."

"He looks none too happy about it."

"He isn't, believe me. I've never known him to be this aloof."

"Because he had to leave behind Fynch?"

"Correct. The two of them are inextricably linked."

"But you told me he was your dog."

Wyl sighed. "It's complicated," he said, smiling sadly. "Knave loves us all and has protected all of us. Now he is having to suffer each of us dying, and me so many times over."

Aremys was eager to get away from the painful subject. "So how can the dog help us?"

"He is of the Thicket. He is our connection to it."

"And?" Aremys was still baffled.

"Remember how you suddenly found yourself between the fringe of Timpkenny and the Razors . . . ?"

Aremys frowned, then understanding dawned. "Oh, no. You jest, surely?"

He saw Cailech's eyes—now settled back to their pale green—sparkle in the light of the flaming torch he carried. "Not this time, my friend."

Aremys began to stutter, words falling out on top of one another. "But how do you summon it, command it, control it?"

Cailech's shoulders shrugged and a twitch of a grin at his mouth disappeared as rapidly as it arrived. "We just have to trust the Thicket."

"That place is no friend of mine, Wyl. It cast me out, remember? What if it hurts me this time?"

"It won't."

"You sound so confident," Aremys blustered.

"I am. The Thicket will not hurt either of us—first, because we travel with Knave, and second, because of our connection to Fynch. The boy means everything to the Thicket, I believe."

"How do we know it can do this?"

"It threw me all the way to Briavel in seconds," Wyl said. Aremys gasped. "I didn't know that."

"There is so much you don't know," Wyl said, his voice laced with regret. "Such as the fact that Fynch will die this night, doing what he has done since I first met him."

"Which is?"

"Acting out of sacrifice, loyalty, love. He has always put others before himself." Wyl sighed, then added, "You also don't know that Valentyna will marry Celimus, come what may."

Aremys felt utterly baffled. "What? But I thought we were going to Briavel to try to prevent it."

He saw Cailech shrug. "I can't read the future," Wyl said. "Elysius told me that she will marry the King of Morgravia."

"Why do we go, then?"

"Because Fynch told me that Myrren's Gift is still subject to randomness."

Aremys looked quizzically at the King of the Mountains. They were moving slowly, often raising an arm to acknowledge scouts and guides on higher ridges who were recognizable only by the flicker of their small fires. A special flame burning on top of the fortress told these guards that their king was passing through the mountains, so the two men had no fear of being attacked or stopped. "I don't understand any of this, Wyl."

"I hardly understand it myself," Wyl admitted. "Fynch believes that random acts can still affect the outcome of Myrren's Gift."

"And so you will try to do something to prevent the Queen marrying Celimus, is that right?"

"In truth I don't see how I can. I think I am going simply so that I may see her before I die again."

Aremys reined in his horse and Wyl followed suit, knowing his statement was too provocative to be ignored. "Why?" his friend demanded. "Stay as Cailech. Just think of all you can achieve. Let's turn back. You say yourself that you cannot affect the outcome of the marriage. We have friends here, loyal people. You are a king. You can live. Stop the gift now!"

"Only one thing will stop it, Aremys," Wyl said, weariness in his tone.

"What?" the Grenadyne asked.

Wyl raised Cailech's head and looked his friend directly in the eye. "When I become the sovereign of Morgravia."

"Celimus?" It came out as a choked exclamation.

Wyl nodded, deadly serious. Aremys was shocked to the core. "Is that what this is all about? Myrren's Gift is to make sure that you become him?"

Cailech's face twisted into a snarl. "It's about revenge. Myrren suffered at Celimus's hands, so she and her father worked out a way to make him suffer in return."

"But why involve you? You did nothing but offer her pity."

"I am nothing but a pawn in this complex game," Wyl said softly. "She has used me to avenge her torture, which Celimus so enjoyed."

The big man's horror was written on his face. Wyl recalled his own despair at the discovery of the truth of Myrren's Gift. Perhaps it was even worse for the mercenary, Wyl thought. Often watching those you love suffer was more intolerable than living through the suffering yourself.

"Wyl," Aremys began, recovering himself. "This is worse than I could ever have imagined, I'll agree, but can you not think of it in the more positive light that you will be King of Morgravia and your queen will be Valentyna? Can the knowledge that you will be together soften the damage that has been done? You cannot bring back those you have lost, but perhaps you can make their lives count by making Morgravia great again. Sire heirs with Valentyna and establish a new dynasty. Imagine it—Morgravia ruled by you, not Ce-

limus. One more death, my friend, that's all it will take."
There was a new brightness in the Grenadyne's voice, as if
suddenly he felt everything could be righted.

Wyl looked down at his new large hands with their prominent knuckles and long, blunt fingers. He had thought of the
same scenario many times since learning of his destiny. And
every time he tried to convince himself that this terrible
episode of his life could end happily, he hit a wall. The wall
was called Celimus. "Aremys," he said softly into the chill
spring night. "I don't want to be him."

Aremys had not considered that. "You have no choice."

"I will not live as Celimus," Wyl said slowly, defiantly. "I
would sooner die."

"But you will have everything—"

Wyl cut him off. "I will have nothing but hate and despair.
You don't understand. When I become someone new, much
of who they are remains with me. I have their memories,
their dreams. I have their ways and mannerisms. I have their
darkness, Aremys. I will not live as the person I hate most in
this world, who in turn has hated the Thirsks for two
decades."

"So what are you going to do—die again?" Aremys's tone
was heavy with sarcasm. Wyl remained silent and continued
staring at Cailech's hands.

The Grenadyne shook his head slowly with disbelief.
"Tell me you're not planning to die once you're him, Wyl?"
he urged, a fresh wave of fear washing across him. He realized that once Wyl became Celimus, he would no longer
have Myrren's protection. He would be as vulnerable to
death as anyone.

Wyl spoke in a grave tone. "When it happens—and it will,
for my destiny is to become the sovereign of Morgravia—
you will end my life once and for all."

Aremys was rocked by Wyl's words. "I won't," he
shouted. "I won't do it."

"You will! You will do it because I demand it. I will be
King of Morgravia, don't forget, and I will command you."

"Command me?! Upon the threat of what—pain of
death?" Aremys yelled.

Wyl ignored him, kept speaking. "We shall set it up as an accident. It doesn't have to be by your hand as such, if that revolts you too much. We can manipulate it through others. But you will help me to achieve my death. I think I would like an arrow, clean and swift, to the heart. I would prefer it to be you, Aremys, as I know you shoot accurately. This is about friendship, love, loyalty."

"No, Wyl. What about Valentyna?"

"I can't think about what might happen after my death. That will be beyond my control. But Valentyna will be released from her sentence of being married to Celimus, free to return to Briavel and begin her life afresh."

"But it's not *him*. It's you."

"Valentyna will not know that. She will look at me with disgust; she will detest my touch and speak my name with loathing. No, Aremys," Wyl said sadly, "I would rather be dead, truly. Elysius said I cannot contrive for others to kill me, but I am counting on the fact that once I have become Celimus, as Elysius and Myrren intended, the gift will have run its course and will no longer be able to hurt me or those I care about."

Aremys shook his head; it was too painful. They had battled against so much, but for what? "Don't make this decision yet," he beseeched. "Fynch warned of the randomness—let's wait and see how it all turns out."

Wyl recalled Fynch begging him to tell Valentyna the truth, and was reminded once again that the boy had never led him astray. Fynch had always been true. "Fair enough," he said. "We will not discuss it again until I become Celimus, after which I will give you one night's grace, which I shall spend with Valentyna, and the next day I will expect you to take my life. Agreed?"

Aremys was cornered. "Agreed," he said, deeply unhappy.

"Good," Wyl replied, feeling suddenly brighter for airing the decision he had been brooding on for so long. Now it was time to ask for the Thicket's help.

"Come, we'll try from here," he said, pointing to a small outcrop of rocks.

"Do you know what you're doing?" Aremys asked, leading his horse in the direction of the rocks.

"Not really, but the journey will take too long by conventional means. I have to try."

Aremys sighed audibly. "So what do we do? Turn the horses loose or remain on them?"

Cailech shrugged his broad shoulders. "I haven't even brought anything for her," he said, his mind elsewhere.

Aremys lifted his eyes to the heavens and asked Shar to help them. "Come on, Wyl, what do we do?"

Wyl collected his thoughts. "Knave," he said, "please, would you call on the Thicket? I need it to send us to Werryl Palace, like it did for me before."

Knave could not explain to his friend that he no longer enjoyed the same contact with the Thicket as he had in the past. There was nothing for it now, he realized; he would have to contact Fynch . . . if the boy was still alive.

Letting his mind flood with the trace that was Fynch, Knave cast out to him, begging him to be alive, to answer him . . . not because he needed his help but because he wanted to hear his sweet voice again.

*Knave.* It sounded more of a groan.

*Always here,* the dog answered, keeping his voice steady even though he was frightened by the pain communicated in the single syllable of Fynch's response.

*Is Wyl safe?*

*Yes.* Knave knew not to waste time on small talk. Fynch was fighting for his life. *We need to use the Thicket to travel quickly to Briavel. I'm sorry to—*

*Wait.* There was a silence and then Fynch was back; his voice sounded even more fractured and filled with pain than just moments earlier. *I've set up a bridge. Use it, but hurry— I can't hold it together for long.*

*Fynch, what's happening?*

*Hurry, Knave. Please.*

Knave closed his eyes in grief. It sounded as though Fynch were near to death. He reached toward the Thicket, feeling guilty at drawing on Fynch's waning reserves. He could not understand it. Fynch was strong in his power. Surely he could easily overcome Rashlyn?

It was Rasmus who answered the unspoken question. *Fynch is following his destiny, Knave. You must do what he has commanded. The Thicket will allow this request.*

*There are horses too,* Knave replied, disguising his rising fear for Fynch.

The owl made a sound of disgust. *Wyl Thirsk never makes it easy,* the bird said testily. *We'll have to be careful how they land. Tell the two men to sit on horseback. Then we only have to control three "parcels."*

*Just two. I plan to return to Fynch.*

*No. You have been commanded. You must do as he wishes. Now make ready.*

Knave cut the link angrily, unused to feeling such emotion. He felt a keen loyalty to Wyl and would give his life for him if asked, but with Fynch it ran much deeper. It was love. Not something you turned your back on.

*Thank you, Fynch,* he sent, filled with sorrow.

He could barely hear the reply, but he felt it. *I love you, Knave. Farewell.*

And then the boy cut their link. Knave whined softly, feeling a deep and irreplaceable loss, then turned to Wyl and gave a low growl.

Aremys shook his head. "Do you understand him?"

Wyl nodded. "Sort of. I've been around him long enough to grasp what kind of message is being communicated."

"And that one meant . . . ?"

"We wait." He turned to Knave. "I know you're hurting, boy, but I need you to come with us."

Wyl's comment was timely. Knave realized, as much as he hated to admit it, that he was not of much use to Fynch right now. But Wyl needed him for to this trip to Briavel. That settled it. He would go.

The men began to dismount, but Knave barked.

Aremys frowned. "What now?"

"Wants us to remain on horseback, I think," Wyl said. "Is that right, Knave?"

The dog gave a familiar growl and Wyl nodded to his friend. "Yes. I guess we're taking the horses."

"This will take some explaining at the other end," Aremys said as the air around them began to thicken.

"Here we go," Wyl cautioned. "It's not pleasant, I warn you."

"I think I remember that much," was all Aremys had time to say before he felt a huge pressure on his body and all went dark.

The blinding golden light that had initially shimmered around the dragon had gradually dimmed to a soft glow, taking on a dirty bronze color. The dragon's wings hung limply and each breath was labored, but still it stood upright, absorbing the magic slamming into its body.

"Die, beast," the barshi screamed, clearly confused as to why the creature would not retaliate. "You came here to destroy me," he yelled. "Yet you can't even shield yourself against my magic."

He blasted the dragon again with a powerful spell and saw the beautiful beast stagger for the first time, its head drooping.

*Fynch!* Lothryn screamed.

*He can't hear you,* Kestrel warned. *He won't listen anyway. He is dying, wants to die . . . has to die, I think.*

*We must do something,* Lothryn cried. He was feeling much stronger, and was restless, frantic to help Fynch.

*We are. We bear witness to his sacrifice.*

*We stand by and let him die? But we could save him! We could all rush at Rashlyn together and destroy him,* Lothryn tried.

Kestrel tutted. *He is already being destroyed.*

*What do you mean?*

*With every spell the sorcerer weakens. He cannot feel it yet, but we can see it. His magic is a filthy brown, tainted and ugly, not bright and golden like that of the Dragon King. The man has been careless—he has used most of it up.*

*And?*

*Fynch will absorb the evil magic until there is no more left in the sorcerer. And in doing so, he sacrifices himself.*

A collective groan echoed around the forest and up to the mountain ridges as the animals saw the dragon slump to one side, its golden light no more than a slight wash of color.

Rashlyn was laughing maniacally. "It is you who dies, you fool. Am I so strong? Can you not fight me? I am the King of the Creatures, not you. I will rule them. I can change them and bend them to my will." He shook his bony fist toward the animals who watched. "You will all hail me as your king. Look at the dragon now. He dies. I have vanquished him and I shall take all of his power and wield it as I will."

It was true. The King of the Creatures had rolled onto his side and was breathing so shallowly that death was surely imminent.

If Lothryn had not been mesmerized and moved by the boy's courage, he would have closed Galapek's eyes. But he could not do that. Instead he focused on Rashlyn, and because he was helplessly linked to him through the evil man's filthy magic, he could feel the barshi summoning everything he had within. Curiously, Lothryn felt himself grow even stronger. The pain had diminished; his flesh no longer twitched and trembled. He sensed Rashlyn gathering all his power to hurl at the dying dragon.

"Finish it!" the animals heard their king whisper. Fynch's words were met by a hysterical cackle from Rashlyn.

The barshi unleashed a primeval howl and launched every ounce of magic he possessed toward the dragon. The animals who had gathered to pay homage bore witness as Fynch, King of the Creatures, rolled back onto his clawed feet again in a last defiant show of strength and will. He too loosed a roar—a death roar—which every creature felt rattle through its chest, and he accepted the powerful killing spell, absorbing the twisted magic. And then, with a mighty effort, he went on sucking hard at the barshi, whose twisted face of triumph turned to surprise. He was no longer giving his magic; it was being stolen from him, pulled in a great and dirty arc into his opponent.

*I will take it all from you, Rashlyn,* the dragon vowed.

Lothryn and Kestrel watched in awed silence as Fynch, howling with anger, dragged the very essence of the barshi's being into himself and consumed it in golden fire. The brilliant light pulsed brightly around the dragon before extinguishing itself.

The King of the Creatures fell, reducing in size and stature until, where the mighty dragon had stood so proudly just hours earlier, the tiny shape of a boy lay curled tightly into himself on the forest floor.

Each creature present cried out in sympathy and then, as if on a given signal, all but the zerkons began to move toward the child, who looked as though he were sleeping. One by one they nuzzled or sniffed the tiny body, each softly giving thanks for the sacrifice that had been given to preserve their lives and their ways.

In Briavel, Knave threw back his head and howled a sound to chill the souls who stood nearby. He did it again and again and Wyl knew the black dog was grieving for Fynch.

He lowered King Cailech's head in grief. "Fynch is dead," he said to Aremys, and the mercenary knew better than to offer hollow words of comfort.

A man staggered between the trees, his body burned and shriveled, his hair flaming. His tangled beard was a blackened mass and patches of charred flesh ate at his face. His eyes were unseeing, scorched black, and he moaned, arms outstretched as he blindly felt his way. He began to scream and his empty cries echoed off the mountain peaks and returned to taunt him.

"Yes, scream, you evil bastard," a voice said.

"Who speaks?" shrieked Rashlyn, swinging around in the direction of the voice.

"It is Gueryn le Gant."

"The dog?" Rashlyn whispered.

"The man," Gueryn said, and it sounded like a threat. "You have no more magic, Rashlyn. You cannot bind me and so I have been freed." He looked at the horse next to him, sorrow knifing through him. "I see his magic was not used with such sophistication on you, my friend. You remain en-trapped."

Having felt his spirit soar with untold joy at seeing Gueryn whole, Lothryn experienced the sickening fall of disappointment at realizing that he, of course, remained as Galapek. He turned his great head toward the man but could no longer communicate with him by sending thoughts.

Gueryn lifted his finger to his lips to calm Lothryn. "We will find a way," he whispered to the horse, knowing the man inside could hear.

"How did this happen?" yelled Rashlyn, his voice trem-bling. "You were stabbed, dead."

"The other dog, Knave, healed me. He licked each of my wounds, sealing them with his own magic. He sensed I would be returned if you lost your power."

"Lost my power?" the barshi echoed.

Gueryn advanced on the wild man. He could smell the charred flesh and took great pleasure in noticing injuries that would normally turn his gut. "Try your magic now," he taunted. "If you can."

Rashlyn reached inside himself and, discovering his loss, screamed in despair.

Gueryn laughed. "Fynch may not have had the desire to kill, but I do, Rashlyn," Gueryn said. "I do." He moved to-ward the staggering man, who was now walking in circles, arms outstretched. But then, looking up, Gueryn had a far better idea. Most of the animals had scattered at the demise of their king, but one type of creature remained. They were gradually closing in on the three that remained in the clear-ing, but Gueryn could see that their attention was focused on the charred man.

"Ah, a better idea," he said gleefully. "A fitting one, Rashlyn."

Spinning toward his voice, Rashlyn began to weep. "What?"

"Do you know what zerkons look like?"

The barshi fell to his knees, pleading for mercy. Gueryn laughed, amazed at the man's audacity. "Go to your god, Rashlyn, and I hope he burns you in eternal fire."

Gueryn bent down to the boy, not wasting time to check for

a pulse. He lifted the tiny mass of limbs and cradled the child
in his arms. Fynch's head rolled against the soldier's chest.
Gueryn called to Galapek and rapidly hefted himself onto the
stallion's broad back, Fynch all but weightless in his arms.
"Lothryn, if you wouldn't mind taking us out of here . . . ?"
he asked.

Galapek's powerful frame carried them swiftly from the
clearing as two massive zerkons descended on the screaming man, who understood all too well, blind or not, that
death had finally arrived. Only one creature remained to
witness the barshi's bloody end—a kestrel, perched high in
a tree's branches.

# 35

AREMYS THOUGHT THAT COMING TO WERRYL WAS A STUPID
idea. It was clear from what Wyl had said that Knave
would prefer to be back in the Razors, and even Wyl's good
sense must have warned him against reentering Briavel. And
yet here they were, taking deep breaths to recover from the
magical travel and preparing to waltz up to the Queen of
Briavel and present King Cailech, sworn enemy of the
southern realms and newly agreed partner-in-crime with the
treacherous Morgravian monarch.

"Do you think the Queen will start screaming like a ban-
shee or do you imagine she'll keep her composure and offer
the Mountain King high tea?" Aremys said sarcastically.
"That is, if we make it past the hail of arrows."

"We'll send Knave," Wyl said, smoothing back Cailech's
long golden hair. "How do I look?"

Aremys laughed, harsh and brief. "Like the fucking King
of the Razors."

"I meant," Wyl replied calmly, "am I untidy?"

Aremys shook his head. "What does it matter? Let's go, Wyl, and get this done with."

"Trust me, my friend. She will see us."

"And kill us," the mercenary growled.

"Not with Knave leading us, she won't. She trusts the dog more than she trusts me."

"Who is 'me,' Wyl?" Aremys asked angrily.

"Romen," Wyl corrected. "You're welcome to remain here," he offered, tiring of the Grenadyne's bitterness even though he understood.

"No, it's always fun watching you die," Aremys cut back swiftly. He regretted the words instantly as he saw pain sweep across Cailech's face, the eyes darkening with barely contained sorrow. "Forgive me, Wyl." He groaned. "I didn't mean that."

"I know you didn't," his friend said softly. "I just have to see her once more, Aremys, before I become Celimus and am forced to see her through his cruel eyes."

"How will it happen, do you think? The Queen will turn you over to him . . . again?"

"Probably," Wyl said, resigned to his fate. "Come, I hope she has not already left for Pearlis."

Valentyna was taking a late supper with Liryk. Conversation was hard won with her this night, just a day before their departure to Pearlis. She was trying, of that the commander was certain, but gradually her gaze had clouded and now she had withdrawn into her private, no doubt grim, imaginings of life as Celimus's queen.

Liryk wished he could spare her the sorrow she was feeling, but he thought of her father and imagined how proud Valor would be of his only child. She was giving Briavel a brilliant gift—the gift of peace.

He watched her pushing food around her plate, her fork never once lifting any of it toward her mouth. The only sound in the room was the clink of cutlery against porcelain. She lifted her beautiful face, aware of his gaze.

"Forgive me, Liryk."

"Nothing to forgive, your highness."

Valentyna smiled wanly. "My thoughts are elsewhere this eve—a bride's prerogative, I think." She tried to widen the smile but failed. Tears welled instead.

They both started at the sound of a knock at the door.

"Let me, your majesty," Liryk offered, rising to answer the messenger. He returned tight-lipped and frowning.

"Important?" she asked, presuming it was for him. "Don't fret, you're excused from my dazzling repartee this evening." He gazed at her, wishing he did not have to tell her anything, wishing they could leave for Pearlis tonight. "What is it? Not bad news, please . . . unless"—she laughed harshly—"it's to tell me that Celimus has unexpectedly and tragically died."

"Far more intriguing, your highness. Knave is on the bridge."

She stood. "Knave's back! Is Fynch with him?"

"No, your majesty." Liryk's hesitant tone snapped her to attention.

"He's not alone, though, is he?"

"He brings with him two men. One is Aremys Farrow."

Valentyna's mouth dropped open. "The man Ylena Thirsk and the Duke of Felrawthy spoke of—the one brokering the peace treaty with the Mountain King?"

Liryk nodded.

"And who accompanies him?" Valentyna asked, then frowned at Liryk's silence. "Come on, Commander, the suspense is irritating."

Liryk wiped away the perspiration coating his forehead. "King Cailech of the Mountains, your majesty."

The silence that met his words felt as heavy as the dread in his own heart. He watched the Queen's hand fly to her throat; to her credit, she gave away nothing more than the initial shock. Visibly gathering her composure, she turned toward the double windows, unlatched and threw them open, then stepped out onto the balcony.

He joined her in looking down upon the famous Werryl Bridge to where three figures stood, surrounded by soldiers. One was familiar; as if on cue, the dog raised his great dark head and looked directly at Valentyna. Valentyna felt that penetrating gaze cross the substantial distance between them and pierce her heart. She had to stop herself from clutching her breast, where an old ache, barely buried, resurfaced to taunt and frighten her.

"He has brought him back to me," she whispered to herself.

"Beg your pardon, your majesty?" Liryk said.

Valentyna closed her eyes momentarily then calmly replied, "Bring them to my study."

"Your majesty, I don't—"

"Now, Liryk, please. Search them and remove their weapons."

"Yes, your highness."

She disappeared from the balcony, leaving Liryk to look down upon the strange trio once more.

"Now what have you sent us, Shar, to disrupt her peace?" he muttered.

Valentyna splashed icy water on her face and took several deep, steadying breaths as she held the drying linen to her cheeks. She groaned. What was happening to her?

She raced through the questions that were alarming her. How could Knave know the Mountain King? Why bring him here? How could they have come so far without encountering the Briavellian Guard? It was impossible, she realized. Unless they materialized out of thin air, two riders and a huge dog would not escape notice.

Knave's return inevitably reminded her of Fynch and she recalled his last conversation with her, when he had implied that the man she loved was not decaying in a tomb within the palace crypt. *If I suggested this was simply a dead body and not really the Romen Koreldy you loved, what would you say?* he had asked, shocking her. And she had replied that it was cruel to ask such a thing. Still, he had tried, dear Fynch, to make her understand something which she could not believe, and yet now felt so deep in her heart. *Although Romen's corpse lies here before us, that the man you knew— the man you loved, your highness—is not dead.*

Looking down at the trio on Werryl Bridge, she had felt as

much, even though neither of the two men looked remotely like Romen. She hesitated even to say the word, but it hovered nevertheless on the tip of her tongue. Magic.

"Magic," she said aloud, recalling Elspyth's warning about being open to different ways of understanding. She had spoken of reincarnation and told her that love might return in the shape of another. Elspyth had been trying to convey a message; Valentyna had heard it in the urgency of her tone, her desperation to imply something important while not actually saying it. Elspyth had said that love might even present itself as a woman and Valentyna had laughed. Yet Ylena Thirsk had tried to give her love. Valentyna had rejected it, disgusted and upset that a woman would make such an approach to her. *But that was no ordinary woman, was it?* she thought to herself now, throwing down the linen and staring at her reflection in the mirror. *If you were truthful to yourself, you would admit there was an attraction there. You could not explain it if you were asked to, but if your life depended on it, you might whisper that Ylena behaved with you as a man would . . . as a particular man would.*

Helpless tears rolled down her face as she permitted the truth of her thoughts to be unleashed for the first time. Ylena Thirsk had walked and talked like a woman but acted like a man. She had even had that curious habit of pulling at her ear and pacing when deep in thought.

*Say it!* she urged herself.

"Like Romen," she whispered to the mirror. "She kissed me like Romen did."

Thoughts clamored and clashed in her head until she could no longer bear it. She heard a gentle tap at the door and gave herself one last look in the mirror. She looked tousled and unsure of herself.

Fynch had connected Romen with Wyl Thirsk too. The boy had told her a long time ago that he believed Romen embodied General Wyl Thirsk, the redheaded, shy, and courageous emissary from Morgravia who had saved her life and given his own in an attempt to save her father. Both her father and Wyl had died, but somehow Romen had survived.

Romen, a mercenary in the pay of King Celimus . . . a mercenary who, upon his return to Pearlis, had searched out and rescued Ylena Thirsk.

Valentyna thought about the men on the bridge. Fynch had told her that Knave responded to no one but those Wyl Thirsk loved. Wyl hardly cared for Romen Koreldy or King Cailech or indeed Aremys Farrow, another stranger. And yet the dog had brought all three of these men to her. Why . . . if they weren't connected to Wyl?

The tap at the door came again. Valentyna dug deep and found enough strength to call out, "Enter." Even so, she was not ready emotionally for the two strapping men who stepped into the room behind Commander Liryk, both towering over him. Knave pushed around their legs and bounded toward her.

Tears came to her eyes at the sight of King Cailech, along with the unshakable, inexplicable feeling that she was once again in the presence of Romen Koreldy. She pretended her tears were for the dog and bent to pat his head and then hugged him fiercely, whispering "Thank you," although she was not sure why.

The rattle of guards' weapons as the door closed behind her visitors reminded her who and where she was. Valentyna straightened, ignoring her wet cheeks, and raised her eyes to meet the warm, dark eyes of Aremys Farrow and the cool yet burning gaze of the Mountain King, who was staring at her hungrily.

"Gentlemen, forgive me. As you can see, I am overwhelmed to see my friend Knave again," she said, amazed that her voice sounded so steady.

"Your majesty," King Cailech said, bowing low, "the apology is all ours for disturbing you at this hour."

Valentyna felt a thrill tingle through her body at the warmth in his tone. His voice was as deep as she had expected, yet also layered with humor and something else . . . affection, she thought fancifully. She curtsied, paying due respect to a king. "You must be Aremys Farrow," she continued, turning to the bear of a man who stood awkwardly beside the king. She stepped forward and extended her hand. "I have heard about you from Lady Ylena Thirsk and the Duke of Felrawthy."

Aremys took her hand and kissed it. "Your highness," he said.

"Come," she said, "are you hungry?" Both men shook their heads. "A drink, then, of my father's finest wine. I cannot imagine the tale I am about to hear about how two men of the Razors—one a king, no less—covered hundreds of leagues of my realm without a single guard spotting them."

"Indeed," Farrow muttered.

"Valentyna."

Something in the way Cailech said her name made her heart leap in her breast.

"Yes, Cailech?" she responded, and they both smiled at the sudden lack of formality.

"May we speak as sovereigns . . . in private?"

She noted how Aremys Farrow glared at the King. It was an odd reaction, unless theirs was a friendship that extended beyond that of monarch and bodyguard.

"Of course," she offered, glancing toward Liryk, who looked astounded at the suggestion.

"Your highness," he began.

Valentyna held a hand in the air to stop her commander, knowing precisely his concerns but somehow not at all daunted by them. "Can we trust you, King Cailech?" she said.

"Far more than you can your husband-to-be, Queen Valentyna," he responded, and Valentyna saw Liryk close his eyes with despair at the King's inflammatory words.

A remys was fuming as Commander Liryk escorted him from the room. Nevertheless, he could not blame his friend. Ever since a treacherous king had sent him on a mission of death, Wyl had known nothing but violence and despair, frustration and sorrow—save a few days in Briavel, as Romen, when he had wooed a queen.

*And here he is doing it again,* Aremys thought, not realizing he had voiced that thought.

"I beg your pardon," Liryk said. He looked as angry as Aremys felt.

"I'm sorry, Commander. It's been a long journey," the mercenary said. He noticed the man's eyes widen in further wrath.

"Yes, I'd like to talk to you about that, Master Farrow."

Aremys sighed. He had no idea how to explain their mysterious arrival. "Actually, first I need to relieve my bowels," he said, knowing this remark would throw off even the most persistent pursuer. "Also, I am famished and I need to bathe and rest. Then I shall attempt to answer all of your questions, I promise. But please remember, I am only a bodyguard to my king. A foot soldier, if you will. It would be best if you saved your wrath for him."

And with that, Aremys Farrow took himself off in the direction Commander Liryk, filled with surprise at the rebuttal, pointed. Aremys just hoped Wyl had some plan to get them out of Werryl as easily.

Valentyna, self-conscious and uncharacteristically blushing, showed the tall Mountain King toward the comfortable sofas in her study. "Are you cold, sire?" she asked, then her face fell as he smirked. "Ah yes, how silly of me, I hear your people don't feel the cold."

He shook his head gently. "I'm sorry. By all means, let us sit by your fire."

She smiled. "I'm afraid I do hate to be cold," she admitted, "although I must give the fire away soon. Each eve is milder than the next these days."

"Which means summer is beckoning," he reminded. She did not miss what he left unspoken.

"Is that why you are here?"

"Yes," but he seemed to hesitate, as if unwilling to broach the subject. "This is a most pleasant room."

"Thank you. Is Farrow your friend?"

He grinned at the odd question. "As a matter of fact he is."

"Which would explain his fury at being asked to leave?"

He nodded. "No doubt, although he has no right to feel that way."

"Indeed, sire. I hear that you don't treat your friends all that well," she baited, handing him a cup of wine.

"I can't imagine what you refer to, Valentyna," the Mountain King responded calmly.

"I refer to Lothryn, your second in command, your closest friend. The man you murdered."

"He is not dead," Wyl answered simply. His mind raced. Why in Shar's name had he come here? How would he explain any of this to her? What could he possibly say—other than that he worshiped her—that would make her listen to him, prevent a courier being sent to Morgravia that night?

"Not dead?" she spluttered. "But Elspyth told me—"

"Elspyth is wrong, your highness. I have left Lothryn alive in the Razors."

Valentyna knew that there was no love lost between Cailech and Elspyth. But every fiber of her being screamed at her that this man was an impostor, in the same curious way Ylena Thirsk had seemed to embody someone else, and she decided to test him. "Elspyth may never live to hear that good news, my lord."

"What?" Cailech said, spilling wine on his hand as he leaned forward in his chair.

Intrigued by his reaction, she continued: "The last I heard, she was near death and being carried to Pearlis—or so Liryk tells me."

The King's face drained of color. "What happened to her?"

"Why do you care? She is a Morgravian slut to you, surely?"

She watched the King hesitate, his gaze darkening as he collected his thoughts.

"I care," was all he said. "Is she alive?"

"Yes," she said. "But that's all I know."

Wyl put the cup down and, without realizing it, began to pull at an earlobe as he thought on this news. He did not see the sudden sick expression that crossed the Queen's face. Presumably Crys Donal was with Elspyth, he decided. He asked as much and the Queen nodded. He could not know that she did not trust her voice to speak, her eyes riveted by the habit she had seen four people demonstrate now, starting with Wyl Thirsk.

"Valentyna," Cailech began, but the Queen was no longer interested in the strange game that was being played out between them. She stood suddenly and demanded, "Why is it that Knave sits at your side? He belonged to Wyl Thirsk and looks kindly only on those Wyl loved. So why does he choose to accompany you?"

Wyl could no longer stand the tension between them. He put down his wine and stood also, facing the woman he so loved. He was very close and a head taller than she. To her credit, he thought, she did not flinch. The defiance in her eyes only fired his desire more and he took her hand and pulled her toward him. This time he would kiss her as a man, and to hell with the consequences.

Valentyna did not fight him. She did not think she could have resisted even if she had wanted to. Cailech, King of the Mountains, had a raw and blistering charisma that burned around him like a halo. If her heartbeat had increased for Romen, it was hammering for Cailech, and if her body had yearned for Romen's touch, it cried for Cailech's so strongly that she was tempted to throw herself down before the hearth and have him take her like the barbarian he was purported to be. The ardor she had felt for Romen was nothing compared with the carnal desire she felt for this golden man who was standing too close, his huge hands gripping her upper arms, their faces a hairbreadth apart, the fire of passion burning between them.

Wyl found his courage. He touched his lips to hers, instantly becoming lost in a sizzling rush of desire and need he had hungered after for too long.

The fire had burned so low it was only glowing embers, but neither noticed the cool of the air. Their naked bodies were still entwined and to Valentyna it was as though they were one. She could not feel where her lean limbs ended and his muscled limbs began. They lay facing each other and she stroked his golden hair while he held her in an embrace she never wanted to leave and stared at her in a way that made her heart leap all over again.

"Perhaps I should have asked first?" he said.

She laughed, full-throated and tinged with a devil-may-care happiness she had never thought she would feel again. "Particularly as it was my first time," she said, pulling a face.

"I'll kill myself if I hurt you," he said fiercely.

"That's not the sort of comment I would expect from a barbarian king."

"We are not barbarians," he said, dropping his hand away.

Her expression betrayed her anguish. "Oh, Cailech, no, I didn't mean it that way. It was a jest. It's just that . . ."

"Just what?" he asked softly, returning his hand to the crook of her back, resting it in the soft dip before the rise of her buttocks.

She felt his fresh arousal and smiled to herself as she realized what power women had over men. Even Kings were vulnerable. No weapon, no threat, no blood; a woman's body was all it took to make an enemy king compliant. Cailech should have come and seen her before to discuss the problem in the north—she and her kind could have solved it in an instant, she thought, delighting in the fact that she had just lost her virginity to him, and did not have to gift it to Celimus.

"It's just that I feel as though I know you," she risked, daring to venture toward her wild thoughts of earlier.

"You do," he said gently, watching her carefully.

She sat up, her breasts high yet irresistibly heavy and rounded. Wyl could not believe he was really here with her, and more, she was not merely returning his affections but was inviting them, loving them. He too sat up and reached toward her, but she took his hands and put them into her lap.

"We've known each other less than two hours, Cailech, and we've spent more than half of that time making love. No preamble, no honeyed words, no romantic gestures. It's impossible that I would act this way—impossible! But I felt a burning for you from the moment we met. Before, in fact. I watched you from my window as you stood on Werryl Bridge, surrounded by guards, and my heart was pounding for you then."

"Valentyna, I—"

"No, wait. I have to say this." She smiled, suddenly embarrassed, and pulled around her the dress she remembered him unbuttoning not so long ago. "There are a lot of voices crowding in my mind—a boy called Fynch, for one, whom I adore." She noticed something dark flicker across his face at the mention of Fynch, but she pressed on, determined to say what had been niggling at her for so long. "He once said something profound to me, which I dismissed as a child's fancy. I think now I was wrong. Then a friend of mine from Yentro, Elspyth, encouraged me to open up my heart to someone else after I was betrayed by the man I loved, Romen Koreldy."

Again Wyl tried to speak and again she hushed him, this time with a hand to his lips. Tears welled in her eyes at the mention of Romen. "A noblewoman called Ylena Thirsk came to me to offer her help and then gave herself up like a sacrifice to King Celimus so that the Legion would be withdrawn from our borders. You were there at Felrawthy, Cailech; you would have met her. It was a lie that I sent her to him. It was all her own selfless idea to walk into the dragon's den."

He nodded and she saw grief in him. "Where is she now?" she asked, almost too frightened to hear the truth.

"She is dead, Valentyna. She showed the courage to match her name. The Thirsks have always been true to Morgravia and yet both Wyl and Ylena pledged themselves to you. They both loved you in their own way."

His words made her weep openly. "Who killed her?"

"I did," he whispered.

She looked at him, not understanding. "You?"

He nodded so sadly she had to believe him. "It was an accident. I rescued her from Celimus—he had planned a horrible death for her, which I won't sully your presence by describing. Suffice to say it was up to his usual cruel and humiliating standard. Aremys and I took her away from Felrawthy and into the Razors."

"What happened there?"

"She did something very brave—may I leave it at that? I find it painful to think on."

Valentyna heard the tremor in his voice. The description Romen had given of Cailech was of a man who was anything but tender as this man was. In fact, nothing she had seen of the Mountain King matched the description she had heard of the arrogant sovereign. But then, all that was hearsay—always secondhand. She needed to find out the truth for herself.

"I will grieve for Ylena. She was my friend."

It was Wyl's turn to take a chance. "She told me you parted on bad terms."

Valentyna pushed her hair back from her face. "We parted amicably, although there was something between us . . . Ylena tried to make love to me," she stammered, surprisingly herself with her candor.

Cailech looked down at their linked hands. "Yes, she told me her error. Wished she could take it back."

"I wish I could have reacted differently. I was flustered and tactless with her." Valentyna paused. "But, Cailech—how is it that Knave favors you in the same way he favored Wyl Thirsk, Fynch, Ylena, and Romen?"

*I could tell her,* he thought frantically, *and see what happens.* Or he could preserve the lie and not trouble her life with talk of magic. Already a plan was forming in his mind. Now that he had possessed her so completely, he knew he could never let her go, never allow her to be with Celimus. The most daring yet logical scenario seemed to be to call the Mountain warriors into Briavel and take their chances on war with the Legion. If Crys Donal had taken his advice, he would be stirring up trouble within the Legion anyway, and with powerful people such as the Benches behind that push, perhaps Celimus would not have so many of his Legionnaires to count on.

Wyl made his decision. "I have a plan, Valentyna, which may prevent your marrying Celimus. It is dangerous, and spells death for some Briavellians, but I believe it is the right path for your realm. You know that Celimus has killed so many, not the least of whom was your father," he said, hating to see how his words brought tears, "and so perhaps it is the way you want to go anyway. Until now I haven't been able to help you. I thought you were as trapped as I am."

She looked at him and frowned. "You're not making sense. Why are you trapped?"

It was time. This had not been his intention when he set out from the Razors, but then he had not expected that he would be holding a naked Valentyna in his arms. Sharing her body had changed everything. He swallowed hard, wondering at how she would react. "I have to tell you something," he said.

"I hear fear in your voice," she replied. "Why does what you are about to say scare you?"

"Because it requires an honesty I have been unable to find before with you. I was scared it would push you away."

She shook her head. "But you have never met me before," she said, feeling the soft hairs lift on her arms and behind her neck. This was it. This was what she had searched her soul for.

"I have met you before, Valentyna. I first met you and fell in love with you in this very chamber. Your father was present and we took supper together and you laughed at me because was I too short in your opinion to be an emissary from the King of Morgravia."

If time could stand still, if a heart could stop beating, if all breath could cease and one could still live, Valentyna believed these things are happening to her now. She kept silent, her eyes riveted on Cailech's.

"And when I met you again, my beloved"—the King reached for his trousers, pulling from them a handkerchief—"you gave me this."

Valentyna started sobbing now, deep, heartfelt sobs. She shook her head in denial. What she had wanted to hear suddenly sounded too frightening to contemplate. "I gave that to Romen Koreldy," she pleaded, squeezing Cailech's hands so tight her own felt numb. "He was a Grenadyne nobleman, a mercenary."

"He was me," Wyl said gently, tears welling in his own eyes. "It was me you loved, Valentyna. Romen was dead— you never knew the real man. I am Wyl Thirsk and I was trapped in Romen's body."

Words failed her. It was as if she were listening to a language she did not understand. He continued, driving the painful understanding deeper into her heart.

"I returned to your life as Ylena, my own sister. My brave girl tried to stand up to Romen's killer."

"Hildyth, the whore," Valentyna whispered.

"Her real name was Faryl. She was an assassin sent by Celimus to kill Romen, which she successfully achieved, except that it was me inside Romen's body and the magic, known as the Quickening, forced me to take her life. She died instead." He pulled Valentyna close, and to his surprise, she permitted it. He went on, determined to tell her everything. "Ylena heard about Faryl. She took her chance at Tenterdyn as I raced to catch up with her and Elspyth, and a lucky blow killed me once again, this time compelling me to take my sister's life."

Valentyna sobbed audibly.

"I had to see you, to try to help you," Wyl went on. "I came back to Werryl and tried so hard not to make a fool of myself, but still I succeeded in doing so. I have loved you, Valentyna, since that very first night. I'm sorry for humiliating you and making you feel so bad about Ylena."

Valentyna took the linen handkerchief from his lap and dried her eyes. She told herself to find some strength. Her father would be ashamed to see her so undone, although it was unlikely he had ever faced anything this daunting in his long life. She sniffed and tried for a watery smile, but failed. She raised her hand to wipe away Wyl's tears, too.

"I think I knew it then. Your sister showed too many masculine traits—habits I recognized as belonging to Romen. But I just couldn't make myself believe something so incredible. And so," she continued for him, "Ylena lost her fight again and became King Cailech; is that right, Wyl?"

To hear her speak his true name was more than he had ever dreamed. He kissed her, stroking her hair. "That's right," he said. "I'm Wyl. I'm so sorry for lying to you, but I was just trying to protect you."

"From myself," she said harshly, "because I wouldn't accept the existence of magic." She thought of all the occasions Fynch had tried so hard to convince her.

"Don't blame yourself," Wyl urged. "I would not have believed it either had it not happened to me."

"But you see, Wyl, others believed you—I presume Aremys knows?" He nodded. "You see. You have people who trust you. I hate that I did not."

"You didn't know!" he said, desperate not to upset her any further.

"I saw the clues. It was all there for me. Knave did everything but speak to me," she cried. "But . . . if you were Romen, does that mean that Romen wasn't real?"

"Oh no, Valentynta, no! Don't cry. Romen was real, as real as I am here. I was Romen; he was me. It's me, Wyl, who loves you, who said all of those things to you as Romen."

"You," the Queen said, dazed. "Wyl Thirsk. Poor red-headed Wyl."

"That's right," he whispered, sad to feel her draw away from him. "It's always been me. I stopped you giving yourself to Romen that night; I planned the feast celebrations; I gave you the dove mask and told you I loved you. I wore the black mask and fought Celimus. I would have killed him too, if not for you. It broke my heart to see my betrayal reflected in your eyes."

She stared back at him, wanting to believe but struggling to absorb such shattering news. He understood.

"Know this, Valentyna. Whatever happens now, I have loved you with all my heart. I love you now and I will love you forever, whoever I am. There is nothing you could ever do to make me feel another way, and I shall never give my heart to another. It is yours."

Valentyna sighed. She was too overwhelmed. She had no more words.

He rescued her. "May I tell you my plan?"

She hesitated, then seemed to relax. "I don't really know how to reply to your sweet words. I . . . I loved Romen, and I cannot give you—whoever you are—up."

Wyl nodded, afraid, yet daring to hope she might be able to love him back.

"Wyl," she began again, but was interrupted by a frantic

knocking. Her soft expression turned to one of terror. "Quick, we must dress!"

Wyl was into his few garments in moments, and was impressed at how quickly and deftly the Queen slipped into her gown despite the intimidating banging on the door. "Stall for time," he hissed, helping her button the back.

Valentyna was about to call some excuse for the delay when the door burst open and Aremys rushed into the room. He took in the scene in a second and a look of deep apology swept across his face, but the palpable sense of fear that entered the room with him caused all three to forget their embarrassment.

Valentyna was at his side rapidly, praying to Shar that none of her men would notice her dishevelment or guess that her gown was still undone at the back. "We'll be fine, thank you," she said, closing the door on the anxious guards.

"What is it?" Wyl asked, stepping to Valentyna's side and finishing off the buttons on her dress.

"Celimus," Aremys answered. He could not hide the distress in his voice.

"What? Here?" Valentyna rushed to the windows.

"I'm afraid so. Come on, Wyl, we leave now!"

"You called him Wyl," Valentyna said, turning from the window and the riders flying Legion colors below. It was true, then. Out of Wyl's affectionate embrace, the intimate moment lost, the reality felt harsh and suddenly ridiculous.

Aremys shrugged, sheepish. "Well, your highness, I assume he has told you the truth. Is that right, Wyl?"

Wyl nodded, glancing toward the Queen with a heavy heart. It was over so soon . . . before he had even had a chance to put his plan into action.

"Wyl!" Aremys repeated. "We must go, now! My apologies, your highness."

Wyl did not move.

"Go!" Valentyna urged, catching Farrow's infectious anxiety. "Please. The Legion is entering the palace."

"Is Celimus here?"

"I don't know. I can't—"

Aremys interrupted, angry now. "He's here in person, Wyl. I beg you, let's go."

King Cailech took some time to right his clothes, then a calm smile broke across the rugged face that truly reflected the mountain region that had raised him. "This is meant to be, Aremys," he said, voice soft and sad. "This is it, the culmination of Myrren's Gift."

"No!" the Grenadyne yelled, striding toward his friend. "We can escape. If you won't think about yourself, think about Valentyna and how your presence here will reflect on her."

Wyl had not considered how Celimus might react to finding him here. Aremys was right: He had to leave, if just to protect Valentyna from any suggestion that she was consorting with the enemy behind the Morgravian King's back.

"What are you talking about?" Valentyna said. "Why is this meant to be?"

Aremys caught the stern glance from Wyl and knew this was one secret he had not shared. The mercenary shrugged; he knew when to keep his own counsel.

Liryk saved them further argument by barging in, all protocol disregarded. He was startled to see Aremys. "Who let you in, Farrow?"

"I let myself in, Commander. I lied to your guards; they let me through."

"This is preposterous, your majesty," Liryk blustered. "I am supposed to be taking care of your security and it seems anyone can come and go as they please."

Valentyna took charge, concerned now that Celimus might catch her in Cailech's company. "Liryk? What did you come here to tell me?" Her tone brooked no further delay.

The Commander adopted a formal tone old Chancellor Krell would have been proud of. "My queen, I am here to tell you that King Celimus has just arrived in the bailey."

Valentyna took a steadying breath. "Thank you. King Cailech cannot be seen here and I need to . . . tidy up."

Liryk frowned, still flustered at finding Farrow in the room with them. *If only he knew what had happened,* Wyl thought. It would have been safer for Valentyna had Farrow been there all along.

"King Cailech," Liryk said, "I will organize an escape

route and divert the Morgravian party, but you must leave now. You have made your peace with Celimus—now let us make ours!" The vehemence in his voice surprised them all. "Your majesty, please go ahead to your chambers. I will let your husband-to-be know that you are not far away." He emphasized the word "husband," taking in her disheveled clothes and the heightened color in her cheeks. Looking around the room, he saw that the rug was crumpled and the lavender stalks strewn on the floor were crushed in one spot. Their fragrance overlay another one he knew well from places like the Forbidden Fruit . . . no, he certainly did not want to take his thoughts down that path. One more day and Valentyna would be on her way to Pearlis, where she would marry King Celimus and finally unite the two realms. Liryk would permit nothing to get in the way of that vision.

Valentyna felt cornered. She nodded at Liryk. "Thank you, Commander." Then: "King Cailech, it has been enlightening," she said, extending a hand. The Mountain King kissed it too long and too tenderly for Liryk's liking.

"Come, gentlemen," the commander urged. "Your highness, I will wait for you in the main salon."

"Use the secret door," she said, and he nodded.

Liryk did not miss the long, meaningful glance exchanged between his queen and the Mountain King, but pretended to ignore it, feeling more relieved with every step he and the two visitors took closer to the door and the passageway that would lead them out of the palace.

Cailech turned just before ducking to enter the secret stairwell. "Valentyna, remember all that I've said. It's the truth." And then he was gone.

Valentyna stared as the door closed behind him, leaving her alone. Leaving her to face Celimus and a desperately unwanted marriage while her heart's light burned fiercely for Wyl Thirsk.

# 36

REMYS HAD PERSUADED WYL AS FAR AS THE GATES, HURRYING Cailech's bulky form down into the bowels of the palace. The guard accompanying them directed them to a little-used gate, which brought them out into a courtyard near the chapel.

When Aremys cursed their lack of weapons, Wyl remembered that Koreldy's blue sword was stored in a secret spot in the chapel. Against the guard's wishes they hurried in, startling Father Paryn.

A familiar voice greeted them. "Aremys!" Turning, they saw young Pil, who had escaped with Ylena from the massacre at Rittylworth.

"You know these men, child?" Father Paryn asked the novice.

"I know Farrow—we met at Felrawthy, Father. But I don't know his friend."

"Pil," Aremys said, his voice spilling its relief. "This is—"

Wyl would not permit it. "I am King Cailech of the Razors," he said, bowing.

Father Paryn's face drained of color. To his credit, young Pil recovered quickly and bowed. "Why are you here, your highness?" the novice asked.

"We're running from King Celimus," Aremys growled, hurling an angry glance Wyl's way.

"King Celimus is here?" Father Paryn asked.

"I'm afraid so," Wyl said calmly. "We must not be found or it will look bad for the Queen, you understand?" Clearly neither of them did, judging from their confused expression.

Wyl pushed on; confusion could be helpful now. "Anyway, we need Romen's sword."

"No fighting in the house of Shar, King or not," the priest cautioned.

"There won't be, Father. We just want to take the sword and leave. I promise no blood will be spilled."

It was too late. There were shouts outside and the guard accompanying them shrugged. "I'm sorry, sire," he said, "I shall have to turn you in. I've been briefed by Commander Liryk not to risk the Queen's reputation."

Wyl nodded. "I understand."

"What?" Aremys roared. "Wait!"

"Be quiet, Aremys," Wyl commanded. He turned quickly to Father Paryn and Pil. "Hide him," he said, indicating the Grenadyne, "and help him escape the palace compound. I ask no more than that you give him Koreldy's weapons. Queen Valentyna will thank you for it," he added, then lied: "She has sanctioned it."

Both holy men nodded dumbly, watching as King Cailech of the Razors strode out to meet the Legionnaires and the Briavellian Guard.

"Quick!" Pil said, and with no choice left to him, Aremys Farrow hung his head and followed the novice.

A few minutes later he heard the soldiers enter and receive a predictable roasting from Father Paryn for bearing arms in the chapel. They tried to explain but achieved nothing but the threat of damnation in Shar's eternal fire if they did not leave at once. "Curse you all for disturbing a man at prayer," the priest called after them.

Pil left Aremys in a small room behind the main chapel while he went for news from Father Paryn. "Where did they take the King?" Aremys asked when Pil returned, wondering how he might free Wyl from a company of Legionnaires and the Briavellian Guard.

"I gather he's in the guardhouse. There are soldiers everywhere. Is he really the King of the Razors?"

Aremys looked sorrowfully at Pil and nodded before adding, "He was also Ylena Thirsk, Faryl of Coombe, and Romen Koreldy."

The boy's eyes widened. "Wyl Thirsk!" he exclaimed in a hushed tone of wonder.

"That's right. And now the King finally has him in his clutches."

"What are we going to do?" Pil asked, terrified.

Aremys knew that trying to rescue Wyl right away was pointless. He needed time to think it through, and Celimus would not do anything too risky on Briavellian soil just before his wedding. No, he would save Cailech for some sort of spectacle after the marriage ceremony, no doubt.

"You're going to stay here and keep our secret," he told the novice. "And I'm going to take Koreldy's sword and make my way to Pearlis."

"That's where he'll be taken, I gather. To Stoneheart."

"Good work, Pil," Aremys said, knowing the praise would help the frightened young monk.

"Is there anything else I can do?"

"Lead me out safely and then let the Queen know that I've escaped."

"Do you need a horse?"

Aremys shook his head. "Too risky and Celimus is too smart. No, I'll go on foot and hitch a ride somehow."

"There are plenty of nobles and merchants headed for Pearlis, Master Farrow," Pil said excitedly. "I'm sure you can get a lift with one of them."

The Grenadyne tried to smile but failed. "That's what I'll do, then."

Most of the nobles making the journey to Pearlis for the royal wedding had their own men for protection, but Aremys was counting on the strata of society below the nobles not having reliable security. A number of middle-class families had decided the opportunity to witness the marriage ceremony combined with the sight of the great city of Pearlis was irresistible, and were also preparing for the trip.

After lying low in the northern part of Werryl for a couple of hours and carefully watching the procession of travelers, Aremys offered his services to three couples who were obviously traveling together. Aremys knew he possessed one of those inherently honest faces, which in this instance won favor with the ladies—along with his suggestion that although Briavel was relatively safe, Morgravia was riddled with bandits who preyed on wealthy merchants.

And so Aremys found himself sitting alongside Mat, a purveyor of fine foods to the nobility, who was driving the carriage that carried the rest of the party, while another man, Bren, brought up the rear, riding one of the two fresh horses they had brought along.

"I've never seen a sword tinged with blue like that," Mat commented.

"Aye," Aremys answered, more sadly than he meant to. "It belonged to a friend who gave it to me as a gift."

Mat whistled. "Some gift. Must have set him back a penny or two. My brother's a craftsman in weapons, but I've never seen him work on anything like that."

"I believe it was made by Master Craftsman Wevyr."

"At Orkyld," the man said in awe.

Aremys nodded. "He was a good friend."

"I guess so," Mat agreed, some irony in the grin he cast the Grenadyne's way. The two men settled into a comfortable silence as the carriage cleared the city and headed onto the main road that led to Morgravia.

## 37

ALENTYNA DESCENDED THE STAIRCASES TO THE MAIN SALON, feeling as though she were now two people: the one who was presently contriving a welcoming smile for her betrothed, whom she despised; and the one who—in mind, certainly—was fleeing with King Cailech and Aremys Farrow.

The truth of the Mountain King's identity had still to sink in fully. It was all she could think about, her mind moving back through the time she'd spent with Wyl as himself, as Romen, as Ylena. As much as she wanted to find holes in the story—just one would do—comparing Romen with Cailech yielded frightening similarities, and when she threw Ylena into the mix, it left her numb. Why had he never tried to tell her?

She answered her own question: She never would have believed it. Not when he was Romen; not even with the miraculous arrival of the chaffinch that had seemed to herald Ylena's visit. She had considered the finch's song a timely coincidence, not magical, but she now realized it must have been magic of some kind. She thought of Fynch; Wyl had not had time to tell her how he was, nor enough of his idea of how she could avoid marrying Celimus. What would she not give to hear it now! She had considered every possible scenario and had not been able to find a way out. Only a few more steps now, she realized, emerging from her disquieted thoughts, and Celimus would be kissing her hand and offering sugary platitudes. What could he be doing here? Well, he could just turn around and go home. She still had one more day before she had to leave for Pearlis.

She took a deep breath and nodded at the guards outside the salon as they pushed open the doors for her entry. Valentyna had already pictured King Celimus bowing elegantly, then striding majestically forward, smiling widely with those perfect teeth. She had already planned her own contrived expression—a delicate balance of surprise and feigned pleasure that he was in Briavel. But she did not have to contrive any surprise. It slapped her hard in the face when she swept into the room only to be confronted by a snarling, struggling Cailech and a smugly grinning King of Morgravia.

"Valentyna, my love," Celimus said expansively, "look what I found sneaking out of your palace like a rat."

Valentyna stopped, unable to breathe. She saw Cailech shake his head, knew what he wanted her to do. Her heart broke. Again; it was happening again. Once more he was offering himself up to save her.

Everyone was waiting for her to speak.

"I've already explained," Wyl yelled, shaking off his captors' hands, "that I never got to speak with the Queen." Valentyna noticed the manacles around his arms and ankles.

"I heard you the first time, Cailech," Celimus spat, turning back toward his bride. "My dear, is this true?"

*Don't hesitate, Valentyna, just agree,* Wyl prayed.

For Briavel then, she decided, rapidly assessing her helplessness in the situation. She summoned her most regal tone and hurled it back at Celimus. "Of course it's true," she answered tersely. "Who is this man?" She pointed toward Wyl—presumably Aremys had escaped. "And how dare you hold anyone against his will in my court, King Celimus."

That startled him. He was not prepared for her wrath, having already decided she was as guilty as the Mountain King in conspiring against him.

"Your majesties." Liryk stepped in. "Allow me to escort the prisoner to a secure place and perhaps then you might discuss—"

"Yes, why don't you do that, Commander," Valentyna agreed, cutting across his words and seizing control. "This is unforgivable, King Celimus. You called him Cailech. I still don't know who he is."

Celimus had also regained some equanimity. "Don't you? Let me introduce you to the treacherous King of the Razors, who just days ago was signing a peace treaty with Morgravia at Felrawthy."

Valentyna feigned shock, hiding her despair as the man she had loved through so many lives was led away.

Cailech turned his head, spoke over his shoulder. "I'm glad you have finally met me, your majesty." The word "me" was loaded with meaning. "We'll meet again," Wyl said.

"Oh, I'm sure you will," Celimus said. "I'll insist my wife is present for your execution."

She saw Cailech's sad smile and did not understand it. Dismissing everyone, she swung around on Celimus the minute the door had closed. "How dare you, sir!"

"Valentyna, please," he cajoled. "I came with only romantic intentions. My chancellor suggested that it would be wonderful for both our peoples if we could be seen together.

His idea was that I bring an escort to accompany you on this symbolic journey across our two realms. I know I should have sent word, but it sounded like such a worthy plan, I was excited and in a hurry to catch you before you left Werryl Palace. I've had a special carriage made, my love, emblazoned with our new heraldic device, which my craftsmen have been designing for months now. It flies the colors of Briavel and Morgravia, sweet Valentyna. We have woven the crimson with the emerald and violet so beautifully, it seems we were always meant to be one."

Valentyna was taken aback by his enthusiasm. She could see that the idea of this marriage had great merit for the people of their realms, but she hated surprises being sprung on her at the best of times, let alone by the hated King of Morgravia.

She had promised herself one day. One final day to mourn the loss of her status. One night to remember with love the touch of Romen, of Cailech . . . of Wyl Thirsk. Now Celimus had taken that from her too.

She wanted to react, to scream her frustration, sob her grief. But the man in front of her was dangerous, and she needed to respond with her head, not her heart. She nodded slowly, affecting calm. "What do you plan to do with Cailech?"

"I'm not sure yet. I shall be taking him with us to Stoneheart."

"Surely you don't mean a trial and execution?" she wondered, a new terror chilling her. He could not die again. She could not lose him as she had lost Romen.

"I said I don't know. Death would be my choice."

"Why must he die?" she demanded.

"That you need to ask such a question baffles me, Valentyna," Celimus replied calmly, but followed it with a condescending smirk.

"But you said yourself that you'd just signed a peace treaty."

The King's famous temper began to stoke. He had done well to get this far without losing his patience. "Which he broke by setting foot into Briavel—and that, I might add, is a whole new mystery. How the King of the Razors can infiltrate your realm and cover almost its entire length without being noticed is a puzzle."

"It certainly is," Valentyna replied abruptly. "Which is why I don't agree to any decision on your part, sire. He is my prisoner, on my land. I will decide his fate."

A new note crept into Celimus's voice, one she had not heard before but one she was very sure was more characteristic of this cruel King of Morgravia. Gone was the affected brightness, the sugary tone. "I'm sorry, Valentyna, you will not. I've noticed how you deal with treachery—you send it off to a brothel for the night."

If only he knew how deep his words cut. "Leave me, Celimus," she commanded, not trusting herself to say more.

He impaled her with a stare, which she returned with defiance, and then he nodded. "Fine. We shall leave tomorrow as you had planned, and Valentyna, you had better wipe that scowl off your face by then. I will marry you, and I will reserve the right to execute my enemies if they are found on my soil."

"You mean my soil, don't you, Celimus?" she spat, trembling from the hate that was threatening to overwhelm her.

He shook his head. "It's mine from now on, Valentyna. Get used to the idea. We can marry and please our realms and I'll provide peace for your people. Or we can do it the hard way and I promise I will slaughter every man, woman, and child of Briavel if it comes to that."

She had not thought he could shock her, but the venom with which he spoke now—in a way she had never been spoken to before—chilled her. She felt the wispy hairs on her arms stand on end. That was no way to speak to a queen, especially in her own palace, but she was powerless to stop him. The only weapons she had left were words. She threw them at him now.

"You are a snake, Celimus. Wyl Thirsk was right."

"Wyl Thirsk is dead, Shar rot him, as you will be if you don't put on a happy face, come serenely to Pearlis, and take those wedding vows as planned."

"I would rather be dead," Valentyna snapped recklessly.

"That's your choice," her fiancé snarled. "No more woo-ing, Valentyna. This is your new life as my queen. You are not my equal. The only good you'll do me is to give me the sons I crave, and believe me, if you won't give them to me willingly, I will take my pleasures as I see fit."

Wyl sat glumly in the guardhouse. Much as he wanted to please Celimus, Liryk could not bring himself to have the King of the Razors incarcerated in the palace dungeons. Legionnaires were posted throughout the guardhouse, one for each Briavellian soldier.

"Did Aremys get away?" Wyl asked Liryk.

The man nodded. "You shouldn't have hesitated, sire."

"It was wrong of me to run."

"Your pride aside, this is all very dangerous for our queen."

"She handled it well. I won't make any further problems for her. Thank you for maintaining our secret."

The old soldier sighed. "I'm not sure I understand your coming here, or now your calm acceptance of what is certain death at the King's hands."

"This is how it is meant to be," Wyl said, resigned to his fate. "This is Myrren's Gift playing out precisely to plan."

"Myrren's Gift?"

Wyl smiled. "Take no notice of me."

Liryk was baffled but his relief that Valentyna seemed to be compromising with Celimus overwhelmed his curiosity. "How did the King know? He sent men looking for you immediately upon his arrival."

"It was my horse," Wyl replied, grateful for Cailech's memories.

"What?"

"I gave Celimus my white stallion as a gift at Felrawthy. He fell in love with it, so I insisted he have it because I had its twin back at the fortress. Identical."

Liryk understood. "He saw your horse, the twin."

"He's probably riding its brother. How could he miss it? You won't tell him about Aremys, will you, Liryk?"

The old man shook his head. "No, sire. I want no further

grief for her majesty. No one needs to know about the mercenary, and the Briavellian Guard can be trusted to keep the secret."

"Thank you."

"I shall see to your comforts, sire. We leave for Pearlis tomorrow at dawn."

Wyl nodded, no longer caring.

Valentyna escaped her anger and Celimus by taking her horse out, refusing to have him accompany her. This would be her last ride as a single woman through the woodland of Briavel and onto the moors. Next time—if there was a next time, she thought, remembering the King's threat—she would be married to Celimus. She would have the grand title of Queen of Briavel and Morgravia, but it would be an empty title.

She glanced back at the odd medley of guards following her, comprising her own men and Legionnaires. Celimus was taking no chances with her. There was nowhere to run and hide anyway, and it would be unseemly for a monarch to flee her own realm. No, Valentyna was made of sterner stuff. She would face this trial, would bestow the gift of peace upon her people as she had promised.

But the memory of Cailech's touch still burned in her mind and on her body. It had been such a rushed, frantic episode and yet she could remember each moment of it, relive it in her thoughts in a delicious slow-moving scene. She could still not quite grasp that she was no longer a virgin; it had all happened so fast. She could never have planned for this, and yet nothing gave her greater satisfaction—nothing!—than knowing her greatest possession had been given to the man she loved, not the one who would steal it from her under false pretenses.

Cailech . . . no, Wyl, she reminded herself, was such an enigma. He had claimed she had known him as Romen and yet she knew so little about him really, other than that he loved her, would die for her—*had* died for her. Poor Wyl, she thought. She could not imagine how he had survived the killing of his sister . . . wished she could ask him, have time with him. That was impossible, she knew, but she would do what she could. She would marry Celimus and give everything of herself toward preserving the life of the King of the Razors. Even if she could never see him again, it would be enough to know that he lived. Celimus would not execute Cailech because she would forbid it.

She had taken the wrong approach with Celimus, she realized. All she had done was anger him, corner him into making rash statements. Her father had always said she must learn to curb her tongue. Being a good royal, he had cautioned, was about diplomacy, careful choice of words, and always giving oneself time to consider. She had ignored his advice in her behavior with Celimus, and it had cost her. He had obviously been shocked to find Cailech in Werryl and, like a wounded animal, had struck back. She should have sensed the danger lurking there; Valentyna admonished herself for such clumsiness. If she was going to survive in the Morgravian court, she would have to play Celimus more intelligently than she had today. She must fuel his vanity, make him feel omnipotent, make herself irresistible. Valentyna slowed Bonny to a walk, in no rush to be back in the palace, and remembered how powerful she had felt just hours before, realizing what a woman could do to a man. For all his strength and stamina, his status and bearing, Cailech had been too vulnerable. Faced with naked desire and a compliant partner, he had become putty. Could she achieve the same with Celimus?

She recalled that Chancellor Krell had intimated that, if she approached the marriage with the right attitude, she could use her feminine wiles to get what she wanted. Her revulsion for Celimus aside, if she could play the role of affectionate Queen, impress his people and thus please him, she might be able to enjoy small wins of importance to her.

Her first priority was Wyl. She understood that there was no changing his status as prisoner; Celimus would want to make an example of him. So be it. But she would put all her efforts into ensuring that this was the extent of the punishment. They had lied once already. No doubt Wyl could dream up some clever reason as to why he had come to Briavel. Surely there must be a feasible explanation. She pondered, found the wisp of an idea. It might work. She would need to get word to Wyl.

# 38

HE JOURNEY ACROSS BRIAVEL AND INTO MORGRAVIA PASSED uneventfully. In any other situation, Valentyna would have truly enjoyed the trip and the chance to mix with her people, for they came out in the hundreds to wave the royal procession through their towns and villages. And what a procession it made: The Briavellian Guard was in full formal dress in emerald and violet, while the Legionnaires looked dashing in their crimson and black. Trailing the rear came a cavalcade of nobles, dignitaries, servants, and attendants, not to mention Madam Eltor's personal retinue in charge of the Queen's wardrobe, as well as cooks, pastry makers, and bakers—all the people required to provide a joint wedding feast that blended Morgravia's culinary specialties with Briavel's fine foods.

And in the midst of the brightly colored entourage rode a smiling king and queen, graciously accepting the crowd's blessings for their happiness.

"You can almost believe it," Valentyna commented, aiming a shy smile toward the King.

He did not look at her, but she heard the softer tone in his voice. Perhaps it was hard work being vicious all of the time, she thought. "Why not? They love you. They love me for marrying you and for bringing peace to the realm."

"It is a good thing, Celimus."

"Do you mean that?"

She caught a posy thrown by a young lad and blew him a kiss, which won a roar of approval from the happy mob. "I regret my behavior of yesterday, and indeed throughout our courtship."

He finally looked away from the mass of happy faces and turned to her. "And?"

"I wish us to start again, here and now. Neither of us has parents to guide our choices, no family to lean upon." She sighed. "We are trying to achieve something extraordinary: two young monarchs, new to their thrones, forging peace and prosperity. I did a lot of soul-searching last night, Celimus, and realized that what you have worked so hard to bring about will become a landmark era in the history books."

Celimus's expression was skeptical. "But last—"

"Yesterday was different. You frightened me and I was rattled to think that King Cailech had infiltrated Briavel without my knowledge. Did he tell you why?"

"No. I thought I'd find out courtesy of Stoneheart's clever men of the dungeons," the King offered unkindly.

Valentyna did not react. Celimus, like any bully, was always looking for ways to hurt others. Instead she planted the first seed of her lie. "Cailech told Liryk that he wanted to meet with me to talk about a surprise festival he was thinking about throwing in your honor."

It was clear that Celimus had not expected this. "My honor!"

"Yes. He wanted to hail you as the region's peacemaker, bringing long life and prosperity to the three realms." She held her breath through the pause that followed, forcing herself to look back and wave to the crowd, smiling calmly despite her fear.

"That might change things," Celimus said softly.

Instead of leaping on his words and giving away her excitement, Valentyna shrugged. "Yes, well, it is of no matter to me, but perhaps you can find out more in due course. It would be a pity to lose a friend in the Razors when you have worked so hard to establish the truce."

"Indeed," he said drily, but it was obvious that the notion

that Cailech had not been in Briavel for sinister reasons had been successfully planted. She would need to water it subtly throughout the journey, Valentyna realized.

"To get back to what I was saying earlier, my lord, you can rely on me to be faithful and dutiful. Let us make this marriage the success everyone wants so badly."

He laughed derisively. "I know you don't love me, Valentyna."

"As you don't me, sire," she countered with care. "But that doesn't mean we cannot be a successful royal couple. Respect, affection, cooperation—surely these are all qualities we can work to achieve?"

"Surely. But I don't understand."

"What puzzles you, sire?"

"The change of heart. One minute you are a spitting cat, the next a kitten."

"I dreamed last night of my parents, Celimus," she lied, trying not to recall her true dream of Cailech's passionate embrace, his ardent yet gentle touch, his kisses so tender and deep, his declarations of love . . . she felt herself going hot in all the wrong places.

"Yes?" the King prompted.

"And . . . they urged me that this was a match made by Shar for the good of the realms. They told me that Shar's angels, if we let them, will guide us to hold our marriage fast and be good to each other. That we will have sons—strong boys—four of them," she said, feeling nauseated by her own creative invention. "Are you superstitious, Celimus?"

"Not really. Why?"

"This morning I found a white rose on the bush my father planted for my mother at her death."

Celimus looked at her quizzically, although she could tell he was intrigued. "What is the significance?"

"Ah, perhaps it is only in Briavel we believe this. Legend has it that if a white rosebush produces a single bloom, which opens before any other buds show themselves, any dream of the previous night is destined to come true."

"No matter whether it is good or bad?" he asked.

"That's correct. That is why I went looking for the rose,

because my dream was so profound, so vivid. I could see our sons, Celimus—dark, strapping boys, like their father."

He grinned. "That's very interesting, Valentyna. I'm pleased that you feel so positive suddenly."

"I intend to be a good wife to you, sire. I will make you proud and happy."

Celimus looked into her clear blue gaze and saw no guile. He reached across the distance between their two horses, his white, hers black, and took her hand. The crowd gasped, then cheered uproariously when King Celimus bent to place his lips against the back of the hand of his queen.

Valentyna felt nothing but revulsion. She was relieved she had chosen to wear gloves.

Wyl was traveling among a different cavalcade but toward the same destination. Tied, gagged, and thrown in a covered wagon, he was driven hard. There were no stops for food or rest. Fresh horses took over at various points until, just by the smell of the air, he knew he was approaching Pearlis. Wyl had lost track of time and thought. His mind felt like a skein of tangled wool.

"Stoneheart ahead!" he heard a soldier cry, and smiled to himself. Death was upon him. Myrren's Gift was reaching its climax and the Quickening would come to an end.

He hoped Aremys had made his own way to Pearlis, and that his friend would keep his solemn promise to end Celimus's life the moment the change occurred. He thought briefly of Fynch's caution about randomness, and took solace from it. It was randomness that had given him Valentyna by the fireside not so long ago. Nothing could ever take away that time of exhilaration, that delicious loss of thought and control, that intense passion that had sealed his love for her.

Valentyna was his. They were one, coupled in love and desire; it had been an exquisite pain when they reached that final dizzying, breathtaking pleasure in each other. He had known her in a way no other had. Her maidenhood had been given gladly, lovingly, and he had taken it with a trembling, feverish joy. Celimus might marry Valentyna but the Queen of Briavel belonged to the King of the Razors . . . to Wyl Thirsk.

He would not swap his lying with Valentyna for anything—not even in exchange for his life. He could die happily now, for he was loved—and loved as Wyl Thirsk. She had uttered his name.

His thoughts were interrupted by soldiers unfastening the hood of the cart. He cast a final thought toward Knave, wished he had had a chance to say goodbye to the faithful dog. He did not struggle as rough hands dragged him from the cart and led him to a place in the depths of Stoneheart from which few people returned.

For the first time in his life Knave had neither mission nor magic to call upon. He was still driven, though, urged by a force more complex than anything he had known before. It went by the name of sorrow.

He had hidden himself in the palace compound, close enough to watch the guardhouse for any movement on Wyl's part. He had made sure that the Grenadyne had gotten safely out of Werryl and had seen him organize transport with some Briavellian folk on their way to the wedding festival in Morgravia. Then he had returned to the palace and kept Valentyna company during her ride, watching her fall so deeply into thought that her horse could have probably stopped and grazed without her realizing it.

He had watched Celimus prowl around the guardhouse, giving orders to his Legionnaires, making sure they remained alert and that nobody visited the prisoner without his express permission—not even the Queen. The palace had finally settled down for the night, although a constant quiet movement of servants prepared for the departure the next day.

Knave had wandered away to the woodland, where he had spent favorite times with Fynch. He found the spot where they had slept the night, where he had heralded the death of Romen Koreldy with a piercing howl into the dark. He lay there, his head on his huge paws, as the hours crawled by, and he mourned the loss of the boy he had come to love, the boy who had given his life to destroy the enemy of all that was good and natural in the world.

Knave threw back his huge head and howled in grief. It seemed the Thicket heard him, for once again he felt himself connected to its magic.

*Knave?* came a voice.

*Rasmus.* He groaned, his throat swelling from the pain of his emotion.

*We promised Faith Fynch we would aid Wyl Thirsk,* the bird said.

Knave waited, his head hung low. He did not want any more instructions.

*Go to Argorn,* Rasmus finally said. *Find Felrawthy's duke and return him to Pearlis, where he will meet Farrow.*

*And then?*

*They will know what to do. Go now. The Thicket will send you.*

Knave closed the connection, too numb to care what happened now that Fynch was gone. Very soon he was hurtling through the dark toward the region of Morgravia that had produced Wyl Thirsk.

# 39

YL SAT ON THE COLD FLOOR OF ONE OF STONEHEART'S DUNgeons, his head resting on his knees. Moments earlier he had turned to prayer, beseeching Shar to watch over and protect Valentyna, to heal Elspyth, to restore Lothryn, and to welcome Ylena and Alyd, Fynch and Gueryn into everlasting life. As the list of souls lengthened he had stopped, overcome by distress. How many lives had been lost or destroyed because of Celimus? Wyl's anguish deepened as he accepted that he was helpless now. There was nothing he could do from the dungeon except wait for Myrren's Gift to mete out its final crushing blow and hope that Aremys would keep his promise.

And so he sat in silence, wishing the guards would come for him and speed his death. A strange tingling sensation coursed through his body and then a blue shimmering light forced him to look up. He recognized the feeling—it was connected to the magic of the Thicket.

"Fynch," he whispered as the shimmering coalesced to reveal a vision of his young friend.

*Hello, Wyl,* the boy said into his mind.

"Are you alive?"

*Not in the way you mean.*

"Then you died during the battle with Rashlyn?"

*Wyl,* Fynch interrupted gently, *my time with you is short.*

"What is it that I must do?"

*Just trust me.*

"To do what?"

*To forge a Bridge of Souls.*

W yl remained baffled by Fynch's visit. It had been inspiring, calming even, to see the ghostly vision of his friend and hear Fynch speak so surely. He had insisted that Wyl trust him, and Wyl did—but that was all Fynch would tell him, other than to promise that the Bridge of Souls would save his life. His instructions to Wyl were simple. When Wyl needed to be saved, all he had to do was call out Fynch's name. But, in truth, Wyl did not believe there was any escape from this dungeon or from his fate. He appreciated Fynch's attempt to soothe him, but he was thinking only of death now—real death. There would be no returning from the end of Aremys's sword.

Wyl looked around the cell, touched the cold black stone that encased him. Not so long ago Stoneheart had been his home, a place that embraced him with the love of Magnus and the security of his title as General. Now it was the lair of his foe and its cold walls would witness his death twice over in the coming hours.

Wyl's gaze roamed absently in the dim light, which filtered through from an outside cresset. It fell upon an inscription scratched into one of the bottom stones. AVENGE ME, WYL, it said. His heart pained. He had come full circle. This was surely the work of Myrren. She must have suffered in this very cell all those years ago. Her touching plea still had the ability to move him.

He hated Celimus for being the cause of so much suffering. As if on some silent signal, he heard the click of boots on flagstones. There was only one person who walked with that arrogant stride. He turned away, did not want to see the King gloating over his rival's downfall.

Liryk had gotten a message through to Wyl from Valentyna, saying that she had found a way to explain Cailech's presence in Briavel. Liryk had watched Cailech shake his head at the idea, but had not had the heart to relay the Mountain King's attitude to the Queen. Wyl had no intention of making excuses.

He soon discovered this was also the reason for the King's visit late into the night.

"Tell me, Mountain King, was there a good reason for your visiting Briavel without an invitation?" Celimus gave a soft, deprecating laugh as he flicked an invisible mote of dust from his jacket. "You see, the Queen seems to think you had very fine intentions of joining forces with her to plan some special festivities on my account." He shook his head with mock embarrassment. "How very jolly."

"I would not plan any festival around you, Celimus, other than your funeral," Wyl enjoyed saying.

The King laughed in obvious delight. He clapped his hands, loving Cailech's bitterness. "You obviously want to die, my friend. Valentyna was surely throwing you a lifeline here."

"Thank her for her generosity," Wyl said. "And I'll wait to see you in Shar's eternal fire. We'll settle our score there, Celimus . . . if not sooner."

Celimus had looked at him quizzically, not understanding his final words, but Wyl did not elaborate. Intent on having the last laugh, the King gave his dazzling smile. "Is there anything I can do for you in the meantime?" he asked.

"Yes. Do it yourself."

"Pardon?"

"You heard me. Kill me yourself."

Celimus made a sound of disapproval. "I might miss and merely injure you—oh dear, that could be messy and painful."

"I'll risk it. Let me feel the touch of your blade."

Celimus smiled and nodded. "Perhaps. We shall see what mood I'm in tomorrow. Sleep well, your highness," he said, leaving with a chuckle.

Wyl felt even more hollow than before. Not once but thrice had he betrayed her. First as Romen, later as Ylena, and now as Cailech. She would never forgive him. He sat in the darkness, the bleak atmosphere matching his thoughts, disturbed first by the scuffling of rats and then by the sound of yet another arrival.

Once again there was no need for introductions. "King Cailech, I regret to find you here, sire," Chancellor Jessom said. "Is there anything I can get you?"

"Other than the key, you mean?" Wyl murmured, refusing to turn toward the King's servant. He would make him speak to his back.

"A rug perhaps, sire?"

"You forget that I am of the Razors, Chancellor. We don't feel the cold."

"A candle, then. Let me at least light this grim space for you, my lord."

"Do what you wish. It matters not to me."

"I meant what I said, King Cailech. I regret to see you incarcerated here. When the rider gave the news of who was being brought here, I thought the man must have been duped, charmed by a hedgewitch."

"Be careful talking of witches in here, Jessom. Or you'll find yourself on this side of the bars."

The Chancellor cleared his throat, sounding abashed, and Wyl heard the rasp of a clay plate being pushed through the bars. Shadows leapt across the bars as a soft light eased the darkness.

"There, that's better, surely," Jessom said.

"What are you looking for, Chancellor? Absolution?"

"What do you mean?"

"All the deaths—you must have so much blood on your hands."

"I don't understand you, sire."

"Why not? I am speaking the same language you do."

"But what could you know of me?" Jessom replied. "We are all but strangers."

Wyl admonished himself to be careful. It was true: Cailech would hardly know the Chancellor, other than by name and sight from Tenterdyn. However, the truth was, he was not of a mind to be careful anymore. He wished Celimus would hurry up and bring about the final death in Myrren's ghastly plan. He ignored Jessom's question and posed his own instead. "Where is your king?"

"Asleep, I hope. He has a big day tomorrow."

"So the wedding goes ahead as planned?"

"Yes, sire. Why would you think otherwise? I'm afraid the city will shortly degenerate into mass celebrations and drunkenness. It is but an hour to dawn."

"The Morgravians want the marriage as badly as the Briavellians," Wyl commented, more to himself than for the Chancellor's hearing.

"Of course. It is a brilliant union."

"Not for Valentyna."

"Why do you say that, sire?"

"He will destroy her."

"He wants her very much."

The words fired a new anger in Wyl and he swung around to face the Chancellor. "He wants what she brings him, Jessom. He wants to own the glittering jewel of Briavel, and everything else that Briavel can give him. He doesn't care about Valentyna. He wants her body and the sons she can provide, the peace and prosperity she brings. The people love her, and because of her they will love him, for surely they hate him right now."

Jessom cleared his throat. "You seem to have a very deep understanding of the south, King Cailech."

Wyl grunted. "It is my business to know these things.

Mark my words, Jessom, if he destroys her—and he will—the people will rise up against him. Already I suspect there are mutterings within the Legion. The right whisper in the right ear and the army will move against the Crown. You know it is powerful enough."

Wyl realized that the Chancellor was actually paying attention to what he was saying. Perhaps the man had not come here to bait him after all. If he could sway this powerful person, he might be able to help Valentyna from beyond the grave.

Jessom interrupted his thoughts. "The King has placed his own people in senior positions in the Legion. They would not move against him," he said.

As far as Jessom was concerned, Celimus had played out his last vicious act. Imprisoning and executing the King of the Razors, with whom only days ago he had signed a peace treaty, was sheer madness. But Jessom's first attempt at arguing against killing the Mountain King had failed and a second could have dire consequences. Jessom knew Celimus saw killing Cailech as a way of ridding himself of the final obstacle to becoming Emperor. But he did not agree. It was a mistake.

"When someone like Eryd Bench knows the truth of what's been going on, his voice alone will be enough to turn the Legionnaires," Wyl assured.

Jessom could not guess how King Cailech could know of Eryd Bench, but that did not matter now. The death and destruction had to stop. Unification and peace were at hand. But Jessom feared Celimus was not the monarch to lead the Morgravians to greatness. Whenever the King took a dislike to someone or felt in any way threatened, he turned to killing. Such a sovereign would ultimately destroy the region. "Lord Bench is dead, sire, I'm sorry to say."

Jessom was astonished to see Cailech react as if he'd been punched. The Mountain warrior's head rocked back, his eyes closed in agony, and he threw his body toward the bars, gripping them with white knuckles. "Dead?"

"I'm afraid so, King Cailech."

"How?" Wyl rasped.

"How else?" Jessom replied, revealing more of his private feelings than he had intended. "Let's just say our king took umbrage at Eryd Bench's gentle inquiries about certain events in the north."

Wyl groaned. His hands fell away from the bars and he slumped against the wall, slowly sliding his tall body to the ground. "His women—Lady Bench, Georgyana?"

"Do you know them?"

"Are they safe?" Wyl yelled, no longer caring how he might be confusing the Chancellor.

Stung by the Mountain King's venom, Jessom answered truthfully. "They escaped. A servant told our men that two guests had arrived, a man and woman. The woman was injured; dark-haired, small, attractive. The man was probably Crys Donal of Felrawthy." He surprised himself by offering so much information. There was something compelling about Cailech. He seemed entirely different to the arrogant, sharp-witted man he had met in the north.

"Elspyth," Wyl whispered. "No sign of where they went?"

Jessom shook his head. "May I ask why this interests you, sire?"

"No. But I will tell you this, Chancellor Jessom: Your days as a powerful adviser to the Crown are numbered. Mark my words, you will be dead at the hands of your king in a matter of days . . . perhaps hours. You will be lucky to see out the next few days." Wyl enjoyed the sudden insecurity that coursed across the angular planes of the Chancellor's pale face.

"He needs me," Jessom said.

"No, he doesn't, Chancellor. I can sense your disgust at his actions. If I can, he already has." Jessom heard the ring of truth in the Mountain King's warning.

"He doesn't know that Lord Hartley still lives," Jessom muttered to himself, his agile mind racing.

"Lord Hartley?"

The Chancellor looked up, his thoughts clearly elsewhere. "Yes, Celimus ordered his death, but I let Hartley go—he's in hiding now. I can call upon his help to rally the other nobles against our king."

"Not before the King kills you," Wyl said cruelly. "But I have an idea, Jessom. It's too late for me—and for you, I fear, unless . . ."

The man's mortified expression was quickly replaced by wrath. It was not death he feared, Wyl realized. It was loss of power, wealth, and position.

"Unless what, sire?" Jessom asked. He was composed again, his tone curious.

"Unless you put your considerable knowledge and influence behind Queen Valentyna. Protect her, befriend her, put your faith in her. Someone else will deal with Celimus. Trust me on this. He will not live to see old age. He may not even live to see out the spring. But the Queen can live to a ripe age if she is given the right defenses. She can win over the Legion, she can woo the nobles. Through her, Morgravia can achieve peace with Briavel and retain the truce with the Razors."

"The Mountain People will make war on Morgravia and Briavel if you are executed." No more diplomatic language, Jessom decided; King Cailech knew he could not escape his fate. There was a bargain being made here. He was not sure he understood it, or why Cailech cared about peace in the region, but Jessom was a pragmatist. Cailech was right: Valentyna was the future, especially if she were to quickly become pregnant by Celimus. Then nothing but the Queen and the heir—the true Crown of the newly unified realms—would matter.

"You echo my thoughts so closely, King Cailech, it is uncanny."

"Come closer, Jessom. I have something to tell you and I do not wish to be overheard."

"I cannot save your life, King Cailech," Jessom warned candidly.

"I understand," Wyl said, extending Cailech's blunt fingers through the bars.

Jessom smiled thinly. He was curious to hear the bargain this imprisoned, doomed King could offer. The Chancellor stepped closer but drew his blade to show the man of the mountains that he was not naive. He would shake hands cautiously.

"No need for that, Jessom. I have no intention of anything but sealing our bargain."

Palm met palm and Cailech's fingers closed around Jessom's hand. The King was smiling, and Jessom suddenly realized there was something unnerving, something predatory, in that expression. The Chancellor balked, tried to release himself from Cailech's grip, but it was too late. A shimmering blue light flowed around their hands. A seal.

# 40

ALENTYNA STOOD FORLORNLY IN A GRAND CHAMBER AT Stoneheart, her heart as cold as the dark stone surrounding her. Madam Eltor had permitted only her most senior and trusted assistant to help her dress the Queen. Valentyna sensed rather than saw the surreptitious glances between the two older women as they took in her grief-stricken expression.

"Come now, my queen," her seamstress tried once more. "Please don't stain your face with tears."

"There are no more tears left within me," Valentyna replied.

"This is your wedding day, your highness. The happiest day ever for the people of Briavel and Morgravia," the assistant risked.

"Not for me, though," the Queen replied, not caring that her words provoked a raising of the assistant's eyebrows and a stern gaze from her superior.

The women had worked fast and fluidly. Valentyna was already stitched into her gown, although Madam Eltor had tut-tutted, warning, "You've lost weight, my girl. This was perfect last week."

Valentyna just shook her head. "Let's get this over with."

"That will be all, Maud," Madam Eltor said, dismissing her assistant. "I hope I don't need to remind you that what is discussed in our presence always remains private."

Maud curtsied and left hurriedly, the news no doubt already spilling out of her that the Queen was going to her wedding as full of grief as when she had attended her father's funeral. "Valentyna!" the seamstress snapped. "Stop this!"

"I don't love him," she said, balling her fists and closing her eyes, trying to get a grip on her spiraling emotions.

"We don't care!" Madam Eltor replied, deciding that harshness was the only solution now. "He brings us peace. I regret that you are the currency with which we buy it, your highness, but it is too late for you to turn back."

Valentyna was stung. "Yes. Of course, you're right. Forgive me."

The seamstress's voice softened. "Be stout of heart, Valentyna. You are Briavel's jewel. The brightest jewel now in Morgravia's crown. Imagine how proud you would make your father today."

"Yes, by marrying the man who murdered him," Valentyna muttered.

Her companion gave a gasp of shock and Valentyna realized too late that hurting Madam Eltor achieved nothing. The truth of Valor's demise did not change the fact of his death or her decision to marry Celimus. She hated the way she veered between courage and weakness: One moment she felt she could make the marriage work, would bear his children, would make Briavel safe and prosperous. The next, she plunged into gloom, remembering that passionate hour in Wyl's arms. How could she wipe that from her thoughts? How could she lie with Celimus this evening and not feel anything but revulsion?

*Because you must,* she told herself in a small, urgent voice. *Because Briavel's future rests upon it.*

"I'm all right," she reassured her seamstress. "My nerves are jangling. I'll be fine once we leave for the cathedral, I promise. Put the veil on."

Madam Eltor did not believe her, but she obediently

draped the exquisite veil over Valentyna's head and face, then stepped back to admire her work. "You are breathtaking, your majesty. The Morgravians will fall in love with you instantly."

Valentyna found a small smile for her lifelong friend. "I'm ready," she said.

Celimus had ordered a glistening white carriage to convey his bride to the cathedral. It sported the new device linking Morgravia and Briavel: the intertwined initials of the King and Queen painted in their national colors. Four stunning white horses, imported from Grenadyne, pulled the carriage. Accompanying the Queen were members of the Briavellian Guard, beautifully outfitted in emerald and violet. A proud Commander Liryk waited, as did all the crowd, for the first glimpse of the Queen.

As if Shar himself had ordained it, the sun appeared from behind a cloud and bathed the main square of Stoneheart in a dazzling golden light. The people screamed their delight as the Queen appeared on the steps of Stoneheart's main entrance in that same moment. Trumpets sounded above the din, and without a male family member to do the honors, it was left to Commander Liryk to walk stiff and proud up those stairs to escort her. He bowed low before her, as did all gathered.

Valentyna was moved. A lump formed in her throat and she recalled the similar tumultuous welcome she had been given on her arrival into Pearlis. She and Celimus had had a deafening, exhausting couple of hours making their way through the cheering city. Everyone had seemed to be waving squares of linen in the colors crimson, black, emerald, and violet, creating a sea of moving color that mingled the two realms more effectively than any device she and Celimus could have arranged.

She curtsied low and long to the people. The gracious acknowledgment drove them into even wilder applause. Liryk smiled at her action. "You are already their queen," he said, his breath catching.

Valentyna thought she might cry again. "I hope my father is watching," she managed to say.

He took her hand and squeezed it. "He will be cheering alongside your beautiful mother, both of them so proud."

"Thank you, Liryk, for all you have done for me. I'm sorry I have been difficult in recent times."

"Your highness," he said with genuine reverence. "I am your servant."

Valentyna was warmed by the sentiment of her commander and the pride his words evoked within her. She vowed once again to somehow exist alongside Celimus without fracturing the peace their two realms considered so very precious.

"Come, Liryk. Lead me to my husband."

Wyl could hear delirious cheering as he was led out of the dungeons into a courtyard he had never seen before.

"Has the Queen left the palace?" he asked one of the senior soldiers, a man he recognized.

"I think so," the man answered, embarrassed by his task. This was a king, after all, and they had been led to believe a peace agreement had been made with the Mountain dwellers.

"And where do you take me now?"

The man hesitated and checked that the manacles were secure on their prisoner. "We have orders to move you, King Cailech."

"That doesn't answer my question, soldier," Wyl insisted. "I asked where."

To his credit, the soldier looked directly into the hard gaze of the Mountain King. "To the block, sire."

Wyl sighed. "I see." Celimus was wasting no time in executing his northern rival. He wondered if the cruel sovereign would force Valentyna to witness the death. He knew that Celimus would revel in the grisly notion. And she would have no choice. Executions were something royalty had to face whether or not they had a stomach for it. And

Valentyna would not be watching a stranger die, as Celimus assumed; she would be watching the head of the man she loved be severed and lifted in triumph above his slumped corpse. He hated to think about how this would hurt her very soul, and did not want to ponder how she would respond to his transference into Celimus.

Wyl heard the crowd cheer again and imagined the Queen of Briavel's procession to the cathedral. She would be serene, he decided; she would rise above her sorrow and do her realm justice. Her gown would be simple, with little if any adornment, as was her way. He imagined she would wear her raven hair loose, and smiled sadly to think how the bridal veil would be a welcome sheath between herself and the reality of her situation, a barrier between herself and Celimus. But not for long. Once their vows were exchanged, the King would claim a kiss to seal the holy pact made before Shar, raising the veil and tearing away Valentyna's last protection.

Wyl could not help but recall how he had fallen in love with Valentyna at first sight. Dusty and dressed in riding breeches, she had had smudges on her cheeks and her hair had been falling about her face. She had reeked of horse and leather. Yet it had been his pleasure to kiss her hand and his heart's desire to ask for it in marriage, even on behalf of another. A smile had broken across her face like new sunlight; he had bathed in its warmth and his heart had become instantly hers.

But that was over now. It had all gone so terribly wrong. Above the roar of the crowd he could hear the cathedral bells pealing, heralding the impending marriage. Soon she would be the Morgravian Queen, married to his enemy, and he himself would be past caring about.

Wyl felt sick. He stumbled slightly and the soldier walking by his side instinctively threw out a steadying hand. "I'm not used to being in chains," Wyl lamented. The man nodded, clearly awkward.

*And so I move between Kings today,* Wyl thought, *and then I die.* He had not lived out the great Thirsk tradition of death on a battlefield; instead he would succumb to death enmeshed in a battle of magic he could not win. He was nothing more than an unwilling puppet.

"Wait." Wyl stopped, suddenly anxious. "The King will be present, I take it?"

"Yes, sire."

Relief flooded him. "Good. I want him to share my death," he said, surprising the Legionnaires around him by smiling fiercely.

Aremys had arrived only hours before the wedding procession, exhausted and dirty but relieved that he had made it to Pearlis in time. He used his strength to bully his way to the front of the crowd, earning disgruntled grumbles. One man risked hurling his displeasure at the bear, who simply turned and scowled at him through dark, hooded eyes. "Shut up!" was his reply, and all within earshot did just that.

Valentyna caught her breath at the first sight of the famed cathedral of Pearlis. Bells were pealing and heralds trumpeted her arrival into its grounds. She tried to imagine what Celimus was feeling inside the cathedral. Satisfaction, she decided. He had won. It seemed he always did where she was concerned.

Meanwhile, inside the hushed cathedral, King Celimus took the nod from Jessom that the Queen's carriage was pulling into the compound. The man looked thinner and more vulturelike than ever. Celimus had heard the whispered jokes about his chancellor's likeness to a carrion bird. It was actually a very good description, particularly today, he thought, wondering what was passing through Jessom's sharp and slippery mind. He did not trust him as he once had. There was defiance lurking behind that well-guarded facade. The King was not fooled: Jessom would switch allegiance in a blink if he thought the cards were going to fall the wrong way. And Celimus had begun to believe that the Chancellor might be considering his future quite carefully.

Jessom's fierce disagreement with the King's latest idea regarding King Cailech's execution had further fueled Celimus's mistrust. Where did the Chancellor's interest lie that he would advise so strongly against taking the Razor King's life?

"Is everything ready?" he whispered.

"Her majesty arrives, sire, yes," Jessom confirmed.

"Not her, you fool. Cailech?"

Jessom nodded in that slow, reptilian manner of his. "As you ordered, sire."

"Good. Now get out of my way. You're blocking the view of my latest conquest. This is a good day, Jessom. A very good day. Two monarchs will be brought to their knees before me." He laughed quietly, straightening the front of his black jacket. He knew he was resplendent in dashing crimson and noir with flashes of gold and a cape of the blackest yarn lined with the fiery red of Morgravia. He was looking forward to claiming Valentyna's maidenhood tonight and did not plan on being gentle about it. A husband must impress on his wife that he was in charge.

Aremys watched with a heavy heart as Valentyna alighted from the carriage, aided by Commander Liryk. He had mixed feelings about the Briavellian who had helped him escape while at the same time aiding in the capture and imprisonment of King Cailech.

The Grenadyne assumed that Wyl was already cooling his heels in Stoneheart's dungeons. During the frenzied dash from Werryl to Pearlis, he had focused only on getting to the capital and finding a way to help Wyl. The promise he had made to Wyl burned brightly in his mind now. Would he be able to do it? Could he murder his closest friend? He had watched Wyl's strange journey through three lives and had come to love him in the way that King Cailech had once described his feelings for Lothryn: brotherhood, friendship, loyalty. Aremys felt an intense sorrow for Wyl's suffering, but he was not sure he could find the courage to kill the man he loved as a brother, even out of kindness.

Aremys pulled himself out of his dark thoughts as Valentyna approached. She looked more beautiful than he could ever have imagined, gliding alongside Commander Liryk, smiling softly to the crowd and carrying herself proud and erect. As she passed, and the cheering around him increased to its highest volume, he roared her name, not really expecting her to hear. Amazingly, she did, swinging around toward his voice.

When she saw him she faltered. "Aremys," she mouthed as she passed, and he lifted a hand in greeting. They were both thinking the same thing: *Wyl.* When she cast a last glance over her shoulder, looking at him through her veil, he nodded his encouragement to her.

And then she was gone in a fanfare of trumpets, through the massive double doors of the cathedral, swallowed into its dark depths and an uncertain future.

Crys Donal had seen the bride too, but had not been able to make eye contact with her—not that she would have recognized him if he had. His yellow hair was now a deep brown and he sported a beard and mustache, also darkened. Gone were the fine clothes, replaced with the uniform of a Legionnaire. He blended into the crowd perfectly, and as neither King Celimus nor those he kept close knew Crys Donal by sight, he felt relatively secure.

He used his height and newly assumed status to shoulder his way through the crowd toward the cathedral. It was acceptable for him, as a Legionnaire, to be seen crossing the unmarked line that separated onlookers from the participants, particularly when an officer hailed him.

"Soldier, are you on duty?"

"No, sir," Crys answered crisply. "Just part of the cheering crowd."

"Well, you're back on as of now. Get down to the cathedral's entrance and move that mob back. The happy couple won't be able to get out of the church if we don't create space for the carriage to come through."

"Understood, sir. Right away."

"Good lad," the officer said, and moved on.

Crys was jogged down the street in front of yet another sparkling new carriage designed for this special day. Black with crimson flourishes, it bore the King's personal device and its gold dragons glinted in the sunlight while bunting in emerald and violet flickered in the spring breeze. Other soldiers had been sent in as well and Crys joined them in pushing back the happy mob.

"If you tread on my foot again, I'll rip that beard off your chin, sonny," one big fellow said.

"Hello, Aremys," Crys murmured, and won the shocked gasp he expected. "It's Crys."

Aremys grinned in spite of his bleak mood. "Good to see you, Donal."

Crys looked around to see that no one was watching them. Not only could no one hear, but no one cared. The mood was festive and fun-filled. All the people wanted was their new queen and they chanted her name ceaselessly.

"The King won't care for that much," Aremys commented.

"He'll have to get used to it. It's her they've turned out in the thousands to see."

"Crys, I heard about your family. Shar, I'm so sorry, lad. I wish—"

"I know," Crys said softly. "Everyone does."

Aremys nodded. "Where's Elspyth?" he asked, then wished he had not when he saw how the youngster's face darkened.

"Come with me," Crys said. "They'll be an age yet and we need to talk."

He dragged Aremys out of the crowd and away from the main entry of the cathedral, finding a slightly more quiet spot around back. Crys told him everything but saved the worst until last. "A new infection has her in its grip. She seemed all right for a while and I assumed she would recover after the physic in Pearlis pronounced her wounds in good shape, but the trip to Argorn was too hard for her. By the time we got there, she was feverish again and high-colored."

"Why did you leave her?"

"Knave arrived—you know, that strange dog of Wyl's?" Aremys nodded. "Out of the blue, just walked into Argorn Manor."

"And . . .?"

"Elspyth rallied slightly at seeing him; she obviously understood better than I that he had come for us. Don't ask me how he knew where we were."

"You don't want to know," Aremys said. "It goes hand in hand with the Quickening and magic." He grimaced at the news of pretty Elspyth's sickness. "Is she under good care?"

"Yes. She had to stay in Argorn, of course, no chance of more travel. Another physic has seen her, but you know, Aremys, it's a bit like she's given up on herself, as though she doesn't want to fight anymore. It was so nasty what she went through." He shrugged awkwardly. "I just think she's accepting death."

"Go back there, then. Make her fight!"

Crys shook his head. "No, I'm no good for her. It's tricky—there are two other women there. Lady Bench and her daughter, Georgyana. The daughter is . . . well, she's lovely, and . . ."

"And what?" Aremys quizzed.

"Shar, but you can be dense sometimes, Farrow. I like her and she likes me. I think being around us makes it worse for Elspyth. She's so in love with Lothryn, as you know, and it hurts her to see us falling for each other."

"But that can't kill her, surely?" the big man growled.

"No, but that infection might, especially when she denies herself food, fights the medication, can't sleep—won't even try. She talks about leaving to find Lothryn, weeps that he's in pain, that he's been changed somehow." Crys ran his hands through his newly dark hair. "But she was lucid when Knave arrived. She seemed to know that he wanted us to go with him. I'm ashamed to say we had to tie her to the bed to stop her trying to accompany us."

"She's no good to anyone here," Aremys said gravely.

"I'm not sure any of us are any good here. She wept when I left, said we'd never see each other again. It's left me hollow, I can tell you."

"You're sure the women are safe there?"

"No one knows they're there, and Argorn has sealed its

collective mouth. What about your story—what's happened since we parted? Where is Wyl? More to the point, *who* is Wyl?"

"Would you believe me if I told you he is currently King Cailech?"

It was Crys's turn for disbelief. Aremys told him the whole story.

"So he's here right now? That's why Knave came for us."

"In the dungeon. I have no idea what's planned for him, though."

The Duke of Felrawthy turned ashen. "I think I do," he said. "Hurry, we must get to the dungeon. But first we need to disguise you as a Legionnnaire."

# 41

THE NEWLYWEDS EMERGED ONTO STONEHEART'S LARGEST balcony, known as the wedding balcony because it was the place where so many Morgravian Kings had presented their new queens to the people.

Valentyna's heart was pounding yet she felt somehow numb. It was done. The ceremony within the cathedral had dragged on, but she had spoken clearly when asked to take her vows, had even found a smile for the despised man beside her as she uttered the words that bound her to him for life. Their exit from the cathedral had provoked a rapturous noise she had not imagined possible. As the royal couple had walked to their new carriage, its dominant colors not lost on Valentyna, she had been showered with rose petals from blooms especially cultivated beneath glass. Their pastel colors joined the fresh whites of spring flowers. Underfoot, just before her, she had noticed a spray of lavender; it was so out of keeping with the roses and so dear to her heart that Valentyna had turned toward the man who'd thrown it. The Legionnaire had grinned, and she had suddenly recognized the Duke of Felrawthy despite his disguise.

"Thank you," she mouthed, but much as she wanted to bend and pick up the purple heads of her favorite flower, she had not wished to draw the King's attention to it. He was far too sharp not to wonder who had thought to throw lavender to the new Queen. She had stepped on it instead, crushing the heads and releasing the fragrance briefly before Celimus had helped her into the open-air carriage.

The noise had been deafening as they had made their slow way back toward the castle. Valentyna had searched for Aremys or Crys but had not seen either again. Inside the carriage the time had seemed right, so she had reached inside the small cream velvet pouch she carried.

"This, my lord, is for you," she had said in the sweetest voice she could muster, knowing she had to preserve the fragile bond they had formed.

Celimus had looked puzzled as he took the small, exquisitely lacquered box. She knew he was captivated by the way his mouth opened when he saw the gift inside.

"It is a lovely ring, Valentyna," he had whispered, and kissed her, much to the people's joy. "Will you put it on me?"

She did so. "I'm glad you like it."

"I will wear it always. I have something for you too," he replied. "It's being readied for you now."

"Oh?"

"A special surprise," he had promised, turning away to wave to the crowd.

And now she found herself waving from the wedding balcony to the sea of people below who had crowded into the main square before the castle.

"They are so proud of you, my lord," she said above the din, leaning close to be heard. She hated her obsequiousness.

"And they love you. I knew they would. You are very good for me," he replied. She knew he did not mean it as a romantic compliment. Celimus meant it literally: Valentyna made him look better; she was good for his image.

There was truly no hope for them, she thought. She would

struggle her entire life to be a sugary-sweet doormat just to keep the peace between them. She could not do it. Just maintaining the delicate truce forged by her careful words on their journey into Morgravia was destroying her soul. She hated him. And tonight she was expected to respond passionately between the sheets with him. As she gazed out across the ocean of smiling faces, Valentyna felt she would rather die than have Celimus touch her intimately.

It seemed he had the same scene on his mind. "Tonight," he began, "when all the formalities are done with and we are finally in bed, I mean to teach you something."

Valentyna tried but failed to sound seductive or indeed even interested. "That sounds rather intriguing, my lord. What can you mean?"

"I mean to teach you that I am not someone to be trifled with."

Valentyna felt her body chill. He meant to hurt her. "I don't understand, my lord." She tried for levity in her voice.

"I will teach you how the King of Morgravia expects his Queen to behave."

"Have I disappointed you during the marriage proceedings?" she asked, all other sounds now fading to the background as she focused on his voice alone.

"You lied to me, barefaced and at a particularly poignant moment. I am hurt by this."

She could not imagine Celimus emotionally hurt by anything, least of all words. "I don't understand, Celimus," Valentyna said, more firmly now, her mind racing. Which particular lie might he be referring to?

"Cailech denied your story to me in person last night. Of course I had hoped it was true, hoped I was the one who had jumped to the wrong conclusion."

Something in Valentyna died. Wyl had refused her gift of life. "I . . ." She struggled to form a response.

"Now," Celimus began brightly, waving to the people and encouraging her to do the same, "I can forgive you this misdemeanor. You have behaved perfectly since our arrival at Pearlis; I believe that you did not invite Cailech to Werryl, nor did you know of his arrival there or his intention to stir up war using Briavel as an ally. My belief is that you lied to save further bloodshed; you hoped to preserve the peace between the three realms. And I am delighted by the wedding gift you have given me. So I forgive you. But you will learn an important lesson tonight."

Valentyna began to say something, but he hushed her with his hateful hand against her mouth, replacing it quickly with his lips, much to the crowd's delight and her disgust.

"Hush, my love. Take your medicine and be pleased it's not more harsh. I appreciate that you are a virgin, though I cannot promise to be as gentle as I might have been a few days ago. Wave farewell to your people now and let me cheer you with my own special wedding gift as promised."

"I—"

"Hush. I shall wait while you change. I want you to wear crimson, the color of Morgravia."

Aremys followed Crys blindly as they made their way to the Legionnaires' barracks. Stoneheart was like a town in itself—a maze of streets and openings, corridors and courtyards. When they finally reached their destination, the barracks were virtually deserted. Everyone was either on duty at the wedding or joining in the celebrations. Crys was able to sneak into the provisions office and take the biggest uniform he could find.

"I have no idea if this will fit," he said, returning to the small outbuilding where he had left Aremys, "but it's genuine Legionnaire, so it should do the trick and get you past security. Everyone's so preoccupied anyway—they'll see the crimson and black and no questions will be asked. Let's face it, it's likely none of the guards on duty around Cailech are going to be proper Legionnaires anyway—they're probably all mercenary impostors."

"I hope you're right," Aremys grumbled. "I'm sensing we have to get into the dungeon, right?" Crys nodded grimly. "Don't you think it will be heavily guarded, no strangers permitted?"

"We're not strangers. We're guards."

Aremys did not have the heart to argue. "Lead on," he said.

At the dungeon Crys discovered that the royal prisoner had been moved.

"We've been sent along to make up extra numbers. King's orders," Crys said to the officer there, trying his best to sound as uninterested as possible. "Who is the prisoner, anyway?"

The man ignored him. "Who sent you?"

Fortunately Crys knew the senior officers and captains of the Legion. "Captain Berryn," he said, giving the name of one of the more aggressive captains.

The man's tone changed instantly. "All right, how many of you?"

"There's two of us but I don't know how many others he is sending. We were told to report to you here," Crys lied.

"Why can't they send a runner and inform us of what they want? I'll tell you, it was different in the days when the Thirsks ran this outfit."

Crys shrugged, feigning indifference.

"Get your companion and follow me. I'm on my way there now. And listen, sonny, this is no sideshow, all right? Today we execute a king and you will behave with due respect. Is that clear?"

"Yes, sir," Crys said, straightening, glad that Wyl was at least being accorded due respect.

Crys and Aremys remained silent as they walked a few steps behind the officer. The man was so preoccupied with what was ahead that he ignored them totally anyway.

They arrived at the courtyard at almost the same time as the King and new Queen, but both had eyes only for the prisoner.

"Cover up, you know the drill," the officer said, handing them black hoods from a small sack he carried. He left immediately to confer with one of the captains on the other side of the courtyard.

Crys explained the hood to Aremys in a low whisper. "It's an old custom dating back to the first persecution of witches and sorcerers. It was held that empowered people had to see a person to cast a spell against them. The mask was introduced to ensure that anyone present at an execution would be impervious to their magic. The belief died out over the centuries, but soldiers are still required by tradition to cover their faces at executions."

"Suits me," said Aremys. "At least we won't risk being recognized by the King or Jessom."

Valentyna stood in the crimson gown Celimus had ordered made for her and then demanded she wear. She did not notice the trio of Legionnaires arrive in the courtyard. Anger, fear, and the hideous injustice of the position she found herself in quickly gave way to a feeling of desolation when her gaze followed the King's pointing finger. Chained to a post like an animal, but still looking proud, was Wyl: tall and golden, fury burning in his eyes and a defiant set to his jaw. Now she felt weak, overcome by a combination of terror and an overwhelming rush of love.

Wyl's light green gaze left her and fell on Celimus. A smirk crossed Cailech's face and he raised a fist and turned the clenched fingers toward his Morgravian counterpart. A northerner would know that this was the sign that the tribes of the Razors gave to indicate a declaration of war.

Crys looked helplessly at his companion, not understanding.

"He's baiting the King," Aremys muttered.

"Why? Surely there's enough bad feeling?" Crys whispered.

"Wyl is trying to ensure that the King will personally kill him, although I'm not sure the Quickening obeys such laws."

Dawning had spread on the Duke's face beneath his hood. "He will be our king, then?"

Aremys nodded as they watched Wyl being unchained from the post. But not for long, he thought in private anguish.

Valentyna felt as though she could no longer breathe. Tears were streaming down her face.

"I didn't know you cared for him that much, my love," Celimus cooed.

"Why must he die?"

"Because he can't be trusted. He will always be a danger to us."

"But killing him will merely enrage the Mountain People

and encourage them to wage their own war against both our realms."

"You have no realm now, beloved."

"What?"

"Briavel is now part of Morgravia. I now rule both our realms—that's my job. Your job is to swiftly become pregnant with my sons and be a smiling, loving wife. You will no longer worry about realms, politics, war, strategy—I shall take care of all that. And I am not in the slightest bit intimidated by the Razor Kingdom."

Valentyna could not stand to be beside him for another moment. With a final glance toward Cailech's granite expression, she feigned weariness and asked to be excused.

"Soon enough," Celimus said. "But first let me deliver my gift to you."

"What do you mean?" she asked, fresh anxiety washing over her.

"You must bear witness, my love. I am executing King Cailech in your honor. He will never trouble you again."

"I refuse—"

"You refuse me *nothing,* wife! Remember, you belong to Morgravia now . . . and to its king."

# 42

Wyl was led up onto a hastily built wooden stage. Despite that touch of theater, it was a lonely scene for a king's end. The only witnesses were the two royals, a few guards, the Chancellor, and, of course, the masked executioner, who had just arrived.

Wyl was not afraid. The truth was, he could not wait to die again, and feel the Quickening release him from Myrren's Gift and the curse she had brought over his life. He would not have to live long as Celimus. Just long enough to be with Valentyna again, to hold her once more.

And if it all went sadly awry, he would still live—this time as a burly man of enormous strength and stature. Wyl had taken the precaution of discovering the executioner's name: Art Featherstone. He wondered briefly how, in the guise of the executioner, he would ever contrive to get close enough to Celimus for Myrren's Gift to come into play again, but gave up the line of thought. Whoever could have thought that Wyl would become Romen, or that Faryl would claim Romen's life, or that Ylena—he faltered on hearing her name in his thoughts—would kill Faryl and become her brother's host. And now here he was, the King of the Razors, about to become the King of Morgravia . . . or the burly executioner.

He had done his best to plant the seed, without actually inviting death—surely Celimus would find the temptation to personally separate King Cailech's head from his body irresistible? It would be another triumph for the Crown.

A huge Legionnaire came up with a cup of water. "Orders," the man said toward the executioner, who nodded, uncaring.

Wyl's spirits lifted at the sound of the man's voice. "Aremys," he whispered as the Grenadyne gave him the cup.

"I beg you, don't make me keep the promise," Aremys muttered beneath his breath.

"You will keep it if you care anything for me," Wyl growled.

Aremys stared into the green eyes, then nodded sadly. "As One," he said, walking away.

A single trumpet sounded and Wyl noticed for the first time that Valentyna was dressed in a crimson gown. The color of Morgravia. The color of blood. She was solemn-faced and looked intensely frightened. He wished he could spare her this—had hoped against hope that Celimus would come without her.

Valentyna would not look at anyone—not even at Wyl. He could not blame her. It must have felt like a shocking betrayal to hear that he had denied her fabricated story. He understood, but it did not make it any easier to see her ignoring him. Was it just two days ago they had been making love at Werryl? As the killing blow fell he would cling to that, remember what it felt like to lie naked with Valentyna and love her as she loved him.

Celimus guided his wife to a pair of thronelike seats hurriedly erected in the courtyard. He kissed her hand, winning a sickly grimace from the Queen. Her expression did not seem to matter to Celimus, who was now announcing why the King of the Mountains was to die.

Wyl looked toward Jessom as the King spoke and remembered the strange blue light entwining their hands in the dungeon, binding them to each other. He wondered if Fynch was right, if the Chancellor might somehow provide that random element that could outwit Myrren's Gift. Turning his attention back to Celimus's speech, Wyl heard that he was to be sacrificed as a wedding gift to Valentyna. At this, he withdrew into himself, praying to Shar that the King of Morgravia would see fit to gift Valentyna by making the killing blow himself.

Valentyna had withdrawn too. There was nothing to live for anymore. Soon she would have to witness the death of the man she loved, his head savagely removed from his neck with, hopefully, one swing of a cruel sword. It was too much for her heart to bear.

And after all of that, all that was left for her was Celimus, who had made his despicable intentions very clear. Her notion that she might be able to dupe him into believing she was true had been naive. Celimus was too sharp to fall for that ruse, although he would still expect her to treat him as she had promised, even if she was pretending every minute of every day.

He would continue to hurt her, she knew—first taking Wyl from her, then Briavel, no doubt ultimately taking away every son she bore. Her life would be utterly controlled by him. Bile rose to her throat as she imagined what he was going to do her tonight. Rape, she was sure, would be the very least of it.

Celimus had finished explaining his reasons for executing the treacherous Mountain King and the sudden silence dragged her out of her thoughts. She looked at Cailech, whose shirt was being cut away to reveal his broad torso, sculpted with muscles. She remembered that body well, riding above her in an urgent rhythm, each thrust taking her to a higher level of pleasure.

Chancellor Jessom, looking appropriately somber in black robes, gravely pronounced the Crown's sentence on the accused. "Have you anything to say, Cailech, King of the Mountains?" he asked finally.

Wyl spoke clearly. "Legionnaires, remember who you are. Remember your oath to protect and serve Morgravians above all others. Above all others," he stressed, "even above your king—"

"Enough!" roared Celimus, enraged.

At the King's signal, the beefy executioner backhanded the prisoner, who stumbled but did not fall, despite his manacled ankles.

Wyl knew the guards were probably not Legionnaires—Celimus would not risk them witnessing such an unlawful execution. Nevertheless, he hoped the insult had been sufficient to provoke Celimus into swinging the death sword himself.

"Get on with it!" the King ordered the executioner. "My wife and I wish to continue our wedding festivities."

"You accuse me of treachery, King Celimus. I'm surprised you aren't carrying out that threat you made in the dungeon! Or are you too squeamish to risk my blood on your fine garments?" Wyl roared, hoping his lie would get lost in the alarm his words would prompt. He knew he must not try to force death, but perhaps he could needle Celimus into picking up a weapon and killing him in wrath, as Cailech had killed Ylena. "My hunch is that you have never killed anyone yourself but always get others to do it for you, you sniveling coward. A poor shadow of your father," he added, sneering.

His challenge was greeted with stunned silence as all gathered turned to watch the young King of Morgravia.

Celimus's voice sounded as cold as the ice from Cailech's own mountains when it finally came. "I made no threat but you should be assured that I have never been scared to spill your blood, Cailech."

"Is that so? I'm sure you'll never prove such a claim," Wyl taunted, laughing.

Valentyna could not bear it. Wyl had already severed the lifeline she had thrown him and now he wanted to make sure that Celimus chopped his head off? Why? Surely he would prefer the accurate swing of an executioner over the perhaps deliberately clumsy hacking by a man whom he'd just publicly scorned? Wyl had gone mad. He would die painfully and then Celimus would—

Valentyna caught her breath audibly as the realization hit hard. And then Celimus would become Wyl!

Oh Shar! He was doing it deliberately so that Celimus would die and Wyl would take over his body, becoming the King, and her husband. Wyl would live on because of Myrren's Gift! Now her breath came hard and fast and her pulse began to race. She stood. "Do it for me, Celimus!" she cried, her cheeks flushed, her heart pounding.

The King swung around in surprise. "You want me to kill him?"

"Yes," she demanded. "He has driven a wedge between us with his underhanded dealings. I hate him. I hate his treachery. Kill him, Celimus. Do it with your own hand so that we are free of his curse on our lives. That would be my ultimate wedding gift, sire." She curtsied low, ensuring that her husband saw the swell of her breasts.

Celimus grinned ferociously. He looked like a wolf closing in on its prey as he peeled off his cloak, the crimson lining reminding everyone of the blood he would shortly spill.

Valentyna could hardly believe it. Her spirits were soaring with the hammering of her heart. She would have Wyl. She would have Romen. She would have Cailech. He would be Celimus, but the real Celimus would be dead. *Thank you, Myrren,* she whispered. *Thank you, Shar.*

"Come, stand closer, my love," Celimus called to her. "You must share in this, my wedding gift to you."

Cailech was forced to his knees. Valentyna, no longer afraid, glided confidently toward the husband she despised, her eyes locked on the man who would soon be her one love. She leaned forward and kissed Celimus, making it as tender as she could. She wanted him to know how much this meant to her.

Wyl felt sickened by the kiss and closed his eyes. He knew Valentyna had guessed what was going to happen; he had seen it reflected in the blaze of her eyes and the hungry expression she suddenly wore. But he did not believe she could live alongside him once he was in the body of the Morgravian King. Celimus had damaged them both too much. *Hurry, Shar damn you,* he thought, opening his eyes and silently urging the King on. He lowered his head to the block and bared his thick neck.

But Celimus hesitated. He too had noted the change in his wife's demeanor. The kiss was a surprise, especially after his threat on the balcony barely an hour ago. He thought about her behavior since: one moment despairing, the next filled with a fervor he did not know she possessed. She looked rejuvenated, excited . . . she looked hungry. What could possibly have had that effect on her? Surely not the mention of blood. Even the little he knew of her confirmed that she was far from bloodthirsty—she was marrying him simply to prevent bloodshed. No, it was not that. Yet her whole manner had changed at the suggestion that he kill Cailech himself, galvanizing her into this lustful creature. Her eyes blazed with a passion he had not seen since that night in Briavel when they had danced together. And even then he had felt sure the fervor had not been for him.

Celimus's sharp mind worked across every possible scenario but came up wanting. He could find no logical explanation for this odd change of heart. Valentyna had lied to save this man's life, had wept at the thought of him dying just moments earlier, yet now she was begging for his execution at the King's own hand. His instincts screamed that there was duplicity here, but he could not get to the truth. He would test her.

"No!" he roared. "The King of Morgravia will not tarnish his wedding day by dirtying his hands with blood."

"But, my lord," Valentyna cried, "this is for me. I want his head."

"And you shall have it, I promise." Celimus turned back to the executioner. "Do your job: Behead the treacherous sovereign on behalf of Morgravia and Briavel," he ordered.

Celimus took Valentyna's hand and led her back to their thrones. She felt breathless with panic. The King had thwarted them. If Myrren's Gift continued, Wyl would become the bald-headed executioner. What a terrible irony, she thought. Only weeks ago she had scorned Fynch for believing in magic, and now here she was pinning everything on the hope of an enchantment. If that hope failed, Valentyna knew in her heart that she would not lie with Celimus tonight . . . or any night. She would take her own life if need be.

She shook her mind clear as the executioner lined up for his single killing blow. The least she could do for Wyl was bear witness to his brave death. She watched the big man raise his sword slowly, carefully, smoothly. It reached the apex of his swing and was about to fall with its severing blow when she heard herself shriek, "Wait!" The man teetered and then stopped, looking angrily toward King Celimus for guidance.

"What is it, Valentyna?" Celimus asked smoothly. Perhaps now the truth of her strange behavior would reveal itself.

"Let me do it, sire," she begged, for his hearing only. It was the only way out for her.

For the first time since she'd known him, Valentyna saw hesitancy and alarm on his face. "You would kill this man?"

"For you, Celimus. It is the only way I can resolve the difficulties between us."

"Through his death?" he queried, wondering if she had gone mad.

"Yes," she whispered. "He will release us. You will know I am true to you if I do this."

Celimus shook his head, baffled. Nevertheless, the shock of her suggestion titillated his sadistic streak. He rather liked the idea of her executing Cailech. Such an act would haunt her forever, offering further opportunity for exploitation. She would be even more easily controlled when her demons rose to remind her of this ugly spectacle. It would also, of course, show her to be a strong person, either terrifying or inspiring the onlookers—either way suited him.

He studied her and she stared back at him hungrily. There was no doubting she meant her words.

"It is not a pleasant thing you request, Valentyna. You will have to live with this memory all of your life."

"You have no idea how important that notion is to me, sire."

He shook his head, as if washing his hands of her. "As you wish."

He turned to the executioner. "Bind the prisoner's mouth," he ordered, knowing Cailech was likely to make a fuss when he learned of this new and exciting turn of events. The idea of his queen killing a man made Celimus feel like rutting. His mind slithered toward the bedchamber. An heir would be made tonight, he was sure of it. He would have his first son before next spring.

Wyl looked around, confused. He watched Celimus stand once again, hoping against hope that the King had had a change of heart and would deliver the killing blow. But it was Valentyna who walked toward him.

"No!" he shouted from beneath the bindings, but it came out as a strangled cry. His eyes were wide with horror at her decision.

Valentyna glided toward him in her bloodred gown and Wyl was suddenly reminded of his dream at Tenterdyn. This was it. No dream, but a premonition. She bent toward him, tears streaming down her face. "Forgive me," she whispered, and he roared his anguish, not caring that it appeared he was about to die cringing like a coward.

The executioner pushed Cailech's head down onto the block again. "Don't make it harder for her," he growled. "She'll never survive it if she misses."

Wyl knew the man spoke the truth and he stopped struggling. He did not want to become Valentyna. He did not want her to sacrifice herself for him. He could hear her shallow, terrified breathing. The courtyard was so silent he was sure he could hear her heartbeat too. It was too much for his own bleeding heart. Wyl closed his eyes and begged for a miracle that might thwart Myrren and her cursed gift.

*Fynch!* he called silently

Valentyna lifted the sword. She took a moment to pray for her own soul before she screamed her despair, pouring her sorrow, pain, and anguish into the downward sweep that severed King Cailech's head from his neck.

She sank slowly to her knees in his blood, her heart aching, tears streaming, and waited for the change to come over her body. She had no idea what to expect or how the magic worked. All she knew was that she would accept him gladly. This would be her ultimate sacrifice, the final demonstration of her love.

Behind her, Celimus's dark olive eyes sparked with the fire of lust for this woman and the joy of knowing his final enemy was slain. He was Emperor now—and perhaps Valentyna had just shown herself worthy of the title of Empress.

Nearby, Chancellor Jessom's body sagged and he hung his head as he struggled slightly to breathe. He would need to gather his composure quickly.

The King of the Razors' body was slumped forward over the block. The executioner bent to pick up the head, which had rolled to his feet. For the umpteenth time he wondered whether the brain remained alive just long enough to know its head had been removed from its body. At the King's nod, Art Featherstone placed the head of the Mountain sovereign in a leather sack. He would take care of the body once the royal party had departed.

Valentyna felt nothing. Not even a single tear. Was she now Wyl? Had her soul left her body? She was confused. Her hands were slick with his blood, and through her wet eyes she could focus on nothing else.

"Come, Valentyna," said the voice she hated more than any in the world, and then she felt the King of Morgravia's touch. She turned away from the headless body to look at Celimus and knew in that instant that something had gone terribly wrong. It had all been a lie. The Quickening was not real. Cailech was dead and the story about Wyl Thirsk must have been some sort of cruel ruse. She was alive and her husband awaited her.

"Jessom," the King said.

The Chancellor looked up and cleared his throat. "Sire?"

"Help Queen Valentyna to her chambers. I will see you both there shortly."

"Yes, your majesty," the Chancellor said, offering his arm to the Queen. Her pale skin was spattered with blood. "You, guard," he called to Aremys, and beckoned. Aremys moved silently toward the Chancellor; he could not risk being recognized. "You look a burly enough fellow. Help the executioner remove the body immediately and lock it away. Bring the key to me. No one is to be permitted entry. Is that clear?" Aremys nodded.

Jessom looked directly at Crys. "And you, take an inventory of all present, including guards and the herald. I want the names brought immediately to me in the Queen's chambers. Is that understood?"

Crys, puzzled, nodded beneath his hood, avoiding speech for the same reason Aremys had.

Jessom looked as stunned as the Queen by the afternoon's events. Moving with uncharacteristic awkwardness but quickly, he hurried Valentyna from the scene of death, and using back corridors that only he seemed to know about, he got the silent, shivering bride to her suite of rooms.

# 43

HANCELLOR JESSOM WAS SURPRISINGLY TENDER WITH HER, but Valentyna was too lost in her own darkness to notice. He wet a square of linen and wiped her face and hands clean of the blood, and tried gently to get her to talk. There were important things she must understand before the King arrived.

"What can I do to help you, my queen?" he whispered,

wondering how to revive her from this stricken state before he began to explain his new situation.

Valentyna was in utter turmoil. What had gone wrong? She was still herself . . . and Cailech was dead. She had killed him, and Wyl had not possessed her. Everyone had lied to her. Fynch, Elspyth, Cailech . . . but why? She groaned involuntarily. It was a sound of such anguish that she saw fear pass across the hook-nosed Chancellor's face. Why was he showing her such concern?

"Your majesty?" Jessom whispered, trying to bring her back to the present.

"Kill me," she whispered. "Before I have to spend a night with him."

"I cannot do that, your highness."

"Then I shall kill myself," she said, color flushing her ghastly, almost yellow complexion.

She saw him flinch. "Please don't, your majesty. Listen to me: I made a promise to King Cailech yesterday that I would offer you my protection. Rest assured, my word is true. I am now your servant, your highness." He broke protocol by taking her hand and placing it on his heart. She tried to pull it back, repulsed, but he held it firmly in place. "You must trust me," he begged her. "King Cailech—"

She cut across his words. "Why do you offer your allegiance to me? You are the King's man."

"You must trust me, please," he repeated. He took her dull silence as agreement. "The King is on his way here, your majesty. I have important information to share with you, but let me organize some refreshment so it arrives before Celimus does. I will be only moments." He swiftly exited the chamber.

Valentyna did not move, knowing he would not leave her alone long enough to end her life. It briefly occurred to her that the Chancellor was treating her far more kindly than she had expected. Perhaps the Mountain King had indeed managed to persuade him to watch over her. Jessom could not protect her, however, from Celimus's attentions tonight. She felt bile rise again, thought she might be sick. It mattered not—by tonight she planned to be dead herself. Jessom returned. He was breathing hard, as if he had been running. "Ah, here we are now, your highness. Please drink this."

"What is it?"

"The King's favorite wine. It has a rich and full flavor. It suits only the heaviest of foods because it tends to overpower other tastes, but then the King does not take a midday meal and thus favors the heaviness."

Valentyna wondered why the Chancellor was giving her such an in-depth description of the wine. Perhaps he thought she needed educating on Celimus's preferences.

The door suddenly opened and the King of Morgravia himself stood before her. His cheeks were flushed and he looked triumphant. "You were magnificent, Valentyna," he said, laughing. "Do you still have his blood on you, you savage Briavellian?"

"I washed it away, your highness," Jessom said softly. He was ignored by both King and Queen.

Valentyna stood and curtsied. "I don't know what came over me, sire."

"I do," Celimus said, taking the proffered goblet of wine from Jessom without even looking at his chancellor. "It was a wonderful demonstration of patriotism. I am proud of you. To us," he said, raising his glass.

"To us," Valentyna echoed. She thought of her father's small dagger, which she had packed and brought with her to Morgravia. It had been for the sake of sentimentality that she had wrapped it so carefully in muslin and laid it among her things. Shortly it would serve a different purpose, bringing welcome death when it opened the arteries at her wrists.

Celimus drained his glass. It was swiftly taken away and refilled by Jessom, then returned as surreptitiously.

"Are you feeling up to the feast, my love?" the King asked.

"I will change, I think," Valentyna replied drily, looking at her stained gown.

The King sniggered at the jest. "Of course, go ahead. The nobles can wait. I'll hang on to the gown for posterity, though; Cailech's dried blood will make an amusing keepsake."

"More wine, sire?" Jessom said, stepping forward.

Valentyna watched Celimus drain his second glass of wine and knew that by tonight he would be intoxicated and even more determined to keep his promise. Jessom filled the glass for a third time and Valentyna grimaced, wishing the Chancellor would stop plying the King with so much liquor.

"I won't be long," she said. She was backing into her dressing chamber when she saw the King stagger slightly.

"Are you all right, sire?" Jessom asked.

"Shar, but I feel a little odd," Celimus said.

"Well, I imagine that's the poison I put in your glass, sire," Jessom offered matter-of-factly.

Valentyna's mouth fell open. "Poison?" she echoed. Her gaze moved from the King's suddenly haggard expression to the victorious face of his chancellor.

"Yes, your majesties," Jessom replied. "Valentyna, you don't love the King, I most certainly don't love the King, the nobles despise him, and Morgravia will hardly miss him—I decided we were all better off without him."

Celimus tried to move toward the Chancellor, but succeeded only in twitching awkwardly.

"Ah yes, I think the paralysis must be setting in by now, and because you drank two . . ."—Jessom gave a soft chortle as he checked the glass decanter in his hand—"almost three glasses, each with a hefty dose of the poison, it will work fast. So let's talk swiftly."

Celimus made to speak, but nothing of sense came from his lips. He spilled the tiny amount of liquid left in his glass down his front, the glass itself rolling off his lap and hitting the edge of the chair before falling to the floor and shattering.

"No matter, sire, we can clean that up along with your corpse. This is a wonderfully lethal potion Jessom discovered just recently. It kills cleanly, without a giveaway smell and no telltale signs left behind on the body. I'm afraid it's not a very pleasant death for the victim—no doubt quite similar to the one Eryd Bench would have experienced," Jessom went on. "A hideously agonizing end, which is less than you deserve, sire, if I might say so."

Valentyna was slowly shaking her head in disbelief; Celimus bared his teeth ferociously.

"Not long now, sire, I promise. Your highness"—Jessom turned to a stunned Valentyna—"if you have anything to say to him, say it now. We have about ten minutes at most before his heart stops."

She had never been more unnerved. "You have really poisoned him?"

The Chancellor nodded. "I had to run back to Jessom's rooms to get the vial, which is why I was so out of breath, your majesty."

She frowned. "Why do you speak of Jessom as though you were elsewhere?"

"Oops. How forgetful of me," the Chancellor replied, clearly enjoying himself. He gave a sly grin that Valentyna did not understand. "Look at me, Celimus," he demanded, his voice no longer playful as he moved to stand in front of the King. "Watch carefully."

Chancellor Jessom closed his eyes; Valentyna could swear she heard him softly call the name Fynch. A blue shimmering light appeared around his body, burning him, dissolving him. Then her hand moved to her mouth to stifle the scream of disbelief, for beneath the shimmering, another man was emerging. As Jessom disappeared into the blue furnace, it was Cailech who lifted his proud head, Cailech's eyes that opened to look into hers, Cailech's beloved face that looked at her with such love.

Valentyna felt herself tremble and she began to weep, unable to understand what was happening. Could this be true?

*Thank you, Fynch,* Wyl whispered across the miles. And deep in the heart of the Thicket, a boy smiled.

"It is I, Valentyna," Wyl said gently.

She shook her head, hardly daring to trust him. "I killed you."

"You killed Jessom."

"How?" Her voice was a groan.

"Fynch made it possible for me to swap places with Jessom temporarily, and for the Chancellor to impersonate Cailech. He called it the Bridge of Souls."

"Magic?" she whispered.

"That's right, my love, a clever glamour and a transference between bodies. Fynch came to me in the dungeon and asked me to trust him. I was not of a mind to grasp what he was offering; I only believed it myself when I realized Cailech was screaming and yet it was not me making that sound. Fynch gave his last reserves for us, Valentyna. He worked out that if Myrren and her father could weave such a curse, though he could not undo it, he could reweave it to truly make it a gift."

"A gift of life?"

Wyl nodded. "In the truest sense. I don't plan on changing again. I hope you like me enough as Cailech." Valentyna put her head in her hands, overwhelmed by emotion. Wyl took her in his arms and kissed her bent head. Then he looked across to Celimus; the King's eyes were disbelieving and glassy, and spittle dribbled through lips pulled back in a rictus of anger.

"I think we just have enough time for me to tell you a story, Celimus," Wyl said coldly. He settled Valentyna in a chair and held her hand, but stared directly at the dying King as he spoke briefly and succinctly, starting in the dungeon of Stoneheart, where a young woman named Myrren was being tortured and a boy named Wyl Thirsk offered her pity.

Valentyna felt awed at hearing the story in its entirety. Somehow it was fitting that its full telling should take place before the man who had been the source of it all. Myrren was truly avenged now.

"And Jessom?" Valentyna asked when Wyl was finished. She needed to understand how the Chancellor's fate had become so closely linked with her future happiness.

"Jessom was a parasite, Valentyna. He might not have made the cruel decisions himself, but he saw that they were carried out. The blood of too many people was on his hands. It was fitting that he should suffer for his sins. I suspect he was ready to swap allegiances, but instead the Bridge of Souls saw to it that he swapped bodies."

"So you knelt there and let me pretend to kill you," she said, aghast.

"It wasn't easy. You must know I was happy to die, and I had hoped to die by Celimus's hand," he said, glancing at the

King. "Fynch warned me once of the power random acts had to affect the Quickening, but I could never have foreseen that you might make such a sacrifice. Fynch could, and he took appropriate precautions."

"He knew I would do such a thing?"

Wyl shook his head. "None of us did. Not even you, I imagine. Fynch just seems to see the larger picture. I think he understood that an unpremeditated action might change the pattern of life, and he put his Bridge of Souls in place so that I might be saved, come what may."

"That child is too clever by half."

Wyl fixed her with his green gaze, knowing he could not hide the truth from her. "I believe Fynch is dead, Valentyna."

Her throat swelled with fresh grief. "No!"

"He used what was left of his spirit to help us. It is a long story, my love—one I shall share with you later. First I must finish my task here."

Celimus groaned. His fingers had shaped themselves into claws and Wyl had no doubt that the King was in pain.

"It's over, Celimus," he said, feeling very little satisfaction at seeing the once-proud sovereign arch in death's paralysis. "Let Shar's Gatherers take you now, and may our god alone have the generosity to show you mercy."

Celimus found one last spurt of energy to gurgle his fury and suddenly Wyl felt a sharp pain, like a blade of ice, cutting through Cailech's body and forcing a cry from him.

"What is it?" Valentyna said, grabbing his arm. Wyl barely felt her touch or heard her; his vision dimmed and he could no longer see the chamber around him. But he knew where he was. He was with Celimus.

*You!* Celimus whispered.

And Wyl understood: This was Myrren's parting gift, her final vengeance. She was showing Celimus the truth.

*I'm glad you can see me at last, Celimus.* It was no longer Cailech before the King, but a short, redheaded man. Wyl Thirsk, General of the Morgravian Legion.

*The Legion and the nobles will not permit it,* Celimus screamed into the mind of his nemesis.

*You forget, they do not see me; they see only a crowned*

*monarch you yourself have forged a truce with. Very few know I was captured and incarcerated, and even fewer know of my death.*

*You will not take my throne. Morgravia will never accept a Mountain King.*

*I don't have to. You gave your throne to Valentyna the moment you married her, Celimus. She is the ruler of both realms now. But I will become sovereign of Morgravia when I marry her. I have to, you see, to fulfill Myrren's Gift and rid myself fully of the Quickening. It demands that I be sovereign.*

The King of Morgravia screamed his despair into his rival's mind as he sighted Shar's Gatherers approaching.

# 44

THERE WAS A KNOCK AT THE DOOR. "CHANCELLOR JESSOM?" A voice called.

"It's Aremys and Crys," Wyl said, closing the eyes of the dead King. He had hoped to have a few minutes alone with the Queen, but the Grenadyne had obviously done his duty quickly. He strode to the door and pulled it open. Instantly the color in the two familiar faces before him drained as they gazed upon the ghost of a man they had watched die just moments before.

"What in Shar's name—" Aremys began.

"Hush, come in quickly," Wyl said. He felt sorry for their shock, but there was no time to spare for niceties. "Shut the door behind you. Hello, Crys. Oh, I think I should say 'carving knife.'" He grinned.

The newcomers entered the chamber tentatively. At the same moment, they spotted the familiar figure slumped in a chair.

"Celimus is dead?" Crys whispered, his gaze moving to Valentyna and then returning with fresh fear to Wyl.

Wyl nodded.

"Wait!" Aremys demanded. "What's going on? Cailech is dead! I watched it happen. I waited for the Quickening but saw no evidence of it. I feared you had died for good."

"As you see, I'm very much alive," Wyl replied, taking a grim pleasure in his friend's shock. "It was Fynch. He worked out a way to channel his own magic to save me without disturbing Myrren's Gift."

"How?" the two men asked at once, awe in their voices. Then Crys nudged Aremys and both bowed to their queen. "Your majesty," they said, embarrassed at their lack of courtesy.

Valentyna smiled and shook her head. "I'm too unsettled to even notice any lapses in protocol."

"Tell us," Aremys said, turning back to Wyl. "What did Fynch contrive?"

"He swapped me with Jessom."

"So Jessom was executed?" Aremys said, his wonder obvious.

"Fynch called it a Bridge of Souls," Wyl answered. "He came to me in the dungeon. He begged me to trust him and mentioned the Bridge of Souls, but he did not explain it and I didn't ask him to elaborate. My mood was grim, and much as I treasured seeing him once more, I didn't think anything could change the course I was on."

"I thought you'd become the Queen," Crys finally said, his relief evident. "No disrespect, your majesty," he said to Valentyna.

And then suddenly Aremys had Wyl in a bearlike hug. Wyl reached out a long arm to encompass Crys in the embrace. Valentyna had to look away, the rush of emotion she felt at witnessing their relief echoing her own. She wished she could join them, but sensed this was a special moment between the three men. There would be time ahead for her and Wyl to share their feelings.

Finally the men pulled apart. The newcomers examined for themselves the cooling corpse of King Celimus.

"What happened?" Aremys asked, delight obvious in his voice.

"Jessom poisoned him—I mean, I did. As soon as the King was as good as dead, I was released from the glamour and could reveal the truth to him."

Aremys scratched his head, unsure of what to say or do. He followed his gut instinct and knelt before the two royals. "Your majesties, my sword is yours to command. Although do not ask me to use it on you now, Wyl."

The King laid a hand on the warrior's bowed head. "I won't, Aremys, my great friend. Only we four know of what has truly occurred today. No one else need ever find out."

"So you will remain as Cailech, is that it?" Aremys asked carefully as he stood. "But Myrren's Gift demands that you become sovereign of Morgravia!"

Valentyna spoke up. "We shall marry as soon as it is feasible. It must be with the nobles' permission, but most blessed my strategic marriage to Celimus. Why not a second union in the name of peace?"

Crys Donal nodded. "That's true. And there are rumblings among the true Legionnaires about a civil uprising backed by key nobles. It doesn't seem to be idle gossip any longer. I just have one question: How will you explain the King's death?"

Wyl began to pace the room. Shocked and overwrought as she was, Valentyna could not help but smile to see Cailech's large hand tug at his earlobe in a gesture unique to Wyl Thirsk.

"Jessom poisoned the King and then fled," Wyl said. "The only other person in the chamber was Valentyna, but she had retired to her dressing room to change into her gown for the wedding banquet. She saw the Chancellor pour the wine for the King before she left the room—and we still have the wine in the decanter to prove that it was poisoned. When Valentyna returned, ready to attend her wedding feast, she found the King in his death throes and raised the alarm. You and I, Aremys, had come to pay our respects to the newly married couple, and so were on hand to hear the Queen's cries. We hunted down the Chancellor and dispatched him quickly and without honor, as befitting a traitor. That will also explain his corpse's headless state, should news of it get out."

Wyl paused and looked at his friend. "Is this all right with you?"

"My pleasure to be responsible for his death," the big man replied. "I'll ensure the body is disposed of carefully too."

"What about the executioner?" Valentyna asked. "He will know that it was Cailech I executed, not Jessom. And there were a few guards in the courtyard too."

"Apparently they were all mercenaries, your majesty," Crys offered, "not true Legionnaires, and I have a list here of their names, as Jessom—I mean, Wyl—ordered. We can easily track them down and either pay them to keep their silence, or use other means. Same for the executioner."

"The executioner need not die. He is a good man," Wyl said, remembering how Featherstone had asked him not to make Valentyna's task any harder. "When you find him, bring him to me. I shall explain." He offered no further explanation and no one pushed him for one.

"What reason do we hazard for Jessom's betrayal of the King?" Crys asked.

Wyl tugged at his ear again. "I can say I had a discussion with Jessom the night before the wedding and shared with him my understanding that Celimus intended to lay the blame for so many deaths at the Chancellor's feet. The King would have needed to explain to the nobles somehow, and that would be an ideal solution. And so they will assume that Jessom killed Celimus out of revenge. Let's be honest, few of the nobles are going to grieve at the news of the King's death."

"They'll probably have to grit their teeth to prevent themselves from cheering, if truth be known," Aremys commented.

"Then we have the perfect opportunity at the wedding feast to explain our position," Wyl continued. "We should be as honest as we can. Celimus is dead—we cannot escape this."

"I shall throw Felrawthy's support behind Valentyna as

the new sovereign of Morgravia," Crys Donal offered. "Hopefully others will follow the Donal lead."

"That's generous of you, Crys," Valentyna said, "but I worry about Morgravia accepting me. Surely there is another family they would argue is more suitable?"

"They might," Crys said, "but that family is my own; we are distantly related to the Crown. And I would not accept— believe me, it's the last thing I wish for. I belong in the north and you, Valentyna, already have one crown on your head. In marrying Celimus, you accepted the second."

"He's right," Wyl said. "And I think they will accept you if the right voices are behind you. We must speak with Lord Hartley too—he is a powerful voice and will probably be the most pleased among the lords to hear of Celimus's death, as he only just escaped being killed himself. We can thank Jessom for that mercy." Wyl turned to Crys. "You can't be seen here. The nobles have been told that Cailech slaughtered your family, so it's unthinkable you would even be in the same room as him. In fact, you should change into your formal wear, get your hair color back to normal, and join the nobles to hear what is said at the wedding feast."

Crys nodded. "So I know nothing of this, right?"

"Correct," Wyl said. "But we shall be revealing the fact of Celimus's death at the banquet, so you can have your say then."

Valentyna said aloud what they were all thinking. "I know this is all a lie, but Celimus and Jessom deserve no better."

Aremys had one last question. "What about the Quickening?"

Wyl smiled and turned to Valentyna. "I believe the magic will be satisfied if I become sovereign of Morgravia through marriage, instead of through Celimus," he said. "That is, if Queen Valentyna will have me?"

Crys and Aremys had left them, and Wyl and Valentyna were finally alone. Wyl took Valentyna's hand, ready to pour out all that was in his heart, when there came a knock at the door. He smiled sadly and nodded at her to answer it. "We have a lifetime ahead of us, my love," he said, kissing her fingers.

The Queen took a moment to compose herself, then called out, "Who is it?"

"It's Renton, your majesty."

*My page,* Valentyna mouthed to Wyl. She went to the door and opened it a crack, to hide the interior of the chamber from curious eyes. "Yes?" she said.

"The nobles are gathered in the banquet hall, your highness. They await their king and queen."

# 45

TALL MAN CLUTCHING A CHILD WALKED INTO A SUNLIT CLEARing, emerging from the tangled mass of the curiosity known as the Thicket. He was followed by a magnificent black horse.

Gueryn looked at the boy in his arms, pale and lifeless, and wanted to cry. To him, the death of young Fynch was the embodiment of all of his sorrows. The passing of the courageous child echoed the bravery of so many who had died since that terrible day the witch Myrren had died, bequeathing Wyl Thirsk a strange and painful gift. Gueryn had no idea what he was doing in this strange place that reeked of magic, but he had been drawn here, with Fynch and Galapek, as if he no longer controlled the direction in which he moved. What must he do next?

His wonderings were answered, somewhat disturbingly, by an oversized owl, who pierced him with a grave yellow gaze and said into his mind, *Put him on the ground, please. The Thicket wishes to feel him.*

Gueryn obeyed. He had seen so much—felt so much—that was strange, not even a huge talking bird could shock him now.

*We of the Thicket are pleased to see you are restored, Gueryn le Gant.*

Gueryn bowed to the bird. "It was Knave, I believe, who saved my life."

*He is here. You can thank him yourself,* Rasmus said, turning his head toward a massive black dog who was bounding out from the shadow of the yews.

"Knave!" Gueryn called, kneeling to greet the dog. "I owe you my life," he whispered to his savior, hugging him close.

The dog barked and then, as he looked at the child on the ground, whined sadly, sniffing every inch of the boy's body.

"Can you help Lothryn?" Gueryn asked, the plea evident in his voice.

*A great evil has been wrought upon this beast,* Rasmus replied. *I cannot undo it.*

Gueryn laid his hand on Galapek's strong neck. Had this journey been for nothing, then? As he mourned the tragic fate of the Mountain Man, the sun-drenched patch where they stood was suddenly darkened by a great shadow. Gueryn looked up and was astounded to see a huge figure descending upon them.

*The King comes,* Rasmus said reverently.

Now Gueryn could make out the shape looming above them. "A dragon?" he whispered, overcome by awe.

The massive creature landed, shaking the ground. Its scales shimmered with dark, seemingly ever-changing colors.

Gueryn was on his knees in veneration in a second. He lifted his head a fraction and dared to stare, goggle-eyed, at the fantastic creature before him.

*Welcome, Gueryn le Gant,* it said. *We owe you our thanks for returning Faith Fynch to us.*

"Can you help him, sire?" Gueryn pleaded.

*Not in the way you would like,* the dragon's deep voice answered gently. *But although Fynch's life among your kind is over, he will live on in a new form.*

The dragon turned its attention to the trembling horse. *Come to me, poor Galapek.*

The stallion moved to stand before the King of the Creatures and effected a gracious bow of sorts. Gueryn instinctively stepped back from the horse and the dragon as he sensed the thrum of a powerful magic gathering. The clearing exploded into a dazzling golden light, which burned for several moments. It blazed like a huge fire; he could feel its warmth and hear its crackle as it flamed around them, then suddenly disappeared. The rays of sunlight seemed dull by comparison.

Standing where Galapek had been was a huge man. His body was shaking and his head was thrown back, mouth open in silent prayer.

"Lothryn!" Gueryn called, tears flowing freely down his face and into his straggly beard. He ran toward the Mountain Man and grabbed him just as he toppled, taking them both heavily to the ground.

*Let him recover for a few moments,* the dragon advised. *He is weak now and will remain so for some time.*

Gueryn nodded. "When I was bringing Fynch here, I thought I heard the boy call Wyl's name. It was the only word he uttered. Did I imagine it?"

*Fynch did not die at Rashlyn's hands, as you suspected. He died because he chose to relinquish his spirit and his power.*

"What do you mean, your majesty?" Gueryn asked.

*Fynch was a sacrifice,* the Dragon King said, and Gueryn heard genuine sorrow in the creature's tone. *We demanded so much and he accepted all that we asked of him, giving his life freely. His one request was that he use his power to aid your Wyl Thirsk. Rashlyn did not kill the boy. Fynch was far stronger than even we had anticipated.*

"But I thought—"

*You heard true; Fynch did call Thirsk's name. He needed to send himself a long way to reach Wyl, and he was so weakened by the fight with Rashlyn that he had to make a decision. He could not maintain life in his body and also send himself to Wyl.*

"He chose Wyl?" Gueryn was shocked. He had assumed that Wyl was dead, but perhaps not all hope was lost.

*Fynch made the ultimate sacrifice for his friend. He gave his life.*

Gueryn bowed his head. He grieved for the child but badly wanted to know that Wyl lived. "And Wyl Thirsk?" he asked, frightened to hear the reply.

*Wyl Thirsk lives, le Gant, as the Mountain King. And Celimus is dead.*

Gueryn's mouth dropped open in shock, but no words came. Finally: "I don't know what to say," he admitted. He could tell that the dragon, along with the strange creatures he now noticed gathering around the fringe of the clearing, was hurting at the loss of Fynch. Even the Thicket itself seemed to be pulsating with a sense of sorrow.

*We shall provide horses to take you and Lothryn from here,* was all the dragon replied.

Lothryn spoke as a man for the first time in a long time. It hurt, just as it hurt to breathe, even to think. "Elspyth?" was all he could manage. The dragon turned to regard him with huge black eyes. *She clings to life, Mountain Man. Go to Argorn in Morgravia, and hurry.*

Both men paid homage once again to the King of the Creatures. But there was still one thing left to ask.

Gueryn cleared his throat and looked at the tiny bundle on the ground beside him. "The boy? Should I take him back to his family or . . ."

*We are Fynch's family now,* the dragon replied gently. *He is one with me and my flesh.*

"I don't understand, sire," Gueryn said, helping Lothryn to his feet.

*Fynch was no ordinary gong boy. He was sired by Magnus, King of Morgravia.*

Gueryn paled. "Did Magnus know?" he asked, astonished he could sound so composed.

*No.*

"What are you telling us, your majesty?"

*That Fynch is the true Dragon King. As you know, the Kings of Morgravia have always been bonded exclusively to the dragon. No one else but they are permitted to claim union with me.*

Gueryn shook his head with wonder. "Do you mean, your majesty, that Fynch was a prince of Morgravia?"

*Now Celimus is dead, he becomes a king.*

"There must be something you can do, great one," Gueryn said, looking around wildly. "Surely Fynch can be saved?"

*There is something I can do, Gueryn,* the dragon said patiently. *Watch.* The two men looked on incredulously as the creature of legend tenderly lifted the tiny boy in its huge claws. A blaze of golden light surrounded Fynch the instant the dragon touched him, and the gold in turn was fringed by a riot of dark iridescent colors that echoed the creature's ever-changing hues.

*We are one—dragon and King united.* The dragon's voice boomed deep in their minds as he wrapped his vast wings about the tiny body, cocooning it. Then he threw back his head and roared in triumph. As he did so, his scales turned to gold, dazzling and sparkling in the drench of sunlight. He opened his wings to their full breadth and both men inhaled sharply. Fynch's body was gone.

And then a new voice spoke to them. *Thank you, Gueryn, Lothryn. Courageous Knave. I shall never forget you.* It was Fynch.

Knave leapt up and let loose with a howl that even the men could tell was one of victory. They clung to each other, tears and laughter mingling as they shared in the creatures' triumph that Fynch lived on.

*Farewell,* Fynch called. *This will be our secret. I trust you will honor it.*

The dragon beat its powerful wings and the resulting wind drove the two men backward. They held on to each other as the great beast lifted effortlessly into the sky, disappearing toward the east, into the Wild.

Rasmus broke the awed silence. *It is time for you to leave us,* he said, looking to where two horses emerged from the yews. *They are yours now.*

Gueryn nodded, still tongue-tied from all the emotions surging through him: sorrow and joy, elation and awe.

*Elspyth is in Argorn, as you have been told, Lothryn,* Rasmus continued matter-of-factly. *Wyl is in Stoneheart, Gueryn. We shall not meet again, although Knave has agreed to accompany you. Brace yourselves, the Thicket is sending you . . .*

They arrived moments later beneath the cover of a small stand of trees. The air was sweet-smelling and Gueryn in-

stantly recognized their surroundings as the region of Argorn. He knew precisely where they were: in a small copse
barely an eighth of a mile from the Thirsk family estate.

He looked at his companion. "How do you feel?"

"I'm not sure. Weak enough to lie down here and never
get up again, yet so energized by the thought that Elspyth is
close that I could run all the way to her."

"Then do that, my friend. And when you reach her, hold
her tight and never let go. Bring her to Stoneheart as soon as
she is well. She may be in a position to bear witness to some
events, and I'm sure you will have things to work out for
your people in the Razors."

Lothryn smiled. It felt strange to be happy, to know pleasure again. "Thank you, Gueryn. May our realms never be
enemies again."

"Between you and Wyl, I'm sure you'll see to it."

"I shall raise Aydrech as a proud ally."

"Hurry to the capital," Gueryn reminded him. "I'll let Wyl
know you are coming."

The two men embraced and then parted to follow separate
paths. The Mountain Man rode toward the grand manor,
where an ailing woman waited for him. The Morgravian,
with a huge black dog coursing beside him, galloped off toward Pearlis.

# EPILOGUE

Cailech's long arms reached around Valentyna and hugged her close. They were standing on the small balcony of Magnus's old war tower. It was the only place Wyl could think of where they might truly be alone.

"Do you have to go to north so soon?" she asked.

There was amusement in his voice. "You'll handle yourself brilliantly and I'll be back before you know it, Valentyna. The meeting with the nobles went better than we could have dreamed. You already have them twirled around your little finger."

She shook her head with wonder. "Thanks to Lord Hartley coming out of hiding and revealing just how treacherous Celimus was, even to his own nobility."

"We shall be married by summer's end, how's that?"

Valentyna nodded glumly, knowing it would not be appropriate any sooner.

Wyl continued. "I know you understand that I want to be with Crys when he returns to Felrawthy. We shall grieve together at Tenterdyn and our prayers will cleanse it."

The Queen sounded uncharacteristically sulky when she replied, "Crys is so smitten with Georgyana Bench, I'm sure he'll hardly notice your presence." She saw his expression turn serious and was instantly contrite. "I'm sorry. I'm just so scared of losing you again."

"I know," he said gently, kissing her head. "You won't lose me again, I promise you."

"How long will you be gone? It was Aremys who told me you'd be going to the Razors. Were you too scared to share that news with me yourself?"

Wyl laughed. "Yes, as a matter of fact. I may be Wyl to you, but I have to make an effort to be Cailech to everyone else. I must return to the Razors and do the right thing by his people."

"You're going to appoint Lothryn to rule in your stead?"

He nodded. "It's fitting. The people will understand that now that I am planning to marry the southern Queen, I will spend a lot of my time here. But an absent king is not good for their needs, so Lothryn will administer the realm—and far better than I can, I'm sure."

"There's a child, though, is that right?"

"Yes. Cailech fathered the boy, but on Lothryn's wife. Loth has always thought of Aydrech as his own and now he can rightfully raise him as his son."

"Will he be King?"

"Yes. Bastard children are recognized as heirs in the Razors."

Valentyna nodded. "It must feel good to put everything back into balance again," she said. "I'm so happy for Elspyth, too. She's glowing. Did you ever think things could work out so right after everything felt so hideously wrong?"

Wyl turned her to him and kissed her softly, his lips lingering on hers so she could feel the tenderness and passion behind his affection. "I never thought I would win you. I told myself that the time at Briavel would be enough, if that was all I could have. Shar has blessed me."

Valentyna pulled him closer still and whispered into his ear, his golden hair tickling her face, "Shar has blessed you with more than you think."

He pulled away and looked at her quizzically.

"Shar, but for a king, you can be thick, Wyl Thirsk!"

"What am I missing?" he begged, laughing at her insult.

"Marry me fast, my lord, for I am pregnant. It seems we shall have the first royal heir to the joint throne of Briavel and Morgravia by the close of next winter."

She watched the light green eyes of the northern King—soon to be a southern king too—fill with tears. She continued talking, knowing he was at a loss for words. "If he's a boy we shall call him Wyl Magnus—then your name shall live on and our son will take a favorite name from both Morgravia and Briavel. And I'd better start remembering to call you Cailech all the time—do you mind?"

Finally Wyl found his voice. "And if we have a princess?"

"Ylena, of course. What else but a name that signifies such courage and represents so much love in both our lives?"

"Valentyna . . ." Whatever else Wyl was going to say was choked by a soft sob of joy. He hugged her tight, showering her hair and face with kisses. "If I died right here and now I couldn't be happ—"

"Don't! We're both going to live until we're so old we will need servants to help us on and off the privy."

They laughed among their shared tears. "That's right," he said. "We shall grow old and creaky together."

"Make Aremys bring you home to me quickly. I can only believe you are safe while I can see you, hold you," she said fervently. Wyl understood. He would have to be very careful with Cailech's body until they were married and he was rightfully King of Morgravia.

Valentyna sighed, looking out across the landscape. "It's beautiful here. I miss my woodlands but this is certainly a wonderful view. I feel like I can see all the way to Briavel."

"That was the point. This war tower was built so it offered a view in all directions, but especially toward Briavel."

"Well, we shall give this tower a new purpose. I shall dream something up by your return, King Cailech."

He grinned, and as he did so a shadow fell across them. "What's that?" he said, shading his eyes against the sharp sunlight as he looked up.

"I can't imagine," Valentyna said, squinting into the sky. "An eagle?"

"Not in these parts, and it's too big anyway."

Knave, who had been slumped drowsily close by, leapt to his feet and began to bark.

"What is it, Knave?" Wyl asked. He was rewarded with an answer from a voice he had never thought to hear again. *Hello, Wyl.*

*Fynch! he sent back. Oh Shar—is it really you?*

*Tell Valentyna. She can't hear us—she's not linked*

*through the Thicket. And fret not, I've made myself invisible
to all but you three.*

"What is it?" Valentyna asked, baffled.

"My love, you won't believe it." Wyl grinned, feeling a
shaft of happiness spear his heart. "It's Fynch! He's alive."

"Where?" Valentyna asked, amazed.

"Up there," he said, pointing. *What are you?* he sent.

*A dragon!* He heard the boy laugh in his head and the
sound was one of pure joy.

Read on for a preview of the
new trilogy from Fiona McIntosh

# ODALISQUE
## Book One of the Percheron Saga

A sweeping new epic fantasy trilogy
set in the famed harem of an exotic palace
and rife with forbidden love, treachery,
betrayal and possession

The prisoners, chained together, shuffled awkwardly into the main square of the slave market of Percheron; six men, all strangers and all captives of a trader called Varanz, who had a reputation for securing the more intriguing product for sale. And this group on offer was no exception, although most onlookers' attention was helplessly drawn to the tall man whose searing, pale-eyed stare, at odds with his long dark hair, seemed to challenge anyone brave enough to lock gazes with him.

Varanz knew it too; knew this one was special, and he sensed a good price coming for the handsome foreigner well worth the effort it had cost six of his henchmen to firstly bring the man down and then rope him securely. It puzzled him why the man had been traveling across the desert, of all places—that in itself a perilous journey—but and also moving alone, which meant almost certain trouble, particularly from slavers renowned in the region.

But Varanz had a policy of not inquiring into the background of his captives; perhaps to ease his conscience he didn't want to know anything about them, save what was obvious to his own eye. And this one, who refused to name himself, or indeed mutter much more than curses, was clearly in good health. That was enough for the merchant.

Trading for this cluster of slaves opened at the sound of the gong. The Master of the Market called the milling crowd of buyers to order: "Brothers, we have here Varanz Set Number Eight." His voice droned on, extolling the virtues of each on offer, but already the majority of potential buyers were in the thrall of the angry-eyed man, clearly the pick of the bunch and the only one of the six who held his head defiantly high. Sensing a lively auction, the Master of the Market decided to state more than the obvious of healthy appearance, strong structure and good teeth. "He was found emerging from the golden sands of our desert alone, not even a camel for company. Brothers, I'd hazard this one will make a fine bodyguard. If he's canny enough to travel our wasteland and remain as well as he looks, then I imagine he has excellent survival skills."

"Can he fight?" one buyer called out.

Varanz arched an eyebrow and looked toward the slave, wondering whether he'd finally get something out of the man. His instincts were right.

"I can fight," the man replied. "In fact," he challenged, "I demand to fight for my freedom."

A fresh murmuring rippled through the crowd. An oddity in Percheron's slave market was its ancient and somewhat quaint rule that a slave who was captured as a free person had one chance to buy his freedom—with a fight to the death. The Crown covered the cost of his loss, either way, to the trader. It was one of the Market's oldest customs, set up by a Zar many centuries earlier who understood that such a contest from time to time would provide entertainment for the otherwise tedious business of trading in human cargo.

Such fights were rare, of course, as most prisoners took their chances with a new life as a slave. But now and then one would risk death in the bid to win back his independence.

Varanz strolled over to the man now that he knew his tongue was loosened. "You understand what you ask for?"

"I do. It was explained to us on the journey here by one of your aides. I wish to fight for my freedom. I also wish to speak with your Zar."

At this Varanz smirked. "I can't imagine he will want to speak with you."

"He might after he watches me best twelve of his strongest warriors."

Varanz was speechless at the man's arrogance. He shook his head and walked to the Master, briefly explaining in a quiet mutter what the slave was proposing. Now both of them returned to stand before the man.

"Don't try and talk me out of it. I want my freedom back. I will pay the price if I fail to win it," the slave warned them.

The Master had no intention of attempting to thwart the proposition of some sport after an already long and wearying day in the market. He could see that Varanz was unfazed, knowing that he would get a good price either way.

"What is your reserve, Varanz?" he asked.

"No less than 200 karels for this one."

The Master nodded. "I will send a message to the palace for authorization," he said; now turning to the man, he insisted, "You must give us your name."

The slave knifed them with a cold gaze. "My name is Lazar."

The palace did more than give authorization. A runner returned swiftly with the news that Zar Joreb, his interest piqued, would be in attendance for the contest. "You understand how unusual it is for The Zar of Percheron to visit the slave traders," Varanz informed Lazar.

The foreigner was unmoved. "I wish to speak with him if I succeed."

Varanz nodded. "That is up to our Zar. We have told him you have offered to fight twelve of his men to the death. This is no doubt why he is coming to witness the contest."

"It is why I suggested so many."

Varanz shook his head, exasperated. "How can you best a dozen fighters, man? There's still time to change your mind and not waste your life. I will ensure a cozy position for you. A fellow like you will find himself in high demand by a rich man to escort his wives, families . . . take care of their security."

Lazar snorted. "I'm no nursery maid."

"All right." Varanz tried again. "I know I can sell you as a high caliber bodyguard to a man who needs protection while he travels. I'll find you a good owner."

"I don't want to be owned," Lazar snarled. "I want my freedom."

The trader shrugged. "Well you'll have it, my friend, but you'll be carried off in a sack."

"So be it. I slave for no-one."

Their conversation was ended by the Master of the Market hissing for silence—a troop of Percheron's guard had arrived, signifying that The Zar's karak was just moments away. Varanz nodded to one of his aides to escort the rest of the prisoners to the holding pen. Trading would resume once this piece of theater was done with.

"I wish you luck, brother," he said to Lazar and moved away to stand with the Master, who was marshaling all the other traders into a formal line of welcome. The Zar finally arrived flanked by several of the Percherese Guard, his karak carried by six of the red-shrouded Elim, the elite guardians of The Zar's harem who also provided bodyguard duties to royalty. The Zar's entry between the slave market's carved pillars of two gryphons was heralded by the trumpeting of several of the curled Percherese horns, and everyone who was not attached to the royal retinue instantly humbled himself. No one dared raise his eyes to The Zar until given formal permission.

No-one but Lazar, that is.

He was on his knees because he had been pushed down but he brazenly watched The Zar being helped out of the karak; their gazes met and held momentarily across the dust of the slave market. Then Lazar dipped his head, just a fraction, but it was enough that The Zar knew the brash young man had acknowledged the person who was the closest thing to the god Zarab that walked the earth.

The Guard quickly set up The Zar's seat and the Elim unfurled a canopy over it. Zar Joreb settled himself. He had a wry smile on his face as the Master of the Market made the official announcement that the prisoner, Lazar, captured by Trader Varanz, had opted to fight for his freedom against a dozen warriors from the Percherese Guard. No-one watched the Master or even The Zar. All eyes were riveted on the dark foreigner, whose wrists and ankles were now unshackled and who was disrobing down to the once white, now gray and dirty loose pants he wore beneath. They watched his measured movements, but mostly they watched him study the twelve men taking practice swipes with their glinting swords, all bearing smirks, none prepared to take the ridiculously outnumbered opposition seriously.

The gong sounded for silence and the Master outlined what was about to happen. It was a superfluous pronouncement but strict protocol was a way of life for Percheron's various markets, especially in the hallowed presence of The Zar.

". . . or to the prisoner's death," he finished somberly. He looked to Zar Joreb who, with an almost imperceptible nod, gave the signal for combat to begin.

Those who were present at the slave market that day would talk about the fight for years to come. Lazar accepted the weapon thrown toward him and without so much as a hurried prayer to his god of choice strode out to meet the first of the warriors. To prolong the sport, the Guard had decided to send out one man at a time—presumably they intended to keep wounding the arrogant prisoner until he begged for mercy and the death blow. However, by the time the first three men were groaning and bleeding on the ground, their most senior man hurriedly sent in four at once.

It didn't make much difference to Lazar, who appeared to the audience to be unintimidated by numbers. His face wore the grim countenance of utter focus; he made no sound, never once backed away, always threatening his enemy rather than the other way around. It was soon obvious that his sword skills could not be matched by any of the Percherese, not even fighting in tandem. His fighting arm became a blur of silver that weaved a path of wreckage through flesh, turning the dozen men, one after another, into writhing, crying heaps as they gripped torn shoulders, slashed legs, or profusely bleeding fighting arms. To their credit, the final two fought superbly, but neither could mark Lazar. He fought without fear, his speed only increasing. Cutting one man down by the ankle, Lazar stomped on his sword wrist, breaking it, to ensure he did not return to the fray, and some moments later, fought the other into exhaustion until the man was on his knees. Lazar flicked the guard's sword away and gave a calculated slash across his chest. The man fell, almost grateful for the reprieve.

The slave market was uncharacteristically quiet, save for the cries of bleeding, paining men. Varanz looked around at the carnage, his nostrils flaring with the raw metallic smell of blood thick in the air, and he raised his eyebrows with surprise. No one was dead. Lazar had mercilessly and precisely disabled each of his rivals but claimed the life of none.

Throwing down his sword, Lazar stood in the circle of hurt warriors, a light sheen of perspiration on his body the only indication that he had exerted himself. His chest rose and sank steadily, calmly. He turned to The Zar and bowed long and deeply.

"Zar Joreb, will you now grant my freedom?" he spoke finally into the hush that had fallen.

"My men would surely seek death than live with the dishonor of losing this fight," was Joreb's response.

Varanz watched Lazar's curiously light eyes cloud with defiance. "They are innocent men. I will not take their lives for a piece of entertainment."

"They are soldiers! This was a fight to the death."

"Zar Joreb, this was a fight to *my* death, not theirs. It was made clear that I either win my freedom through death or through survival. I survived. No one impressed upon me that anyone had to die as part of the rules of this custom."

"Arrogant pup," Joreb murmured into the silence. Then, impossibly, he laughed. "Stand before me, young man."

Lazar took two long strides and then went down on one knee, his head finally bowed.

"What is it you want, stranger?" The Zar demanded.

"I want to live in Percheron as a free man," Lazar replied, not lifting his head.

"Look at me." Lazar did so. "You've humiliated my Guard. You will need to rectify that before I grant you anything."

"How can I do that, Zar Joreb?"

"By teaching them."

Lazar stared at The Zar, a quizzical look taking over his heretofore impassive expression, but he said nothing.

"Become my Spur," Zar Joreb offered. "Our present Spur must retire soon. We need to inject a fresh approach. A young approach. You fight like you're chasing away demons, man. I want you to teach my army how to do that."

Lazar's gaze narrowed. His tone sounded guarded. "You're offering to pay me to live as a free man in Percheron?"

"Be my Spur," Zar Joreb urged. This time there was no humor in his voice, only passion.

The crowd collectively held its breath as Lazar paused. Finally, he nodded once, decisively. "I accept, but first you owe Varanz over 200 karels apparently."

Joreb laughed loudly in genuine amusement. "I like you, Lazar. Follow me back to the palace. We have much to speak of. I must say, I'm impressed by your audacity. You put your life in danger to get what you want."

"It was never in danger," Lazar replied and the semblance of a smile twitched briefly at his mouth.

# ST. MARTIN'S

# MINOTAUR

## MYSTERIES

## THE MERMAIDS SINGING

"Compelling and shocking."                    —Minette Walters

"A dark tale . . . Complex, carefully crafted, and disturbing
. . . powerful . . . psychologically terrifying . . . impossible to
put down."                                      —*Publishers Weekly*

"Exciting, rapid-fire . . . A satisfying descent into the territory of a twisted mind."                          —*Booklist*

"[A] terrific chiller from Manchester's answer to Thomas
Harris."                                      —*The Guardian* (UK)

"Truly, horribly good."                        —*Mail on Sunday* (UK)

## KILLING THE SHADOWS

"Vivid and adept . . . mounts in tension while at the same
time making readers aware of their complicity in craving
the grisly shocks the genre provides . . . as Stephen King
did in *Bag of Bones*, McDermid is trying to address the
inhumanity that's all too easy for popular writers to lapse
into as they seek to titillate an increasingly jaded readership
. . . McDermid is a whiz at combining narrative threads . . .
and ending chapters with cliffhangers that propel you to
keep reading. In terms of hooking her readers and carrying
them along out of sheer desire to find out what happens
next, McDermid is as smooth a practitioner of crime fiction
as anyone out there . . . *Killing the Shadows* is further proof
that she's the best we've got."
                              —*The New York Times Book Review*

**MORE . . .**

# THE MERMAIDS
# SINGING

## VAL McDERMID

St. Martin's Paperbacks

First published in Great Britain by HarperCollins*Publishers*.

THE MERMAIDS SINGING

Copyright © 1995 by Val McDermid.

Cover photograph © Roine Magnusson/Image Bank/Getty Images

Excerpt from *The Wire in the Blood* © 1997 by Val McDermid.
Excerpt from *Killing the Shadows* © 2000 by Val McDermid.

Extract from "The Love Song of J. Alfred Prufrock" from the *Collected Poems 1909–1962* by T. S. Eliot (published by Faber and Faber Ltd.) is reproduced by permission of Faber and Faber Ltd.

Val McDermid asserts the moral right to be identified as the author of this work.

ISBN: 0-312-98360-3

Printed in the United States of America

St. Martin's Paperbacks edition / June 2002

St. Martin's Paperbacks are published by St. Martin's Press, 175 Fifth Avenue, New York, NY 10010.

10   9   8   7   6   5   4   3

# Acknowledgments

It's always disturbing when life seems to imitate art. I started planning this book in the spring of 1992, long before the killings that shook the gay community in London. I sincerely hope that there is nothing in these pages that will cause grief or offence to anyone.

As ever, I have picked brains galore and thoroughly exploited my friends while researching and writing *The Mermaids Singing*. I'd particularly like to thank senior clinical psychologist and offender profiler Mike Berry of Ashworth Top Security Psychiatric Hospital in Liverpool for giving so generously of his time and expertise in the preparation of this book. The insights and information I gleaned from him have been invaluable, as well as stopping the conversation at dinner parties dead in its tracks.

Thanks too to Peter Byram of the Responsive College Unit in Blackburn, who gave me advice on the finer points of computer technology. Alison Scott and Frankie Hegarty provided helpful information on matters medical. Detective Superintendent Mike Benison of the Sussex Police generously made time in his busy schedule to fill me in on the handling of major murder enquiries. Jai Penna, Diana Cooper and Paula Tyler demonstrated yet again that some lawyers are generous with their time and knowledge.

For their support, patience and advice throughout, I'd particularly like to thank Brigid Baillie and Lisanne Radice. It can't be easy putting up with someone who spends her days inside the head of a serial killer . . .

The northern city of Bradfield is entirely a creature of my imagination. In particular, the attitudes and behaviour attributed to assorted professionals, including police officers, were chosen for reasons of fictional necessity rather than verisimilitude. In Britain, we are fortunate to have few serial killers; that's because most of them are caught after their first murder. Let's hope the profilers and the police can keep it that way.

For Tookie Flystock, my beloved serial insect killer.

I have heard the mermaids singing, each to each.
I do not think that they will sing to me.

"The Love Song of J. Alfred Prufrock"
T. S. Eliot

The soul of torture is male.

Comment on exhibit card
*The Museum of Criminology and Torture,*
*San Gimignano, Italy.*

All chapter epigraphs are taken from
"On Murder considered as one of the fine arts"
by Thomas De Quincey (1827)

# THE MERMAIDS SINGING

*You always remember the first time. Isn't that what they say about sex? How much more true it is of murder. I will never forget a single delicious moment of that strange and exotic drama. Even though now, with the benefit of experience and hindsight, I can see it was an amateurish performance, it still has the power to thrill, though not any longer to satisfy.*

*Although I didn't realize it before the decision to act was forced upon me, I had been paving the way for murder well in advance. Picture an August day in Tuscany. An air-conditioned coach whisking us from city to city. A busload of Northern culture vultures, desperate to fill every moment of our precious fortnight's package with something memorable to set against Castle Howard and Chatsworth.*

*I'd enjoyed Florence, the churches and art galleries filled with strangely contradictory images of martyrdom and Madonnas. I had scaled the dizzy heights of Brunelleschi's dome surmounting the immense cathedral, entranced by the winding stairway that leads up from the gallery to the tiny cupola, the worn stone steps tightly sandwiched between the ceiling of the dome and the roof itself. It was like being inside my computer, a real role-playing adventure, working my way through the maze to daylight. All it lacked were monsters to slay on the way. And then, to emerge into bright day and amazement that up here, at the end of this cramped ascent, there was a postcard and souvenir seller, a small, dark, smiling man stooped from*

*years of lugging his wares aloft. If it had really been a
game, I would have been able to purchase some magic from
him. As it was, I bought more postcards than I had people
to send them to.*

*After Florence, San Gimignano. The town rose up from
the green Tuscan plain, its ruined towers thrusting into the
sky like fingers clawing upwards from a grave. The guide
burbled on about "a medieval Manhattan," another crass
comparison to add to the list we'd been force-fed since
Calais.*

*As we neared the town, my excitement grew. All over
Florence, I'd seen the advertisements for the one tourist
attraction I really wanted to see. Hanging splendidly from
lampposts, gorgeous in rich red and gold, the banners insisted that I visit the Museo Criminologico di San Gimignano. Consulting my phrasebook, I'd confirmed what I'd
thought the small print said. A museum of criminology and
torture. Needless to say, it wasn't on our cultural itinerary.*

*I didn't have to search for my target; a leaflet about the
museum, complete with street plan, was thrust upon me less
than a dozen yards inside the massive stone gateway set in
the medieval walls. Savouring the pleasure of anticipation,
I wandered around for a while, marvelling at the monu-
ments to civic disharmony that the towers represented. Each
powerful family had had its own fortified tower which they
defended against their neighbours with everything from
boiling lead to cannons. At the peak of the city's prosperity,
there were supposedly a couple of hundred towers. Compared to medieval San Gimignano, Saturday night down the
docks after closing time seems like kindergarten, the sea-
men mere amateurs in mayhem.*

*When I could no longer resist the pull of the museum, I
crossed the central piazza, tossing a bicoloured 200-lire
coin in the well for luck, and walked a few yards down a
side street, where the now familiar red and gold hangings
adorned ancient stone walls. Excitement buzzing in me like
a blood-crazed mosquito, I walked into the cool foyer and*

*calmly bought my entrance ticket and a copy of the glossy, illustrated museum guide.*

*How can I begin to describe the experience? The physical reality was so much more overwhelming than photographs or videos or books had ever prepared me for. The first exhibit was a ladder rack, the accompanying card describing its function in loving detail in Italian and English. Shoulders would pop out of their sockets, hips and knees separate to the sound of rending cartilage and ligament, spines stretch out of alignment till vertebrae fell apart like beads from a broken string. "Victims," the card said laconically, "often measured between six and nine inches taller after the rack." Extraordinary minds the inquisitors had. Not satisfied with interrogating their heretics while they were alive and suffering, they had to seek further answers from their violated bodies.*

*The exhibition was a monument to the ingenuity of man. How could anyone not admire the minds that examined the human body so intimately that they could engineer such exquisite and finely calibrated suffering? With their relatively unsophisticated technology, those medieval brains devised systems of torture so refined that they are still in use today. It seems that the only improvement our modern post-industrial society has been able to come up with is the additional frisson provided by the application of electricity.*

*I moved through the rooms, savouring each and every toy, from the gross spikes of the Iron Maiden to the more subtle and elegant machinery of pears, those slender, segmented ovoids which were inserted into vagina or anus. Then, when the ratchet was turned, the segments separated and extended till the pear had metamorphosed into a strange flower, petals fringed with razor-sharp metal teeth. Then it was removed. Sometimes the victims survived, which was probably a crueller fate.*

*I noticed unease and horror on the faces and in the voices of some of my fellow visitors, but recognized it for the hypocrisy it was. Secretly, they were loving every minute of their pilgrimage, but respectability forbade any public display of their excitement. Only the children were honest in their ardent fascination. I would have happily bet that I was far from the only person in those cool, pastel rooms who felt the surge of sexual desire between their legs as we drank in the exhibits. I have often wondered how many holiday sexual encounters have been spiced and salted by the secret recollection of the torture museum.*

*Outside, in a sun-drenched courtyard, a skeleton crouched in a cage, bones clean as if stripped by vultures. Back in the days when the towers stood tall, these cages would have hung on the outer walls of San Gimignano, a message to inhabitants and strangers alike that this was a city where the law exacted a harsh penalty if it was not respected. I felt a strange kinship with those burghers. I too respect the need for punishment after betrayal.*

*Near the skeleton, an enormous metal-shod spoked wheel leaned against the wall. It would have looked perfectly at home in an agricultural museum. But the card fixed to the wall behind it explained a more imaginative function. Criminals were bound to the wheel. First, they were flayed with scourges that ripped the flesh from their bones, exposing their entrails to the eager crowd. Then, with iron bars, their bones were broken on the wheel. I found myself thinking of the tarot card, the wheel of fortune.*

*When I realized I was going to have to become a killer, the memory of the torture museum rose before me like a muse. I've always been good with my hands.*

*After that first time, part of me hoped I wouldn't be forced to do it again. But I knew that if I had to, the next time it would be better. We learn from our mistakes the imperfections of our actions. And luckily, practice makes perfect.*

# 1

*Gentlemen, I have had the honour to be appointed by your committee to the trying task of reading the Williams' Lecture on Murder, considered as one of the Fine Arts; a task which might be easy enough three or four centuries ago, when the art was little understood, and few great models had been exhibited; but in this age, when masterpieces of excellence have been executed by professional men, it must be evident, that in the style of criticism applied to them, the public will look for something of a corresponding improvement.*

Tony Hill tucked his hands behind his head and stared up at the ceiling. There was a fine web of cracks around the elaborate plaster rose which surrounded the light fitting, but he was oblivious to it. The faint light of dawn tinged with the orange of sodium streetlamps filtered in through a triangular gap at the top of his curtains, but he had no interest in that either. Subconsciously, he registered the central-heating boiler kicking in, readying itself to take the edge off the damp winter chill that seeped in round door and window frames. His nose was cold, his eyes gritty. He couldn't remember the last time he'd had a straight night's sleep. His concerns about what he had to get through that day was part of the reason for the night's interrupted dreams, but there was more than that. Much more.

As if today wasn't more than enough to worry about. He knew what was expected of him, but delivering it was another story. Other people managed these things with nothing more than a short-lived flutter in the stomach, but not Tony. It required all his resources to maintain the façade he'd need to get through the day. In circumstances like these, he understood how much it took out of method actors to produce the fraught, driven performances that captivated their audiences. By tonight, he'd be good for nothing except another vain attempt at eight hours' sleep.

He shifted in bed, pulling one hand out and running it through his short dark hair. He scratched the stubble on his chin and sighed. He knew what he wanted to do today, but equally, he was well aware it would be professional suicide if he did. It didn't matter that he knew there was a serial killer loose in Bradfield. He couldn't afford to be the one to say it first. His stomach clenched on emptiness and he winced. With a sigh, he pushed the duvet back and got out of bed, shaking his legs to unfurl the concertina folds of his baggy pyjamas.

Tony trudged off to the bathroom and snapped on the light. As he emptied his bladder, he reached out with his free hand and switched on the radio. Bradfield Sound's traffic announcer was revealing the morning's projected bottlenecks with a cheerfulness that no motorist could have equalled without large doses of Prozac. Thankful that he wouldn't be driving that morning, Tony turned to the sink.

He gazed into his deep-set blue eyes, still bleary with sleep. Whoever said the eyes were mirrors of the soul was a true bullshit merchant, he thought ironically. Probably just as well, or he wouldn't have an intact mirror in the house. He undid the top button of his pyjama jacket and opened the bathroom cabinet, reaching out for the shaving foam. The tremor he spotted in his hand stopped him short. Angrily, he slid the door shut with a loud crack and reached up for his electric razor. He hated the shave it produced, never leaving him with the fresh, clean feeling that came from a wet shave. But better to feel vaguely scruffy than to turn up looking like a walking illustration of the death of a thousand cuts.

The other disadvantage of the electric razor was that he didn't have to concentrate so hard on what he was doing, leaving his mind free to range over the day ahead. Sometimes it was tempting to imagine that everybody was like

him, getting up each morning and selecting a persona for
the day. But he had learned over years of exploring other
people's minds that it wasn't so. For most people, the available selection was severely limited. Some people would
doubtless be grateful for the choices that knowledge, skill
and necessity had brought Tony. He wasn't one of them.

As he switched off the razor, he heard the frantic chords
that preceded every news summary on Bradfield Sound.
With a sense of foreboding, he turned to face the radio,
tense and alert as a middle-distance runner waiting for the
starting pistol. At the end of the five-minute bulletin, he
sighed with relief and pushed open the shower curtain.
He'd expected a revelation that would have been impossible
for him to ignore. But so far, the body count was still three.

On the other side of the city, John Brandon, Bradfield Metropolitan Police's Assistant Chief Constable (Crime)
stooped over the washbasin and stared glumly into the bathroom mirror. Not even the shaving soap covering his face
like a Santa Claus beard could give him an air of benevo-
lence. If he hadn't chosen the police, he'd have been an
ideal candidate for a career as a funeral director. He was
two inches over six feet, slim to the point of skinny, with
deep-set dark eyes and prematurely steel-grey hair. Even
when he smiled, his long face managed to sustain an air of
melancholy. Today, he thought, he looked like a blood-
hound with a head cold. At least there was good reason for
his misery. He was about to pursue a course of action that
would be as popular with his Chief Constable as a priest
in an Orange Lodge.

Brandon sighed deeply, spattering the mirror with foam.
Derek Armthwaite, his Chief, had the burning blue eyes of
a visionary, but there was nothing revolutionary in what
they saw. He was a man who thought the Old Testament a
more appropriate handbook for police officers than the Police And Criminal Evidence Act. He believed most modern
police methods were not only ineffective but also heretical.

In Derek Armthwaite's frequently aired opinion, bringing back the birch and the cat-o'-nine-tails would be far more effective in reducing crime figures than any number of social workers, sociologists and psychologists. If he'd had any idea of what Brandon had planned for that morning, he'd have had him transferred to Traffic, the present-day equivalent of Jonah being swallowed by a whale.

Before his depression could overwhelm his resolve, Brandon was startled by a banging on the bathroom door. "Dad?" his elder daughter shouted. "You going to be much longer?"

Brandon snatched up his razor, dunked it in the basin and scraped it down one cheek before replying. "Five minutes, Karen," he called. "Sorry, love." In a house with three teenagers and only one bathroom, there was seldom much opportunity for brooding.

Carol Jordan dumped her half-drunk coffee on the side of the washbasin and stumbled into the shower, nearly tripping headlong over the black cat that wound himself round her ankles. "In a minute, Nelson," she muttered as she closed the door on his interrogative miaow. "And don't waken Michael."

Carol had imagined that promotion to detective inspector and the concomitant departure from the shift rota would have granted her the regular eight hours' sleep a night that had been her constant craving since the first week she joined the force. Just her luck that the promotion had coincided with what her team were privately calling the Queer Killings. However much Superintendent Tom Cross might bluster to the press and in the squad room that there were no forensic connections between the killings, and nothing to suggest the presence of a serial killer in Bradfield, the murder teams thought differently.

As the hot water cascaded over Carol, turning her blonde hair mouse, she thought, not for the first time, that Cross's attitude, like that of the Chief Constable, served his prej-

udices rather than the community. The longer he denied that
there was a serial killer attacking men whose respectable
façade hid a secret gay life, the more gay men would die.
If you couldn't get them off the streets any longer by arresting them, let a killer remove them. It didn't much matter
whether he did it by murder or by fear.

It was a policy that made a nonsense of all the hours
she and her colleagues were putting in on the investigation.
Not to mention the hundreds of thousands of pounds of
taxpayers' money that these enquiries were costing, particularly since Cross insisted each killing be treated as an entirely separate entity. Every time one of the three teams
came up with some detail that seemed to link the killings,
Tom Cross dismissed it with five points of dissimilarity. It
didn't matter that each time the links were different and the
dissimilarities the same tired quintet. Cross was the boss.
And the DCI had opted out of the strife completely, taking
sick leave with his opportunistic bad back.

Carol rubbed the shampoo to a rich lather and felt herself gradually wake under the warm spray. Well, her corner
of the investigation wasn't going to run aground on the
rock of Popeye Cross's bigoted prejudice. Even if some of
her junior officers were inclined to grasp at the boss's tunnel vision as an excuse for their own uninspired investigations, she wasn't going to stand for anything less than
one hundred per cent committed action, and in the right
direction. She'd worked her socks off for the best part of
nine years, first to get a good degree and then to justify her
place on the promotion fast track. She didn't intend her
career to hit the buffers just because she'd made the mistake
of opting for a force run by Neanderthals.

Her mind made up, Carol stepped out of the shower,
shoulders straight, a defiant glint in her green eyes. "Come
on, Nelson," she said, shrugging into her dressing gown
and scooping up the muscular bundle of black fur. "Let's
hit the red meat, boy."

\*    \*    \*

Tony studied the overhead projection on the screen behind him for a final five seconds. Since the majority of his audience had expressed their lack of commitment to his lecture by pointedly not taking notes, he wanted at least to give their subconscious minds the maximum opportunity to absorb his flow chart of the criminal profile generating process.

He turned back to his audience. "I don't have to tell you what you already know. Profilers don't catch criminals. It's bobbies that do that." He smiled at his audience of senior police officers and Home Office officials, inviting them to share his self-deprecation. A few did, though most remained stony faced, heads on one side.

However he dressed it up, Tony knew he couldn't convince the bulk of the senior police officers that he wasn't some out-of-touch university boffin there to tell them how to do their jobs. Stifling a sigh, he glanced at his notes and continued, aiming for as much eye contact as he could achieve, copying the casual body language of the successful stand-up comics he'd studied working the northern clubs. "But sometimes we profilers see things differently," he said. "And that fresh perspective can make all the difference. Dead men do tell tales, and the ones they tell profilers are not the same as the ones they tell police officers.

"An example. A body is found in bushes ten feet away from the road. A police officer will note that fact. He'll check the ground all around for clues. Are there footprints? Has anything been discarded by the killer? Have any fibres been snagged on the bushes? But for me, that single fact is only the starting point for speculations that, taken in conjunction with all the other information at my disposal, may well lead me to useful conclusions about the killer. I'll ask myself, was the body deliberately placed there? Or was the killer too knackered to carry it further? Was he hiding it or dumping it? Did he want it to be found? How long did he expect or want it to stay hidden? What is the significance of this site for him?" Tony lifted his shoulders and held out his hands in an open, questioning gesture. The audience looked on, unmoved. God, how many tricks of the trade was he going to have to pull out of the hat before he got a response? The prickle of sweat along the back of his neck was becoming a trickle, sliding down between his skin and his shirt collar. It was an uncomfortable sensation that reminded him of who he really was behind the mask he'd assumed for his public appearance.

Tony cleared his throat, focused on what he was projecting rather than what he was feeling, and continued. "Profiling is just another tool that can help investigating officers to narrow the focus of their investigation. Our job is to make sense of the bizarre. We can't give you an offender's name, address and phone number. But what we *can* do is point you in the direction of the kind of person who has committed a crime with particular characteristics. Sometimes we can indicate the area where he might live, the kind of work we'd expect him to do.

"I know that some of you have questioned the necessity for setting up a National Criminal Profiling Task Force. You're not alone. The civil libertarians are screaming about it too." At last, Tony thought with profound relief. Smiles and nods from the audience. It had taken him forty minutes to get there, but he'd finally cracked their composure. It didn't mean he could relax, but it eased his discomfort. "After all," he went on, "we're not like the Americans. We don't have serial killers lurking round every corner. We still have a society where more than ninety per cent of murders are committed by family members or people known to the victims." He was really taking them with him now. Several pairs of legs and arms uncrossed, neat as a practised drill-hall routine.

"But profiling isn't just about nailing the next Hannibal the Cannibal. It can be used in a wide variety of crimes. We've already had notable success in airport anti-hijacking measures, in catching drug couriers, poison-pen writers, blackmailers, serial rapists and arsonists. And just as importantly, profiling has been used very effectively to advise police officers on interview techniques for dealing with suspects in major crime enquiries. It's not that your officers lack interviewing skills; it's just that our clinical background means we have developed different approaches that can often be more productive than familiar techniques."

Tony took a deep breath and leaned forward, gripping the edge of the lectern. His final paragraph had sounded good in front of the bathroom mirror. He prayed it would hit the right spot rather than stamp on people's corns. "My team and I are now one year into a two-year feasibility study on setting up the National Criminal Profiling Task Force. I've already delivered an interim report to the Home Office, who confirmed to me yesterday that they are committed to forming this task force as soon as my final report is delivered. Ladies and gentlemen, this revolution in crime fighting is going to happen. You've got a year to make sure it happens in a form that you feel comfortable with. My team and I have all got open minds. We're all on the same side. We want to know what you think, because we want it to work. We want violent, serial offenders behind bars, just like you do. I believe you could use our help. I know we can use yours."

Tony took a step backwards and savoured the applause, not because it was particularly enthusiastic, but because it signalled the end of the forty-five minutes he'd been dreading for weeks. Public speaking had always been firmly outside the boundaries of his comfort zone, so much so that he'd turned his back on an academic career after achieving his doctorate because he couldn't face the constant spectre of the lecture theatre. The ability to perform was not a reason in itself for doing so. Somehow, spending his days poking around in the distorted recesses of the minds of the criminally insane was far less threatening.

As the short-lived clapping died away, Tony's Home Office minder bounced to his feet from his front-row chair. While Tony provoked a wary distrust in the police section of his audience, George Rasmussen generated more universal irritation than a flea bite. His eager smile revealed too many teeth and a disturbing resemblance to George

Formby that was at odds with the seniority of his Civil Service post, the elegant cut of his grey pinstripe suit and the yammering bray of a public-school accent so exaggerated that Tony was convinced Rasmussen had really been educated in some inner-city comprehensive. Tony half listened as he shuffled his notes together and replaced his acetates in their folder. Grateful for fascinating insight, blah, blah . . . coffee and those absolutely delicious biscuits, blah, blah . . . opportunity for informal questions, blah, blah . . . remind you all submissions to Dr. Hill due by . . .

The sound of shuffling feet drowned out the rest of Rasmussen's spiel. When it came to a choice between a civil servant's vote of thanks and a cup of coffee, it was no contest. Not even for the civil servants. Tony took a deep breath. Time to abandon the lecturer. Now he had to be the charming, well-informed colleague, eager to listen, to assimilate and to make his new contacts feel he was really on their side.

John Brandon stood up and stepped aside to allow the other people in his row to move out of their seats. Watching Tony Hill's performance hadn't been as informative as he'd hoped. It had told him a lot about psychological profiling, but almost nothing about the man, except that he seemed self-assured without being arrogant. The last three quarters of an hour hadn't made him any more certain that what he was planning was the right course of action. But he couldn't see any alternative. Staying close to the wall, Brandon moved forward against the flow until he was level with Rasmussen. Seeing his audience vote with its feet, the civil servant had sharply wound up his speech and switched off his smile. As Rasmussen gathered up the papers he'd dumped on his seat, Brandon slipped past him and crossed the floor towards Tony, who was fastening the clasps on his battered Gladstone bag.

Brandon cleared his throat and said, "Dr. Hill?" Tony looked up, polite enquiry on his face. Brandon swallowed his qualms and continued. "We haven't met before, but you've been working on my patch. I'm John Brandon . . ."

"The ACC Crime?" Tony interrupted, a smile reaching his eyes. He'd heard enough about John Brandon to know he was a man he wanted on his side. "I'm delighted to meet you, Mr. Brandon," he said, injecting warmth into his voice.

"John. It's John," Brandon said, more abruptly than he'd intended. He realized with a spurt of surprise that he was nervous. There was something about Tony Hill's calm assurance that unsettled him. "I wonder if we can have a word?"

Before Tony could reply, Rasmussen was between them. "If you'd excuse me," he interjected without any note of humility, the smile back in place. "Tony, if you'd just come through now to the coffee lounge, I know our friends in the police will be eager to chat to you on a more intimate basis. Mr. Brandon, if you'd like to follow us."

Brandon could feel his hackles rising. He felt awkward enough about the situation without having to fight to keep their conversation confidential in a room full of coffee-swilling coppers and nosy Home Office mandarins. "If I could just have a word with Dr. Hill in private?"

Tony glanced at Rasmussen, noting the slight deepening of the parallel lines between his eyebrows. Normally, it would have tickled him to wind up Rasmussen by continuing his conversation with Brandon. He always enjoyed pricking pomposity, reducing the self-important to impotent. But too much hung on the success of his encounters with other police officers today, so he decided to forego the pleasure. Instead, he turned pointedly away from Rasmussen and said, "John, are you driving back to Bradfield after lunch?"

Brandon nodded.

"Perhaps you could give me a lift, then? I came on the train, but if you don't mind, I'd rather not wrestle with British Rail on the way back. You can always drop me at the city limits if you don't want to be seen fraternizing with the Trendy Wendies."

Brandon smiled, his long face creasing into simian wrinkles. "I don't think that'll be necessary. I'll be just as happy to drop you at force headquarters." He stood back and watched Rasmussen steer Tony to the doors, fussing all the way. He couldn't shake off the slightly disconcerted feeling that the psychologist had given him. Maybe it was simply that he'd grown so accustomed to being in control of everything in his world that asking for help had become an alien experience that automatically made him feel uncomfortable. There was no other obvious explanation. Shrugging, Brandon followed the crowd through to the coffee lounge.


Tony snapped the seat belt closed and savoured the comfort of the unmarked Range Rover. He said nothing as Brandon manoeuvred out of the Manchester force headquarters' car park and headed for the motorway network, unwilling to interfere with the concentration necessary to avoid missing the way in an unfamiliar city. As they cruised down the slip road and joined the fast-flowing traffic, Tony broke the silence. "If it helps, I think I already know what it is you wanted to talk to me about."

Brandon's hands tensed on the wheel. "I thought you were a psychologist, not a psychic," he joked. He surprised himself. Humour wasn't his natural mode; he normally resorted to it only under pressure. Brandon couldn't get used to how nervous he felt asking this favour.

"Some of your colleagues would take more notice of me if I was," Tony said wryly. "So, do you want me to have a guess and run the risk of making a complete fool of myself?"

Brandon snatched a quick look at Tony. The psychologist looked relaxed, hands palm down on his thighs, feet crossed at the ankles. He looked as though he'd be more at home in jeans and a sweater than in the suit which even Brandon recognized as well past its fashionable sell-by date. He could relate to that, remembering the scathing comments his daughters routinely passed on his own plain clothes. Brandon said abruptly, "I think we've got a serial killer operating in Bradfield."

Tony released a small, satisfied sigh. "I was beginning to wonder if you'd noticed," he said ironically.

"It's by no means a unanimous opinion," Brandon said, feeling the need to warn Tony before he'd even asked for his help.

"I'd gathered as much from the press coverage," Tony said. "If it's any comfort to you, I'm as certain as I can be from what I've read that your analysis is right."

"That's not entirely the impression you gave in those quotes of yours I saw in the *Sentinel Times* after the last one," Brandon said.

"It's my job to cooperate with the police, not to under mine them. I assumed you had your own operational reasons for not going public with the serial-killer angle, did stress to them that what I was saying was no more than an informed guess based on the information that was in the public domain," Tony added, his genial tone contradicting the sudden tensing of his fingers that ruched the material of his trousers into loose pleats.

Brandon smiled, aware only of the voice. "Touché. So are you interested in giving us a hand?"

Tony felt a warm rush of satisfaction. This was what he had craved for weeks now. "There's a service area a few miles down the road. D'you fancy a cup of tea?"


Detective Inspector Carol Jordan stared at the broken chaos of flesh that had once been a man, determinedly forcing her eyes to remain out of focus. She wished she hadn't bothered to snatch that stale cheese sandwich from the canteen. Somehow, it was acceptable for young male officers to throw up when they were confronted with victims of violent death. They even got sympathy. But in spite of the fact that women were supposed to lack bottle any way, when female officers chucked up on the margins of crime scenes they instantly lost any respect they'd ever won and became objects of contempt, the butts of locker-room jokes from the canteen cowboys. Pick the logic out of that Carol thought bitterly as she clamped her jaws tighter together. She thrust her hands deep into the pockets of her trench coat and clenched her fists, the nails pressing into her palms.

Carol felt a hand on her arm, just above the elbow. Grateful for the chance to look away, she turned to find her sergeant looming above her. Don Merrick towered a good eight inches over his boss, and had developed a strange hunchbacked stoop when he spoke to her. At first, she'd found it amusing enough to regale friends with over drinks or the occasional dinner party when she managed to squeeze a night off. Now, she didn't even notice. "Area's all cordoned off now, ma'am," he said in his soft Geordie accent. "Pathologist's on his way. What d'you think? Are we looking at number four?"

"Don't let the Super hear you say that, Don," she said, only half joking. "I'd say so, though." Carol looked around. They were in the Temple Fields district, in the rear yard of a pub which catered primarily to the gay trade, with an upstairs bar that was lesbian three nights a week. Contrary to the jibes of the macho men she'd overtaken in the promotion stakes, it wasn't a bar Carol had ever had reason to enter. "What about the gate?"

"Crowbar," Merrick said laconically. "It's not wired into the alarm system."

Carol surveyed the tall rubbish dumpsters and the stacked crates of empties. "No reason why it should be," she said. "What's the landlord got to say?"

"Whalley's talking to him now, ma'am. Seems he locked up last night about half past eleven. They've got bins on wheels behind the bars for the empties, and at closing time they just wheel them into the yard back there." Merrick waved over towards the back door of the pub, where three blue plastic bins stood, each the size of a supermarket trolley. "They don't sort them out till the afternoon."

"And that's when they found this?" Carol asked, gesturing over her shoulder with her thumb.

"Just lying there. Open to the elements, you might say."

Carol nodded. A shudder ran through her that was nothing to do with the sharp north-eastern wind. She took a step towards the gate. "OK. Let's leave this to the SOCOs for now. We're only in the way here." Merrick followed her into the narrow alley behind the pub. It was barely wide enough for a single vehicle to squeeze down. Carol looked up and down the alley, now closed off by police tapes and guarded at either end by a pair of uniformed constables. "He knows his turf," she mused softly. She walked backwards along the alley, keeping the gate of the pub in constant view. Merrick followed her, waiting for the next set of orders.

At the end of the alley, Carol stopped and swung round to check out the street. Opposite the alley was a tall building, a former warehouse that had been converted into craft workshops. At night, it would be deserted, but in mid-afternoon, almost every window framed eager faces, staring out from the warmth within at the drama below. "Not much chance of anyone looking out of a window at the crucial time, I suppose," she remarked.

"Even if they had, they wouldn't have taken any notice," Merrick said cynically. "After closing time, the streets round here are jumping. Every doorway, every alley, half the parked cars have got a pair of poofs in them, shagging the arse off each other. It's no wonder the Chief calls Temple Fields Sodom and Gomorrah."

"You know, I've often wondered. It's pretty clear what they were up to in Sodom, but what do you suppose the sin of Gomorrah was?" Carol asked.

Merrick looked bewildered. It increased his resemblance to a sad-eyed Labrador to a disturbing degree. "I'm not with you, ma'am," he said.

"Never mind. I'm surprised Mr. Armthwaite hasn't got Vice pulling them all in on indecency charges," Carol said.

"He did try it a few years back," Merrick confided. "But

the police committee had his bollocks barbecued for it. He fought them, but they threatened him with the Home Office. And after the Holmwood Three business, he knew he was already on thin ice with the politicians, so he backed down. Doesn't stop him slagging them off every chance he gets, though."

"Yeah, well, I hope this time our friendly neighbourhood killer has left us a bit more to go on, or our beloved leader might just pick another target for his next slagging off." Carol straightened her shoulders. "Right, Don. I want a door-to-door of the businesses, now. And tonight, we're all going to be out on the streets, talking to the trade."

Before Carol could complete her instructions, a voice from beyond the tapes interrupted. "Inspector Jordan? Penny Burgess, *Sentinel Times*. Inspector? What have you got?"

Carol closed her eyes for a brief moment. Dealing with the recalcitrant bigots in the chain of command was one thing. Dealing with the press was infinitely worse. Wishing she'd stayed in the yard with the grisly corpse, Carol took a deep breath and walked towards the cordon.


"Let me get this straight. You want me to come on board for the duration of this murder enquiry, but you don't want me to tell anyone?" The look of amusement in Tony's eyes masked his anger at the reluctance of influential policemen to accept the value of what he could do.

Brandon sighed. Tony wasn't making it easy for him, but then, why should he? "I want to avoid any suggestions in the press that you are helping us. The only chance I have of getting you formally involved with the investigation is to persuade the Chief Constable that you're not going to be stealing the limelight from him and his coppers."

"And that it won't become public knowledge that Derek Armthwaite, the Hand Of God, is turning to the mumbo-jumbo men for help," Tony said, an edge in his voice betraying more than he wanted to.

Brandon's face twisted in a cynical smile. It was good to see that it was possible to ruffle that smooth surface. "If you say so, Tony. Technically, it's an operational matter, and he's not really supposed to interfere unless I'm doing something that's counter to force and Home Office policy. And it is the policy of BMP to use expert assistance whenever it is appropriate."

Tony snorted with laughter. "And you think he'll accept me as 'appropriate'?"

"I think he doesn't want another confrontation with the Home Office or the police committee. He's due to retire in eighteen months, and he's desperate for the knighthood." Brandon couldn't believe what he was saying. He didn't even voice this kind of disloyalty to his wife, never mind to a virtual stranger. What was it about Tony Hill that had made him open up so swiftly? There must be something in this psychology lark after all. Brandon comforted himself that at least he had harnessed that something in the service of justice. "So what do you say?"

"When do I start?"

*Even that first time, I planned the event more carefully than a theatre director plans the first production of a new play. In my mind, I crafted the experience, till it was like a bright and shining dream, there every time I closed my eyes. I checked and rechecked every choreographed move, making sure I hadn't missed some vital detail that would endanger my freedom. Looking back on it now, the mental movie I created was almost as pleasurable as the act itself.*

*The first step was to find a place where I could safely take him, a place we could be private together. I immediately dismissed my home. I can hear my neighbours' squalid arguments, the barking of their hysterical German shepherd and the irritating thud of their stereo's bass; I had no desire to share my apotheosis with them. Besides, in my terraced street, there are too many curtain twitchers. I wanted no witnesses to Adam's arrival or his departure.*

*I considered renting a lock up garage, but rejected that for the same reasons. Besides, it seemed too seedy, too much of a cliché from the world of television and film. I wanted something in keeping with what was going to happen. Then I remembered my mother's Auntie Doris. Doris and her husband Henry used to farm sheep on the moors high above Bradfield. Then, about four years ago, Henry died. Doris tried to keep things going for a while, but when her son Ken invited her out last year for an extended holiday with his family in New Zealand, she sold the sheep and packed her bags. Ken had written to me at Christmas, saying his mother had suffered a mild heart attack and wouldn't be coming back for the foreseeable future.*

*That night, I took advantage of a lull in work to call Ken. At first, he sounded surprised to hear from me, then muttered, "I suppose you're using the phones at work."*

*"I've been meaning to ring for ages," I said. "I wanted to know how Auntie Doris was doing." It's much easier to appear solicitous via satellite. I made the appropriate noises while Ken bored on about his mother's health, his wife their three kids and their sheep.*

*After ten minutes, I decided I'd had enough. "The other thing is, Ken, I was worried about the house," I lied. "It's so isolated up there, someone should keep an eye on the place."*

*"You're not wrong," he said. "Her solicitor's supposed to be doing that, but I don't reckon he's been near it."*

*"Do you want me to pop out and check it over? Now I'm back living in Bradfield, it would be no bother."*

*"Would you? That'd be a hell of a load off, I don't mind telling you. Between ourselves, I'm not sure Mum's ever going to be well enough to go back home again, but I'd hate to think of anything happening to the family home," Ken said eagerly.*

*Hate to think of anything happening to his inheritance more like. I knew Ken. Ten days later, I had the keys. On my next day off, I drove out there to check the accuracy of my recollection. The rutted track leading to Start Hill Farm was much more overgrown than the last time. I'd been there, and my four-wheel drive jeep struggled to climb the three miles from the nearest single-track lane. I cut the engine a dozen yards from the grim little cottage and sat listening for five minutes. The biting wind from the high moors rustled the overgrown hedges, occasional birds sang. But there were no human sounds. Not even the distant thrum of traffic.*

*I got out of the jeep and had a look round. One end of the sheep shed had collapsed into a random pile of mill-*

*stone grit, but what pleased me was that there was no sign
of casual human visitations; no picnic remains, no corrod-
ing beer cans, no crumpled newspapers, no cigarette butts,
no used condoms. I walked back to the house and let myself
in.*

*It was little more than a two-up, two-down. Inside, it
was very different from the cosy farmhouse I remembered.
All the personal touches—photographs, ornaments, horse
brasses, antiques—were gone, packed up in crates in storage, a very Yorkshire precaution. In a way, I was relieved;
there was nothing here that could trigger off memories that
would interfere with what I had to do. It was a blank tablet,
with all humiliations, embarrassments and pain erased.
Nothing of my past lurked to surprise me. The person I had
been was absent.*

*I walked through the kitchen towards the pantry. The
shelves were empty. God knows what Doris had done with
her serried ranks of jams, pickles and home-made wines.
Maybe she'd shipped them to New Zealand as a hedge
against being fed alien food. I stood in the doorway, and
stared at the floor. I could feel a foolish grin of relief spread
across my face. My memory hadn't let me down. There was
a trapdoor in the floor. I squatted down and pulled the rusty
iron ring. After a few seconds, the door swung back on
creaking hinges. As I sniffed the air from the cellar, I grew
more convinced that the gods were with me. I had feared
it would be damp, fetid and stale. But instead, it was cool
and fresh, slightly sweet.*

*I lit my camping gas lamp and carefully descended the
flight of stone stairs. The lamp revealed a sizeable room,
about twenty feet by thirty. The floor was flagged with stone
slabs, and a broad stone bench ran the length of one wall.
I held the lamp high and saw the solid beams of the roof.
The lath and plaster ceiling was the only part of the cellar
that showed any signs of disrepair. I could easily fix that
with plasterboard, which would serve the double purpose
of preventing any light escaping through the bare floorboards above. At right angles to the stone bench was a slop*

sink. I remembered the farm was served by its own spring. The tap was stiff, but when I finally managed to turn it, the water ran out pure and clear.

Near the stairs stood a scarred wooden workbench, complete with vices and G-clamps, Henry's tools hanging in neat rows above. I sat on the stone bench and hugged myself. A few hours' work was all that was needed to turn this into a dungeon far superior to anything the games programmers had ever come up with. For a start, I didn't have to think about creating an in-built weakness so my adventurers could escape.

By the end of the week, coming out to the farm in my time off, I had completed the job. Nothing sophisticated; I'd fixed padlock and internal bolts to the trapdoor, I'd repaired the ceiling, and covered the walls in a couple of coats of whitewash. I wanted the place as light as possible to improve the quality of the video. I'd even run a spur off the ring main to provide me with electricity.

I'd thought long and hard before I'd decided how to punish Adam. Finally, I'd fixed on what the French call the chevalet, the Spanish escalero, the Germans the ladder, the Italians veglia and the poetic English "The Duke of Exeter's Daughter." The rack got its euphemistic name from the resourceful John Holland, Duke of Exeter and Earl of Huntingdon. After a successful career as a soldier, the duke became Constable of the Tower of London and somewhere around 1420 he introduced that splendid instrument of persuasion to these shores.

The earliest version consisted of an open rectangular frame raised on legs. The prisoner was laid underneath it, fastened by ropes round his wrists and ankles. At each corner, the ropes were attached to a windlass operated by a warder pulling on levers. This inelegant and labour-intensive device became more sophisticated over the years, ending up more like a table or a horizontal ladder, often incorporating a spiked roller in the middle so that, as the prisoner's body moved, his back was shredded on the spikes. Pulley systems had also been designed which linked *all four ropes together, making it possible for the machine to be used by one person alone.*

*Fortunately, those who have applied punishment through the ages have been thorough in their descriptions and drawing. I also had the photographs in the museum handbook to refer to, and with the assistance of a CAD program, I'd designed my very own rack. For the mechanism, I'd cannibalized an old-fashioned clothes wringer that I picked up in an antique shop. I'd also bought an old mahogany dining table in an auction. I took it straight up to the farm and dismembered it in the kitchen, admiring the craftsmanship that had gone into the solid timber. It took a couple of days to build the rack. All that remained was to test it.*

# 2

*Let the reader then figure to himself the pure frenzy of horror when in this hush of expectation, looking, and indeed, waiting for the unknown arm to strike once more, but not believing that any audacity could be equal to such an attempt as yet, whilst all eyes were watching . . . a second case of the same mysterious nature, a murder on the same exterminating plan, was perpetrated in the very same neighbourhood.*

As soon as Brandon started the engine, the mobile phone mounted on the dashboard trilled. He grabbed the handset and barked, "Brandon." Tony could hear the computerized voice say, "You have messages. Please call 121. You have messages . . ."

Brandon took the phone from his ear, hit the keys and jammed it back again. This time, Tony couldn't hear what was said. After a moment, Brandon dialled another number. "My secretary," he explained briefly. "Sorry about this . . . Hello, Martina? John. You were looking for me?"

A few seconds into the answer, Brandon squeezed his eyes shut, as if in pain. "Where?" he asked, his voice dull. "OK, got it. I'll be there within the half-hour. Who's dealing? . . . Fine, thanks, Martina." Brandon opened his eyes and ended the call. He carefully replaced the handset and twisted in his seat to face Tony. "You wanted to know when you could start? How about now?"

"Another body?" Tony asked.

"Another body," Brandon agreed grimly, turning back and slamming the car into gear. "How do you feel about scenes of crime?"

Tony shrugged. "I'll probably lose my lunch, but it's a

bonus for me if I get to see them in a fairly pristine state."

"There's nothing pristine about the way this sick bastard leaves them," Brandon growled as he shot on to the motorway and made straight for the outside lane. The speedo read ninety-five before he eased back on the accelerator.

"Has he gone back to Temple Fields?" Tony asked.

Taken aback, Brandon shot him a quick look. Tony was staring straight ahead, his dark eyebrows corrugated in a frown. "How did you know?"

That was a question Tony wasn't prepared to answer. "Call it a hunch," he stalled. "I think last time out he was scared that Temple Fields might be getting a bit too hot. Dumping the third body in Carlton Park shifted the focus, maybe stopped the police concentrating on one area, probably relaxed people's vigilance a bit. But he likes Temple Fields. Either because he knows the patch really well, or else it's important to his fantasy. Or maybe it makes some kind of statement for him," Tony mused aloud.

"Do you always come up with half a dozen different hypotheses every time someone tosses you a fact?" Brandon asked, flashing his lights at a BMW that was reluctant to give up possession of the fast lane. "Shift, you bastard, before I get Traffic out to you," he snarled.

"I try," Tony said. "That's how I do the job. Gradually, the evidence makes me eliminate some of my initial thoughts. Eventually, some sort of pattern begins to form." He fell silent, already fantasizing about what he would find at the scene of the crime. His stomach felt hollow, muscles fluttering like a musician before a concert. Normally, all he ever got to see were the second-hand, sanitized versions of crime scenes. No matter how good the photographer and the other forensic officers, it was always someone else's vision he had to translate. This time, he was going to be as close to a killer as he'd ever been. For a man who lived his life behind the shield of learned behaviours, penetrating a killer's façade was the only game in town.

\*    \*    \*

Carol said, "No comment," for the eleventh time. Penny Burgess's mouth tightened and her eyes flicked round the scene, desperate for someone who would be less of a stone wall than Carol. Popeye Cross might be a male chauvinist pig, but in between the patronizing comments he always salted a few memorable quotes. Drawing a blank, she focused on Carol again.

"What happened to sisterhood, Carol?" she complained. "Come on, give us a break. Surely there must be something you can tell me apart from 'No comment'."

"I'm sorry, Ms. Burgess. The last thing your readers need to hear is ill-informed off-the-cuff speculation. As soon as I've got anything concrete to say, I promise you'll be the first to know." Carol softened her words with a smile.

She turned to walk away, but Penny grabbed the sleeve of her mac. "Off the record?" she pleaded. "Just for my guidance? So I don't end up writing something that makes me look a pillock? Carol, I don't have to tell you what it's like. I work in an office full of guys that are running a book on when I'll make my next cock-up."

Carol sighed. It was hard to resist. Only the thought of what Tom Cross would make of it in the squad room kept her mouth closed. "I can't," she said. "Anyway, as far as I'm concerned, you've been doing just fine so far." As she spoke, a familiar Range Rover turned the corner. "Oh shit," she muttered, pulling her arm away from the reporter. All she needed was John Brandon deciding she was the police source behind the *Sentinel Times*'s serial-killer hysteria. Briskly, Carol walked towards Brandon's car as it jerked to a halt, waiting for someone to shift the tapes keeping the crowd at bay. She stopped and waited while the constables rushed to impress the ACC with their efficiency. The Range Rover nosed forward, giving Carol the opportunity to spot the stranger in Brandon's passenger seat. As the two men climbed down, she scanned Tony, committing the details to the memory bank she'd trained herself to develop. You never knew when you'd need to come up with a photofit. Around five-eight, slim, good shoulders, narrow hips, legs and trunk in proportion, short dark hair, side parting, dark eyes, probably blue, shadows under the eyes, fair skin, average nose, wide mouth, lower lip fuller than upper. Shame about the dress sense, though. The suit was even more out of fashion than Brandon's. It didn't look worn, however. Deduction: this was a man who didn't spend his working life in a suit. Equally, he didn't like throwing money away, so the suit was going to be worn till it fell to bits. Second deduction: he probably wasn't married or in a permanent relationship. Any woman whose partner needed a suit occasionally would have pitched him into buying a timelessly classic style that wouldn't look so absurd five years after its purchase.

By the time she'd reached this conclusion, Brandon was by her side, gesturing to his companion to join them. "Carol," he said.

"Mr. Brandon," she acknowledged.

"Tony, I'd like you to meet Detective Inspector Carol Jordan. Carol, this is Dr. Tony Hill from the Home Office."

Tony smiled and held out his hand. Attractive smile, Carol added to her list of particulars as she shook the hand. Good handshake, too. Dry, firm without the macho need to crush the bones that so many senior officers exhibited. "Pleased to meet you," he said.

A surprisingly deep voice, faintly northern. Carol kept her own smile tight. You never knew with the Home Office. "Likewise," she said.

"Carol's heading up one of the murder teams we've got on these killings. Number two, is it, Carol?" Brandon asked, already knowing the answer.

"That's right, sir. Paul Gibbs."

"Tony's in charge of the Home Office National Crime Profiling Task Force feasibility study. I've asked him to take a look at these murders, to see if his experience can give us any pointers." Brandon's eyes bored into Carol's, making sure she realized there were lines to be read between.

"I'd appreciate any help Dr. Hill can give us, sir. From

the brief look I've had at the scene of the crime, I don't think we've got any more to go on than in the previous similar cases." Carol signalled that she understood what Brandon was saying. They were both walking the same tightrope, but from different ends. Brandon could not be seen to undermine Tom Cross's operational authority, and if Carol wanted a tolerable existence in the Bradfield force, she couldn't openly contradict her immediate superior, even if the ACC agreed with her. "Would Dr. Hill like to see the crime scene?"

"We'll all have a look," Brandon said. "You can fill me in as we go. What have we got here?"

Carol led the way. "It's in the back yard of the pub here. The scene of crime is obviously not the scene of death. No blood at all. We have a white male, late twenties, naked. ID unknown. He appears to have been tortured before death. Both shoulders seem to have been dislocated, and possibly his hips and knees. Some tufts of hair are missing from the scalp. He's lying on his front, so we've not had a chance to see the full extent of his injuries. I'd guess the cause of death is a deep wound to the throat. It also looks like the body had been washed before it was dumped." Carol ended her flat recitation at the yard gate. She glanced back at Tony. The only difference her words had made was a tightening of his lips. "Ready?" she asked him.

He nodded and took a deep breath. "As I'll ever be," he said.

"Stay outside the tapes please, Tony," Brandon said. "The SOCOs will still have a lot to do, and they don't need us dumping forensic traces all over their murder scene."

Carol opened the gate and waved the two of them through. If Tony had thought her words had prepared him for the sight inside, one look told him otherwise. It was grotesque, made all the more so by the unnatural absence of blood. Logic screamed that a body so broken should be an island in a lake of gore, like an ice cube in a Bloody Mary. He had never seen a corpse so clean outside a funeral parlour. But instead of being laid out calm as a marble statue, this body was twisted into a loose-limbed parody of the human frame, a disjointed puppet left lying where it fell when the strings were cut.

When the two men entered the yard, the police photographer stopped snapping and gave John Brandon a nod of recognition. "All right, Harry," Brandon said, seemingly undaunted by the sight before him. No one could see the hands clenched into tight fists in the pockets of his waxed jacket.

"I've done all the long- and medium-range stuff, Mr. Brandon. I've just got the close-ups to go," the photographer said. "There's a lot of wounds and bruising; I want to make sure I've got it all."

"Good lad," Brandon said.

From behind them, Carol added, "Harry, when you've done that, can you snap all the cars parked up in the immediate area?"

The photographer raised his eyebrows. "The lot?"

"The lot," Carol confirmed.

"Good thinking, Carol," Brandon chipped in before the scowling photographer could say anything more. "There's always the outside chance that me laddo left the scene on foot or in the victim's car. He might have left his here to collect later. And photographs are that much harder for the defence brief to argue with than a bobby's notebook."

With a sharp snort of breath, the photographer turned back to the corpse. The brief exchange had given Tony time to get a grip on his churning stomach. He took a step closer to the body, trying to glean some primitive understanding of the mind that had reduced a man to this. "What's your game?" he said inside his head. "What does this mean to you? What translations are going on between this broken flesh and your desire? I thought I was the expert in keeping things battened down, but you're something else, aren't you? You are truly special. You're the control freak's control freak. You are going to be one of the ones they write books about. Welcome to the big time."

Recognizing that he was dangerously close to admiration

for a mind so disturbingly complex, Tony forced himself to focus on the realities of what lay before him. The deep slash to the throat had virtually decapitated the man, leaving the head tilted as if hinged at the back of the neck. Tony took a deep breath and said, "The *Sentinel Times* said they all died from having their throats cut. Is that right?"

"Yes," Carol said. "They were all tortured while they were still alive, but it's the throat wounds that have been fatal in each case."

"And have they all been as deep as this?"

Carol shook her head dubiously. "I'm only completely familiar with the second case, and that was nowhere near as violent a gash as this. But I have seen the photographs of the other two, and the last one was nearly this bad."

Thank God for something recognizably textbook, Tony thought. He took a couple of steps back and scanned the area. The body aside, there was nothing to distinguish it from the back yard of any other pub. Crates of empties were stacked against the walls, the lids on the big industrial wheelie bins were firmly closed. Nothing obvious taken away, nothing obvious left behind except for the corpse itself.

Brandon cleared his throat. "Well, everything seems to be under control here, Carol. I'd better go and have a word with the press. I saw Penny Burgess trying to rip the sleeve out of your coat when I got here. No doubt the rest of the pack are baying at her heels by now. I'll see you back at HQ later. Drop by my office. I want to have a chat with you about Dr. Hill's involvement. Tony, I'll leave you in Carol's capable hands. When you're finished here, maybe you can arrange a session with Carol so she can go through the case files."

Tony nodded. "Sounds good. Thanks, John."

"I'll be in touch. And thanks again." With that, Brandon was gone, closing the gate behind him.

"You do profiling, then," Carol said.

"I try," he said cautiously.

"Thank God the powers that be have finally seen sense,"

she said drily. "I was beginning to think they'd never get round to admitting we've got a serial killer on our hands."

"You and me both," Tony said. "I was worried after the first one, but I've been convinced since the second one."

"And I suppose it's not your place to tell them that," Carol said wearily. "Bloody bureaucracy."

"It's a sensitive point. Even when we have a national task force set up, I suspect we're still going to have to wait for the individual police forces to come to us."

Carol's reply was cut off by the banging of the yard gate as it was thrown open. They both swung round. Framed in the doorway was one of the biggest men Tony had ever seen. He had the solid brawn of a prop forward run to seed, his beer gut preceding his massive shoulders by a good half-dozen inches. His eyes protruded like boiled gooseberries from a fleshy face, the source of Detective Superintendent Tom Cross's nickname. His mouth, like that of his cartoon namesake, was an incongruously small cupid's bow. Mousey hair fringed a bald spot like a monk's tonsure. "Sir," Carol greeted the apparition.

Pale eyebrows furled in a discontented scowl. Judging by the deep lines between his brows, it was a familiar expression. "Who the bloody hell are you?" he demanded, waving a stubby finger at Tony. Automatically, Tony noted the bitten nail. Before he could respond, Carol spoke smartly. "Sir, this is Dr. Tony Hill from the Home Office. He's responsible for the National Crime Profiling Task Force feasibility study. Dr. Hill, this is Detective Superintendent Tom Cross. He's in overall charge of our murder enquiries."

The second half of Carol's introduction was drowned out by Cross's booming response. "What the hell are you up to, woman? This is a murder scene. You don't let any old Tom, Dick or Home Office penpusher walk all over it."

Carol closed her eyes fractionally longer than a blink. Then she said in a voice whose cheerful tone astonished Tony, "Sir, Mr. Brandon brought Dr. Hill with him. The ACC thinks Dr. Hill can help us profile our killer."

"What d'you mean, killer? How many times do I have to tell you? We've not got a serial killer loose in Bradfield. We've just got a nasty bunch of copycat queers. You know what the trouble is with you fast-track graduates?" Cross demanded, aggressively leaning towards Carol.

"I'm sure you'll tell me, sir," Carol said sweetly.

Cross stopped momentarily, with the slightly baffled air of a dog who can hear the fly but can't see it. Then he said, "You're all desperate for glory. You want glamour and headlines. You don't want the bother of proper coppering. You can't be arsed grafting on three murder enquiries so you try to knock 'em all into one to minimize the effort and maximize the press coverage. And you," he added, wheeling round towards Tony. "You can remove yourself from my crime scene right now. The last thing we need is bleeding-heart liberals telling us we're looking for some poor sod who wasn't allowed to have a teddy bear when he were a lad. It's not mumbo jumbo that catches villains, it's police work."

Tony smiled. "I couldn't agree more, Superintendent. But your Assistant Chief Constable seems to think that I can help you target your police work more effectively."

Cross was too old a hand to fall for civility. "I run the most effective team in this force," he retorted. "And I don't need some bloody doctor telling me how to catch a bunch of homicidal poofters." He turned back to Carol. "Escort *Doctor* Hill off the premises, Inspector." He managed to make her rank sound like an insult. "And when you've done that, you can come back here and fill me in on what you've managed to find out about our last killer."

"Very good, sir. Oh, by the way, you might like to join the ACC. He's giving an impromptu press conference round the front." This time, the sweetness was tinged with acerbity.

Cross gave a perfunctory glance at the body lying exposed in the yard. "Well, *he*'s not going any place, is he?" he remarked. "Right, Inspector, I'll expect a report just as soon as I've finished with the ACC and the press." He turned on his heel and stormed out as noisily as he'd arrived.

Carol put a hand on Tony's elbow and steered him out of the gate. "This is going to be worth seeing," she muttered in his ear as she ushered him down the alley in Cross's wake.

Half a dozen reporters had joined Penny Burgess behind the yellow plastic tapes. John Brandon faced them. As they grew closer, they could hear the cacophony of questions the press were hurling at the ACC. Carol and Tony hung back as Cross pushed past a constable standing at Brandon's shoulder and shouted, "One at a time, ladies and gentlemen. You'll all get heard."

Brandon half turned towards Cross, his face expressionless. "Thank you, Superintendent Cross."

"Have we got a serial killer loose in Bradfield?" Penny Burgess demanded, her voice cutting through the momentary quiet like the cry of some bird of ill omen.

"There's no reason to suppose . . ." Cross started.

Brandon cut across him icily. "Leave this to me, Tom," he said. "As I said a moment ago, this afternoon we have found the body of a white male in his late twenties or early thirties. It's too soon to be one hundred per cent certain, but there are indications that this killing may be connected to three previous homicides that have taken place in Bradfield over the last nine months."

"Does that mean you're treating these murders as the work of one serial killer?" asked a young man with a tape recorder thrust forward like a cattle prod.

"We are examining the possibility that one perpetrator is responsible for all four crimes, yes."

Cross looked as if he wanted to hit someone. His hands were bunched into fists at his sides, his brows so low they must have cut his vision to a slit. "Though it's only a possibility at this stage," he said mutinously.

Penny chipped in ahead of the opposition again. "How will this affect your approach to the investigation, Mr. Brandon?"

"As of today, we will be amalgamating the three previous murder enquiries with this latest one into a single major incident task force. We will be making full use of the Home Office Large Major Enquiry System computer to analyse the available data, and we are confident that this will enable us to develop new leads," Brandon said, his lugubrious face belying the optimism in his voice.

"Yo, go for it," Carol muttered under her breath.

"Haven't you left it a bit late? Hasn't the murderer had a head start because you wouldn't acknowledge he was a serial killer?" a voice from the rear of the pack shouted angrily.

Brandon squared his shoulders and looked stern. "We're policemen, not clairvoyants. We don't theorize ahead of the evidence. Rest assured, we will be doing everything within our power to bring this killer to justice as swiftly as is humanly possible."

"Will you be using a psychological profiler?" It was Penny Burgess again. Tom Cross shot Tony a look of pure hatred.

Brandon smiled. "That's all for now, ladies and gentlemen. There will be a statement later from the force press office. Now, if you'll excuse us, we've got a lot of work to do." He nodded benevolently towards the press, then he turned away, taking Cross firmly by the elbow. They walked back towards the alley, Cross's back rigid with fury. Carol and Tony followed a few paces behind. As they went, Penny Burgess's voice rang out behind them. "Inspector Jordan? Who's the new boy?"

"God, that woman doesn't miss a trick," Carol muttered.

"I'd better keep out of her way, then," Tony remarked. "Me ending up front-page news could be a serious health hazard."

Carol stopped in her tracks. "You mean the killer could target you?"

Tony grinned. "No. I mean your Chief Constable would have an apoplexy."

The irresistible urge to mirror his smile hit Carol. This

man was unlike any Home Office Jobsworth she'd ever encountered. Not only did he have a sense of humour, he didn't mind being indiscreet. And close up, he definitely fell into the category her friend Lucy described. as "a bit chewy." He was showing signs of being the first interesting man she'd met in the Job for a very long time. "You could be right," was all she said, managing to sound noncommittal enough for her words not to be held against her.

They reached the corner of the alley in time to see Tom Cross round on Brandon. "With respect, sir, you just contradicted everything I've been telling them buggers since this sideshow started."

"It's time for a different approach, Tom," Brandon said coolly.

"So why not discuss it with me instead of making me look a dickhead in front of that mob? Not to mention my own men." Cross leaned forward belligerently. His hand strayed upwards, index finger pointed, as if he were going to stab Brandon in the chest with it. But common sense careerism prevailed, and the hand dropped back by his side.

"You think if I'd had you in my office and suggested a different approach I'd have got one?" There was steel beneath the mildness in Brandon's voice, and Cross recognized it.

His lower jaw jutted. "At the end of the day, operational decisions are down to me," he said. Beneath the belligerence, Tony pictured a small boy, an aggressive bully resenting the adults who still had the power to sort him out.

"But I'm the ACC Crime and the buck stops with me. I make the policy decisions, and I've just made one that happens to impact on your sphere of operations. From now on, this is one single major incident enquiry. Is that clear, Tom? Or do you want to take it further?" For the first time, Carol saw for herself how John Brandon had climbed so far up the greasy pole. The threat in his voice was no empty posturing. He was clearly prepared to do whatever it took to achieve his ends, and he acted with all the assurance of a man used to winning. There was nowhere left for Tom Cross to go.

Cross rounded on Carol. "Have you got nothing better to do, Inspector?"

"I'm waiting to make my report, sir," she said. "You told me to wait for you after the press conference."

"Before you get into that . . . Tom, let me introduce you to Dr. Tony Hill," Brandon said, motioning Tony to come forward.

"We've met," Cross said, sullen as a schoolboy.

"Dr. Hill has agreed to work closely with us in this investigation. He's got more experience in profiling serial offenders than just about anybody else in the country. He's also agreed to keep his involvement under wraps."

Tony gave a self-deprecating, diplomatic smile. "That's right. The last thing I want is to turn your enquiry into a sideshow. If there's any credit going when we nail this bastard, I want it to go to your team. They'll be the ones doing the work, after all."

"You're not wrong there," Cross muttered. "I don't want you under our feet, getting in the road."

"None of us want that, Tom," Brandon said. "That's why I've asked Carol to act as liaison officer between Tony and us."

"I can't afford to lose a senior officer at a time like this," Cross protested.

"You're not losing her," Brandon said. "You're gaining an officer with a unique overview of all the cases. Could prove invaluable, Tom." He glanced at his watch. "I better be off. The Chief's going to want a briefing on this one. Keep me posted, Tom." Brandon sketched a wave and stepped back into the street and out of sight.

Cross pulled a packet of cigarettes out of his pocket and lit up. "You know your trouble, Inspector?" he said. "You're not as smart as you like to think you are. One step out of line, lady, and I'll have your guts for a jock strap." He took a deep drag of his cigarette and leaned forward to blow smoke in Carol's direction. The gesture was ruined by the gust of wind that snatched the smoke away before it reached her. Looking disgusted, Cross turned on his heel and marched back to the scene of the crime.

"You meet a nice class of person in this job," Carol said.

"At least I know now which way the wind blows," Tony replied. As he spoke, he felt a drop of rain on his face.

"Oh shit," Carol said. "That's all we need. Look, can we meet tomorrow? I can grab the files tonight and skim them beforehand. Then you can get stuck in."

"Fine. My office, ten o'clock?"

"Perfect. How do I find you?"

Tony gave Carol directions, then watched as she hurried back down the alley. An interesting woman. And attractive too, most men would agree to that. There were times when he almost wished he could find an uncomplicated response in himself. But he'd long since gone beyond the point where he would allow himself to be attracted to a woman like Carol Jordan.

It was after seven when Carol finally made it back to headquarters. When she rang John Brandon's extension, she was pleasantly surprised to find him still at his desk. "Come on up," he told her.

She was even more surprised when she walked through his secretary's door and found him pouring two steaming mugs from the coffee maker. "Milk and sugar?" he asked her.

"Neither," she said. "This is an unexpected pleasure."

"I gave up smoking five years ago," Brandon confided. "Now it's only the caffeine that holds me together. Come through."

Carol walked into his office, fired with curiosity. She'd never been across the threshold before. The decor was regulation cream paint, the furniture identical to Cross's office, except that here the wood was gleaming, free from scuffs, scratches, cigarette burns and the telltale rings left by hot cups. Unlike most senior officers, Brandon hadn't decorated his walls with police photographs and his framed commendations. Instead, he'd chosen half a dozen reproductions of turn-of-the-century paintings of Bradfield street scenes. Colourful yet moody, often rain-soaked, they mirrored the spectacular view from the seventh-floor window. The only item in the room that ran true to expectation was the photograph of his wife and children on the desk. Even that was no posed, studio shot, but an enlargement of a holiday snap on board a sailboat. Deduction: in spite of the impression Brandon strove to give as a bluff, straightforward, conventional copper, he was actually far more complex and thoughtful under the surface.

He waved Carol to a pair of chairs in front of his desk, then sat down in the other one. "One thing I want to be clear about," Brandon said without preliminary. "You report to Superintendent Cross. He's in charge of this operation. However, I want to see copies of your reports and Dr. Hill's, and I want to know any theories the pair of you come up with that you're not ready to commit to paper. Think you can handle that balancing act?"

Carol's eyebrows rose. "There's only one way to find out, sir," she said.

Brandon's lips twitched in a half smile. He'd always preferred honesty to bullshit. "OK. I want you to make sure you are given access to everybody's files. Any problems with that, any sense that anyone's trying to stall you and Dr. Hill, and I want to know about it, no matter who's responsible. I'll talk to the squad myself in the morning, make sure nobody's in any doubt about what the new rules of the game are. Anything you need from me?"

Another twelve hours in the day would be a start, Carol thought wearily. Loving a challenge was all very well. But this time, it looked like love was going to be an uphill struggle.

Tony closed his front door behind him. He dropped his briefcase where he stood and leaned against the wall. He'd got what he wanted. It was a battle of wits now, his insight against the killer's stockade. Somewhere in the pattern of these crimes there lay a labyrinthine path straight to a murderer's heart. Somehow, Tony had to tread that path, wary of misleading shadows, careful to avoid straying into treacherous undergrowth.

He shrugged away from the wall, feeling suddenly exhausted, and headed for the kitchen, pulling off his tie and unbuttoning his shirt on the way. A cold beer, and then he could go through his scanty collection of press clippings on the three previous murders. He had just opened the fridge to grab a can of Boddingtons when the phone rang. He slammed the door shut and snatched up the extension, juggling with the cold can. "Hello?" he said.

"Anthony," the voice said.

Tony swallowed hard. "This isn't a good time," he said, cutting coldly across the husky contralto coming down the line. He dumped the can on the worktop and popped the ring pull with one hand.

"Playing hard to get? Oh, well, that's part of the fun, isn't it? I thought I'd cured you of trying to avoid me. I thought we'd left all that behind us. Don't say you're going to regress and hang up on me again, that's all I ask." The voice was teasing, laughter bubbling just beneath the surface.

"I'm not playing hard to get," he said. "It really isn't a good time." He could feel the slow burn of anger rising from the pit of his stomach.

"That's up to you. You're the man. You're the boss. Unless, of course, you want things different for a change. If you catch my drift." The voice was almost a sigh, teasing him with its elusive quality. "After all, this is strictly between you and me. Consenting adults, as they say."

"So don't I have the right to say no, not right now? Or is it only women who have that right?" he said, hearing the tension in his voice as the anger rose like bile in his throat.

"God, Anthony, your voice gets so sexy when you're angry," the voice purred.

Nonplussed, Tony held the phone away from his ear, staring at it as if it were an artefact from another planet. Sometimes he wondered if what came out of his mouth were the same words that arrived in his listeners' ears. With a clinical detachment he couldn't bring to his caller, he noted that his grip on the phone was so tight his fingers were white. After a moment, he put the receiver back to his ear. "Just listening to your voice makes me wet, Anthony," she was saying. "Don't you want to know what I'm wearing, what I'm doing right now?" The voice was seductive, the breathing more audible than it had been at first.

"Look, I've had a hard day, I've got a load of work to do and much as I enjoy our little games, I'm not in the mood tonight." Agitated, Tony looked desperately round his kitchen as if searching for the nearest exit.

"You sound so tense, my darling. Let me soothe all that pressure away. Let's play. Think of me as a relaxation technique. You know you'll work better afterwards. You know I give you the best time you've ever had. With a stud like you and a sex queen like me, there's nothing we can't do. And for starters, I'm going to give you the dirtiest, sexiest, horniest phone call we've ever shared."

Suddenly, his anger found a weakness in the dam and burst free. "Not tonight!" Tony yelled, slamming the phone down so hard the can of beer jumped. Creamy froth swelled up through the triangular hole in the top. Tony stared at it in disgust. He picked up the can and threw it in the sink. The can clattered against the stainless steel, then rolled from side to side. Beer and foam spurted out in brown and cream gouts as Tony dropped into a crouch, head down, hands over his face. Tonight, faced with staring into the depths of someone else's nightmares, he absolutely did not want the inevitable confrontation with his own deficiencies that the phone calls always brought in their wake. The phone rang again, but he remained motionless, eyes squeezed shut. When the answering machine picked up, the caller disconnected the line. "Bitch," he said viciously. "Bitch."

*When my neighbours go out to work in the morning, they leave their German shepherd loose in the back yard. All day long, he lopes restlessly up and down the yard, quartering the poured concrete with the diligence of a prison officer who really loves the work. He's heavy-set, black and brindle, with a shaggy coat. Whenever anyone enters the yards on either side of his, he barks, a long, deep-throated cacophony that lasts far longer than any intrusion. When the bin men come down the back alley to trundle our wheelie bins to their truck, the dog becomes hysterical, standing on his hind legs, forepaws scrabbling uselessly against the heavy wooden gate. I've watched him from the vantage point of my back-bedroom window. He's nearly as tall as the gate itself. Perfect, really.*

*Next Monday morning, I bought a couple of pounds of steak and cut it into one-inch cubes, like all the best recipes say. Then I made a small incision in each cube and inserted one of the tranquillizers my doctor insists on prescribing for me. I never wanted them, and certainly never use them, but I'd had the feeling they might come in useful one day.*

*I came out of my back door and listened cheerfully to the dog's salvo of barks. I could afford to be cheerful; it would be the last time I'd have to endure it. I plunged my hand into the bowl of moist meat, enjoying its cool, slippery*

*feel. Then I tossed it over the wall in handfuls. I returned
indoors, washed up and went upstairs to my vantage point
by the computer. I chose the atmospheric world of Dark-
seed, calming my excitement with the gothic and macabre
underworld I had come to know so well. In spite of my
absorption in the game, though, I couldn't help glancing
out of the window every few minutes. After a while, he
slumped to the ground, tongue lolling out of his mouth. I
exited from my game and picked up my binoculars. He
seemed to be breathing, but wasn't moving.*

*I ran downstairs, picking up the holdall I'd prepared
earlier, and got into the jeep. I reversed it down the alley
till the tailgate was level with next-door's yard gate. I
turned off the engine. Silence. I couldn't resist a certain
smug satisfaction as I picked up my crowbar and jumped
down. It took moments to force next-door's gate. As it
swung open, I could see the dog hadn't stirred. I opened
the holdall and crouched down beside him. I shoved his
tongue back into his mouth and taped his muzzle shut with
a roll of surgical tape. I bound his legs together, front and
back, and dragged him to the jeep. He was heavy, but I
keep myself in shape, and it wasn't too hard to manhandle
him into the back.*

*His breath was coming in soft snores when we got to the
farmhouse, but there was no flicker of consciousness, even
when I thumbed back his eyelids. I tipped him into the
wheelbarrow I'd left out there, wheeled him through the
cottage and emptied him down the flight of steps. I switched
on the lights and hauled the dog on to the rack like a sack
of potatoes, then turned to study my knives. I'd fitted a
magnetic strip to the wall, and there they hung suspended,
each sharpened to a professional edge; cleaver, filleting
knife, carving knife, paring knife and craft knife. I chose
the craft knife, cut away the tape from the dog's legs and
spread him out on his stomach. I fastened the strap round
his middle to hold him tightly against the rack. That's when
I realized I had a problem.*

*Sometime in the past few minutes, the dog had stopped*

breathing. I thrust my head against the rough hairs of his chest, searching for a heartbeat, but it was too late. I'd obviously miscalculated the drug dosage, and given him too much. I was furious, I have to admit. The dog's death wouldn't affect the practicalities of scientifically testing my apparatus, but I had been looking forward to his suffering; a small revenge for the dozens of times his demented barking had woken me up, especially when I'd come off a hard night shift. But he'd died without a moment's suffering. The last thing he'd known was a couple of pounds of steak. It didn't please me that he'd died happy.

That wasn't all; I soon discovered a second problem. The straps I'd fitted were fine for human ankles and wrists. But the dog didn't have hands or feet to stop his limbs slipping free.

I didn't puzzle for long. It was a far from elegant solution, but it served my purpose. I still had some six-inch nails left over from the repairs and modifications I'd made to the cellar. I carefully placed his left front paw so it straddled a gap in the timbers. I felt for the space between the bones and, with one blow of my club hammer, I drove the nail through at right angles to the paw, just above the last joint. I fixed the strap below the nail, and tugged at it. I reckoned it would hold for long enough.

I'd fixed the other legs within five minutes. Once he was securely strapped down, I was finally able to get started on the business of the day. Even with the bare prospect of a purely scientific experiment, I could feel the excitement rising in me till it was like a hard lump in my throat. Almost, it seemed, without conscious thought, my hand strayed to the handle of the rack. I watched it, detached, as if it were the hand of a stranger. It caressed the cogs, ran lightly over the wheel, and finally came to rest on the handle. The aroma of lubricating oil still hung lightly on the air, melding with the faint smell of paint and the stale, doggy smell of my assistant in the experiment. I took a deep breath, shivered in anticipation, and slowly began to turn the handle.

# 3

*I do not stick to assert, that any man who deals in murder must have very incorrect ways of thinking, and truly inaccurate principles.*

Don Merrick unzipped his flies. With a sigh of relief, he relaxed his muscles and let his bursting bladder empty. Behind him, the cubicle door opened. His pleasure was abruptly shattered when a heavy hand descended on his shoulder. "Sergeant Merrick. Just the man I wanted to see," Tom Cross boomed. Inexplicably, Merrick discovered he couldn't finish what he'd started.

" 'Morning, sir," he said cautiously, shaking himself and quickly tucking his manhood out of Cross's sight.

"Told you about her new assignment, has she, your guv'nor?" Cross asked, all lads-together bonhomie.

"She mentioned it, yes, sir." Merrick looked longingly at the door. But there was no escape. Not with Cross's hand still clamped on his shoulder.

"I hear you're planning on taking your inspector's exams," Cross remarked.

Merrick's stomach clenched. "That's right, sir."

"So you'll be needing all the friends in high places you can find, eh, lad?"

Merrick forced his lips apart in what he hoped was a smile to match Cross's. "If you say so, sir."

"You've got the makings of a good officer, Merrick. As long as you remember where your loyalties lie. I know Inspector Jordan's going to be a very busy lady over the next few weeks. She might not always have time to keep me fully *abreast* of things." Cross leered suggestively. "I'll be relying on you to keep me informed of all developments. You understand, lad?"

Merrick nodded. "Aye, sir."

Cross dropped his hand and made for the door. Opening it, he turned back to Merrick and said, "Especially if she starts shagging our doctor friend."

The door sighed shut behind Cross. "Fuck and bollocks," Merrick said softly to himself as he moved to the washbasin and started scrubbing his hands vigorously under the hot tap.

Tony had been at his desk since eight. So far, all he'd done was make some photocopies of the Crime Analysis Report form he'd devised for the projected task force. Heavily based on the FBI's Violent Criminal Apprehension Program questionnaire, it aimed to produce a standard classification of every aspect of the crime, from the victim through to the forensic evidence. He shuffled the forms absently, then rearranged his newspaper cuttings into a neat pile. He justified his lack of activity by telling himself that until Carol arrived with the police files, there was little he could do. But that was merely an excuse.

The truth was, there was good reason why concentration was eluding him. She was in his head again. The mystery woman. At the start, he'd felt vulnerable, unwilling to take part in her games. Just like his patients, he thought ironically. How many times had he uttered the maxim that everybody was reluctant to cooperate with therapy at some level? He'd lost count of the number of times he'd slammed the phone down in the early days. But she had persisted, patiently continuing to administer her soothing persuasions till he had started to relax, even to join in.

She had completely thrown him off balance. She had seemed from the first to have an instinct for his Achilles heel, yet she never attacked it. She was everything anyone could desire in a fantasy lover, from gentle to raunchy. The key question for Tony was whether he was pathetic because he managed to relate to pornographic phone calls from a stranger, or whether he should congratulate himself on being so well adjusted that he understood what he needed and what worked for him. But he could not escape the fear that, if not yet dependent on the phone calls, he was at risk of succumbing to that danger. Already incapable of sustaining a normal sexual relationship, was he colluding in the worsening of his condition, or was he moving towards recovery? The only way to test which was correct was to attempt the shift from fantasy to reality. But he was still too wary of fresh humiliation for that. For now, it seemed he'd have to settle for the mysterious stranger who managed to make him feel like a man for long enough to drive the demons underground.

Tony sighed and picked up his mug. The coffee was cold, but he drank it anyway. In spite of himself, he began replaying past conversations in his mind. As if he hadn't run through it enough during the early hours of the morning when sleep had been as elusive as the Bradfield serial killer. The woman's voice buzzed in his ears, inescapable as someone else's Walkman in a train carriage. He tried to close off his emotions and treat the calls with the intellectual objectivity he brought to his work. All he had to do was shut himself off, the way he did when he was examining the perverse fantasies of his patients. He'd certainly had enough experience of refusing to recognize echoes in himself.

Stop the voice. Analyse. Who was she? What drove her? Maybe, like him, she simply enjoyed digging around in messy heads. That at least would explain how she'd wormed her way through his barricades. She was certainly a different animal from the women who worked for the sleazy telephone sex chatlines. Before he'd started this study for the Home Office, he'd been engaged in a piece of research into those chatlines. A significant number of the recently convicted offenders he had dealt with had admitted they were regular callers to the premium-rate phone lines where they could pour their sexual fantasies, however bizarre, obscene or perverse, into the ears of dismally paid women who were encouraged by their bosses to indulge the callers for as long as they were prepared to pay. He'd actually phoned some of the lines himself, just to sample what was on offer, and to discover, using the transcripts of some of his interviews, just how far it was possible to go before disgust overcame the profit motive or the desperate need to earn a living.

Finally, he'd interviewed a selection of the women who worked the phones. The one thing they all held in common was a sense of being violated and degraded, however some of them dressed it up in the contempt they voiced for their clients. He'd come to several conclusions, but the paper he'd subsequently written hadn't included all of them. Some he'd left out because they were too off the wall, others because he feared they might reveal too much about his own psyche. That included his conviction that the response of a man who had previously called a chatline to a dirty phone call from a member of the opposite sex would be radically different to that of a woman in the same situation. Instead of slamming down the receiver, or reporting it to Telecom, most of these men would be either amused or aroused. Either way, they'd want to hear more.

All he had to work out now was why, unlike the chatline workers, this woman found telephone sex with a stranger so appealing. What he needed was to satisfy the intellectual curiosity that was at least as strong as his urge to explore the sexual playground she had opened up for him. Maybe he should consider suggesting a meeting. Before he could go any further, the phone rang. Tony started, his hand stopping halfway in its automatic journey to the receiver. "Oh, for God's sake," he muttered impatiently, shaking his head like a high-diver surfacing. He picked up the phone and said, "Tony Hill."

"Dr. Hill, it's Carol Jordan here."

Tony said nothing, relieved that his thoughts had failed to conjure up the mystery woman.

"Inspector Jordan? Bradfield Police?" Carol continued into the silence.

"Hello, yes, sorry, I was just trying to . . . clear a space on my desk," Tony stumbled, his left leg starting to jitter like a cup of tea on a train.

"I'm really sorry about this, but I'm not going to be able to make it for ten. Mr. Brandon's called all the squad together for a briefing, and I don't think it would be politic to miss it."

"No, I can see that," Tony said, his free hand picking up a pen and unconsciously doodling a daffodil. "It's going to be hard enough for you to act as go-between without making it look like you're not part of the team. Don't worry about it."

"Thanks. Look, I don't think this briefing is going to last that long. I'll be with you as soon as I can. Probably around eleven, if that doesn't interfere with your schedule."

"That's fine," he said, relieved he wouldn't have too long to brood before they could get down to work. "I've no meetings in the diary for today, so take your time. You're not putting me out."

"OK. See you then."

Carol replaced the phone. So far, so good. At least Tony Hill didn't seem a prisoner of his professional ego, unlike several of the experts she'd had dealings with. And, unlike most men, he'd perceived her potential difficulty, sympathized without patronizing her, and had happily gone along with a course of action that would minimize her problems. Impatiently, she pushed away the memory of the attraction she'd felt for him. These days, she had neither the time nor the inclination for emotional involvement. Sharing a flat with her brother and finding the time to sustain a few close friendships took as much of her energy as she could spare. Besides, the ending of her last relationship had dealt her self-esteem too serious a blow for her to enter on another one lightly.

The affair with a casualty surgeon in London hadn't survived her move from the Met to Bradfield three years before. As far as Rob was concerned, it was Carol's decision
to move to the frozen north. So travelling up and down
motorways to spend time together was down to her. He had
no intention of wasting any of his valuable off-duty time
putting unnecessary mileage on his BMW just to go to a
city whose only redeeming feature was Carol. Besides,
nurses were a lot less stroppy and critical, and they understood long hours and shift work just as well as a copper, if
not better. His brutal self-interest had shaken Carol, who
felt cheated of the emotion and energy she'd invested in
loving Rob. Tony Hill might be attractive, charming, and,
if his reputation was correct, intelligent and intuitive, but
Carol wasn't about to risk her heart again. Especially not
with a professional colleague. If she was finding it hard to
get him out of her mind, it was because she was fascinated
by what she could learn from him about the case, not because she fancied him.

Carol ran a hand through her hair and yawned. She'd
been home for precisely fifty-seven minutes in the previous
twenty-four hours. Twenty of those had been spent in the
shower in a futile attempt to inoculate herself against the
effects of no sleep. She'd spent a large chunk of the evening
out on the knocker with her CID team, pursuing fruitless
enquiries among the nervous inhabitants, workers and regular customers of Temple Fields and its gay businesses. The
men's reactions had ranged from total noncooperation to
abuse. Carol felt no surprise. The area was seething with a
mass of contradictory feelings.

On the one hand, the gay businesses didn't want the area
swarming with police because it was bad for cash flow. On
the other hand, the gay activists were angrily demanding
proper protection now the police had belatedly decided that
there was a gay serial killer on the loose. One group of
customers were horrified to be questioned, since their gay
life was a deep secret from wives, friends, colleagues and
parents. Another group were happily playing macho men,

boasting that they'd never get into a situation where they were slaughtered by some glassy-eyed maniac. Yet another group were eager for details, obscurely and, in Carol's eyes, obscenely excited by what could happen when one man went out of control. And there was a handful of hardline lesbian separatists who made no secret of their glee that this time, men were the targets. "Maybe now they'll understand why we were so outraged during the Yorkshire Ripper hunt when men suggested single women should have a curfew," one had sneered at Carol.

Exhausted by the turmoil, Carol had driven back to headquarters to begin her trawl of the files of the existing enquiries. The murder room was strangely quiet, since most of the detectives were out in Temple Fields, pursuing different lines of enquiry or taking advantage of a few hours off to catch up on their drinking, their sex lives or their sleep. She'd already had a quick word with her opposite numbers on the other two murder investigations, and they had reluctantly agreed to give her access to their files provided she had the material back on their desks first thing in the morning. It was exactly the response she'd expected; superficially cooperative, but, in real terms, calculated to cause her even more problems.

When she'd walked through her office door, she'd been appalled by the sheer volume of paper. Stacks of interview statements, forensic and pathology reports, files of photographs virtually buried her office. Why, in God's name, hadn't Tom Cross decided to use the HOLMES computer system for the earlier murders? At least then all the material would be accessible in the computer, indexed and cross-referenced. All she'd have had to do then was to persuade one of the HOLMES indexers to print out the relevant stuff for Tony. With a groan, she closed her door on the mess and walked through the empty corridors to the uniform sergeant's office. The time had come to test the ACC's instruction to all ranks to cooperate with her. Without another pair of hands, she'd never get through the night's work.

Even with the grudgingly granted help of a PC, it had

been a struggle to get through the material. Carol had skimmed the investigation reports, extracting everything that seemed to hold the possibility of significance and passing it on to the constable for copying. Even so, there was a daunting pile of material for Tony and her to work through. When her assistant knocked off at six, Carol wearily loaded the photocopies into a couple of cardboard cartons and staggered down to her car with them. She helped herself to full sets of photographs of all the victims and scenes of crime, filling in a form to requisition fresh copies for the investigating teams to replace the ones she'd taken.

Only then had she headed home. Even there, she had no respite. Nelson waited behind the door, miaowing crossly as he wove his sinuous body round her ankles, forcing her to head straight for the kitchen and the tin opener. When she dumped the bowl of food in front of him, he stared suspiciously at it, frowning. Then hunger overcame his desire to punish her and he wolfed down the whole bowl without pause. "Nice to see you missed me," Carol said drily as she made for the shower. By the time she emerged, Nelson had clearly decided to forgive her. He followed her around, purring like a dialling tone, sitting down on every garment she selected from the wardrobe and placed on the bed.

"You really are the pits," Carol grumbled, pulling her black jeans out from under him. Nelson carried on adoring her, his purr not disrupted in the slightest. She pulled on the jeans, admiring the cut in her wardrobe mirror. They were Katharine Hammett, but she'd only paid £20 for them in a seconds shop in Kensington Church Street, where she went on a twice-annual trawl for the designer clothes she loved but couldn't afford, even on an inspector's wages. The cream linen shirt was French Connection, the ribbed grey cardigan from a chain store men's department. Carol picked a few black cat hairs from the cardigan and caught Nelson's reproachful stare. "You know I love you. I just don't need to wear you," she said.

"You'd get a shock if he answered you," a man's voice said from the doorway.

Carol turned to face her brother, who leaned against the doorjamb in his boxer shorts, blond hair tousled, eyes bleary with sleep. His face had a strange congruence with Carol's, as if someone had scanned her photograph into a computer and subtly altered the features away from the feminine and towards the masculine. "I didn't wake you, did I?" she asked anxiously.

"Nope. I've got to go to London today. The money man cometh." He yawned.

"The Americans?" Carol asked, crouching down and scratching the cat behind the ears. Nelson promptly rolled over on to his back, displaying his full stomach to be stroked.

"Correct. They want a full demo of what we've done so far. I've been telling Carl that nothing looks very impressive right now, but he says they want some reassurance that they're not just pouring their development money into a black hole."

"The joys of software development," Carol said, rumpling Nelson's fur.

"Leading-edge software development, please," Michael said, self-mockingly. "How about you? What's happening down the murder factory? I heard on the news last night that you'd copped for another one."

"Looks like it. At least the powers that be have finally admitted that we've got a serial killer on the loose. And they've brought in a psychological profiler to work with us."

Michael whistled. "Fuck me, Bradfield police enter the twentieth century. How's Popeye taking it?"

Carol pulled a face. "He likes it about as much as a poke in the eye with a sharp stick. He thinks it's a total waste of bloody time," Carol said, dropping her voice and affecting Tom Cross's Bradfield accent. "Then when I was appointed liaison officer with the profiler, he perked up."

Michael nodded, a cynical expression on his face. "Two birds with one stone."

Carol grinned. "Yeah, well, it'll need to be over my dead body." She stood up. Nelson gave a small miaow of protest. Carol sighed and headed for the door. "Back to work, Nelson. Thanks for taking my mind off the bodies," she said.

Michael swung out of the doorway to let her pass and gave her a hug. "Take no prisoners, sis," he said.

Carol snorted. "I don't think you've quite grasped the principle of policing, bro."

By the time she was behind the wheel, the cat and Michael were forgotten. She was back with the killer.

Now, a couple of hours and a stack of overnight murder team reports later, home seemed a memory as distant as her summer holiday in Ithaca. Carol forced herself out of her chair, picked up the paperwork and walked into the main CID office.

It was standing room only by the time she arrived, detectives normally based in other stations jockeying for position in the crowd. A couple of her detective constables shifted to make room for her, one offering his chair. "Fucking brown nose," a voice said audibly from the other side of the room. Carol couldn't see who had spoken, but recognized it wasn't one of her own team. She smiled and shook her head at her junior officer, choosing instead to perch on the edge of his desk beside Don Merrick, who nodded a morose greeting. The clock read nine-twenty-nine. The room smelled of cheap cigars, coffee and damp coats.

One of the other inspectors caught Carol's eye and started to move towards her. But before they could speak, the door opened and Tom Cross barrelled in, followed by John Brandon. The superintendent looked disturbingly benign as he marched in. The troops parted automatically before him, leaving a clear path for him and Brandon to walk to the whiteboard at the far end of the room.

" 'Morning, lads," Cross said genially. "And lasses," he added as an obvious afterthought. "There's nobody here that doesn't know we've got four unsolved murders on our hands. We've got IDs for the first three bodies—Adam Scott, Paul Gibbs and Gareth Finnegan. So far, we've not made any progress on the fourth victim. The lads down the path lab are working on him now, trying to come up with a face that won't frighten the horses when we release the picture to the press." ·

Cross took a deep breath. If anything, his expression became even more benevolent. "As you all know, I'm not a man given to theorizing ahead of the evidence. And I've been reluctant officially to connect these killings because of the media hysteria that would bring down about us. Judging by this morning's papers, I was right about that." He pointed to several of the newspapers the detectives held.

"However, in the light of this latest killing, we're going to have to revise our strategy. As of yesterday afternoon, I have amalgamated the four murder enquiries into one major investigation."

There was a murmur of support. Don Merrick leaned forward and murmured in Carol's ear, "Changes his tune more often than a juke box."

She nodded. "I wish he changed his socks as often."

Cross glared in their direction. He couldn't have heard the remarks, but seeing Carol's lips move was enough of an excuse. "Settle down," he said sternly. "I'm not finished yet. Now, it doesn't take much in the way of detective abilities to see that this place is too small for us *and* the normal activities of the station, so as soon as we're finished here this morning, we'll be moving this operation to the former station in Scargill Street, which some of you will remember was mothballed six months ago. Overnight, there's been a team of maintenance workers, computer whizz kids and British Telecom engineers getting it back to temporary operational status."

A groan went up. No one had shed a tear when the old Victorian building in Scargill Street had been closed down. Draughty, inconvenient, short of parking spaces, ladies' toilets—everything except cells—the building had been earmarked for demolition and redevelopment. Typically, there hadn't been enough money in the budget to push ahead with the project. "I know, I know," Cross said, cutting across their complaints. "But we'll all be under one roof, so I'll be able to keep an eye on you. I will be in overall charge of the enquiry. You'll have two inspectors to report to—Bob Stansfield and Kevin Matthews. They'll be sorting out your assignments in a minute. Inspector Jordan will be otherwise engaged on an initiative of Mr. Brandon's." Cross paused. "Which I'm sure you'll all want to cooperate with."

Carol kept her head high and looked around. The faces she could see mostly showed open cynicism. Several heads turned towards her. There was no warmth in their stares. Even those who might support the profiling initiative were brassed off that the prime job had gone to a woman rather than one of the lads.

"So Bob will take over Inspector Jordan's operational responsibilities for Paul Gibbs and Adam Scott, and Kevin will handle yesterday's body as well as Gareth Finnegan. The HOLMES team have been called in, and they'll be starting to input their data just as soon as the boffins have got the wires in place. Inspector Dave Woolcott, who some of you will remember from when he was a sergeant here, will be the enquiry manager in charge of the HOLMES team. Over to you, Mr. Brandon." Cross stepped back and waved the ACC forward. His gesture was only just on the right side of the border between insolence and politeness.

Brandon took a moment to look around the room. He'd never had to make a more important pitch. Most of the detectives in the room were jaded and frustrated. Many of them had been working on one of the previous murders for months now, with precious little to show for it. Tom Cross's powers of motivation were legendary, but even he was facing an uphill struggle, not least because of his pig-headed refusal to admit before now that the crimes were connected. It was time to beat Tom Cross at his own game. Bluntness had never been Brandon's strong suit, but he'd been practising all morning. In the shower, in front of the shaving mirror, in his head while he ate his egg on toast, in the car on the way to the station. Brandon thrust one hand in his trouser pocket and crossed his fingers.

"This is probably the toughest task of any of our careers. As far as we're aware, this guy is only operating in Brad-field. In a way, I'm glad about that, because I've never seen a better bunch of detectives than we've got here. If anyone can nail this bastard, it's you lot. You've got a hundred and ten per cent support from your senior officers, and all the resources you need are going to be made available, whether the politicians like it or not." Brandon's note of belligerence won a murmur of agreement from the room.

"We're going to be blazing a trail here in more ways than one. You all know about the Home Office plans for a national task force for profiling repeat offenders. Well, we're going to be the guinea pigs. Dr. Tony Hill, the man who's going to be telling the Home Office what to think, has agreed to work with us. Now, I know there are some amongst you who think that profiling is a load of crap. But like it or not, it's part of our future. If we cooperate and work with this guy, we're a lot more likely to see this task force end up something like we want it to be. If we piss him off, we're liable to be lumbered with a bloody great millstone round our neck. Is that clear to everyone here?"

Brandon looked sternly round the room, not missing out Tom Cross. The nods varied from enthusiastic to barely perceptible. "I'm glad we all understand one another. Dr. Hill's job is to assess the evidence we provide him with and to come up with a profile of the killer to help us focus our enquiries. I've appointed Inspector Carol Jordan as the liaison officer between the murder squad and Dr. Hill. Inspector Jordan, can you just stand up a minute?"

Startled, Carol scrambled to her feet, dropping her files on the way. Don Merrick immediately got down on his knees and grabbed the spilling papers. "For those of you from other divisions who don't know Inspector Jordan, there she is." Nice one, Brandon, thought Carol. As if there were squads of female detectives to choose from.

"Inspector Jordan is to have access to each and every piece of paper on this enquiry. I want her kept fully informed of any developments. Anyone who is pursuing a promising lead should discuss it with her as well as with their own inspector, or Superintendent Cross. And any requests from Inspector Jordan must be treated as urgent enquiries. If I hear that anybody's being a smartarse, trying to freeze Inspector Jordan or Dr. Hill out of the investigation, I won't be taking prisoners. The same goes for anybody who leaks anything about this aspect of the investigation to the media. So think on. Unless you've got a burning ambition to climb back into uniform and walk the streets of Bradfield in the rain for the rest of your career, you'll do everything in your power to help her. This isn't a competition. We're all on the same side. Dr. Hill isn't here to catch the killer. That's your—'

Brandon stopped in mid-sentence. No one had noticed the door opening, but the words of the communications room sergeant captured everyone's attention faster than a gunshot. "Sorry to interrupt, sir," he said, his voice tight with suppressed emotion. "We've got an ID on yesterday's victim. Sir, he's one of ours."

*It was an American journalist who said, "I have seen the future and it works." I know just what he meant. After the dog, I knew Adam wouldn't be any problem.*

*I spent the rest of the week in a state of nervous tension. I was even tempted to try one of the tranquillizers myself, but I resisted. This wasn't the time to give in to weakness. Besides, I couldn't afford to be anything less than completely in control of myself. My years of self-discipline paid off; I doubt if any of my colleagues noticed anything unusual in my behaviour at work, except that I couldn't bring myself to do the weekend overtime I usually volunteer for.*

*By Monday morning, I was at a peak of readiness. I was primed and polished, the perfect killer-in-waiting. Even the weather was on my side. It was a crisp, clear autumnal morning, the kind of day that brings a smile even to the lips of commuters. Just before eight, I drove past Adam's home, a new terraced three-storey town house with integral garage on the ground floor. His bedroom curtains were closed, the milk bottle still sitting on his doorstep, half a* Daily Mail *protruding from his letter box. I parked a couple of streets away outside a row of shops and retraced my journey. I walked down his street, satisfied that so far I was right on time. His bedroom curtains were drawn back, the milk and newspaper gone. At the end of the street, I crossed to the little park opposite and sat on a bench.*

*I opened my own* Daily Mail *and imagined Adam read-*

*ing the same stories that I was staring at unseeingly. I shifted my position so I could see his front door without craning round the paper, and put my peripheral vision on alert. Right on schedule, the door opened at eight-twenty, and Adam appeared. Casually, I folded up my paper, dumped it in the litter bin by the bench and strolled off down the street in his wake.*

The tram station was less than ten minutes' walk away, and I was right behind him as he strode on to the crowded platform. The tram glided into the station moments later and he moved forward with the flow of passengers. I hung back slightly and let a couple of people come between us; I was taking no chances.

He was craning his head as he entered the carriage. I knew exactly why. When their eyes met, Adam waved and squirmed through the crowd so they could chatter mindlessly all the way into town. I watched him as he leaned forward. I knew every expression on his face, every angle and gesture of his lean, muscular body. His hair; the little curls in the nape of his neck still damp, his skin pink and glowing from his shave, the scent of his Aramis cologne. He laughed aloud at something in their conversation, and I felt the sour taste of bile rise in my mouth. The taste of betrayal. How could he? It should have been me talking to him, making his face light up, bringing that beautiful smile to his warm lips. If my fixity of purpose had ever wavered, the sight of the pair of them enjoying their Monday-morning encounter would have turned my resolve to granite.

As usual, he left the tram in Woolmarket Square. I was less than a dozen yards behind him. He turned back to wave to his soon-to-be bereaved lover. I swiftly turned away, pretending to read the tram timetable. The last thing I wanted right then was for him to notice me, to realize I was dogging his steps. I gave it a few seconds, then took up the pursuit. Left into Bellwether Street. I could see his dark hair bobbing among the shop and office workers crowding the pavements. Adam cut down an alley to his right, and I *emerged in Crown Plaza just in time to see him enter the Inland Revenue building where he worked. Satisfied that this was just another Monday, I carried on through the plaza, past the squat glass and metal office block, and into the newly restored Victorian shopping arcades.*

*I had time to kill. The thought brought a smile to my lips.*

*I went off to do some studying in the Central Library. They had nothing new in, so I settled for an old favourite,* Killing for Company. *Dennis Nilsen's case never ceases both to fascinate and repel me. He murdered fifteen young men without anyone ever missing them. No one had the faintest idea that there was a gay serial killer stalking the homeless and rootless. He befriended them, took them home, gave them drink, but he could only cope with them once they had been perfected in death. Then, and only then, could he hold them, have sex with them, cherish them. Now that is sick. They'd done nothing to deserve their fate; they had committed no betrayal, no act of treachery.*

*The only mistake Nilsen made was in the disposal of the bodies. It's almost as if subconsciously he wanted to be caught. Chopping them up and cooking them was fine, but flushing them down the toilet? It must have been obvious to a man as intelligent as he was that the drains wouldn't be able to handle that volume of solids. I've never understood why he didn't just feed the meat to his dog.*

*However, it's never too late to learn from the mistakes of others. The blunders of killers never cease to amaze me. It doesn't take much intelligence to understand how the police and forensic scientists operate and to take appropriate precautions, especially since the men who earn their living trying to catch the killers have obligingly written detailed textbooks about the precise nature of their work. On the other hand, we only ever hear about the failures. I knew I was never going to appear in those catalogues of incompetence. I had planned too well, every risk minimized and balanced against the benefits it would bring. The only account of my work will be this journal, which will not see printer's ink until my last breath is a distant memory. My only regret is that I won't be around to read the reviews.*

*I was back at my post by four, even though I'd never known Adam leave work before a quarter to five. I sat in the window of Burger King on Woolmarket Square, perfectly placed to watch the mouth of the alley leading to his office. Right on cue, he emerged at 4:47 and headed for the tram stop. I joined the knot of people waiting on the raised platform, smiling quietly to myself as I heard the tram hoot in the distance. Enjoy your tram ride, Adam. It's going to be your last.*

# 4

*The fact was, I "fancied" him, and resolved to commence
business upon his throat.*

When Damien Connolly failed to turn up at the start of his
shift as local information officer in F Division's station on
the south side of the city, the duty sergeant hadn't been
unduly worried. Although PC Connolly was one of the best
collators in the force, and a trained HOLMES officer, he
was a notoriously bad timekeeper. At least twice a week,
he came hurtling through the doors of the station a good
ten minutes after his shift was due to start. But when he
still hadn't shown up half an hour after he was due on duty,
Sergeant Claire Bonner felt a twinge of irritation. Even
Connolly had enough sense to realize that if he was going
to be more than fifteen minutes late, he had to phone in.
Today of all days as well, when headquarters were demanding a full turnout of HOLMES officers on the serial-
killer investigation.

Sighing, Sgt. Bonner checked Connolly's home number
in her files and dialled it. The phone rang and rang, till
finally it was automatically disconnected. She felt a prickle
of concern. Connolly was something of a loner outside the
job. He was quieter and maybe more thoughtful than most
of the officers on Sgt. Bonner's relief, always keeping his
distance when he joined in the social life of the station. As
far as she was aware, there was no girlfriend in whose bed
Connolly might have overslept. His family were all up in
Glasgow, so there were no relatives to try locally. Sgt. Bonner cast her mind back. Yesterday had been a day off for
the relief. When they'd knocked off from the previous night
shift, Connolly had come for breakfast with her and half a

dozen of the other lads. He'd not said anything about having plans for his time off other than catching up on his kip and working on his car, an elderly Austin Healey roadster.

Sgt. Bonner went through to the control room and had a word with her opposite number, asking him to have one of the patrol cars swing round by Connolly's house to check he wasn't ill or injured. "See if they can check the garage, make sure that bloody car of his hasn't come off the jack with him underneath," she added as she went back to her desk.

It was after eight when the control room sergeant appeared in her office. "The lads have checked Connolly's house. No answer to the door. They had a good scout round, and all the curtains were open. Milk on the doorstep. No sign of life as far as they could make out. There was only one thing a bit odd that they could see. His car was parked on the street, which isn't like him. I don't have to tell you, he treats that motor like the crown jewels."

Sgt. Bonner frowned. "Maybe he's got somebody stopping with him? A relative, or a girlfriend? Maybe he's let them stick their car in the garage?"

The control room sergeant shook his head. "Nope. The lads had a look in the garage window, and it was empty. And don't forget the milk."

Sgt. Bonner shrugged. "Not a lot more we can do, then, is there?"

"Well, he's over twenty-one. I'd have thought he'd have more sense than to go on the missing list, but you know what they say about the quiet ones."

Sgt. Bonner sighed. "I'll have his guts for garters when he shows his face. By the way, I've asked Joey Smith to stand in for him in the collator's office for this shift."

The control room sergeant cast his eyes upwards. "You really know how to make a man's day, don't you? Couldn't you have got one of the others? Smith can barely manage the alphabet."

Before Sgt. Bonner could argue the toss, there was a

knock at the door. "Yeah?" she called. "Come in."

A PC from the control room entered hesitantly. She looked faintly sick. "Skip," she said, the worry in her voice obvious from the single word. "I think you'd better have a look at this." She held out a fax, the bottom edge ragged where it had been torn hastily off the roll.

Being nearer, the control room sergeant took the flimsy sheet and glanced at it. He drew in his breath sharply, then closed his eyes for a moment. Wordlessly, he handed the fax to Sgt. Bonner.

At first, all she saw was the stark black and white of the photograph. For a moment, her mind automatically protecting her from horror, she wondered why someone had gone over her head and reported Connolly missing. Then her eyes translated the marks on the paper into words. *"Urgent fax to all stations. This is the unidentified murder victim discovered yesterday afternoon in the back yard of the Queen of Hearts public house, Temple Fields, Bradfield. Photograph to follow later this a.m. Please circulate and display. Any information to DI Kevin Matthews at Scargill Street Incident Room, ext. 2456."*

Sgt. Bonner looked bleakly at the other two officers. "There isn't any doubt about it, is there?"

The PC looked at the floor, her skin pale and clammy. "I don't think so, skip," she said. "That's Connolly. I mean, it's not what you'd call a good likeness, but it's definitely him."

The control room sergeant picked up the fax. "I'll get on to DI Matthews right away," he said.

Sgt. Bonner pushed her chair back and stood up. "I'd better go round to the morgue. They're going to need a formal identification as soon as possible so they can get weaving."

"This makes it a whole new ball game," Tony said, his face sombre.

"It certainly ups the stakes," Carol said.

"The question I'm asking myself is whether or not Handy Andy knew he was giving us a bobby," Tony said softly, swinging round in his chair to stare out of the window at the city rooftops.

"Sorry?"

He gave a twisted smile and said, "No, it's me who should apologize. I always give them a name. It makes it personal." He swung back to face Carol. "Does that bother you?"

Carol shook her head. "It's better than the station nickname."

"Which is?" Tony asked, eyebrows raised.

"The Queer Killer," Carol said, her distaste clear.

"That begs a lot of questions," Tony said noncommittally. "But if it helps them deal with their fear and anger, it's probably no bad thing."

"I don't like it. It doesn't feel personal to me, calling him the Queer Killer."

"What does make it personal to you? The fact that he's taken one of yours now?"

"I felt like that already. As soon as we got the second murder, the one I was handling, I was convinced we were dealing with a serial offender. That was when it got personal for me. I want to nail this bastard. I need to. Professionally, personally, whatever." The cold vehemence in Carol's voice gave Tony confidence. This was a woman who was going to pull out all the stops to make sure he had what he needed to do his job. Her tone of voice and the words she'd chosen were also a calculated challenge, showing him she didn't give a damn what he made of her desire. She was just what he needed. Professionally, at any rate.

"You and me both," Tony said. "And together, we can make it happen. But only together. You know, the first time I got directly involved in profiling, it was a serial arsonist. After half a dozen major fires, I knew how he was doing it, why he was doing it, what was in it for him. I knew exactly the kind of mad bastard he was, yet I couldn't put

a name or a face to him. It drove me crazy with frustration
for a while. Then I realized it wasn't my job to do that.
That's your job. All I can do is to point you in the right
direction."

Carol smiled grimly. "Just point, and I'll be off like a
gun dog," she said. "What did you mean when you said
you wondered whether he knew Damien Connolly was a
bobby?"

Tony ran a hand through his hair, leaving it spiky as a
punk's. "OK. We've got two scenarios here. Handy Andy
may not have known Damien Connolly was a bobby. It may
be nothing more than a coincidence, a particularly unpleasant coincidence for his colleagues, but a coincidence nevertheless. That's not a scenario I'm happy with, however,
because my reading, based on the little I know so far, is
that these aren't random victims snatched by chance. I think
he chooses his victims with care, and plans thoroughly.
Would you agree with that?"

"He doesn't leave things to chance, that's obvious,"
Carol said.

"Right. The alternative is that Handy Andy knows full
well that his fourth victim is a policeman. That in itself
leads to two further possibilities. One: Handy Andy knew
he'd killed a copper, but that fact is supremely irrelevant
to the meaning of the killing for him. In other words, Damien Connolly fulfilled all the other criteria that Andy
needs from his victims, and he would have died at this point
whether he was a bobby or a bus driver.

"The other scenario is the one I like best, though. The
fact that Damien was a copper is a crucial part of the reason
why Handy Andy *chose* him as his fourth victim."

"You mean he's thumbing his nose at us?" Carol asked.

Thank God she was quick. That was going to make the
job so much simpler. She'd done well to get as far up the
ladder as she had, given she had looks as well as brains.
Either attribute without the other would have made promotion easier. "That's certainly a possibility," Tony acknowledged. "But I think it's more likely to be about

vanity. I think he'd started to get pissed off with Detective Superintendent Cross's refusal to acknowledge his existence. In his own eyes, he's very successful at what he does. He's the best. And he deserves recognition. And that desire for recognition has been thwarted by the police's refusal to admit there's only one offender behind these killings. OK, so the *Sentinel Times* has been speculating about a serial killer since the second victim, but that's not the same as being given the official accolade by the police themselves. And I may have unwittingly added fuel to the fire after the third killing."

"You mean, the interview you did with the *Sentinel Times*?"

"Yeah. My suggestion that it was possible there were two killers at work will have made him angry that he wasn't being acknowledged as the master of his craft."

"Dear God," Carol said, torn between revulsion and fascination. "So he went out and stalked a police officer so we'd take him seriously?"

"It's a possibility. Of course, it can't have been just any police officer. Even though making his point to the powers that be is important to Handy Andy, the prime directive is still to go for victims who fulfill his very personal criteria."

Carol frowned. "So what you're saying is that there's something about Connolly that makes him different from most other coppers?"

"Looks like it."

"Maybe it's the sexuality thing," Carol mused. "I mean, there aren't many gays in the force. And those that there are tend to be so deep in the closet you could mistake them for a clothes hanger."

"Whoa," Tony laughed, holding up his hands as if to fend her off. "No theorizing without data. We don't know yet whether Damien was gay. What might be useful, though, is to find out what shifts Damien worked recently. Say, the last two months. That'll give us some idea of the times he was at home, which might help the officers who'll be questioning his neighbours. Also, we should be asking around the other officers on his relief, to check out whether he always left alone, or if he ever gave anyone a lift home. We need to find out everything there is to know about Damien Connolly both as a man and as a bobby."

Carol pulled out her notebook and scribbled a reminder to herself. "Shifts," she muttered.

"There's something else this tells us about Handy Andy," Tony said slowly, reaching for the idea that had just swum into his consciousness.

Carol looked up, her eyes alert. "Go on," she said.

"He's very, very good at what he does," Tony said flatly. "Think about it. A police officer is a trained observer. Even the thickest plod is a lot more alert to what's going on around them than the average member of the public. Now, from what you've told me, Damien Connolly was a bright lad. He was a collator, which means he was even more on the ball than most officers. As I understand it, a collator's job is to act like the station's walking encyclopaedia. It's all very well having all the local information about known villains and MOs on file cards, but if the collator isn't sharp, then the system's worthless, am I right?"

"Spot on. A good collator is worth half a dozen bodies on the ground," Carol said. "And by all accounts, Connolly was one of the best."

Tony leaned back in his chair. "So if Handy Andy stalked Damien without setting any alarm bells ringing, he must be bloody good. Face it, Carol, if somebody was tailing you on a regular basis, you'd pick them up, wouldn't you?"

"I bloody hope so," Carol said drily. "But I'm a woman. Maybe we're just a bit more on our guard than the blokes."

Tony shook his head. "I think a copper as smart as Damien would have noticed anything other than a very professional tail."

"You mean we might be looking for someone who's in the Job?" Carol demanded, her voice rising as she spoke the unthinkable.

"It's a possibility. I can't pitch it more strongly than that till I've seen all the evidence. Is that it?" Tony asked, nodding towards the cardboard box Carol had deposited by the door of his office.

"That's some of it. There's another box and some folders of photographs still in the car. And that's after some serious editing."

Tony pulled a face. "Rather you than me. Shall we go and fetch it, then?"

Carol stood up. "Why don't you get started while I go and get the rest?"

"It's the photographs I want to look at first, so I might as well come and help," he said.

"Thanks," Carol said.

In the lift, they stood on opposite sides, both conscious of the other's physical presence. "That's not a Bradfield accent," Tony remarked as the doors slid shut. If he was going to work successfully with Carol Jordan, he needed to know what made her tick, personally as well as professionally. The more he could find out about her, the better.

"I thought you said you left the detective work to us?"

"We're good at stating the obvious, us psychologists. Isn't that what our critics on the force say?"

"Touché. I'm from Warwick, originally. Then university at Manchester and into the Met on the fast track. And you? I'm not great on accents, but I can spot you're a Northerner, though you don't sound like Bradfield either," Carol replied.

"Born and bred in Halifax. London University, followed by a DPhil at Oxford. Eight years in special hospitals. Eighteen months ago, the Home Office head-hunted me to run this feasibility study." Give a little to get a lot, Tony thought wryly. Who exactly was probing whom?

"So we're both outsiders," Carol said.

"Maybe that's why John Brandon chose you to liaise with me."

The lift doors slid open and they walked through the underground car park to the visitors' parking area where Carol had left her car. Tony hefted the cardboard box out of the boot. "You must be stronger than you look," he gasped.

Carol picked up the folders of photographs and grinned. "And I'm a black belt in Cluedo," she said. "Listen, Tony, if this maniac is in the Job, what sort of stuff would you expect to find?"

"I shouldn't have said that. I was theorizing ahead of data, and I don't want you to place any weight on it, OK? Strike it from the record," Tony panted.

"OK, but what would the signs be?' she persisted.

They were back in the lift before Tony answered her. "Behaviour that exhibits a familiarity with police and forensic procedure," he said. "But in itself, that proves nothing. There are so many true-crime books and TV detectives around these days that anyone could know that sort of stuff. Look, Carol, please put it out of your head. We need to keep an open mind. Otherwise the work we do is valueless."

Carol stifled a sigh. "OK. But will you tell me if you still think that way after you've seen the evidence? Because if it's more than a slim possibility, we might need to rethink the way we're dealing with the enquiry."

"I promise," he said. The lift doors slid open, as if placing their own full stop on the conversation.

Back in the office, Tony slid the first set of photographs out of their folders. "Before you start, could you fill me in on how you want to pursue this?" Carol asked, notebook at the ready.

"I'll go through all the pictures first, then I'll ask you to take me through the investigation so far. When we've done that, I'll work through the paperwork myself. After that, what I usually do is draw up a profile of each of the victims. Then we have another session with these," he said, brandishing his forms. "And then I walk out on the high wire and do a profile of the offender. Does that sound reasonable to you?"

"Sounds fine. How long is all that likely to take?"

Tony frowned. "It's hard to say. A few days, certainly.

However, Handy Andy seems to work on an eight-week cycle, and there's no sign that he's accelerating. That's unusual in itself, by the way. Once I've studied the material I'll have a better idea of how in control he is, but I think we've probably got a bit of time to spare before he kills again. Having said that, he may well have already selected his next victim, so we've got to make sure that we keep any progress we make well away from the press. The last thing we want is to be the catalyst for him speeding up the process."

Carol groaned. "Are you always this optimistic?"

"It goes with the territory. Oh, and one more thing? If you develop any suspects, I'd prefer not to know anything about them at this stage—there's a danger that my subconscious will alter the profile accordingly."

Carol snorted. "We should be so lucky."

"That bad, is it?"

"Oh, we've pulled in anybody who's got form for indecent assault or violent offences against gay men, but none of them looks even a remote possibility."

Tony pulled a sympathetic face then picked up the photographs of Adam Scott's corpse and slowly started going through them. He picked up a pen and moved his A4 pad nearer to him. He glanced up at Carol. "Coffee?" he asked. "I meant to ask earlier, but I was too interested in what we were talking about."

Carol felt like a co-conspirator. She had been enjoying their conversation too, in spite of a twinge of guilt that multiple murders shouldn't be a source of pleasure. Talking with Tony was like talking to an equal who had no axe to grind, whose primary concern was finding a path to the truth rather than a way to boost the ego. It was something she'd missed on this case so far. "Me too," she admitted. "I'm probably approaching the point where coffee is a necessity. Do you want me to go and fetch some?"

"Good God, no!" Tony laughed. "That's not what you're here for. Wait there, I'll be right back. How do you take yours?"

"Black, no sugar. In an intravenous drip, preferably."

Tony took a large Thermos jug out of his filing cabinet and disappeared. He was back inside five minutes with two steaming mugs and the jug. He handed Carol a mug and gestured towards the Thermos. "I filled it up. I figured we might be some time. Help yourself as and when."

Carol took a grateful sip. "Will you marry me?" she asked, mock romantic.

Tony laughed again, to cover the lurch of apprehension that shifted his stomach, a familiar response to even the most idle of flirtations. "You won't be saying that in a few days' time," he said evasively, turning his attention back to the photographs.

"Victim number one. Adam Scott," he said softly, making a note on his pad. He went through the photographs one by one, then went back to the beginning. The first picture showed a city square, tall Georgian houses on one side, a modern office block on a second and a row of shops, bars and restaurants on the third. In the centre of the square was a public garden, crossed by two diagonal paths. In the middle was an ornate Victorian drinking fountain. The park was surrounded by a three feet high brick wall. Along two sides of the garden was deep shrubbery. The ambience was slightly seedy, the stucco of the houses peeling in places. He imagined himself standing on the corner, taking in the view, smelling the fumid city air mixed with the stink of stale alcohol and fast food, hearing the night sounds. The rev of engines, the sound of high heels on pavements, occasional laughs and cries borne on the wind, the twitter of starlings, conned out of sleep by the sodium light of streetlamps. Where did you stand, Andy? Where did you watch your ground from? What did you see? What did you hear? What did you *feel*? Why here?

The second photograph showed a section of the wall and the shrubbery from the street side. The photograph was clear enough for Tony to make out the little iron squares on the top of the wall, which were all that remained of railings that had presumably been removed during the war to make guns and shells. A section of the bushes showed broken branches and crumpled leaves. The third shot showed the body of a man, face down on the earth, his limbs splayed at strange angles. Tony let himself be drawn into the picture, trying to put himself in Handy Andy's shoes. How did it feel, Andy? Were You proud? Were you scared? Were you exultant? Did you feel a spasm of regret at abandoning the object of your desire? How long did you allow yourself to drink in this sight, this strange tableau that you created? Did the sound of footsteps move you on? Or did you not care?

Tony looked up. Carol was watching him. To his surprise, for once he didn't feel uncomfortable to have a woman's eyes on him. Perhaps because their relationship had so firm a professional base, but without direct competition. The tension in him relaxed a notch. "The place where the body was found. Tell me about it."

"Crompton Gardens. It's at the heart of Temple Fields, where the gay village and the red-light district overlap. It's poorly lit at night, mostly because the streetlights are always being vandalized by the sex vendors who want a bit of darkness to cover their activities. There's a lot of sex goes on in Crompton Gardens, in the bushes and on the park benches under the trees, in the office doorways, in the basement areas of the houses. Rent, prostitution and casual pick-ups. There are people around throughout the night, but they're not the sort who are going to come forward about anything unusual they might have seen, even if they noticed it," Carol explained while Tony took notes.

"The weather?" he asked.

"Dry night, though the ground was pretty damp."

Tony returned to the photographs. The body was shot from various angles. Then, following the removal of the body, the dumping ground was pictured in close-up sections. There were no visible footprints, but some scraps of black plastic were lying under the body. He pointed at them with the tip of his pen. "Do we know what these are?"

"Bradfield Metropolitan Council bin bags. Standard issue to businesses, blocks of flats . . . anywhere wheelie bins are inappropriate. That grade of bag has been in use now for the last two years. There's apparently nothing to indicate whether they were already there or if they were dumped at the same time as the body," Carol said.

Tony raised his eyebrows. "You seem to have assimilated a helluva lot of detail since yesterday afternoon."

Carol grinned. "It's tempting to pretend I'm Superwoman, but I have to confess that I'd already made a point of finding out what I could about the other two enquiries. I was convinced they were linked, even if my boss wasn't. And in fairness to my colleagues, the inspectors leading the other two enquiries had an open mind. They didn't object to me making the occasional trawl through their stuff. Ploughing through it all overnight just refreshed my memory, that's all."

"You've been up all night?"

"Like you said, it goes with the territory. I'll be fine till about four this afternoon. Then it'll hit me like a sledgehammer," Carol admitted.

"Message received and understood," Tony replied, turning back to the photographs. He moved on to the series of shots from the postmortem. The body lay on its back on the white slab, the hideous wounds visible for the first time. Tony went slowly through the whole sequence of pictures, sometimes flicking back to previous shots. When he closed his eyes, he could picture Adam Scott's intact body, slowly breaking out in wounds and bruises like alien blooms. He could almost conjure up the slo-mo vision of the hands that brought flesh to such a pass. After a few moments, he opened his eyes and spoke again. "These bruises on the neck and chest—what did the pathologist say?"

"Suck marks. Like love bites."

A head descending, predatory, a bizarre parody of love. "And these sections of the neck and chest. Three places where the flesh has been cut away?" Tony asked distantly.

"They were removed postmortem. Maybe he likes to eat them?"

"Maybe," Tony said doubtfully. "Was there any trace of bruising in the remaining tissues, can you remember?"

"I think there was." Carol's surprise showed in her voice.

Tony nodded. "I'll check the pathologist's report. He's a clever lad, our Handy Andy. My first reaction is that these aren't souvenirs, or indications of cannibalism. I think they might have been bite marks. But Handy Andy knows enough about forensic dentistry to realize that identifiable bite marks would be enough to put him away. So once the frenzy's spent, he's cooled down and removed the evidence. These cuts to the genitals—pre or postmortem?"

"Post. The pathologist remarked that they seemed quite tentative."

Tony gave a small smile of satisfaction. "Did the pathologist say what has caused the trauma to the limbs? The shots at the site look like a rag doll."

Carol sighed. "He didn't want to be pushed to an official conclusion. All four limbs were dislocated, and some of his vertebrae were out of alignment. He said . . ." She paused and imitated the pathologist's portentous delivery, " 'Don't quote me, but I'd expect to see injuries like this after the Spanish Inquisition had put someone on the rack.' "

"The rack? Shit, we're really dealing with a messy mind here. OK. Next set. Paul Gibbs. This one's yours, I think?" Tony asked as he replaced Adam Scott's photographs and took out the contents of the second folder. He repeated the process he'd gone through before. "So where is this scene in relation to the first one?" Tony asked.

"Hang on a minute. I'll show you." Carol opened one of the boxes and picked out the large-scale map she'd thought to bring with her. She unfolded it and spread it out on the floor. Tony got up from his desk and crouched down beside her. She was instantly aware of the smell of him, a mixture of shampoo and his own faint, animal scent. No macho aftershave, no cologne. She watched his pale, square hands on the map, the short, almost stubby fingers, with their neatly trimmed nails and a sparse scattering of fine black hairs on the bottom section of each finger. Appalled, she felt a stirring of desire. You're pathetic as an adolescent, she savagely chided herself. Like a teenager who fancies the first teacher who says anything nice about your work. Grow up, Jordan!

Under the guise of pointing out the sites on the map, Carol inched away. "Crompton Gardens is here," she said. "Canal Street is about half a mile away, over here. And the Queen of Hearts pub is just along here, about midway between the two."

"Is it safe to assume he knows the area well?" Tony asked, making his own mental map of the murder sites.

"I think so. Crompton Gardens is a pretty obvious dumping ground, but the other two imply quite a high degree of familiarity with Temple Fields." Carol sat back on her haunches, trying to work out if the pattern of sites implied an approach from one specific direction.

"I need to take a look at the scenes. Preferably around the time the bodies were dumped. Do we know when that was?" Tony said.

"We don't know about Adam. Estimated time of death is an hour either side of midnight, so not before then. With Paul, we know the doorway was clear just after three A.M. Gareth's time of death is estimated at between seven and ten P.M. the evening before his body was found. And with Damien, the yard was clear at half past eleven," Carol recited, closing her eyes to recall the information.

Tony found himself staring at her face, glad of the freedom her shuttered eyelids gave him. Even without the animation of her blue eyes, he could see that she'd be classified beautiful. Oval face, broad forehead, clear pale skin, and that thick blonde hair, cut slightly shaggy. A strong, determined mouth. A furrow that appeared between her brows when she concentrated. And his appreciation was as clinical as if she were a photograph in a casebook. Why was it that, faced with a woman any normal man would regard as attractive, something in him closed down? Was it because he refused to allow himself to feel the first stirrings that might lead him to a place where he was no longer in control, where humiliation lurked? Carol's eyes opened, registering surprise when she saw him watching her.

He felt his ears tingle with a blush and turned back to the map. "So he's a night owl," he said abruptly. "I'd like to take a look at the area tonight, if I can. Maybe you can get someone else to show me round so you can catch up on your sleep."

Carol shook her head. "No. If we can get through here by five, I'll go home and grab a few hours' shut-eye. I'll pick you up around midnight and we can go then. Is that OK?" she asked, belatedly.

"Perfect," Tony said, getting to his feet and retreating behind his desk. "As long as you don't mind." He picked up the photographs and forced himself back behind Handy Andy's eyes. "He's made a real mess of this one, hasn't he?"

"Paul's the only one who's been beaten up like this. Gareth has cuts to his face, but nothing as extreme. Paul's face has been smashed to a pulp—broken nose, broken teeth, broken cheekbone, dislocated jaw. The anal injuries are horrendous as well; he's been partially disembowelled. The degree of violence is one of the reasons why the Super felt we were looking at a different perpetrator. Also, none of his limbs are dislocated, unlike the other three."

"This is the one the papers said was covered up with bin bags?"

Carol nodded. "Same variety as the scraps found under Adam's body."

They moved on to Gareth Finnegan. "I'm going to have to give some serious thought to this one," he said. "He's changed his pattern in at least two significant ways. First, the dumping ground moves from Temple Fields to Carlton Park. It's still a gay cruising area, but it's an aberration." He stopped himself short and gave a hollow laugh. "Listen to me. As if his whole behaviour isn't wildly aberrant. The second thing is his letter and video to the *Sentinel Times*. Why did he decide to announce this body and none of the others?"

"I've been thinking about that," Carol said. "And I wondered if it had something to do with the fact that it could have lain there for days, even weeks, otherwise."

Tony made a note on his pad and gave her the thumbs-up sign with the other hand. "These wounds to the hands and feet. I know it sounds off the wall, but it almost looks like he was crucified."

"The pathologist wasn't crazy about going on the record with that one either. But the hand wounds, coupled with the dislocation of both shoulders, makes crucifixion a conclusion that's hard to resist, especially when you remember this probably happened on Christmas Day." Carol got to her feet, rubbing the sleep out of her eyes. She couldn't manage to stifle a jaw-cracking yawn. She paced round the small office, shrugging her shoulders to loosen the taut muscles. "Sick bastard," she muttered.

"The genital mutilations are getting more severe," Tony observed. "He's virtually castrated this one. And the fatal wounds, the cutting of the throat. That's getting deeper too."

"Does that tell us anything?" Carol asked, almost unintelligible through another yawn.

"Like your pathologist, I'm reluctant to speculate just yet," Tony said. He moved on to the final set of pictures. For the first time, Carol saw his professional mask slip. Horror swept across Tony's face, widening his eyes, drawing his lips back in a hissed intake of breath. She wasn't surprised. When they'd turned Damien Connolly over, a six-foot rugby-playing detective had keeled over in a dead faint. Even the experienced police pathologist had turned away momentarily, visibly struggling not to be sick.

Rigor mortis had frozen Damien Connolly's limbs in a parody of human gesture. The dislocated joints stuck out at crazy angles. But there was more, and worse. His penis had been severed and thrust into his mouth. His torso was branded from chest to groin in a bizarre, random pattering of starburst burns, none more than half an inch across.

"Dear God," Tony breathed.

"He's really getting the hang of this, isn't he?" Carol said bitterly. "Takes a pride in his work, doesn't he?"

Tony said nothing, forcing himself to study the appalling photographs as closely as he'd done with the previous sets. "Carol," he eventually said. "Has anybody come up with any theories as to what he's used to make these burn marks?"

"Not a one," she said.

"They're odd," he said. "The patterns vary. It's not like he's used some random object and kept on using it. There are at least five different shapes. Have you got anybody who can do computer pattern analysis? To see if there's any hidden message here? There must be dozens of these bloody burns!"

Carol rubbed her eyes again. "I don't know. Me and computers are about as compatible as the Prince and Princess of Wales. I'll ask when I go back to the office. And if we don't have someone, I'll ask my brother."

"Your brother?"

"Michael's a computer genius. He works in games software development. You want a pattern analysed, manipulated, turned into a shoot-'em-up arcade game, he's your man."

"And he can keep his mouth shut?"

"If he couldn't, he wouldn't be doing the job he does. Millions of pounds depend on his company getting on the next rung of the ladder before anybody else. Believe me, he knows when to button his lip."

Tony smiled. "I didn't mean to sound offensive."

"You didn't."

Tony sighed. "I wish to God I'd been brought in sooner on this. Handy Andy's not going to stop here. He's too much in love with his work. Look at these pictures. This bastard's going to carry on capturing and torturing and killing until you catch him. Carol, this guy's a career killer."

*I walked boldly up the path and pressed Adam's doorbell. In the seconds before he answered the chime, I composed my face into what I believed was an apologetic smile. I could see the fuzzy outline of his head and shoulders as he walked down the hall. Then the door opened and we were face to face. He half smiled quizzically. As if he'd never noticed me before in his life.*

*"I'm sorry to bother you," I said. "Only my car's broken down, and I don't know where there's a pay phone, so I wondered if I might use your phone to call the AA? I'll pay for the call, of course . . ." I let my voice trail away.*

*His smile broadened and relaxed, his dark eyes crinkling at the corners. "No problem. Come in." He stepped back and I moved inside the door. He gestured down the hall. "There's a phone in the study. Just on the right there."*

*I moved slowly down the hall, ears alert for the sound of the front door closing behind me. As the lock snapped back into place, he added, "There's nothing worse, is there?"*

*"I'll just look up the number," I said, pausing in the doorway to reach in my backpack. Adam kept on walking, so that when I pulled out the Mace spray, he was only a couple of feet away from me. It couldn't have been more perfect. I let him have it full in the face.*

*He roared in pain and stumbled back against the wall, hands clawing at his face. I moved in swiftly. One foot between his ankles, hands on his shoulders, a quick twist and down he went, face crushed into the carpet, gasping for breath. I was down on top of him in seconds, gripping one wrist and twisting his arm up his back while I snapped the handcuff over it. He was struggling against me by now, tears streaming down his face, but I managed to grab his other flailing arm and snap the other half of the cuffs on it.*

*His legs were thrashing under me, but my weight was enough to keep him pinned to the floor while I took a ziplock plastic bag from my backpack. I opened it, extracted a pad soaked in chloroform and clamped it over his nose and mouth. The sickly odour drifted upwards into my nostrils, making me feel slightly light-headed and queasy. I hoped the chloroform hadn't gone off; I'd had the bottle for a couple of years, ever since I'd stolen it from the dispensary on a Soviet ship where I'd spent the night with the first officer.*

*Adam struggled even harder when he felt the cold compress cut off his access to the air, but within minutes his legs stopped their pointless thrashing. I waited a little longer, just to be on the safe side, then I rolled off and fastened his legs together with surgical tape. I returned the chloroform pad to its secure bag, then I taped Adam's mouth shut.*

*I stood up and took a deep breath. So far, so good. Next, I pulled on a pair of latex gloves and took stock. I am familiar with the theory of the French forensic scientist Edmond Locard, first demonstrated in a murder trial in 1912, that every contact leaves a trace; a criminal will always take something away from the scene of his crime and leave something behind. With this in mind, I had carefully chosen my wardrobe for today. I was wearing Levi 501s, the same brand I'd seen Adam wear often. I'd topped it with a baggy V-necked cricket sweater, the exact double of one I'd watched him buy in Marks and Spencer a couple of weeks before. Any stray fibres I left behind would inevitably be ascribed to the contents of Adam's own wardrobe.*

*I took a quick look round the study, pausing by his answering machine. It was one of the old-fashioned ones, with a single cassette tape. I opened the machine and helped myself to the tape. It would be nice to have a memory of his voice sounding normal; I knew that the soundtrack on the video wouldn't have that same relaxed quality.*

*The door to the garage was locked. I headed off up the stairs, where I found the jacket of his suit tossed over the back of a chair in the kitchen diner. The bunch of keys was in the left-hand pocket. Back downstairs, I opened the garage door and unlocked the hatchback of his two-year-old Ford Escort. Then I went back for Adam. He had, of course, come round. His eyes were filled with panic, muffled grunts came from behind the gag. I smiled down at him as I pressed the chloroform pad over his nose again. This time, of course, he couldn't struggle effectively at all.*

*I pulled him into a sitting position, then brought a chair through from the study. I managed to get him on to the chair, and from there I was able to sling him over my shoulder and stagger through into the garage. I dumped him in the luggage space, and slammed the tailgate shut. Not a trace of his body was visible.*

*I checked my watch. Just after six. It would be another hour till it was dark enough to be certain none of the neighbours passing casually would notice a stranger driving out of Adam's garage. I filled the time by browsing through his life. Packets of photographs revealed friends, a family Christmas dinner. I would have fitted into this life perfectly. We could have had it all, if he hadn't been such a fool.*

*I was startled out of my reverie by the phone. I let it ring, and went through to the kitchen. I helped myself to a bottle of creme cleanser and a cloth and carefully washed down all the paintwork in the hall. I put the used cloth in my backpack, then fetched the vacuum cleaner. I went over the entire hall slowly and carefully, erasing all traces of the struggle from the hard-wearing Berber carpet. I trailed the vac behind me, right into the garage, where I left it in a corner, looking as if it had always lived there. Satisfied I'd removed all traces of me, I climbed into Adam's car, pressed the remote-control button on his keyring and started the engine as the garage door rose smoothly before me.*

*I shut the door behind me, and drove off. I could hear muffled noises from the back of the car. I raked around in the glove box till I found a Wet, Wet, Wet cassette. I shoved it into the player and turned the volume up high. I sang along with the music as I drove out of the city and on to the moors.*

*I'd been worried that Adam's car might not make it all the way up the track, and I'd been right. About half a mile from home, the road became too overgrown and rutted. With a sigh, I got out and walked up to collect the wheelbarrow. When I opened the tailgate to tip him into the barrow, his eyes were wide and staring. His muffled calls were wasted on me, however. I dragged him unceremoniously out of the car and into the barrow. It was a hard half-mile up the track, since his constant struggling made steering more difficult. Luckily, Auntie Doris had had the foresight to buy a proper builder's barrow, one with two wheels in front.*

*When we reached the farmhouse, I opened the trapdoor. The cellar below looked dark and welcoming. Adam's eyes widened in terror. I stroked his soft hair and said, "Welcome to the pleasure dome."*

# 5

*As to ... the mob of newspaper readers, they are pleased with anything, provided it is bloody enough. But the mind of sensibility requires something more.*

After he'd seen Carol to her car, Tony walked across the campus to the general stores and bought a copy of the evening paper. If publicity was what Handy Andy craved, he'd finally achieved it. Fear and loathing stalked the pages of the *Bradfield Evening Sentinel Times*. Five of them, to be precise. Pages 1, 2, 3, 24 and 25, plus an editorial, were devoted to the Queer Killer. If the nickname was anything to judge by, the police were already leaking like a Cabinet committee.

"You're not going to like being called the Queer Killer, are you, Andy?" Tony said softly to himself as he walked back to his office. Back behind his desk, he studied the paper. Penny Burgess had had a field day. The front page screamed, QUEER KILLER STRIKES AGAIN! in banner headlines. In smaller headline type, readers were told, POLICE ADMIT SERIAL KILLER STALKS CITY. Beneath was a lurid account of the discovery of Damien Connolly's body, and a photograph of him at his passing-out parade. The turnover on pages two and three was a sensationalist summary of the three previous cases, complete with sketch map. "Bricks without straw, right enough," Tony said to himself as he flicked through to the centre spread. GAYS TERRIFIED BY QUEER KILLER MONSTER left the reader in no doubt who the *Sentinel Times* had decided were at risk. The copy focused on the supposed hysteria gripping Bradfield's gay community, complete with interior shots of cafés, bars and clubs that made the scene look seedy enough to pander to the readers' prejudices.

"Oh boy," Tony said. "You're really going to hate this, Andy." He turned back to the editorial.

"At last," he read, "police have admitted what many of us have believed for some time. There is a serial killer on the loose in Bradfield, his target the young, single men who frequent the city's sordid gay bars.

"It's a disgrace that the police have not warned the city's homosexuals to be on their guard before now. In the twilight world of anonymous pick-ups and casual sex, it cannot be difficult for this predatory monster to find willing victims. The police's silence can only have made it easier for the killer.

"Their reluctance to speak out has probably increased the gay community's existing suspicion of the police, making them fear that the authorities value the lives of gay men less than those of other members of the community.

"Just as it took the murders of 'innocent' women rather than prostitutes to make the police pay full attention to the Yorkshire Ripper, it is wrong that a police officer has had to be murdered before Bradfield Metropolitan Police takes this Queer Killer seriously.

"In spite of this, we urge the gay community to cooperate fully with the police. And we demand that the police investigate these horrific killings diligently and with compassion for the concerns of Bradfield's homosexuals. The sooner this vicious killer is caught, the safer we all will be."

"The usual mixture of self-righteousness, indignation and unrealistic demands," Tony said to the Devil's Ivy on his windowsill. He clipped the articles and spread them across the desk. He switched on his micro-cassette recorder and spoke.

"*Bradfield Evening Sentinel Times*, February 27th. At last, Handy Andy has made the big time. I'm wondering how important that is to him. One of the tenets of profiling serial offenders is that they crave the oxygen of publicity. But this time, I'm not so sure he's too bothered about that. There were no messages after the first two killings, neither of which received that much publicity after the initial discovery of the bodies. And although there was a message directing the police to the third body via a newspaper, that note made no claims about the earlier killings. I had puzzled over that until Inspector Carol Jordan offered an alternative explanation for the note and accompanying video, namely that without direction, the body may have lain undiscovered for some time. So, while Handy Andy may not be obsessive about creating headlines and panic, it's clear he wants the bodies found while they are still recognizably his work." He switched off the cassette with a sigh. Although he'd turned his back on the academic circus years before, he couldn't escape his training; every stage of the process had to be on record. The prospect of this investigation providing the raw material for articles or even a book was something Tony found hard to resist.

"I'm a cannibal," he said to the plant. "Sometimes I disgust myself." He shovelled the clippings together and tucked them into his press-cuttings folder. He opened the boxes and took out the stacks of document wallets they contained. Carol had labelled them all neatly. Fluent capitals, Tony noted. A woman comfortable with the written word.

Each victim had a pathology report and a preliminary forensic report. The witness statements were divided into three groups: Background (victim), Witness (scene of crime) and Miscellaneous. Selecting the Background (victim) files, he walked his wheeled chair across to the table where his personal computer stood. When he'd arrived at Bradfield, the university had offered him a terminal linked into their network. He'd declined, not wanting to waste time learning a new set of protocols when he was perfectly at home with his own PC. Now, he was glad he didn't have to add data security to the list of worries that kept him awake at nights.

Tony called up the customized software that would allow him to make comparisons between the victims, and started the long slog of inputting the data.

Five minutes in the Scargill Street station was enough to make Carol wish she'd gone straight home. To get to the office she'd been allocated for the duration of the investigation, she had to walk the length of the main squad room. Copies of the evening paper were strewn over half the desks, mocking her with their thick black headlines. Bob Stansfield was standing with a couple of DCs halfway down the room and he called to her as she passed. "The good doctor knocked off already, has he?"

"From what I've seen of the good doctor, Bob, he could give some of our bosses a few lessons in working overtime," Carol said, wishing she could think of some sharper put-down. Doubtless it would come to her hours later in the shower. On the other hand, maybe it was as well she hadn't come up with something too devastating. Better not alienate the lads any more than her assignment had already done. She stopped and smiled. "Anything new?" she asked.

Stansfield detached himself from his juniors, saying, "Right, lads, get on with it." He moved over to Carol's side and said, "Not as such. The HOLMES team are working flat out, smacking all we've got so far into the computer, see what correlations they can come up with. Cross has ordered us to pull in all the nonces again. He's convinced one of them's our best bet."

Carol shook her head. "Waste of time."

"You said it. This bastard's not got form, I'd put money on it. Kevin's got a team going out tonight to try something a bit different, though," he added, taking out and lighting his last cigarette. He tossed the packet in a nearby bin, an expression of disgust on his face. "If we don't get a fucking break soon, I'm going to have to put in for a raise to cover my bloody nicotine consumption."

"Me, I'm drinking so much coffee I've got a permanent case of the jitterbug boogies," Carol said ruefully. "So what's this idea of Kevin's?" Gently does it. First the rapport, then the question. Funny how getting information out of colleagues followed the same rules as interrogating suspects.

"He's got an undercover team going out on the gay scene, concentrating on the clubs and pubs with a reputation for S&M." Stansfield snorted. "They've all been down Traffic this avvy, scrounging leather trousers off the bike boys."

"It's worth a try," Carol said.

"Yeah, well let's hope Kevin's not sending in a bunch of closet pansies like Damien Connolly turned out to be," Stansfield said. "Last thing we want is a bunch of CID fairies ending up wearing their own handcuffs."

Carol refused to dignify the comment with a reply and moved off towards her office. She'd got her hand on the door when Cross's voice boomed down the room. "Inspector Jordan? Get your body in here."

Carol closed her eyes and counted to three. "Coming, sir," she said cheerfully, turning back and walking the length of the room to Cross's temporary office. He'd only been in there a day, but already he'd marked it like a tomcat spraying his territory. The room reeked of cigarette smoke. Half-drunk polystyrene cups of coffee strategically placed on window ledge and desk top had butts floating in them. There was even a girlie calendar on the wall, proof that sexism was alive and well and working in the advertising industry. Hadn't they realized *yet* that it was the women who stood in the supermarkets deciding which brand of vodka to buy?

Leaving the door open in a bid for air, Carol walked into Cross's office and said, "Sir?"

"What's Wonder Boy come up with then?"

"It's a bit early for conclusions, sir," she said brightly.

"He's got to read through all the reports I copied for him."

Cross grunted. "Oh aye, I forgot he's a bloody professor." He spat the word out sarcastically. "Everything in writing, eh? Kevin's got some more stuff on the Connolly business; you'll have to catch up with him. Was there anything else, Inspector?" he asked belligerently, as if she were the one who had imposed herself on him.

"Dr. Hill has a suggestion, sir. About the burn marks on PC Connolly's body. He wondered if there was anyone on the HOLMES team who could do statistical pattern analysis."

"What the bloody hell is statistical pattern analysis?" Cross said, dumping the end of his cigarette into a coffee cup.

"I think it means—"

"Never mind, never mind," Cross interrupted. "Go and see if anybody down there knows what the hell you're on about."

"Yes, sir. Oh, and sir? If we can't do it here, my brother works in computers. I'm sure he could do it for us."

Cross stared at her, his expression unreadable for once. When he spoke, he was all affability. "Fine. Go ahead. Mr. Brandon gave you carte blanche, after all."

So that's what a passing buck sounds like, Carol thought as she headed downstairs to the HOLMES room. A five-minute conversation with a harassed Inspector Dave Woolcott confirmed what she'd already suspected. The HOLMES team had neither the software nor the expertise to carry out the analysis Tony wanted. As Carol walked down to the canteen in search of Kevin Matthews, she hoped Michael could deliver in complete confidence. Keeping quiet about technological developments was very different from resisting the urge to gossip about a high-profile murder enquiry. If he let her down, she could kiss goodbye to a future outside Personnel.

Kevin was hunched alone over a cup of coffee, a plate with the remains of a fry-up next to him. Carol pulled out the chair opposite him. "Mind if I join you?"

"Be my guest," Kevin said. He looked up and gave her the ghost of a grin, pushing his unruly ginger curls back from his forehead. "How's it going?"

"Probably a lot easier than it is for you and Bob."

"What's this Home Office boffin like, then?"

Carol considered for a moment. "He's cautious. He's quick, he's sharp, but he's not a know-all, and he doesn't seem to want to tell us how to do our job. It's really interesting watching him work. He looks at things from a different perspective."

"How do you mean?" Kevin asked, looking genuinely interested.

"When we look at a crime, we look for physical clues, leads, things that point us to who we might want to talk to or where we might want to look. When *he* looks at a crime, he's not interested in all that stuff. He wants to know why the physical clues happened the way they did so he can work out who did it. It's as if we use information to move us forward and he uses it to move him backwards. Does that make sense?"

Kevin frowned. "I think so. You think he's got what it takes?"

Carol shrugged. "It's early days yet. But yeah, on first impressions, I'd say he's got something to offer."

Kevin grinned. "Something to offer the investigation or something to offer you?"

"Piss off, Kevin," Carol said, tired of the innuendo that followed her round the job. "Unlike some, I never shit on my own doorstep."

Kevin looked momentarily uneasy. "Only joking, Carol, honest."

"Jokes are supposed to be funny."

"OK, OK, sorry. What's he like to work with, though? Nice bloke, or what?"

Carol spoke slowly, measuring her words. "Considering he spends his working life getting inside the minds of psychopaths, he seems pretty normal. There's something quite . . . closed off about him. He keeps his distance. Doesn't give much away. But he treats me like an equal, not like some thick plod. He's on our side, Kevin, and that's the main thing. I'd guess he's one of those workaholics who's more interested in getting the job done than anything else. And speaking of getting the job done, Popeye says you've turned something up on PC Connolly?"

Kevin sighed. "For what it's worth. One of the neighbours came home from work at ten to six. She knows the time because the shipping forecast had just started on the car radio. Connolly was on his drive, closing the bonnet of his car. He had overalls on. The neighbour says he must have been working on the car, he was always at it. By the time the neighbour got out of her car and into the house, Damien was reversing his car into the garage. The same neighbour came out about an hour later on her way to a game of squash, and she noticed Connolly's car parked on the street. She was a bit surprised, because he never left the car sitting out, especially after dark. She also noticed that the light was on in Connolly's garage. And that's about the size of it."

"Is it an integral garage?" Carol asked.

"No, but it's attached to the house, and there's a door from the garage leads into the kitchen."

"So it looks like he was snatched from the house?"

Kevin shrugged. "Who knows? There's no sign of a struggle. I spoke to one of the SOCOs who turned the place over, and he said not to hold our breath."

"Sounds just like the first two."

"That's what Bob says." Kevin pushed his chair back. "I better get weaving. We're going out on the town to-night."

"I might bump into you later," Carol said. "Dr. Hill wants a tour of the crime scenes at the sort of time when the bodies were dumped."

Kevin got to his feet. "Just don't let him talk to any strange men."

\*     \*     \*

Tony took the plastic container of lasagne out of the microwave and sat down at the breakfast bar in his kitchen. He'd input all the data that he could find on the four victims, then he'd transferred the files to a floppy disk so he could work on it at home while he waited for Carol to arrive. As soon as he'd reached the tram stop, he'd realized he was ravenous. Then he remembered he'd eaten nothing since his breakfast cereal. He'd been working with such concentration, he hadn't even noticed. He found the hunger curiously satisfactory. It meant he was too involved in what he was doing to be conscious of himself. He knew from long experience that his best work came when he lost self-consciousness, when he could immerse himself in the patterns of another human being, locked into that other's idiosyncratic logic, in tune with a different set of emotions.

He attacked the food with gusto, shovelling it down as quickly as possible so he could get to his computer and carry on with his victim profiles. There were still a couple of forkfuls left in the dish when the phone rang. With no pause for thought, Tony snatched up the phone. "Hello?" he said cheerfully.

"Anthony," the voice said. Tony dropped the fork, tipping the pasta out on the worktop.

"Angelica," he said. He was back in his own world, anchored within his own head at the sound of her voice. "Feeling more sociable today?" the sweet huskiness asked.

"I wasn't feeling anti-social yesterday. I just had things to do I couldn't ignore. And you distract me," Tony said, wondering why he bothered to justify himself to her.

"That's the general plan," she said. "But I missed you, Anthony. I was so horny for you, and when you discarded me like an old sock, all my pleasure in the day was over."

"Why do you do this with me?" he demanded. It was a question he'd asked before, but she had always deflected him.

"Because you deserve me," the voice said. "Because I want you more than anyone in the world. And because you don't have anyone else in your life to make you happy."

It was the same old story. Cut off the question with some flannel. But tonight, Tony wanted answers, not flattery. "What makes you think that?" he asked.

The voice chuckled softly. "I know more about you than you can possibly dream. Anthony, you don't have to be alone any more."

"What if I like being alone? Isn't it fair to assume that I'm alone because I want to be?"

"You don't look like a happy boy to me. Some days, you look like you need a hug more than anything in the world. Some days, you look like you haven't slept for more than a couple of hours. Anthony, I can bring you peace. Women have hurt you before, we both know that. But I won't. I can stop it hurting. I can make you sleep like a baby, you know that. All I want is to make you happy." The voice was soothing, gentle.

Tony sighed. If only . . . "I find that hard to believe," he stalled. Right from the start of these conversations, part of him had wanted to slam the phone down on this exquisite torture. But the scientist in him wanted to hear what she had to say. And the damaged man inside had enough self-awareness to know he needed to be cured, and that this might just be the way. He reminded himself of his earlier resolve not to let her get under his skin, so that when the time came, he could walk away without pain.

"But you let me try." The voice was so self-assured. She was confident of her power over him.

"I listen, don't I? I join in. I haven't put the phone down yet," he said, forcing artificial warmth into his voice.

"Why don't you do just that? Why don't you put down this phone and go upstairs to your bedroom and pick up the extension there? So we can be comfortable?"

A cold stab of fear hit Tony in the chest. He struggled to frame the question professionally. Not, "How do you know that?," but, "What makes you think I've got a phone in the bedroom?"

There was a pause, so brief that Tony couldn't be certain he wasn't imagining it. "Just guessing," she said. "I've got you sussed. You're the kind of man who has a phone by the bed."

"Well guessed," Tony said. "OK. I'm going to put the phone down and I'll pick up in the bedroom." He replaced the receiver and hurried through to his study, where he switched the answering machine over to "record" mode. Then he picked up the phone again. "Hello? I'm back," he said.

"Are we sitting comfortably? Then I'll begin." Again that low, sexy chuckle. "We are going to have some real fun tonight. Wait till you hear what I've got lined up for you tonight. Oh, Anthony," she said, her voice dropping almost to a whisper. "I've been dreaming about you. Imagining your hands on my body, running your fingers over my skin."

"What are you wearing?" Tony asked. It was, he knew, the standard question.

"What would you like me to be wearing? I have an extensive wardrobe."

Tony bit back the crazy urge to say, "Fishermen's waders, a tutu and a rainmate." He swallowed hard and said, "Silk. You know how I like the feel of silk."

"That's why you love my skin. I take a lot of trouble to keep myself in perfect condition. But just for you, I've covered some of my skin with silk. I'm wearing a pair of black silk French knickers and a sheer black silk camisole. Oh, I love the feeling of silk against my body. Oh, Anthony," she groaned. "The silk's rubbing against my nipples, gently, like your fingers would. Oh, my nipples are hard as rocks, sticking up, inflamed with you."

In spite of himself, Tony began to feel the stirrings of interest. She was good, no two ways about it. Most of the women he'd heard on the chatlines had sounded stale and bored, their responses predictable and stereotypical. Nothing in their conversations had aroused anything other than scientific interest in him. But Angelica was different. For one thing, she sounded like she meant it.

She moaned softly. "God, I'm wet," she breathed. "But

you can't touch me yet, you've got to wait. Just lie back, that's a good boy. Oh, I love to undress you. I've got my hands under your shirt, my fingers are running over your chest, stroking you, touching you, feeling your nipples under my fingers. God, you're wonderful," she sighed.

"That's nice," Tony said, enjoying the caress of her voice.

"That's just the beginning. Now I'm straddling you, unbuttoning your shirt. I'm leaning over you, my nipples inside the silk brushing against your chest. Oh, Anthony!" her voice exclaimed in pleasure. "You really are pleased to see me, aren't you? You're hard as a rock underneath me. Oh, I can't wait to get you inside me."

Her words froze Tony. The erection he'd felt hardening inside his trousers died like a snowflake in a puddle. They were there again. "I think I'm going to disappoint you," he said, his voice cracking.

That sexy chuckle again. "No way. You're already more than I dreamed. Oh, Anthony, touch me. Tell me what you want to do to me."

Tony could find no words.

"Don't be shy, Anthony. There are no secrets between us, nowhere we can't go. Close your eyes, let the feelings flow. Touch my breasts, go on, suck my nipples, eat me, let me feel your hot wet mouth all over me."

Tony groaned. This was almost more than he could bear, even in the interests of science.

Angelica's voice was more breathy now, as if her words were arousing her as much as they should have been arousing him. "That's right, oh God, Anthony, that's wonderful. Oh-oh-oh," she said in a shuddering moan. "See, I told you I was wet. That's right, plunge your fingers deep into my cunt. Oh God, you're the best . . . Let me . . . let me, oh God, let me get at you."

Tony heard the sound of a zipper down the phone line. "Angelica . . ." he started to say. It was falling apart again, just as it always did, spiralling out of control like a wounded bird.

"Oh, Anthony, you're beautiful. That's the most beautiful cock I've ever seen. Oh, let me taste you . . ." Her voice tailed off with the sound of sucking.

The blood rushed to Tony's face in a sudden wave of shame and anger. He slammed the phone down and immediately took it off the hook again. Jesus, what kind of a man couldn't even get it up over the phone? And what kind of scientist couldn't divorce his own pathetic failings from the exercise of objective data collection?

The worst of it was, he recognized his own behaviour. How many times had he sat across the table from a multiple rapist, arsonist or killer and watched them reach the point in their reliving of events where they could no longer face themselves. Just like him, they closed down. They couldn't disconnect a phone, but they closed down just the same. Eventually, of course, with the right therapy, they breached the walls and managed to confront what had brought them there. That was the first step towards recovery. Part of Tony prayed that Angelica knew enough about the theory and practice of psychology to stick with him till he too could break down the barriers and stare into the face of whatever it was that had bred this sexual and emotional cripple.

But the other part of him hoped she'd never call again. Never mind "no pain, no gain." He just wanted no pain.

John Brandon scrupulously wiped his plate with the last piece of nan bread and smiled at his wife. "That was great, Maggie," he said.

"Mmm," his son Andy agreed through a mouthful of lamb and aubergine curry.

Brandon shifted awkwardly in his chair. "If it's all right with you, I think I'll pop back down to Scargill Street for an hour. Just to see how things are going."

"I thought ranking officers like you didn't have to work evenings," Maggie said good-humouredly. "I thought you said the troops didn't need you breathing down their necks?"

Brandon looked sheepish. "I know. But I just want to see how the lads are going on."

Maggie shook her head, a resigned smile on her face. "I'd rather you went down and got it out of your system than you sat all night fidgeting in front of the telly."

Karen perked up. "Dad, if you're going back into town, can you drop me at Laura's? So we can work on our history project?"

Andy snorted. "Work on how you're going to get off with Craig McDonald, more like."

"You know nothing," Karen huffed. "Will you, Dad?"

Brandon got up from the table. "Only if you're ready now. And I'll pick you up on my way back."

"Oh, Dad," Karen complained. "You said you were only going to be gone an hour. That's not nearly long enough for us to do all we want to."

It was Maggie Brandon's turn to snort with laughter. "If your father's back before half past nine, I'll make Scotch pancakes for supper."

Karen looked at each parent in turn, the anguish of choice written on her fourteen-year-old face. "Dad?" she said. "Can you pick me up by nine o'clock?"

Brandon grinned. "Why do I feel like I've been stitched up?"

It was just after half past seven when Brandon arrived in the HOLMES room. Even that late, every terminal was occupied. The sound of fingers hitting keyboards clicked away under the quiet conversations taking place at a few of the desks. Inspector Dave Woolcott sat beside one of the collators, who was pointing out some detail on the screen. No one looked up when Brandon entered.

He walked over behind Woolcott and waited till he had finished talking to the constable on the terminal. Brandon suppressed a sigh. It was definitely time he started thinking about retirement. It wasn't just the bobbies that looked young to him now; even the inspectors didn't look old enough to be out of probationer's cap bands. "Keep trying for a match, Harry, cross-ref with the CROs," he heard

Woolcott say. The lad on the keyboard nodded and stared into his screen.

" 'Evening, Dave," Brandon said.

Woolcott swung round in his chair. Registering who the newcomer was, he got to his feet. " 'Evening, sir."

"I was on my way home, and I thought I'd swing by and see how you were doing," Brandon lied smoothly.

"Well, sir, it's early days. We'll have teams working round the clock for the next couple of days, feeding in all the statement details from the earlier cases as well as PC Connolly's. I'm also liaising with the team manning the hot-line phones. Most of it's the usual spite, vengeance and paranoia, but Sergeant Lascelles is doing a good job of prioritizing the messages."

"Anything coming out yet?"

Woolcott rubbed his bald spot in the reflex gesture which his second wife claimed had caused the problem in the first place. "Bits and pieces. We've got a few names of blokes who were out and about in Temple Fields on at least two of the nights in question, and those are being actioned. We've also been hammering the PNC with car index numbers that have shown up regularly around the times of the killings. Luckily, ever since the second killing, Inspector Jordan's had somebody clocking car numbers round the gay village. It's a long job, sir, but we'll get there."

If he's in there, Brandon thought. It was he who had been adamant that this was a case for the HOLMES team. But this killer was unlike any he'd seen or read about. This killer was careful.

Brandon didn't know much about computers. But one adage had stuck: garbage in, garbage out. He hoped fervently that he hadn't given his men a job that should have gone to the Cleansing Department.


Carol's eyes snapped open, heart pounding. In her dream, a heavy cell door had slammed shut, leaving her a prisoner of cold, sweating windowless walls. Still groggy from sleep, it took her a moment to realize that the familiar weight of Nelson's body wasn't lying across her feet. She heard footsteps, the rattle of keys being thrown on a table. A narrow sliver of light spilled through the few inches of open door Nelson required for his comings and goings. She rolled over with a groan and grabbed the clock. Ten past ten. Robbed of twenty minutes' precious sleep by Michael's noisy return.

Carol stumbled out of bed and pulled on her heavy towelling bathrobe. She opened her bedroom door and walked into the enormous room that made up most of the third-floor flat she shared with her brother. Half a dozen floor-mounted up-lights of different heights cast a warm and elegant glow on the room. Nelson appeared from the kitchen doorway, bouncing lightly on the stripped-wood flooring. Then he crouched and, in a leap that seemed to defy gravity, bounded into the air, touching briefly on a tall thin speaker before landing delicately on top of a blond wood bookcase. From there, he stared superciliously across the room at Carol, as if to say, "I bet you can't do that."

The room was about forty feet by twenty-five. At one end, a group of three two-seater sofas covered with quilted throws surrounded a low coffee table. At the opposite end stood a dining table with six chairs in the style of Rennie Mackintosh. Near the sofas was a TV and video on a black trolley. About half of the back wall was occupied by shelves crammed with books, videos and CDs.

The walls were painted a cool dove-grey, except for the far wall, which was exposed brickwork, with five high arched windows looking out over the city. Carol walked across the room till she could just see the edge of the black ribbon of the Duke of Waterford canal below. The city lights glittered like a cheap jeweller's window. "Michael?" she called.

Her brother stuck his head out of the narrow galley kitchen, looking surprised. "I didn't realize you were home," he said. "Did I wake you?"

"I was getting up soon anyway. I've got to go back to

work. I was just grabbing a few hours," she said resignedly. "Is the kettle on?" She walked across to the kitchen and perched on a high stool while Michael made tea and carried on building himself a sandwich with ciabatta, beef tomatoes, black olives, spring onions and tuna.

"Eat?" he asked.

"I could handle one of those," Carol admitted. "How was London?"

Michael shrugged. "You know. They like what we're doing, but could we have it finished yesterday."

Carol pulled a face. "Sounds just like the *Sentinel Times*'s editorials about the serial killer. What exactly is it you're doing at the moment anyway? Is it explainable in words of one syllable to a techno-illiterate?"

Michael grinned. "The next big thing is going to be computer adventure games with the same quality as videos. You film real stuff and digitize it and manipulate it to produce gameplay that's as real as a movie. So we're on to the next, next big thing. Imagine you're playing a computer adventure, but all the characters are people you know. You're the hero, but not just in your imagination."

"You've lost me now," Carol said.

"OK. When you install the game on your computer, you'll plug in a scanner and scan photographs of yourself and anybody else you want in your game. The computer reads that information, and translates it into screen images. So instead of Conan the Barbarian leading the quest, it's Carol Jordan. You can import pics of your best friends or your lust objects to be your companions in the game. Anybody you don't like, you turn into the baddies. So, you could have an adventure with Mel Gibson, Dennis Quaid and Martin Amis, and fight enemies like Saddam Hussein, Margaret Thatcher and Popeye," Michael explained enthusiastically as he stuffed the ingredients into the bread. He dumped the sandwiches on plates and together they walked back into the living room and sat staring out over the canal as they ate.

"Clear?" he asked.

"As it needs to be," Carol said. "So once you've got this software up and running, presumably you could use it to put people in compromising positions? Like blue movies?"

Michael frowned. "Theoretically. Your average computer nerd wouldn't even know where to begin. You'd need to know what you were doing and you'd also need seriously expensive hardware to get decent quality stills or videos off your computer."

"Thank God for that," Carol said, with feeling. "I was beginning to think you were creating a Frankenstein's monster for blackmailers and tabloid journalists."

"No chance," he said. "Anyway, close analysis would show it up. So what about you? How's your quest coming along?"

Carol shrugged. "I could do with a few superheroes to help out, to be honest."

"What's this profiler like? He going to shake things up a bit?"

"Tony Hill? He already has. Popeye's going around with a face like a melted wellie. But I'm hopeful we might get something constructive out of him. I've had one session with him already, and he's bursting with ideas. He's a nice guy as well, no hassle to work with."

Michael grinned. "That must be a refreshing change."

"You're not kidding."

"And is he your type?"

Carol pulled a piece of crust off her bread and threw it at Michael. "God, you're as bad as the sexist pigs I work with. I haven't got a type, and even if I did and Tony Hill was it, you know I won't mix work with pleasure."

"Given the fact that you work all hours and spend all your spare time asleep, I guess you're looking at a lifetime of celibacy," Michael replied drily. "So is he gorgeous, or what?"

"I hadn't noticed," Carol said stiffly. "And I doubt whether he's even noticed I'm female. The man's a workaholic. In fact, he's the reason I'm working again tonight. He wants to see the scenes of crime at around the time the bodies were dumped so he can get a feel for it."

"Shame you've got to go out again," Michael said. "It's ages since we've had a night in with the telly and a few bottles of wine. We see so little of each other just now, we might as well be married."

Carol smiled ruefully. "The price of success, eh, bro?"

"I guess so." Michael got up. "Oh well, if you're going to work, I might as well do a couple of hours before I sack out."

"Before you go . . . I need a favour."

Michael sat down again. "As long as it doesn't involve doing your ironing."

"What do you know about statistical pattern analysis?"

Michael frowned. "Not a lot. I did a little bit when I was doing part-time jobbing work while I was doing my PhD, but I don't know what's state of the art right now. Why? You want something looking at?"

Carol nodded. "It's a bit grisly, I'm afraid." She outlined the sadistic injuries to Damien Connolly. "Tony Hill has an idea they might yield some kind of a message."

"Sure, I'll have a look for you. I know a bloke who's almost certainly got the latest software in the field. I'm sure he'd let me have some time on his machine to fiddle about with this," Michael said.

"Not a word to anybody what it's about," Carol said.

Michael looked offended. "Of course not. What do you take me for? Listen, I'd rather get on the wrong side of a serial killer than you. I'll keep my mouth shut. Just get the stuff to me tomorrow, and I'll do my best, OK?"

Carol leaned over and rumpled her brother's blond hair. "Thank you. I appreciate it."

Michael grabbed her in a quick hug. "This is seriously weird territory, little sis. Be careful out there, huh? You know I can't afford the mortgage on this place alone."

"I'm always careful," Carol said, ignoring the small voice inside her warning not to tempt fate. "I'm a survivor."

"I wanted you the first time I saw you," I said softly. "I've wanted you for so long."

Adam's lolling head straightened slightly. I pressed the remote record button on the tripod-mounted video camera. I didn't want to miss a thing. Adam's eyelids, heavy from all that chloroform, struggled open to a slit, then suddenly snapped wide as memory kicked in. His head thrashed from side to side as he tried to see where he was, how he was restrained. As he took in his nakedness, spotted the details of the soft leather wrist and ankle cuffs, and realized that he was fastened to my rack, a moan of what sounded like panic escaped from behind the tape over his mouth.

I stepped out of the shadows behind him and moved into his line of vision, my body oiled and shining in the bright lights. I had stripped down to my underwear, carefully chosen to show off my superb body to its best advantage. When he saw me, his eyes opened even wider. He attempted to speak, but all that came out was a strained mumble.

"But you decided you couldn't allow yourself to want me, didn't you?" I said, my voice hard and accusing. "You betrayed my love. You didn't have the courage to choose a love that would have exalted us both. No, you ignored your real self and went for a stupid little bimbo, that trashy tart. Don't you realize? I'm the only one in the world who understands, really understands, what you need. I could have given you ecstasy, but you chose the safe, pathetic option.

*You didn't have the nerve for a marriage of true minds and bodies, did you?"*

*Drops of sweat were trickling down his temples, in spite of the coolness of the cellar. I moved forward and stroked his body, running my hand over his pale, muscular chest, fluttering my fingers over his groin. He flinched convulsively, his dark-blue eyes pleading. "How could you betray what I know is in your heart?" I hissed, digging my nails into the soft flesh above the wiry curls of his dark pubic hair. He tensed against me. I thrilled to the sensation. I took my hand away and admired the scarlet half-moons my nails had left in his skin. "You know you belong to me. You told me. You wanted me, we both know you did."*

*Another groan from behind the gag. Now the sweat had spread to his chest, droplets matting the thick dark hair that tapered down his abdomen into a thin line pointing to his cock lying curled and useless as a slug between his legs. Even though it was obvious that he didn't want me, the very sight of his vulnerable nakedness aroused me. He was beautiful. I could feel the blood flowing faster, feel my flesh expanding, ready to take him, ready to explode. I hated myself for that weakness, and I turned away before he could see the effect he was having.*

*"All I wanted was to love you," I said quietly. "I didn't want it to be like this." My hand strayed to the handle of the rack and caressed the smooth wood. I turned my head and gazed at Adam's beautiful face. Slowly, infinitely slowly, I started to turn the handle. His body, already taut, tightened against the pull of the straps. His effort was wasted. The gears on the winding mechanism multiplied my small exertion till it equalled the strength of several men. Adam was no match for my machine. I could see the muscles of his arms and legs bulge, his chest heaving as he struggled for breath.*

*"It's not too late," I said. "We could still be lovers. Would you like that?"*

*Desperately, he moved his head. There was no mistaking it, it was a nod. I smiled. "That's more like it," I said. "Now all you have to do is show me you mean it."*

*I ran one hand over his damp chest, then rubbed my face against the fine dark hairs. I could smell his fear, taste it in his sweat. I buried my head in his neck, sucking and biting, nibbling his ears. His body stayed rigid, but I felt no trace of an erection beneath me. Frustrated, I pulled away. I leaned over him and, in one swift agonizing movement, I yanked the tape away from his mouth.*

*"Aagh!" he yelled as the adhesive ripped his skin, rasping on the faint stubble. He licked dry lips. "Please, let me go," he whispered.*

*I shook my head. "I can't do that, Adam. Maybe if we were really lovers . . ."*

*"I won't tell anyone," he croaked. "I promise."*

*"You betrayed me once," I said sadly. "How can I trust you now?"*

*"I'm sorry," he said. "I didn't realize . . . I'm sorry." But there was no penitence in his eyes, only desperation and fear. I'd played this scene so many times in my head. Part of me exulted that I'd predicted the shape of it so well, that the dialogue was almost identical to the scenario I'd conjured up. Part of me felt an inexpressible sadness that he was exactly as weak and faithless as I'd feared. And yet another part of me was almost uncontrollably excited by what lay ahead, whether love or death, or both.*

*"It's too late for words," I said. "It's time for actions. You said you wanted us to be lovers, but that's not what your body's saying. Maybe you're scared. But there's no need to be. I'm a generous person, a loving person. You could find that out for yourself. I'm going to give you one last chance to atone for your betrayal. I'm going to leave you now for a while. When I come back, I expect you to be able to control your fear and show me how you really feel about me."*

*I let him go and walked over to the camcorder. I took out the tape that had been recording our encounter and replaced it with a fresh one. At the top of the stairs, I turned* back. "*Otherwise, I'll be forced to administer punishment for your treachery.*"

"*Wait!*" he howled desperately as I disappeared from sight. "*Come back,*" I heard as I dropped the trapdoor into place. I expect he carried on yelling. But I couldn't hear him. I went upstairs to Auntie Doris and Uncle Henry's bedroom. I slotted the video into the player I'd set up on the chest at the end of the bed, switched on the TV and climbed between the cold cotton sheets. Even if Adam didn't want me, I couldn't escape my desire for him. I watched him on his rack, my hand stroking me, touching myself with all the skill and ingenuity I wanted from him, imagining his beautiful cock swelling in my mouth. Every time I reached the point of orgasm, I stopped, gripping myself tight, forcing myself not to come, to save myself for what lay ahead. After I'd gone through the video for the fourth time, I decided he'd had long enough.

I slipped out of bed and went back downstairs. I looked at him spread-eagled on the rack. "*Please,*" he said. "*Let me go. I'll do anything you want, but let me go. I'm begging you.*"

I smiled and gently shook my head. "*I will take you back to Bradfield, Adam. But first, it's time to party.*"

# 6

*People begin to see that something more goes to the com-
position of a fine murder than two blockheads to kill and
be killed—a knife—a purse—and a dark lane. Design, gentlemen, grouping, light and shade, poetry, sentiment, are
now deemed to be indispensable to attempts of this nature.*

Work might not solve anything, but it was a great diver-
sionary tactic. Tony stared into the screen, scrolling down
through the tabulated information he'd gleaned from the
police reports. Satisfied that he'd incorporated everything
useful, he switched on the printer. While it chattered and
stuttered its way through the print-out, Tony opened another
file and started to sketch out the conclusions he had drawn
from the raw data. Anything, anything to keep her at bay.

He was so absorbed in his work he barely registered the
doorbell's first peal. When it rang out a second time, he
looked up, startled, at the clock. Five past eleven. If it was
Carol, she was earlier than he'd anticipated. They'd already
agreed that there was little point in beginning their trip before midnight. Tony got to his feet, uncertain. Since she
knew his phone number, it wouldn't be too hard for Angelica to discover his address too. He arrived at the front
door just as the bell rang for the third time. Wishing he'd
installed a peephole, Tony cautiously inched the door open.

Carol grinned. "You look like you're expecting Handy
Andy," she said. When Tony said nothing, she added,
"Sorry I'm a bit early. I did try ringing, but you were en-
gaged."

"Sorry," Tony mumbled. "I must have accidentally left
it off the hook from earlier. Come on in, it's no problem."
He found a smile from somewhere and led Carol into his

study. As he reached his desk, he slid the phone back on the hook.

Carol registered that the phone's engaged signal had been no accident. Deduction: he didn't want to be disturbed, not even by the answering machine. Probably, like her, he couldn't resist a ringing phone. She glanced at the sheets of paper sitting on the printer table. "You've obviously been busy," she said. "And there was me thinking you were taking your time answering the door because you'd gone for a quick zizz."

"Did you get some sleep?" Tony asked, noting that she looked more clear-eyed than she had done earlier.

"Four hours. Which is about ten too few. I've got a couple of bits of information for you, by the way." She filled him in succinctly on the results of her visit to Scargill Street, leaving out Cross's hostility.

Tony listened carefully, making a couple of notes on his pad. "Interesting," he said. "I don't think there's a lot of point in pulling in the sex offenders again, though. If Handy Andy's got form, it's more likely to be juvenile offences, petty burglary, minor violence, that sort of thing. Still, I've been wrong before."

"Haven't we all? By the way, I checked with the HOLMES room, and there's no one there who knows anything about statistical pattern analysis, so I've asked my brother to see what he can do for us. Should I just give him a set of the photographs, or is there some other way of presenting the raw data?"

"I suppose there's less chance of a mistake if he works directly from the photographs," Tony said. "Thanks for sorting that out for me."

"No sweat," Carol said. "Secretly, I think he's quite chuffed to be asked. He thinks I don't take him seriously. You know, he writes games software, I do the real thing."

"And do you?" Tony asked.

"What? Take him seriously? You bet I do. I respect anybody that understands something as far beyond my grasp

as computers. Besides, he earns about twice what I do. That
has to be serious."

"I don't know about that. Andrew Lloyd Webber probably earns more in a day than I do in a month, but I still
don't take him seriously." Toby stood up. "Carol, do you
mind if I abandon you for ten minutes? I need a quick
shower to wake me up."

"Fine, feel free. It's me that's early."

"Thanks. D'you want a brew while you're waiting?"

Carol shook her head. "I'll pass, thanks. It's cold out
there, and there aren't many places a woman can have a
pee in Temple Fields in the early hours."

Almost shyly, Tony picked up the sheaf of a print-out
and proffered it to Carol. "I've started the work on the
victims. Maybe you'd like to take a look while I'm gone?"

Eagerly, Carol took the paper. "I'd love to. I'm fascinated by this whole process."

"This is just very preliminary," Tony stressed, backing
towards the door. "I mean, I've not drawn any conclusions
yet. I'm working on that."

"Relax, Tony, I'm on your side," Carol said as he left
the room. She stared after him momentarily, wondering
what it was that had unsettled him. By the time they parted
in the afternoon, they had built up an easy camaraderie,
she'd thought. But now, he was edgy, abstracted. Was it
that he was tired, or was it that he was uncomfortable to
have her sitting in his home? "God, does it matter?" she
muttered to herself. "Concentrate, Jordan. Pick the man's
brains." She focused on the first sheet and studied the data.

|  | Adam S. | Paul G. | Gareth F. | Damien C. |
|---|---|---|---|---|
| Victim No. | 1 | 2 | 3 | 4 |
| Date of crime | 6/7.9.93 | 1/2.11.93 | 25/26.12.93 | 20/21.2.94 |
| Bradfield resident? | Yes | Yes | Yes | Yes |
| Sex | M | M | M | M |
| Ethnic origin | Caucasian | Caucasian | Caucasian | Caucasian |
| Nationality | British | British | British | British |

| Age | 28 | 31 | 30 | 27 |
|---|---|---|---|---|
| Star sign | Gemini | Cancer | Scorpio | Capricorn |
| Height | 5'10" | 5'11" | 5'11" | 6' |
| Weight | 147lb | 136lb | 151lb | 160lb |
| Built | Medium | Slim | Medium | Medium |
| Musculature | Good | Average | Average | Excellent |
| Hair length | Abv collar | Collar | Abv collar | Abv collar |
| Hair colour | Brown | Dark brown | Brown | Reddish brown |
| Hair type | Wavy | Straight | Straight | Curly |
| Tattoos | No | No | No | No |
| Clothing | None | None | None | None |
| Occupation | Civil servant | University lecturer | Solicitor | Police officer |
| Place of work | City centre | South of city centre | City centre | Southern suburbs |
| Car owned | Ford Escort | Citroën AX | Ford Escort | Classic Austin Healey |
| Hobbies | Working out, angling | Walking | Working out, theatre, cinema | Car restoration |
| Residence | Modern terraced town house; integral garage | Edwardian terraced house; no garage | Thirties semi; no garage | Modern detached estate house; attached garage |
| Relationship status | Divorced Lived alone NCP RP | Single Lived alone NCP NRP | Single Lived alone CP NRP | Single Lived alone NCP NRP |
| Personal items missing? | Wedding ring, watch | Watch | Signet ring, watch | Watch |
| Items missing from home? | Answering-machine tape | Answering-machine tape | None known | None known |
| Known sexual history | Hetero | Hetero | Hetero | Not known |
| Last seen by previous acquaintance | Tram home from work, 6 P.M. approx. | Leaving work, 5:30 P.M. approx. | Home, 7:15 P.M. | Home, 6 P.M. |
| Criminal record | None | None | None | None |
| Connection to scene of crime | None known | None known | None known | None known |
| Status of body-recovery site | Urban | Urban | Suburban/rural | Urban |

| | | | | |
|---|---|---|---|---|
| Site of first contact with killer | Unknown | Unknown | Unknown | Unknown |
| Site of death | Unknown | Unknown | Unknown | Unknown |
| Disposition of body | Semi-hidden to cause short delay before discovery | Semi-hidden to cause short delay before discovery | Hidden; note to police via newspaper required | Openly displayed but in area unattended until specific time |
| Body posed? | No | No | No | No |
| *Has the body been washed? | Yes | Yes | Yes | Yes |
| Cause of death | Throat cut | Throat cut | Throat cut | Throat cut |
| **Ligatures? | Wrists Ankles Adhesive gag | Wrists Ankles Adhesive gag | Wrists Ankles Adhesive gag | Wrists Ankles Adhesive gag |
| Bite marks | No | No | No | No |
| Putative bite marks (i.e., flesh removed) | Yes | Yes | Yes | Yes |
| Location of marks | Neck(2) Chest (1) | Neck (2) | Neck (3) Abdomen (4) | Neck (3) Chest (2) Groin (4) |
| Signs of torture or unusual assault? | Yes (see A) | Yes (see B) | Yes (see C) | Yes (see D) |

*BODY WASHING: No fragranced materials appear to have been used, suggesting that the offender is not using the washing process as a means of denial; rather, in line with the rest of his cautious behaviour, I suggest that this washing is intended to obliterate forensic clues, especially since the killer appears to have taken particular care with the fingernails. Scrapings on all four victims showed nothing except traces of unperfumed soap.

**LIGATURES: None were found on bodies, but postmortems reveal bruising consistent with handcuffs on wrists, slight traces of adhesive, missing hairs and bruising round ankles consonant both with parcel tape and with separate ligatures, and traces of adhesive on face around mouth. No traces of blindfolds.

A: *Adam Scott*. Dislocation of ankles, knees, hips, shoulders, elbows and several vertebrae. Consistent with being stretched on a rack. Tentative postmortem cuts to penis and testicles.

B: *Paul Gibbs*. Severe lacerations to rectum, virtual destruction of anal sphincter and partial disembowelment. Suggestive of spiked object repeatedly inserted via anus. Also some burnt tissue internally, suggesting the possibility of heat or electric shock. Face badly beaten before death; bruising, broken facial bones and teeth. Postmortem cuts to genitals, more pronounced than in A.

C: *Gareth Finnegan*. Irregular pierce wounds to hands and feet, ½" diameter approx. Lacerations to left cheek and nose, suggestive of glass or bottle being broken across face by right-handed assailant. Shoulders dislocated. ?Possible crucifixion? Postmortem wounds to genitals, virtually castrated.

D: *Damien Connolly*. Dislocations similar to A, but no major spinal trauma, ruling out the idea of a rack. Large number of small, star-shaped burns to torso. Penis severed postmortem and inserted in victim's mouth.

Query: Were Damien Connolly's handcuffs still in his home or police locker?

Query: Why are the bodies always dumped Monday night/Tuesday morning? What happens on Monday that allows him to be free? Does he work nights and have Monday off? Is he perhaps a married man who has Monday free because his wife does things with friends, e.g., girls' night out? Or is it that Monday isn't a traditional "going out" night and he can be more sure of finding his victims at home?

Carol was aware that Tony had returned, but she carried on reading, simply raising one hand and waving her fingers to indicate she knew he was there. When she reached the end of the report, she took a deep breath and said, "Well, Dr. Hill, you *have* been busy."

Tony smiled and shrugged himself away from the doorjamb he'd been leaning against. "I can't believe there's anything in there that you didn't already have filed neatly away in your head."

"No, but seeing it laid out like that somehow makes it clearer."

Tony nodded. "He has a very specific type."

"Do you want to talk about it now?"

Tony looked down at the floor. "I'd rather leave most of it for now. I need to let it sink in, and I need to go through all the rest of the witness statements before I can think about a profile."

Carol couldn't help feeling disappointed. "I understand," was all she said.

Tony smiled. "Were you expecting more?"

"Not really."

His smile broadened. "Not even a smidgen?"

The smile was infectious. Carol grinned back. "Hoping, maybe. Expecting, no. By the way, there was one thing I didn't understand. NCP? CP? NRP? I mean, we're not talking National Car Parks and the Communist Party here, are we?"

"No current partner. Current partner. No recent partner. Acronymitis. It's the disease that afflicts all of us in the soft sciences like psychology, sociology. We have to mystify the uninitiated. Sorry about that. I try to keep things as jargon-free as possible."

"So you don't confuse us thick plods, eh?" Carol teased.

"It's more about self-preservation. The last thing I want is to give the sceptics another big stick to hit me with. It's hard enough getting people to accept that my reports are even worth reading without alienating them with all that unnecessary pseudo-scientific mumbo jumbo."

"I believe you," Carol said ironically. "Shall we go?"

"Sure. There is one thing I would like to bounce off you now," Tony said, suddenly serious again. "The victims. Everybody's assuming this killer is targeting gay men. Now, there are hundreds, probably thousands of openly gay men in Bradfield. We've got the biggest gay scene in the country outside London. Yet every one of those victims has no known history of homosexuality. What does that say to you?"

"He's in the closet himself and he only goes for men who are closeted too?" Carol hazarded.

"Maybe. But if they're all busily passing as straight, how does he meet them?"

Carol straightened the edges of the papers to give herself a moment. "Contact magazines? Small ads? Multi-user phone chatlines? The Internet?"

"OK, all possibilities. But there was no evidence of any of those interests, according to the reports of the officers who searched their houses. Not in one single case."

"So what are you trying to say here?"

"I don't think Handy Andy gets turned on by gay men. I think he likes them straight."

Sergeant Don Merrick decided he'd never felt more fed up. As if it wasn't bad enough that he had Popeye on his back over the guv'nor's new assignment, he was now a servant of three masters. He was supposed to make sure that Inspector Jordan's orders were carried out when she wasn't around, and he was also supposed to be working for Kevin Matthews on the Damien Connolly case as well as liaising with Bob Stansfield on the work that he and Inspector Jordan had already completed on the Paul Gibbs case. To top it all, he was spending his evening in the Hell Hole.

Never, in his opinion, was a club more aptly named. The Hell Hole advertised itself in the gay press as "The club that dominates Bradfield. One visit and you'll be enslaved. You're *bound* to have the time of your life in the Hell

Hole!" All of which was a coy way of saying that the Hell Hole was the place to go to pick up partners if sado-masochism and bondage was how you got your rocks off.

Merrick felt like Snow White at an orgy. He didn't have a clue how he was supposed to behave. He wasn't even sure if he looked right. He'd opted for an old, ripped pair of Levis that normally only saw the light of day when he was doing odd jobs around the house, a plain white T-shirt and the battered leather jacket he used to wear on his motorbike in the days before the kids came along. In his back pocket were his official handcuffs, there in the hope they'd lend some verisimilitude to his pose. Looking round the dimly lit bar, Merrick spotted so much distressed denim and leather that he expected to see an SOS flare rising above the dance floor. Superficially, at least, he thought he might just look the part. Which was worrying in itself. As his eyes grew accustomed to the low lighting, he caught sight of a few of his colleagues. Mostly, they looked as uncomfortable as he felt.

The club had been virtually empty when he'd first arrived just after nine. Feeling incredibly conspicuous, Merrick had asked for a pass-out and gone back on to the streets. He'd wandered round Temple Fields for the best part of an hour, stopping in a café-bar for a cappuccino. He'd wondered why some of the gay clientele had been giving him strange looks until he realized that he was the only customer wearing leather and denim. Clearly he'd transgressed some unwritten dress code. Uncomfortable, Merrick had swallowed the scalding coffee as quickly as he could and got back out on to the streets.

He felt seriously vulnerable, alone on the pavements and walkways of Temple Fields. The men who passed him, either singly, in couples or in groups, all eyed him up and down speculatively as he passed, most glances pausing at his crotch. He squirmed inside, wishing he'd picked a pair of jeans that didn't hug his body quite so tightly. As a couple of black youths walked past, arms entwined, he heard one say loudly to the other, "Great ass for a white guy, huh?" Merrick felt the blood rise to his cheeks, unsure whether it was anger or embarrassment. In a moment of dreadful clarity, he realized what women meant when they complained of being treated as objects by men.

He returned to the Hell Hole, relieved that the place had filled up now. Loud disco music throbbed, the beat so strong Merrick seemed to feel it inside his chest. On the dance floor, men in leather adorned with chains, zips and peaked caps moved energetically, showing off their Nautilus-hardened muscles, thrusting their groins into empty air in bizarre parodies of sex. Stifling a sigh, Merrick pushed his way through the crowd to the bar. He ordered a bottle of American beer that tasted unbelievably insipid to a palate trained to expect the nutty sweetness of Newcastle Brown.

Turning round to face the dance floor again, Merrick leaned against the bar and surveyed the room, desperately trying to avoid eye contact with anyone in particular. He'd been standing like that for about ten minutes when he became aware that the man standing next to him wasn't actually trying to be served. Merrick glanced round to discover the man's eyes fixed on him. He was almost as tall as the detective, but with a broader, more muscular build. He wore tight black leather trousers and a white vest. His blond hair was cut short at the sides, longer on top, and his body was as tanned and smooth as a Chippendale. He raised his eyebrows and said, "Hi. I'm Ian."

Merrick grinned weakly. "Don," he replied, raising his voice to combat the music.

"I've not seen you in here before, Don," Ian said, moving closer so that his naked arm pressed against the worn leather of Merrick's sleeve.

"It's my first time," Merrick said.

"You new in town, then? You don't sound local."

"I'm from the North East," Merrick said carefully.

"That explains it. A bonny laddie from Geordieland," Ian said, with a bad imitation of Merrick's accent.

Merrick felt his smile grow sick and die. "You a regular here, then?" he asked.

"Never miss it. Best bar in town for the kind of guy I like." Ian winked. "Can I buy you a drink, Don?"

The sweat trickling down Merrick's back had nothing to do with the warmth of the bar. "I'll have another one of these," he said.

Ian nodded and turned round to the bar, using the crowd around him as an excuse to thrust himself against Merrick. Merrick stared across the room, his jaw set. He noticed one of the other murder squad detectives watching him. His colleague gave a grotesque wink and mimed one finger pumping into the closed fist of his other hand. Merrick turned away, coming face to face with Ian, who had been served. "There you go, bonny laddie," Ian said. "So, you looking for a bit of fun tonight, Geordie?"

"Just checking out the scene," Merrick said.

"What's the scene like up in Newcastle, then?" Ian asked. "Bit lively? Cater for all tastes, does it?"

Merrick shrugged. "I don't know. I'm not from Newcastle. I come from a little village up on the coast. It's not the kind of place where you can be yourself."

"I get you," Ian said, laying a hand on Merrick's arm. "Well, Don, if you want to be yourself, you've come to the right place. And you've found the right guy."

Merrick prayed he didn't look as terrified as he felt. "It's certainly busy enough," he tried.

"We could go somewhere quieter, if you like. There's another room through the back there, where the music isn't so loud."

"No, I'm fine here," Merrick said quickly. "I like the music, if I'm honest."

Ian moved forward so his torso leaned against Merrick's. "What is it you're into, Don? Top or bottom?"

Merrick choked on his beer. "I'm sorry?" he gasped.

Ian laughed and rumpled Merrick's hair. His light-blue eyes glinted wickedly, holding Merrick's stare. "You really are an innocent abroad, aren't you? What I'm saying is, what do you like best? Handing it out or taking it?" His hand strayed down to Merrick's trousers. Just when the detective thought he was going to be groped in a way that no one apart from his wife had ever done, Ian's hand slid to one side and moved round to stroke Merrick's buttock.

"That depends," Merrick croaked.

"On what?" Ian asked suggestively, moving so close that Merrick could feel the other man's erection against his leg.

"On how much I trust the person I'm with," Merrick replied, trying not to let his revulsion show in voice or expression.

"Oh, I'm very trustworthy, me. And you look like the reliable kind too."

"Are yez not a bit worried, like, about strangers? With this serial killer doing the rounds?" Merrick asked, using the opportunity of putting his empty bottle back on the bar to move away slightly from Ian's insistent body.

Ian's smile was cocky. "Why should I be? These guys that are getting topped don't hang out in places like this. Stands to reason that this isn't where this mad bastard's picking them up."

"How do you know that?"

"I've seen the pictures in the papers, and I've never spotted a single one of them out on the scene. And believe me, I know the scene. That's how I knew you were the new kid in town." Ian moved closer again and thrust a hand in Merrick's back pocket. He ran his fingers over the hard outline of the handcuffs. "Hey, that feels interesting. I'm starting to get a picture of what you and me could be like."

Merrick forced a laugh. "For all you know, I could be the killer."

"So what if you are?" Ian said, all self-assurance. "I'm not the type this fucking nutter goes for. He likes closet queens, not macho men. If he picked me up, he'd want to fuck, not commit murder. Besides, a good-looking guy like you doesn't need to kill somebody to get a fuck."

"Yeah, well, maybe so, but how do I know you're not the killer?"

"Tell you what, just to prove I'm not, I'll let you top tonight. You'll be in charge. I'll be the one with handcuffs on."

Carry on like this and you won't be wrong, Merrick thought to himself. He reached down and gripped Ian's wrist hard, removing his hand from the pocket. "I don't think so," he said. "Not tonight. Like you said, I'm the new kid in town. I'm not going home with anybody till I know a bit more about them." He released Ian's wrist and stepped back. "Nice talking to you, Ian. Thanks for the drink."

Ian's face altered in an instant. His eyes narrowed and the smile changed to a snarl. "Wait a minute, Geordie. I don't know what sort of poxy Watch With Mother clubs you're used to, but in this city, you don't get into a clinch with somebody and take drinks off him if you're not prepared to come across."

Merrick tried to get away, but the press of bodies round the bar made any movement difficult. "I'm sorry if there's been a misunderstanding," he said.

Ian's arm shot out and gripped Merrick firmly just below his bicep. The pain was excruciating. Merrick found a moment to wonder what sort of person actively sought out pain like this as part of their sexual pleasure. Ian thrust his face so close that Merrick could smell the bad breath he'd learned to associate with amphetamine abuse. "It's not a misunderstanding," Ian said. "You came here tonight for sex. There's no other reason to be here. So sex is what we're going to do."

Merrick swivelled on the balls of his feet and jabbed his elbow sharply underneath Ian's ribcage. His breath burst out of him in a sudden "whoosh," and he doubled over, letting go of Merrick's arm in the reflex of clutching at his solar plexus. "No, we're not," Merrick said mildly, moving away through the space that had cleared around him as if by magic.

On his way across the room, one of the other undercover officers fell into step beside him. "Nice one, Sarge," he said out of the corner of his mouth. "You did what we've all been wanting to do ever since we got in here."

Merrick stopped and smiled at the constable. "You're supposed to be doing an undercover. Either fucking dance with me or fuck off and let one of these poofters chat you up."

Leaving the constable open mouthed, Merrick walked over to the far side of the dance floor and leaned against the wall. The commotion he'd left at the bar had died down. Ian pushed his way through the crowd, still holding his stomach, and left the club, shooting venomous glares at Merrick.

Before long, Merrick had company again. This time, he recognized his companion as a detective constable from one of the other divisions who had only joined the murder squad that day. He was sweating under the weight of heavy leather jacket and trousers that looked suspiciously like standard police motorcycle issue. He leaned close to Merrick, so he wouldn't be overheard in the crowd round the dance floor and said urgently, "Skip, there's a guy I think we should take a look at."

"Why?"

"I overheard him mouthing off to a couple of blokes that he knew the dead guys. He was boasting about it. Reckoned there weren't many that could say that. And I heard him say that the killer must be a body-builder like him, on account of lugging bodies around. He was saying he bet there were people here tonight who didn't know they knew a murderer. Boasting, like, all the way."

"Why don't you bring him in yourself?" Merrick asked, his interest quickened by what he'd heard, but reluctant to deprive the constable of the credit of pulling in a suspect.

"I tried to strike up conversation with him, but he gave me the brush-off." The constable gave a wry smile. "Maybe I'm not his type, skip."

"And what makes you think I am?" Merrick demanded, not sure whether he was being subtly insulted here.

"He's wearing the same kind of gear as you."

Merrick sighed. "You better point him out to me."

"Don't look now, sir, but he's standing over by the disco speakers. IC1 male, five foot six, short dark hair, blue eyes, clean shaven, heavy Scottish accent. Dressed like you. Drinking a pint of lager."

Merrick leaned back against the wall and slowly scanned the room. He got the suspect on the first pass. "Got him, I think," he said. "OK, son, thanks. Look fucked off when I go."

He shrugged away from the wall and left the constable practising his depressed look. Slowly, Merrick moved round the room until he found himself next to the man who'd been pointed out to him. He had the bulky build of a weightlifter and the face of a boxer. His outfit was almost identical to Merrick's, save that his jacket had more buckles and zips. "Busy in here tonight," Merrick said.

"Aye. Lots of new faces. Half of them probably polis," the man said. "See that jerk you were just talking to? He might as well have come in his Panda car. Did you ever see a more obvious busy in all your born days?"

"That's why I fucked him off sharpish," Merrick replied.

"I'm Stevie, by the way," the man said. "Busy night you're having with the unwanted solicitations. I saw you sort that toerag out earlier. Nicely done, pal."

"Thanks. I'm Don."

"Nice to meet you, Don. You new about here, then? Accent like that, you're obviously not a local."

"Does everybody know everybody else here?" Merrick asked with a wry smile.

"Pretty much. It's a real village, Temple Fields. 'Specially the S&M scene. Let's face it, if you're gonnae let somebody tie you up, you want to know what you're getting into."

"You're not wrong, Stevie," Merrick said with feeling. "Even more so when there's a killer on the loose."

"My point exactly. I mean, I don't suppose these guys that got themselves killed thought they were up for anything more than a bit of rough. I knew them, you know. Adam Scott, Paul Gibbs, Gareth Finnegan and Damien

Connolly. Every last one of them, and let me tell you, I wouldn't have had them pegged for that sort of scene. Just shows you, doesn't it? You can never tell what goes on in people's heads."

"How come you knew them, then? I thought the paper said they weren't known on the scene," Merrick said.

"I run a gym," Stevie said proudly. "Adam and Gareth, they were members. We used to go out for a drink now and again. That Paul Gibbs, I knew him through a mate of mine, used to have a pint with him and all. And that copper, Connolly, he came round the gym after we had a burglary."

"I bet there's not many around here that can say they knew all the poor sods," Merrick said.

"You're right there, pal. Mind you, I don't suppose the killer had anything more in mind than a wee bit of fun."

Merrick's eyebrows rose. "You think it's fun to murder folk?"

Stevie shook his head. "Naw, you're no' following me. See, I don't think he sets out to kill these guys. Naw, it's kind of an accident, if you get my meaning. They're playing their games, and your man just gets carried away, and it all gets out of hand. He's obviously strong, he carts these bodies about and dumps them in the middle of the city, for God's sake. He's not going to be a seven-stone weakling, now is he? If he's a real body-builder like me, he maybe doesn't know his own strength. Could happen to anybody," he added after a moment's pause.

"Four times?" Merrick demanded incredulously.

Stevie shrugged. "Maybe they asked for it. Know what I mean? Prick teases and that? Promising what they didnae want to deliver when push came to shove? I've been there, Don, and let me tell you, there've been times when I've wanted to strangle the wee bastards."

The detective in Merrick was straining at the leash. Carol Jordan wasn't the only Bradfield copper who'd been reading up on the psychology of the serial killer. Merrick had read cases where killers got off on this kind of justification, swaggering in front of a third party. The Yorkshire

Ripper, he knew, had boasted to his male cronies about "doing" prostitutes. He wanted Stevie in an interview room. The only problem was how to get him there.

Merrick cleared his throat. "I suppose the only way to avoid that is to get to know the people you go to bed with before you get there."

"My point exactly. You fancy getting out of here? Maybe going for a cup of coffee down the diner? Getting to know each other a wee bit better?"

Merrick nodded. "Sure," he said, dumping the remains of his beer on a nearby table. "Let's go." Soon as they got outside, he could switch his radio to "transmit only" and one of the back-up teams would pick them up. Then they could test Stevie's bravado in Scargill Street.

Although it was after midnight, the street outside the Hell Hole was far from deserted. "This way," Stevie said, pointing to his left. Merrick slid his hand into his jacket and adjusted the radio switch.

"Where is it we're going?" he asked.

"There's an all-night diner in Crompton Gardens."

"Great. I could murder a bacon butty," Merrick said.

"Very bad for your health, all that grease," Stevie said seriously.

As they rounded the corner into the alley leading into the square, Merrick sensed someone stepping out of a darkened doorway behind him. He started to turn towards the sound of footsteps.

Just like Bonfire Night, was his last conscious thought as a starburst of light erupted behind his eyes.

*It didn't last as long as I'd expected. Surprisingly, Adam proved more fragile than the German shepherd. Once he'd lapsed into unconsciousness following the dislocation of his limbs, he proved impossible to rouse. I waited for hours, but nothing seemed to bring him round; not pain, not cold water, not warmth. I was disappointed, I admit it. His pain had been a mere shadow of mine, his punishment not enough for the betrayal that occasioned it.*

*I finished what I had to do, neatly and swiftly, just after midnight. Then I took him off the rack and folded him into a heavy-duty garden rubbish sack. I put that inside a black Bradfield Metropolitan Council bin bag. It was a struggle to get the dead weight back up the cellar steps and into the wheelbarrow, but my hours pumping iron paid off.*

*I couldn't wait to get home to my computer, to transform the evening into something transcendent. But I still had work to do before I could relax and indulge myself. I drove into the city centre just above the legal speed limit—not so fast I'd get pulled for speeding, and not so slow that I'd be stopped on suspicion of being a careful drunk driver. I made for the gay cruising area behind the university. Temple Fields used to be a student area, filled with small cafés, restaurants, shops and bars with low prices and standards. Then, about ten years ago, a couple of the bars became gay. Our left-wing city council responded to pressure and funded a gay and lesbian centre, which moved into the* basement of an Indian restaurant. That seemed to trigger a domino effect, and within a year or two, Temple Fields had become Cruising City and the straight students had moved over to Greenholm on the far side of campus. Now, Temple Fields was home to gay bars, clubs, chichi bistros, shops selling leather and bondage gear, and a nightly rent rack right along the canal.

By half past one on a Tuesday morning, there were still quite a few men out on the streets. I drove around a couple of times, concentrating on the area round Crompton Gardens. The square was dark; most of the streetlights had been vandalized for reasons of sexual privacy, and the council was too strapped for cash to repair them. Besides, none of the local businesses was complaining; the darker the square, the more desirable the area, the bigger their profits.

I looked around cautiously. Nothing stirred. I wrestled the bag to the lip of the boot, then half rolled, half carried it on to the low wall. I tipped it over the edge with a rustling thud and closed the tailgate as quietly as I could. I took a penknife out of my pocket, leaned over the wall and slit the bags open. I pulled them free of the body and crumpled them into a ball.

Just after two, I parked Adam's car a couple of streets away from his house then walked back to my jeep, stuffing the bags in a litter bin on the way. I was in bed by three. In spite of my burning desire to carry on with my work, I was overwhelmed with exhaustion. Not surprising, considering the effort I'd expended. I was asleep as soon as I switched off the light.

When I woke, I rolled over and looked at the clock. Then I checked with my watch. I had to accept its corroboration. I'd been asleep for thirteen and a half hours. I don't think I've ever slept for that length of time, not even after general anaesthetic. I was furious with myself. I'd been looking forward to sitting down at my computer to relive and rebuild my encounter with Adam till it more closely resembled

*my deepest fantasies. But now I barely had enough time to
shower and eat.*

*On my way into work, I picked up a late city final edition
of the* Bradfield Evening Sentinel Times. *I'd made page
two of the paper:*

## NAKED BODY FOUND

*The mutilated body of a naked man was found in
Bradfield's gay village early this morning.*

*Council worker Robbie Greaves made the grisly
discovery as he made a routine rubbish collection in
the Crompton Gardens area of Temple Fields.*

*Now the city's gay community fears this may be
the first act of a gay serial killer like the man who
recently terrorized London's homosexuals.*

*The body was found among shrubs behind a wall
in the park, a notorious night-time meeting place for
gay men looking for casual sex.*

*The man, said to be in his late twenties, has not
yet been identified. Police describe him as white, 5ft
10ins, muscular build, with short dark wavy hair and
blue eyes. He has no distinguishing marks or tattoos.*

*A police spokesman said, "The man's throat had
been cut and his body mutilated. Whoever committed
this callous crime is a violent and dangerous man.
The nature of the victim's injuries mean the killer
must have been covered in blood.*

*"We believe the man was killed elsewhere and the
body dumped in the park sometime during the night.*

*"We would urge anyone who was in the Crompton
Gardens area of Temple Fields last night to come
forward for the purposes of elimination. All
information will be treated in the strictest
confidence."*

*Robbie Greaves, 28, the council worker who
discovered the body, said, "I'd only just started work.*

*It was just after half past eight. I was using my grab to pick up litter. When it touched the body, I thought at first it was a dead cat or dog. Then I lifted up the bushes and saw the body.*

*"It was horrible. I threw up, then I ran to the nearest phone box. I've never seen anything like it in my life and I hope I never do again."*

Well, at least they'd got one thing correct. The body was killed somewhere else and dumped in Crompton Gardens. As for the rest of it . . . If this was any indication of the police's skills, I didn't think I'd have too much to worry about. That was fine by me. The last thing I wanted was to be arrested, since I'd already chosen Adam's successor. Paul, I knew, was going to be different. This time, it wouldn't have to end in death.

# 7

*All his acquaintances afterwards described his dissimulation as so ready and so perfect, that if, in making his way through the streets . . . he had accidentally jostled any person, he would . . . have stopped to offer the most gentlemanly apologies: with his devilish heart brooding over the most hellish of purposes, he would yet have paused to express a benign hope that the huge mallet, buttoned up under his elegant surtout, with a view to the little business that awaited him about ninety minutes further on, had not inflicted any pain on the stranger with whom he had come into collision.*

Carol turned off the main drag and cut through the back doubles to emerge in Crompton Gardens. "Adam Scott was found just there," she said, pointing to a spot halfway down one side of the shrubbery.

Tony nodded. "Can you drive slowly round the square, then park up against the wall where the body was found, please?"

Carol did as he asked. As they cruised round the square, Tony gazed out intently, swinging round in his seat a couple of times to snatch a second look. When the car stopped, he got out. Without waiting for Carol, he crossed to the pavement and prowled round the edge of the square. Carol got out of the car and followed in his wake, trying to see what Tony saw.

Neither the murders nor the freezing weather had changed the habits of those who frequented Temple Fields. Doorways and basement areas still held grunting couples, heterosexual and homosexual alike. A few froze momentarily at the sound of Carol's heels on the pavement, but most ignored it. A great place to hang out if you were into voyeurism, Carol thought cynically.

Tony reached the end of the houses and crossed the street to the shop and bar fronts. Here, there were no copulating couples. The city's crime rate dictated heavy shutters and grilles for windows and doors. Ignoring them, Tony looked over towards the gardens in the centre of the square, matching what he'd seen on the photographs with the reality. There were no bushes on this side, only the low wall. He barely noticed two men walking past, wrapped round each other like competitors in a three-legged race. He wasn't interested in anyone else but Handy Andy.

"You've been here," he said to himself. "This isn't a place you just happened on, is it? You've walked this pavement, watched these parodies of love and affection that people pay for. But that's not what you were after, was it? You wanted something different, something a lot more intimate, something you didn't have to pay for." How had they felt, those voyeuristic adventures of Handy Andy? Tony concentrated.

"You've never had a normal relationship with another person," he thought. "The prostitutes don't bother you, though. Or the rent boys. You're not killing them. You're not interested in what you can do with them. It's the couples that get to you, isn't it? I know, you see, I know that for myself. Am I projecting? I don't think so. I think you're looking for coupledom, the perfect relationship, the one where you can be yourself, the one that will value you as highly as you think you should be valued. And then it will be all right. The past won't matter. But it does matter, Andy. The past is what matters most of all."

He was suddenly aware of Carol standing by his side, looking at him curiously. Probably his lips were moving. He'd better be careful, or she'd be consigning him to the bin marked "nutter" too. He couldn't afford that, not if he was to keep her on his side long enough to achieve the result he needed.

The last building on that side was an all-night diner, its

windows opaque with condensation. In the bright light inside, shapes moved like creatures of the deep. Tony moved forward and pushed open the door. A handful of customers glanced up at him before returning to their fry-ups and chat-ups. Tony stepped back on to the street and let the door sigh shut behind him. "I don't think you go in there," he decided. "I don't think you want to be seen to be alone in a place that's meant for companionship."

The third side of the square consisted of a couple of modern office blocks. In the doorways, a clutch of homeless teenagers slept, bundled in clothes, newspapers and cardboard boxes. By now, Carol had caught up with him. "Have they been interviewed?" Tony asked.

Carol pulled a face. "We tried. My dad used to do a bit of folk singing. When I was a kid, he used to sing me a song with the chorus, 'Oh, but I may as well try and catch the wind.' Now I know what it means."

"That good, eh?"

They crossed to the houses on the fourth side of the square, passing a pair of hookers on the corner. "Hey, gorgeous!" one of them shouted. "I could give you a better time than that tight-arsed bitch."

Carol snorted with laughter. "Now there's a triumph of hope over experience," she said wryly.

Tony said nothing. The words had barely penetrated his reverie. He continued slowly down the pavement, pausing every few steps to drink in the atmosphere. Conflicting music filtered out faintly into the night from the flats and bedsits. The smell of curry wafted on the breeze that rustled the litter and sent polystyrene fast-food trays tumbling along the gutters. The square was never entirely empty, he noted. "You despise their messy lives, don't you?" he said to himself. "You like things clean and neat and orderly. That's partly why you wash the bodies. That's at least as important to you as erasing the forensic traces." He turned the final corner and walked across to the rear of Carol's car, feeling the first stirrings of confidence that he was capable of mapping this complex and fatally skewed mind.

"He probably had to sit here for a few minutes to make sure he wasn't being watched," Tony said. "Depending on what kind of vehicle he's using, it could have taken as little as a minute to get the body out and over the wall. But he'd want to be sure no one was watching."

"We did a full door-to-door across the street, but nobody admitted to seeing anything out of the ordinary," Carol replied.

"Let's face it, Carol, when you look at what's ordinary round here, it leaves plenty of scope for a serial killer. OK, I've seen enough. Shall we go?"


Cross bounded into the squad room, surprisingly light on his feet as fat people often are, as if somehow moving lightly negates the bulk of their body. "All right, then, where is the scumbag?" he bellowed. Then he caught sight of the thin figure leaning against the wall, his conversation with Kevin Matthews interrupted by Cross's entrance.

"Sir?" Cross said, stopping in his tracks. "I wasn't expecting you in." He threw a look of pure venom at Kevin Matthews.

Brandon straightened up. "No, Superintendent, I don't suppose you were." He took a couple of steps towards Cross. "I left instructions with the control room that if any arrests were made in connection with the serial killings I was to be informed at once. This is going to be a high-profile case when it comes to court, Tom. I want us to be seen to be squeaky clean."

"Yes, sir," Cross said mutinously. However Brandon dressed it up, what he was saying was that he didn't believe Cross was the man to make sure that over-zealous detectives didn't go too far. With Brandon pacing the corridors, no serial-killer suspects were going to have unfortunate accidents in custody. Cross turned to Kevin Matthews. "What exactly happened?"

Kevin, so pale with tiredness and stress that his freckles stood out on milk-white skin like some vicious pox, said,

"As far as we can make out, Don Merrick came out of the Hell Hole with some bloke. One of the back-up teams saw them. Don switched his radio on to transmit, so we're assuming he wanted this bloke picked up for questioning. They were heading for the all-night diner in Crompton Gardens, according to the back-up boys. There's an alley that's a short cut through to the gardens, and they went down there. Next thing the back-up hear is a scuffle going on. They leg it round there and find Don on the floor and two blokes slugging it out. They arrested the pair of them and they're kicking their heels in the cells."

"What about Merrick?" Cross demanded. For all his faults, Cross was a copper's copper. His men were almost as important to him as his own career.

"He's down Casualty getting stitches in a sore head. He came round in the ambulance. I've got one of my lads down there with him taking a statement." Kevin glanced at his watch. "He should be back any time now."

"So what are we looking at here?" Cross demanded. "Have we got a suspect, or what?"

Brandon cleared his throat. "I think we can assume that Merrick thought the man he was with was worth a chat. As for the man who attacked them, I suspect we'll need to wait for Merrick's statement. I suggest Inspector Matthews and one of his team talk to the attacker while you and I have a preliminary chat with Merrick's target. That OK with you, Tom?"

Cross nodded, disgruntled. "Yes, sir. And as soon as your lad gets back from Casualty, Kevin, I want to see him." He moved towards the door, looking over his shoulder expectantly at Brandon.

Brandon said, "Before we go, Tom, I think we need Inspector Jordan and Dr. Hill in here."

"With respect, sir, it's the middle of the night. Do we really need to bugger up the man's sleep?"

"I don't want to get into questioning anyone about the murders until I've had the chance to take Dr. Hill's advice about how the interview should proceed. Besides, the two of them are probably still out working. DI Jordan was planning to show Dr. Hill the crime scenes tonight. Can you fix that, Inspector?"

Kevin glanced at Cross, who nodded slightly. "No problem, sir. I'll page Inspector Jordan right away. I'm sure she'll be delighted to lend a hand."

Brandon smiled and walked past Cross into the corridor. "Just shows what happens to your bottle when you get behind a desk," Cross muttered, shaking his head in mock-sorrow. "You get so's you need a bloody psychologist to tell you how to interview some scumbag off the streets."

Canal Street was still busy. People came in and out of clubs, taxis dropped off and picked up, couples shared their kebabs and chips on street corners, rent boys and hookers watched the slow-moving traffic, pouncing on the least opportunity. "Interesting, isn't it, how areas become defined?" Tony said to Carol as they walked briskly along the street.

"You mean this is the zone for public encounters, while Crompton Gardens is for the dark side?"

"And ne'er the twain shall cross over," Tony said. "It's really quite lively for the time of night, isn't it? Are Monday nights quieter?"

"A bit," Carol said. "A couple of the clubs shut on Mondays. And one of the others has a women-only night."

"So there's probably not as much street traffic," Tony mused. As they'd driven round the streets, speculating on Handy Andy's approach route, Tony had been struck by how very public an area he'd chosen for his first two victims. Almost as if he were setting himself challenges. Now, at the corner of the alley leading to the side door of Shadowlands, he looked along the street and mused. "He's desperate to be the best," he said softly.

"Sorry?"

"Handy Andy. He just doesn't go for the easy options. His victims are all in the high-risk category. His dumping grounds aren't obscure, deserted hiding places. The bodies are cleaned of forensic clues. He's smarter than us, he thinks, and he has to keep proving it to himself. I'd hazard a guess that the next body's going to be dumped somewhere very, very public."

Carol felt a shiver run through her that was nothing to do with the cold. "Don't talk about the next body as if we're not going to find him before then," she pleaded. "It's just too depressing to think about."

Carol led the way into the short dark cul-de-sac. "Now, the second body, Paul Gibbs, was found just down here. All there is down here is the fire exit for the Shadowlands club."

"It's dark enough," Tony complained, stumbling over the edge of a disintegrating cardboard carton.

"We did suggest to the manager that a security light would be a good idea, if only to prevent him being mugged when he's locking up at night, but you can see how seriously he's taken the idea," Carol replied, raking through her handbag to find her mini-torch. She snapped it on and the narrow beam revealed Tony silhouetted against a hooker in a red rubber dress giving a blow-job to a bleary-eyed businessman in the fire-exit doorway.

"Hoy!" the outraged man shouted. "Bugger off, Peeping Tom!"

Carol sighed. "Police. Zip your dick or you're nicked." Before she'd even finished the sentence, the hooker was on her feet and heading for the mouth of the alley as fast as her stilettoes would let her. Realizing it wasn't worth arguing now the whore had gone, the man quickly fastened his trousers and pushed past Tony. As he turned the corner, he shouted, "Frigid cunt!" back at her.

"You all right?" Tony asked, his genuine concern obvious.

Carol shrugged. "When I started in the job, it really shook me when punters abused me like that. Then I realized it was them that had the problem, not me."

"The theory's sound. How does it work in practice?"

Carol pulled a face. "Some nights I go home and stand

in the shower for twenty minutes and I still don't feel clean."

"I know exactly what you mean. Some of the messy heads I have to poke about inside leave me feeling like I'll never have a normal relationship with another human being again." Tony turned away, not wanting his face to betray him. "So this is where you found Paul?"

Carol moved forward to stand beside him. She shone her torch into the doorway. "He was lying there, with a couple of bin bags tucked around him so he wasn't immediately obvious. Judging by the condoms lying around, the working girls had been screwing the night away smack bang next to a corpse."

"I take it you've talked to the girls?"

"Yes, we've had them all in. The one that scuttled out of here like a cockroach when the light goes on uses this spot most nights. She says she had a punter some time around four in the morning. She knows it was then because this bloke is a regular who comes off his shift at the newspaper-printing plant about then. Anyway, she was going to bring him down here, but there was a car in the way." Carol sighed. "We thought we'd cracked it, because she could remember the make, model and the numbers on the licence plate, because it was the same as the number of her house. Two-four-nine."

"Don't tell me. Let me guess. It was Paul Gibbs's car."

"Got it in one."

The insistent bleep of Carol's pager cut into the conversation, demanding as a baby's cry. "I have to find a phone," Carol said.

"What is it?"

"One thing you can always say for sure," Carol said, hurrying back out of the alley. "It's never good news."

"Look, I've told youse all I know. I'd just met this guy Don in the Hole, we was going for a cup of tea and suddenly there's footsteps and Don hits the ground like Vinny Jones just tackled him and I turn round and there's this bampot with a brick. So I give him the citizen's arrest with the left hook, and that's when your boys turn up mob-handed, and here I am." Stevie McConnell spread his hands out in front of him. "Youse should be giving me a commendation, no' the third degree."

"And you expect us to believe this . . ." Cross consulted his notes. "This Ian attacked this Don just because he'd turned him down earlier in the evening?"

"That's about the size of it. Look, this Ian, he's known about the town. He's a heidbanger. He gets out of his brain on speed and thinks he's God Almighty. This Don gave him a right showing up, you know, made him look like a big jessie instead of macho man, so your man was for getting his own back. Look, you gonnae let me go, or what?"

Cross was spared from replying by a knock on the door. Brandon shrugged away from the wall he'd been leaning against and opened the door. He exchanged a few murmured words with the constable outside then came back in. "Interview suspended at 1:47 A.M.," he said, leaning past Cross to turn off the tape recorder. "We'll be back shortly, Mr. McConnell," Brandon promised.

Outside the interview room, Brandon said, "Inspector Jordan and Dr. Hill are upstairs. And DS Merrick has come back from Casualty. Apparently, he says he's well enough to run through the evening's events himself."

"Right. Well, we'd better hear what he's got to say, and then we can have a proper go at Jock." Cross marched upstairs to the squad room, where a concerned Carol was hovering over Merrick. Tony sat a few feet away, feet propped up on the rim of a wastepaper bin.

"Bloody hell, Merrick!" Cross roared, seeing the dramatic bandage that turbanned his head. "You've not turned into one of them bloody Sikhs, have you? Christ, I knew it was a risk sending a team into poofterville undercover, but I wasn't expecting religious mania."

Merrick smiled weakly. "I figured that way you couldn't send me back into uniform for cocking up, sir."

Cross gave a grudging smile in return. "Let's be hearing it, then. Why have I got a bolshie little sporran-sucker in my nick?"

Brandon, standing a couple of feet behind Cross, interrupted. "Before DS Merrick runs through the evening's events for us, I just want to explain to Dr. Hill why we've dragged him in here at this time of night." Tony straightened up in his chair and pulled a sheet of paper towards him. "When you were giving your lecture the other day," Brandon continued, moving past Cross and sitting on the edge of a desk, "you mentioned that psychologists can often give pointers to detectives about interview approaches. I wondered if you could apply that to this situation."

"I'll do my best," Tony said, uncapping his pen.

"How do you mean, interview approaches?" Cross said suspiciously.

Tony smiled. "A recent example from my own experience. A force I'd been advising had arrested a suspect in two rape cases. He was the macho type, all bluster and muscle. I suggested that they send in a woman CID officer to interview him, preferably a small, very feminine woman. That made him angry right from the start, because he held women in contempt and thought he wasn't being treated with the appropriate respect. I'd briefed her in advance to suggest in her line of questioning that he couldn't possibly be the rapist since, frankly, she didn't think he had it in him. The result was, he blew his stack and coughed to the two rapes they had him in the frame for, as well as three other offences they didn't even know about."

Cross said nothing. "DS Merrick?" Brandon asked.

Merrick took them through his experiences in the bar with frequent pauses for thought. At the end of his recital, Brandon and Carol looked expectantly towards Tony. "What do you think, Tony? Are either of them a possible?" Brandon asked.

"I don't think Ian Thomson is a starter. This killer is far too careful to get involved in something as ridiculously high profile as a street brawl. Even if Don hadn't been a police officer, the chances are that Thomson would have ended up in trouble for going after someone with a half-brick. Even in a city where attacks on gays are not noted for their high priority in policing terms," he added drily.

Cross scowled. "Gays get treated same as everybody else by the lads," he blustered.

Tony wished he'd kept his mouth shut. The last thing he wanted was to get into a head-to-head with Tom Cross on Bradfield police's "gays and blacks don't count" policy. He decided to ignore the comment and forged on. "Also, there's nothing in what we know about the killer's behaviour to suggest that he's an upfront S&M gay man. It's clearly not from the gay scene that he's selecting victims. However, McConnell sounds more interesting from your point of view. Do we know what he does for a living?"

"He's the manager of a gym in the city centre. The same gym that Gareth Finnegan used," Cross said.

"Hasn't he been questioned before?" Brandon asked. Cross shrugged.

"One of Inspector Matthews's team has spoken to him," Carol butted in. "I noticed the report when I was preparing the material for Dr. Hill," she added hastily, when she saw the beginnings of a scowl on Cross's face. God forbid he should think she was trying to undermine him. "My dustbin memory," she continued, trying to make a joke of it. "As far as I can remember, it was simply a routine enquiry, checking up on whether Gareth had had any particular buddies or contacts at the gym."

"Do we know McConnell's domestic arrangements?" Tony asked.

"He shares a house with another couple of shirt-lifters," Cross said. "He says they're both in the body-building game too. So, is he in the frame or not?"

Tony doodled in the margin of his notes. "It's possible," he said. "What are the chances of getting a search warrant?"

"On what we've got at the moment? Not good. And we've no grounds for a search without one. Not even in our wildest dreams can we claim that a street assault gives us grounds to search McConnell's house for evidence relating to serial killings," Brandon said. "What would we be looking for in particular?"

"A camcorder. Any indication that he has access to somewhere isolated and deserted like an old warehouse, factory, derelict house, lock-up garage." Tony ran a hand through his hair. "Polaroid photographs. Sado-masochistic pornography. Souvenirs of his victims. The jewellery missing from the bodies." He looked up and met Tom Cross's sneer. "And you should check the deep freeze just on the off chance that he's kept the pieces of flesh he removed from the bodies." He felt a moment's gratification when Cross's expression changed to disgust.

"Charming. But first we have to get something more to go on. Any suggestions?" Brandon asked.

"Send DS Merrick and Inspector Jordan in to interview him. The realization that the man he tried to pick up is a police officer will unsettle him, make him feel that his instincts can't be trusted. There's a chance too that he has problems with women—'

"Of course he's got problems with women," Cross interjected. "He's a bloody arse bandit."

"Not all gay men dislike women," Tony said mildly. "But a lot do, and McConnell may be one of them. At the very least, Carol will make him feel threatened. All-male situations offer him the opportunity for camaraderie, so we take that off him."

"Let's try it, then," Brandon said. "If DS Merrick is up to it."

"I'm game, sir," Merrick said.

Cross looked as if he couldn't decide whether to hit Brandon or Tony. "I might as well bugger off home, then," he blustered.

"Good idea, Tom. You've had more than your fair share of all-nighters lately. I'll hang on here, see what comes out of McConnell's interview."

Cross stomped out of the squad room, passing Kevin Matthews on the way. The atmosphere visibly lightened in

Cross's absence. "Sir?" Kevin said. "Ian Thomson—it looks like he's out of the frame on the murders."

Brandon frowned. "I thought I told you not to bring the murders up? At this stage, all we want to front Thomson with is the assault."

"I didn't bring up the murders, sir," Kevin said defensively. "But it emerged during the interview that Thomson works three nights a week as a DJ in Hot Rocks. That's a gay club in Liverpool. He does Monday, Tuesday and Thursday. It should be easy enough to check whether he was working on the nights of the murders."

"OK, get someone on it," Brandon said.

"Which leaves McConnell," Carol said thoughtfully.

"Let's do it," Brandon said.

"Any tips?" Carol asked Tony.

"Don't be afraid to patronize him. Stay sweetness and light, but make it clear that you're the ranking officer. And DS Merrick—you can afford to play the gratitude card a bit."

"Thanks," Carol said. "OK, Don?"

They left Brandon and Tony together. "How is it going?" Brandon asked, getting up and stretching.

Tony shrugged. "I'm starting to get a feel for his victims. There's a definite pattern there. He's a stalker, I'm sure of it. I should have a rough profile in a day or two. It's just bad timing that you've pulled in a suspect now."

"How do you mean, bad timing?"

"I understand why you wanted my input. But I don't like knowing about suspects before I draw up my profile. The danger is that I skew the profile subconsciously so that it's a better fit for the suspect."

Brandon sighed. He'd always found it hard to be optimistic in the small hours. "We'll cross that bridge when we come to it. By this time tomorrow, our suspect might just be a distant memory."

*Getting to know Paul was somehow more exciting than Adam had been. Partly, I suppose, because I knew now I could handle it if things didn't work out the way I wanted. Even if Paul didn't have the insight to see that I could give him more than anyone else, even if he rejected my love, even if he went as far as Adam and actually betrayed the inevitability of our partnership with someone else, I knew that there was an alternative scenario that could give me almost as much satisfaction as the achievement of what I deserved.*

*But this time, I felt sure that I would get what I wanted. Adam, I now saw, had been immature and weak. Paul was neither of those, I could tell at once. For a start, he hadn't chosen to live in the yuppie part of town like Adam. Paul lived on the south side of the city in Aston Hey, a leafy suburb beloved of university lecturers and alternative therapists. Paul's house was in one of the more inexpensive streets. Like mine, it was terraced, though his two-up and two-down rooms were obviously far bigger. Unlike mine, he had a small garden at the front, and his back yard was twice the size, scattered with terracotta planters and tubs filled with flowers and dwarf shrubs. The perfect place to sit together for a preprandial drink after work on summer evenings.*

*Now with Paul, I'd have the chance to live in Aston Hey, to enjoy those quiet streets, to walk in the park together, to*

*be just like other couples. He had an interesting job, too—
lecturer at Bradfield Institute of Science and Technology,
specializing in CAD programs. We already had so much in
common. It was a shame I'd never be able to show him
what I'd achieved with Adam.*

*One of the major advantages of having no mortgage is
that I have virtually all of my salary to play with. It's a
substantial disposable income for someone of my age and
with my lack of dependants. That means I can afford a
state-of-the-art computer system, with regular upgrades to
keep me out there at the leading edge. Given that one software program alone cost me nearly three thousand pounds,
it's just as well I don't have anyone leeching off me. With
my new CD-ROM system, video digitizer and special-effects
software, it took me less than a day to import the videos
into my computer. Once they were digitized and installed
there, I could manipulate and morph the images to tell any
story I wanted to see. Thanks to other video erotica I'd
already installed on my system, I was even able to give
Adam the erection he'd failed to achieve in life. Finally, I
could fuck him, suck him, fist him, and watch him do the
same to me. But the knowledge that I would be able to do
that still hadn't been enough to save him. Not even my
computer and my imagination could give me the joy and
satisfaction he could have done if he'd only been honest
with himself about his desire for me. And so, every day he
had to die all over again. The ultimate fantasy, constantly
changing, shaped to fit my every mood and whim. At last,
Adam was performing everything he could ever have fan-
tasized about. It was a shame he couldn't share in my pleasure.*

*It wasn't perfect, but at least I was having more fun than
the police. From what I read, it was clear they were getting
nowhere. Adam's death barely merited a mention in the national media, and even the* Bradfield Evening Sentinel
Times *gave up after five days. Adam's body was identified
after four days, when anxious colleagues reported him
missing after failing to get any reply from his phone or his*

doorbell. I was interested in their tributes (popular, hard-working, well liked, etc.) and I felt a moment's regret that his stupidity had deprived me of their friendship. The Sentinel Times's crime reporter had even managed to track down Adam's ex-wife, a mistake he'd made at twenty-one which he'd extricated himself from by his twenty-fifth birthday. Her comments made me laugh out loud.

Adam Scott's ex-wife Lisa Arnold, 27, fought back the tears as she said, "I can't believe this could have happened to Adam.

"He was a friendly man, really sociable. But he wasn't a big drinker. I can't imagine how this weirdo managed to get hold of him."

Lisa, a primary-school teacher who has since remarried, went on, "I've no idea what he was doing in Crompton Gardens. He never showed any gay tendencies when we were married. Our sex life was quite normal. If anything, it was a bit boring.

"We married too young. Adam's mother had brought him up to expect a wife who waited on him hand and foot, and that just wasn't me.

"Then I met someone else and I told Adam I wanted a divorce. He was really upset, but I think it was more that his pride was hurt.

"I haven't seen him since the divorce, but I heard he was living on his own. I know he's had a few affairs over the last three years, but nothing serious as far as I know.

"I just can't get used to the idea that he's dead. I know we hurt each other, but I'm still devastated that he's been murdered like this."

I didn't rate the chances of Lisa's second marriage lasting the course if she still had as little insight into the workings of the male mind. Boring? Lisa was the only reason sex with Adam could be boring.

And as for calling me a weirdo! She was the one who had turned her back on a charming, handsome man who *loved her so much that he was still talking about her to complete strangers three years after she'd rejected him. I knew all about it; I'd listened to him. If anyone was a weirdo, it was Lisa.*

# 8

*No unpractised artist could have conceived so bold an idea as that of a noon-day murder in the heart of a great city. It was no obscure baker, gentlemen, or anonymous chimney-sweeper, be assured, that executed this work. I know who it was.*

Stevie McConnell ran both hands through his hair in a gesture of desperation. "Look, how many times do I have to tell you? I was telling porkies. I was trying to make myself sound the big man. I wanted to cop off, I was trying to make myself interesting. I never knew Paul Gibbs or Damien Connolly. I never saw either of them in my life."

"We can prove you knew Gareth Finnegan," Carol said coldly.

"OK, I admit I knew Gareth. He was a member down the gym, I can't pretend I'd never met him before. But Christ, woman, the man was a lawyer. He must have known thousands of people in the city," McConnell said, thumping the table with a solid fist.

Carol didn't even flinch. "And Adam Scott," she went on relentlessly.

"Yeah, yeah," he said wearily. "Adam Scott had a trial one-month membership down the gym about two years ago. He never joined up. I bumped into him a couple of times in my local pub, we had a jar together, that's all there was to it. I have a drink with a lot of people, you know. I'm not a bloody hermit. Christ, if I killed everybody I've ever stood at a bar with, youse bastards would be busy from now till the next century."

"We will prove you knew Paul Gibbs and Damien Connolly. You know that, don't you?" Merrick chimed in.

McConnell sighed. His hands clenched, forcing the muscles in his powerful forearms into sharp relief. "If you do, you'll have to make it up, because you can't prove what isn't true. You're not going to do a Birmingham Six on me, you know. Look, if I was really this mad bastard, do you think I'd have hung around to help you? First sign of trouble, I'd have legged it. Stands to reason."

Sounding bored, Carol said, "But you didn't know then that Sergeant Merrick was a police officer, did you? So give us your alibi for Monday night."

McConnell leaned back in the chair and stared at the ceiling. "Mondays is my day off," he recited. "Like I said, the guys that share my house are on their holidays, so I was on my tod. I got up late, went down the supermarket for my messages, then I went for a swim. About six o'clock, I drove out to the multi-screen off the motorway, and I went to see the new Clint Eastwood film."

Abruptly, he lurched forward in the chair. "They'll be able to confirm it. I paid by credit card, and their system's all computerized. They can prove I was at the pictures," he said triumphantly.

"They can prove you bought a ticket," Carol said laconically. From the cinema to Damien Connolly's house would take no more than half an hour round the motorway, even allowing for rush-hour traffic.

"I can tell you the whole plot, for fuck's sake," McConnell said angrily.

"You could have seen it any time, Stevie," Merrick said gently. "What did you do after the pictures?"

"I went home. Cooked myself a steak and some vegetables." McConnell paused and stared at the table. "Then I went into town for the last hour. Just for a quick drink with a few mates."

Carol leaned forward, sensing McConnell's reluctance. "Where in town?" she demanded.

McConnell said nothing.

Carol leaned further forward, the tip of her nose an inch from his. Her voice was quiet but icy cold. "If I have to stick your face on the front page of the *Sentinel Times* and send a team into every pub in the city, I'll do it, Mr. McConnell. Where in town?"

McConnell breathed in heavily through his nose. "The Queen of Hearts," he spat.

Carol leaned back, satisfied. She stood up. "Interview terminated at 3:17 a.m.," she said, leaning over to switch off the tape recorder. She looked down at McConnell. "We'll be back, Mr. McConnell."

"Wait a minute," he protested as Merrick got up and the two of them made for the door. "When am I going to get out of here? You've got no right to keep me!"

Carol turned back in the doorway, smiled sweetly and said, "Oh, I have every right, Mr. McConnell. You've been arrested for assault, let's not forget. I have twenty-four hours to make your life a misery before I even have to think about charging you."

Merrick gave an apologetic smile as he backed out of the room in Carol's wake. "Sorry, Stevie," he said. "The lady's not wrong."

He caught up with Carol as she was asking the custody sergeant to return McConnell to the cells. "What do you think, ma'am?" Merrick asked as they walked off together.

Carol stopped and eyed Merrick critically. His skin was pale and clammy, his eyes feverishly bright. "I think you need to go home and get some sleep, Don. You look like shit on a stick."

"Never mind me. What about McConnell, ma'am?"

"We'll see what Mr. Brandon has to say." Carol set off for the stairs, Merrick trailing behind her.

"But what do *you* think, ma'am?"

"On the face of it, he could be our man. He's got nothing approaching an alibi for Monday night, he runs the gym where Gareth Finnegan worked out, he knew Adam Scott and by his own admission he was in the Queen of Hearts on Monday night for the last hour. He's certainly strong enough to have carted the bodies in and out of a car. He's got form, even if it is only a couple of breaches of the peace and a Section 18 wounding. And he's into S&M. But that's all circumstantial. And I still don't think we've got grounds for a search warrant," Carol rattled off. "What about you, Don? Got a feeling in your water about this one?"

They turned down the corridor towards the murder squad room. "I kind of like him," Merrick said grudgingly. "I can't imagine that I'd take a liking to the bastard that's been doing these murders. But then, I suppose that's a pretty daft reaction. I mean, he's not the two-headed man, is he? He's got to have something about him that lets him get close enough to his victims to do the business. So maybe it *is* Stevie McConnell."

Carol opened the door to the squad room, expecting to find Brandon and Tony still sitting there, fuelled by coffee and canteen sandwiches. The room was empty. "Where's the ACC got to now?" Carol said, tiredness lending her voice a note of exasperation.

"Maybe he's left a message at the front desk," Merrick suggested.

"And maybe he's done the sensible thing and buggered off home to bed. Well, that's us for tonight, Don. McConnell can stew for a bit. See what the bosses have to say in the morning. Maybe we can try for a search warrant now we know McConnell was in the Queen of Hearts. Now, get out of my sight and go home to bed before your Jean accuses me of leading you off the straight and narrow. Get some sleep. I don't want to see you before noon, and if your head's hurting, stay in bed. That's an order, Detective Sergeant."

Merrick grinned. "Yes, ma'am. See you."

Carol watched Merrick walk back down the corridor, worried at the slow deliberation of his movements. "Don?" she called. Merrick turned enquiringly back to her. "Get a taxi. My authorization. I don't want you wrapped round a lamppost on my conscience. And that's an order, too." Merrick grinned, nodded and disappeared down the stairs.

With a sigh, Carol walked down the squad room to her

temporary office. There was no message on her desk. Bloody Brandon, she thought. And bloody Tony Hill. Brandon at least should have waited till she'd finished her interrogation of McConnell. And Tony might have left some indication of when he expected them to meet to discuss his profile. Muttering under her breath, Carol followed Merrick out of the building. As she reached the foyer, the officer minding the front desk called, "Inspector Jordan?"

Carol turned back. "I'm what's left of her."

"The ACC left a message for you, ma'am."

Carol approached the desk and took the envelope the constable handed her. She ripped it open and pulled out a single sheet of paper. "Carol," she read. "I have taken Tony off on a little mission. I'll drop him at home afterwards. Please be in my office for ten this morning. Thanks for your hard work. John Brandon."

"Great," Carol said bitterly. She gave the constable a tired smile. "I don't suppose you know where Mr. Brandon and Dr. Hill were headed?"

He shook his head. "Sorry, ma'am. They didn't say."

"Wonderful," she muttered sarcastically. Turn your back for a minute and they were off playing their boys' games. Little mission, indeed. Bollocks to that, Carol thought as she marched back to her car. "Three can play at that game," she said as she turned the ignition key.


Tony flicked through the last of the magazines and returned it to the box file in the bedside storage cube. "S&M always leaves me feeling faintly queasy," he remarked. "And this lot's particularly nasty."

Brandon agreed. McConnell's collection of hard-core pornography consisted mostly of magazines crammed with glossy colour pictures of well-muscled young men torturing each other and masturbating. A few were even more disturbing, with their graphic shots of male couples indulging in full sex with an array of sado-masochistic trappings. Brandon couldn't remember seeing nastier examples, even when he'd done a six-month attachment with Vice.

They were sitting on the bed in Stevie McConnell's room. As soon as Carol and Merrick had left for their interrogation, Brandon had said, "Would it be helpful to you to see where McConnell lives?"

Tony picked up his pen again and started to doodle on the sheet of paper. "It might give me some insight into the man. And if he is the killer, there could be evidence that ties him into the crimes. I don't mean murder weapons, or anything like that. I'm thinking more of the souvenirs. Photographs, newspaper clippings, as well as the stuff I was talking about before. But it's academic, isn't it? You said there was no chance of getting a search warrant."

Brandon's melancholy face lit up in a strange smile, almost a leer. "When you've got a suspect in custody, there are things you can do to circumvent the rules. You game?"

Tony grinned. "I'm fascinated." He followed Brandon downstairs to the cells. The custody sergeant hastily dropped the Stephen King novel he'd been reading and jumped to his feet.

"It's all right, Sergeant," Brandon said. "If I only had a couple of prisoners to think about, I'd be enjoying a good read, too. I'd like to have a look at McConnell's property."

The sergeant unlocked the property cupboard and handed the transparent plastic bag to Brandon. There was a wallet, a handkerchief and a bunch of keys inside. Brandon opened it and removed the keys. "You haven't seen me, have you, Sergeant? And you won't see me when I come back in a couple of hours, will you?"

The sergeant grinned. "You couldn't possibly have been here, sir. I'd have been bound to notice."

Twenty minutes later, Brandon was parking the Range Rover outside McConnell's terraced house. "Lucky for us McConnell happened to mention that the two blokes he shares the house with are away on holiday." He took a cardboard box out of the glove compartment and gave Tony a pair of latex gloves. "You'll need these," he said, slipping a pair over his own hands. "If we do get a search warrant, it would be a bit embarrassing when the fingerprint team turn up you and me as prime suspects."

"There's one thing I'm curious about," Tony said as Brandon inserted the key in the mortice lock.

"What's that?"

"This is an illegal search, right?"

"Right," Brandon said, opening the door and stepping into the hall. He groped for the light switch, but didn't turn it on when he found it.

Tony followed him, closing the door behind him. Only then did Brandon snap the light on, revealing a carpeted hall and stairs. There were a couple of framed posters of body-builders on the walls. "So if we find any evidence, presumably it's inadmissible?"

"Also right," said Brandon. "But there are ways round that. For example, if we find a bloodstained cut-throat razor under McConnell's bed, it will mysteriously find its way on to the kitchen table. Then we go to the magistrate, explain that we went to McConnell's house to check he was telling the truth when he said his house-mates were on holiday, and we happened to look through the windows and we spotted what we have reason to believe is the weapon used to kill Adam Scott, Paul Gibbs, Gareth Finnegan and Damien Connolly."

Tony shook his head in amusement. "Bent? Us? Never, your honour!"

"There's bent and there's bent," Brandon said grimly. "Sometimes you need to give things a shove in the right direction."

Tony and Brandon moved through the house, room by room. Brandon was intrigued by Tony's method. He would walk into a room, stand in the middle of the floor and slowly scan the walls, the furniture, the floor coverings, the shelves. He almost sniffed the air. Then, meticulously, he opened cupboards and drawers, lifted cushions, examined magazines, checked titles of books, CDs, cassettes and videos, handling everything he touched with the care and precision of an archaeologist. Within seconds, his mind was

busy, analysing everything he saw and touched, slowly
building a picture in his mind of the men who lived here,
constantly matching it against the embryonic picture of
Handy Andy that was developing in his mind like a pho-
tographic print in developer fluid.

"Have you been here, Andy?" he asked himself. "Does
this feel like you, smell like you? Would you watch these
videos? Are these your CDs? Judy Garland and Liza Minnelli? The Pet Shop Boys? I don't think so. You're not
camp, I know that much about you. And there's nothing
camp or chichi about the house. This place is so aggressively masculine. A living room furnished in eighties
chrome and black. But it's not a straight man's house, is
it? No girlie magazines, not even car magazines. Just body-
building periodicals stacked under the coffee table. Look at
the walls. Men's bodies, oiled and shining, muscles like
carved wood. The men who live here know who they are,
they know what they like. I don't think this is you, Andy.
You're controlled, Andy, but not this controlled. It's one
thing to keep yourself buttoned up, it's another thing altogether to be strong enough to project so coherent an image.
I should know, I'm the expert. If you were as firmly rooted
in your identity as the guys who live here, you wouldn't
have to do what you do, would you?

"Look at the books. Stephen King, Dean R. Koontz, Stephen Gallagher, Iain Banks. Arnold Schwarzenegger's bi-
ography. A couple of paperbacks about the Mafia. Nothing
soft, nothing gentle, but nothing off the wall either. Would
you read these books? Maybe. I think you'd like to read
about serial killers, though, and there's none of that here."

Tony turned slowly towards the door. It was a small
shock to see Brandon standing there. He'd become so absorbed in his scrutiny that he'd lost all sense of being in
company. Watch yourself, Tony, he warned himself. Stay
inside your head.

In silence, they trooped through to the kitchen. It was
spartan, but well equipped. In the sink there was a dirty
soup bowl and a mug half full of cold tea. A small shelf

of cookery books testified to the occupants' obsession with healthy eating. "Fart city," Tony observed wryly, opening a cupboard filled with jars of pulses. He opened the drawers, noting the kitchen knives. There was a small vegetable knife with a blade worn thin from sharpening, a bread knife whose blade was pitted with age, and a cheap carving knife, the handle bleached from the dishwasher. "These are not your tools, Andy," Tony said to himself. "You like knives that do their work properly."

Without consulting Brandon, he walked out of the kitchen and up the stairs. Brandon watched him stick his head round the first bedroom door and reject it. As he passed, he saw that it was obviously the couple's room. He followed Tony through the door across the landing. In McConnell's bedroom, Tony seemed to drift away altogether into a world of his own. The room was simply furnished with modern pine bed, chest of drawers and wardrobe. An array of weightlifting trophies sat on the deep windowsill. A tall bookcase was crammed with pulp science fiction and a handful of gay novels. On a small table, there was a games computer and a television monitor. On a shelf above was a collection of games. Tony browsed through Mortal Kombat, Streetfighter II, Terminator 2, Doom and a dozen other games whose keynote was violent action.

"This is more like it," he murmured. He stood by the chest of drawers, hand poised to open one. "Maybe it's you after all," he thought. "Maybe you leave the living room to the other two. What if this is your only domain? What would I expect to find here? I'd want your souvenirs, Andy. You need to keep something by you, otherwise the memory disintegrates too fast. We all need something tangible. The discarded perfume spray that holds her fragrance and summons her before my eyes like a hologram; the theatre programme from the night we first made love and it was all right. Keep the good memories, throw away the bad. What have you got for me?"

The first three drawers were disappointingly innocuous:

underwear, T-shirts, socks, jogging suits and shorts. When Tony opened the bottom drawer, he sighed in satisfaction. The drawer contained McConnell's S&M gear—handcuffs, leather restraint straps, cock rings, whips, and a clutch of items that looked to Brandon as if they ought to be in some kind of laboratory or mental institution. As Tony calmly took them out and examined them, Brandon shuddered.

Tony sat down on the bed and looked around. Slowly, cautiously, he tried to construct a picture of the man who lived in this room. "You like to exercise power through violence," he thought. "You enjoy the flow of pain in your sexual experience. But there's no subtlety here. No sign that you're a man who plans things with care and detail. You worship your body. It's a temple to you. You've achieved things, and you're proud of that. You're not socially inadequate. You manage to share a house with two other men, and you're not obsessive about your privacy, since there's no lock on the door. You don't have a problem with your sexuality, and you're comfortable with the idea of picking up a man in a club, provided you have the chance to get to know him a bit first."

His picture-building was interrupted by Brandon. "Look at this, Tony!" he said excitedly. The ACC had been painstakingly going through a shoebox full of papers, mostly receipts, electrical guarantees, bank and credit-card statements. The box was almost empty, but now, he held out a flimsy slip of paper.

Tony took it. It was some kind of official police form. He frowned. "What's this?"

"It's the form you get when an officer stops you in a car and you haven't got your documents with you. You have to take them to a police station within a fixed period, so they can check everything's in order. Look at the name of the officer," Brandon urged.

Tony looked again. The name that had at first seemed a scrawled jumble suddenly resolved itself into "Connolly."

"I recognized his number," Brandon said. "You can hardly make out the name."

"Shit," Tony breathed.

"Damien Connolly must have stopped him for some minor traffic offence, or just on a spot check, and asked him to produce his documents," Brandon said.

Tony frowned. "I thought Connolly was a local information officer? What was he doing dishing out a traffic ticket?"

Brandon looked over Tony's shoulder at the slip of paper. "It was nearly two years ago. Connolly obviously wasn't a collator then. Either he was doing a stint with Traffic or he was on duty in the area car when he saw McConnell doing something he shouldn't have been."

"Can you check that out discreetly?"

"No problem," Brandon said.

"You've cracked it, then, haven't you?"

Brandon looked astonished. "You mean . . . you think that clinches it? McConnell's the man?"

"No, no," Tony said hastily. "Not at all. All I meant was that if you can track that back from the other end, you should be able to get a magistrate to grant you an official search warrant on the basis that McConnell knew three of the four victims, which goes beyond mere coincidence."

"Right," Brandon said, sighing. "So you're still not convinced McConnell's the killer?"

Tony stood up and paced to and fro across the carpet, its jagged geometric pattern of grey, red, black and white reminding him of the one and only migraine he'd ever had. "Before you found this, I'd come to the conclusion you'd got the wrong man," he said after a few moments. "I know I've not had time to sit down and write out a full profile yet, but I felt like I was beginning to get a sense of what this killer's like. And there are too many things here that don't fit that picture. But this is a hell of a coincidence. This is a big city. We've established that Stevie McConnell knew or at least had met three out of the four victims. How many people are going to be in that position?"

"Not many," Brandon said grimly.

"I still don't like McConnell for the killer, but it's possible that the killer is someone he knows, someone who's met Adam Scott and Gareth Finnegan through him," Tony said. "Maybe even somebody who was with him when he got that traffic ticket, or someone that he pointed Damien out to. You know the kind of thing: 'That's the bastard who nicked me for speeding.' "

"You really don't think it's him, do you?" Brandon said flatly, disappointment in his voice. "I suppose it's thin. After all, there's no evidence as such to connect the house to the killings," he said cautiously. "But you said yourself, he's more likely to be doing his killing somewhere else. That might be where he keeps his souvenirs."

"It's not just the absence of souvenirs," Tony said. "Putting it crudely, John, serial murderers kill to turn their fantasies into reality. Typically, they have fantasies developed to the point where they are more real to them than the world around them. There's nothing here to suggest McConnell is that type of personality. Sure, he's got a stack of porn mags. But so have most single men of his age, regardless of sexual orientation. He's got violent computer games, but so have thousands of teenagers and grown men too. What there is is plenty of evidence to suggest that Stevie McConnell isn't a sociopath. Look around you, John. This whole house reeks of normality. The kitchen calendar has dates for people coming round for dinner. Look at that pile of Christmas cards on his bookshelf. There must be fifty there. Look at his holiday snaps. He was obviously with the same partner for four or five years, judging by the locations and hairstyle changes. Stevie McConnell doesn't seem to have problems forming relationships with people. OK, so there doesn't seem to be anything relating to his family, but a lot of gay people get cut off by their families when they come out. It doesn't mean that his family were dysfunctional in the ways that typically lead to the development of a serial killer. I'm sorry, John. I wasn't sure at first, but the more I've seen, the more this guy just doesn't smell right to me."

Brandon got to his feet and carefully replaced the slip

of paper exactly where he'd found it. "It grieves me to say so, but I think you're right. When I interviewed him earlier, I thought he was way too calm to be our man."

Tony shook his head. "Don't let that mislead you. Chances are when you do pull the right guy, he'll be calm too. Don't forget, this is something he's planned carefully. Although he thinks he's the best, he'll still have made contingency plans. He'll expect to be brought in for questioning sooner or later. He'll be ready for you. He'll be reasonable, pleasant. He won't look like a con. He'll be bland, helpful, and he won't ring alarm bells with your detectives. His alibi will be no alibi. He'll probably say he's been with a tart, or been to an away football match on his own. He'll end up being eliminated from your enquiries because other suspects will be superficially far more appealing."

Brandon managed to look even more depressed than normal. "Thanks, Tony. You've really cheered me up now. So what do you suggest?"

Tony shrugged. "Like I said, it's a possibility that he knows the killer. He may even have his own suspicions. I'd hang on to him for a bit longer, sweat him for what and who he does know. But I wouldn't call off the team. Get a warrant. Do a proper search, under the floorboards, in the loft. You never know what you might turn up. Don't forget, I could be completely wrong."

Brandon glanced at his watch. "Right. I'd better get these keys back before the end of the custody sergeant's shift. I'll drop you off on the way."

With a last look to check they'd left nothing out of place, Brandon and Tony left McConnell's house. As they approached the Range Rover, a voice from the shadows said, "Good morning, gentlemen. You're nicked." Carol stepped forward into the light of the streetlamp. "Dr. Anthony Hill, and Assistant Chief Constable John Brandon, I am arresting you on suspicion of breaking and entering. You do not have to say anything . . ." At that point, the giggles took over.

Brandon's heart had thudded into his throat at her first

words. "Hellfire, Carol," he protested. "I'm too old for tricks like that."

"But not for ones like this, I see," Carol said drily, gesturing with her thumb towards McConnell's house. "Unauthorized search, and with a civilian? Just as well for you I'm off duty, sir."

Brandon gave a weary smile. "So why are you loitering with intent around the suspect's house?"

"I'm a detective, sir. I thought I might find you and Dr. Hill here. Any joy?"

"Dr. Hill thinks not. What about your interview?" Brandon asked.

"Your suggestions worked really well, Tony. McConnell's got no alibi to speak of for Damien Connolly's murder, apart from one hour late on in the evening, by which time Damien could have been dead already. The significant thing is where he was for that hour. Sir, he was drinking in the pub where the body was dumped."

Tony's eyebrows climbed and he sucked his breath in sharply. Brandon turned to him. "Well?"

"It's exactly the cheeky sort of thing Handy Andy could pull. You might want to get someone to check if he's a regular in there. If he isn't, it makes it significant," Tony said slowly. Before he could say more, he was overwhelmed by a huge yawn. "Sorry," he yawned. "I'm not a night bird."

"I'll drive you home," Carol said. "I think the ACC has something to drop off at the station."

Brandon looked at his watch. "Fine. Make it eleven, not ten, Carol."

"Thank you, sir," Carol said with feeling as she unlocked her car for Tony. He slumped into the passenger seat, unable to stop the wave of yawns that had engulfed him.

"I'm really sorry," she made out through a jaw-cracker. "I can't stop yawning."

"Did you find anything to make it worthwhile?" Carol said, her tone more sympathetic than her words.

"Damien Connolly nicked him a couple of years ago for a traffic offence," Tony said heavily.

Carol whistled. "Gotcha! We've caught him in a double lie, Tony! McConnell originally told Don Merrick he'd met Connolly after a burglary at the gym. Then in the interview he denied ever having seen him. He said he'd been lying to make himself seem interesting. But now it turns out he really had met him! What a break!"

"Only if you believe he's the killer," he said. "I'm sorry to disappoint you, Carol, but I don't think he's the one. I'm too tired to go through it all now, but once I've drawn up my profile and we go through it, you'll see why I can't get excited about Stevie McConnell." He yawned again and leaned his head on his hand.

"When can we do that?" Carol asked, fighting the urge to shake his thoughts out of him.

"Listen, give me the rest of today to myself, and by tomorrow morning I'll have a draft profile for you. How's that?"

"Fine. Anything else you need in the meantime?"

Tony said nothing. Carol gave him a quick sidelong glance and realized he had dozed off. All right for some, she thought. Forcing herself to concentrate, she drove across town to Tony's house, a turn-of-the-century brick-built semi in a quiet street a couple of tram stops away from the university. Carol pulled up outside. The car's slow glide to immobility did nothing to disturb Tony, whose breathing had become audible.

Carol undid her seat belt and leaned over to shake him gently. Tony's head came up in a startled gesture, his eyes wide and frantic. He stared uncomprehendingly at Carol. "It's all right," she said. "You're home. You fell asleep."

Tony rubbed his eyes with his fists, muttering something unintelligible. He looked blearily at Carol and gave a sleepy, lopsided smile. "Thanks for bringing me home."

"No problem," Carol said, still twisted round in her seat, fiercely aware of his closeness. "I'll give you a ring this afternoon, we can fix up a time to meet tomorrow."

Tony, awake now, felt claustrophobic. "Thanks again," he said, retreating hastily, opening the car door and almost tumbling on to the pavement, thanks to the combination of haste and sleepiness.

"I can't believe I wanted him to kiss me," Carol said to herself as she watched Tony open his gate and walk up the short path. "Dear God, what is happening to me? First I treat Don like a mother hen, then I start fancying the expert witnesses." She saw the front door open, stuffed a cassette in the stereo and drove off. "What I need," she told Elvis Costello, "is a holiday."

"You tease, and you flirt, and you shine all the buttons on your green shirt," he sang back.

"Last night, we were practically sticking the champagne on ice. Now you're telling me you want to let McConnell go?" Cross shook his head in a gesture of exasperation so ancient it probably appeared on a Greek vase. "What's happened to change everything? Come up with a cast-iron alibi, has he? Out on the razz with Prince Edward and his body-guards, was he?"

"I'm not saying let him go this minute. We need to question him closely about his associates, check if he introduced anyone to both Gareth Finnegan and Adam Scott. And after that, we have to let him walk. There's no real evidence, Tom," Brandon said wearily. Lack of sleep had transformed his face into a grey mask that wouldn't have looked out of place in a Hammer Horror film. Cross, on the other hand, looked and sounded as fresh as a toddler who's just had a nap.

"He was in the Queen of Hearts that night. For all we know, he had Damien Connolly's body in the boot of his car, just waiting for closing time. It's got to be grounds for searching his gaff."

"As soon as we've got enough evidence to get a search warrant, we'll do it," Brandon said, reluctant to admit that he'd already taken that unorthodox step. Earlier, he'd asked

Sergeant Claire Bonner to check all Damien Connolly's arrests and traffic tickets, supposedly on the off chance of a connection to McConnell, but so far, she hadn't unearthed the crucial information that he knew was lurking there.

"I suppose this is all down to Boy Wonder," Cross said bitterly. "I suppose the shrink says McConnell's childhood wasn't unhappy enough."

Carol bit her tongue. It was bad enough being the fly on the wall in this clash of the titans without reminding either of her bosses she was witnessing their conflict.

Brandon frowned. "I have consulted with Dr. Hill, and yes, he does feel that on the basis of what we've got so far, McConnell probably isn't our man. But that's not the main reason why I think we should let him loose. The lack of evidence is a hell of a lot more important to me."

"And to me. That's why we need time to collect some more. We need to interview these poofters he was drinking with on Monday night, to see what kind of state he was in. And we need to take a look at what McConnell's got under his mattress," Cross said forcefully. "We've had him in custody for less than twelve hours, sir. We're entitled to keep him till gone midnight. Then we can charge him with the assault for now, and ask the magistrates for a lie-down in police custody, which gives us another three days. That's all I'm asking for. I'll have nailed him by then. You can't say no to that, sir. You'll have the lads up in arms."

Wrong, Carol thought. You were doing fine up till then, but the emotional blackmail just scuppered you.

Brandon's ears flushed scarlet. "I hope no one thinks that because we are questioning someone the work stops," he said, a dangerous edge in his voice.

"They're dedicated, sir, but they've been working on this a long time without a break in the case."

Brandon turned away, staring out of the window at the city below. His instincts said to let McConnell go after they'd had one last attempt at digging his contacts out of him, but he had known without Cross's clumsy comments that having a suspect had given the murder squad a new lease of energy. Before he could make a decision, there was a knock at the door. "Come in," Brandon called, swinging round and dropping heavily into his chair.

Kevin Matthews's carrot curls appeared round the door. He looked like a kid who's been promised a trip to Disneyland. "Sir," he said. "Sorry to interrupt, sir, but we've just had a report from Forensic on the Damien Connolly killing."

"Come in and tell us, then," Cross invited genially.

Kevin gave an apologetic smile and slid his slim frame round the door. "One of the SOCOs found a scrap of torn leather caught on a nail on the gate," he said. "It's a secure area, the public can't just walk in, so we thought it might be significant. Obviously, we had to eliminate the people who work at the pub, and the draymen who deliver there. Anyway, it turns out that the yard was whitewashed and the gates were painted only a month ago, so we didn't have to chase too many bodies. Bottom line is, no one admitted owning anything made from leather like this, so we sent it off to Forensic and asked them to look at it double urgent. The report's just come back." He proffered the report to Brandon, eager as a Boy Scout.

The relevant passage had been highlighted in yellow. It leapt off the page at Brandon. "The fragment of dark-brown leather is extremely unusual. For a start, it appears to be deerskin of some sort. More significantly, analysis indicates that it has been cured in sea water rather than a specialist chemical-curing medium. I know of only one source of such leather: the former Soviet Union. Because regular supplies of the correct chemicals are difficult to come by, many tanners there still use the old method of curing with sea water. I would guess that the fragment has come from a leather jacket that originated in Russia. Leather like this is not available commercially elsewhere, since it does not meet the quality levels required by Western retail outlets." Brandon read it, then tossed it across the desk towards Cross.

"Bloody hell!" Cross said. "You mean we're looking for an Ivan?"

*I read somewhere that murder enquiries cost a million pounds a month. When Paul demonstrated he was every bit as stupid and treacherous as Adam, I began to realize the actions I'd been forced to take might start to have a significant impact on local taxes. Not that I minded a few extra pence a year on my council-tax bills; it was a small price to pay for the satisfaction I gained from dealing with their perfidy.*

*I was devastated by Paul's defection. Just as I'd set the scene for the triumphant celebration of our love, he turned his back on me and chose another. The night he made his first approach, I don't know how I got home. I can't remember a single detail of the journey. I sat in my jeep outside the farm, raging against his shallowness, his failure to recognize that I was the one he truly loved. My anger was so strong I'd lost all physical coordination. I virtually fell out of the driver's seat and staggered like a drunk towards the haven of my dungeon.*

*I climbed on to the stone bench and hugged my knees to my chest while the unfamiliar tears rolled down my cheeks and splashed on the raw stone, staining it dark as Adam's blood. What was wrong with them? Why couldn't they let themselves have what I knew they wanted?*

*I wiped my eyes. I owed it to both of us to make the experience as rich and as perfect as possible. It was time*

*for new toys. Adam had been the dress rehearsal. Paul was
going to be the first night.*

*The ploy of the car that wouldn't start had served me well
with Adam, so I used it on Paul. It worked like a dream.
Before I was three steps down the hall, he'd even invited
me to have a drink while I was waiting for the AA man.
But I didn't fall for his blandishments; he'd had his chance,
and it was too late now for me to abort my plans for our
union on my terms.*

*When he came round, he was strapped into a Judas chair.
It had taken me a few days to construct it, since I'd had to
start from scratch. The Judas chair was one of my San
Gimignano discoveries. I'd only ever seen a couple of ref-
erences to it in my books, none of which made it at all clear
how exactly it was constructed. But there in the museum,
they had their very own working model. I had taken a couple of photographs to augment the one in the museum catalogue, and equipped with those, I had worked out a
practicable design on my computer.*

*It's not a machine that inquisitors have used much,
though I can't quite see why. The San Gimignano museum
puts forward a theory which frankly seems absurd to me.
Coupled with some of the other descriptions on the cards,
this daft theory convinces me that the cards have been written by some blinkered, obsessive feminist. The theory goes
thus: it was OK to use implements of torture on women
such as vaginal pears that shredded the cervix and vagina,
so-called "Chastity" belts which ripped their labia to a
bloody pulp, implements that chopped nipples as efficiently
as a cigar cutter, because women were a separate species
from the inquisitors, and indeed were often creatures of the
devil. On the other hand, so this demented theory goes,
torture instruments used on men tend not to be directed
against their sexual organs, in spite of the tenderness of*

those areas, because—wait for it—the torturers felt sub-consciously connected to their victims and therefore any mutilation inflicted on their cocks and balls were unthink-able. Clearly, the caption writer in San Gimignano is far from au fait with the refinements of the Third Reich.

My Judas chair, even if I say so myself, is a masterpiece of the type. It consists of a square frame with a leg at each corner, with arm supports for the forearms and a thick plank up the back. Much like a primitive carving chair, except that there is no seat. Instead, below the gap where the seat should be, there is a sharply barbed conical spike, attached to the chair legs at its base by a cross-brace of strong wooden struts. For the spike, I'd used one of the large cones that cotton yarn used to be wound round on industrial looms. You can pick them up in the souvenir shop of any outpost of the heritage industry. I'd covered it with a thin, flexible sheet of copper, and fastened thin strands of razor wire in a spiral round the outside. I'd added my own refinement to the example in the torture museum; my spike was wired up to the electrical supply via a rheostat, allow-ing me to apply electric shocks of varying intensity. The whole thing is bolted to the floor to prevent accidents.

While he'd still been unconscious, Paul had been held above the spike by a strong leather strap under his armpits, binding him to the back of the chair. I'd also strapped each ankle to one of the front legs of the chair. As soon as I unfastened the strap, he'd be thrown on his own resources, relying on the muscles in his calves and his shoulders to keep him from the savage spike, carefully sited immediately below his anus. Since the chair was so high that only his toes could reach the floor, I didn't expect him to hold out too long.

His eyes registered the same panic I'd already seen in Adam. But his situation was entirely of his own making. I told him so before I ripped the tape away from his mouth.

"I had no idea, no idea," he gabbled. "I'm sorry, I'm so sorry. You've got to let me make it up to you. Just let *me out of this thing, and I promise we can make a fresh start."*

I shook my head. "Robert Maxwell got one thing right. He said trust is like virginity; you can only lose it once. You have a treacherous soul, Paul. How can I believe in you?"

His teeth began chattering, though not, I suspect, from cold. "I made a mistake," he forced out. "I know that. Everybody makes mistakes. Please, all I ask is the chance to make it right. I can make it right, I promise."

"Show me, then," I said. "Show me you mean it. Show me you want me." I stared at his shrivelled cock, dangling with his balls in the space where the seat should have been. I had looked forward to beauty, but he had failed me there, too.

"N-not here, not like this. I can't!" His voice rose in a pathetic wail.

"It's this or nothing. Here or nowhere," I told him. "By the way, in case you're wondering, you're strapped into a Judas chair." Carefully, I explained how the chair worked. I wanted him to make an informed choice. As I talked, his skin turned grey and clammy with fear. When I explained about the electricity, he lost it completely. Piss dribbled from his cock, splashing on the floor beneath him. The stink of warm urine rose and choked me.

I slapped him so hard his head cracked against the back board of the Judas chair. He cried out, and tears sprang into his eyes. "You dirty, filthy baby," I shouted at him. "You don't deserve my love. Look at you, pissing and crying like some little girl. You're not a man."

Hearing my mother's words coming from my mouth shattered my self-control as nothing else could have done. I kept hitting him, revelling in the crunch of cartilage as his nose collapsed under my fist. I was beside myself with anger. He'd fooled me into thinking he was something he wasn't. I'd thought Paul was strong and brave, intelligent and sensitive. But he was just a stupid, cowardly, lecherous pig, a pathetic excuse for a man. How had I ever let myself *imagine he could be a worthy partner? He wasn't even resisting, just sitting there mewing like a kitten, letting me hit him.*

*Panting with exertion and anger, I finally stopped. I stepped back and stared contemptuously at him, watching his tears wash lines through the blood on his face. "You brought this on yourself," I hissed. All my careful plans had gone up in smoke.*

*But now, I didn't want to give him the second chance I'd given Adam. I didn't want Paul's love, not under any circumstances. He didn't deserve me. I stepped round to the back of the chair and grasped the tongue of the strap. "No," he whimpered. "Please, no."*

*"You had your chance," I said angrily. "You had your chance and you blew it. You've no one to blame but yourself, coming here and pissing on the floor like a baby who can't control itself." I pulled the strap, tightening it enough to let me slip it free of the buckle. Then I let it slide free.*

*Paul's muscles instantly clenched, holding him rigidly in place, a scant half-inch above the spike. I moved round into his line of vision and slowly stripped off, caressing my body, imagining what his hands would have felt like. His eyes bulged with effort as he tried to keep himself in place. I sat down and slowly, deliciously began to rub myself, irresistibly turned on by his fight to stay away from the agonizing spike.*

*"You could have been doing this," I sneered, aroused still further by the quivering of his thighs and calves. "You could have been making love instead of fighting to keep your arse in working order."*

*If he'd worked out like Adam had, the pleasure would have lasted longer. As it was, his screams of agony mingled with my groans of pleasure. I came like a Guy Fawkes rocket, fire flashing through me and erupting in an orgasm that had me buckling at the knees.*

*He tried to pull free, but the barbs just cut deeper into his tender flesh. I lay back in the chair, savouring the waves of pleasure that flowed through me after my orgasm, Paul's moans and screams an extravagant counterpoint to my sexual satisfaction.*

*As time passed, he sank lower on the spike, and his screams moderated to whimpering groans. To my surprise, I felt sexual desire rise in me again. After the exquisite pleasure of my first orgasm, I wanted my excitement matched again. I reached for the control box for the electrical current to the spike, and pressed the button that completed the circuit. Even with a relatively low current, Paul's body convulsed in an arc that wrenched him almost clear of the spike, a fine spray of blood spattering the floor for a couple of feet around.*

*I matched the rhythms of our two bodies, the speed and intensity of our mutual excitement keeping perfect pace. I felt my muscles quiver like his as I thrust against my hand. As I came, my body arched in sync with his, my gasps echoed by his last agonized cries before unconsciousness came.*

*I have to confess I was surprised by how much I enjoyed Paul's punishment. Perhaps because he had deserved so much more than Adam, perhaps because I had had higher expectations of him in the first place, or perhaps simply because I was getting better at what I had to do. Whatever the reason, my second excursion into murder left me feeling as if I'd found my true vocation at last.*

# 9

*We dry up our tears, and ... discover that a transaction which, morally considered, was shocking, and without a leg to stand upon, when tried by principles of Taste, turns out to be a very meritorious performance.*

"OK, Andy, it's showtime," Tony said to the blank screen of his computer. After Carol had dropped him off, he'd stumbled upstairs, kicking off his shoes and letting his quilted baseball jacket lie where it fell on the landing. Pausing only to empty his bladder, he'd burrowed under the duvet and fallen into the deepest sleep he'd known for months. When he'd woken, it had been after noon. But for once, he felt no guilt about the work he should have been doing. He felt refreshed, excited, elated even. Searching Stevie McConnell's house had given him a new certainty that he really did understand what he was doing. He had known, with absolute clarity, that Handy Andy did not live like that. And although it wasn't something he could admit to anyone outside the tight circle of fellow profilers, there was a real rush in realizing that he could probably find his way into Handy Andy's head and map a path through the tortured labyrinth of his unique logic. All he had to do now was find the key to the door.

In the office, Tony powered his way through the remaining piles of documents, making notes as he went along. Then he closed the blinds and told his secretary to hold all his calls. He moved his own chair round the desk so that it faced the visitor's chair. On the desk to one side, he placed his tape recorder, still switched off. He walked over to the door and stood with his back to it, contemplating the room. Some poem he'd once read echoed in his mind. Something about a road that divided in a wood, and the importance of choosing the branch less travelled by. For as long as he could recall, his fascinations had led him down the road less travelled by. It was the road that his patients walked, the dark path that led into the undergrowth, away from the dappled sunshine of the broad path. "I need to understand why you chose that road, Andy," Tony murmured. "This is what I do best, Andy. You see, I know what draws me to that road. But I'm not like you. I can go back when I want to. I can choose the sunny path. I don't have to be here. All I'm doing is studying your footsteps. Or at least, that's what I tell the world.

"But we know the truth, don't we? You can't hide from me, Andy," he said softly. "I'm just like you, you see. I'm your mirror image. I'm the poacher turned gamekeeper. It's only hunting you that keeps me from being you. I'm here, waiting for you. Journey's end." He stood for a moment longer, savouring the admission he'd made to himself.

Finally, he sat down in his chair and leaned forward, elbows on knees, hands loosely linked. "OK, Andy," he said. "It's just you and me. We're going to skip the preliminaries; all that stuff where we do the verbal arm wrestling and you eventually decide to talk to me. We're going straight for it. First off, I want to say how impressed I am. I've never seen a cleaner job. I don't just mean the bodies, I mean the whole thing. Sweet as a nut, you did it. Never a witness. Let me rephrase that. Never anybody seeing any significance in what they saw or heard, because there must have been people who saw or heard something, but they didn't make the connection. How did you manage to be so invisible?" He pressed "record" on the cassette recorder, then stood up and stepped across to the other chair.

Tony took a deep breath and deliberately relaxed his body. He used breathing techniques to put himself into a light state of trance. He instructed his conscious mind to let go, to allow his higher self to access directly all he knew about Handy Andy and to answer for him. When he spoke, even his voice was different. The timbre was rougher, the tones deeper. "I blended in. I took care. I watched and I learned."

Tony swapped chairs again. "You obviously did a good job of it," he said. "How did you choose them?"

Back into Andy's chair. "I liked them. I knew it would be special with them. I wanted to be like them. They all had good jobs, a nice life. I'm good at learning things, I could have learned to be like them. I could have fitted into their lives."

"So why kill them?"

"People are stupid. They don't understand me. I was the one they always laughed at, then they learned to be afraid of me. I don't like being laughed at, and I'm tired of people being wary of me, like I'm some animal that's going to go for them. I gave them a chance, but they didn't give me any choice. I had to kill them."

Tony sank back in his own chair. "And after you'd done it once, you realized that was the best thing in the world."

"I felt good. I felt in control. I knew what was going to happen. I'd planned it all out, and it worked!" Tony surprised himself by the degree of enthusiasm that came out. He waited, but nothing more seemed to emerge.

He returned to his own chair. "Didn't last for long, did it? The pleasure? The sense of power?"

In Andy's chair, he felt at a loss for the first time. Usually, he found role play loosened up his ideas, let his thoughts flow free. But something was clogging this up. That something was clearly at the heart of the issue. Tony moved back to his own seat and thought about it. "Serial killers act out their fantasies in their crimes. The crime itself never lives up to the fantasy, so it has limited power. Its details are incorporated into the fantasies, which are then realized in a second, often more ritualistic killing. And so on. But as time goes by, the fantasies have less and less staying power. The killings have to get closer and closer together to keep the fantasies fuelled. But your killings don't get closer together, Andy. Why is that?"

He moved across, not hopeful. He allowed his mind to

blank, letting his consciousness drift off, hoping it would
come up with an answer that might satisfy his idea of Andy.
After a few moments, Tony felt himself slipping away from
consciousness. All at once, from what felt like a long way
away, a deep chuckle rumbled through him. "That's for me
to know and you to find out," his own voice mocked him.

Tony shook his head like a diver coming to the surface.
Dazed, he got to his feet and snapped the blinds open. So
much for alternative techniques. What was interesting,
however, was the point at which his brain had snagged.
This was one of the factors about Handy Andy that was
unique. The gaps stayed constant. Even allowing for his
use of a camcorder, it was still remarkable.

The line of thought restored Tony's earlier vigour and
he decided to take a side trip to the university library's
media-studies section where he went through the back numbers of the *Bradfield Evening Sentinel Times* for the
appropriate dates. A careful scrutiny of the entertainments
pages revealed little in common between the four evenings
in question, unless he was prepared to consider that the
local art cinema always showed classic British black-and-
white comedies on Mondays. Somehow, he couldn't imagine *Passport to Pimlico* fuelling homicidal sexual fantasies.
Finally, just after seven, he was ready to start on the profile.

He started with the usual caveat.

The following offender profile is for guidance only and
shouldn't be regarded as an identikit portrait. The offender
is unlikely to match the profile in every detail, though I
would expect there to be a high degree of congruence between the characteristics outlined below and the reality. All
of the statements in the profile express probabilities and
possibilities, not hard facts.

A serial killer produces signals and indicators in the
commission of his crimes. Everything he does is intended,
consciously or not, as part of a pattern. Uncovering the
underlying pattern reveals the killer's logic. It may not appear logical to us, but to him it is crucial. Because his logic

is so idiosyncratic, straightforward traps will not capture him. As he is unique, so must be the means of catching him, interviewing him and reconstructing his acts.

Tony continued the profile with a detailed account of the four victims. He included everything he'd gleaned from the police reports about their domestic circumstances, employment history, reputation among friends and colleagues, habits, physical condition, personality, family relationships, hobbies and social behaviour. Next, he wrote a short résumé of the pathologist's report on each man, the nature of their injuries and a description of the crime scenes. Then he began the crucial process of organizing and arranging his information into meaningful patterns so he could start to draw his conclusions.

None of the four victims had any history of homosexual relationships, as far as can be ascertained. (We cannot exclude a secret homosexual/bisexual orientation, but there is no evidence in any of the four cases to suggest this.) Yet each body was dumped in an area known primarily for its use by the gay community. In particular, the bodies were dumped in spots which are notorious for the consummation of casual sexual encounters. What does this say about the killer?

1. He is a man who is not comfortable with his own sexuality. He deliberately chooses men who are not openly gay-identified. It may well be that he has made a sexual approach to his victims in the past and has been rebuffed. The killer is almost certainly not an out gay; he probably represses his own sexuality at some personal cost. He probably grew up in an environment where masculinity was highly prized and praised and homosexuality condemned, possibly on religious grounds. If he is in a sexual/domestic relationship, it will be with a woman. And he will almost certainly have sexual problems within that relationship, probably ones of potency.

Tony stared bleakly at the screen. Sometimes he hated the way his job constantly forced him to confront his own problems. Did his own sexual failings mean he was really stuck on the road less travelled by? Was there going to be a night when some woman went too far, when her determination to translate his problem into a comment on her womanhood tipped him over the edge? For Tony, it was a scenario that was all too vivid. That's why Angelica was safe. When she drove him to distraction, he could slam the phone down, rather than slap her face. Or worse. Best stay out of risk, he thought. Don't even think about thinking about Carol Jordan. You've seen it in her eyes, she's interested in more than your mind. Don't even think about it, fuck-up. Get back to work.

2. He despises those who express their homosexuality openly. At least part of his motivation in using these dumping grounds is to show his contempt for them, as well as to frighten them. He's also demonstrating his superiority: "Look at me, I can come and go among you and none of you know me. I can desecrate your places, and you can't stop me."

3. He is nevertheless familiar with areas where gay men go to socialize and to pick up sexual partners. It may be that his job takes him into the Temple Fields area from time to time, perhaps to make deliveries or to provide some service to businesses. He is fascinated with the gay culture, to the extent that he has scouted out the specific area in Carlton Park where gay cruising goes on.

4. He has a high degree of self-control. He is driving into a populous area and dumping bodies without behaving in a way that draws attention to himself.

"Tell me about it," Tony said bitterly. He got up and stalked a path from the window to the door. "I could have written the manual." Ever since the bullies had started to pick on him, the smallest boy in the street and in his class, he'd learned the harsh lessons of self-control. "Never show you're hurt, it only encourages them. Never show they've hit the mark, it only reveals your weak points. Learn to be one of the lads. Learn the vocabulary, learn the body language, acquire the attitude. Mix it all together and what do you get? You get a man who hasn't got the remotest idea of who he is. You have a consummate actor, a human impostor who can take on local colour like a chameleon." The miracle was that it fooled so many people. Brandon clearly thought he was a good bloke. Carol Jordan obviously fancied him. Claire, his secretary, thought he was the best boss she'd ever had. He was passing for human, all right. The only one he couldn't fool was his mother, who still treated him with the thinly disguised contempt which was all he'd ever known from her. His fault his father had left them, and no wonder, according to her. She'd have dumped him in some children's home if it hadn't been for her need to keep in with her parents, the ones who held the purse strings. As it was, she'd dived head first into a career as soon as she'd been able to persuade her mother to mind little Tony. He'd done his best to be good, as Granny had instructed him, but it wasn't always easy. She wasn't a bad woman, just constrained by her own upbringing into the belief that children should be seen and not heard. His grandfather's response to domestic tyranny was to escape to the betting shop, the bowling green and the Legion. Tony had swiftly learned self-control the hard way. Was that what had happened to Andy, too? Rubbing his hand across eyes surprisingly damp, Tony threw himself back into his chair and started typing frantically.

5. His domestic and work situation allows him to be free on Monday evenings, and he does not expect to be spotted in Temple Fields by anyone who knows him. This throws up several possibilities: he may have chosen Monday nights specifically because it's his night off work or because his wife/girlfriend is away from home on Monday nights; he may have decided to kill on Mondays because the first time was a Monday and it worked out for him and

now has superstitious power; or he may have decided to keep on killing on Mondays in the hope that it will skew the investigation. He is obviously intelligent, and such careful planning should not be presumed to be beyond him.

Tony paused for thought, flicking through the pages of notes he'd made. He wasn't thinking like Handy Andy yet, but the elusive mind was getting closer and closer. He wondered again if his involvement in the twisted logic of killers was a surrogacy, the only thing that prevented him from joining their number. God knows, there were times when the inevitable drive that surged through their heads seemed attractive. And there were times enough when he'd felt murderous rage, though it was usually turned against himself rather than the person he was in bed with. "Enough, already," Tony said aloud, and returned to the glowing screen.

The offender is an organized serial killer, who is managing to maintain a constant eight-week gap between killings. This consistency is unusual in itself, since the normal pattern is that the space between murders decreases as they lose their power to satisfy the killer's fantasies. One reason for the maintenance of this gap may be that he spends so long stalking his victim before the kill. Thus the delights of anticipation, coupled with the savour of his previous kills, act as a brake. I also believe that the killer is using his camcorder to record his activities and that this is also fuelling his fantasies between kills.

Tony stopped to consider what he had written. The stumbling block. His analysis probably looked good enough to convince the lay person, but he was far from satisfied with it. But no amount of dredging of his mind or his data could come up with a better explanation. With a sigh, he continued.

What is the primary intent of his killings? We can rule out killing in the course of criminal activity, such as armed robbery or burglary. We can also rule out emotional, selfish or cause-specific killings, such as self-defence, compassion, assassination or domestic disputes. This places the killings in the category of sexual homicides.

The chosen victims all fall into the low-risk category. In other words, they all had occupations and lifestyles that didn't make them vulnerable targets. The flip side of this is that the killer has to take high-level risks to capture and kill them. What does this tell us about the killer?

1. He is operating under extremely high stress levels.

2. He plans his kills very carefully. He cannot afford to make mistakes, because if he does, his victims will escape and put him at risk, both physically and legally. He is almost certainly a stalker. He chooses his victims carefully, and studies their lives in detail. Interestingly, so far he has not been thwarted in his choice of evening. Is this a result of careful planning, prearrangement or just luck? We know that the third victim, Gareth Finnegan, told his girlfriend he was going on a lads' night out, but none of his male friends or colleagues seemed to know anything about it, and it is not clear whether he was abducted from his home or if the contact took place at a prearranged point. It may be that the killer has had prior arrangements to meet each of his victims, either at their homes or elsewhere. He may even be posing as an insurance salesman or something similar, though I feel it's unlikely that he would have the people skills to do such a job successfully for a living.

3. He likes the extra excitement that walking out on the high wire gives him. He needs that buzz.

4. He must have some areas of emotional maturity in his make-up that allow him to hold himself under control in these highly stressful situations. This may also allow him to buck the poor work-history pattern so common among serial offenders. (See below.)

Most serial offences demonstrate a degree of escalation, indicating the killer's need for more thrills, better execution of his fantasies. Like a roller coaster, each high needs to be bigger to compensate for the inevitable low that has preceded . . .

Tony looked up, startled. What was that noise? It had sounded like the door to the open-plan outer office, but at this time of night, there shouldn't be anyone on this floor. Nervously, he pushed himself away from the computer desk, steering his chair across the carpet on silent castors till he was behind his desk and out of the pool of light shed by the lamp beside the computer. He held his breath and listened. Silence. The tension gradually began to ooze away. Then, abruptly, a line of light appeared under his office door.

The metallic taste of fear gripped Tony. The nearest thing to an offensive weapon on his desk was a chunk of agate he used as a paperweight. He snatched it up and moved stealthily out of his chair.

When Carol opened the door, she was taken aback to find Tony halfway across the room, hefting a rock in his hand. "It's me," she yelped.

Tony's arms dropped to his side. "Oh shit," he said.

Carol grinned. "Who were you expecting? Burglars? Journalists? The bogeyman?"

Tony relaxed. "I'm sorry," he said. "You spend all day trying to get inside some nutter's head and you end up as paranoid as he is."

"Nutter," Carol mused. "Now would that be some technical term you psychologists use?"

"Only inside these four walls," Tony said, walking back to his desk and putting the agate back where it belonged. "To what do I owe the pleasure?"

"Since British Telecom don't seem to be able to connect us, I thought I'd better come round personally," Carol replied, pulling up a chair. "I left a message on your machine at home this morning. I assumed you'd already left for work, but you weren't here either. I tried again around four, but there was no reply from your extension. At least, I assume that's why the switchboard operator said, 'I'm putting you through now,' and I ended up in a black hole. And, of course, now the switchboard have all gone home and I never thought to ask for your direct line."

"And you a detective," Tony teased.

"That's my excuse, anyway. Actually, I couldn't face another minute in Scargill Street."

"Want to talk about it?"

"Only if I can talk with my mouth full," Carol said. "I'm starving. Could you go a quick curry?"

Tony glanced at his computer screen, then back at Carol's drawn face and tired eyes. He liked her, even though he didn't want to get close, and he needed her on his side. "Just let me save this file, and I'm out of here. I can come back later and finish this."

Twenty minutes later they were attacking onion bhajis and chicken pakora in an Asian café in Greenholm. The other customers were students and those of the terminally right-on tendency who hadn't quite adjusted to the fact they were no longer studying anything except political correctness. "It's not exactly Good Food Guide, but it's cheap and cheerful, and the service is quick," Tony apologized.

"Fine by me. I'm more egg on toast than Egon Ronay. My brother got the gourmet genes in our family," Carol said. She glanced quickly around her. Their table for two was less than a foot away from the next. "Did you bring me here deliberately so we couldn't talk about work? Some psychologist's ploy to refresh my mind?"

Tony's eyes widened. "I didn't even think of that. You're right, of course, we can't talk about it in here."

Carol's smile lit up her eyes. "You can have no idea how much pleasure that gives me."

They ate in silence for a few minutes. Tony broke the silence. That way, he stayed in control of the subject. "What made you decide to be a copper?"

Carol raised her eyebrows. "Because I like oppressing the underprivileged and hassling racial minorities?" she tried.

Tony smiled. "I don't think so."

She pushed her plate to one side and sighed. "Youthful idealism," she said. "I had this crazy idea that the police should be there to serve and protect society from lawlessness and anarchy."

"It's not such a crazy idea. Believe me, if you dealt with the people I used to handle, you'd feel relieved that they weren't on the streets."

"Oh, the theory's fine. It's just the practice that's such a bummer. It all started when I read sociology at Manchester. I specialized in the sociology of organizations, and all my contemporaries despised the police force as a corrupt, racist, sexist organization whose sole role was to preserve the illusory comfort of the middle classes. To some extent, I agreed with them. The difference was that they wanted to attack institutions from the outside, whereas I've always believed that if you want fundamental change, it has to come from inside."

Tony grinned. "You little subversive, you!"

"Yeah, well, I guess I didn't realize what I was getting into. David knocking out Goliath was a piece of piss compared with trying to change things in the police."

"Tell me about it," Tony said with feeling. "This national task force could revolutionize the clear-up rate on serious crimes, but the way some senior officers carry on, you'd think I was setting up a scheme to allow paedophiles to retrain as child minders."

Carol giggled. "You mean, you'd rather be back in the locked ward with your nutters?"

"Carol, sometimes I feel like I've never left. You've no idea what a refreshing change it is to work with people like you and John Brandon."

Before Carol could reply, the waiter arrived with their main courses. As she spooned out lamb and spinach, chicken karahi and pilau rice, Carol said, "Does your job create the same problems with having a private life as the police service does?"

Instantly defensive, Tony answered with a question. "How do you mean?"

"Like you said earlier, you get obsessed with the job. You spend your time dealing with shitheads and animals—'

"And that's just your colleagues," Tony butted in.

"Yeah, right. And you come home at night after dealing with broken bodies and fractured lives and you're expected to sit down and watch the soaps and act like normal people do."

"And you can't because your head's still plugged into the horrors of the day," Tony finished. "And with *your* job, you have the added complication of shift work."

"Exactly. So, do you get the same problems?"

Was she asking out of idle curiosity or was this an oblique way of finding out about his private life? Sometimes Tony wished he could just switch off the part of his head that had to analyse every statement, every gesture, every intricate piece of body language and just revel in the pleasure of eating dinner with someone who seemed to enjoy his company. Suddenly aware that he had left too long a pause between the question and the answer, Tony said, "I'm probably even worse at switching off than you. Men generally seem to get much more obsessive than women. I mean, how many female train spotters, stamp collectors or football fanatics do you know?"

"And that interferes in your personal relationships?" Carol persisted.

"Well, none of them have ever gone the distance," Tony said, struggling to keep his voice light. "I don't know if that's down to the job, or to me. Mostly, the last thing they've screamed at me as they walked out the door hasn't been, 'you and your bloody nutters,' so I guess it must be me. How about you? How do you handle the problems of the job?"

Carol's fork continued its journey to her mouth and she chewed and swallowed her mouthful of curry before she answered. "I've found that men aren't very sympathetic towards shifts unless they do them too. You know, you're never there with the tea on the table when they've got to rush out to that vital squash match. Add to that the difficulty of getting them to understand why the job drives you inside your head and what are you left with? Junior doctors, other coppers, fire fighters, ambulance drivers. And in my experience, there aren't many of them who want a relationship with an equal. I guess the job takes too much out of us for us to have much left over. The last guy I was involved with was a doctor, and all he wanted to do when he wasn't working was sleep, fuck and party."

"And you wanted more?"

"I wanted the occasional conversation, maybe even a movie or a night out at the theatre. But I put up with it because I loved him."

"So what made you end it?"

Carol stared down at her plate. "Thanks for the compliment, but I didn't. When I moved up here, he decided that driving up and down the motorway was a waste of good shagging time, so he dumped me for a nurse. Now it's just me and the cat. He doesn't seem to mind the irregular hours."

"Ah," Tony said. He had heard the real pain under the surface, but for once, all his professional skills didn't seem adequate to the response.

"How about you? You involved with anyone?" Carol asked.

Tony shook his head and carried on eating.

"Nice bloke like you, I'd have thought you'd have been snapped up ages ago," Carol said, the tease in her tone covering something Tony wished he was imagining.

"Ah, but you've only seen the charming side. When the moon's full, I sprout hair on the palms of my hands and bay at the moon." Tony leered melodramatically at Carol. "I am not what I appear to be, young woman," he growled.

"Oh, Grandmamma, what big teeth you've got!" Carol said in falsetto.

"All the better to eat my curry with," Tony laughed. He knew this was the point where he could have moved the relationship forward, but he had spent too long constructing his defences against precisely these moments of weakness to let them down that easily. Besides, he told himself, he had no need of a relationship with her. He had Angelica and bitter experience had taught him that was all he could handle and still function.

"So how did you get into this soul-destroying line of work?" Carol asked.

"I discovered while I was working on my DPhil that I hated getting up on my hind legs and talking to an audience, which kind of ruled out academic work. So I went into clinical practice," Tony said, slipping easily into a flow of anecdotes about his work. He felt himself relax, like a man walking on a frozen lake who realizes he's back on dry land.

They spent the rest of the meal on the safer ground of their careers, and Carol asked the waiter for the bill when he came to clear off the table. "I'm picking up the tab, OK? Nothing to do with feminism; you're a legitimate business expense," Carol said.

As they walked back to Tony's office, he said, "So, back to work. Tell me about your day."

The swift switch away from the personal back to the case confirmed to Carol the need to play it cool with Tony. She'd never seen anyone back off so fast at gentle flirtation. It was puzzling, all the more since she sensed he liked her. And she had no doubts about her capacity to attract men. At least tracking Handy Andy with him gave her space and time to build a bridge between them. "We got a break this morning. At least, that's what we're all hoping."

Tony stopped abruptly and turned to face Carol. "What kind of a break?" he demanded.

"Don't worry, you're not being ignored," Carol said. "It's something that would be a minor detail in most investigations, but because we've got so little to go on here, it's got everybody excited. There was a torn fragment of leather on a nail by the gate in the Queen of Hearts's yard. Forensic did a rush job on it, and it turns out that it's very unusual. It's deerskin, and it comes from Russia."

"Oh, my good God," Tony said softly. He turned away and took a couple of steps. "Don't tell me, let me guess. You can't get it in this country, and you'd probably need to send someone to Russia to source it, it's so obscure. Am I right?"

"How the hell did you know that?" Carol asked, catching him up and grabbing his sleeve.

"I've been expecting something like this," he said simply.

"Like what?"

"An outrageous red herring that'll have the entire police force running around like headless chickens."

"You think this is a red herring?" Carol almost shouted. "Why?"

Tony rubbed his hands over his face and ran them through his hair. "Carol, this guy has been so careful. He's been almost clinical in his obsession with leaving no clues. Serial killers have typically got high IQs, and Handy Andy is certainly one of the cleverest I've ever come across, either personally or in the whole literature. Yet suddenly, out of nowhere we get not just any old clue, but a clue so obscure that it could only possibly be left by a tiny segment of the population. And you're standing here telling me you think this is for real? That's exactly what he's trying to achieve. I bet the lot of you have been running around like blue-tailed flies all day trying to suss out where this obscure piece of Russian leather came from, haven't you? Oh, and don't tell me, let me guess. I bet there's now a whole squad tracking back through Stevie McConnell's life trying to establish where the hell he got it from."

Carol stared at him. It seemed so blindingly obvious when he explained it like that. Yet not one of them had questioned the validity of the leather scrap.

"Am I right?" Tony asked, more gently this time.

Carol pulled a face. "Not a whole squad. Just me and Don Merrick and a couple of DCs. I've spent most of the day on the phone talking to governing bodies in weightlifting and body-building, trying to establish if McConnell's ever been on a national or regional team that either competed in Russia or competed against Russians. And Don and the lads have been grilling travel agencies trying to check if he's ever been on holiday there."

"Oh, Christ," Tony groaned. "And?"

"Five years ago, he was one of a team of weightlifters from the North West who competed in an event in what was then Leningrad."

Tony took a deep breath. "The poor unlucky bastard," he said. "I don't expect the idea that this was deliberately planted to have occurred to any of you," he added. "I don't mean that patronizingly. I realize how much closer you are to all of this and how desperately you want to catch this bastard. I just wish someone had told me earlier, before it assumed this major significance for everyone."

"I did *try* to phone you this morning," Carol said. "You still haven't said where you were."

Tony held his hands up. "I'm sorry. I'm overreacting. I was in bed, asleep, with the phones turned off. I was exhausted after last night, and I knew I couldn't concentrate on writing the profile unless I had some sleep. I should have checked my answering machine when I got up. Sorry, I shouldn't have had a go."

Carol grinned. "I'll let you off this time. Just save the fearsome bit for when we catch Handy Andy, huh?"

Tony pulled a face. "Shouldn't that be 'if'?"

He looked so vulnerable and fallible, his shoulders slumped, his head down, that Carol's impulses overrode the decision she'd taken only minutes before to play it cool. She stepped forward and pulled Tony into a tight hug. "If anyone can do it, you can," she whispered, rubbing the side of her head against his chin like a cat marking its territory.

Brandon stared at Tom Cross, his face a mask of horror. "You did *what*?" he demanded.

"I searched McConnell's house," Cross said belligerently.

"I thought I said categorically that we had no right to do that? No judge in the land is going to accept that arrest for common assault in the street gives sufficient grounds for suspicion of murder."

Cross smiled. It was a rictus that would have raised a Rottweiler's hackles. "With respect, sir, that was then. Once Inspector Jordan had established that McConnell had been to Russia, the picture changed. Not a lot of people have had access to obscure Russian leather jackets, after all. It puts him in the frame. And there's more than one JP around that owes me one."

"You should have cleared it with me," Brandon said. "The last order I gave on the subject was no search."

"I tried, sir, but you were in a meeting with the Chief," Cross said sweetly. "I thought I'd better strike while the iron was hot, being as how we don't have him banged up indefinitely."

"So you wasted more time searching McConnell's house," Brandon said bitterly. "Don't you think you and your men could have been better employed?"

"I haven't told you yet what we found," Cross said.

Brandon felt his chest constrict. He wasn't a man given to premonitions, but the sinking foreboding that gripped him now was as palpable as any solid fact he'd ever examined. "Think very carefully about what you say next, Superintendent," he said cautiously.

A momentary frown of puzzlement flashed over Cross's features, but he was too full of the message he bore to worry about the ACC's words. "We've got him, sir," he said. "Bang to rights. We found one of Gareth Finnegan's firm's Christmas cards in McConnell's bedroom, and a sweater that's a dead ringer for the one Adam Scott's bird says was missing from his house. Plus a traffic ticket with Damien Connolly's badge number on it. Add that to the Russian connection, and I think it's time to charge the little arse bandit."

*Of course, the discovery that one has a natural bent for something does not necessarily mean one should pursue it blindly. While I was disposing of Paul's body, this time in a dark doorway in an alley in Temple Fields, I had already decided who my next target would be. But even after so magnificent an experience as the one I'd just shared with Paul, I had no intention of repeating it with Gareth.*

*It was going to be third time lucky. Gareth, I already knew, was a man of rich and fertile sexual imagination. Even as I was digitizing Paul's pathetic performance into the computer, I was mourning the fact that, thanks to Gareth, I would never have the opportunity to perfect the extraordinary talent I had discovered in myself. With the resources at my command, I've been making movies like I've never seen. The ultimate snuff stuff. If I could have marketed them, I would have made a fortune. I know there's a market out there. Plenty of people would pay a lot of money to watch Paul fuck me in his death spasms on the Judas chair. And as for what I've done with Adam . . . Let's just say that no one's ever seen sixty-nine like it.*

*As a treat, I went to the cemetery where Adam had been buried a few weeks before. The funeral had featured on the local television news, which I'd video-taped and studied so I could be fairly sure where the grave was. After dark, I made my way through the graves, and found Adam's within twenty minutes. I opened the can of red spray paint I'd brought with me and sprayed "WANKER" on one side of the grey granite, and "POOFTER" on the other side. That should give the police something to occupy their minds.*

*The following evening, while I was waiting for Gareth to emerge from the firm of solicitors where he was a salaried partner, I whiled away the time with the hyperbole of the* Bradfield Evening Sentinel Times. *This time, I'd made the front page.*

### GAY KILLER STRIKES AGAIN?

*The mutilated body of a naked man was found this morning in Bradfield's gay village.*

*The murder victim had been dumped in the fire-exit doorway of the gay club Shadowlands in an alley off Canal Street in the notorious Temple Fields district.*

*This is the second time in two months that the body of a naked man has been discovered in the gay cruising area.*

*Now locals fear a perverted serial killer is stalking the city's large homosexual community.*

*Today's gruesome discovery was made by nightclub owner Danny Surtees, 37, as he arrived for a meeting with his accountant.*

*He said, "I always go into the club through the fire door at the side. I park my car in the alley. This morning, the door was blocked by something covered by a couple of black bin bags.*

*"When I grabbed hold of the bags to try and pull them away from the door, they just came away in my hands and I saw there was a body under them.*

*"He was horribly injured. There was no way he was still alive. I'm going to have nightmares about this for the rest of my life."*

*Mr. Surtees said the doorway had been clear when he locked up his club just after three this morning.*

*The victim, said to be in his early thirties, has not yet been identified. Police describe him as white, 5ft 11ins, slightly built, with dark-brown collar-length hair and hazel eyes. He has an old scar from an appendicectomy.*

*A police spokesman said, "We believe the man was killed elsewhere and the body dumped in the alley between three and eight a.m.*

*"We would urge anyone who was in the Temple Fields area last night to come forward for the purpose of elimination. All information will be treated in the strictest confidence.*

*"At this stage of our enquiry, there is no evidence to connect this killing with the murder two months ago of Adam Scott."*

*Carl Fellowes, the full-time worker at the Bradfield Gay and Lesbian Centre, said today, "The police say that they don't think there's a connection between these two murders.*

*"I don't know what makes me more worried on behalf of the city's gay community—the thought that there's one nutter out there killing gay men, or the thought that there are two of them."*


I didn't know whether to laugh or cry. One thing was clear, though. PC Plod was a long way from covering himself in glory over this case. I'd obviously done a good job covering my tracks.

I folded up my newspaper, finished my cappuccino and signalled for my bill. Any minute now, Gareth would emerge from his office and walk through the rush-hour streets to the tram. I wanted to be ready for him. I had something really special planned for him tonight, and I wanted to make sure he was home alone to enjoy it.

# 10

*The world in general, gentlemen, are very bloody-minded;
and all they want in a murder is a copious effusion of
blood; gaudy display in this point is enough for them. But
the enlightened connoisseur is more refined in his taste.*

Penny Burgess topped up her glass of Californian Char-
donnay from the bottle in the fridge and walked back
through to her living room in time to hear the headlines on
the BBC local news. Nothing fresh to worry about, she
thought with relief. An armed robbery she could catch up
with first thing in the morning. The police were still questioning a man in connection with the gay serial killings, but
no charges had been laid yet. Penny sipped her wine and
lit a cigarette.

They were going to have to move soon, she thought. By
morning, they'd either have had to charge him with something or let him go. So far, no one had got a sniff of the
suspect's identity, which was pretty remarkable. The whole
pack had been leaning heavily on their personal police contacts, but for once, the reservoir of information had reso-
lutely refused to leak. Penny decided she'd better take a
look at the magistrates' court lists in the morning. There
was an outside chance that the cops had something fairly
innocuous to charge their suspect with so they could hang
on to him while they dug around for the evidence they
needed to make the serial killing charges stick.

As the news cut away to the weather forecast, the phone
rang. Penny reached over to the occasional table by the sofa
and grabbed the receiver. "Hello?" she said.

"Penny? It's Kevin."

Hallelujah, Penny thought, sitting up and grinding out

her cigarette. All she said, however, was, "Kevin, my man. How's it hanging?" She raked in her handbag for a pencil and her notebook.

"Something's come up you might be interested in," the police inspector said cautiously.

"It wouldn't be the first time," Penny said suggestively. Her occasional sexual encounters with the very married Kevin Matthews had provided her with more than an inside track on Bradfield Metropolitan Police. He'd turned out to be one of the best lovers she'd ever had. She just wished he could overcome his Catholic guilt more often.

"This is serious," Kevin protested.

"So was I, superstud."

"Listen, do you want this info or not?"

"Definitely. Especially if it's the name of the guy you've got in custody for the Queer Killings."

She heard the sharp intake of breath. "You know I can't tell you that. There are limits."

Penny sighed. It was the story of their relationship. "OK, so what can you tell me?"

"Popeye's been suspended."

"He's off the case?" Penny asked, her mind racing. Tom Cross? Suspended?

"He's off the *job*, Pen. He's been sent home pending disciplinary action."

"Who by?" Jesus, this was a story and a half. Just what had Popeye Cross been up to this time? She felt a momentary panic. What if he'd been caught out giving the suspect's name to one of her rivals? She almost missed Kevin's reply.

"John Brandon."

"What the hell for?"

"Nobody's saying," Kevin said. "But the last thing he did before he saw Brandon was to carry out a search of our suspect's house."

"A legal search?" Penny probed.

"Far as I know he had grounds under PACE," Kevin said cautiously.

"So what's going on, Kevin? Has Popeye been planting evidence, or what?"

"I don't know, Pen," Kevin said plaintively. "Look, I've got to go. If I hear anything else, I'll call you, OK?"

"OK. Thanks, Kev. You're a star, you know."

"Yeah, well. I'll speak to you soon."

The line went dead. Penny dumped the phone back on the base unit and jumped to her feet. She hurried through to her bedroom, pulling off her dressing gown on the way. Five minutes later, she was running down the two flights of stairs from her flat to the underground garage. In the car, she checked the address in her A-Z, then set off, mentally rehearsing what she was going to say on the doorstep.

It was Tony who had pulled away from the clinch first. His body withdrew from hers in a gesture that rendered four inches forty.

Trying to keep it light, to cover the awkwardness that had sprung up between them, Carol said, "Sorry, you just looked like you needed a hug."

"Nothing wrong with that," Tony said stiffly. "We use it all the time in group therapy."

They stood for a moment, eyes not quite meeting. Then Carol moved to Tony's side, slipped a hand through his unyielding arm and steered him forwards across the university courtyard. "So when do I get to look at this profile?"

The conversation was on safe ground again, but Carol was still too close to comfort. Tony could feel the tension inside him, like a cold hand squeezing his chest. He forced himself to speak in a calm, normal voice. "I want to do another couple of hours' work now, and I'll get stuck into it again first thing in the morning. I should have a draft ready for you by early afternoon. How does three o'clock sound to you?"

"Fine. Look, do you mind if I stick around now while you're working? I could do with rereading some of those statements, and I'll get no peace if I go back to Scargill Street."

Tony looked doubtful. "I suppose."

"I promise not to molest you, Dr. Hill," Carol teased.

"Damn," Tony said, snapping his fingers in mock-disappointment. Look at you, he thought cynically. Passing for human, sure of all the moves. "Actually, it's not that. I'm only hesitating because I'm not used to working with someone else in the room."

"You won't know I'm there."

"I doubt that very much," Tony said. She might read that as a compliment, but he knew the truth.

Penny pressed the doorbell of the mock-Tudor detached house in one of south Bradfield's more select streets. Even on a superintendent's salary, it should have been beyond Tom Cross's reach. But Popeye's reputation for being lucky had been enhanced a few years back when he'd won a high five-figure sum on the pools. The subsequent party had passed into police mythology. Now, it looked like he'd dropped his lucky pixie somewhere along the road.

A light snapped on in the hallway and someone lumbered towards the door, turned into an amorphous lump by the stained glass. "*Friday the Thirteenth* meets *Hallowe'en*," Penny muttered under her breath as she heard the lock turn. The door cracked open a suspicious few inches. Penny angled her head round to smile at the shape behind the door.

"Superintendent Cross," she said, the white cloud of her breath meeting the swirl of smoke issuing from the door. "Penny Burgess, *Sentinel Times*."

"I know who you are," Cross snarled, the slur of drink evident in those few words. "What the hell do you want, coming round here this time of night?"

"I hear you've had a bit of a problem at work," Penny tried.

"You hear wrong then, madam. Now, bugger off."

"Look, it'll be all over the media tomorrow. You're going to be under siege. The *Sentinel Times* has always supported you, Mr. Cross. We've been on your side all through this investigation. I'm not some visiting fireman from London, up here to put the boot in. If you've been sidelined, our readers have got a right to hear your side of the story." The door was still open. If she'd managed to say that much without him slamming it shut in her face, the chances were that she was going to get something usable out of him.

"What makes you think I'm off the case?" Cross asked defiantly.

"I heard you've been suspended. I don't know why, and that's the reason I wanted to hear your side of it, before we get fed the official line."

Cross scowled, his gooseberry eyes seeming to pop even further out. "I've got nothing to say," he told her, grudging every syllable.

"Not even off the record? You're willing to stand by and let them trash your reputation after all you've done for the force?"

Cross opened the door wider and looked down his drive towards the street. "You on your own?" he asked.

"Not even my newsdesk know I'm here. I only just heard."

"You'd better come in a minute."

Penny stepped across the threshold into a hall that looked like a Laura Ashley sample book. At the far end of the hall, a door was half open, the television voices distinct even at that distance. Cross steered her in the opposite direction, into a long sitting room. When he switched the lights on, Penny's eyes were assaulted by more patterns than a knitting shop. The only thing the curtains, carpets, rugs, wallpaper, frieze and scatter cushions had in common was that they were all shades of green and cream. "What a lovely room," she stammered.

"You think so? I reckon it's bloody hideous. The wife says it's the best money can buy, which is the only argument I've heard for staying potless," Cross grumbled, heading for a cocktail cabinet. He poured himself a stiff drink from a decanter, then, as an afterthought, said, "You'll not be wanting one, with you having the car."

"That's right," Penny said, forcing the warmth into her voice. "Can't take chances with your lads out on the roads."

"You want to know why them gutless bastards have suspended me?" he demanded belligerently, thrusting his head forward like a hungry tortoise.

Penny nodded, not daring to take out her notebook.

"Because they'd rather listen to some poncey bloody doctor than a proper copper, that's why."

If Penny had been a dog, her ears would have been standing to attention. As it was, she settled for a polite raise of the eyebrows. "A doctor?" she said.

"They've brought this wanker of a shrink in to do our job. And he says the arse bandit we've got banged up is innocent, so it's bollocks to the evidence. Now, I've been a copper for twenty-odd years, and I trust my instincts. We've got the bastard, I can feel it in my water. All I did was try to make sure he stayed behind bars till we nail down all the bloody loose ends." Cross downed his drink and banged his empty tumbler on the cabinet. "And they've got the fucking nerve to suspend *me*!"

Manufacturing evidence, then. Although she was desperate to know more about the mysterious doctor, Penny sensed that she'd better let Cross air his grievances first. "What did they say you'd done?" she asked.

"I've done nothing wrong," he said, pouring another massive slug from the decanter. "Trouble with bloody Brandon is he's been flying a desk for so long, he's forgotten what the job's about. Instinct, that's what it's about. Instinct and hard bloody work. Not some fucking trick cyclist with a head full of daft bloody notions like a fucking social worker."

"Who is this guy, then?" Penny asked.

"Dr. Tony bloody Hill. From the fucking Home Office. Sits in his ivory tower and tells us how to catch villains. He's got no more idea of coppering than I have of nuclear bloody physics. But the good doctor says, let the poofter go, so Brandon says yes, sir, no, sir, three bags full, sir. And just because I don't agree, I'm out on my arse." Cross swallowed more whisky, his face flushed with anger and drink. "Anybody'd think we were dealing with bloody Mastermind here, not some fucking dumbshit arse bandit who's had a bit of luck so far. You don't need smartarses with bloody 'doctor' in front of their name to catch scum like this. All you do is give the homicidal little fairy ideas above his station."

"It's fair to say, then, that you don't agree with the line the investigation's taking?" Penny asked.

Cross snorted. "That's one way of putting it. You mark my words, if they let this little fucker back on the streets, we'll be looking at another body."

To Tony's surprise, Carol proved to be true to her word. She sat at his desk, working her way through the pile of statements while he carried on working at his computer. Far from distracting him, he found her presence curiously soothing. He had no trouble picking up the profile where he'd left off earlier.

> Like a roller coaster, each high needs to be bigger to compensate for the inevitable low that has preceded it. In this instance, there are three principal signs of escalation. The wounds to the throat have become increasingly deep and assured. The sexual mutilation has developed from a few tentative cuts in the genital region to full-scale amputation. And the bites he inflicts then cuts away have increased in number and in depth. Yet he has managed to stay sufficiently in control to cover his tracks.
>
> It is difficult to assess whether or not the level of torture he is administering is escalating, since he seems to be using different torture methods in each case. The fact that he needs the stimulus of these different methods is, however, in itself a form of escalation.

Judging by the pathologist's report, the sequence of events would seem to be:

1. Capture, using handcuffs and ligatures round the ankles.
2. Torture, including sexually motivated acts such as biting and sucking.
3. The fatal blow to the throat.
4. Postmortem genital mutilation.

What does this tell us about the killer?

1. He has sophisticated and highly developed fantasies, which he is exploring through his torture methods.
2. He has a killing place. The amounts of blood and other bodily fluids generated by his activities could not be readily cleaned away from a normal domestic environment; it would be taking far more of a chance than his other cautious behaviour indicates. It will almost certainly have facilities for him to clean himself up after his killings, and power so he can run lights and a camcorder. We should be looking for something like a lock-up garage, a building that is secure but probably has running water and electricity. It may also be in an isolated location, thus avoiding the possibility of his victims' screams being overheard. (He will almost certainly remove any gags while he is torturing them; he will want to hear them scream and plead for mercy.)
3. He is obsessed with torture, and obviously has enough manual skills to construct his own engines of torture. He does not appear to have either medical or butchery skills, judging by the clumsy and tentative nature of the early throat-cutting and genital mutilation.

Tony turned away from the screen and glanced across at Carol. She was totally absorbed in her reading, the familiar frown line between her eyes. Was he being crazy to back off from what she appeared to be offering? More than anyone he'd ever been involved with she would understand the pressures of his job, the highs and lows that accompanied getting inside the head of a sociopath. She was intelligent and sensitive, and if she committed herself as thoroughly to a relationship as she did to her career, she might just be strong enough to work through his problems with him rather than use them as a stick to beat him with.

Suddenly aware of his eyes on her, Carol looked up and flashed him a tired smile. In that instant, Tony made his mind up. No way. He had enough problems dealing with the crap in his head without allowing anyone else to make it a hostage to fortune. Carol was just too sharp to let her any nearer. "Going OK?" she asked.

"I'm starting to get a feel for him," Tony admitted.

"That can't be a very pleasant place to be," Carol said.

"No, but it's what I'm paid for."

Carol nodded. "And I guess it's satisfying. And exciting?"

Tony smiled wryly. "You could say that. I sometimes wonder if that makes me as twisted as them."

Carol laughed. "You and me both. They say the best thief-takers are the ones who get inside the heads of the villains. So if I'm going to be the best at what I do, I have to think like a villain. That doesn't mean I want to do what they do, though."

Strangely comforted by her words, Tony turned back to his screen.

The time the killer spends with his victims can also provide pointers. In three of the four cases, the killer appears to have made contact in the early evening and to have dumped the bodies in the early hours of the following morning. Interestingly, in the third case, he spent far longer with his victim, apparently keeping him alive for the greater part of two days. This was the killing that took place over Christmas.

It may be that he is normally unable to spend long with his victims because of the other demands of his life, demands which altered over the Christmas period. These are more likely to be work-related demands than domestic ones, though it is possible that he is in a relationship with someone who returned alone to their family at Christmas, thus giving him time to spend with his victim. Another possibility is that the extended time he spent with Gareth Finnegan was a bizarre Christmas present to himself, a reward for the good performance of his previous "work."

The short space of time that elapses between the killings and the dumping of the bodies suggests that he does not use drink or drugs to any significant degree during the torture and murders. He would not risk being stopped by the police for erratic driving while he has a body in the boot, whether alive or dead. Also, although he appears to have used his victims' cars on occasion, it is clear that he also has a vehicle of his own. The chances are that this is a reasonably new vehicle in good condition, since he can't afford to take the chance of being stopped in a routine police check.

Tony hit the "save" key on his computer and sat back with a satisfied smile. This was as good a place to stop as any. Tomorrow morning, he'd complete the detailed checklist of characteristics he'd expect to find in Handy Andy, and outline proposals for potential courses of action by the police officers on the case.

"You done?" Carol asked.

He turned to see her leaning back in the chair, her pile of folders closed. "I didn't realize you'd finished," he said.

"Ten minutes ago. I didn't want to disturb the flying fingers."

Tony hated others studying him the way he studied them. The idea of being a patient on the receiving end of his own probing was one of those nightmares that he woke from in a sweat. "I've had it for tonight," he said, making a copy of his file on a floppy disc which he then pocketed.

"I'll give you a lift home," Carol said.

"Thanks," Tony said, getting to his feet. "I can never be bothered bringing the car into town. To tell you the truth, I don't much like driving."

"Can't say I blame you. The city traffic's hell on wheels."

When Carol pulled up outside Tony's house, she said, "Any chance of a cup of tea? Not to mention a pee?"

While Tony put the kettle on, Carol slipped upstairs to the bathroom. She came downstairs to the sound of her own voice issuing from his answering machine. She paused at the foot of the stairs, spying on him as he leaned against his desk, pen and paper in hand, listening to his messages. She enjoyed her growing sense of familiarity with his face and the lines of his body. Her voice ended and the machine beeped. "Hi Tony, it's Pete," the next voice announced. "I've got to be in Bradfield next Thursday. Any chance of a bed and a beer Wednesday night? Congratulations on getting on board the Queer Killer investigation, by the way. Hope you catch the bastard." Beep. "Anthony, my darling. Wherever can you be? I'm lying here, longing for you. We've got some unfinished business, lover boy."

At the sound of the voice, Tony straightened up and he turned to stare at the machine. The voice was husky, sexy, intimate. "Don't think you can—' Tony's hand shot out and cut the voice off abruptly.

So much for not being involved with anyone, Carol thought bitterly. She stepped forward through the doorway. "Let's just forget the tea. I'll see you tomorrow," she said, her voice cold and brittle as ice on a winter puddle.

Tony whirled round, panic in his eyes. "It's not what it seems," he blurted out without thought. "I've never even met the woman!"

Carol turned out of the doorway and walked down the hall. As she fumbled with the lock, Tony spoke coldly. "I'm telling you the truth, Carol. Even though it's actually none of your business."

She half turned, found a smile from somewhere and said, "You're quite right. It *is* none of my business. Till tomorrow, Tony."

The closing of the door reverberated through Tony's

head like a jackhammer. "Thank God you're a psychologist," he said bitterly as he slumped against the wall. "A layman might have really buggered that one up. You really believe in making the job a piece of piss, don't you, Hill?"

*When Gareth half smiled at me on the tram, I was convinced that my dreams were on the point of fulfilment. Because of an unexpected crisis at work, and all the extra overtime that entailed, I hadn't been able to follow him for more than a week.*

*His image had lulled me to sleep when I came home at all hours from work, and his voice throbbed hungrily in my ears, but I needed to see him in the flesh. I'd set my alarm clock to give me plenty of time to be outside his house before he left for work, but I was so exhausted I slept right through it. When I started into wakefulness, I realized my only chance was to catch up with his tram a couple of stops further down the line.*

*The tram was pulling in as I ran on to the platform. I eagerly scanned the first section, but couldn't see him. Anxiety rose in my throat like bile. Then I saw his gleaming head, sitting right by the door of the second carriage. I pushed through the crowd and managed to stand right next to him, my knees brushing his. At the physical contact, he looked up. His grey eyes crinkled at the corners and a smile flickered on his mouth. I smiled back and said, "Sorry."*

*"No problem," he said. "This tram gets busier by the day."*

*I wanted to continue the conversation, but for once I could think of nothing to say. He returned to the Guardian and I had to settle for watching him out of the corner of my peripheral vision while I pretended to stare out at the passing cityscape. It wasn't much, I know, but it was a start. He had acknowledged me; he knew I existed. Now, it could be only a matter of time.*

Shakespeare got it right when he said, "The first thing we do, let's kill all the lawyers." That way at least there would be fewer liars at large. Even the words sound the same: lawyer, liar. I should have expected nothing else from a man who speaks one day for the plaintiff, the next for the defendant.

I'd parked just round the corner from Gareth's house, where I could watch him come home without being seen, thanks to the tinted windows of my jeep. His house had no hedge, so I could see right into his living room from my vantage point.

I knew his habits by now. He arrived home just after six, went through to the kitchen for a can of Grolsch, and returned to the living room where he drank his beer and watched TV. After about twenty minutes, he'd fetch some food from the kitchen—pizza, TV dinner, baked potato. Cooking clearly wasn't his forte. When we were together, I'd have to take over responsibility for that side of our life.

After the news, he'd leave the room, presumably to do some work in another room of the house. I imagined law books arrayed on pine shelves. Then, he'd either return to the TV later in the evening, or walk down to the pub on the corner for a couple of lagers.

Gareth needed someone to share his life, I thought as I waited for him to come home. I was just the person to do that. Gareth was going to be my Christmas present to me.

At a quarter past five, a white Volkswagen Golf slipped into a parking place just beyond Gareth's house and a woman got out. She leaned back into the car and picked up a briefcase bulging with files and a shoulder bag. I thought she looked vaguely familiar as she walked down the pavement. Petite, light-brown hair pulled back in a *heavy plait, big tortoiseshell glasses, black suit, white blouse with a froth of lace at the throat.*

*When she turned in at Gareth's gate, I couldn't quite believe it. For the few seconds it took her to get to the door, I told myself she was his estate agent, his insurance agent, a colleague dropping off some papers. Anything. Anything.*

*Then she opened the flap of her bag and took out a key. My mind screamed "No!" as she inserted the key into the lock and let herself in. The living-room door opened and she dumped her briefcase by the settee. Then she was gone again. Ten minutes later, she was back, wrapped in Gareth's big white towelling dressing gown.*

*Frankly, I was with Shakespeare all the way.*


*'Twas the season to be jolly, so I forced myself not to let my disappointment colour my mood. Instead, I concentrated on researching my next project. I wanted something appropriate to the season, some good old barbaric Christian symbolism. There's not really a lot you can do with a manger and swaddling clothes, so I allowed myself some artistic licence and went for the other end of the life.*

*Crucifixion as a form of punishment was probably borrowed by the Romans from the Carthaginians. (Interesting, isn't it, how the Romans referred to everyone else as the barbarians . . . ) The Romans adopted it round about the time of the Punic Wars, and initially, it was a punishment reserved for slaves only. Which seems appropriate enough, since that was the only role I expected Gareth to be fit for now. Later in the days of empire, it became a more general punishment, meted out to any locals who had the temerity to misbehave after the Romans had kindly come along and conquered—sorry, civilized—them.*

*Traditionally, the felon was flagellated, then forced to carry the crossbeam through the streets to the place where a tall stake had been driven into the ground. Then he was nailed to the crossbeam and hauled up by a system of pulleys. His feet were sometimes nailed, sometimes tied to the* stake. On occasion, death by exhaustion was given a help-ing hand by the soldiers, who broke the legs of the victim, which must have allowed him a merciful lapse into uncon-sciousness. For my purposes, however, I decided to opt for the more decorative St. Andrew's Cross. For one thing, it would place more interesting stresses on Gareth's muscles. For another, should he rise to the occasion, it would make access a lot easier.

Interestingly, crucifixion was never used as a punishment for soldiers except for the crime of desertion. Maybe the Romans had the right idea after all.

# 11

*But who meantime was the victim, to whose abode he was hurrying? For surely he could never be so indiscreet as to be sailing about on a roving cruise in search of some chance person to murder? Oh, no: he had suited himself with a victim some time before, viz., an old and very intimate friend.*

Brandon stared bleakly at the sheet of paper in the typewriter. Tom Cross might have been a long way from the ACC's idea of the perfect copper, but he'd always appeared to be a good thief-taker. Antics like tonight's served only to raise a question mark over his whole career. Just how many other people had Cross fitted up over the years without anyone being any the wiser? If Brandon hadn't himself bent the rules and taken Tony on their illicit search, no one would have doubted the "evidence" Tom Cross had turned up. No one except Stevie McConnell would have known that two of Cross's three "finds" had arrived with him. The mere thought of the consequences of that was enough to send a prickle of cold sweat down Brandon's back.

Cross had left Brandon with no option but to suspend him. The disciplinary hearing that would inevitably follow would be painful for all concerned, but that was the least of Brandon's worries. He was far more troubled about the effect on the murder squad's morale. The only way to combat it was to take direct responsibility for the enquiry himself. Now, all he had to do was convince the Chief that he was right. With a sigh, Brandon pulled the last sheet of paper out of the machine and inserted another page.

His memo to the Chief Constable was brief and to the point. That only left one task before he could crawl home to bed. Sighing, Brandon glanced at the clock. Thirty minutes to midnight. He pushed the typewriter away from him and started writing on a sheet of his personal memo paper. "To Detective Inspector Kevin Matthews. From John Brandon, ACC (Crime). Re: Steven McConnell. Following the suspension of Superintendent Cross, I will assume direct command of the murder squad. There are no grounds for charging McConnell with anything other than assault. McConnell should be released on bail pending a court date for the assault charge, and on separate bail to return to Scargill Street in a week so that we can question him further if more evidence arises. In view of his refusal to give us any information about his contacts, or any names of people he might have introduced to Gareth Finnegan and Adam Scott, we should pursue any contacts he does make. A warrant for a tap on his phone should also be obtained, on the basis of his connection to Scott and Finnegan, and the contact we now know he had with Damien Connolly in a professional capacity. Our enquiries into the four related murders should continue on a broad front, though I suggest that, following his release on bail, we maintain close surveillance of McConnell. There will be a case conference of senior officers tomorrow at noon." He signed the memo and sealed it in an envelope. How to make friends and influence people, he thought as he walked downstairs to the desk sergeant. Brandon prayed that Tony Hill was right about Stevie McConnell. If Tom Cross had been right to follow his instinct, it would be more than the morale of the CID that would be at risk.

Carol slumped over the dining table, chin resting on her folded forearms, one hand tickling Nelson's belly. "What do you think, boy? Is he just another lying bastard, or what?"

"Prrrt," the cat said on a rising intonation, his eyes closed to slits.

"I thought you'd say that. I agree, I know how to pick

them," Carol sighed. "You're right, I should have kept my distance. That's what happens when you make the running. You get the knockbacks. They don't usually come from that far out of left field, though. At least now I know why he kept backing off. Better off without him, cat. Life's tough enough without playing second fiddle."

"Mrrr," Nelson agreed.

"He must think I'm brain dead, expecting me to believe that a total stranger leaves messages like that on his answering machine."

"Rowrr," Nelson complained, rolling over on to his back, batting her fingers with his paws.

"All right, so you think it's ridiculous too. But the man's a psychologist. If he was going to make something up to explain the fact that he'd lied to me, he'd make it a damn sight more plausible than funny phone calls. All he had to say was that it was somebody he'd finished with who wouldn't take the message." Carol rubbed the sleep out of her eyes, yawned and stood up in one languid movement.

The door to the boxroom Michael used as a study opened and he stood framed in the doorway. "I thought I heard voices. You could talk to me, you know. At least I answer you."

Carol gave a tired smile. "So does Nelson. It's not his fault we don't speak cat. I didn't want to disturb you; I could see you were working."

Michael walked over to the drinks cabinet and poured himself a small Scotch. "I was only play-testing, trying to spot the glitches in what we've done so far. No big deal. How's your day been?"

"Don't ask. They've moved us over to Scargill Street. It's a hellhole. Imagine going back to doing your calculations on an abacus, and you get the picture of my current working environment. The atmosphere's shit, and Tony Hill's spoken for. Apart from that, everything's magic." Carol followed Michael's example and poured herself a drink.

"Want to talk about it?" he asked, perching on the arm of one of the sofas.

"Thanks, but no thanks." Carol swallowed her drink in one, shuddered at the kick of the spirit and said, "I've brought you a set of pictures, by the way. How soon can you take a look at them?"

"I've scrounged some computer time with the software tomorrow evening. That do you?"

Carol put her arms round Michael and gave him a hug. "Thank you, bro," she said.

"My pleasure," he said, returning the embrace. "You know how I love a challenge."

"I'm going to bed," she said. "It's been a long one."

No sooner had Carol turned out the light than she felt the familiar thud of Nelson landing on the foot of the bed. It was reassuring to feel his warmth against her legs, though it was no substitute for the body she'd hoped for earlier in the evening. Of course, as soon as her head hit the pillow, her sleepiness vanished. The exhaustion was still there, but her mind was racing. Please God, by tomorrow afternoon, the awkwardness between her and Tony would have evaporated. The sting of humiliation would still be there for her, but she was a grown-up and a professional. Now she knew he was off limits, she wouldn't place him in a difficult position again, and now he knew she knew, maybe he'd be able to relax. Either way, the profile should provide more than enough neutral ground between them. She could hardly wait to see what he'd come up with.


On the other side of the sleeping city, Tony too lay in bed, staring at the ceiling, tracing imaginary road maps in the cracks round the plaster rose. He knew there was no point in switching out his bedside lamp. Sleep would elude him, and in the darkness, he'd start to feel the slow choke of claustrophobia closing in on him. Counting sheep had never appealed; the slow watches of the night were when Tony Hill became his own therapist. "Why did you have to ring tonight?" he murmured. "I *like* Carol Jordan. I know I don't want her in my life, but I didn't want to hurt her either. Hearing your blandishments on the answering machine must have felt like a smack in the face, after me saying there wasn't anybody in my life.

"An outsider would say we hardly know each other, everything that happened tonight was an overreaction. But outsiders don't understand the bonding, the intimacy that springs out of nowhere when you're working closely together on a manhunt, when the clock's ticking the next victim's life away."

He sighed. At least he hadn't blurted out the one thing that might have convinced Carol he wasn't lying, the truth he'd so carefully kept locked inside himself. What was it he told his patients? "Let it out. It doesn't matter what it is, speaking it is the first step in taking away the pain."

"What a load of crap that is," he said bitterly. "It's just another one of the tricks in my magic bag, designed to legitimize my prurient curiosity, tailored to unleash the twisted minds of the fuck-ups who are driven to act out their fantasies in a way society can't accommodate. If I'd told Carol the truth, said the i-word, it wouldn't have taken my pain away. It would only have made me feel even more of a worthless piece of shit. It's all very well for old men to be impotent. Men my age who can't get it up are a joke."

The phone rang, startling him. He rolled over, scrambling for the receiver. "Hello?" he said, his voice tentative.

"Anthony, at last. Oh, how I've missed you!"

His surge of anger at the languid, husky voice died as soon as it flared. What was the point in raging at her? She wasn't the problem. He was. "I got your message," he said, resigning himself. She hadn't caused the awkwardness with Carol; there would have been no grounds for awkwardness at all if he hadn't been such a pathetic excuse for a man. No point in even thinking about relationships with nice, normal women. He would have blown it with Carol, just as he'd always blown it with women as soon as they got close. The best he could hope for was telephone sex. At least it generated a kind of equality; it allowed men to fake not just orgasm but erection too.

Angelica chuckled. "I thought I'd leave you something nice to come home to. I hope you're not too tired for some recreation."

"I'm never too tired for your kind of recreation," Tony said, swallowing the self-disgust that threatened to overwhelm him. Think of it as therapy, he told himself. Tony lay back and let the voice flow over him, his hand straying down his chest towards his groin.

The cleaners were gossiping by the lift as Penny Burgess emerged on the third floor of the *Bradfield Evening Sentinel Times* office. She walked down the newsroom, snapping on lights as she passed, humming tunelessly under her breath. She tossed her bag on the desk by her computer terminal and logged on. She executed the commands that took her into the library database, and pressed the key for "search." Five options were offered: 1. Subject; 2. Name; 3. By-line; 4. Date; and 5. Pictures. Penny hit 2. At the "surname" prompt, she typed "Hill." At the "forename" prompt, she keyed in "Tony," and at the "title" prompt, she entered, "Dr." Then she sat back and waited while the computer sorted through the gigabytes of information stored in its huge memory. Penny flipped open her cigarette packet and pulled out her first cigarette of the day. She was only a couple of drags into it when the screen flashed "Found (6)."

Penny retrieved the six items and called them up on her screen. They appeared in reverse order of date. The first was a two-month-old cutting from the *Sentinel Times*. It had been written by one of the news reporters. Although she'd read it at the time, she'd completely forgotten about it. As she read it, Penny whistled softly.

### INSIDE THE MIND OF A KILLER

*The man the Home Office have chosen to spearhead the hunt for serial killers spoke today about the latest slaying that has terrified the city's gay community.*

*Forensic psychologist Tony Hill is one year into a major study funded by the government which will lead to the setting up of a criminal profiling task force similar to the FBI unit featured in* The Silence of the Lambs.

*Dr. Hill, 34, was formerly the chief clinical psychologist at Blamires Hospital, the maximum-security mental unit which houses Britain's most dangerous criminally insane offenders, including mass murderer David Harney and serial killer Keith Pond, the Motorway Madman.*

*Giving his verdict, Dr. Hill said, "I have not been called in by the police to consult on any of these cases, so I know no more than your readers do about them."*

Either Dr. Hill had been lying to her colleague, or his formal involvement with the case came after the interview. If that was the case, Penny could see how to exploit it in a way that would appeal to her editor. She could picture the headline now. "POLICE FOLLOW *BEST*'S LEAD IN MURDER HUNT." She quickly flicked through the rest of the piece. It didn't tell her anything she didn't already know, although she was interested that Dr. Hill had speculated that the discrepancies in the third killing might mean there were two killers out on the streets. That was an idea that seemed to have sunk without trace. It was something to ask Kevin about next time she managed to get him on the end of a phone.

The next cutting was from the *Guardian*, and announced the setting up of the Home Office programme for developing a national task force to deal with serial offenders. The project was to be based at Bradfield University. The article gave her more background on Dr. Hill, and she jotted down his career details in her notebook. No dummy, this guy. She'd have to handle him carefully. She tapped her teeth with her pen and wondered why the *Sentinel Times* hadn't run a feature on the study, with a profile of Dr. Hill.

Maybe they tried and had been knocked back. She'd have to check with her colleagues on Features.

The next two cuttings were from a national tabloid, a two-part series on serial killers that had been timed to coincide with the general release of *The Silence of the Lambs*. Dr. Hill was quoted in both articles, talking in general terms about the work of psychological profilers.

The last two cuttings dealt with one of his most prominent patients, Keith Pond, the so-called Motorway Madman. Pond had abducted five women from motorway service areas, then savagely raped and murdered them. At the time of his trial, only two of the bodies had been found. But after extensive therapy with Dr. Hill, Pond had revealed the whereabouts of the other three bodies. Dr. Hill had been hailed as a worker of miracles by the bereaved family of one of the victims. One of the two pieces had attempted a profile of Dr. Hill, but they had scant information to go on. As usual, the journalist hadn't let that stand in the way of a good story.

*Tony Hill, who has never married, is devoted to his work. A former colleague said, "Tony's a workaholic. He's married to the job.*

*"He's totally driven by the desire to understand what makes his patients tick. There's probably not another psychologist in the country who has his knack of getting inside their twisted minds and working out what makes them do what they do.*

*"I sometimes thought he related better to mass murderers than he did to normal punters."*

*The reclusive Dr. Hill lives alone and is notorious for not mixing socially with colleagues. Apart from studying the minds of serial killers, the only hobby he apparently indulges in is hill-walking. On weekends off, he regularly drives to the Lakes or the Yorkshire Dales and tramps the fells.*

"Sounds like a real barrel of laughs," Penny said aloud, scribbling more notes on her pad. She returned to the main menu, where she selected the fifth option. Again, she entered Tony's name for a picture search. The data banks revealed there was one stock picture on file. Penny called it up and stared at the face that appeared on her screen. "Gotcha!" she exclaimed. She had only seen him once before, but now she knew who Carol Jordan's new sidekick was.

Penny leaned back in her seat, savouring her third cigarette, and registered that the newsroom was starting to fill up. One quick phone call, then she could afford the time to treat herself to a fry-up in the canteen. Reaching for the phone, she dialled Kevin Matthews's home number. He picked up on the second ring. "DI Matthews," came the sleepy mumble.

"Hi, Kev, it's Penny," she said, savouring the stunned silence that greeted her announcement. "Sorry to bother you at home, but I thought you'd rather answer my questions there than in the office."

"Wh-what?" he stuttered. Then, muffled, "Yeah, it's work. Go back to sleep, love."

"How long has Dr. Tony Hill been on the team?"

"How did you hear about that? Shit, that's supposed to be top secret!" he exploded, his nervousness transforming itself into anger.

"Tut, tut. Kev, she'll never get back to sleep if you yell like that. Never mind how I know, just be grateful you can put your hand on your heart and deny it came from you. How long, Kev?"

He cleared his throat. "Just a couple of days."

"Was it Brandon's idea?"

"That's right. Look, I really can't talk about this. It's supposed to be kept under wraps."

"He's doing a profile, right?"

"What do *you* think?"

"Working with Carol Jordan? Brandon's blue-eyed girl on this one, is she?"

"She's the liaison officer. Look, I've got to go. I'll talk to you about this later on, OK?" Kevin tried to sound menacing, but failed.

Penny smiled and slowly exhaled a mouthful of smoke. "Thanks, Kev. I owe you a very special one." She replaced the handset, cleared her screen and opened a story file.

"Exclusive. By Penny Jordan," she typed. Never mind breakfast. She had far more interesting stuff to do.


Tony was back in front of his screen by half past eight. Instead of the guilt he'd expected to feel about his erotic encounter, he felt refreshed. Giving himself permission to indulge himself with Angelica had somehow released and relaxed him. Surprising though he found it under the circumstances, he'd actually become aroused as she'd talked him through an outrageous, imaginative sexual encounter. He hadn't actually managed to sustain his erection as far as orgasm, but because there was no one there to share his failure, it hadn't seemed to matter. Maybe a few more calls from Angelica would be all he needed to contemplate the reality with something less than abject panic.

But not at work. What he needed now was complete peace. He'd already instructed his secretary to hold all his calls, and he turned off the ringer on his direct line. Nothing and nobody was going to interrupt the flow of his thoughts. His feeling of satisfaction continued as he read through the work he'd done the day before. He was ready now to put himself on the line and commit his conclusions about Handy Andy to paper. Tony poured himself a cup of coffee from his Thermos and took a deep breath.

We are dealing with a serial killer who will certainly kill again unless he is caught. The next killing will take place on the eighth Monday following the death of Damien Connolly unless some trigger accelerates this. What might push him over the edge into extreme escalation could be some catastrophic event that causes him to lose whatever it is he is using to keep the fantasy alive. Since, for example, he is using videos, loss of or damage to his tapes could lead to loss of control. Another possible scenario is that an innocent person is charged with the killings. That would be such an affront to his sense of himself that he might commit his next murder ahead of schedule.

I believe it is likely that he has already selected his next victim and is familiarizing himself with that victim's movements and lifestyle. The chances are that the chosen victim is a man not known to the gay community. He will be, to all intents and purposes, a straight man living a heterosexual lifestyle.

The fact that his last victim was a police officer is disturbing. It is highly probable that this was choice, not accident or coincidence. The killer is sending a message to the investigation. He is demanding that we take notice of him, that we take him seriously. He is also telling us that he is the best; he can catch us but we can't catch him. There is a theory that such behaviour is a way of inviting capture, but I do not believe that is what is going on in this case.

It is possible that his next target may also be a police officer, perhaps even one who is working on the investigation. This alone will not be sufficient motive for the killer to choose them; they must also fit the victim criteria that he has drawn up in his own mind in order for the killing to assume its full meaning for him. I would strongly recommend that any officers who fit the victim profile employ extra vigilance at all times, noting any suspicious vehicles parked near their homes, and checking to see whether they are being followed to and from work and social events.

The stalking and preparation serves two main purposes for the killer: it cuts down on the potential surprise elements when he comes to carry out the killing, and it also fuels the fantasy that is the all-important area of the killer's life.

Our killer is probably a white male, aged between 25 and 35. He is likely to be at least 5ft 10ins tall, well muscled, with considerable upper-body strength. In spite of this, he probably has a poor body image. He may work out in a gym, but if he can afford it, he would prefer to use his own equipment in the privacy of his home. He is right-handed.

He won't look like a con. He'll look deeply, deeply average. He will have a demeanour that doesn't provoke suspicion. He's the sort of bloke you wouldn't look at twice, and certainly wouldn't suspect of being a multiple murderer. He may have tattoos and/or self-inflicted scars, but these are likely to be fairly discreet.

He is familiar with Bradfield, and his knowledge of Temple Fields is clearly current. This implies someone who lives and probably works in the city. I don't think he's a casual visitor, nor a former resident who simply comes back here to kill. There is no obvious geographical pattern to the homes or workplaces of his victims, except that they all lived in reasonably close proximity to a tram line. The first victim's home is most likely to be geographically clos-est to where the killer lives or works. Looking at the gen-eral background and style of the victims, and working on the principle that he's sticking to the kind of environment he knows and understands, I would suspect that the killer lives in privately owned property rather than rented, a house rather than a flat, in a suburban area of similar prop-erties to those of the victims. The victims' houses are prob-ably worth more than the killer's; these are men that in some way he aspires towards.

He is probably of above average intelligence, though I would not expect him to have a university degree. His school record is probably quite patchy, with poor atten-dance and highly variable marks. He will never have lived up to his potential or to other people's expectations of him. Most serial killers have a bad employment record, flitting from job to job, being sacked more often than resigning. But this man exhibits an extraordinary level of control in the commission of his murders, so I would expect him to be capable of holding down a steady job, possibly even one with some degree of responsibility and forward planning.

However, I don't think his job will involve much contact with his fellow human beings, since his relationships with others will be characterized by their dysfunctional nature. His victims are all white-collar workers, with the marginal exception of Damien Connolly, which indicates to me that he probably operates in a similar working environment. I wouldn't be surprised to find him working in a technology-related area, possibly computers. This is an employment area where people can hold down good jobs without having significant people skills. People who don't fit in are accepted and acceptable in the weird world of software engineers; indeed, they are often highly prized since they are hard to replace. I doubt if our killer is a leading-edge creative person in the software world, but I wouldn't be surprised to find him as a systems manager or a program tester. He probably doesn't get on well with his bosses, being inclined to be insubordinate and argumentative.

He will be middle class in terms of his job, his aspirations, his clothes and his home, although he may be working class in background. He is good with his hands, but I am inclined to think he is not in a manual occupation, if only because of the high degree of planning involved in these murders.

Socially, he feels isolated. He may not necessarily be a loner, but he does not connect with people. He feels like an outsider. He probably has developed superficial social skills, but somehow his behaviour always strikes the wrong note. He's the one who laughs too loudly, the one who thinks he's making jokes when he's actually being deeply offensive, the one who sometimes seems to have drifted off in a daydream all of his own. He's the one who doesn't really have any friends, who will join in with the group but never pair off with one buddy in particular. He has little insight into his social failings. He prefers to be alone with his fantasies, because when others are involved socially, he can't fully control what's happening around him.

It's entirely possible that he does not live alone. If he lives with someone, it will be a woman rather than a man.

Because he is sexually attracted to men and cannot accept that, he will not under any circumstances be living with a man, not even in a platonic relationship. His relationships with women may well be sexual, but he will not be an enthusiastic or successful lover. His performance will be barely adequate, and he may regularly experience problems in achieving and/or sustaining an erection. However, he will not be impotent during the commission of his crime, and will almost certainly be able to complete a full sexual act of some sort with his victims.

Tony paused and stared out of the window. Sometimes it felt like the chicken and the egg. Did he empathize with his patients because he too knew the frustrations and anger of impotence, or had his sexual problems increased precisely so that he could do his job better? "Does it matter?" he said impatiently. He ran a hand through his hair and concentrated once again on the screen.

If he is living with someone, she will almost certainly have no suspicion whatsoever that her partner is the killer. It's therefore quite likely that her first instinct will be to alibi him, since in her heart, she knows it couldn't possibly be him. Any suspects solely alibied by girlfriends or wives should therefore not be eliminated on those grounds alone.

He is mobile, with his own car, which is in good condition (see above). And on Monday nights, he's free to roam without hindrance or obligation to be somewhere.

He is a highly structured personality, a control freak. The sort who has a tantrum because his girlfriend has forgotten to buy his favourite cereal. He believes he's absolutely justified; he thinks that in his crimes, all he is doing is actually committing the actions that everybody else wants to but lacks the bottle for. He has a big chip on his shoulder and feels that the world has conspired against him; how come, since he's so bright and talented, he's not running the company instead of doing this poxy job? How come, since he's so charming, he's not going out with some supermodel? The answer is, the world is out to do him down. He has the egocentric world view of the spoiled child, and has no insight into the impact of his behaviour on others. All he sees is the way events affect him.

He is a persistent fantasist and daydreamer. His fantasies are elaborately constructed and seem more significant to him than reality. His fantasy world is where he retreats both from choice and also whenever he faces any kind of setback or obstacle in his day-to-day life. The fantasies are likely to involve violence as well as sex and may also be fetishistic. These fantasies don't remain static; they lose their power and have to be developed further.

He is certain that he can act out his violent fantasies without anyone being able to stop him. He has supreme confidence that he is smarter than the police. He is not planning for the day he will be caught. He thinks he's too clever for that. He has been very careful to erase forensic traces, which is why, as I have already outlined to Inspector Jordan, I am convinced that the fragment of Russian deerskin left at the scene of the fourth killing is a red herring of the grossest kind. He is almost certainly keeping a close eye on the investigation, and will doubtless be laughing his socks off as we run round trying to source the leather. Even if the police do trace it, I suspect that when we find the killer there will be nothing among his possessions that will remotely connect to it.

If he has any criminal record at all, it is likely to be a juvenile one. Possible offences include: vandalism, minor arson, stealing, cruelty to younger children or animals, assault on teachers. However, somewhere along the line, our killer has learned enormous self-control, and he's unlikely to have an adult record.

He will keep abreast of the investigation as much as possible, and will thrive on publicity as long as it appears to accord him the glamour and respect he craves. It is interesting that Adam Scott's grave was desecrated shortly after the second murder. This may have been an attempt to raise the profile of his crimes. He is possibly someone who has contacts with police officers, and if he does, he will endeavour to use this to gain information about the progress of the investigation. Any officer who feels they are being pumped in this way should be encouraged to report it to senior officers in the murder squad.

Tony saved his file and read the whole thing through again. Some of the psychologists he'd worked with incorporated great slabs of background about the likely childhood background of the killer, as well as a checklist of behaviours that the killer would possibly have exhibited when he was growing up. Not Tony. There was time enough for that sort of information once there was a suspect ripe for interrogation. Tony never forgot that he was dealing with coppers who were out there at the sharp end. Men like Tom Cross, who didn't give a toss what kind of hideous childhood their suspect had endured.

Thinking of Tom Cross sharpened Tony's critical eye. Convincing him of the value of the profile was going to be a nightmare.

The first edition of the *Bradfield Evening Sentinel Times* hit the street just before noon. The eager searchers after flats, jobs and bargains snatched the first copies from the street vendors without even looking at the front page. They turned straight to the section of small ads that they hoped would meet their needs, holding the front and back pages up to the advantage of passers-by. Anyone curious enough to glance at the banner headlines on the front page would have discovered "MURDER HUNT BOSS DUMPED. Exclusive, by our Crime Correspondent, Penny Burgess." Further down the page, the bottom right-hand quarter was taken up with a photograph of Tony, saying, "MURDER COPS FOLLOW *BEST* LEAD. Exclusive by Penny Burgess." If they'd been intrigued enough to buy their own copy, they could have read a sub-headline saying, "Top shrink we chose joins Queer Killer hunt, see story p. 3."

In an office high above the bustling streets of Bradfield, a murderer stared at the paper, excitement churning inside. Things were working out beautifully. It was as if the police were acting out the killer's own fantasies, proving that wishes do come true.

*The world was out in the city streets, buying Christmas presents they'd still be paying for at Easter, the fools. I was in my dungeon, making sure I would have a Christmas I'd never forget. Even though it was to be Gareth's last on this earth, I was sure every detail of it would be as clearly etched on his memory as it was going to be on my video tape.*

*I'd arranged our meeting with all the care and precision I could. The advent of the bitch meant I couldn't take the chance of capturing him at home as I'd done with Adam and Paul. I'd had to make alternative plans.*

*I sent him an invitation. I reasoned that Christmas Eve would be spoken for, either by family or by the bitch, so I chose December 23rd. I couched it in terms. I knew he wouldn't be able to resist and that he'd never dare show the bitch. The final sentence read, "Admission by invitation only." A clever touch, that. It meant he'd have to bring with him the only evidence of contact between us.*

*The directions on the back led, if he cared to check it out in advance, to an isolated holiday cottage high up on the moors between Bradfield and the Yorkshire Dales; the opposite side of the city to Start Hill Farm and my dungeon. I anticipated that the cottage would be let over Christmas. But I had no intention of allowing Gareth to get that far.*

\* \* \*

*It was a Christmas-cliché sort of night; bone-white crescent moon, stars twinkling like diamond chips on a cocktail watch, grass and hedgerows heavy with rime. I pulled over on to the verge of the single-track moorland road that led up to the holiday cottage and a couple of farms. In the distance, I could see the dual carriageway leading into Bradfield like a ribbon of fairy lights strung across the Pennines.*

*I turned on my hazard lights, got out of the jeep and opened the bonnet. I placed what I needed near at hand, then I leaned against the front wing and waited. It was freezing, but I didn't care. I'd calculated well. I'd only been waiting for about five minutes when I heard the sound of an engine straining up the steep incline. The lights swung round the bend below me and I stepped out, waving furiously, looking frozen and worried.*

*Gareth's elderly Escort stopped abruptly in front of the jeep. I took a couple of hesitant steps towards him as he opened the door and got out. "Some kind of a problem?" he asked. "I'm afraid I know next to nothing about cars, but if I can maybe give you a lift . . . ?"*

*I smiled. "Thanks for stopping," I said. There was no flicker of recognition in his face as he drew nearer. I hated him for that.*

*I stepped back towards the jeep, gesturing under the bonnet. "It's not a big problem," I said. "Only, I need three hands. If you can just hold this part in place so I can get a spanner on this nut . . ." I pointed into the engine. Gareth leaned over the bonnet. I picked up the spanner and let him have it.*

*Within five minutes, he was trussed tighter than a turkey in the boot of his own car. I had his car keys, his wallet and the invitation I'd sent him. I drove back down through the city to the farm, where I dumped the unconscious body unceremoniously down the cellar steps. I didn't have time to do any more then, not if I was going to get back to the jeep.*

*I drove Gareth's car into the centre of Bradfield, leaving it in Temple Fields in a back alley off Crompton Gardens. Nobody noticed me; they were all too busy partying. It was a mere ten minutes' walk across town to the railway station.*

*A twenty-minute train ride and a brisk fifteen-minute walk brought me back to the jeep. Cautiously, I approached. There was no sign of life, no suggestion that anyone had been poking around. I drove back to Start Hill Farm whistling "Hark The Herald Angels Sing."*

When I switched the cellar light on, Gareth's dark-grey eyes flashed angry fire at me. I liked that. After the pathetic terror of Adam and Paul, it was refreshing to see a man who had some guts. The muffled sound that came from behind the tape on his mouth was more like an angry grunt than a plea.

I stooped over him and stroked his hair back from his forehead. At first, he jerked away from me, then he became calm and still, calculation in his eyes. "That's more like it," I said. "No need to fight, no need to resist."

He nodded, then grunted, signalling down towards his gag with his eyes. I kneeled beside him and picked at one corner of the surgical tape. Once I had a good grip, I ripped it free in one swift movement. It's kinder than doing it gradually.

Gareth worked his jaw, licking his dry lips. He glared at me. "Some fucking party," he snarled, his voice a little shaky.

"It's exactly what you deserve," I said.

"How the fuck do you work that out?" he demanded.

"You were meant for me. But you took up with that slag. And you tried to keep it a secret."

Light dawned in his eyes. "You're . . ." he started.

"That's right," I interrupted. "So now you know why you're here." My voice was as cold as the stone floor. I stood up abruptly and walked over to the bench where I'd laid out my equipment.

Gareth was talking again, but I shut out the sound of

his voice. I know how persuasive lawyers can be, and I wasn't about to be deflected from my course by any amount of sweet talking. I opened the ziplock bag and took out the chloroform pad. I turned back to Gareth and kneeled beside him. With one hand, I gripped his hair and with the other I applied the pad to his mouth and nose. He struggled so convulsively that I ended up with a clump of hair in my hand before he subsided into unconsciousness. Just as well I was wearing my latex gloves, otherwise his hair would have cut me. The last thing I needed was my blood mingling with his.

When he was out cold, I cut his clothes off. I took the strap from the Judas chair and fastened it round his chest, under the armpits. I'd fixed a rudimentary pulley and hoist to one of the ceiling beams, and I attached the hook to the strap. I raised Gareth's body with the hoist till he swung like mistletoe in a draught. Once he was up in the air, it was the work of moments to undo the handcuffs and fasten him to my Christmas tree.

I'd bolted two planks to the wall in the shape of a St. Andrew's Cross, and covered them thickly with prickly boughs of blue Norwegian spruce. To each arm of the cross, I'd attached leather straps, which I fastened around his wrists and ankles. I opened up Gareth's curled fists and taped his hands open to the cross. Finally, I removed the hook and let the wrist straps take the strain. His body slumped alarmingly, and for a moment I was concerned that I hadn't fitted strong enough straps. There was a brief creaking of leather on wood, then silence. He hung like a martyred apostle on the dungeon wall.

I laid out my club hammer and the sharpened cold chisels I'd chosen for the job. We'd be together now till Christmas night. I intended to savour every minute of our forty-eight hours.

# 12

*Very few men commit murder upon philanthropic or patri-*
*otic principles . . . As to the majority of murderers, they are*
*very incorrect characters.*

The four detective inspectors sat stony-faced in what had been Tom Cross's office as John Brandon gave them the official version of the superintendent's suspension. Sometimes, Brandon wished he was one of the lads again, able to explain his reasons without appearing to undermine his own position by doing so. "What we've got to do is put this behind us and move this enquiry forward," he said briskly. "Now, what's the score with McConnell?"

Kevin leaned forward in his seat. "I did as you instructed, sir. He left our custody just before midnight, and I've had a team on him ever since. He hasn't put so much as a toe out of line so far. He went straight home, seemed to go to bed, judging by the lights. He was up at eight this morning, and he's gone off to work. I've got one lad in the gym, posing as a new member, and another one out on the street."

"Stick with it, Kevin. Anything else? Dave, anything interesting coming out of the computer yet?"

"We're following up a lot of car numbers and blokes with previous for any gay-related offences, both on the gay-bashing and the gross indecency side. We're also about to cross-check those lists with the ones Don Merrick's been getting from travel agents of people who have booked holidays in Russia. Once we get the profile, we might be able to develop some suspects, but it's uphill at the moment, sir."

Carol chipped in. "Some of the weightlifting associations said they'd supply us with lists of their members who'd either been to Russia or competed against Russian teams."

Dave pulled a face. "Oh goody, more bloody lists," he said.

"I've got a contact in the leather business," Stansfield said. "Biggest importer in the UK. I asked him about the leather scrap and he said that with it being deerskin, it's probably not your common-or-garden labourer's jacket. He said it was likely to be someone with a bit of clout but not real power. You know. Somebody like a DI," he grinned. "Or a town-hall official halfway up the greasy pole. A deputy stationmaster. The second mate on a ship. That sort of thing."

Dave grinned. "I'll tell HOLMES to keep an eye out for ex-KGB men."

Brandon started to say something, but he was cut off by the peal of the telephone. He grabbed it and said, "Brandon here . . ." His face lost all expression, turning as wooden as the coffins he looked as if he should be carrying. "Yes, sir. I'll be there right away." He put the phone down gently and stood up. "The Chief Constable is interested in hearing how this evening's paper came to look the way it does." He crossed the room and paused by the door, one hand on the handle. "I'm sure the person who washed our dirty linen in Ms. Burgess's sink will be hoping I can persuade him not to make an example of him." He gave Carol a frosty smile. "Or her, come to that."

Tony locked his office door behind him and gave the project secretary a happy wave and smile. "I'm going out for a bite of lunch, Claire. I'll probably go to Café Genet in Temple Fields. Inspector Jordan's due at three, but I'll be back by then. OK?"

"You're sure you don't want to return one of these calls from the journalists?" Claire called after him.

Tony swung round, continuing to walk backwards across the office. "What journalists?" he asked.

"First off, that Penny Burgess from the *Sentinel Times*. She's been trying every half-hour since I came in. Then, in the last hour, they've been on from all the national newspapers, and Radio Bradfield."

Tony frowned, baffled. "Why?" he asked. "Did they say what they wanted?"

Claire held up the copy of the *Sentinel Times* she'd nipped out to buy from the campus newsagent. "I'm no psychologist, Tony, but I think it might have something to do with this."

Tony stopped in his tracks. Even across the office he could read the headlines and make out his own photograph splashed across the front page of the paper. Like an iron filing pulled by a magnet, Tony moved closer to the paper till he could read Penny Burgess's name on both stories. "May I?" he said hoarsely, reaching out for the paper.

Claire relinquished it and watched his reaction. She liked her boss, but she was human enough to relish his discomfort at being exposed in the evening paper. Tony hastily flicked the front page over, hunting for the full story about himself. With a mounting sense of horror, he read:

Dr. Hill is well equipped to enter the twisted mind of the Queer Killer. As well as his two university degrees and a wealth of experience in dealing directly with the criminal perverts who have terrorized society, he has a reputation for dogged determination.

A colleague said, "He's married to the job. It's all he lives for. If anyone can catch the Queer Killer, it's Tony Hill.

"It's only a matter of time now, I'm convinced. Tony is relentless. He won't give up till this bastard is nailed down tight.

"Let's face it, Tony's got a top-class brain. These serial killers might have high IQs, but they're never very smart when it comes to staying out of custody."

"Dear Christ," Tony groaned. Apart from the fact that no self-respecting colleague would ever have given quotes like that, the article was tantamount to throwing down the gauntlet to Handy Andy. It read like a challenge. He felt sure Handy Andy would find a way to respond to that. Tony threw the paper down on the desk and scowled at it.

"It is a bit over the top," his secretary said sympathetically.

"It's bloody irresponsible, never mind over the top," Tony raged. "Oh, bollocks to it. I'm going for lunch. If the Chief Constable rings, tell him I've left for the day." He walked off again towards the door.

"What about Inspector Jordan? What if she rings?"

"You can tell her I've left the country." With the door open, he paused. "No, only joking. Tell her I'll be here for our meeting."

As he stood waiting for the lift, Tony realized nothing in his experience had prepared him for a direct confrontational challenge with a killer. This was one he'd have to fly by the seat of his pants.


Kevin Matthews drained his pint glass and waved it at the barmaid. "Even if it is a red herring, he's still got to have had access to this bloody obscure bit of leather in the first place, hasn't he?" he demanded stubbornly of Carol and Merrick. "Same again?"

Merrick nodded. "I'll have a coffee this time, Kevin," Carol said. "And chuck us a menu, would you? I've got a feeling I'm in for a long session with the doc, and he's got a nasty habit of forgetting about food."

Kevin ordered the drinks then turned back to Carol. With the persistence that had won him promotion, he said, "I'm right though, aren't I? To plant the leather like that, not only has he had access to it, he also knows how unusual it is."

"Agreed," Carol said.

"So it's not a waste of time trying to source it, is it?"

"I never said it was," Carol said patiently. "Now, are you going to fill me in on what happened with Tom Cross, or do I have to copy our murderer and bring out the torture gear?"

While Kevin explained what had happened, Merrick's attention drifted. He'd already heard the tale more times than enough. He leaned against the bar and surveyed the clientele. The Sackville Arms wasn't the nearest pub to the Scargill Street station, but it sold draught Tetleys from Yorkshire and Boddingtons from Manchester, which inevitably made it the police local. The pub was on the outer fringes of Temple Fields, which had given it an added attraction for the local officers when Scargill Street had still been open. The location had meant that hookers or petty villains who wanted to drop a word in the ear of their personal contact on the force could manage it unobtrusively. However, in the few months that Scargill Street had been mothballed, the pub had subtly changed. The regulars had got used to having the place to themselves, and there was a clearly discernible distance between the coppers and the rest of the customers. The officers who'd been using the pub in an attempt to recruit new sources from the community's underbelly had met with a chilly reception. Even with a serial killer on the loose, no one wanted to get back into the habit of informing now they'd kicked it.

With his policeman's eyes, Merrick slowly scanned the room, classifying the drinkers. Hooker, dealer, rent boy, pimp, rich man, poor man, beggar man, wimp. He was jolted out of his scrutiny by Carol's voice. "What do you think, Don?" he caught.

"Sorry, ma'am, miles away. What do I think about what?"

"That it's about time we developed some of our own snouts among the toms, instead of having to rely on the Vice Squad's girls. They've been round the houses so many times, I'd go outside to check if they told me it was raining."

"Never mind the hookers," Merrick said. "We need to

know a damn sight more about how the gay community works. I don't mean the lads that are out of the closet and down the Hell Hole. I mean the secretive ones. The ones that don't flaunt it. They're the ones who might have come across this guy before. I mean, from all I've ever read about serial killers, sometimes they don't actually kill the first time, they just have a go. Like the Yorkshire Ripper did. So maybe there's some frightened little guy in the closet who's been on the receiving end of a bit of violence that got out of hand. That might be the road to a break."

"And God knows we need a break," Kevin said. "But if we don't know how the connections are made, how do we connect?"

Carol said thoughtfully, "When in doubt, ask a policeman."

"Do what?" Kevin asked.

"There are gay officers in the Job. More than most, they must know about keeping a low profile. They'd be able to tell us."

"That doesn't answer the question," Kevin protested doggedly. "If they're so busy keeping it quiet, how do we know who they are?"

"The Met has an association of gay and lesbian police officers. Why don't we get in touch with them, in confidence, and ask for their help? Somebody must have some contacts in Bradfield."

Merrick stared at Carol with admiration, Kevin with frustration, both wondering silently how it was that Inspector Jordan always had an answer.


Tom Cross glanced down at the front page of the *Sentinel Times*, a smirk of satisfaction twitching his cigarette up and down. Ms. Burgess might have thought she was in control of their little encounter the night before, but Tom Cross knew different. He'd played the spider to her fly, and she'd done exactly what he expected of her. No, credit where it's due. She'd done better than he'd expected. That line about the police staggering lamely in the wake of the *Sentinel Times* when it came to seeking out Dr. bloody Hill was a corker.

There were going to be a lot of angry men in Bradfield police today. That was the revenge element of Tom Cross's game with Penny Burgess. But someone else was going to be angry too. When he read tonight's paper, the killer was going to be more than a little put out.

Tom Cross stubbed out his cigarette and slurped from his mug of tea. He folded his paper and placed it on the table in front of him and stared out of the café window. He lit another cigarette. He'd set out to provoke the Queer Killer. Provoked, he'd start to get careless, to make mistakes. And when Stevie McConnell did that, Tom Cross would be ready and waiting. He'd show those sorry bastards in command how to catch a killer.


Tony was back in the office by ten to three. Even so, he wasn't early enough to beat Carol. "Inspector Jordan's here," Claire said as soon as he opened the outer office door. She gestured with her head towards his office. "She's in there waiting. I told her you'd be back."

Tony's responding smile was strained. As he gripped the door handle, he clenched his eyes tightly and took a deep breath. Nailing what he hoped was a welcoming smile on his face, Tony opened the door and stepped into his office. At the sound of the door, Carol turned away from the window she'd been staring out of and gave him a cool, appraising look. Tony closed the door behind him and leaned against it.

"You look like a man who's just stepped in a puddle that's deeper than his shoe," Carol remarked.

"That's an improvement, then," Tony said with more than a trace of irony. "Usually I feel like I've stepped in a puddle that's deeper than my head."

Carol took a step towards him. She'd rehearsed what she was going to say. "There's no need to feel like that with me. Last night . . . well, you were less than candid and I misread the signals. So can we please forget the whole thing and concentrate on what's important between us?"

"Which is?" Tony sounded impersonal as a therapist, his question conversational rather than challenging.

"Working together to nail this killer."

Tony pushed himself away from the door and made for the safety of his seat, careful to keep the desk between them at all times. "That's fine by me." He gave a crooked smile. "Believe me, I'm far better at professional relationships than the other kind. Think of it as a lucky escape."

Carol walked round to the opposite side of the desk and pulled up a chair. She crossed her trouser-clad legs and folded her hands in her lap. "So let's have a look at this profile."

"We don't have to behave as if we're strangers," Tony said quietly. "I respect you, and I admire the way you're so open to learning new aspects of the job. Look, before . . . before what happened last night, we seemed to be moving towards a friendship that went beyond work. Was that such a bad thing? Couldn't we settle for that?"

Carol shrugged. "It's not easy making friends after you've exposed your weaknesses."

"I don't think showing someone you're attracted to them is necessarily a weakness."

"I feel foolish," Carol said, not quite sure why she was opening up like this. "I had no right to expect anything from you. Now, I'm angry with myself."

"And with me too, I expect," Tony said. This was proving less traumatic than he had imagined. His counselling techniques hadn't rusted over from lack of use, he thought with relief.

"Mostly with myself," Carol said. "But I can deal with that. The important thing for me is that we get the job done."

"Me too. It's pretty rare for me to find a police officer who seems to have a grasp of what I'm trying to do." He picked up the papers on his desk. "Carol . . . This isn't about you, you know. It's about me. I have problems of my own that I need to deal with."

Carol stared at him long and hard. He felt a quick twitch of panic as he realized he could not read her eyes. He had no idea what she was feeling. "I hear what you're saying," she replied, her voice cold. "Speaking of problems," she added, "haven't we got some work to do?"

Carol sat alone in Tony's office with his profile of the serial killer. He had left her to read it while he worked next door with his secretary, catching up on the correspondence that had piled up since Brandon had hijacked him only a handful of days before. She couldn't remember ever having been so fascinated by a report in her entire career. If this was the future of policing, she desperately wanted to be part of it. At last, she came to the end of the main body of text and turned to a separate sheet.

Points to pursue:

1. Had any of the victims ever mentioned to a friend/relative that they had been the subject of an unwanted homosexual approach? If so, when, where and from whom?

2. The killer is a stalker. His first encounter with his victims probably takes place quite a long time before he kills—weeks rather than days. Where is he encountering them? It may be something as banal as where they take their dry-cleaning, where they have their shoes heeled, where they buy sandwiches, where they have tyres or exhausts put on their cars. Given that they all lived close to the tram network, I think we should check whether the victims regularly used the trams to go to and from work, or to go out in the evenings. I suggest that in-depth background checks are done, going through bank accounts, credit-card statements and anecdotal evidence from colleagues, girlfriends and family members. This may help develop suspects.

3. Is there any indication that the victims were keeping

the night in question free for any particular purpose? Gareth Finnegan lied to his girlfriend about it—did any of the others?

4. Where is he doing his killing? It's unlikely to be in his home, since he will have calculated the possibility of being arrested, and will have taken pains to avoid leaving forensic traces there. It's also got to be big enough for him to build and use the torture engines we are assuming in these cases. It may be an isolated lock-up garage, or a unit on an industrial estate which is deserted at night. Bearing in mind that he almost certainly lives in Bradfield, it's possible that there exists an isolated rural property that he has undisturbed access to.

5. He must have found out about instruments of torture somewhere so that he could construct his own. It might be worth checking with bookshops and libraries to see if any of their customers has enquired about or ordered books on torture.

Carol flicked back a few pages, rereading a couple of paragraphs which had particularly struck her first time through. She found it hard to credit how quickly Tony had assimilated the stacks of files she'd delivered. Not only that, but he'd drawn out of them the key points that created for the first time in Carol's mind a picture, albeit shadowy, of the man she was hunting.

But the profile raised questions in her mind. At least one of those questions didn't seem to have occurred to Tony. She wondered if it wasn't referred to because he had dismissed it out of hand. Either way, she had to know. And she had to find a way of asking that didn't sound like an attack.

*I hated to keep Gareth hanging on, but I had to leave him for one little errand. In his car, I'd found a few of the Christmas cards his company sent out to favoured clients, already signed by all the partners. Inside one, with a fountain pen, a stencil set and Gareth's blood, I'd written in block capitals,* A MERRY CHRISTMAS TO ALL YOUR READERS; YOUR EXCLUSIVE CHRISTMAS GIFT IS WAITING IN THE SHRUBBERY OF CARLTON PARK BEHIND THE BANDSTAND. COMPLIMENTS OF THE SEASON FROM SANTA CLAWS. *It wasn't easy to write with the blood; it kept congealing on the nib, which I had to clean every few letters. Luckily, there was no shortage of ink.*

*I addressed a Jiffy bag to the editor of the* Bradfield Evening Sentinel Times *and put the card in it, along with a video I'd made a couple of weeks before, when I'd started to plan what to do with Gareth. I'd already decided to change my modus operandi slightly. Temple Fields was bound to be risky now; even if the queens were too drunk or stoned to be vigilant, the police would be keeping an eye open for more than the occasional cottaging poof. But the nature trail through the shrubbery of Carlton Park is almost as notorious a pick-up area.*

*Early on a rainy Sunday morning, when there was nobody about, I'd driven out to Carlton Park with my camcorder. I started off by the wrought-iron bandstand. I walked around it, filming it from every angle. It wouldn't* take long before somebody in the BEST office recognized the landmark. After all, Carlton Park is the biggest park within the city boundaries, and there's a brass-band concert there every Sunday from April to September. I deliberately kept the camcorder at chest level rather than on my shoulder; I've read of instances where correct estimates of height have been made simply from the angle photographs have been taken from. If some forensic scientist was going to draw any conclusions from this video, I wanted to be sure they would be the wrong ones.

Leaving the bandstand behind, I walked down the nature trail towards the shrubbery. I panned across the general area where I thought I'd dump the body, then stopped filming. I passed nobody on my way back to the jeep. That was probably just as well, since I was grinning from ear to ear at the thought of the news editor puzzling over my Christmas message.

The message would also serve two other functions. It would minimize the time it took to identify Gareth's body, which meant the publicity machine would have plenty of fodder to keep it going through what was always a slack news period. Secondly, it would send the police on a wild goose chase, working out who could have had access to the Christmas cards.

The police might even decide that someone connected with Gareth through work had decided to bump him off and make it look like a copycat killing by dumping the body in a gay cruising area. Just the sort of thing a deranged and disillusioned client would do. If I got really lucky, they might even give the bitch a hard time, too.

I drove into the city centre to post the packet at the main post office. There were enough last-minute panicking gift-givers for me to be unremarkable. I stopped at an off licence on the way back to buy a bottle of champagne. I don't normally drink when I'm working, but this was a special occasion.

When I got back, Gareth was semi-conscious, mumbling incomprehensibly. "Santa's here," I said cheerfully as I *came down the stairs. I popped the cork on the champagne and poured two glasses. I took one over to Gareth and, standing on tiptoe, I gently lifted his lolling head. I held the glass to his lips and tilted it. "You'll enjoy this," I said. "It's vintage Dom Perignon."*

*His eyes snapped wide open. For a moment, he looked bewildered, then he remembered and he fixed me with a look of pure hatred. But he was parched, and couldn't resist the champagne. He swallowed it greedily, not savouring it at all. Then he belched in my face, a look of strange satisfaction in his eyes.*

*"Wasted on you," I said angrily. "Like all the fine things in life." I stepped back and slashed the glass across his face. It shattered against his nose, cutting his cheek to ribbons. I was glad Auntie Doris wouldn't be coming back. She'd had that set of six fragile crystal glasses as a silverwedding present, and she'd never used them, terrified that someone would break one. She'd been right to be concerned.*

*Gareth shook his head. "You're evil," he slurred. "Pure evil."*

*"No, I'm not," I said softly. "I'm justice. Remember justice? It's what you're supposed to stand for."*

*"Twisted, evil bastard," he replied.*

*I couldn't believe he still had the stamina for bravado. It was time to show him who was boss. I'd already pinned his hands to the cross with a couple of cold chisels. The blood had congealed around them, black and hard. Now it was the turn of his feet.*

*When he saw me pick up my tools from the workbench, he finally cracked. "There's no need for this," he said desperately. "Please. You could still let me go. They'd never find you. I've no idea where we are. I don't know who you are, where you live, what you do for a living. You could move away from Bradfield and they'd never find you."*

*I took a step closer. Tears welled up in his eyes and spilled over, trickling through the blood on his cheek. They must have stung, but he never flinched. "Please," he whis-*

pered. "It's not too late. Even if you killed those other men. Was it you who killed them?"

He was smart, I had to give him that. Too smart for his own good. He'd just earned himself some more suffering. I turned away and dropped the chisel and club hammer on the workbench. Let him think I was having second thoughts. Let him spend the night convinced I was going to have mercy. That would make Christmas Day all the sweeter.

I shut the cellar door behind me and went upstairs to bed, armed with my videos and the best part of a bottle of vintage champagne. I was having the best Christmas I'd ever had. I remembered all those years of desperate hope, praying that this would be the year my mother would buy me presents like other children got. But all she'd ever done was let me down. Now I'd worked out that the only person who could give me what I craved was myself; I knew that for the first time in my life, I could look forward to the kind of Christmas other people have, filled with surprises, satisfaction and sex.

# 13

*Reading his acts by the light of such mute traces as he left behind him, the police became aware that latterly he must have loitered. And the reason which governed him is striking; because at once it records—that murder was not pursued by him simply as a means to an end, but also as an end for itself.*

The Wunch of Bankers was one of the few city-centre watering holes where Kevin Matthews felt safe meeting Penny Burgess. A fun pub with blaring rap music and decor modelled on soap operas—the Rover's Return Snug, the Woolpack Eaterie, the Queen Vic Lounge, and the Cheers Beer Bar—was the last place he was likely to see another copper or Penny another journalist.

Kevin made a face as his taste buds clenched on the strong bitter coffee that lurked under a swirl of foam that looked more like industrial effluent than a cappuccino. Where the hell was she? He glanced at his watch for the twentieth time. She'd promised she'd be here by four at the latest, and now it was ten past. He pushed the half-empty cup away from him and grabbed his fashionable raincoat from the banquette beside him. He was about to stand up when the pub's revolving door hissed round and disgorged Penny. She waved and headed straight over to his table.

"You said four o'clock," Kevin greeted her.

"God, Kevin, you're getting really anal in your old age," Penny complained, giving him a peck on the cheek as she subsided on to the seat beside him. "Get me one of those mineral waters with a hint of fruits of the forest, there's a love," she said, her voice mocking the pretensions of her chosen drink.

When Kevin returned with a glass already sweating with condensation, Penny immediately put a proprietorial hand on the inside of his thigh. "Mmm, thanks," she said, sipping her drink. "So what's new? Why the urgent meeting?"

"Today's paper," he said tonelessly. "The shit's really hit the fan."

"Oh, good," Penny said. "Maybe we'll get some positive action. Like a suspect you've got some evidence against."

"You're not understanding. They're hunting for the mole. The Chief had Brandon on the carpet this morning, and the upshot is that Internal Affairs have mounted a leak enquiry. Penny, you've got to cover my back," Kevin said desperately. Penny took her time lighting a cigarette. "Are you listening to me?" Kevin demanded.

"Of course I am, sweetheart," Penny soothed automatically, her mind already planning her story for the morrow. "I just don't understand why you're getting so worked up. You know a good journalist never reveals her sources. What's the problem? You think I'm not a good enough journalist?" With an effort, Penny forced herself to listen to Kevin's reply rather than the voice in her head reeling off headlines.

"It's not that I don't trust you," Kevin said impatiently. "It's inside the force I'm worried about. Everybody will be desperate to put themselves in the clear, so anybody that knows about us will be falling over themselves to tell Internal Affairs. And once they know that we're, well, you know? That'll be it. I'll have had it."

"But nobody knows about us. Or not from me, they don't," Penny said calmly.

"I thought nobody knew too. Then Carol Jordan said something that made me think she does."

"And you think Carol's going to shop you to Internal Affairs?" Penny said, failing to hide the incredulity she felt. She hadn't had many dealings with the CID's most glamorous officer, but what she knew of the inspector didn't incline her to cast her in the role of grass.

"You don't know her. She's totally bloody ruthless. She

wants to go all the way, that one, and she'd drop me in it soon as look at me if she thought it would take her a rung up the ladder."

Penny shook her head in exasperation. "You're over-reacting. Even if Carol Jordan has mysteriously discovered that we're seeing each other, I'm sure she's too busy covering herself with glory from her liaison with Dr. Hill to be bothered with shopping you. Besides, if you think about it rationally, she's got nothing to gain from getting herself a reputation with the lads as a grass."

Kevin shook his head dubiously. "I don't know, Penny, you've no idea what it's like on this job. We're all working eighteen-hour days, and we're getting nowhere."

Penny stroked the inside of his thigh. "Sweetheart, you're under a lot of pressure. Look, tell you what. If it all comes on top and somebody fingers you, Internal Affairs are bound to come to us and front us up. They'll be looking for corroboration. If that happens, I'll make it look like Carol Jordan's my source, OK? That should muddy the waters."

Kevin's smile was worth the flannel, she decided. That, and one or two other things about him. Reassured, he bounced to his feet. "Thanks, Pen. Listen, I've got to be a place. I'll call you soon so we can get together, OK?" He leaned over and kissed her deep and hard.

"Keep me posted, lover boy," Penny said softly to his retreating back. Before he even reached the doors, her intro was taking shape. Oh yes, she could see it now.

Bradfield police are devoting new resources to the hunt for the serial killer who has claimed four victims and placed men in jeopardy as never before.

But the extra officers will not be joining the search for the monstrous Queer Killer. Their job will be to police the police themselves.

Top brass in the force are so alarmed by the accuracy of the *Sentinel Times*'s stories on the killings that they have set up a full-scale mole hunt to uncover the source of our stories. Instead of catching the killer, the mole-catchers will be tracking down fellow officers who subscribe to the view that the terrified public have a right to know what's going on.

Carol opened the door to the outer office and said, "I'm all done. Can we talk?"

Tony looked up from the computer screen absently, held up one finger and said, "Yeah, sure, give me a minute," and finished what he was doing.

Carol retreated and took a deep breath. No matter how professional she tried to be, she couldn't help the surge of attraction she felt for this man. Ignoring it was easier said than done. Moments later, Tony joined her. He perched on the edge of his desk, his hair standing on end like Dennis the Menace from thrusting his fingers through it while he concentrated. "So," he said. "What's the verdict?"

"I'm impressed," she said. "It really pulls everything together. There were a couple of things, though."

"Only a couple?" Tony asked, his voice close to a chuckle.

"You talk a lot about how he must be strong, to overpower his victims and move them around. Also, you speculate about how he gets them into a vulnerable position in the first place. I was wondering if maybe there were two of them."

"Go on," Tony said, no hint of frost in his voice.

"I don't mean two men. I mean a man and someone else who appears vulnerable. Maybe an adolescent boy or, more likely, a woman. I don't know, maybe even a person in a wheelchair. A partner in crime. Like Ian Brady and Myra Hindley." Carol shuffled the papers, putting them back in order. Still Tony said nothing. After a few moments watching his expressionless face, she added, "I know you've probably thought about it already, I just wondered if it was a possibility we should still bear in mind."

"Sorry, I didn't mean to look like I was ignoring you," Tony said hurriedly. "I was reviewing the thought, weighing it against what we know and against the profile. One of the first things I considered was whether or not it was a solo. On the balance of overwhelming probability, I decided it was. Cases like the Moors Murders where you have two people acting in tandem to carry out atrocities are incredibly rare, for a kick off. Also, I'd expect to find more variation in the methodology and the pathology if there were two people involved; it's hard to believe their fantasies would coincide so exactly. But it's interesting that you've come up with it. You're right in one respect. If he's working with a woman it does explain how he gets close to his victims without them putting up a fight." Tony sat staring straight ahead, brows lowered in thought.

Carol stayed motionless in her seat. Eventually, Tony turned to face her and said, "I'm going to stick with my soloist. Yours is an interesting idea, but I can't see evidence that convinces me I should shift from the most highly probable scenario."

"OK, point taken," Carol said calmly. "Moving on from that, have you considered the possibility of a transvestite? Like you just said, a woman could get close without them putting up a fight. What about if the woman was a man in drag? Wouldn't that have the same effect?"

Tony looked startled for a moment. "Maybe you should think about applying to join the national task force when it's set up," he stalled.

Carol grinned. "Flattery will get you nowhere."

"I mean it. I think you've got what it takes to do this kind of work. You see, I'm not infallible. I hadn't actually considered a transvestite. Now, why did I ignore that possibility?" he mused, thinking aloud. "There must be some subconscious reason why I rejected it before it even got to the front of my mind . . ." Carol opened her mouth to speak, but he said, "No, wait a minute, please, let me work this out." His hands ran through his hair again, rearranging the dark spikes.

She subsided, telling herself he was just as arrogant as all the rest, unable to accept he might just have missed something. Stop kidding yourself he's different, she told herself sternly.

"Right," Tony said, his voice rich with satisfaction. "We're dealing with a sexual sadist, agreed?"

"Agreed."

"Sado-masochism is the power trip of sexual fetishes. But transvestism is the diametric opposite of that. TVs want to assume the supposedly weaker role that women have in society. What underpins transvestism is the belief that women have a subtle power, the power of their gender. It couldn't be further removed from the brute transaction of pain and power that sado-masochists crave. That's not part of a TV's fantasy at all. To convince the victims that they're dealing with a woman and not a man in drag, the killer would have to be an accomplished cross-dresser. But, uniquely in my experience of clinical psychology, he'd also have to be a sexual sadist. The two just don't go together," Tony explained with an air of finality. "The same goes for a transsexual. Probably more so, in fact, because of the counselling they have to go through before they're accepted for treatment."

"So you're ruling it out, then," Carol said, feeling unreasonably crushed.

"I never rule anything out. That's asking to make a fool of yourself in this game. What I think is that it's so unlikely that I would be loath to include it in a profile because its very inclusion might push people in the wrong direction. But by all means keep it in mind. You're thinking along the right lines." He smiled, unexpectedly, taking the sting of patronage out of his words. "Like I said at the start, Carol, together we can crack it."

"And you're absolutely convinced that it isn't a woman?" she asked.

"The psychology's all wrong. Taking the most obvious point, this killer's an obsessive, and that tends to be a male trait. How many women do you know who hang about station platforms in the rain in anoraks writing down train numbers?"

"But what about that syndrome, what's it called, where people get obsessed with someone else to the point where they make their lives a misery? I thought it was mainly women who suffer from that?"

"De Clerambault's Syndrome," Tony said. "And yes, it is principally women who suffer from it. But they only focus on one person, and the only person who's likely to get dead as a result is the sufferer, who sometimes commits suicide. The thing is that women's obsessions and compulsions are different from men's. Men's obsessions are about control; they collect stamps and catalogue them, they collect a pair of knickers from every woman they've slept with. They need trophies. Women's obsessions are about submission; in eating disorders, it's the obsession that takes them over and controls them rather than the other way about. A sufferer from de Clerambault's Syndrome who married the object of her desire would probably be the chauvinist's ideal of the perfect wife. That pattern doesn't fit our killer."

"I see what you mean," Carol said, loath to give up the one fresh idea she felt she'd contributed to the profiling process.

"Add to that the sheer physical strength involved here," Tony continued, seeing her reluctance. "You're fit. You're probably quite strong for your height. I'm only a couple of inches taller than you. But how far do you think you could carry me? How long would it take you to pick my body up from the boot of a car and dump it over a wall? Could you throw me over your shoulder and carry me through Carlton Park to the shrubbery? Now bear in mind that all the victims have been taller and heavier than me."

Carol gave a rueful smile. "OK, you win. I'm convinced. There was one other thing that occurred to me."

"Let's hear it."

"Reading your profile, it seems to me that the reason you advance for the maintenance of the gaps between the killings just isn't strong enough," she started tentatively.

"You noticed that too," he said wryly. "It didn't convince

me either. But I couldn't think of anything else to explain it. I've never encountered anything quite like it, either face to face or in the literature. All the serial offenders I know about go through escalation."

"I've got a theory that might cover the problem," Carol said.

Tony leaned forward, his expression absorbed. "Speak to me, Carol," he said.

Feeling like a goldfish in a bowl, Carol took a deep breath. She'd wanted his attention, but she wasn't quite sure if she liked it now she had it. "I remember what you said to me a couple of days ago about the intervals." She closed her eyes and recited, " 'With most serial killers, the gap between the killings tends to decrease quite dramatically. It's their fantasies that trigger off the killings in the first place, and the reality never quite matches up to the fantasy, no matter how much they refine their killing procedures. But the more extreme they get, the more blunted their sensibilities become and the more stimulus they need to get the sexual buzz that killing provides. So the kills have to become more frequent. Shakespeare said it. "As if increase of appetite had grown by what it fed on.' " Am I right?"

"Remarkable," Tony breathed. "Can you do that with visuals as well, or is it only auditory?"

Exasperated, Carol cast her eyes upwards. "Auditory only, I'm afraid. Anyway, when I read the bit in the profile where you suggest he might work with computers, something clicked. The question you didn't actually put but is obviously bothering you is, why isn't he getting desensitized to the videos faster as time goes by?"

Tony nodded. The point she'd raised was powerful, and it was precisely what was troubling him. He searched to find an answer that would satisfy them both. Groping for the solution as he went along, he said, "Suppose, for the sake of argument, that the first video had the potential to keep him stable for twelve weeks. But he'd already set in train the process of capturing his second victim, and the opportune moment came along before he was actually compelled to kill again. He just couldn't resist the chance when it presented itself so perfectly. Afterwards, he realizes he's left eight weeks between the killings and he decides that eight weeks is going to be his pattern. So far, the videos have allowed him to maintain that. Maybe that is going to change now."

Carol shook her head. "It's plausible, but I'm not convinced."

Tony grinned. "Thank God for that. Neither am I. There's got to be a better explanation, but I don't know what it is."

"How much do you know about computers?" she asked.

"I know where the on/off switch is and I know how to use the software I need to work with. Other than that, I'm a moron."

"Well, that makes two of us. My brother, however, is a computer whizz kid. He's a partner in a games software house. The stuff he works on is leading-edge technology. Right now, he and his partner are developing a low-cost system that will allow games players to put images of themselves in the games that they're playing. In other words, instead of it being Arnie kicking the shit out of the bad guys on the screen in *Terminator* 2, it would be Tony Hill. Or Carol Jordan. The point is that there's already the hardware and software around that allows you to scan video tape and import the images into a computer. I think they call it digitized images. Anyway, once you've got that into the computer, you can manipulate it exactly how you want to. You can incorporate still photographs, or bits from other videos. You can superimpose things. When they first got the original hardware about six months ago, Michael showed me this sequence he'd made up himself. He'd taped some of the Tory Party conference and he'd also imported a video sex guide. He'd selected all these government ministers' faces while they were giving their speeches and superimposed them on the sex video." Carol snorted with laughter at the memory. "It was a bit choppy, but believe me, you've never seen John Major and Margaret Thatcher getting on so well! It gave a whole new meaning to the word 'gobbledegook'!"

Tony stared at Carol in stunned silence. "You're kidding me," he said.

"It's the perfect explanation of why the videos manage to keep him under control."

"Wouldn't that mean he'd have to be a real boffin, like your brother?"

"I don't think so," Carol said. "From what I gathered, the actual techniques involved are fairly simple. But the software and the peripherals that you need to do it are incredibly expensive. You could be talking two or three grand just for one piece of software. So he's either working for a company where he has that sort of equipment on tap and the privacy to work on his own stuff, or else he's a computer hobbyist with a lot of disposable income."

"Or a thief," Tony added, only half joking.

"Or a thief," Carol agreed.

"I don't know," Tony said dubiously. "It does answer the problem, but it's totally off the wall."

"And Handy Andy isn't?" Carol said belligerently.

"Oh, he's off the wall, all right, but I'm not sure he's that together."

"He builds torture machines. That would be a lot easier with a computer design program. Tony, something's keeping him stable on his eight-week cycle. Why not this?"

"It's a *possibility*, Carol, no more than that at this stage. Look, why don't you make some preliminary enquiries, see how feasible what you're suggesting would be in practice?"

"You don't want to include it in the profile?" Carol asked, bitterly disappointed.

"I don't want to undermine the things I feel are strongly probable by including something that's really only a bit of kite-flying at this stage. You said yourself, it was triggered off by one of the few bits in the profile that is little more than speculation. Don't get me wrong, I'm not knocking the idea. I think it's brilliant. But we're going to have to work bloody hard as it is to overcome the resistance in some quarters to the profile as a whole. Even people who are broadly in support of the idea aren't necessarily going to agree with some parts of it. So let's not give them any easy targets. Let's bottom it, present it to them gift-wrapped so the snipers can't just knock it straight off the perch. OK?"

"Fine," she said, knowing in her heart he was right. She picked up a sheet of paper and a pen. "Check out software manufacturers and consultancies in Bradfield area," she muttered to herself as she wrote. "Check with Michael about manufacturers of necessary hardware/software then check sales records. Check recent thefts."

"Computer clubs," Tony added.

"Thanks, yes," Carol said, adding that to her list. "And bulletin boards. Oh boy, I'm going to be really popular with the HOLMES team." She got to her feet. "It's going to be a long job. I'd better get cracking. I'll take this down to Scargill Street now and give it to Mr. Brandon. We'll need you to come in and go through it."

"No problem," Tony said.

"I'm glad something isn't."


Tony stared out of the window of the tram, watching the city lights pass in a blur of rain. There was something cocoon-like about the gleaming white interior of the tram. Graffiti-free, warm, clean; it felt like a safe place to be. As the driver approached traffic lights, he gave a blast on the breathy horn. It sounded like a noise from childhood, the sort of hooting that a cartoon train would produce, he decided.

He turned away from the window and covertly studied the half-dozen other passengers on the tram. Anything to take his mind off the curious emptiness he felt now he had delivered his profile. It wasn't as if this would be the end of his involvement with the case. Brandon had told Carol that she was to have a daily briefing with him.

He wished he could have been more encouraging about

her computer theory, but years of training and practice had rendered the habit of caution ingrained. The idea itself was brilliant. Once she had done some research into the practicability of what she was suggesting, he'd be only too happy to endorse it with her fellow officers. But for the sake of his profile's credibility, he had to keep his distance from ideas that the average copper would dismiss as science fiction.

He wondered how the police were faring that evening. Carol had called him to say that teams were going out in Temple Fields, trawling the area's regulars, trying to see if the profile suggestions produced any recognition. With luck, they might get some names that would cross-reference to data already in HOLMES, either from previous criminal records or from the car index numbers whose registered keepers had been fed into the system.

"The next stop will be Bank Vale station. Bank Vale station next stop," the electronic voice from the speakers announced. With a start, Tony realized they had left the city centre far behind and were emerging on the far side of Carlton Park, less than a mile from his home. Bank Vale came and went, and Tony swung round in his seat, ready to make for the exit doors when the next stop was announced.

He walked briskly through the neat suburban streets, past the school playing fields, skirting the small copse that was all that remained of the plantation that had given the Woodside area its name. Tony glanced at the trees as he hurried past, thinking wryly that the path cutting diagonally through the wood would almost certainly be completely deserted. First it was the women walking home alone who had abandoned it. Then it was the children, kept away by anxious parents. Now, in Bradfield, it was the men who were learning the bitter lessons of life in jeopardy.

Tony turned into his street, relishing the quiet of the cul-de-sac. He'd get through the evening somehow. Maybe drive down to the supermarket and buy the ingredients for a chicken biryani. Pick up a video. Catch up on his reading.

As he turned the key in the lock, the phone started ringing. Dropping his briefcase, Tony ran for the phone, kicking the door to behind him. He picked up the phone, but before he could say anything, her voice trickled into his ear like warm olive oil soothing an earache. "Anthony, darling, you sound like you're panting for me."

He'd managed to avoid thinking about it all the way home, but he knew this was what he'd been hoping for.

Brandon had turned out the bedside light less than a minute before the phone rang. "You should have known better," Maggie murmured as he dragged himself away from her complaisant warmth and reached for the receiver.

"Brandon," he growled.

"Sir, it's Inspector Matthews," the tired voice said. "We've just picked up Stevie McConnell. The lads have just lifted him at the ferry port in Seaford. He was about to get on a ship for Rotterdam."

Brandon sat up in a tangle of duvet, ignoring Maggie's protests. "What have they done?"

"Well, sir, they didn't think there was a lot they could do, being as how he's on police bail and there's no conditions for him to breach."

"Are they holding him?" Brandon was out of bed and reaching for his underwear drawer.

"Yes, sir. They've got him in the Customs lads' office."

"What on?"

"Assaulting a police officer." Kevin's voice somehow summoned up the image of a smirk as disembodied as the Cheshire Cat's smile. "They rang me to ask what they should do next, and since you've taken such a personal interest in the case, I thought I should ask you first."

Don't push it, Brandon thought savagely. All he said, however, was, "I'd have thought it was pretty obvious. Arrest him for attempting to pervert the course of justice and bring him back to Bradfield." He wrestled into a pair of boxer shorts and leaned over to pick up his trousers from the back of a chair.

"I take it we show him to the magistrates this time and ask that they refuse bail?" Kevin's voice was so sweet it was on the border of costing him his teeth, and not from decay.

"That's what we normally do when we have grounds, Inspector. Thanks for keeping me informed."

"One other thing, sir," Kevin said unctuously.

"What?" Brandon growled.

"The lads have also had to make another arrest."

"*Another* arrest? Who the hell else have they had to arrest."

"Superintendent Cross, sir. Apparently, he was trying rather forcibly to prevent McConnell from boarding the ferry."

Brandon closed his eyes and counted to ten. "Is McConnell hurt?"

"Apparently not, sir, just a bit shaken up. The super has a black eye, though."

"Fine. Tell them to let Cross go home. And tell them to ask him to call me tomorrow, OK, Inspector?" Brandon replaced the phone and leaned over to kiss his wife, who had reclaimed the duvet and was rolled up tight as a hibernating dormouse.

"Mmm," Maggie murmured. "Are you sure you have to go in?"

"It's not my idea of a good time, believe me, but I want to be there when they bring this prisoner in. He's just the sort of bloke who might fall downstairs."

"A problem with his balance?"

Brandon shook his head grimly. "Not *his* balance. Other people sometimes get a bit unbalanced, love. We've already had one maverick on the prowl tonight. I'm not taking any more chances. I'll see you when I see you."

Fifteen minutes later, Brandon walked into the murder squad room. Kevin Matthews was slumped over a desk at the far end of the room, his head cradled in his arms. As

Brandon approached, he heard the soft snore of Kevin's breathing. He wondered when any of the squad had last had a straight night's sleep. It was when officers got tired and edgy at the lack of results that the serious mistakes happened. Brandon desperately wanted to avoid his name in lights ten years down the road as the man who masterminded a sensational miscarriage of justice, and he'd go to any lengths to avoid it. There was only one problem with that, he wryly acknowledged to himself as he sat down opposite Kevin. In order to keep his finger on the pulse of the investigation, he had to work the same kind of ridiculous hours that led to the very misjudgements he wanted to avoid. *Catch-22*. He'd read that, a few years back now, when Maggie had decided to go to evening classes and take the A Levels she'd never got round to at school. She'd said it was a wonderful book, funny, savage, sharply satirical. He'd found it almost too painful. It reminded him too strongly of the Job. Especially on nights like tonight when previously sane men turned desperado.

The phone rang. Kevin stirred, but didn't wake. Pulling a sympathetic face, Brandon reached over and lifted it. "CID. Brandon speaking."

There was a momentary, confused silence. Then a strained voice said, "Sir? Sergeant Merrick here. Sir, we've copped for another body."

Getting Gareth to Carlton Park was less easy than I'd anticipated. I'd done my reconnaissance carefully, I thought, and I'd counted on being able to drive down the access road used by the gardeners. What I hadn't taken into account was the long Christmas break. The road was blocked off by two metal posts slotted into the asphalt and locked in place with heavy padlocks. I could probably have squeezed through on the verge, since the jeep would have had no problem flattening the small shrubs that lined the road. But I would inevitably have left tyre tracks and probably tiny traces of paint. I had no intention of allowing Gareth to deprive me of my liberty, so that option was closed to me.

I parked the jeep round the back of the storage shed where the park staff kept their equipment. At least there I was out of sight both from the road and the park. There weren't many people around at two o'clock on Boxing Day morning, but success is all about taking pains.

I got out of the jeep and scouted around. The shed was out; it had a burglar alarm. But the gods were smiling on me now. Around the side of the shed, there was a low wooden trolley, the kind that porters used to wheel along station platforms in the days when there were railway porters who didn't think shifting luggage was beneath them. The gardeners probably used it to transport plants round the park. I pushed it back to the jeep and tipped Gareth's naked body on to it. I tucked a couple of black plastic bin liners round the body and sprayed the axles with a quick blast of lubricating oil to cure a nasty squeak, then stealthily I set off towards the shrubbery.

Again, I was lucky. I saw no one. I steered the trolley round to the rear of the bandstand towards the shrubs that covered the steep slope behind. At the edge of the path, I pushed the trolley on to the grass verge and into the edge of the shrubs. Then, wary of leaving footprints on the soft ground, I clambered on to the trolley and rolled Gareth's body off the end and into the bushes. I stepped back and jumped down, pulling the trolley after me. The bushes looked a little battered, but there was no sign of Gareth. With luck, he'd remain undiscovered until the postman delivered my Christmas message to the BEST.

Ten minutes later, the trolley was back in place and I was nosing out of the park's rear entrance on to a quiet lane opposite the churchyard. Even though the chances of being spotted were slim, I waited until the main road was in sight before I turned my lights on. Unlike Temple Fields, this was exactly the sort of area where some nosy insomniac would notice a strange vehicle in the early hours.

I drove home and slept for twelve hours, waking up in time for an interesting couple of hours on my computer before I went in to work. Luckily, it was a busy night, so I had plenty of complex problems to take my mind off the anticipation of the following day's Sentinel Times.

They'd done me proud, in spite of the short time they'd had to deal with my message. They'd obviously got on to the plod right away, and managed to persuade them to take it seriously. They'd given me the front page, complete with a photograph of my message, though without anything that would identify who the card had come from.

### KILLER ALERTS BEST!

The naked and mutilated victim of a twisted killer has been discovered in a city park following a bizarre message sent to the Sentinel Times.

*The killer, who signed himself "Santa Claws," revealed in a grisly Christmas message that he had dumped the body in Carlton Park.*

*The sick communiqué appeared to be written in blood. It was scrawled on the company Christmas card of one of the city's leading firms of solicitors.*

*It was accompanied by a home video of the body's location, which BEST staff immediately recognized from the distinctive bandstand on Park Hill.*

*Alerted by BEST reporters, police dispatched a squad of uniformed and plain-clothes officers to the area of the park mentioned in the Christmas card.*

*After a short search among bushes off the nature trail near the bandstand, as indicated in the video, a uniformed constable discovered the body of a man.*

*According to police sources, the body was naked. The man's throat had been cut and his body mutilated.*

*It is believed that he may have been tortured before his death.*

*Although this area of Carlton Park is known as a pick-up area for predatory homosexuals, police are not presently connecting this killing with the murders earlier this year of two young men whose bodies were dumped in the Temple Fields "gay village" area of the city.*

*The body has not yet been identified, and police have not released a description of the victim, who is believed to be in his late twenties or early thirties.*

*The package, which had been posted on Christmas Eve in Bradfield, arrived at the offices of the* Sentinel Times *in this morning's post, addressed to the news editor, Matt Smethwick.*

*Mr. Smethwick said, "My first thought was that someone was playing a sick joke, especially since I know one of the solicitors in the firm concerned.*

*"Then I realized my friend was out of the country on a skiing holiday, so it couldn't have been him who posted the package.*

*"I rang the police right away, and luckily they took it
seriously."*

I should think they did. I'd never been more serious in
my life. In spite of what the police were saying, the thought
that Gareth was the third in a series must have made the
short journey across their minds. It had certainly not escaped the attention of the journalists, who used the latest
discovery as an excuse to rehash the killings of Adam and
Paul. By the time the City Final edition hit the streets,
they'd even found a rent-a-quote academic to spout forth.

### INSIDE THE MIND OF A KILLER

The man the Home Office have chosen to spearhead the
hunt for serial killers spoke today about the latest slaying
that has terrified the city's gay community.

Forensic psychologist Tony Hill is one year into a major
study funded by the government which will lead to the setting up of a criminal profiling task force similar to the FBI
unit featured in The Silence of the Lambs.

Dr. Hill, 34, was formerly the chief clinical psychologist
at Blamires Hospital, the maximum-security mental unit
which houses Britain's most dangerous criminally insane
offenders, including mass murderer David Harney and serial killer Keith Pond, the Motorway Madman.

Giving his verdict, Dr. Hill said, "I have not been called
in by the police to consult on any of these cases, so I know
no more than your readers do about them.

"I'm reluctant to make a snap judgement, but if pushed,
I'd say it was certainly possible, and possibly likely that
the murders of Adam Scott and Paul Gibbs were committed
by the same person.

"On the surface, this latest killing looks similar, but
there are certain crucial differences. For a start, the body
has turned up in a very different sort of location. Even
though Carlton Park is also known as a gay cruising area,

*it's got a very different ambience from the urbanized Temple Fields.*

*"Also, the sending of the message to the* Sentinel Times *is a significant variation. Nothing similar happened in the earlier cases, and the killer makes no reference to previous killings.*

*"That inclines me to think we may be dealing with at least two separate individuals here."*

*And so on and so forth, all of it in much the same vein. All of it saying in neon lights, "We haven't got the faintest idea where to start looking." I didn't think that worrying about Dr. Tony Hill was going to keep me awake at nights. I decided it was time to teach the powers that be a couple of lessons they wouldn't forget in a hurry.*

# 14

*A man is not bound to put his eyes, his ears, and under-standing into his breeches pocket when he meets with a murder. If he is not in a downright comatose state, I sup-pose he must see that one murder is better or worse than another, in point of good taste. Murders have their little differences and shades of merit, as well as statues, pictures, oratorios, cameos, intaglios or what not.*

Tony lay sprawled in his bath, a snifter of brandy close at hand. Languid, relaxed, spent, he couldn't remember the last time he'd felt this comfortable, this optimistic. His ex-periences on the phone with Angelica, coupled with his conviction that he'd done a good job on the profile, had given him fresh hope. Maybe he didn't have to be dys-functional. Maybe he could join the rest of the world, the ones who handled things, who assimilated the past and shaped their world according to what they wanted to see. "I can change my life," he announced.

The cordless phone rang. In a slow, flowing movement, Tony reached for it. It held no terrors for him now. Strange how he had grown to welcome rather than fear Angelica's calls. "Hello," he said cheerfully.

"Tony, it's John Brandon. I'm sending a car round for you. We've got another one."

Tony sat up, the water swilling up and down like an experiment in a marine laboratory. "You're sure?"

"Carol Jordan and Don Merrick were at the scene within five minutes of the shout."

Tony squeezed his eyes shut. "Oh God," he groaned. "Where is it?"

"The public toilets in Clifton Street. Temple Fields."

Tony stood up and stepped out of the bath. "I'll see you there," he said heavily.

"OK, Tony. The car should be with you in five minutes or thereabouts."

"I'll be ready." Tony cut off the connection and walked out of the bathroom, towelling himself dry as he went. His mind racing, he pulled on jeans, T-shirt, shirt, sweater and leather jacket, adding an extra pair of socks as he remembered how bitter the night had been earlier. The doorbell rang just as he was tying the laces of his boots.

In the squad car, the atmosphere of tension wrecked any possibility of constructive thought as they sped through the night streets, blue light strobing against the unearthly orange of the streetlights. His escort, a pair of macho traffic cops, maintained a taciturn pose of absolute control that didn't lend itself to conversation. Tyres squealing, they swept into Clifton Street, the driver slamming on the anti-lock brakes at the sight of the police tapes that cut off access to the central section of the street.

The tape was lifted for Tony, who headed for the middle of the street where a cluster of police vehicles and an ambulance were parked at seemingly random angles. As he drew closer, he could see the sign for the public toilets, lit up against the looming dark of the building. By the ambulance, he spotted the conspicuous figure of Don Merrick, unmistakable with his bandaged head. Ignored by the milling officers, Tony pushed his way through to Merrick, who was deep in conversation on a mobile phone. He gave Tony a quick wave to signal he'd spotted him, and wound up his phone conversation with, "All right, thanks, sorry to have bothered you."

"Sergeant," Tony said. "I'm looking for Mr. Brandon. Or Inspector Jordan."

Merrick nodded. "They're both inside. You'll be wanting a look too, I suppose."

"Who found the body?"

"One of the street girls. She claims all the ladies loos were full, and that's why she went into the disabled cubicle.

Me, I'd lay money she was with a client. He'll have legged it at the first sight of trouble."

Out of the corner of his eye, Tony saw Carol emerge from the toilets. She made straight for the pair of them. "Thanks for turning out," she said as Merrick moved away and continued making his phone calls.

"If I said I wouldn't have missed it for the world, someone would almost certainly take it the wrong way," Tony replied wryly. "What makes you think it's Handy Andy?"

"The victim's naked, and his throat's been cut. He'd obviously been brought there in a wheelchair, but he'd been tipped out on to the floor. And lying on top of him, there was a copy of last night's *Sentinel Times* front page," Carol replied, her voice strained, her eyes haggard. "We provoked him, didn't we?"

"We didn't. The newspaper might have, but we didn't," Tony said bleakly. "I didn't expect him to react this fast, though."

Merrick approached again and said cheerfully, "Looks like I've tracked down the wheelchair. One went walkabout from the maternity hospital reception earlier on tonight. With a bit of luck, somebody might have seen it."

"Good work, Don," Carol said. "Shall we take a look, then?" she asked Tony. He nodded and followed her as she shouldered her way through the milling officers towards the toilet entrance. Tony slowly walked into the lavatories, making a mental inventory as he looked around him, conscious of the black rubber tiled floor with its raised circles, the apparently random pattern of the grey and black tiles on the wall, the defiant graffiti, the raw dank air, the smell of disinfectant barely masking the piss. Inside the entrance, the toilets split in two, men to the left, women to the right. The disabled toilet was to the right, just by the entrance to the women's toilets. Brandon and Kevin Matthews stood by the door, looking in through the wide doorway. Tony walked up and joined their glum and silent communion. A photographer was standing just inside the door, off to one side, recording a scene that would shake some jury to the core, provided Brandon's men could deliver Handy Andy to them. Every few seconds, the stark white light of the flash etched the scene on the retinas of the watching men.

Tony stared intently at the body lying sprawled on the floor. It was, as Carol had said, naked, but it was not clean. There were smears of some sort of dark, oily substance on knees, elbows and one ankle. And there were bloodstains on the body too. The cut to the throat was wide, but not, Tony suspected, deep enough to have caused death. As far as he could see, the sexual organs themselves were undamaged, but the man's rectum and anus and the soft flesh around there had been savagely removed with deep cuts from a sharp blade. A warm surge of relief flowed through him, forcing him to recognize what he'd been refusing to think about. Like Carol, he too had been afraid that somehow his activities had provoked Handy Andy to break his cycle and to strike again. Ever since Brandon's phone call, that horror had been sitting on his shoulder like a malevolent bird of prey.

Tony turned to Brandon and said bluntly, "It's not him. You've got a copycat."

From the shadows at the far end of Clifton Street, coat collar turned up, Tom Cross joined the ghouls who seemed to spring from under the pavement itself and watched the familiar ritual dance of a murder-scene investigation. His lips pursed in a tight smile and he moved further back into the shadows. He took his diary out of his inside pocket and ripped out a page for notes. In the dim light from a streetlamp, he wrote, "Dear Kevin, I bet you a bob to a gold clock that the Queer Killer didn't do this one. All the best, Tom."

Seaford had been embarrassing as well as painful, but Tom Cross was not a man who allowed humiliation to stand in the way of his purpose. He folded the note in four and wrote, "Detective Inspector Kevin Matthews. Personal," on it. He pushed his way through the crowd till he caught the eye of one of the constables behind the tape. "You know who I am, don't you, lad?" Cross demanded.

The constable nodded hesitantly, casting a quick glance to either side, to see who was watching his encounter with the force's current leper.

Cross proffered the note. "See that Inspector Matthews gets this, there's a good lad."

"Yes, sir," the constable said smartly, enclosing the note in his gloved fist, finding a moment to wonder who'd had the bottle to give Popeye Cross a shiner like that.

"I'll remember you when I'm back in harness," Cross said over his shoulder as he pushed back through the spectators.

Cross cut back through an alley to the Volvo, parked in front of a nightclub's fire exit. The day had been far from satisfactory, and the morning held no promises of improvement. But the conviction that his message to Kevin Matthews was the truth made Tom Cross feel there had been some point to his activities.

"The postmortem will back me up," Tony said stubbornly. "Whoever killed this guy, it wasn't our serial killer."

Bob Stansfield scowled. "I don't see how you can be so sure, just because of a few oil stains."

"It's not just that the body wasn't clean." Tony ticked the points off on his fingers. "He's the wrong age group. He's barely twenty, if that. Far from being in the closet, he was well known on the gay scene. You'd identified him by three this morning."

Kevin Matthews nodded. "Well known to Vice. Chaz Collins. An ex-rent boy who worked in a bar and liked rough sex."

"Exactly," Tony said. "Also, there's not a mark on his penis or his testicles, whereas our killer has been progressively violent with those organs. All the press have been told so far is that the victims have been sexually mutilated. We haven't indicated how or where. This killer has interpreted that as a justification for getting rid of the whole anal area. I suspect he's done that because he buggered the victim before he killed him and he wanted to make sure Forensic didn't pick up any semen." Tony paused to collect his thoughts, and to pour another cup of coffee from the pot that the canteen had sent up with the breakfast trolley John Brandon had ordered for their morning conference.

"The wheelchair," Carol said. "He took a big risk stealing that from the maternity hospital. I don't think that fits with the cautious behaviour the serial killer has always displayed so far."

"And he's not been tortured," Kevin added, through a mouthful of sausage-and-egg roll. "Or not obviously, anyway." He had a note in his pocket that would determine his view as much as anything that was said inside this room. Popeye might be off the job, but Kevin would back his instinct against anyone's.

But Bob Stansfield wasn't giving up. "OK, what if he's doing it differently to make us think it's a copycat? What if he's deliberately trying to confuse us? After all, you can't ignore the newspaper lying there. And Dr. Hill's profile warned us that the stress of inaccurate newspaper coverage might throw his pattern out."

Tony carried on meticulously building a bacon-and-egg roll. He squirted an aureole of brown sauce round the yolk, closed the lid, squashed it so the yolk broke, then said, "There's nothing wrong with that as a theory. It's perfectly feasible that he might kill just to flaunt his skills. It wouldn't be planned so far ahead as the others, so his choice of victim might well be very different. But the underlying pattern would be the same."

"But it is," Stansfield insisted. "This kid had his throat cut, same as the other ones. And this bastard had made a right mess of him. How can you say he wasn't tortured when you look at the state of his arse?"

"If I was a betting man, I'd lay you a hundred to one that Chaz Collins didn't die from having his throat cut. I'd bet he was manually strangled and his throat cut afterwards to make it look like he's one of the serial-killer victims. I think what happened here is that some rough sex got a bit out of hand. Chaz was struggling while he was being sodomized, and his sex partner grabs him round the throat to get him to calm down. In the frenzy of orgasm, he squeezes too tight and he has a corpse on his hands. He figures his only chance of getting away with it is making it look like the serial killer's handiwork, and just in case we don't get the message, he dumps last night's paper on the body."

"It's certainly plausible," Brandon said, fastidiously wiping his greasy fingers on a paper tissue from a pack in his pocket.

"I think Tony's right," Carol said decisively. "My first reaction was that this was the fifth victim, but the more I think about it, the more I think I was wrong. You know what really clinches it for me?" Four pairs of eyes looked quizzically at her. She felt under as much pressure as she ever had in the witness box. "Last night wasn't Monday."

Tony grinned. Stansfield cast his eyes upwards. Kevin nodded reluctantly, and Brandon said, "You think the night of the week's that important to him?"

Carol nodded. "There's obviously some very strong reason why he goes for Monday, whether it's practical or superstitious. And whatever it is, it means a lot to him. I don't think he'd break it just to stick two fingers up to us."

"I agree with Carol," Kevin chipped in. "Not just because of the night of the week. The other stuff, too."

Stansfield looked surprised. "Well, I'm obviously outvoted here," he said good-naturedly. "Separate job it is. Who's going to handle it, then?"

Brandon sighed. "I'll have a word with Chief Superintendent Sharples at Central, pass the buck on to him. If it's not one of ours, it'll be down to their chief inspector."

"He's off sick," Kevin reminded him absently.

"So he is. Well, it'll be passed on to whichever inspector drops unlucky this morning. Now, I know the events of last night deprived us of the chance to give Dr. Hill's profile the attention it demands, but I think we should—' Brandon was cut short by a knock at the door. "Come in," he said, trying to keep the irritation out of his voice.

The uniformed desk sergeant came in with a couple of envelopes. "These have just come in, sir. One from Forensic, one from the path lab," he said, laying them on the desk in front of Brandon. He was gone by the time Brandon had taken a sheaf of papers from each.

The others hid their impatience as Brandon skimmed through the pathologist's preliminary findings. " 'Dear John'," he read out, ' 'I know you'll be screaming for something on this one, since on the face of it, it looks like your serial killer has finally left some forensic traces. The bad news is, I don't think this is your man's handiwork. The victim was already dead from asphyxiation before his throat was cut. He was probably strangled manually. Also, I don't think he was cut with the same blade as your four earlier victims. From the look of it, this was a longer and thicker blade, more like a chef's vegetable chopping knife. Whereas, as you know, I reckon the earlier ones were done with something more like a filleting knife. Time of death I'd put between eight and ten p.m. last night. I'll let you have a full report as soon as . . .' blah, blah, blah. Well, looks like you were right, Tony."

"Just as well I'd agreed to go along with you in time, otherwise I'd have looked a right prat," Bob Stansfield said, extending a hand to Tony. "Nice one, Doc." Carol smiled secretly. Thank God the rest of the team were finally starting to accept Tony had something worth saying. It was amazing how different the atmosphere was now that Cross had gone.

Kevin shifted uncomfortably in his chair and said, "What have Forensic got to say? Anything about our cases, or is it all preliminary stuff on Chaz Collins?"

Brandon flicked through the other papers. "Prelims . . . prelims . . . prelims . . ." He drew his breath in sharply. "Jesus Christ," he said, baffled disgust in his voice.

"What is it, sir?" Carol asked.

Brandon rubbed a hand over his long face and stared at

the paper again, as if checking that he hadn't misread it. "They've been looking at the burns on Damien Connolly's body. Trying to work out what caused them."

Tony stopped moving, the last bite of his sandwich half-way to his mouth. "So what's the verdict?" Bob Stansfield demanded bluntly.

"This is totally bloody mental," Brandon said. "The only thing the lads in Forensic can come up with is the attachments for a cake-icing kit."

"Of course," Tony breathed dreamily, a distant smile lighting up his eyes. "All the different star shapes. It's obvious, once it's pointed out." He was suddenly aware that the other four were staring at him. Carol alone looked concerned. On the other faces, he saw expressions he'd seen before. Wariness, repugnance, disgust, incomprehension.

"Twenty-four-carat head banger," Stansfield said bitterly. No one was quite certain whether he meant the killer or Tony.


The day Penny Burgess took over the *Bradfield Evening Sentinel Times*'s crime beat, she resolved that she was going to have better contacts than any of her male predecessors had managed. She realized that the male rituals of the masonic lodge and the smoker were going to remain closed worlds to her, but she determined that nothing was going to happen of any significance even there without her knowledge.

It wasn't surprising, then, that her home phone had rung twice between six and seven that morning. Both calls were from police officers, telling her that the man who'd been questioned earlier in connection with the Queer Killings had been arrested trying to skip the country. No names, no pack drill, but the anonymous suspect would be up before the magistrates that morning to be remanded in custody on a charge of attempting to pervert the course of justice. Following on from the discovery of a fifth body that had kept

Penny out of her bed till gone two that morning, the connection was obvious.

Penny smiled dreamily to herself over her second cup of strong Earl Grey. It would be another front page for her tonight. Provided the editor and the lawyer didn't lose their bottle. She dumped her cup and cereal bowl in the sink and picked up her coat. Either way, it was going to be an interesting day.


Carol had drawn the short straw when it came to going to court to make sure everything went according to plan before the magistrates. Stansfield and Kevin had a backlog of routine enquiries to pursue, and Tony had gone to Leeds to keep a long-standing appointment with a Canadian academic psychologist who was attending a conference in the city. They needed, said Tony, to discuss some esoteric aspect of his task-force study. "Conceptual mapping," he'd told her as they'd snatched a few moments together after the group briefing.

He might as well have said "quantum mechanics," she thought ironically as she ran up the steps of the court building, her collar turned up against an east wind that promised sleet before dinner. She was going to have to learn a lot if she was going to get anyone to consider her seriously for this task force, that much was clear.

Any thoughts of the task force vanished as soon as she cleared the security check and turned into the long corridor that housed half of the dozen magistrates' courts. Instead of the usual disgruntled and defiant knots of low-level law breakers and their depressed families, she came face to face with a milling mob of journalists. She'd never seen that kind of media turnout at a Saturday-morning court, normally the quietest of the week. At the heart of the crowd, she could see Don Merrick, his back to the courtroom door, looked harassed.

Carol immediately wheeled round on her heel. But she was too late. She'd not only been spotted but also recognized by one of the handful of journalists who weren't visiting firefighters sent up by the national media networks at the sniff of a good tale. As she rounded the corner, they shot after her. All except Penny Burgess, who leaned against the wall and gave Don Merrick a tired smile.

"You weren't the only one that got the early-morning phone call, then," he said cynically.

"Unfortunately not, Sergeant. At least the lads seem more interested in your guv'nor than they do in you."

"She's better looking," Merrick said.

"Oh, I wouldn't say that."

"So I've heard," Merrick said drily.

Penny's eyebrows climbed. "You must let me buy you a drink sometime, Don. Then you can find out for yourself if the gossip's true."

Merrick shook his head. "I don't think so, pet. The wife wouldn't like it."

Penny grinned. "Not to mention the guv'nor. Well, Don, now the pack's gone off in full cry after Inspector Jordan, are you going to let me exercise my democratic right to report the proceedings of the magistrates?"

Don Merrick stood clear of the door and waved her in. "Be my guest," he said. "Just remember, Ms. Burgess, the facts, and nothing but the facts. We don't want innocent people put at risk, do we?"

"You mean, like the Queer Killer's been doing?" Penny asked sweetly as she slipped past him and into the court.

Brandon stared in disbelief at Tom Cross. His face was knit in an expression of deep complacency, his multi-coloured eye socket the only disruption to a picture of smug self-satisfaction. "Just between ourselves, John," he was saying, "you have to admit I was bang on the button about McConnell. That stiff last night—it wasn't down to the Queer Killer at all, was it? Well, it couldn't have been, could it, on account of you had me laddo banged up downstairs." Ignoring the absence of ashtrays in the ACC's office, Cross lit a cigarette and puffed a happy cloud of smoke into the air.

Brandon struggled, but he couldn't find the words. For once, he was speechless.

Cross looked around vaguely for somewhere to flick his ash, and settled for the floor, rubbing it into the carpet with the toe of his shoe. "So when do you want me to start back on the job?" he asked.

Brandon leaned back in his chair and stared at the ceiling. "If it was up to me, you'd never work in this town again," he said pleasantly.

Cross choked on a mouthful of smoke. Brandon looked back down and savoured the moment. "By heck, you like your joke, John," Cross spluttered.

"I've never been more serious in my life," Brandon said coldly. "I called you here this morning to warn you off. What you did to Steven McConnell yesterday afternoon was assault. The file stays open, Superintendent. If you come anywhere near this investigation again, I'll have no hesitation in charging you. In fact, I'll enjoy it. I will not have this force brought into disrepute by any officer, serving or under suspension." As Brandon's words sank in, Cross paled, then turned puce with anger and humiliation. Brandon stood up. "Now get out of my office and my station."

Cross got to his feet like a man concussed. "You'll regret this, Brandon," he stuttered furiously.

"Don't make me, Tom. For your own sake, don't make me."

Thinking on her feet, Carol led the journalists round to the small lounge outside the lawyers' cafeteria. "OK, OK," she said, trying to damp down their baying with exaggerated hand movements. "Look, if you'll just give me two minutes, I'll come right back and answer your questions, OK?"

They looked uncertain, one or two at the back showing

a tendency to drift back towards the courts. "Look, people," she said, gently massaging her jaw, "I'm in agony. I've got a raging toothache, and if I don't ring my dentist before ten, I've got no chance of him fitting me in today. Please? Give me a break? Then I'm all yours, promise!" Carol forced a pained smile and slipped through to the cafeteria. There was a phone on the far wall, which she picked up. She made great play of taking out her diary and looking up a page, while dialling the familiar number of the court. "Court one, please." She waited for the connection, then said to the clerk, "This is Inspector Jordan here. Can I speak to the CPS solicitor?"

Moments later, she was talking to the Crown Prosecution Service lawyer. "Eddie? Carol Jordan. I've got about thirty hacks here waiting for Steven McConnell to come up. They're dying to jump to all the wrong conclusions, and I think you might prefer to get him on now while I've got them tied up at an impromptu press conference. Can you swing it with the clerk?" She waited while the solicitor muttered with the court clerk.

"Can do, Carol," he said. "Thanks."

Keeping up the pretence, Carol put the phone down and scribbled something in her diary. Then she took a deep breath and headed back towards the pack.

*Damien Connolly, the ultimate PC Plod. I couldn't have found a better person to teach the police a lesson if I'd searched for a year. But he was already there, on my list, one of my own personal Top Ten. He was harder to stalk than the others, because his shift pattern was often in conflict with the hours I work. But, as my grandmother always used to say, nothing worth having comes easy.*

*I trapped him in the usual way. "I'm sorry to trouble you, but my car's broken down and I don't know where the nearest call box is. Can I use your phone to ring the AA?" It's almost laughably easy to get across the threshold of their homes. Three men dead, and still they fail to take the most elementary precautions. I almost felt sorry for Damien, since of all of them, he is the only one who had not betrayed me. But I needed to make an example of him, to show the police how pathetically useless they are. It was galling to find myself in agreement with the so-called "gay community," but they were one hundred per cent correct when they said that while supposedly gay men were being killed, the police would do nothing. Killing one of their own would be the one thing that would make them sit up and notice. At last, they'd be forced to give me the recognition and respect I deserve.*

*To mark this, I had devised something a bit special for Damien. An unusual method of punishment, used occasionally to act as a terrible example* pour discourager les autres.

*It seems to have been most commonly used in cases of high treason, where men had plotted to kill the king. Appropriate, I thought. For what was Damien if not an integral part of the group that would bring me down if only they could?*

*The earliest record of this treatment in England was in 1238, when some minor nobleman broke into the royal lodge at Woodstock intent on killing Henry III, there on a hunting trip. To demonstrate to any other potential traitors that the king was serious about attempts on his life, the man was sentenced to be torn limb from limb by horses then beheaded.*

*Another would-be royal assassin met the same fate in the mid-eighteenth century. The aspiring assassin's name just had to be an omen. François Damiens stabbed King Louis XV at Versailles. His sentence read that "his chest, arms, thighs and calves be burned with pincers; his right hand, holding the knife with which he committed the said attack, burned in sulphur; that boiling oil, melted lead, and rosin and wax mixed with sulphur be poured into his wounds; and after that his body be pulled and dismembered by four horses."*

*According to reports of the execution, Damiens's dark-brown hair turned white during the torture. Casanova, that other great lover, reported in his memoirs, "I watched the dreadful scene for four hours, but was several times obliged to turn my face away and to close my ears as I heard his piercing shrieks, half the body having been torn away from him."*

*Obviously, I couldn't get a team of horses down into the cellar, so I'd had to come up with my own arrangement. I'd built a system of ropes and pulleys, attached to floor and ceiling and linked with one of those powered winches that are used on yachts. Each rope ended in a steel shackle that would fasten round wrist or ankle. By adjusting the lengths and tensions on the ropes, I had suspended Damien in midair, his limbs spread in a massive, human X, his pathetic genitals dangling in the middle like something in a butcher's shop.*

*The chloroform had a worse effect on him than it did on any of the others. As soon as he came round, he vomited violently, not an easy thing to achieve when you're hanging upright four feet above the floor. It was just as well I'd removed his gag, or he'd have choked on his own vomit, which would have cheated me out of my satisfaction in his punishment.*

*He was completely bewildered. He had no idea why he was there. "Because I chose you," I told him. "You were just unlucky enough to choose the wrong job. Now I'm going to question you the way you question your suspects."*

*While I'd been poking around in Auntie Doris's kitchen, vaguely looking to see if she had anything I might find useful, I'd come across her icing set. I remembered that icing set. Every year, her Christmas cakes were a miracle of artistry that any of Bradfield's bakers would have been hard pressed to equal. Once, she'd been called away by Uncle Henry while she was doing the big cake, and I'd picked up the icing bag, determined to help. I can't have been more than six.*

*When she came back from whatever disgusting farmyard task she'd been helping with and saw my efforts, she went berserk. She grabbed the weighted leather strop that Uncle Henry used to keep his cut-throat razors sharp and beat me so hard she tore my shirt. Then she locked me in my room without any supper, leaving me there for the best part of twenty-four hours with nothing but a bucket to piss in. I knew I had to find an appropriate use for her treasured icing set.*

*There was a blowlamp in the cellar which I used to heat up the icing attachments so I could leave my mark on Damien, just as the executioner had on his namesake Damiens two hundred and forty years before. There was something quite beautiful about the way his skin blossomed into scarlet starbursts as the red-hot piping rosettes came into contact with his pale flesh. It was also astonishingly effective. He told me everything I wanted to know and lots of rubbish I didn't give a damn about. I was just sorry he wasn't*

*directly involved in the investigation into my previous work.
I could have confirmed at first hand how hopelessly at sea
the police are.*

*I decided to deposit the remains in Temple Fields again.
I'd used the time since Gareth to find additional safe sites
for the disposition of my handiwork. The back yard of the
Queen of Hearts was perfect for my purpose; secluded and
isolated at night. But it would come alive the next day,
ensuring Damien wouldn't be left out in the cold for too
long.*

*The time was ripe for a new game. In preparation for
this, shortly after Adam, I went up into the loft and opened
the trunk that contains those parts of my past I have re-
tained. One of the things I'd kept as a souvenir was a
leather jacket that was given to me by the engineer on a
Soviet factory ship, in lieu of payment for a night he won't
forget in a hurry. It looks and feels different from anything
I've ever seen in this country. I ripped strips of leather from
the sleeve until I was satisfied that I'd got something that
could have been snagged on a nail or the sharp corner of
a lock. I tucked the scrap in a drawer, then I chopped the
rest of the jacket into shreds, stuck it in a plastic bag with
eggshells and vegetable peelings, and drove into town until
I found a skip to dump it in. By the time I needed to use
the red herring, the remains of the jacket would be long
buried in some anonymous landfill.*

*I couldn't help feeling a thrill at the thought of how
many man-hours the police would waste trying to track
down where this strange little piece of leather had come
from, but they'd never tie it in to me. Apart from anything
else, no one in Bradfield has ever seen me wear it.*

*This time, the publicity outshone everything I'd achieved
so far. At last, the police admitted that one mind was behind
all four killings. Finally, they had realized it was time to
take me seriously.*

*With Damien off the planet and in my computer, I still
had one more person to deal with before I could return to
my original project. I couldn't settle to the task of finding*

*a man worthy of me, a man to share my life as an equal and respectful partner, not until I had punished the man who had publicly treated me with such contempt.*

*Dr. Tony Hill, the fool who hadn't even realized that Gareth Finnegan was one of my bodies, was the target. He had insulted me. He had poured scorn on me, refusing to acknowledge the extent of my achievements. He had no idea of the calibre of the mind he was up against. He was going to have to pay for his arrogance.*

*I couldn't help but see his disposal as a challenge. Wouldn't anyone?*

# 15

*Can they not keep to the old honest way of cutting throats, without introducing such abominable innovations . . . ?*

The sound of a roaring crowd greeted Carol as she closed the door of the flat behind her. Michael, sprawled on one of the sofas, didn't even take his eyes off the rugby match on the television. "Hi, sis," he said. "Needle match. Ten minutes, and I'm all yours."

Carol glanced at the screen where muddy giants in England and Scotland's colours were sprawled across the turf in a collapsed scrum. "Very hi-tech," she muttered. "I need a shower."

Fifteen minutes later, brother and sister were sharing a celebratory bottle of cava. "I have some print-out for you," Michael said.

Carol perked up. "Anything significant?"

Michael shrugged. "I don't know what's significant to you. Your killer used five different-shaped objects to make the marks. I separated them out into five separate patterns. You've got what looks like a heart and some rudimentary letters. A, D, G and P. Mean anything to you?"

Carol shivered involuntarily. "Oh, yes. Plenty. You got the print-out here?"

Michael nodded. "It's in my briefcase."

"I'll look at it in a bit. Meanwhile, can I pick your brains again?"

Michael drained his glass and refilled it. "I don't know. Can you afford me?"

"Dinner, bed and breakfast at the country-house hotel of your choice, first weekend I have off," Carol offered.

Michael pulled a face. "At this rate, I could be collecting

my pension before I collect on that one. How about you do my ironing for a month?"

"A fortnight."

"Three weeks."

"Consider it a done deal." She offered her hand and Michael shook it.

"So, what do you want to know, sis?"

Carol outlined her theory about the computer manipulation of the killer's videos. "What do you think?" she asked anxiously.

"It's a can-do," he said. "No question about that. The technology's available, and it's not difficult software to use. I could do it standing on my head. But you're talking serious money. Say three hundred for a video capture card, four hundred for a ReelMagic card, another three to five for a decent video digitizer, plus at least a grand for a state-of-the-art scanner. The real killer is the software, though. There's only one package that will do what you're talking about to any real quality. Vicom 3D Commander. We've got it, and it set us back nearly four grand, and that was six months ago. The last upgrade cost us another eight hundred. Manual thick as a house brick."

"So it's not a piece of software that many people would have?"

Michael snorted. "Damn right it isn't. It's a serious bit of kit, that. Professionals like us, video production studios and very serious hobbyists only."

"How readily available is it? Could you buy it over the counter?" Carol asked.

"Not really. We dealt directly with Vicom, because we wanted them to run us a full demo before we committed ourselves to laying out that much dosh. Obviously, some specialist business suppliers sell it, but they wouldn't be shifting it in bulk. That would be mail order, anyway. Most computer stuff is."

"The other stuff you mentioned—are they things that lots of people would have?" Carol asked.

"They're not uncommon. Off the top of my head, say

two or three per cent market penetration on the video stuff, maybe fifteen per cent on the scanner. But if you're thinking of tracking down your man, I'd start with the Vicom end," Michael advised.

"How do you think they'd be about letting us look at their sales records?"

Michael pulled a face. "Your guess is as good as mine. You're not a competitor, and this is a murder investigation. You never know, they might be happy to cooperate. After all, if this guy is using their stuff, it'd be bad PR if they didn't. I can dig out the name of the guy we dealt with. He was their sales director. Scottish bloke. One of those names you can't tell which is the Christian name. You know, Grant Cameron, Campbell Elliott . . . It'll come to me . . ."

While Michael searched through his contacts book, Carol refilled her glass and savoured the prickle of bubbles against her palate. Lately, pleasure seemed to have been in short supply. But if she could come up with some leads on her theory, all of that might change.

"Got it!" Michael exclaimed. "Fraser Duncan. Give him a ring Monday morning and mention my name. Time you got a break, sis."

"You're not wrong," Carol said with feeling. "Believe me, I deserve it."


Kevin Matthews lay sprawled across the rumpled king-sized bed, smiling up at the woman straddling him. "Mmm," he murmured. "That was a bit nice."

"Better than home cooking," Penny Burgess said, running her fingers through the dark auburn hair that curled across Kevin's chest.

Kevin chuckled. "Just a bit." He reached for the remains of the hefty vodka and Coke Penny had poured for him earlier.

"I'm surprised you could get away tonight," Penny said, moving forward languidly so her nipples brushed his.

"We've had so much overtime lately she's given up expecting me home for anything except for a bit of kip."

Penny let her upper body fall heavily on Kevin, thrusting the breath out of his body. "I didn't mean Lynn," she said, "I meant work."

Kevin grabbed her wrists and wrestled her off him. When they subsided, lying side by side, giggling breathlessly, he finally said, "There wasn't much to do, tell you the truth."

Penny snorted incredulously. "Oh yeah? Last night Carol Jordan finds body number five, the suspect is arrested trying to leave the country and you tell me there's nothing much doing? Come on, Kevin, this is me you're talking to."

"You've got it all wrong, darling," Kevin said magnanimously. "You and all the rest of your media cronies." It wasn't often he got the chance to put Penny right and he intended to make the most of it.

"What do you mean?" Penny propped herself up on one elbow, unconsciously covering her body with the duvet. This wasn't a bit of fun any more; this was work.

"Number one. The body Carol found last night wasn't one of the serial killer's victims. It was a copycat job. The postmortem proved that beyond reasonable doubt. It was just another seedy little sex murder. Central should clear it up in a few days with a bit of help from Vice," Kevin said, the self-satisfaction obvious in his voice.

Penny bit on the bullet and said sweetly through clenched teeth, "And?"

"And what, darling?"

"If that was number one, there must be a number two."

Kevin smiled, so smug that Penny made the instant decision that he was on the out just as soon as she had an acceptable alternative lined up. "Oh yes, number two. Stevie McConnell isn't the killer."

For once, Penny ran out of words. The information was shocking in itself. But more shocking was the fact that, knowing this, Kevin had said nothing. He had remained silent and let her paper run a story that was eventually going to make her look an ill-informed pillock. "Really?" she said, in the superior accent she hadn't used since the day she'd gratefully quit boarding school and made the decision to go vocally downmarket.

"That's right. We knew that before he legged it." Kevin lay back on the pillows, blissfully unaware of the look of distilled hatred that Penny was beaming in his direction.

"So what exactly was that pantomime at court this morning in aid of?" she demanded in tones her elocution mistress would have been proud of.

Kevin smirked. "Well, most of us had already decided that McConnell wasn't our man. But Brandon had put a tail on him, so when he tried to skip the country, we were more or less obliged to pull him in. By that time, it was starting to look definite that McConnell isn't the Queer Killer. Plus, he doesn't fit the profile that Tony Hill came up with."

"I don't believe I'm hearing this," Penny said sharply.

Kevin finally registered that all was not well. "What? You got a problem, darling?"

"Just a fucking bit," said Penny, enunciating each syllable crisply. "You mean to tell me you've not only put an innocent man on remand, you've also let the world's press broadcast the assumption that this man is quite probably the Queer Killer?"

Kevin propped himself up and took another swig of his drink, reaching out to rumple Penny's hair with his other hand. She pulled away with a jerk. "It's no big deal," he said patronizingly. "Nobody can get a lynch mob together and go round his house while he's inside. And we reckon that telling the world between the lines that we've got the killer banged up might just provoke the real killer into getting in touch with us to make sure we know he's still out there."

"You mean you want to drive him to kill again?" Penny demanded, her voice rising.

"Of course not," Kevin said indignantly. "I mean, to get in touch. Like he did after he'd killed Gareth Finnegan."

"My God," Penny said wonderingly. "Kevin, how can

you sit there and tell me that nothing bad can happen to
Stevie McConnell while he's locked up in prison?"

While Penny Burgess and Kevin Matthews were arguing
the morality of Stevie McConnell's remand, in C Wing of
Her Majesty's Prison Barleigh, three men were taking turns
to show Stevie McConnell what happens to sex cases in
prison. At the end of the landing, a warden stood impassively, appearing as oblivious to McConnell's screams and
entreaties as a deaf man with his hearing aid switched off.
And on the moors above Bradfield, a ruthless killer put the
finishing touches to the torture instrument that would help
show the world that the man in prison was not the person
responsible for four perfectly executed serial punishments.

The HOLMES room was a quiet hum of activity, operators
staring into screens and tapping keys. Carol found Dave
Woolcott sitting in his office picking listlessly at fish and
chips. He looked up when she entered and managed a wan
smile. "Thought you were having a night off," he said.

"I'm still hoping to. My brother promised to buy me a
bucket of popcorn all to myself if I make it to the multi-
screen before the film begins. I just wanted to swing by
and run something past you." She dumped two plastic bags
on Dave's desk. Glossy computer magazines spilled out.

"I've got this theory," she said. "Well, more of a hunch."
For the third time, Carol outlined her idea about the killer
importing videos and transforming them into supports for
his fantasies.

Dave listened carefully, nodding as Carol's ideas sank
in. "I like it," he said simply. "I've read that profile a couple
of times now, and I really can't accept what Dr. Hill says
about keeping stable just by using videos of the killings. It
doesn't make sense. Your idea does. So what do you want
from me?"

"Michael reckons that tracing the buyers of Vicom 3D

Commander might lead us to him if we're right. I'm not so sure. It's possible that the company the killer works for has the software, and he does the manipulation work there. To be on the safe side, though, he'd need to do all the scanning and digitizing at home. So I thought it would also be worthwhile doing a trawl of the suppliers of video digitizers and video capture cards. We can find suppliers via the ads in these magazines, since virtually all computer stuff comes mail order. We should also contact local computer clubs too. If you've got any bodies to spare, that is."

Dave sighed. "Dream on, Carol." He picked up a magazine and flicked through the pages. "I suppose I could draw up a list tonight and tomorrow, and first thing Monday morning we could get a couple of DCs to do a ring-round. When my operators will have time to input the data, I don't know, but I will see that it gets done. OK?"

Carol grinned. "You're a star, Dave."

"I'm a bloody martyr, Carol. My youngest's cut two teeth that I haven't even seen yet."

"I could stay and help you go through the magazines," Carol said reluctantly.

"Oh, bugger off. Go and enjoy yourself. It's about time one of us did. What are you going to see?"

Carol pulled a face. "It's a Saturday Special double bill—*Manhunter* and *The Silence of the Lambs*."

Dave's laughter echoed in her ears all the way to the car.

The long howl seemed to come from the pit of his stomach. As his orgasm shuddered through him like a runaway train, Tony felt a glorious sense of release. "Oh, God," he groaned.

"Oh, yeah, yeah," Angelica gasped. "I'm coming again, again, oh, Tony, Tony . . ." Her voice faded in a gulping sob.

Tony lay back on his bed, chest heaving, the smell of sweat and sex heavy around him. He felt as if he'd been suddenly detached from a burden he had been carrying for so long he had ceased to notice its weight. Was this what being cured felt like, this sense of light and colour, this sensation of having dumped the past like sacks of coal in a bunker? Was this how his patients felt when they'd unloaded their mess on him?

In his ear, he could hear the ragged sound of her breathing. After a few moments, she said, "Wow. Just wow. That was the best ever. I just love the way you love me."

"It was good for me, too," Tony said, meaning it for once. For the first time since they had started this strange combination of therapy and sexual gameplaying, he'd had no trouble with his erection. Right from the start, he'd been hard as a rock. No fading, no wilting, no shame. Just the first problem-free sex he'd had for years. OK, so Angelica wasn't actually in the room with him, but it was a giant step in the right direction.

"We make the sweetest music," Angelica said. "Nobody's ever turned me on like you do."

"Do you do this often?" Tony asked languidly.

Angelica chuckled, a husky, sexy gurgle of laughter. "You're not the first."

"I could tell that. You're far too much of an expert," Tony flattered, not entirely insincerely. She'd been the perfect therapist for him, that much was certainly true.

"I'm very choosy about the men I allow to share with me," Angelica said. "It's not everyone who appreciates what I have to offer," she added.

"They'd have to be very strange not to enjoy it. I know I do."

"I'm glad, Anthony. You'll never know how glad. I have to go now," she said, her tone changing abruptly to the businesslike one Tony had come to associate with the end of their calls. "Tonight has been really special. We'll talk soon."

The line went dead. Tony switched off the phone and stretched out. Tonight, with Angelica, for the first time in his life, Tony had felt a protective care that succoured without smothering. His grandmother, he knew intellectually, had loved him and cared for him, but theirs had never been a demonstrative family, and her love had been brusque and practical, meeting her needs rather than his. The women he'd been involved with in the past had, he now realized, been her emotional doppelgangers. Thanks to Angelica, he dared hope the pattern had been broken. It had caused him enough pain over the years.

His sexual life had started later than most of his contemporaries, in part because his body had been reluctant to mature. Until his seventeenth year, he'd been by far the smallest boy in his class, condemned to dating the thirteen- and fourteen-year-olds who were even more scared of sex than he was. Then, suddenly, he'd shot up five inches in as many months. By the time he'd gone to university, he'd lost his virginity in a clumsy fumble on a single bed, the candlewick bedspread leaving him with uncomfortable friction burns for days afterwards. His girlfriend, relieved to be rid at last of the encumbrance of her virginity, had dumped him days later.

At university, he'd been too shy and hard-working to improve his experience by much. Then, when he'd started work on his doctorate, he'd fallen head over heels with a young philosophy tutor in his college. Because he was bright and interesting, he captured her interest. Patricia made no secret of the fact that she was a woman of the world, just as she made no secret of the fact that she had ended their relationship because of his lacklustre performance between the sheets. "Face it, sweetheart," she'd told him, "your brain might be DPhil material, but your fucking wouldn't earn you an O level."

It had been downhill from then. The last couple of women Tony had been involved with had thought he was a perfect gentleman, never pressurizing them into bed. Until they got him there and discovered how seldom he could actually deliver. He had long ago discovered how hard it was to convince a woman that the fact that he couldn't get it up had nothing whatsoever to do with her. "They just got fed up with having their egos bashed," he said aloud.

Maybe now he had finally found a way to confront the past and move forward. A few more nights like tonight with Angelica and maybe, just maybe, he'd be ready to try the real thing. He wondered if her services extended to that. Perhaps he should start thinking about dropping a few hints.

Brandon read the sheet of paper on his desk and rubbed the grit of sleep from his eyes. He and Dave Woolcott had spent the evening going through the dozens of reports that had flowed in from the actions Dave had ordered in response to the correlations thrown out by the HOLMES computer. In spite of their determined efforts to find some slender thread of evidence to unravel back to the killer, there was nothing that either of them could identify as a lead.

"Maybe this idea of Carol's will do the business for us," Dave yawned.

"We've tried everything else," Brandon said, his voice as depressed as his face. "It can't hurt to run with it."

"She's a smart operator, that one," Dave remarked. "She'll be running the shop one of these days." There was no bitterness in his tone, only a tired admiration. Another yawn split his face.

"Go home, Dave. When was the last time you saw Marion awake?"

Dave groaned. "Don't you start, sir. I was going to knock off anyway, there's not a lot doing. I'll be in tomorrow, finish off listing these computer suppliers."

"OK, but not too early, you hear? Give your family a treat. Eat breakfast with them." Before he took his own advice, Brandon wanted to go through the witness statements and officers' impressions once more, unable to believe that there wasn't something lurking in there that would give them their first serious break. By the time he was halfway through he was finding it almost impossible to motivate himself to get through the rest of the pile. The prospect of tucking himself round Maggie's warm body was overwhelmingly appealing.

Brandon sighed and focused on the next sheet of paper. His scrutiny was interrupted by the insistent trill of his telephone. "Brandon," he sighed.

"Sergeant Murray here, front desk. Sorry to interrupt you, sir, but none of the inspectors are in the station at the moment. Thing is, there's a gentleman down here I think you'll want to talk to. He's a neighbour of Damien Connolly's, sir."

Brandon was already out of his chair. "I'm on my way," he said.

The man at the front desk was sitting on the wooden bench that ran along the wall, head down, the rough blur of stubble dark along his jaw. As Brandon came round from behind the counter, he looked up. Late twenties, Brandon estimated. Sun-bed tan, bruised circles under his eyes. Some sort of businessman, judging by the expensive but sombre suit and the silk tie hanging askew under the open top button of the shirt. He had the rumpled, red-eyed look of someone who's been travelling so long they've forgotten which day or which city it is. Seeing someone more tired than himself seemed to inject Brandon with fresh energy. "Mr. Harding?" he said cheerfully. "I'm John Brandon, the Assistant Chief Constable in charge of the investigation into Damien Connolly's death."

The man nodded. "Terry Harding. I live a couple of doors down from Damien."

"My sergeant tells me you might have some information for us."

"That's right," Terry Harding said, his voice thick with exhaustion. "I saw a stranger driving out of Damien's garage the night he was killed."

*I had already started work on Dr. Tony Hill even before I had dispatched Damien Connolly. It seemed poetic justice to me that, like Damien, his name was already on my list as a potential partner. If I had needed any kind of reinforcement that I was doing the right thing by punishing him, that was it.*

*So, I already knew where he lived, where he worked and what he looked like. I knew what time he left the house in the morning, what tram he caught to work, and how long he stayed in his little office in the university.*

*I only realized how smoothly everything had gone up till now when things started to move in directions I hadn't predicted and didn't like. I suppose I'd made the mistake of underestimating the stupidity of the forces opposed to me. I'd never thought there was much brain power shared out among the officers of Bradfield police, but the latest developments shook even me. They arrested the wrong man!*

*Their incredible lack of intelligence and perception was matched only by the media, following uncritically like sheep. I couldn't believe it when I picked up the* Sentinel Times *to read that a man was in custody helping police enquiries into my killings. The arrest came after a street assault involving a police officer. How on earth could they imagine that someone who had taken as much care as I had would end up in some street brawl in Temple Fields?*

*It was an insult to my intelligence. Did they really think I was some out-of-control street yob?*

*I read and reread the article, unable to credit the depths of their foolishness. Anger burned inside me. I could feel it in my guts like indigestion and wind cramps rolled into a spiky ball. I wanted to do something vicious and dramatic, something that would prove to them how wrong they were.*

*I worked out with my weights till my muscles were trembling from effort and my kit was saturated with sweat, but still the anger refused to abate. I stormed upstairs to my computer and worked on the videos of Damien that I'd imported into my system. By the time I'd finished, we'd performed sexual gymnastics that the Russian national team would have been proud of. But nothing satisfied me. Nothing took the anger away.*

*Luckily, unlike them I'm not stupid. I know how dangerous uncontrolled anger could be for me. I needed to harness my anger, to be creative with it and make it work for me. I forced myself to channel my rage into constructive pathways. I planned in meticulous detail how I would capture Dr. Tony Hill, and what I would do with him when I got him. I'd be keeping him in suspense—literally.*

*Squassation and strappado. The Spanish Inquisition knew exactly how to make the most of what was available. They simply harnessed the most powerful force on the planet, the force of gravity. All you need is a winch, a pulley, a few ropes and a lump of stone. You fasten the victim's hands behind his back and run a rope from them through the pulley. Then you tie the stone to his feet.*

*In his book* The Horrid Cruelties of the Inquisition, *published in 1770, John Marchant described this efficient torture most eloquently:*

He is then drawn up on high, till his head reaches the pulley. He is kept hanging in this manner for some time, that by the greatness of the weight hanging at his feet, all his joints and limbs may be dreadfully stretched, and on a *sudden he is let down with a jerk, by the slacking of the rope, but is kept from coming quite to the ground, by which terrible shake, his arms and legs are disjointed, whereby he is put to the most exquisite pain; the shock which he receives by the sudden stop of his fall, and the weight at his feet stretching his whole body more intensely and cruelly.*

The Germans added a refinement that attracted me. Behind the victim, they placed a spiked roller, so that as he descended, the rollers cut into and excoriated his back, leaving his body a bloody, dislocated mass. I considered reproducing this effect, but even after a lot of juggling with the layout, I couldn't come up with a design on the computer that I was satisfied would work smoothly, unless I cuffed his hands in front of him, which makes the squassation and strappado far less effective. Keep it simple, that's my motto.

While I was planning and constructing, I took steps to draw my web even tighter around Dr. Hill. He might think he could climb inside my head, but he'd got things the wrong way round.

I couldn't wait to get started. I was counting the hours.

# 16

*"Now, Miss R., supposing that I should appear at about midnight at your bedside, armed with a carving knife, what would you say?" To which the confiding girl had replied, "Oh, Mr. Williams, if it was anybody else, I should be frightened. But as soon as I heard your voice, I should be tranquil." Poor girl; had this outline sketch of Mr. Williams been filled in and realized, she would have seen something in the corpse-like face, and heard something in the sinister voice, that would have unsettled her tranquillity forever.*

When the phone rang, Carol's first reaction was outrage. Ten past eight on a Sunday morning could only mean work. She stirred, a long, low growl of discontent making Nelson's ears prick. Carol's arm appeared from under the covers, groping around on the bedside table. She connected with the phone and grunted, "Jordan," into it.

"This is your early-morning alarm call." The voice was far too cheerful, Carol decided, before the identity of her caller registered.

"Kevin," she said. "This better be good."

"It's better than good. What would you say to a witness who saw the killer drive away from Damien Connolly's house?"

"Say again?" she mumbled. Kevin repeated his announcement. The second time round, his voice catapulted Carol into a sitting position, on the edge of the bed. "When?" she demanded.

"The guy walked in late last night. He's been out of the country on business. Brandon interviewed him. He's called a meeting for nine," Kevin said, excited as a Christmas child.

"Kevin, you bastard, you might have called me before now . . ."

He chuckled. "I thought you needed your beauty sleep."

"Bollocks to beauty sleep . . ."

"No, I've only been in five minutes myself. Can you bring the doc in with you? I just tried calling him, but there was no reply."

"OK, I'll swing round by his place and see if I can raise him. He seems to have a habit of switching the phones off. Fancy thinking he could get away with a decent night's sleep. You can tell he's not a copper," she added. Carol replaced the phone abruptly and headed for the shower. The thought that Tony might have switched off his phone because he was with the woman on the answering machine crossed her mind. The idea made her stomach hurt. "Silly bitch," she muttered to herself as the water cascaded over her.

By twenty to nine, she was leaning on Tony's doorbell. After a couple of minutes, the door opened. Bleary eyed, struggling with the belt of his dressing gown, Tony peered out at her. "Carol?"

"Sorry to wake you," she said formally. "You weren't answering your phone. Mr. Brandon asked me to pick you up. There's a meeting at nine. We've got a witness."

Tony rubbed his eyes, looking bemused. "You better come in." He walked down the hall, leaving Carol to close the door behind her. "Sorry about the phones. I was late getting to sleep, so I switched them off." He shook his head. "Can you hang on while I have a shower and a shave? Otherwise, I'll make my own way in. I don't want you to be late on my account."

"I'll wait," Carol said. She picked the paper off the mat and flicked through it, leaning against the wall, alert for the telltale signs of a third person's presence. She felt unreasonably pleased when she heard none. Even though she knew her reaction was childish, it didn't mean these responses were going to stop overnight. She was just going to have to learn to disguise them until they died away, as she felt sure they would eventually, starved out of existence by Tony's lack of interest.

Ten minutes later, Tony reappeared in jeans and rugby shirt, hair damp and neatly brushed. "Sorry about that," he said. "My brain doesn't work until I've had a shower. Now, what's all this about a witness?"

Carol told him the little she knew on the way to the car.

"That's great news," Tony enthused. "First big break-through, isn't it?"

Carol shrugged. "It depends how much he can tell us. If the guy was driving a red Ford Escort, it doesn't take us a lot further forward. We'd need something solid to cross-match. Maybe something like the computer angle."

"Oh yes, the computer theory. How goes that?"

"I discussed it with my brother. He reckons it's perfectly feasible," Carol said coldly, feeling patronized.

"Great!" Tony enthused. "I really hope that works out. I wasn't trying to pour cold water on it, you know. I have to work with the balance of probabilities, and your idea's way beyond my parameters. But it's the kind of investigative brainwave that we're going to need on the national task force. I really think you should seriously consider signing up when we get the show on the road."

"I didn't think you'd be comfortable with the idea of working with me after this," Carol said, eyes firmly fixed on the road.

Tony took a deep breath. "I've never met a police officer I'd rather work with."

"Even if I do trespass on your personal space?" she asked bitterly, hating herself for picking at the hurt like an old scab.

Tony sighed. "I thought we'd agreed we could be friends? I know I . . ."

"Fine," she interrupted, wishing she'd never opened up the conversation. "I can do friends. What do you think of Bradfield Victoria's chances in the Cup?"

Startled, Tony twisted in his seat and stared at Carol. He

saw a smile twitching at the corner of her mouth. Suddenly, they were both laughing.

The latest government threats to the prison service meant the officers at HM Prison Barleigh had started to work to rule. That in turn meant that prisoners were banged up for twenty-three hours in every twenty-four. Stevie McConnell lay on his side on his bunk bed in the cell he had to himself. Following the attack that had left him with two black eyes, a couple of cracked ribs, more bruises than he could count, and the kind of sexual damage that made sitting down an option too painful to contemplate readily, he had asked for and been granted solitary confinement.

It didn't matter how much he protested that he wasn't the Queer Killer. Nobody cared, neither cons nor screws. He'd realized that the warders held him in as much contempt as his fellow prisoners when he'd heard the sounds of slopping-out all along the wing. But no officer had unlocked his cell door to allow him to empty the stinking bucket of his sewage that sat in the corner, its smell insistent and somehow more disgusting than any of the dozens of public toilets where Stevie had picked up strangers for sex.

As far as he could see, his prospects were bleak. The very fact that he was behind bars was enough to condemn him in most people's eyes. Probably the whole world was convinced that the Queer Killer had taken his last victim now that Stevie McConnell was in jail. After he'd been released following his first stretch of questioning, he'd been painfully aware that everyone at work, staff and clients, were giving him a wide berth, refusing to meet his eyes. One drink in a Temple Fields bar where he'd been a regular for years had been enough to show him that gay solidarity had mysteriously deserted him too. The police and the press clearly thought he was their psychopath. And until they caught the Queer Killer, Bradfield wasn't going to be a welcoming place for Stevie McConnell. The decision to

move out to Amsterdam where an ex-lover ran a gym had
seemed to make sense at the time. It hadn't occurred to him
that they'd be tailing him.

The irony that this had all happened to him because he'd
rushed to the defence of a police officer in the first place
was not lost on Stevie. He gave a bitter bark of laughter.
That big Geordie sergeant was probably counting his blessings that he'd been smacked with a half-brick, figuring that
that was the only thing that had saved him from being the
Queer Killer's next victim. The reality was that Stevie
McConnell was the only victim around that night. And it
wasn't going to get any better. Even his shocked family
didn't want to know, according to his solicitor.

Lying there, examining his future dispassionately, he
came to a decision. Grimacing with pain, Stevie rolled off
the bunk and took off his shirt, wincing at the stab of pain
from his ribs. With his teeth and nails, painstakingly he
unpicked the seams that held the denim together. On the
sharp end of a bed spring, he ripped the edges of the material so he could tear it into thin strips, which he plaited
together for extra strength. He tied one end of the makeshift
ligature round his neck in a tight noose, then climbed on
to the top bunk. He fastened the other end of his short rope
to the bottom rail of the upper berth.

Then, at seventeen minutes past nine on a sunny Sunday
morning, he threw himself head first over the edge.


Like an ailing company which has won a life-saving tender
against all odds, Scargill Street was buzzing with excited
activity. At the heart of it all was the HOLMES room,
where officers stared into screens, manipulating the new
information, evaluating the new correspondences the system was throwing out.

In his office, Brandon held a council of war with his
four inspectors and Tony, all of them clutching a photocopy
of Brandon's notes on his interview with Terry Harding.
The ACC had only had five hours' sleep, but the prospect

of movement on the enquiry had given him a new energy, betrayed only by the heavy shadows around his deep-set eyes. "To recap, then," Brandon said. "At about quarter past seven the night Damien Connolly was killed, a man drove out of his garage in some kind of big four-wheel drive jeep, dark in colour. He got out of the jeep to close the garage door, and that's when our witness got his best look at him. The description we've got is white, five ten to six feet, aged between twenty and forty-five, possibly with his hair tied back in a ponytail. Wearing white trainers, jeans and a long waxed coat. Overnight, the HOLMES team have been going through the vehicles clocked in Temple Fields that fit the description. Most of these drivers have already been interviewed, but they're all going to be followed up and questioned more thoroughly now we've got Terry Harding's evidence. Bob, I want you to take charge of that, and I want alibis checking too."

"Right, boss," Stansfield said, flicking the ash off his cigarette with a determined motion.

"Oh, and Bob? Can you get someone to check that Harding really has been in Japan all week on a business trip? I want to make sure we cover all the bases on this one." Stansfield nodded.

"I'm sending a car round for Harding at eleven o'clock," Brandon went on, checking the list he'd made in the kitchen at seven. "Carol, I want you to do the interview. Check what taxi firm Harding used to take him to the airport; let's see if we can get that time narrowed down a bit more. Tony, I'd like you to sit in on it. Maybe you can help us with strategies to improve his recollection, see if we can get any firm description of what this character looks like."

"I'll do my best," he said. "At least I can probably distinguish between what he really remembers and what he thinks he remembers."

Brandon gave him an odd look, but carried on regardless. "Kevin, I want you to organize a team to hit the car showrooms, get as many brochures and posters as you can of four-wheel drive jeeps, so we can show them to Mr.

Harding and see if he can give us a positive ID."

"Will do, sir. Do you want us to go back to the neighbours in the earlier cases, see if anyone noticed the same vehicle there?" Kevin asked eagerly.

Brandon considered for a moment. "Let's see how we go on today," he said after a few moments. "It'll take a lot of bodies and time to go over the old ground again, and we might not need it. It's probably worth having a word with the rest of the neighbours in Connolly's street, though. Now we've got something positive to hit them with. Good idea, Kevin. Now, Dave. What can you do for us?"

Woolcott outlined the actions the HOLMES team were already carrying out. "With it being Sunday, I'm holding back on contacting Swansea until we've tried to get the vehicle narrowed down. The more information we can give them, the fewer possibilities we'll have to deal with. If this Harding bloke can give us make, model and year, or at least eliminate some models, we can ask DVLC to let us have a list of all the matches throughout the UK. Then we can start interviewing registered keepers, starting with Bradfield and moving out from there. It's a helluva big job, but we should get there in the end."

Brandon nodded his acknowledgement. "Anybody got anything else?"

Tony lifted a hand. "If you're questioning neighbours anyway, it might be worth extending the enquiries slightly." All eyes were on him, but he was only aware of Carol's. What had happened between them had sharpened his desire to be instrumental in capturing Handy Andy. "This guy is a stalker, I don't think anyone would dispute that now. I think he'd been watching Damien Connolly for a while. Given that we're in the middle of winter and it's not the ideal weather for standing around in the open, chances are he did the bulk of his spying from his car. He probably didn't park up in the close itself, since he'd be too noticeable in such a short street. I'd guess he parked on the street that runs along the bottom, somewhere that he had the house in his line of sight. Maybe someone there noticed an unfamiliar vehicle parked outside for long stretches."

"Good thinking," Brandon said. "Kevin, can you cover that?"

"Will do, sir. I'll get the lads on to it."

"And the lasses," Carol said sweetly. "And maybe we should ask them not to concentrate on the four-wheel drive motor. If this guy's as careful as we think he is, he might only use the jeep for the actual snatches and go for something different when he's doing the stalking, just in case a nosy neighbour has clocked him."

"What do you think, Tony?" Brandon asked.

"It wouldn't surprise me," he said. "It's important we don't forget how competent this killer is. He might even be using hired cars."

Dave Woolcott groaned. "Oh God, don't do this to me."

Bob Stansfield looked up from the pad where he'd been scribbling the names of his team. "I take it that the other lines of enquiry that Dr. Hill suggested are on the back burner for now?"

Brandon pursed his lips grimly. The euphoria had died somewhere during the briefing. The weight of the work ahead seemed unbearable, the idea of finding the killer almost as distant as it had before Terry Harding walked into the station. "That's right. No disrespect, Tony, but your suggestions are hypotheses, and what we've got now is our first solid set of facts."

"No problem," Tony said. "Hard evidence always comes first."

"And Carol's idea about the computer stuff? Should we still pursue that?" Dave asked.

"Same thing applies," Brandon said. "It's a hunch, not a fact, so yes, it goes on the back burner."

"With respect, sir," Carol chipped in, determined not to be sidelined. "Even if Terry Harding gives us a positive ID on the make and model of the vehicle, we might be no further forward. We need other elimination factors before we can narrow things down. If I'm right about the computer, we'd be looking at such a small segment of the population that it would be significant if we did get a cross-match."

Brandon considered for a moment. Then he said, "Point taken, Carol. OK, we can pursue it, Dave, but not as a priority. Only as and when we have bodies freed up from the main enquiry. Right, are we all clear what we've got to do?" He looked around expectantly, registering the series of nods. "OK, team," Brandon said, his voice stern. "Let's go for it."

"And may the force be with you," Kevin said under his breath to Carol as they emerged from the office.

"I'd rather have the force than the gutter press," she said drily, turning her back on him. "Tony, can we find a quiet corner and plan our strategy for this interview?"

"The only way you're going to get more out of him is by hypnosis," Tony told Carol as they talked in the corridor after an hour with Terry Harding.

"Can you do that?" Carol asked.

"I've got the basic technique. Judging by his eye movements and body language, he was telling the truth about what he saw, not making anything up or exaggerating, so he might come across with more detail under hypnosis, particularly if we have pictures to show him."

Ten minutes later, Carol was back with a sheaf of car brochures that Kevin's team had scavenged from city dealerships. "This what we need?"

Tony nodded. "Perfect. You sure you want me to give this a go?"

"It's got to be worth a try," Carol said.

They walked back into the interview room, where Terry Harding was finishing a mug of coffee. "Can I go now?" he said plaintively. "Only I'm due to fly out to Brussels tomorrow and I haven't even unpacked my bag."

"Not much longer, sir," Carol said, sitting down to one side of the table. "Dr. Hill would like to try something with you."

Tony smiled reassuringly. "We've got some pictures of the kind of jeep you saw leaving Damien's garage. What I'd like to do, if you're agreeable, is to put you in a light hypnotic trance and ask you to look at them."

Harding frowned. "Why can't I just look at them as I am?"

"The chances are better that you'd recognize the particular model," Tony explained soothingly. "Thing is, Mr. Harding, you're obviously a very busy man. Since you saw the incident, you've travelled to the other side of the world, you've had a series of important business meetings, and you've probably not had enough sleep. All of that means your conscious mind has probably filed away the details of what you saw last Sunday. Using hypnosis, I can help you retrieve that information."

Harding looked dubious. "I don't know. Always supposing you could get me to go under, you could make me say anything."

"Unfortunately, that's not the case. If it was, hypnotists would all be millionaires," Tony joked. "Like I said, all it does is free up the stuff you've buried because it's not important."

"What do I have to do?" Harding said suspiciously.

"Just listen to my voice and follow what I tell you," Tony said. "You'll feel a little strange, a little spaced out, but you'll be in control at all times. I use a technique called neuro-linguistic programming. It's very relaxing, I promise you."

"Do I have to lie down, or what?"

"Nothing like that. And I'm not going to wave a watch in front of you. Are you prepared to give it a try?"

Carol held her breath, watching Harding as an assortment of expressions chased each other across his face. Finally, he nodded. "I doubt you'll be able to get me under," he said. "I'm a man who knows his own mind. But I'm willing to try."

"OK," said Tony. "I want you to relax. Close your eyes

if it feels more comfortable. Now, I want you to go deep down inside yourself . . ."

Elated with their success, Tony and Carol bounced into the murder squad room. Bob Stansfield was standing by the window, staring out at the rain-drenched street below, his shoulders slumped, a cigarette burning unheeded in his hand. He glanced round and Carol called, "Cheer up, it might never happen."

Stansfield swung round and said bitterly, "You obviously haven't heard the news."

"What news?" Carol asked, walking over to him.

"Stevie McConnell topped himself."

Carol rocked on her heels and stumbled against a desk. Her ears were ringing and she thought she was going to faint. Instinctively, Tony moved forward and steered her into a chair. "Deep breaths, Carol. Deep and slow," he said softly, leaning over her, staring intently at her white face.

She closed her eyes, dug her nails into her palms and obeyed. "Sorry," Stansfield said. "It knocked me for six too."

Carol looked up and pushed her hair away from a forehead suddenly clammy. "What happened?"

"Apparently he took a beating yesterday. A sex-case special, by all accounts. So, this morning he tore up his shirt and hung himself. The fucking warders never noticed, on account of they're playing at work to rule," he added savagely.

"The poor bastard," Carol said.

"There's going to be hell to pay," Stansfield predicted. "I'm glad it was fuck all to do with me. At least it won't be my arse in the fire. I mean, Brandon's bombproof, so it's going to be some poor fucker of an inspector who's going to carry the can."

Carol looked at him as if she'd like to hit him. "Sometimes, Bob, you really fuck me off," she said coldly. "Where's Brandon?"

"Down in the HOLMES room. Probably hiding from the Chief."

They found Brandon and Dave Woolcott closeted in the inspector's cubby hole off the main room. "We've got a positive make, sir," Carol said, her initial exuberance flattened by Stansfield's news. "We know what car he was driving."

Penny Burgess turned off the main road on to the Forestry Commission track that led deep into the heart of the woodland. She was aiming for a car park and picnic area in the middle of the woods. It was one of her favourite spots from which to strike off through the trees and up on to the bare gritstone edges where the wind could blow away all the accumulated dross of the week. She certainly needed it after the last few days of hard graft, big stories and not enough sleep.

The record on the radio finished and the announcer said, "And now, over to the newsroom for the headlines on the hour." The news ident followed, then a woman said in a voice altogether too bright for her subject matter, "Northern Sound news on the hour. A man who was questioned by Bradfield police in connection with the serial killings that have terrorized the city was found dead this morning in his cell at Barleigh jail."

In her shock, Penny took her foot off the accelerator and pitched forward as the car stalled. "Shit!" she exclaimed, her hand shooting out to twist the volume higher.

"Steven McConnell is thought to have committed suicide by hanging himself with a noose made from his own clothes. McConnell, the manager of a body-building gym in the city, was arrested last week after a street brawl involving an undercover police officer in the city's gay village," the newsreader continued, sounding for all the world as if she were announcing the results of the Eurovision Song Contest. "He was released on bail, but rearrested after attempting to flee the country. A Home Office spokesman said there would be a full enquiry into the circumstances of his death.

"The economy has never been in a better position, the Prime Minister said today . . ." Penny turned the key in the ignition and did a perilous five-point turn in the narrow lane before stamping on the gas and shooting back towards the road. It was just as well, she thought, that she'd already decided to dump Kevin. After the story she was about to write, she couldn't imagine him ever wanting to see her again anyway.

Tony drummed his fingers on the back of the cab's seat, a curious restlessness possessing him. Leaving Scargill Street hadn't been easy, but he knew he had no role while the police worked on their one piece of solid evidence. The last thing they needed in that maelstrom of reproach and driven activity was for him to sit around reminding them of all the reasons why he'd never been convinced that Stevie McConnell was their man.

His consolation was that he felt certain that Angelica would phone tonight. As the taxi hissed through the wet and empty streets, Tony rehearsed the conversation. He felt a new confidence, a certainty that tonight he would have no problems, that he had finally wrestled his demon into submission thanks to her strange erotic therapy. He would tell her she had no idea how much her phone calls had meant to him. That she had helped him more than she could know. Satisfied that he had things under control, Tony sighed comfortably and cleared his mind of Handy Andy.

Penny Burgess popped the top on a can of Guinness, lit a cigarette and switched on her computer. After making a handful of phone calls to firm up the version of events she'd heard on the radio, she was fired with the self-righteous enthusiasm that only politicians, journalists and fundamentalist preachers seem capable of harnessing for professional advancement.

She inhaled a long stream of smoke, thought for a moment, then started to hammer the keys.

Bradfield's serial killer claimed his fifth victim yesterday (Sunday) when gay body-builder Stevie McConnell killed himself in a prison cell.

Police had implied that McConnell was himself the Queer Killer in a cynical bid to force the real killer's hand.

But their twisted exercise ended in tragedy when McConnell, 32, hung himself with a makeshift rope woven from his own torn shirt. He tied it to the top bunk in his solitary-confinement cell at Barleigh prison and threw himself off, strangling himself.

And last night, a police officer involved in the Queer Killer investigation admitted, "We've known for several days that Stevie McConnell wasn't the killer."

McConnell had pleaded with prison staff to put him in solitary after a barbaric attack by fellow inmates the previous day.

A source inside Barleigh prison said, "He took a real beating. The word on the grapevine when he arrived was that he was the Queer Killer, only the police didn't have enough evidence to charge him yet.

"Prisoners don't like sex killers, and they tend to make their feelings known. McConnell got a brutal hammering. He was badly beaten up, and sexually assaulted too."

Warders are said to have turned a blind eye to McConnell's savage battering. Then yesterday (Sunday) because of a prison officers' work to rule, he was left unattended in his cell for long enough to end his life. A Home Office spokesman said there would be a full enquiry into the incident.

McConnell managed Bodies gym in the city centre, where the killer's third victim, solicitor Gareth Finnegan, was a member.

McConnell faced a minor assault charge after coming to

the rescue of an undercover police sergeant who was attacked by a third man in the Temple Fields gay village.

He then tried to flee the country while he was out on bail. Police rearrested him as he was about to board a ferry for Holland, and persuaded magistrates to remand him in custody.

A police source revealed, "What we did made people think that McConnell was the killer, and that's what we wanted.

"Serial killers are very vain, and we thought that the killer would be so outraged that we had pointed the finger at the wrong person that he would break cover and make contact.

"It's all gone horribly wrong."

A friend of McConnell's said last night, "Bradfield police are murderers. As far as I'm concerned, they killed Stevie.

"The police really grilled him about the serial killings. They put him under all kinds of pressure.

"Even though they let him go afterwards, mud like that sticks. He got the cold shoulder at work, and out in the gay bars.

"That's why he decided to leg it. It's a tragedy. Worse than that, it's a pointless tragedy.

"This hasn't taken the police an inch closer to finding the killer."

Penny lit another cigarette and read through her copy. "Pick the bones out of that, Kevin," she said softly, hitting the keys that would save the file and transmit it via her modem to the office computer. Then, as an afterthought, she typed:

*Memo to newsdesk.*
    *From Penny Burgess, Crime Desk.*
    *I am taking tomorrow (Monday) as time off in lieu of working extra hours last week and today. Hope this doesn't pose too many problems!*

*       *       *

"A Land Rover Discovery, metallic grey or dark blue?" Dave Woolcott confirmed, making a note on a pad.

"That's what the man said," Carol agreed.

"Right. With it being Sunday, I can't get a full run-down from Swansea on every vehicle like that on our patch," Dave said.

"What we could do, though, is get a team going round the main dealerships and the quality second-hand dealers asking for their records of anyone who's bought one," Kevin suggested. Like all of them, he was fired with an excitement only slightly tempered by the tragic news from Barleigh.

"No," Brandon said. "That's a waste of time and personnel. There's no guarantee that the killer bought his vehicle locally. We wait until tomorrow morning. Then we go flat out."

Everyone looked disappointed, even though they recognized the force of Brandon's argument. "In that case, sir," Carol said, "I'd like to work with Dave compiling lists of computer hardware and software suppliers so we're ready to roll with that as soon as there are some spare bodies to hit the phones."

Brandon nodded. "Good thinking, Carol. Now, why don't the rest of us go home and rediscover what our houses look like?"


Tony was stretched out on the sofa, trying to persuade himself he was enjoying the luxury of watching TV when the doorbell rang. The hope of company come to rescue him from his restless boredom catapulted him to his feet and down the hall. He opened the door, a smile already spreading across his face.

The smile died halfway as he registered that he was out of luck. There was a woman on the doorstep, but she wasn't one of his friends or colleagues. She was tall, big-boned, with heavy, blunt features and a strong, square jaw. She pushed her long dark hair away from her face and said, "I'm really sorry to trouble you, only my car's broken down and I don't know where there's a pay phone. I wondered if I might use your phone to call the AA? I'll pay for the call, of course . . ." Her voice trailed off and she smiled apologetically.

FROM 3½" DISC LABELLED: BACKUP.007; FILE LOVE.017

*When I clocked Sergeant Merrick in the Sackville Arms, I thought I was going to pass out. I'd only gone there because I knew the detectives from Scargill Street use it. I wanted to hear what the gossip was among the murder squad. I wanted to hear them talk about me and my accomplishments. The last thing I expected was to see so familiar a face staring out at me.*

*I was sitting unobtrusively in the corner when I saw Merrick come in. I debated whether to leave, but I decided that might make me noticeable. The last thing I wanted was for him to recognize me and follow me for whatever reasons of his own. Besides, why should I let a policeman drive me away from my lunch break?*

*But I couldn't stop the churning in my stomach in case he caught sight of me and moved across to speak to me. I wasn't afraid of him, but I just didn't want to draw attention to myself. Luckily, he was with two of his colleagues, and they were too busy discussing something—me, probably, had they but known it—to pay much attention to anybody else. I recognized the woman from the papers. Inspector Carol Jordan. She looks better in the flesh than in print, probably because her hair's a lovely shade of blonde. The other man I hadn't seen before, but I filed his face away for future reference. Carroty-red hair, pale skin, freckles, boyish features. And of course, Merrick, head and shoulders above the others, some kind of dressing on his head. I wondered how he'd come by that.*

*I'd never hated Merrick the way I hated some of the others, even though he'd taken me into custody a couple of times. He'd never treated me with the contempt they had. He'd never sneered at me when he arrested me. But I could see he still saw me as an object, someone not worthy of respect. He never understood that when I sold my body to sailors it was for a purpose. But whatever I did then is irrelevant now. I am different now, I am a changed person. What happened back in Seaford feels as irrelevant and remote as something I'd seen at the cinema.*

*In a strange way, being in the presence of the very officers who are trying to track me down was quite exciting. I got a real buzz out of being only feet away from my hunters, who didn't sense their prey. They didn't even have enough sixth sense to realize there was something extraordinary happening, not even Carol Jordan. So much for women's intuition. I see it as a sort of test, a measure of my ability to delude my pursuers. The notion that they can catch me is so absurd, it's unthinkable.*

*I felt so strong after that encounter that the next day's paper hit me like a blow with a sandbag. I was walking through the main computer room when I saw an early edition of the* Sentinel Times *lying on some junior engineer's desk.* FIFTH BODY IN QUEER KILLER'S RAMPAGE *screamed out at me.*

*I wanted to rage and shout, to throw things through windows. How dare they? My handiwork is so individual, how could they mistake some blundering copycat's body for one of mine?*

*I was trembling with suppressed fury when I made it back to my own office. I'd wanted to ask the engineer if I could have a look at his paper, but I didn't trust myself to speak. I wanted to rush out of the office to the nearest newsagent's and snatch a copy off the counter. But that would have been unforgivable weakness. The secret of success, I told myself, was to behave normally. To do nothing that would make my colleagues think there was something peculiar going on in my life.*

*"Patience," I told myself, "is the cardinal virtue." So I sat at my desk, fiddling with the intricacies of a piece of software that needed rewriting. But my heart wasn't in it, and I know I wasn't justifying my salary that afternoon. By four o'clock, I could stand it no longer. I grabbed my phone and dialled the special number that broadcasts Bradfield Sound to callers.*

*The story was the lead item on the news bulletin, as it ought to have been. "The body of a man found in the Temple Fields area in the early hours of the morning is not the fifth victim of the serial killer who has brought terror to Bradfield's gay community, police revealed this afternoon." As the newsreader's words sank in, I felt my anger depart, the hollowness inside me whole once more.*

*Without waiting for more, I slammed the phone down. They'd got something right at last. But I'd gone through four hours of hell because of their mistake. Every hour I'd suffered would be an hour added on to the agonies of Dr. Tony Hill, I vowed.*

*Because the Bradfield police have now committed the ultimate absurdity, Dr. Tony Hill, the stupid man who hadn't even recognized that all my crimes belonged to me, has been appointed the official police consultant to the serial-killer enquiry. The poor, deluded fools. If that's their best hope, then they clearly have no hope.*

# 17

*In a murder of pure voluptuousness, entirely disinterested,
where no hostile witness was to be removed, no extra booty
to be gained and no revenge to be gratified, it is clear that
to hurry would be altogether to ruin.*

The agony was so extreme Tony wanted to believe he was
in a nightmare. He had never understood before how many
different kinds of pain there were. The dull throb in his
head; the harsh rasp in his throat; the screaming, wrenching
rip in his shoulders; and the knives of cramps in his thighs
and calves. At first, the pain blocked all his other senses.
His eyes screwed up tight, all he knew was suffering so
stark it made the sweat pop out on his forehead.

Gradually, he learned to bear the extremes of his pain,
realizing that if he took his weight on his feet, the cramps
would slowly subside and the excruciating tearing in his
shoulders grow less. As the torment became more tolerable,
he grew aware that he felt nauseous, a deep queasiness that
sat in his stomach and threatened to spill over at any moment. God alone knew how long he'd been hanging here.

Slowly, fearfully, he opened his eyes and raised his head,
a movement which sent a spasm of agony through his neck
and shoulders. Tony looked around. Instantly, he wished he
hadn't. He knew immediately where he was. The room was
brightly lit, spotlights mounted on the ceiling and walls
revealing a whitewashed room, its rough stone floor marked
with dark stains that he knew without examination were the
visible remains of the blood that had pooled and splashed
there. Facing him was the blind eye of a camcorder on a
tripod, a red light on the side indicating that his scrutiny
was not going unrecorded. Fixed to the far wall was a mag-

netic strip with a selection of knives hanging neatly on it.
In one corner of the room, he saw the unmistakable implements of torture. A rack; a strange contraption like a chair
which he recognized but could not name at first. Something
religious? Something vaguely Christian? Something treacherous, not what it seemed? A Judas chair, that was it. And
on the wall, a huge wooden saltire, like some hideously
perverted holy relic. A soft moan escaped from his dry lips.

Now he knew the worst, he took stock of his own position. He was naked, his skin gooseflesh in the chill of the
cellar. His hands were fastened behind his back; judging by
the hard edges cutting into his wrists, by handcuffs, held
taut in their turn by a rope or chain or something that was
obviously fastened to the ceiling. This hawser was tight
enough to force his upper body forward, leaving him doubled over at the waist. Tony managed to push himself on
to the tips of his toes and twist his body sideways. Out of
the corner of his eye, he could see a strong nylon rope
leading from behind him, through a pulley, along the ceiling, through another pulley on to a winch.

"Jesus Christ," he croaked. He was afraid to look at his
feet, lest his worst fears should be confirmed, but he forced
his eyes downwards nevertheless. As he had feared, each
ankle was encased in a leather strap. The straps in their
turn were attached to a rope cradle that held a heavy stone
flag. An involuntary shudder of fear rippled through him,
stressing his tortured muscles even further. He knew about
torture; to treat his patients he'd had to study the history
of sadism. Not even in his worst moments had he imagined
he would face so inhuman a fate.

His mind was already racing ahead. He would be winched
up till he reached the ceiling. His muscles would wrench
and tear, his joints strain to their utmost limit. Then the
winch would be released, letting him drop a few feet before
the brake was applied. The weight of the stone flag, still
hurtling downwards accelerating at thirty-two feet per second, would finish the job, ripping his joints apart, leaving
him dangling in a jumble of dislocated limbs. If he was

lucky, the shock and pain would thrust him into unconsciousness. Strappado, brought to a fine art by the Spanish Inquisition. No need for high tech in torture.

In a bid to escape the blind panic his knowledge had brought him to, he forced himself to cast his mind back to what had happened. The woman at the door, that was where it had started. As he had let her into the house, Tony had felt a niggle of familiarity. He felt sure he'd seen her somewhere, but he couldn't imagine having seen someone so distinctively ugly and not remembering. He'd walked ahead of her down the hall and into his study. Then, the faintest whiff of a strangely medicinal, chemical smell, before a hand had sneaked round his neck and clamped a cold, disgusting pad on his face. A kick behind his knee to buckle his legs and bring him down. He'd struggled, but with her weight on top of him, it had only lasted for moment before he had lost consciousness.

Then he had drifted in and out of a half-world of light and dark, aware only of the pad that seemed constantly to send him out as soon as he struggled into consciousness. Until, finally, he had come round. In Handy Andy's torture chamber. Out of nowhere, a quotation sprang into his mind. "Depend upon it, sir, when a man knows he is to be hanged in a fortnight, it concentrates his mind wonderfully." Somewhere, he knew there was a clue in what had happened that might just allow him to escape what seemed inevitable. All he had to do was to find it.

Had he been completely wrong in his profile? Was the woman who had kidnapped him Handy Andy? Was she the one? Or was she just the decoy, the willing accomplice who got off on her master's vice? Again, he replayed what his memory would allow him to snatch back. He summoned up the woman's image again. Clothes first. Beige mac, cut continental style, just like Carol's, swinging open to reveal a white shirt, enough buttons undone to reveal the swell of full breasts and a deep cleavage. Jeans, trainers. Trainers. They were the same make and model as his own. But none of this was significant, Tony told himself. They were only

outward symbols of the care Handy Andy took not to be
caught. The woman's garb had been chosen so that if she
did leave any stray fibres, they wouldn't show up as having
any significance, being identifiable as having come from
either Carol's clothes or his. And Carol had been in his
house often enough now for her to have left stray fibres.

The woman's face didn't really ring any bells either. She
was tall for a woman, at least five feet ten, with chunky
bone structure to match. Not even her mother could have
called her attractive, with her heavy jaw, slightly bulbous
nose, wide mouth and eyes set curiously far apart. Even
though she was skilfully, if heavily, made up, there wasn't
a lot she could do with the basic building materials. He was
sure they'd never been in a room together, though he
couldn't rule out having passed her in the street, at the tram
station or on campus.

The trainers. For some reason he kept coming back to
the trainers. If only the pain would stop long enough for
him to focus properly. Tony locked his legs straight, trying
to relieve the agonizing strain on his shoulders. The fraction
of an inch he gained wasn't nearly enough. Again, visceral
fear gripped him and he blinked away a tear.

What was it about the trainers? Tony summoned every
ounce of concentration he could master, and called up the
image of the woman again. With a slow gasp of understanding, he realized what it was. The feet were too big. Even
for a woman of that height, the feet were too big. As soon
as he grasped that, he remembered the hands too. First,
black leather, later thin latex gloves covering big hands,
fingers thick and strong. The person who had brought him
here had not always been a woman.


Carol pressed the doorbell again. Where the hell was he?
The lights were on, the curtains drawn. Maybe he'd nipped
out to pick up a pizza, post a letter, buy a bottle of wine,
rent a video? With a frustrated sigh, she turned away and
walked down to the end of the street, turning into the ginnel

that ran between Tony's street and the houses behind. She walked down to his back yard, where a previous owner had demolished the wall and concreted half the area to provide the hard standing where Tony had told her he always kept his car.

The car was in place, exactly where it should have been. "Oh, bloody hell," Carol complained. Edging past the car, she walked up to the house and peered through the kitchen window. The light from the open door into the hall cast a pale glow over the room. No sign of life. No dirty dishes, no empty bottles.

On the off chance, Carol tried the back door. No joy. "Bloody men," she grumbled as she strode back to her car. "Five minutes, pal, then I'm off," she said, throwing herself into the driver's seat. Ten minutes crawled by, but no one appeared.

Carol started the engine and drove off. At the end of the street, she glanced across at the pub on the other side of the main road. It was worth a try, she supposed. It took less than three minutes to check the smoky, crowded rooms and discover that wherever Tony Hill was, it wasn't in the Farewell to Arms.

Where else could he be within walking distance at nine o'clock on a Sunday night? "Anywhere," she told herself. "You can't be his only friend in the world. He wasn't expecting you; you only called round to arrange a meeting for tomorrow."

Giving up, Carol drove home. The flat was empty. Michael, she remembered, was out to dinner with some woman he'd met at a trade fair. She decided to give up on the world and go to bed. But first, she'd better leave a message on Tony's machine. If she turned up two mornings running without warning, he might start to get twitchy. The answering machine checked in after a couple of rings, but there was no outgoing message, just a series of clicks followed by the tone. "Hi, Tony," she said. "I don't know if your machine's working properly, so I don't know if you'll get this message. It's twenty past nine, and I'm about to

have an early night. I'll be in the office first thing, working
on the computer supplies stuff. Mr. Brandon's called a case
conference for tomorrow at three. If you want to get together before then, give me a call. I'll be in the HOLMES
room if I'm not in the squad room."

Sitting down with Nelson on her lap and a stiff drink by
her side, Carol thought about the job that lay ahead. The
list of computer supplies companies who sold the peripherals and hardware Handy Andy would need to construct
his own images was depressingly long. She had told Dave
not to start work on it until she'd had a chance to check
out the software company. Their list of customers would be
. shorter, and they would have the Discovery to cross-
reference that list with. Only if that came up blank would
she set Dave's team loose on the dozens of numbers she'd
painstakingly compiled that evening. "We'll get there, Nelson," she told the cat. "It just better be worth the trip."


The clatter of high heels on stone cut through the delirium
of pain like a wire through cheese. So everyday a sound,
translated by its location into a threat. He had no idea
whether it was day or night, or how long had passed since
he had been snatched from his life. Tony forced himself
into alertness as the sound approached him from behind.
She was coming downstairs. At the foot of the stairs, the
clicking ended. He heard a low chuckle. Slowly, one step
at a time, the footsteps crossed behind him. He could sense
the scrutiny he was under.

She took her time, skirting round his trussed body until
she moved into his line of vision. Tony was momentarily
taken aback by the magnificence of her body. From the
neck down, she could have been a model for a soft-porn
magazine. She stood with legs apart, arms akimbo. She
wore a loose red silk kimono, which fell open to reveal an
extraordinary red leather basque with peephole nipples and
a split crotch. Black stockings sheathed shapely, muscular
legs which ended in black stilettoes. Even under the ki-

mono, he could see the clear outline of strong, well-muscled arms and shoulders. From where he was hanging, she was as erotic as a kaolin poultice.

"Worked it out yet, *Anthony*?" she drawled, the warmth of suppressed laughter evident in her voice.

The stressing of his full name was the last turn in the Rubik's cube of his memory. His mind racing, Tony said, "I suppose a couple of paracetamol would be out of the question, Angelica?"

The low chuckle again. "Glad to see you haven't lost your sense of humour."

"No, only my dignity. I wasn't expecting this, Angelica. Nothing in our phone conversations led me to imagine this is what you had in mind for me."

"You had no idea who I was, did you?" Angelica said, pride unmistakable in her tones.

"Yes and no. I didn't know you were the person who killed those men. But I did know you were the woman for me."

Angelica frowned, as if uncertain how to respond. She turned away and checked the camcorder. "You took long enough to get that far. Do you have any idea how many times you slammed the phone down on me?" Her voice was angry, not hurt.

Tony sensed the danger and tried to find emollient words. "That was because I had a problem, not because of you."

"You had a problem with me," she said, moving over to the stone benches that ran along one wall. She picked up another cassette and walked back to the camera.

Tony tried again. "Quite the opposite," he said. "I've always had trouble with relationships with women. That's why I didn't know how to treat you in the beginning. But it got so much better. You know it did. You know we were wonderful together. Thanks to you, I feel like all my problems are behind me." He hoped she wasn't alive to the unintentional irony in his words.

But Angelica was no fool. "I think you can safely say that, Anthony," she said with a wry smile.

"You outsmarted me, you know. I was convinced the killer was a man. I should have known better."

With her back to him, Angelica swapped the cassettes in the camcorder. Then she wheeled round and said, "You'd never have caught me. And with you out of the way, no one else will either."

Ignoring the threat, Tony continued to chat, straining to keep his voice warm and even. "I should have realized you were a woman. The subtlety, the attention to detail, the care you took to clear up after yourself. It was stupid of me not to grasp that those were the hallmarks of a woman's mind, not a man's."

Angelica smirked. "You're all the same, you psychologists." She spat the word out as though it were an obscenity. "You've got no imagination."

"But I'm not like them, Angelica. OK, I made that one crucial mistake, but I bet I know more about you than any of them ever did. Because you've shown me the inside of your mind. And not just through the killings. You've shown me the real woman, the woman who comprehends love. But I guess they didn't understand you, did they? They didn't believe you when you told them you had a woman's spirit trapped in a man's body. Oh, I expect they pretended to, I expect they patronized you and talked down to you. But deep down, they wrote you off as a freak, didn't they? Believe me, I've never done that." Tony's voice cracked as he reached the end of his speech, his mouth dry with a mixture of fear and chloroform. At least the adrenaline coursing through his veins seemed to be acting as an analgesic.

"What do you know about me?" she said roughly, the pain on her face a strange contrast with the coquettish pose she had adopted.

"I need a drink if we're going to talk," Tony said, gambling that her narcissism would demand that she share her exploits, that she needed to hear his version of herself. If he was to have any chance of escaping with his life, he needed to build up a relationship with her. A drink would be the first brick in the wall. The more he could get her to see him as an individual, not as a cipher, the higher his chances rose.

Angelica scowled suspiciously. Then, with a toss of her head that sent her long hair swirling, she turned away and walked to a slop sink set against the wall. She turned on the tap and looked around vaguely for a drinking vessel of some kind. "I'll get a glass," she muttered, passing him and clattering up the steps again.

Tony felt a surge of relief at his small victory. Angelica was gone for less than thirty seconds, returning with a thick white mug. Kitchen above, Tony deduced as she walked back to the sink. She moved well in the heels, her stride measured and feminine. It was interesting, since she had obviously reverted to more masculine movements under the stress of kidnapping and killing. That was the only way to account for Terry Harding's conviction that he'd seen a man driving off from Damien Connolly's.

Angelica filled the mug and approached Tony cautiously. She gripped his hair, pulled his head back agonizingly and tipped freezing water into his mouth. As much went down his chin as his throat, but the relief was palpable. "Thanks," he gasped as she withdrew.

"One should always be hospitable to one's guests," she said sardonically.

"I hope to remain one for some time," Tony replied. "You know, I admire you. You've got style."

She frowned again. "Don't bullshit me, Anthony. You won't get round me with stupid flattery."

"It's not bullshit," he protested. "I've spent days and nights poring over the details of what you've achieved. I'm so deep inside your head, how could I not admire you? How could I not be impressed? The other ones you brought here, they didn't have a clue about who you are, what you can do."

"That's true, I'll grant you that. They were like babies,

frightened, stupid babies," Angelica said contemptuously. "They didn't appreciate what a woman like me could do for them. They were treacherous, lecherous fools."

"That's because they didn't know you like I know you."

"You keep saying that. Prove it. Prove you know anything about me."

The gauntlet was well and truly down now, Tony thought. Never mind singing for your supper, talk for your life. This was the proving ground, the place where he would discover if his psychology was indeed a science or just bullshit.

"Fraser Duncan? Hello, this is Detective Inspector Carol Jordan of Bradfield police," she said. Carol had never grown used to referring to herself by her full title. She felt as if, any moment, someone was going to jump out and shout, "Oh no, you're not! We found you out at last." Luckily, that didn't seem to be happening today.

"Yes?" The voice was cautious, the single syllable drawn out in a question.

"Actually, it was my brother, Michael Jordan, who suggested you might be able to help me with an enquiry we're pursuing."

"Oh, yes?" The climate was getting warmer. "How is Michael? Is he enjoying the software?"

"I think it's absolutely his favorite toy," Carol replied.

Fraser Duncan laughed. "An expensive toy, Inspector. Now, what can I do for you?"

"It's the Vicom 3D Commander I wanted to talk to you about. In strictest confidence, you understand. We're pursuing a major murder investigation, and one of the theories I'm looking at is that our killer might be using your software to edit his own videos, maybe even to import other material into them. That would be possible, wouldn't it?"

"More than possible. It would be perfectly straightforward."

"So, do you keep records of all your customers?" Carol asked.

"We do. We don't sell all the packages direct, obviously, but anyone who buys the Commander should register their purchase with us since that gives them access to a free customer helpline and also means they get priority mailings when we develop upgrades." Duncan was positively expansive now. "Do I detect a request for access to our customer database, Inspector?"

"You do indeed, sir. This is a murder enquiry and the information could be crucial to us. Can I stress too that it would be completely confidential? I would personally undertake to ensure that your data is removed from our system as soon as we have finished with it," Carol said, trying not to sound as if she was begging.

"I don't know," Duncan said hesitantly. "I'm not sure I like the idea of you and your colleagues hammering on the doors of my customers."

"It wouldn't be like that, Mr. Duncan. No way. What we would do is input the list into our Home Office Major Large Enquiry System and cross-match it against existing data. We would only act on any correlations that came up with people who are already in there."

"Is this the serial killer you're after?" Duncan asked abruptly.

What did he want to hear, Carol wondered momentarily. "Yes," she said, taking a gamble.

"Let me call you back, Inspector. Just to make sure you are who you say you are."

"No problem." She gave him the main police switchboard number. "Ask them to put you through to me in the HOLMES room at Scargill Street."

The next five minutes passed in a fever of impatience. The phone barely chirruped before Carol had it to her ear. "Inspector Jordan?"

"You owe me, sis."

"Michael!"

"I've just been telling Fraser Duncan what an honourable little person you are and despite what he's heard about the police, he can trust you."

"I love you, bro. Now get off the phone and let the man talk to me!"

Within the hour, Vicom's data was inside the HOLMES computer network, thanks to Dave Woolcott and the miracles of modern technology. Carol had passed Fraser Duncan on to him after they had agreed the ground rules for the data use, and Carol had listened uncomprehendingly to Dave's end of a conversation which consisted of alien expressions like "baud rate" and "ASCII files."

Carol sat by Dave's side as he worked on one of the terminals. "OK," he said. "We've got the list from Swansea of everyone within a twenty-mile radius of Bradfield who has one of these Discoveries. We've also got the list of names from Vicom of people who have bought their software. I hit this key, and go down this menu to this option, wild-card match, and now we sit back and let the machine talk to itself."

For an agonizing minute, nothing happened. Then the screen cleared and a message flashed up. "[2] matches found. List matches?" Dave hit the "y" key and two names and addresses appeared on the screen.

1: Philip Crozier, 23 Broughton Crag, Sheffield Road, Bradfield BX4 6JB
2: Christopher Thorpe [sort criterion I]/Angelica Thorpe [sort criterion 2], 14 Gregory Street, Moorside, Bradfield BX6 4LR

"What does that mean?" Carol asked, pointing to the second option.

"The Discovery is registered to Christopher Thorpe and the software was bought by Angelica," Dave explained. "Using the wild-card option means that the machine sorted by address as well as by name. Well, Carol, you've got something. Whether it means anything or not, we'll have to see."

\*    \*    \*

Penny Burgess strode over the rough, fissured limestone of Malham Pavement. The sky was the bright blue of early spring, the rough moorland grasses starting to look more green than brown. From time to time, larks shot out into the air and poured their songs into her ears. There were two occasions when Penny really came alive. One was on the trail of a hot story. The other was up on the high moorlands of the Yorkshire Dales and the Derbyshire Peak District. Out in the open air, she felt free as the skylarks, all pressure gone. No newsdesk demanding copy by an hour ago, no contacts to be appeased, no looking over her shoulder to be sure of staying ahead of her rivals. Just the sky, the moors, the extraordinary limestone landscape, and her.

For no reason, Stevie McConnell burst into her thoughts. He'd never see the sky again, never walk a moor and watch the turning of the seasons. Thank God she had the power to make sure that someone would pay for that inhuman deprivation.

Philip Crozier's house was a narrow, terraced three-storey modern town house, the ground floor consisting mainly of an integral garage. Carol sat in the car, eyeing it up and down. "We going in, ma'am?" the young detective constable in the driving seat asked.

Carol thought for a moment. Ideally, she'd wanted Tony to be with her when she interviewed the people whose names the computer had spat out. She'd tried ringing him at home. No reply. Claire said he hadn't come into the office yet, which surprised her since he'd had a nine-thirty appointment. Carol had swung round by the house, but it looked exactly the same as it had the night before. Off having fun with his lady friend, she'd decided. Serves him right if he misses out on the showdown with Handy Andy, she thought maliciously, then immediately regretted her childishness. Failing Tony, she'd have liked to have had

Don Merrick with her. But he was out pursuing other lines of enquiry that had flowed from the identification of the Discovery. The only person she could find who wasn't urgently involved with something else was DC Morris, on the third month of his secondment to CID.

"We might as well see if he's in," Carol said. "Though he's probably at work."

They walked up the path, Carol taking in the details of the neatly trimmed lawn and the smart paintwork. The house didn't really fit Tony's profile. It was more like the victims' houses in terms of value and status, rather than the home of someone who aspired to their lifestyles. Carol pressed the bell and stepped back. They were about to give up and return to the car when Carol heard feet pounding downstairs. The door swung open to reveal a stocky black man dressed in grey sweat pants and a scarlet T-shirt, his feet bare. He couldn't have looked more different from Terry Harding's description. Carol's heart sank momentarily, then she reminded herself that Crozier might not be the only person with access to his software and his Discovery. He was still worth interviewing. "Yeah?" he said.

"Mr. Crozier?"

" 'S right. Who wants to know?" His voice was relaxed, the Bradfield accent strong.

Carol produced her warrant card and introduced herself. "I wonder if we could come in and have a word, sir?"

"What about?"

"Your name has cropped up in some routine enquiries and I'd like to ask you some questions for the purposes of elimination."

Crozier's brows furrowed. "What sort of enquiries?"

"If we could just come in, sir?"

"No, hang on, what's all this about? I'm trying to get some work done here."

Morris stepped to Carol's side. "There's no need to be difficult, sir, it's just routine."

"Mr. Crozier isn't being difficult, Constable," Carol said coolly. "I'd feel just the same in your shoes, sir. A car answering the description of yours has been involved in an incident, and we need to eliminate you from our investigation. We're speaking to several other people in connection with this enquiry, sir. It won't take long."

"All right then," Crozier sighed. "You'd better come in."

They followed him up stairs carpeted in functional cord carpet into an open-plan living room-cum-kitchen. It was furnished in expensive but minimalist style. He waved them to two leather and wood armchairs and dropped into a leather bean bag on the polished wood floor. Morris pulled out his notebook and ostentatiously opened it to a fresh page.

"You work from home, then?" Carol asked.

" 'S right. I'm a freelance animator."

"Cartoons?" Carol said.

"I do mostly science animations. You want something for your Open University course that shows how atoms collide, I'm your man. So what's all this about?"

"You drive a Land Rover Discovery?"

" 'S right. It's in the garage."

"Can you tell me if you were driving it last Monday night?" Carol asked. God, was it only a week ago?

"I can. I wasn't. I was in Boston, Massachusetts."

She went through the routine questions that established precisely what Crozier had been doing, and who she could check the information with. Then she stood up. Time for the key question, but it was important to keep it looking casual. "Thanks for you help, Mr. Crozier. One more thing—is there anyone else who has access to your house while you're away? Someone who could have borrowed your car?"

Crozier shook his head. "I live on my own. I don't even have a cat or plants, so nobody has to come in when I'm away. I'm the only one with keys."

"You're sure of that? No cleaning lady, no colleague who drops in to use your system?"

"Sure, I'm sure. I do my own cleaning, I work alone. I split up with my girlfriend a couple of months back and I

changed the locks, OK? Nobody's got keys except me."
Crozier was starting to sound tetchy.

Carol persisted. "And no one could have borrowed your
keys without your knowledge and had them copied?"

"I don't see how. I'm not in the habit of leaving them
lying around. And the car's only insured for me, so nobody
else has ever driven it," Crozier said, his irritation clearly
mounting. "Look, if somebody did anything criminal in a
car with my number on, they were using faked-up plates,
OK?"

"I accept what you're saying, Mr. Crozier. I can assure
you that if the information you've given me checks out, you
won't be hearing from us again. Thanks very much for your
time."

Back at the car, Carol said, "Find me a phone. I want
to try Dr. Hill again. I can't believe he's gone AWOL the
one time we really need him."

*It's laughable. They pick a man who can't even tell whether I've carried out a particular punishment or not and they employ him to help them catch me. They could at least have shown me the respect of employing someone who has some reputation, an opponent worthy of my skills, not some idiot who has never encountered someone of my calibre.*

*Instead, they insult me. Dr. Tony Hill is supposed to be producing a profile of me, based on his analysis of my killings. When this account is published, years hence, after my death in my bed from natural causes, historians will be able to compare his profile with the reality and laugh at the gross inaccuracies of his pseudo-science.*

*He will never come close to the truth. For the record, I set down that truth.*

*I was born in the Yorkshire port of Seaford, one of the busiest fishing and commercial docks in the country. My father was a merchant seaman, the first officer on oil tankers. He went all over the world, then he would come home to us. But my mother was as bad a wife as she was a mother. I can see now that the house was always in chaos, the meals irregular and unappetizing. The only thing she was good at, the only thing they could share, was the drinking. If there was an Olympic pairs event for pissheads, they'd have walked off with the gold.*

*When I was seven, my father stopped coming home. Of course, my mother blamed me for not being a good enough* son. She said I'd driven him away. She told me I was the man of the house now. But I could never live up to her expectations. She always wanted more from me than I was capable of, and ruled me by blame rather than praise. I spent more time locked in the cupboard than most people's coats do.

Without my father's pay cheque, she was thrown on the resources of the welfare system, which was barely enough to live on, never mind get drunk on. When the building society repossessed the house, we went to live with relatives in Bradfield for a while, but she couldn't handle their disapproval, so we moved back to Seaford, when she turned to the town's other boom industry, prostitution. I grew accustomed to the procession of disgusting, drunken sailors traipsing through the succession of grubby flats and bedsits where we lived. We were always behind with the rent, usually doing a moonlight flit just before the bailiffs got really heavy.

I grew to hate the ugly, grunting copulation that I was a constant witness to, and stayed out of the house as much as I possibly could, often sleeping rough down by the docks. I used to pick on kids that were younger than me to get their money off them so I could afford to eat. I moved schools almost as often as we moved house, so I never did too well there, in spite of the fact that I knew I could run rings round most of the other kids, who were just stupid.

As soon as I was 16, I left Seaford. It wasn't a wrench; it wasn't as if I'd ever managed to make many friends, what with moving all the time. I'd seen enough of men to know that I didn't want to grow up like them, and I felt different inside. I thought if I moved back to a big city like Bradfield I'd find it easier to work out what I wanted. One of my mother's cousins got me a job at the electronics firm where he worked.

About that time, I discovered that dressing in women's clothes made me feel good about myself. I got my own bedsit so I could do it whenever I wanted to, and that calmed me down a lot. I started studying computer science

*at evening classes, and eventually got some proper quali-
fications. About that time, my mother got left a house in
Seaford in her brother's will.*

*I got the chance of a job back in Seaford, working in
computer systems for the local private phone company. I
didn't really want to go back there, but the job was too
good to turn down. I never went near my mother. I don't
think she even knew I was there.*

*One of the few good things about Seaford is that it's
handy for the ferry to Holland. I used to go there every
other weekend, because in Amsterdam I could go out
dressed as a woman and nobody batted an eyelid. Over
there, I met a lot of transsexuals as well as transvestites,
and the more I talked to them, the more I realized that I
was just like them. I was a woman trapped in a man's body.
That explained why I'd never had much sexual interest in
girls. And although I found men attractive, I knew I wasn't
a poof. They disgust me, with their pretence at normal relationships when everybody knows that it's only men and
women that can fit together properly.*

*I went to see the doctors at Jimmy's in Leeds, where they
do all the sex-change operations in the north, and they
turned me down. Their psychologists were as stupid and
blinkered as all the rest of their brotherhood. But I managed
to find a private doctor in London who prescribed the hormone treatment I needed. Of course, I couldn't go on working while this was going on, but I spoke to the boss and he
said he'd give me a good reference for another job when
I'd had the operation and I was a woman.*

*I had to go abroad for the operation, and it was all much
more expensive than I expected. I went to my mother and
asked her if she'd mortgage the house to lend me the money
and she just laughed at me.*

*So I did what I'd learned from her. I sold myself on the
docks. It's amazing how much money sailors will pay for a
travesti. They get out of their heads with excitement at the
thought of someone who has breasts and a cock. I wasn't
like the other hookers either; I didn't blow it all on drink*

or·drugs or a pimp. I stashed it all away till I could afford the operation.

When I came to Seaford, not even my own mother recognized me at first. I'd only been back a few days when she took that tragic accidental overdose of drink and pills. Nobody was surprised. Yes, Doctor, you can add her to the list.

With my qualifications, experience and reference, I had no trouble getting a job as a senior systems analyst with the phone company in Bradfield. The money I made from the sale of the house in Seaford bought me my home in Bradfield, and I started the task of finding a worthy man to share my life.

And Dr. Tony Hill presumes to understand me, without knowing any of this? Well, in a very short time, I'll share it all with him. Such a shame he won't have the chance to write it down for himself.

# 18

*The truth is, I am a very particular man in everything relating to murder; and perhaps I carry my delicacy too far.*

Don Merrick walked into the HOLMES room munching a two-inch-thick double cheese and Bar-B-Q bacon burger. "How do you do it?" Dave Woolcott asked. "How do you get those slack Alices down the canteen to cook you edible food? They could burn a cup of tea, that lot, but you always manage to twist them round your little finger."

Merrick winked. "It's my natural Geordie charm," he said. "I just pick on the ugliest one and tell her she reminds me of my mother when she was in her prime." He sat down and stretched his long legs. "I've checked out the half-dozen Discoveries your sergeant gave me. They're all in the clear. Two of them are women, two of them have got rock-solid alibis for at least two of the nights in question, one's got multiple sclerosis, so he couldn't have done the jobs, and the sixth sold his to a dealership in the Midlands three weeks ago."

"Great," Dave said heavily. "Give the list to one of the operators so we can update the file."

"Where's the guv?"

"Carol or Kevin?"

Merrick shrugged. "I still think of Inspector Jordan as my guv'nor."

"She's off chasing wild geese," Dave said.

"She got a result, then?" Merrick asked.

"Two cross-matches."

"Let's have a look," Merrick said.

Dave rummaged among his papers and found three sheets of paper stapled together. The first listed the two correlations. Merrick frowned and flicked over a page. The second was a print-out of the result of a criminal records search on Philip Crozier. Nothing known. Hurriedly, he turned to the third page, which listed two Christopher Thorpes. One had a last-known address in Devon and several convictions for burglary. The second had a last-known address in Seaford. There were a string of juvenile convictions; assaulting a football referee, breaking windows at a school, shoplifting. There were half a dozen adult convictions, all for soliciting prostitution. Merrick sucked in his breath sharply and turned back to the front page. "Fuck," he said.

"What is it?" Dave asked, suddenly alert.

"This here. Christopher Thorpe, the Seaford one?"

"Yeah? Carol reckoned it wasn't the same one as ours. I mean, he's got convictions for being a male prostitute, but this one in Bradfield looks to be married, because the woman at the same address has his surname. And let's face it, you don't get dockland rent boys driving around in serious motors like the Discovery."

Merrick shook his head. "No, you've got it all wrong. I know this Christopher Thorpe from Seaford. I worked on Vice in Seaford before I came here, remember? I was the arresting officer on two of these charges in soliciting. Christopher Thorpe was halfway to a sex change at the time. He had the tits and everything, he was trying to earn enough money to get the operation. Guess what his working name was? Dave, Christopher Thorpe isn't *married* to Angelica Thorpe, he *is* Angelica Thorpe."

"Fuck," Dave echoed.

"Dave, where the hell is Carol?"


Angelica stood in front of him, hands on hips, chewing one corner of her mouth. "You can't, can you? You can't prove it because you know nothing about my life."

"In one sense you're absolutely right, Angelica. I don't know the facts of your life," Tony said carefully, "but I think I know a bit about the shape of it. Your mother didn't do a very good job of loving you. Maybe she had a problem with drink or with drugs, or maybe she just didn't understand what a little kid needed. Either way, she didn't make you feel loved when you were little. Am I right?"

Angelica scowled. "Go on. Dig yourself a hole."

Tony felt a prickle of fear tingle at the base of his skull. What if he'd got it wrong? What if this woman was the exception to every statistical near certainty Tony had held at the front of his mind during the whole enquiry? What if she was the one serial killer who had come from a happy, loving family? Dismissing his doubts as a luxury he couldn't afford right now, Tony ploughed on. "Your father wasn't around much when you were growing up, and he never showed you he was proud of his son, even though you did everything you knew how to make him feel that pride. Your mother expected too much of you, kept telling you you were the man of the house, and giving you a bad time when you behaved like the child you were instead of the man she wanted to pretend you were." Angelica's face twitched in a spasm of recognition. Tony paused.

"Go on," she grated between clenched teeth.

"It's not easy for me to talk, doubled over like this. Can't you slacken the rope a bit, let me stand upright?"

She shook her head, her mouth sulky as a child's.

"I can't look at you properly like this," Tony tried. "You've got a fabulous body, you must know that. If it's going to be the last thing I see, at least let me appreciate it."

She cocked her head to one side, as if replaying his words to check them for truth or trickery. "All right," she conceded. "It doesn't mean anything's changed, though," she added as she moved to the winch and released it. She let out about a foot of slack.

Tony couldn't bite back the scream of pain that shot through his shoulders as the muscles were released from the strain that had stretched them to their limit. "It'll wear off," Angelica said roughly as she returned to her station by the camcorder. "Keep talking," she instructed him. "I've always enjoyed fantasy fiction."

He eased himself upright, struggling against the pain. "You were a bright kid," he gasped. "Brighter than the rest of them. It's never easy making friends when you're so much smarter than the other kids. And maybe you moved around a bit. Different neighbours, maybe even different schools."

Angelica was back in control of herself, her face impassive as he continued. "It wasn't easy to make friends. You knew you were different from everybody else, special, but you couldn't work out why at first. Then as you grew up, you realized what it was. You weren't the same as the other boys because you weren't a boy at all. You had no interest in girls sexually, but it wasn't because you were gay. No way. It was because you were really a girl yourself. What you discovered was that dressing up in women's clothes made you feel like you'd come home, like this was how you were meant to be." He paused and gave her a crooked smile. "How am I doing so far?"

"Very impressive, Doctor," she said coldly. "I'm fascinated. Carry on."

Tony flexed his shoulder muscles, relieved to discover that the damage so far seemed to be only temporary. The pins and needles that raged across his back seemed no more than a minor irritation after what he'd been through. He took a deep breath and carried on. "You decided to become the person you were inside, the woman you knew you really were. God, Angelica, I've got so much respect for you, putting yourself through that. I know how hard it is to get the medical profession to take the idea seriously. All the hormone therapy, the electrolysis, living as a half-man, half-woman while you waited for the operations, and then all the pain of the surgery." He shook his head, wonderingly. "I know I wouldn't have the courage to put myself through all that."

"It wasn't easy." The words escaped from Angelica's lips, almost against her will.

"I believe you," Tony said sympathetically. "And after all that, to find yourself wondering if it had been worth it after all, when you realized that the stupidity, the insensitivity, the lack of insight you'd identified in men didn't just disappear because you were a woman. They were still the same old bunch of bastards, incapable of recognizing an exceptional woman when they were offered her love and affection on a plate." He paused, studying her face, deciding if the time was right for the big gamble. The coldness had left her eyes, replaced by a look almost of misery. He softened his voice and lowered the volume. Please God, let his training pay off.

"They rejected you, didn't they? Adam Scott, Paul Gibbs, Gareth Finnegan, Damien Connolly. They turned you down."

Angelica shook her head violently, as if by activity she could deny the past. "They *let* me down. They *let* me down, they didn't turn me down. They betrayed me."

"Tell me about it," Tony said softly, praying that his hard-earned techniques weren't going to fail him now. "Tell me about it."

"Why should I?" she shouted, stepping forward and slapping him so hard he tasted blood as his cheek impacted against his teeth. "You're no better than them. What about that slag? That blonde bitch, that fucking plonk you've been giving one to?"

Tony swallowed the warm salty blood that filled his mouth. "You mean Carol Jordan?" he said, playing for time. How should he play this? Should he lie or tell the truth?

"You know full well who I mean. I know you've been with her, don't fucking try lying to me," she hissed, raising her hand again. "You treacherous, faithless bastard." Her hand cracked him across the face again, so hard he heard his neck crick under the force of it.

Tears sprang to his eyes involuntarily. The truth wasn't going to work. It would only earn him more punishment. Praying he could lie with conviction, Tony pleaded, "Angelica, she was just a fuck, just someone to scratch the itch.

You'd got me so horny with your phone calls. I didn't know when you were going to call again, or even if you were." He allowed anger to creep into his voice. "I wanted you and you didn't tell me how I could get hold of you. Angelica, it's like you with the other ones. I was filling in time, waiting for my equal. You can't believe that a mere cop would answer my fantasies, do you? You should know, you've had one too."

Angelica stepped back, shock on her face. Sensing he had made some kind of a breakthrough, Tony pursued her with his words. "We were different, you and me. They weren't worthy of you. But we were special. You must know that, from our phone calls. Didn't you sense that we had something extraordinary? That this time it would be different? Isn't that what you really want? You don't want the killing. Not really. The killing only happened because they weren't worthy, because they let you down. What you really want is a worthy partner. What you want is love. Angelica, what you want is me."

For a long moment she stared at him, eyes wide, mouth open. Then confusion took over, as obvious to Tony as a hooker's come-on. "Don't use that word to me, you worthless scumbag," she stuttered. "Don't fucking say it!" Her voice was a low, throaty scream. Suddenly, she turned on her heel and ran from the room, her heels clattering up the stairs.

"I love you, Angelica," Tony shouted desperately after her retreating footsteps. "I love you."


Carol and DC Morris stood on the doorstep of the small terraced house in Gregory Street. She didn't need to be a psychologist to read his body language. Morris was fed up at trailing round pursuing Carol's daft hunch. "They must be out at work," he remarked after their fourth assault on the doorbell.

"Looks that way," Carol agreed.

"Shall we come back later?"

"Let's go on the knocker," Carol suggested. "See if any of the neighbours are around. Maybe they can tell us when the Thorpes get back from work."

Morris looked as if he'd rather be on crowd control at a student demo. "Yes, ma'am," he said in a bored voice.

"You take across the street, I'll go for this side." Carol watched him trudge across the street as wearily as a miner at the end of his shift, shook her head with a sigh and turned her attention to number twelve. This was much more the kind of territory Tony had suggested for their killer. Thinking of Tony just made Carol cross again. Where the hell was he? She really needed his input today, not to mention a bit of support for an idea that everybody else seemed to think was a complete waste of time. He couldn't have picked a worse moment to go on the missing list. It was unforgivable. At least he could have phoned his secretary and not left her having to field his calls and make excuses for him.

There was no bell on the door of number twelve, so Carol bruised her knuckles on the solid wood. The woman who opened it looked like a caricature from a soap opera. In her forties, her make-up would have been over the top for dinner in LA, never mind mid-afternoon in a Bradfield back street. Her dyed platinum blonde hair was piled high in a lopsided beehive. She wore a tight black sweater with a scoop neck revealing a cleavage the texture of crumpled tissue, shiny blue skin-tight leggings, white stilettoes and a thin gold ankle chain. A cigarette dangled from a corner of her mouth. "What is it, love?" she said nasally.

"Sorry to trouble you," Carol said, flashing her warrant card. "Detective Inspector Carol Jordan, Bradfield police. I'm trying to get in touch with your next-door neighbours at number fourteen, the Thorpes, but there doesn't seem to be anybody home. I wonder if you happen to know what time they get in from work."

The woman shrugged. "Search me, love. That cow comes and goes at all hours."

"What about Mr. Thorpe?" Carol asked.

"What Mr. Thorpe? There's no Mr. Thorpe next door, love." She gave a croak of laughter. "It's easy seen you've never clapped eyes on her. Any man that married that ugly cow would have to be blind and bloody hard up. So what've you got her for?"

"It's just routine enquiries," Carol said.

The woman snorted. "Don't give me that fanny," she said. "I've watched enough episodes of *The Bill* to know they don't send inspectors out on routine enquiries. It's about time you put that cow behind bars, if you want my opinion."

"Why is that, Mrs . . . ?"

"Goodison, Bette Goodison. As in Bette Davis. Because she's an ugly, anti-social cow, that's why."

Carol smiled. "I'm afraid that's not a crime, Mrs. Goodison."

"No, but murder is, isn't it?" Bette Goodison crowed triumphantly.

Carol swallowed, hoping the effect of the word wasn't as visible as it was palpable. "That's a very serious accusation."

Bette Goodison took a final drag of her cigarette and expertly flipped the dog end across the narrow pavement and into the gutter. "I'm glad you think so. It's more than your mates at Moorside nick did."

"I'm sorry you feel you've not been well served by my colleagues," Carol said in a concerned tone. "Perhaps you could tell me what you're talking about?" Please God, let this not be a rerun of the Yorkshire Ripper case, where the killer's best friend told the police they suspected he was the Ripper and the police paid no attention.

"Prince, that's who we're talking about."

For one wild moment, Carol had a vision of the diminutive American rock star buried in the back yard of a Bradfield terrace. Pulling herself together, she said, "Prince?"

"Our German shepherd. Always complaining about him, that Angelica Thorpe was. And she had no grounds. That dog was doing her a service. Anybody so much as walked down our ginnel and that dog let you know about it. She'd have paid a fortune for a burglar alarm as efficient as that dog. Any road up, a few months back . . . August, it were, weekend before Bank Holiday, we come home from work, Col and me, and Prince is gone. Now, there's no way he could have got out of that yard, and he'd have gone for anybody that came in. There's only one way he could have disappeared, and that's if he was murdered," Mrs. Goodison said, stabbing Carol in the chest with her finger for emphasis. "She poisoned him and then she got rid of the body so there would be no proof. She's a murderer!"

Normally, Carol would have walked a mile barefoot to avoid this conversation, but she was in pursuit of Handy Andy, and any oddity was something to be grasped eagerly. "How can you be so sure it was Mrs. Thorpe?" she asked.

"Stands to reason. She were the only one that ever complained about him. And the day he went missing, me and Col were out at work, but she were home all day. I know that for a fact, because she were on nights that week. And when we knocked on her door to ask did she know anything about him going missing, she just smiled all over that ugly gob of hers. I could have put her face in for her," Mrs. Goodison said emphatically. "So what are you going to do about it?"

"I'm afraid that without evidence, there's not much we can do," Carol said sympathetically. "You're sure, are you, that Mrs. Thorpe lives alone?"

"Nobody'd want to live with an ugly cow like that. She never even has visitors. Not surprising, mind, she looks like a brick shithouse in drag."

"Do you happen to know what kind of car she drives?" Carol asked.

"One of them bloody yuppie jeep things. I ask you, who needs a bloody great jeep in the middle of Bradfield? It's not like we live up some farm track, is it?"

"And do you know where she works?"

"I don't know and I don't care." She glanced at her watch. "Now, if you don't mind, my serial's starting."

Carol watched the door close behind Bette Goodison, an unpleasant suspicion starting to form in her mind. Before she could try number ten, her pager bleeped insistently. "Phone Don at Scargill Street. Double urgent," she read.

"Morris!" Carol shouted. "Get me to a phone. Pronto monto." Whatever was going on in Gregory Street could wait. Don clearly couldn't.

Exhausted, Tony had slipped into some nightmare delirium doze. A gout of freezing water thrown in his face smacked him straight to agonized attention, his head snapping back painfully. "Augh," he groaned.

"Wakey, wakey," Angelica said roughly.

"I was right, wasn't I?" Tony said through swollen lips. "You've had time to think about it, and you know I'm right. You want the killing to stop. They had to die, they deserved to die. They let you down, they betrayed you, they didn't deserve you. But all that can change now. It can be different with me, because I love you."

The rigid mask of her face crumpled before his eyes, becoming softer, more tender. She smiled at him. "It's never been about sex, you know. I could always have sex. Men paid me for sex. They paid me a lot of money for sex. That's how I paid for the surgery, you know. They always wanted me." Her voice was filled with a strange mixture of pride and anger.

"I can see why," Tony lied, arranging his face in what he hoped was an expression of hunger and admiration. "But what you really wanted was love, wasn't it? You wanted more than loveless sex on the streets or faceless sex down the phone. You deserve that. God, you deserve it. That's what I can give you, Angelica. Love isn't just physical attraction, though God knows you're attractive. But love's about respect, admiration, fascination, and I feel all of that for you. Angelica, you can have what you want. You can have it with me."

Her warring emotions were written plainly on her face.

He could see that part of her desperately wanted to believe him, wanted to escape into the normal world of relationships. But that part had to contend with a level of self-esteem that was so low she couldn't imagine anyone worth loving wanting to love her. And, underlying it all, suspicion that he was trying to entrap her. "How can we?" she demanded harshly. "You've been trying to hunt me down. You're with the police. You're on their side."

Tony shook his head. "That was before I realized you were the same woman I'd fallen in love with on the phone. Angelica, love is the one emotion that overrides duty. Yeah, I've worked with the police, but I'm not one of them."

"You lie down with dogs, you get up with fleas," she sneered. "You've been trying to put me away, Anthony. You expect me to believe you? You must think I'm really stupid."

"Quite the opposite. If you want to talk about stupid, talk about the police. Mostly, they're one-dimensional, boring bigots who couldn't keep a psychologist interested for more than five minutes. I don't have anything in common with them," he argued desperately.

She shook her head, more in sorrow than in anger. "You work for the Home Office. Your whole career, you've spent catching serial offenders and treating them. And you expect me to believe you'd suddenly change sides and stay loyal to me? Come on, Anthony, I'm not going to fall for crap like that."

Tony felt his powers flagging. His brain just wasn't fast enough any longer to keep her at bay. Wretchedly, he said, "I've not made a career of catching people, only treating them. I had to do that, don't you understand? Inside the places where I've worked is the only place where I can find minds that are complex enough to be interesting. It's like going to see animals at the zoo. You want to watch them in their natural habitat, but if the only way you are ever going to see them is at the zoo, you go. I've always had to wait till they were in captivity before I could study them. But you, you're still in the wild, still the way you want to be, perfected in your craft. And compared to them, you're the cream of the crop. You're exceptional. I want to spend the rest of my life being excited by your mind. I can't imagine ever finding you boring." Terrifying, maybe, but never boring.

Her lower lip thrust out, bringing an expression of calculating petulance to her face. She nodded in the direction of his groin, where his penis hung limp. "So if you find me that attractive, how come it doesn't show?"

It was the one question to which Tony had no answer at all.

"What have we actually got, Carol?" Brandon challenged.

Carol paced the floor of Brandon's office, ticking off her points on her fingers. "We've got a transsexual. Not a transsexual who went through the controlled, counselled National Health Service process, but one who, according to Don, was turned down for a sex change here and had to finance an operation abroad by selling sex. So right from the start, we know we've got someone who has been examined by psychiatrists and found to be unstable. We've got this transsexual driving a vehicle identical to the one driven by a suspect in Damien Connolly's murder. We've got a neighbour who's convinced that Angelica Thorpe offed her dog. The dog was killed a fortnight before the first murder. Angelica Thorpe bought software that would allow her to manipulate videos in her computer system, which fits a theory of the killer's behaviour developed by me and endorsed by our psychological profiler. She even lives in the kind of house Tony said she would," Carol argued vehemently.

"When she was Christopher, she was definitely a few butties short of a picnic," Don chipped in.

"I wish we could ask Tony about this," Brandon said, stalling.

"So do I," Carol said through her teeth. "But he's obviously found something more important to do today." A sudden thought hit Carol like a sandbag to the neck. Her knees started to buckle and she collapsed into the nearest chair. "Oh, my God," she gasped.

"What is it?" Brandon asked, concerned.

"Tony. He hasn't been in touch with anybody since he left here yesterday. He had two task-force meetings arranged for today, according to his secretary, but he hasn't shown up at work, and he hasn't phoned in. He wasn't home last night, and he's not there now." Carol's words hung in the air like a cloud of poisonous smoke. A wave of nausea lurched up from her stomach, almost choking her. Somehow, she maintained her composure under Brandon's concentrated stare.

With fingers that trembled, Carol picked up Brandon's copy of the profile from his desk. Urgently, she flicked through the pages till she found what she was looking for. " 'It is possible that his next target may also be a police officer, perhaps even one who is working on the investigation. This alone will not be sufficient motive for the killer to choose them; they must also fit the victim criteria that he has drawn up in his own mind in order for the killing to assume its full meaning for him. I would strongly recommend that any officers who fit the victim profile employ extra vigilance at all times, noting any suspicious vehicles parked near their homes, and checking to see whether they are being followed to and from work and social events.' Think about it, sir. Think about the victim profile. Sir, Tony fits it perfectly."

Not wanting to believe what Carol was suggesting, Brandon said, "But it's not eight weeks. It's not time!"

"But it *is* a Monday. Don't forget, Tony also pointed out that his timetable could be accelerated if something happened to traumatize him. Stevie McConnell, sir. Think of all the publicity. Someone else was getting the credit for his crimes. Look, it's in here, sir: 'Another possible scenario is that an innocent person is charged with the killings. That would be such an affront to his sense of himself that he might commit his next murder ahead of schedule.' Sir, we've got to move on this now!"

Brandon's hand was on the phone before she'd even started her last sentence.


The front door opened directly into the house. Downstairs couldn't have looked more normal. The small living room was furnished inexpensively but comfortably with a two-seater sofa and matching chair upholstered in moss-green Dralon. There was a TV, video, mid-priced stereo system and a coffee table complete with a copy of *Elle*. A pair of framed posters of whales in the ocean hung on the walls. The single bookshelf contained a selection of science-fiction classics, a couple of Stephen King novels and a trio of Jackie Collins bonkbusters. Carol, Merrick and Brandon moved cautiously through the room, past the stairs and into the kitchen diner. It was surgically neat as a showroom, work surfaces clean and uncluttered. On the drainer, one mug, one plate, one fork, one knife.

With Brandon leading the way, they climbed the narrow stairs built between the two downstairs rooms. The front bedroom was pink and frothy as a strawberry milkshake. Even the kidney-shaped dressing table, with its skirt of lace, was pink. "Barbara Cartland, eat your heart out," Merrick muttered. Brandon opened the wardrobe and flicked through the array of women's clothes. Carol headed for the drawers in a pink tallboy and worked her way down. They contained nothing more disturbing than a selection of tacky underwear, much of it in red satin.

It was Merrick who first broached the back bedroom. As soon as he opened the door, he knew no one was going to be screaming to the papers about magistrates granting warrants on non-existent evidence. "Sir?" he shouted. "I think we've cracked it."

The room was arranged as an office. A large desk held a computer and assorted peripherals that none of them could identify. To one side was a telephone linked to a sophisticated tape recorder. A small video-editing desk was in one corner, next to a filing cabinet. A wheeled trolley carried a television and video, both state of the art and top of the range. Shelves lined two walls, filled with computer games, videos, cassettes and computer disks, each box labelled neatly in firm capitals. The only alien object in the room was a leather recliner, the material slung hammock-like on a steel frame.

"Bingo," Brandon breathed. "Well done, Carol."

"Where the fuck do we start?" Merrick said.

"Do either of you know how to work the computer?" Brandon asked.

"I think we should leave that to the experts," Carol said. "It might be programmed to crash the data if someone else tries to log on."

"OK. Don, you take the filing cabinet, I'll take the videos, and Carol, you take the cassettes."

Carol moved across to the shelves of cassettes. The first couple of dozen seemed to be music tapes, ranging from Liza Minnelli to U2. Next were a dozen marked "AS" and numbered from one to twelve. Fourteen marked "PG" followed, then fifteen with "GF," eight eight "DC" and six with "AH." The concatenation of initials was far beyond the boundaries of coincidence. Carol picked the first "AH" tape and, heart heavy with misgivings, slotted it into the cassette player. She picked up the headphones plugged into the machine and gingerly pushed them into her ears. She heard the sound of a telephone ringing, then a voice so familiar she could have wept. "Hello?" Tony said, his voice reduced by the telephone line.

"Hello, Anthony," a voice not entirely strange to her said.

"Who is this?" Tony asked.

A chuckle, low and sexy. "You'll never guess. Not in a million years." Got it, thought Carol, grim foreboding gripping her. The voice on the answering machine.

"OK, so tell me," Tony said, his voice curious, friendly, joining in the game.

"Who would you like me to be? If I could be anyone in the world?"

"Is this some kind of wind-up?" Tony demanded.

"I've never been more serious in my life. I'm here to make your dreams come true. I'm the woman of your fantasies, Anthony. I am your telephone lover."

There was a moment's silence, then the phone slammed down at Tony's end. Over the dialling tone, Carol heard the strange woman say, "*Hasta la vista*, Anthony."

She stabbed the stop button and violently pulled out the headphones. She turned round to see Brandon transfixed by the image of Adam Scott stretched out on a rack, naked and apparently unconscious. Part of her mind could not comprehend what she was seeing. Evil, she thought, should be drenched in blood, not prosaically displayed on a suburban television screen.

"Sir," she forced out. "The tapes. She's been stalking Tony."

Tony tried a laugh. It came out more like a sob, but he carried on regardless. "You expect me to get an erection? Trussed up like this? Angelica, you chloroformed me, kidnapped me and left me to come round alone in a torture chamber. I'm sorry to disappoint you, but I've got no experience of bondage. I'm too bloody scared to get a hardon."

"I'm not letting you go, you know. Not to run straight back to them."

"I'm not asking you to let me go. Believe me, I'm happy to be your prisoner if that's the only way I can spend time with you. I want to get to know you, Angelica. I want to prove my feelings to you, I want to show you what love feels like. I want to show you whose side I'm really on here." Tony tried to turn on the kind of smile he'd learned that women responded to.

"So show me," Angelica challenged, letting one hand

run caressingly down her body, lingering over her nipples and edging towards her crotch.

"I'm going to need your help. Just like I needed you on the phone. You made me feel so good, like a real man. Please, help me now," Tony pleaded.

She took a step towards him, moving sinuously as a stripper. "You want me to turn you on?" she drawled in a ghastly parody of seduction.

"I don't think I can do it like this," Tony said. "Not with my arms pinned behind me like this."

Angelica stopped dead and scowled. "I said, I'm not letting you go."

"And I said I'm not asking you to. All I'm asking is that you cuff my hands in front of me. So I can touch you." Again, he forced the gentle smile.

She looked at him consideringly. "How do I know I can trust you? I'd have to set your hands free so I could cuff them in front of you. Maybe you're trying to double-cross me."

"I won't. I give you my word. If it makes you feel safer, chloroform me again. Do it while I'm unconscious," Tony said, gambling again. Her reaction would tell him all he needed to know about his chances.

Angelica moved behind him. An exultant voice in his head screamed "Yes!" He felt the warmth of her hand between his as she gripped the cuffs and painfully jerked them up. "Shit!" Tony yelled as new arrows of pain shot up his arms and through his shoulders. He heard a click of metal as the shackle connecting the rope to the handcuffs snapped free. Angelica released the handcuffs and Tony collapsed to his knees, his legs buckling under him. "Jesus Christ!" he swore as he crashed forwards on to his face, feeling the rough stone graze his cheek.

Moving swiftly, Angelica unlocked one side of the handcuffs, seized the back of his hair and pulled him upwards. Still holding the arm with the handcuffs attached, she stepped in front of him and roughly gripped his other arm just below the bicep, dragging it across his body. Seconds later, his hands were cuffed again, this time in front of him. He knelt like a supplicant, his discomfort doubled by the tight leather straps round his ankles. "You see?" he gasped. "I told you I wouldn't try anything."

Panting slightly, Angelica stood in front of him, legs apart. "So show me," she demanded.

"You'll have to help me up. I can't do it by myself," he protested weakly.

She bent down and grabbed his hair again, hauling him up on to legs whose muscles trembled with the effort of staying upright. They stood, inches apart, the silk of her kimono brushing his hands. He could feel the warmth of her breath on the raw flesh of his grazed cheek. "Kiss me," he said softly. Whores never get to kiss, he told himself. This'll make it different.

Something flickered in Angelica's eyes, but she leaned over him, releasing his hair and pulling his face to hers. It took every ounce of his willpower not to flinch as her lips met his, her tongue invading his mouth, exploring his teeth and tongue. Your life depends on it, he told himself. You've got a plan. Tony forced himself to kiss her back, thrusting his tongue into her mouth, telling himself there were worse things in the world, and this woman had made her previous victims endure some of them.

After what felt like the longest kiss of his life, Angelica pulled away, looking critically down to his groin. "I'm going to need some help here," Tony said. "It's not been an easy day."

"What kind of help?" Angelica asked, panting slightly through parted lips. It was clear that she was having no difficulty with the sexual arousal that was beyond him.

"Give me head. That's the one thing that always works when I'm having trouble. I've felt your mouth now; I just know you'll be terrific. Please, I really want to make love to you."

Almost before he'd finished speaking, she was on her knees, hands flickering over his balls. Tenderly, she lifted his flaccid penis and slipped it into her mouth, not taking

her eyes from his face. Tony reached out and began to
stroke her hair. Then, with what felt like infinite slowness,
he pulled her head forward on to him, forcing her head
down, her eyes away from him.

Then, summoning up what remained of his strength,
Tony raised his hands and brought the handcuffs crashing
down on the back of Angelica's head.

The blow caught her completely off guard and she went
crashing forward between his legs, her teeth snagging agonizingly on him. Tony let himself fall backwards, feeling
a tearing in his ankles as they protested against a movement
they were never designed to make. As he hit the ground,
he doubled forwards and grabbed Angelica's head, banging
it hard on the stone floor till her body stopped thrashing.

He dragged himself over her prone figure till his numb
fingers could reach the ankle straps. With maddening clumsiness, he struggled to unfasten the sets of buckles that
fixed him to the stone slab. After what felt like hours, he
was finally free. As he tried to stand, his ankles refused the
challenge, turning over and catapulting him to the floor
again, sending excruciating daggers of pain up his legs.
Moaning, he dragged himself across the floor towards the
steps. He had barely travelled a couple of yards when the
body on the floor groaned. Angelica lifted her head, blood
and mucus turning her face into a grisly Hallowe'en mask.
When she saw him, she roared like a wounded animal and
started scrambling to her feet.


The search for a clue to Angelica's killing ground was
growing more desperate as their fear and concern for Tony
grew. They had emptied out the contents of the filing cabinet on to the floor. Every scrap of paper was scrutinized
for any hint of the location of the cellar revealed in the
video. Invoices, guarantees, bills and receipts all got the
treatment. Carol was wading through a file of official correspondence, hoping to come across some lease or mortgage details, anything that related to another property.

Merrick was ploughing through the files relating to Thorpe's sex change. Brandon had already had one false alarm, coming across a stack of solicitor's letters relating to a property in Seaford. It soon became clear, however, that they concerned the sale of Thorpe's late mother's home in the town.

It was Merrick who found the key. He'd finished with the sex-change files and started on a bundle of assorted letters, filed under "Tax." When he came across the letter, he had to read it twice to make sure wishful thinking wasn't making him imagine things.

"Sir," he said cautiously. "I think this might be what we're looking for."

He handed the letter to Brandon, who read the letterhead of Pennant, Taylor, Bailey and Co., Solicitors. "Dear Christopher Thorpe," it said. "We have received a letter from your aunt, Mrs. Doris Makins, in New Zealand, authorizing us to pass on to you the keys for Start Hill Farm, Upper Tontine Moor, by Bradfield, W. Yorkshire. As her agents, we are empowered to allow you access to said property for the purposes of maintenance and security. Please make arrangements with this office to collect the keys at your convenience . . ."

"Access to an isolated rural property," Carol said, looking over Brandon's shoulder. "Tony said that's what the killer might have. And now she's got him there." A wave of anger poured through her, displacing the slow burn of fear that had been eating through her from the moment they'd unlocked the macabre secrets of that superficially normal office.

Brandon closed his eyes momentarily then said tightly, "We don't know that, Carol."

"And even if she has got him, he's a clever bloke. If anyone can keep himself out of trouble with his gob, it's Tony Hill," Don chipped in.

"Never mind whistling in the bloody dark," Carol said sharply. "Where the hell is Start Hill Farm? And how soon can we get there?"

\*    \*    \*

Tony looked around in desperation. The rack of knives was over to his left, impossibly high up. As Angelica got to her knees, he clawed at the stone bench and hauled himself upright. His hand closed on the haft of the knife as she staggered to her feet and threw herself at him, still bellowing like a cow bereft of its calf.

Her weight and the momentum of her charge bent Tony backwards over the bench. Her hands scrabbled for his throat, gripping his windpipe so tightly that white lights started to dance in front of his eyes. Just when he thought he could hold on no longer, he felt the warm, sticky gush of blood against his stomach and Angelica's grasp became flabby as a wet newspaper.

Before he could take it all in, he heard footsteps crashing down the stone steps. Like a mad vision of paradise, Don Merrick crashed downstairs, rapidly followed by John Brandon, his jaw dropping at the tableau in front of him.

"Fucking hell," Brandon breathed.

Carol pushed past the two men and stared uncomprehendingly at the carnage before her.

"You lot took your time," Tony gasped. As he passed out, the last thing he heard was his own hysterical laughter.

# Epilogue

Carol pushed open the door of the side ward. Tony was propped up on a pile of pillows, the left side of his face swollen and bruised.

"Hi," Tony said, a wan half-smile the best he could manage without too much pain. "Come on in."

Carol closed the door behind her and sat down on a chair by the bed. "I brought you some bits and pieces," she said, dumping a plastic bag and a padded envelope on the coverlet.

Tony reached out for the bag. Carol winced inside as she saw the bracelet of bruises round his inflamed wrists. He took out a copy of *Esquire*, a can of Aqua Libra, a tin of pistachio nuts and a Dashiel Hammett omnibus. "Thanks," he said, surprised by how her choice touched him.

"I wasn't sure what you liked," she said defensively.

"Then you're obviously a good guesser. The perfect task-force officer."

"If a little slow on the uptake," Carol said bitterly.

Tony shook his head. "John Brandon was here earlier. He told me how you worked it all out. I don't see how you could have got there any quicker."

"I should have realized sooner that you wouldn't have done a disappearing act at such a crucial time. Come to that, I should have realized as soon as I saw that profile that you could be a target and taken steps to protect you."

"Bollocks, Carol. If anyone should have realized that, it was me. You did a bloody good job."

"No. If I'd been on the ball, we'd have got there in time to save you having to . . . to do what you did."

Tony sighed. "You mean, you'd have saved Angelica's life? For what? Years in a secure mental hospital? Look on the bright side, Carol. You've saved the state a fortune. No expensive trial, no years of incarceration and treatment to pay for. Shit, they'll probably give you a medal."

"That's not what I meant, Tony," Carol said. "I meant you wouldn't have to live with the knowledge that you've killed someone."

"Yes, well, I can't pretend it was the perfect outcome, but I'll learn to live with it." He forced a smile. "Don't take this the wrong way, but the first thing I'm going to do when I can walk again is go out and buy you a new mac," he said. "Every time I look at that coat of yours, I get the urge to scream."

"Why?" Carol frowned in puzzlement.

"Didn't you know? She was wearing the identical mac when she turned up on the doorstep. That way, if she left any fibres at the scene, Forensic would assume they'd come from you."

"Terrific," Carol said ironically. "How are the ankles, by the way?"

Tony pulled a face. "I don't think I'll ever play the violin again. I managed to make it to the loo on crutches, but I had to sit on the edge of the bath to pee. They're saying there probably won't be any permanent damage, but it'll take a while for the torn ligaments to heal. How was your day?"

Carol pulled a face. "Grisly. I suspect you'd have been in your element. You were right about keeping the fantasy alive. She, he, it, had tapes of all the telephone-sex conversations she'd had with her victims, and she'd stolen the outgoing message tapes from the men who had answering machines.

"It took the boffins a little while to crack the computer stuff. We didn't have anybody who really knew what they were doing, but my brother Michael came in and sorted it out for us."

Tony gave a twisted smile. "I didn't want to say anything at the time, but for a wild moment, I actually wondered about your brother."

"Michael? You're kidding!"

Embarrassed, Tony nodded. "It was when you posited the idea of the computer manipulation of the videos. Michael had the expertise to do that, no question. He's in the right age group, he lives with a woman but not in a sexual relationship, he's got access to all the information the killer needed about the way the police and forensic scientists work, his job is in the general area where I'd expect the killer to work, and he was in a position to know exactly what the police were up to and be involved in the investigation. If we hadn't caught Angelica when we did, I'd have been scrounging an invitation to dinner to check him out."

Carol shook her head. "See what I mean about being slow on the uptake? I had access to all the same information as you, and Michael never even crossed my mind as a possibility."

"Not so surprising. You know him well enough to know he's not a psychopath."

Carol shrugged. "Do I, though? It wouldn't be the first time a close family member, a wife even, has made the same mistake."

"Usually, they're either deluding themselves or they're emotionally unstable and dependent on the killer in some way. Neither of which would have applied in this case." He gave a tired smile. "Anyway, tell me about what your Michael uncovered."

"The computer was a total goldmine. She'd kept her own diary of the stalking and the murders. It even says that she wanted it published after her death. Can you beat that?"

"Easily," Tony said. "Remind me to show you some of the academic papers I've got on the subject of serial killers."

Carol shivered. "Thanks, but no thanks. I got a print-out of the diary for you. I figured you'd be interested." She gestured to the envelope. "It's in there. Also, as you'd surmised, she had video-taped the killings, and as I suggested, she'd imported them into her computer and manipulated the images to keep the fantasy alive. It was absolutely gruesome, Tony. It went way beyond nightmare."

Tony nodded. "I won't say you get used to it, because you never do if you're going to be any use at this job. But you do get to the stage where you can lock it away, so it doesn't jump out and wreck your head unawares."

"Oh, yeah?"

"That's the theory. Ask me again in a few weeks," he said grimly. "Was there anything in there about how she chose her victims?"

"Just a fucking bit," Carol said bitterly. "She'd been at this for months before she even picked out the first victim. She worked for the phone company, a computer systems manager. Apparently, she used to work for a small private phone company back in Seaford, which gave her the experience to get the job in Bradfield. She was what they call a super-user of the computer system, so she had access to every piece of data in there. She used the phone company's computer to extract all the residential numbers who had made regular calls to sex chatlines in the past year." Carol paused, letting the obvious question hang in the air.

"It was research," Tony said wearily. "I published a paper on the role of chatlines in the development of fantasies among serial offenders. Someone should have told Angelica not to jump to conclusions."

Reading his remark as a veiled reproach, Carol moved on. "She cross-referenced that against the electoral roll and came up with men who lived alone. Then she just checked them out by watching their houses. She had a clear picture of the physical type she wanted, and she wanted one with his own house, a decent income and good career prospects. Can you believe it?"

"Only too well," Tony said grimly. "Her rationale was that she never wanted to kill them, she only wanted to love them. But they made her murder because they betrayed her. She kept telling herself that what she really wanted was a man who would love her and live with her."

Don't we all, Carol thought but didn't say. "Anyway, once she'd decided on the likely candidate, she paved the way with the dirty phone calls. She got them on the hook that way, on account of all you sleazy men can't resist anonymous sex."

"Ouch," Tony said, wincing. "In my defence, I'd have to say that a large part of my interest was purely academic. I was interested in the psychology of a woman who would do what she did on the phone."

Carol smiled tightly. "At least I know now that you were telling the truth when you said you didn't know the woman who was leaving the sexy messages on your answering machine."

Tony looked away. "And the discovery that a man you were attracted to was getting his rocks off in kinky telephone sex with a stranger must have been delightful for you."

Carol was silent, unsure what to say. "I've heard the tapes now," she admitted. "Yours are very different from the others. You were clearly uncomfortable a lot of the time. Not that it's any of my business."

Still unable to meet her eyes, Tony spoke, his voice clipped and clinical. "I have a problem with sex. To be precise, I have problems with achieving and maintaining an erection. The honest truth is that only part of me was treating the calls with professional interest. The other part of me was trying to use them as a kind of therapy. I know that makes me sound like a pervert, but part of the trouble with doing the job I do is that it's virtually impossible to find a therapist I can respect and trust who isn't connected in some way to the world I work in. And however much they verbally espouse the principle of client confidentiality, I've always been reluctant to expose myself to the risk."

Realizing the difficulty Tony had had in making his confession, Carol reached out for his hand and covered it lightly with hers. "Thank you for telling me that. It won't go any further. And if it makes you feel any better, the only people who have heard the tapes in full are me and John Brandon. You don't have to worry about what people are saying about you behind your back within the force."

"That's something, I suppose. So, go on. Tell me about

Angelica's phone calls to the other victims."

"It was obvious that the men thought this was sex without any commitment or comeback. Angelica's analysis was completely different. She'd convinced herself that their responses meant they were falling in love with her. Unfortunately for the guys, they decided otherwise. As soon as they showed any interest in another woman, they signed their death warrants. Apart from Damien, that is. She killed him to teach us a lesson. You were going to be the other lesson."

Tony shuddered. "No wonder she had to go abroad for the sex-change operation. The NHS psychologists she saw must have had a field day with her attitudes and aspirations."

"Apparently, they decided she was not an appropriate candidate for a sex change because of her lack of insight into her sexuality. They concluded that she was a gay man who couldn't cope with his sexuality because of cultural and family conditioning. They recommended counselling with a sex therapist rather than a sex change. There was an ugly scene at the time. He threw one of the psychologists through a glass door," Carol revealed.

"Pity they didn't press charges," Tony said.

"Yes. And you'll be pleased to hear they're definitely not going to charge you."

"I should think not! Like I said, think of the taxpayers' money I've saved. Maybe we should have dinner to celebrate when I get out of here?" he asked tentatively.

"I'd like that. There is one other good thing that came out of all of this," Carol said.

"What's that?"

"Penny Burgess took the day off yesterday to go walking in the dales. Apparently, her car broke down and she got stranded in the middle of a forest all night. She missed the whole shooting match. There's a dozen by-lines in the *Sentinel Times* tonight, and not a single one of them is hers!"

Tony lay back and stared at the ceiling. Papering over the cracks, that's what they were doing. He suspected Carol knew that as well as he did, and he wasn't sorry for the effort she was making. But he'd had enough for now. He closed his eyes and sighed.

"Oh God, I'm sorry," Carol said, getting to her feet. "I wasn't thinking. You must still be exhausted. Look, I'm out of here. I'll leave you this stuff to read when you feel up to it. I could drop in tomorrow if you like . . ."

"I think I'd like that," Tony said wearily. "It just comes over me in waves sometimes."

He heard her feet cross the floor and the click of the door opening. "Take care," Carol said.

The door closed behind her and Tony pushed himself back up till he was leaning against the pillows. He reached for the padded envelope. While he couldn't cope with conversation, his curiosity wouldn't let him ignore Angelica's diary. He pulled out a thick wedge of A4 paper. "Let's see what you were really made of," he said softly. "What's the story? How did you justify, what did you hide behind?" Hungrily, he began to read.

Wading through the outpourings of the psychologically damaged was normally a routine exploratory experience for Tony. But this was different, he realized after only a few paragraphs. At first, he couldn't pin down what it was. The writing was more literate, more controlled and more immediate than most of their ramblings, but that didn't explain why his response was so different. He moved on a few pages, fascinated and repelled equally. It was no more or less self-obsessed than other things he'd read, but there was a chilling relish here that was unusual. Most killers whose writings he'd read had gloried far more in their own bloody role, reflecting less on what they'd done to their victims and its effect on them, but here was someone who identified herself as much in terms of them. But even that couldn't entirely explain why he felt so unsettled by what he was reading. Whatever it was, it was making him more reluctant to continue the more he read, the opposite to his normal response. He'd been so obsessively keen to get inside the head of the killer he'd dubbed Handy Andy, but now it was laid out before him, it was as if he didn't want to know.

As he forced himself to read on, mentally chalking up the correct assumptions he'd made in his profile, it eventually dawned on him that what he was feeling was personal. These words were touching him in ways he'd never experienced before because the life outlined in these pages had touched him with a directness he'd never known before. These were the footsteps of his own personal nemesis that he was tracing, and it was an uncomfortable journey.

He tossed the papers to one side, unable to keep going, seeing his own fate mirrored in the broken bodies Angelica had meticulously described. The trouble with being a psychologist was that he knew exactly what was happening to him. He knew he was still in shock, still deep in denial. Although he couldn't get the events in the cellar out of his mind, there was still a distance between him and the memory, as if he were watching them from a long way off. One day the horror of the previous night was going to come roaring back in stereo, splashed across his inner eye in Cinemascope. Knowing that, this numbness was a blessing. Already, he knew, his answering machine would be crammed with lucrative offers for the story of how the hunter turned killer. One day, he was going to have to tell that story. He hoped he'd have the strength to save it for a psychiatrist.

It was no comfort to rationalize that having been the target of one serial killer, he was statistically unlikely ever to find himself in that position again. All he could think of was the hours in the cellar, dredging his experience and knowledge for the magic words that would give him a few minutes longer to try for the key to his freedom.

Then that kiss. The whore's kiss, the killer's kiss, the lover's kiss, the saviour's kiss, all rolled into one. A kiss from the mouth that had been seducing him for weeks, the mouth whose words had given him hope for his future, only to leave him finally stranded in this place. He had spent his working life worming his way into the heads of those who kill, only to end up one of them, thanks to a Judas kiss.

"You've won, haven't you, Angelica?" he said softly. "You wanted me, and now you've got me."

Keep reading for a thrilling excerpt
from Val McDermid's

# THE WIRE IN THE BLOOD

Now available from St. Martin's / Minotaur Paperbacks!

Murder was like magic, he thought. The quickness of his hand always deceived the eye, and that was how it was going to stay. He was like the postman delivering to a house where afterwards they would swear there had been no callers. This was the knowledge that was lodged in his being like a pacemaker in a heart patient. Without the power of his magic he'd be dead. Or as good as.

He knew just from looking at her that she would be the next. Even before the eye contact, he knew. There had always been a very particular combination that spelled perfection in his thesaurus of the senses. Innocence and ripeness, mink-dark hair, eyes that danced. He'd never been wrong yet. It was an instinct that kept him alive. Or as good as.

He watched her watching him, and under the urgent mutter of the crowd, he heard echoing in his head the music. *"Jack and Jill went up the hill to fetch a pail of water. Jack fell down and broke his crown..."* The chiming tune swelled and burst then battered his brain like a spring tide against a breakwater. And Jill? What about Jill? Oh, he knew what happened to Jill. Over and over again, repetitious as the barbaric nursery rhyme. But it was never enough. He had never quite been satisfied that the punishment had fit the crime.

And so there had to be a next one. And there he was, watching her watching him sending her messages with his eyes. Messages that said, "I've noticed you. Find your way

to me and I'll notice you some more." And she read him.
She read him, loud and clear. She was so obvious; life
hadn't scarred her expectations with static yet. A knowing
smile quirked the corners of her mouth and she took the
first step on the long and, for him, exciting journey of ex-
ploration and pain. The pain, as far as he was concerned,
was not quite the only necessity but it was certainly one of
them.

She worked her way towards him. Their routes varied,
he'd noticed. Some direct, bold; some meandering, wary in
case they'd misread what they thought his eyes were telling
them. This one favoured the spiral path, circling ever in-
ward as if her feet were tracing the inside of a giant nautilus
shell, a miniature Guggenheim Gallery compacted into two
dimensions. Her step was measured, determined, her eyes
never wavering from him, as if there were no one else between, neither obstacle nor distraction. Even when she was
behind his back, he could feel her stare, which was precisely how he thought it should be.

It was an approach that told him something about her.
She wanted to savour this encounter. She wanted to see him
from every possible angle, to imprint him on her memory
forever, because she thought this would be her only chance
for so detailed a scrutiny. If anyone had told her what the
future truly held, she'd have fainted with the thrill of it.

At last, her decaying orbit brought her within his grasp.
Only the immediate circle of admirers stood between them,
one or two deep. He locked on to her eyes, injected charm
into his gaze and, with a polite nod to those around him,
he took a step towards her. The bodies parted obediently
as he said, "Delightful to have met you, do excuse me?"

Uncertainty flitted across her face. Was she supposed to
move, like them, or should she stay in the ambit of his
mesmerizing stare? It was no contest; it never was. She was
captivated, the reality of this evening outstripping her every
fantasy. "Hello," he said. "And what's your name?"

She was momentarily speechless, never so close to fame,
dazzled by that spectacular dental display all for her benefit.

My, what big teeth you've got, he thought. All the better to eat her with.

"Donna," she finally stuttered. "Donna Doyle."

"That's a beautiful name," he said softly. The smile he won in response was as brilliant as his own. Sometimes, it all felt too easy. People heard what they wanted to hear, especially when what they were hearing sounded like their dream come true. Total suspension of disbelief, that's what he achieved every time. They came to these events expecting Jacko Vance and everyone connected to the great man to be exactly what was projected on TV. By association, anyone who was part of the celebrity's entourage was gilded with the same brush. People were so accustomed to Vance's open sincerity, so familiar with his very public probity, it never crossed their minds to look for the catch. Why should it, when Vance had a popular image that made Good King Wenceslas look like Scrooge? The punters listened to the words and they heard Jack and the Beanstalk—from the little seed Vance or his minions planted, they pictured the burgeoning flower of a life at the top of the tree right alongside his.

In that respect, Donna Doyle was just like all the others. She could have been working from a script he'd written for her. Having moved her strategically into a corner, he made as if to hand her a signed photograph of Vance the megastar. Then he did a double take so exquisitely natural it could have been part of De Niro's repertoire. "My God," he breathed. "Of course. Of course!" The exclamation was the verbal equivalent of smiting himself on the forehead with the heel of his hand.

Caught with her fingers inches from his as she reached out to take what had been so nearly offered, she frowned, not understanding. "What?"

He made a twisted little *moue* of self-disparagement. "Ignore me. I'm sorry, I'm sure you've got much more interesting plans for your future than anything we superficial programme makers could come up with." The first time he'd tried the line, hands sweating, blood thudding in his ears, he'd thought it was so corny it couldn't fool a drunk one sip from catatonia. But he had been right to go with his instincts, even when they had led him down the path of the criminally naff. That first one, just like this next one, had grasped instantly that something was being offered to her that hadn't been on the agenda for the insignificant others he'd been talking to earlier.

"What do you mean?" Breathless, tentative, not wanting to admit she already believed in case she'd misunderstood and left herself open to the hot shaming flush of her misapprehension.

He gave the faintest of shrugs, one that hardly disturbed the smooth fall of his immaculate suiting. "Forget it," he said with a slight, almost imperceptible shake of the head, disappointment in the sad cast of his eye, the absence of his gleaming smile.

"No, tell me." Now there was an edge of desperation, because everybody wanted to be a star, no matter what they said. Was he really going to snatch away that half-glimpsed magic carpet ride that could lift her out of her despised life into his world?

A quick glance to either side, making sure he wasn't overheard, then his voice was both soft and intense. "A new project we're working on. You've got the look. You'd be perfect. As soon as I looked at you properly, I knew you were the one." A regretful smile. "Now, at least I have your image to carry in my head while we interview the hundreds of hopefuls the agents send along to us. Maybe we'll get lucky . . ." His voice trailed off, his eyes liquid and bereft as the puppy left behind in the holiday kennels.

"Couldn't I . . . I mean, well . . ." Donna's face lit up with hope, then amazement at her forwardness, then disappointment as she talked herself out of it without saying another word.

His smile grew indulgent. An adult would have identified it as condescending, but she was too young to recognize when she was being patronized. "I don't think so. It would be taking an enormous risk. A project like this, at so delicate a stage . . . Just a word in the wrong ear could wreck it commercially. And you've no professional experience, have you?"

That tantalizing peep at what could have been her possible future uncapped a volcano of turbulent hope, words tumbling over each other like rocks in the lava flow. Prizes for karaoke at the youth club, a great dancer according to everybody, the Nurse in her form's reading of *Romeo and Juliet*. He'd imagined schools would have had more sense than to stir the tumultuous waters of adolescent desire with inflammatory drama like that, but he'd been wrong. They'd never learned, teachers. Just like their charges. The kids might assimilate the causes of the First World War but they never grasped that clichés got that way because they reflected reality. Better the devil you know. Don't take sweets from strangers.

Those warnings might never have set Donna Doyle's eardrum vibrating if her present expression of urgent eagerness was anything to go by. He grinned and said, "All right! You've convinced me!" He lowered his head and held her gaze. Now his voice was conspiratorial. "But can you keep a secret?"

She nodded as if her life depended on it. She couldn't have known that it did. "Oh, yes," Donna said, dark blue eyes sparkling, lips apart, little pink tongue flickering between them. He knew her mouth was growing dry. He also knew that she possessed other orifices where the opposite phenomenon was happening.

He gave her a considering, calculated stare, an obvious appraisal that she met with apprehension and desire mingling like Scotch and water. "I wonder . . ." he said, his voice almost a sigh. "Can you meet me tomorrow morning? Nine o'clock?"

A momentary frown, then her face cleared, determination in her eyes. "Yes," she said, school dismissed as irrelevant. "Yes, I can. Whereabout?"

"Do you know the Plaza Hotel?" He had to hurry now.

People were starting to move towards him, desperate to recruit his influence to their cause.

She nodded.

"They have an underground car park. You get into it from Beamish Street. I'll be waiting there on level two. And not a word to anyone, is that clear? Not your mum, not your dad, not your best friend, not even the family dog." She giggled. "Can you do that?" He gave her the curiously intimate look of the television professional, the one that convinces the mentally troubled that news-readers are in love with them.

"Level two? Nine o'clock?" Donna checked, determined not to screw up her one chance of escape from the humdrum. She could never have realized that by the end of the week she'd be weeping and screaming and begging for humdrum. She'd be willing to sell what remained of her immortal soul for humdrum. But even if someone had told her that then, she would not have comprehended. Right then, the dazzle and the dream of what he could offer was her complete universe. What could be a finer prospect?

"And not a word, promise?"

"I promise," she said solemnly. "Cross my heart and hope to die."

Best-selling Anthony Award-winning author Val McDermid is back with her haunted psychological profiler Dr. Tony Hill — hero of the mermaids singing and the wire in the blood. Set in the dark and brooding, crime-streaked world of post-Cold War Eastern Europe, McDermid's latest is an unrivaled tour de force…

# THE LAST TEMPTATION
Val McDermid
Bestselling Author of a place of execution

A serial killer is hunting psychologists, subjecting them to vicious torture before dispatching them with vengeance. Dr. Tony Hill has been called in to track the madman and, though the wounds from his last harrowing case are still raw, Hill agrees to help when a friend, and colleague, ends up as one of the victims. Now, as the killer's trail leads to Berlin, the danger is closing in on both Hill and Detective Chief Inspector Carol Jordan—Hill's partner in crime solving, and perhaps in life as well. But, as each narrows in on the criminals they chase, they realize that in the complexities of one investigation lines the solution to the other. Confronting heinous crimes and the sadists who commit them, and struggling to unravel roots that lie deep in the tormented past of Nazi atrocities and Stasi abuse, Tony and Carol are forced to battle for survival against overwhelming odds…

"McDermid is the best we've got."
— *The New York Times Book Review*

"A pleasure…as smart concept, skillfully executed… [McDermid] tells this wicked tale with style, intelligence, and the blackest of humor."
— *The Washington Post* on *Killing the Shadows*

AVAILABLE WHEREVER BOOKS ARE SOLD
FROM ST. MARTIN'S/MINOTAUR PAPERBACKS

And now here's another exciting excerpt
from a Val McDermid novel:

# KILLING THE SHADOWS

Now available from St. Martin's / Minotaur Paperbacks!

*The haar moves up from the steel-grey waters of the Firth
of Forth, a solid wall of mist the colour of cumulus. It
swallows the bright lights of the city's newest playground,
the designer hotels and the smart restaurants. It becomes
one with the spectres of the sailors from the docks who used
to blow their pay on eighty-shilling ale and whores with
faces as hard as their clients' hands. It climbs the hill to
the New Town, where the geometric grid of Georgian ele-
gance slices it into blocks before it slides down into the
ditch of Princes Street Gardens. The few late revellers staggering home quicken their steps to escape its clammy grip.*

*By the time it reaches the narrow split-level streets and
twisting vennels of the Old Town, the haar has lost its dead-
ening solidity. It has metamorphosed into wraiths of pale
fog that turn tourist traps into sinister looming presences.
Peeling posters advertising recent Festival Fringe events
flit in and out of visibility like garish ghosts. On a night
like this it's easy to see what inspired Robert Louis Steven-
son to create* The Strange Case of Dr. Jekyll and Mr. Hyde.
*He may have set the book in London, but it's unmistakably
Edinburgh that comes eerily off the page.*

*Behind the soot-black facades of the Royal Mile lie the
old tenements surrounding their barren courts. Back in the
eighteenth century, these were the equivalent of today's
council-housing schemes—overcrowded with the dispos-
sessed of the city, home to drunks and laudanum addicts,*

*haunts of the lowest whores and street urchins. Tonight, like a tormented replay of the worst historical nightmare, a woman's body lies close to the head of a stone staircase that provides a steep short cut from High Street down the slope of The Mound. Her short dress has been pulled up, the cheap seams splitting under the strain.*

*If she had screamed when she was attacked, it would have been smothered by the blanket of foggy air. One thing is certain. She will never scream again. Her throat is a gaping scarlet grin. To add insult to injury, the gleaming coils of her intestines have been draped over her left shoulder.*

*The printer who stumbled over the body on his way home from a late shift cowers in a crouch at the mouth of the close leading to the court. He is close enough to the pool of his own vomit to gag on the rancid stench held hovering by the oppression of the haar. He has used his mobile phone to call the police, but the few minutes it is taking them to arrive feel like an eternity, his recent vision of hell stamped ineradicably on his mind's eye.*

*Flashing blue lights loom suddenly before him as two police cars swoop to a halt at the kerb. Running footsteps, then he has company. Two uniformed officers gently help him to his feet. They lead him towards their squad car where they hand him into the rear seat. Two others have disappeared down the close, the woolly sound of their footsteps swallowed almost immediately by the clinging mist. Now the only sounds are the crackling of the police radio and the chattering of the printer's teeth.*

*Dr. Harry Gemmell hunkers by the body, his gloved fingers probing things that Detective Inspector Campbell Grant doesn't want to think about. Rather than study what the police surgeon is doing, Grant looks instead at the scene-of-crime officers in their white overalls. They are taking advantage of the portable lights to search the area round the body. The haar is eating into Grant's very bones, making him feel like an old man.*

*Eventually, Gemmell grunts and pushes himself to his feet, stripping the blood-streaked latex from his hands. He studies his chunky sports watch and gives a satisfied nod. "Aye," he says. "September the eighth, right enough."*

*"Meaning what, Harry?" Grant asks wearily. He is already irritated by the prospect of enduring Gemmell's habit of forcing detectives to drag information out of him piecemeal.*

*"Your man here, he likes to play follow-my-leader. See if you can figure it out for yourself, Cam. There are marks on her neck that indicate manual strangulation, though I reckon she died from having her throat cut. But it's the mutilations that tell the story."*

*"Is all this supposed to mean something to me, Harry? Apart from a good reason to lose my last meal?" Grant demands.*

*"Eighteen eighty-eight in Whitechapel, nineteen ninety-nine in Edinburgh." Gemmell raises an eyebrow. "Time to call in the profilers, Cam."*

*"What the fuck are you on about, Harry?" Grant asks. He wonders if Gemmell's been drinking.*

*"I think you've got a copycat killer, Cam. I think you're looking for Jock the Ripper."*

\*     \*     \*

Dr. Fiona Cameron stood on the very lip of Stanage Edge and leaned forward into the wind. The only kind of sudden death she might have to contemplate here would be her own, and then only if she was more careless than she thought she could manage. But just supposing for a moment she lost concentration on the wet millstone grit, she'd plunge down thirty or forty helter-skelter feet, her body bouncing like a plastic doll on the jutting blocks of rock, bones and skin broken and violated.

She'd end up looking like a victim.

No way, Fiona thought, letting the wind push her back from the edge just far enough to take the danger out of her position. Not here of all places. This was the place of pilgrimage, the place where she came to remind herself of all the reasons why she was who she was. Always alone, she returned here three or four times a year, whenever the need grew in her to touch the face of her memories. The company of another living, breathing human would be impossible to bear up on this bleak stretch of moorland. There was only room for the two of them; Fiona and her ghost, that other half of herself who only ever walked beside her on these moors.

It was strange, she thought. There were so many other places where she'd spent far more time with Lesley. But everywhere else was somehow marred by the consciousness of other voices, other lives. Here, though, she could sense Lesley without interference. She could see her face, open in laughter, or closed in concentration as she negotiated a tricky scramble. She could hear her voice, earnest with confidences or loud with the excitement of achievement. She almost believed she could smell the faint musk of her skin as they huddled together over a picnic.

Here, more than anywhere, Fiona recognized the light she had lost from her life. She closed her eyes and let her mind create the picture. Her mirror image, that same chestnut hair and hazel eyes, that same arc of the eyebrows, that same nose. Everyone had always marvelled at the resemblance. Only their mouths were different; Fiona's wide and full-lipped, Lesley's a small cupid's bow, her bottom lip fuller than the upper.

Here, too, the discussions had been had, the decision taken that had ultimately led to Lesley being wrenched from her life. This was the place of final reproach, the place where Fiona could never forget what her life lacked.

Fiona felt her eyes watering. She snapped them open and let the wind provide the excuse. The time for vulnerability was over. She was here, she reminded herself, to get away from victims. She looked out across the brown bracken of Hathersage Moor to the clumsy thumb of Higger Tor and beyond, turning back to watch a wedge of rain drench one end of Bamford Moor. In this wind, she had twenty minutes before it reached the Edge, she reckoned, rolling her shoulders to shift her backpack to a more comfortable position. Time to make a move.

An early train from King's Cross then a connection to a local train had brought her to Hathersage just after ten. She'd made good time on the steep hike up to High Neb, enjoying the stretch in her muscles, savouring the bunching of her calves and the tautness of her quads. The final scramble that brought her to the northern end of Stanage had left her short of breath and she'd leaned against the rock, taking a long drink from her water bottle before she set off along the flat slabs of gritstone. The connection to her past had grounded her more firmly than anything else she knew. And the wind at her back had exhilarated her, setting her thoughts loose from the jumbled knot of irritation that had woken her. She'd known then that she had to get out of London for the day or else accept that by evening her shoulders would be a tight plane sending waves of pain up her neck and across her head.

The only appointment in her diary had been a supervision meeting with one of her PhD students, and that had been easily rearranged with a phone call from the train. Up here on the moors, no tabloid hack could find her, no camera crew could thrust their equipment into her face and demand to know what Candid Cameron had to say about the day's courtroom events.

Of course, she couldn't be certain that things would turn out in line with her expectations. But when she'd heard on last night's news that the sensational trial of the Hampstead Heath Killer was still on hold after a second day of legal arguments, all her instincts told her that by the end of today, the red-top brigade would be screaming for blood. And she was the perfect weapon for them to use to draw that blood from the police. Better to keep well out of it, for all sorts of reasons.

She'd never courted publicity for the work she'd done with the police, but it had dogged her regardless. Fiona hated to see her face splashed across the newspapers nearly as much as her colleagues resented it. What was almost worse than the loss of privacy was that her notoriety had somehow diminished her as an academic. Now when she published in journals and contributed to books, she knew her work was scrutinized with more scepticism than before, simply because she had applied her skills and knowledge in a practical way that met with pursed lips of disapproval among the purists.

The silent condemnation had only grown harsher when one of the tabloids had revealed that she was living with Kit Martin. It was hard to imagine who, in the eyes of the academic establishment, could have been a less respectable partner for an academic psychologist engaged in developing scientific methods that would help police to catch repeat offenders than the country's leading writer of serial killer thrillers. If Fiona had cared enough about what her peers thought of her, she might have bothered to explain that it was not Kit's novels she was in love with but the man who wrote them, and that the very nature of his work had made her more cautious about starting the relationship than she might otherwise have been. But since no one dared challenge her to her face, she chose not to leap into the trap of self-justification.

At the thought of Kit, her sadness shifted. That she had found the one man who could save her from the prison of her introspection was a blessing she never ceased to find miraculous. The world might never see behind the tough-guy charm he turned on in public, but beyond his sharp-edged intelligence, she had discovered generosity, respect and a sensitivity she'd all but given up hope of ever finding. With Kit, she had finally arrived at a kind of peace that mostly kept the demons of Stanage Edge at bay.

As she strode on, she glanced at her watch. She'd made

good time. If she kept up her pace, she'd have time for a drink in the Fox House pub before the bus that would carry her back down into Sheffield for the London train. She'd have had five hours in the open, five hours when she had seen scarcely another human being, and that was enough to sustain her. Until the next time, she thought grimly.

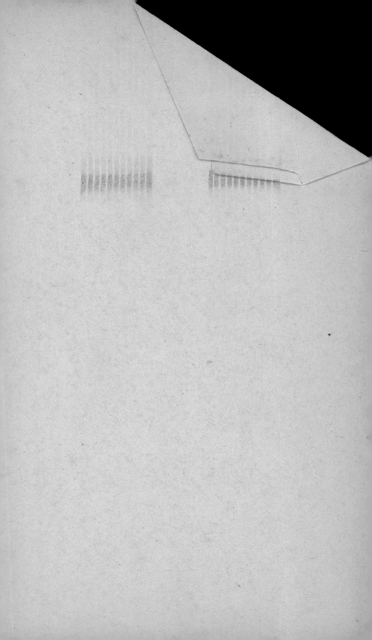